About the Author

After growing up with a love of reading, it has made her a proud bookworm. Tazz can usually be found with her nose buried in a book when she isn't writing. Residing in Northamptonshire, England, she is never far from a pen and paper to jot down ideas to use in her stories.

Her hope is for readers to enjoy the stories told and forget any stress for a few hours and if they laugh at the silly humour, bonus.

Mystic Being: Creation and Him

Tazz Davies

Mystic Being: Creation and Him

Olympia Publishers
London

www.olympiapublishers.com

OLYMPIA PAPERBACK EDITION

A CIP catalogue record for this title is
available from the British Library.

ISBN: 978-1-78830-355-2

This is a work of fiction.
Names, characters, places and incidents originate from the writer's imagination. Any
resemblance to actual persons, living or dead, is purely coincidental.

First Published in 2019

Olympia Publishers
60 Cannon Street
London
EC4N 6NP

Printed in Great Britain

Dedication

To my mum, Heidi — for encouraging me to keep on going with all the craziness that resides in my brain. For not getting aggravated for the countless times I've asked if something sounds right. As well as your contribution on characters, and helping me with names when my head has a temporary blip.

I love you. More today than yesterday, but not as much as tomorrow. Forever and always.

Prologue

Hi there. So you've decided to divulge yourself in the story of Creation and Him. Well, that's brilliant but we've got to start at the very beginning, so you get an idea of what is going on and how it all came to be and so you don't get a little confused with everything.

So get comfortable… Done that? Good. Are you ready? OK, then let's get started!

So let us journey back in time. A good twenty thousand years in fact, but not on Earth as you know it to be. We're heading back in time to a place many of us can only dream about! Hillsides covered in thick, richly luminescent bright green grass that pretty much just begs you to curl your toes in. Mountains of all shapes and sizes that rule the land. They might seem close to one another, but in reality, they're very far apart. Some take a good day just to get from one to the other. Tall, thick-trunked trees of all shapes and sizes with bulging, broad, different coloured leaves scattered around the island, dominating the land. Closer to the ground are bushes in all sizes and many have vicious, poisonous plants in striking displays of colours attached to them, along with stunning dazzling flowers that give off rich fragrances. Many creatures called the forests, mountains and the small assorted villages home. Even part of the coastline with engorged, towering cliffs housed things. As well as many of the small islands dotted off of the coast also housed creatures.

A vast, sweeping shadow glides overhead taking the form of a magnificently graceful, yet powerful black and green dragon. He soars effortlessly on the wind, heading for a monstrous hill, which is away from the mountains and other parts that resides near the coast, and lands elegantly, which is ironic considering his sheer bulk. Other dragons bow their heads in respect for this ancient beast; apart from just one. She didn't bow her head; just stood blending into the shadows; staring into the magic orb that she used to see the other beings of their world; a worried expression marring her features. She didn't interact with many of them, because majority deemed her an 'outcast' due to her unusual foresight. She was what was called a Dragon Seer. Powerful in her own way, and one this dragon trusted.

"Sarhsha; what do you see?" the colossal one asked, drawing her white gaze to his rich, beautiful, liquescent emerald green eyes. He stepped closer to her, the sunshine reflecting off of his magnificent body and making his eyes practically gleam. Thick black scales, with deeply creviced, battle-scarred, velveteen green spines down his back. Chunks and scales were missing, which were the results of numerous bouts of fights to state his dominance and leadership. He towered over them all at a brutal seventy feet high and a scary fifty feet long. He also happened to be the Supreme Ruler; Dragon Lord of all and he'd held his position already for an astounding ten thousand years! And he'd earned his place the only way it was possible for them, via combat. The Supreme Ruler of all Dragons. Basically, their king. His name was Gélio.

"My lord, we need to find something which can stop the Evil Ones. If we don't, we will lose to them and life as we know it will end. The forces of good will be wiped out completely."

"So what do you suggest?"

"There is a fey walking around not far from here that I managed to lock onto a few days past, stumbling, bloody, confused and absolutely petrified. She also happens to be pregnant. Take the foetus, place it in the stone egg and it will be our salvation."

"Downside?" There was always a downside.

"In order for it to work properly, we need creatures from the forces of good and bad to sacrifice themselves. I know it is a lot to ask for, but alas that is the only way in which it will work."

"OK, so we need to spread word about this then." Time was of the essence after all.

"Gélio, do you really think the forces of darkness would willingly sacrifice themselves for this? You know as much as I do that they're all for wiping out the forces of light." His Dragon Soul, the love of his life, Nyhkohl, enquired from where she was flicking a lone claw into one of the small pools of scented oils Sarhsha used for whatever it was she used them for, but he did know that occasionally Nyhkohl came back to their cave smelling of them — not that he complained. She was a tower of strength and beauty; a curvaceous dragon that was a striking shade of fuchsia. Her eyes were a shimmering flash of magenta. Large spines danced down her back and tail in a sharp black. She was a stark contrast to his darkness. But he wouldn't change her for anything. She was after all the light to his dark;

the other half of his being. And he was hopelessly and unconditionally in love with her. And he didn't shun away from that; he wasn't one to muck around with a powerful emotion such as love, and she knew it. Well should do after them being together this long.

"We'd have no choice, Nyhkohl. We have captives who we can use for that. They're sentenced to death anyway, so what better way to do it than this? The sooner we have more help, the better."

"But to train an adolescent up to be nothing but a brutal killing machine? Surely they should at least have a childhood first?"

"I'm sorry Nyhkohl; but we need them to be the best that they can be. No time for a childhood or whatnot, as the whole of Mystic Being needs them. Hell, we need them. We can't keep on living as we do with everyone fighting each and every day. The Good vs. the Bad. Innocents being killed just for spite. Even children are being killed, just because of who their parents are or if they sadly are in the wrong place at the wrong time." He watched as what he said registered with her. She rolled her eyes and walked off, but not before she swung her head around and pierced his gaze with her own intense one.

"Just be careful no matter what you decide to do. I'll see you later." And with that, she spread those magnificent wings and leapt into the sky; disappearing quickly. Gélio waited until she had disappeared and turned his gaze to one of his retriever dragons who stood to the side.

"I need you and a scout to go and retrieve this fey who is pregnant. Sarhsha, where about is she? Details for what she looks like so as not to get confused with the wrong one."

"Yes, my lord." She again plunged her snout into the bowl and for an impatient minute or so he waited as the dragon scoured for the fey. She suddenly reared her head up, splashing the water everywhere, eyes wide as they gazed upon his warriors.

"Get to the snow mountain here on this island; she's there. Quickly now as she's cornered by Rogue Lycanthropes who want a taste of her flesh, and by the harsh energy I can feel, they want her all over again; if she's willing or not. You won't be able to miss her!" The retriever dragons leapt into the sky at the bark of the order to retrieve her from Gélio.

He watched as they soared into the sky and out of his line of vision and then he turned back to Sarhsha.

"How will we make this creation? Do we have someone capable to perform this task?"

"Yes. As a matter of fact, we do. Klmarnau, can you please go and collect the witch who is to help us. She's down on the private beach."

"Certainly." Klmarnau, a rich cerulean blue dragon left to do as she was asked, not even enquiring as to how she knew the witch was at the beach.

"What will this witch do? How can she help?" Gélio asked, drawing Sarhsha's gaze.

"We've already spoken about what needs to be done. We have the 'sacrifices' as I told you about, and she'll know what do to, whereas I don't." She wasn't one to not be honest, that was for sure.

"Why can't you tell me? Thought you were the Dragi for a reason?"

"I might be the dragon equivalent of the witches, but I've never seen this spell before. I don't know the words either. Let alone the power it would take to use the spell even if I did know it, milord. As for the 'sacrifices', I am sorry I went behind your back without consulting you first, but we are desperate. I'm tired of seeing our kind destroyed or changed over to the bad side," Sarhsha replied, her scaled body shimmered with a pulsing blue magic thanks to the breed of dragon that she was. Thank God there were only four breeds of dragon. The Warriors, the Dragi, the Keepers and just simple Dragons, who had no intention of ever doing anything apart from singing, dancing, being happy and raising young that were then selected into their own sections for the remainder of their lives. Gélio himself was the Warrior kind. Lord of them all, but Warrior all the same as were his father and grandfather before him.

"How does this witch know them?"

"You will have to ask her. Here she comes with Klmarnau. And again I apologise for going behind your back and discussing and sorting this with her before you." Gélio nodded his acceptance for her apology, knowing she meant well. Plus this was the very first time she had done so. He turned his head to the side and sure enough this wee tiny thing of a witch came striding along the grassland, next to Klmarnau, right up to him. Not a single ounce of fear marked her features. And he wasn't at all surprised considering the power that flowed through her veins. While she was tiny compared to them, she was probably considered a tall woman amongst her own people.

"Gélio." She nodded her head respectfully to him. She stood no higher than his knee joint, but the power she wielded in her was extraordinary, he could feel it from where he stood. Her eyes were thickly lashed and shone intensely from her raw power. They were brilliantly coloured, like a rainbow shot through with glitter with intricate black lines either side that drew attention to them. Lips were a succulent red colour begging to be nibbled on. Skin was flawless and every inch of her was tanned golden from countless hours, no days, spent kissed by the sun's unrelenting hot rays. Hair was thick, glossy, waist length and multi-coloured. It was kept off of her face by two braids intertwined with glass beads and tied at the back of her head by a gorgeous clip made from black stones interlaced with pure gold swirling vines. Her dress was of multi-coloured material which shimmered like dragon scales with every step she took and hugged her body like a second skin. It ended roughly mid-thigh. Swirling vines of pure gold arm bands adorned her biceps. Multi-coloured blades with glass handles were attached to each thigh and one at her ankle. Feet were bare and her toenails a dusky shade of shell pink. All in all, she was a gorgeous witch; but he didn't think she realised just how pretty she was.

"Khrysalia, how are you?" He nodded back.

"Pretty good. I know what it is you are after, Sarhsha has already filled me in. Let's get this over and done with. Do you have a foetus?" He forgot how blunt she could be from the few times he had met with her to discuss some things.

"Yes. The fey that is pregnant should be on her way now. I sent my best warriors to get her."

"OK. Do you have any place we can do this?"

"What do you think would be the most ideal place?"

"The Sacred Stones will work."

"They're just stones; how will they work?" Gélio knew they had power, but just how much did the collection of eight giant stones have? And how did they work? Long before he became Dragon Lord, he had wondered as to how it all worked, even from when he was a Dragoling. But no one had the true knowledge as to just what they were capable of or the magic that was apparently stored inside. Only that they were protected and set with a spell that anything evil that tried to use their power was immediately killed.

"If you follow me, I'll show you. And Sarhsha, when the fey arrives, please send her along."

"Of course," the old one said and turned away as her name was called, which gave Gélio and Khrysalia time to get away. They didn't talk until they'd reached the stones and away from nosy eavesdroppers.

"Look Gélio, I'm going to be honest with you. We need equal bodies of good and evil. How many of each do you have? We need at least one from each species here."

"Easily done. We have at least every single species here in bad, and I'm sure it won't take much convincing for the good either. Actually, Sarhsha has already put word out and those who have agreed are spending the last day with their families."

"When did she put the word out?"

"Yesterday." He noticed she didn't enquire as to why the word had been put out yesterday. But then again, Sarhsha had said she had already had this extensive conversation for needing the help to combat everything which was going on in their beloved world, so they were preparing for anything.

"How long do they have left?" She wasn't really paying that much attention to him. She was creating magic balls of intense light about the size of a bowling ball, each with vast different colours of glitter water inside of them. They were dazzling colours of red, purple, green, blue, yellow, pink and orange. Once she had created one, she had placed it on the floor until each stone had one in front of it. But the last stone; the biggest of them all that stood ten feet high by five feet wide and a good three feet thick, had a bright ball of magic in front of it with each and every colour swirling inside. It was an amazing thing to see. He couldn't look directly into it from the brightness but from the side, it really was remarkable. The balls themselves were easily fifty centimetres wide and fifty centimetres tall.

"They'll be here within the next thirty minutes or so."

"So they'll be here by mid-afternoon at the latest?" she asked, gazing up at the sky with the huge flaming ball that beat down on them with penetrating heat, her skin soaking up the rays, covertly fuelling her powers.

"Yes. Now what are you doing?" He watched, transfixed as she drew a small blade from a sheath that was on her upper thigh and drew it across her palm, causing blood to rise. But it wasn't a normal colour. Hers was a rich red that was highlighted by glitter and swirls of magic that caused it to glow a lot brighter than usual! Gélio's eyes bulged as she smeared the blood onto the surface in front of her and it seemed to sink into the rock.

"You know how precious these collections of stones are, don't you?" She looked over at him.

"Yes; everyone does."

"Do you know exactly why?"

"Actually, no. Not sure many actually do." She turned to fully look at him then.

"Well, there's a small group of witches, the coven I am from, who know the full extent of what's so special with these rocks. If I had our Elder with us, we could do this with ease, but because she sadly passed away a couple of years back, you'll have to deal with just me."

"So you know what these stones are for?"

"Yep. Good ol' Marlànya taught me everything she knows. This is why I'm the most powerful witch that's lived, as of yet."

"I can tell that isn't your ego talking. Just stating fact."

"Of course. I don't see the point in bragging. Facts serve a lot more purpose." Damn, he could like this tiny witch; could see they'd be vast friends. Too bad she was willing to sacrifice herself. The tell-tale noise of dragons' wings in flight came over them then and they both turned their heads as they watched as Gélio's trusted Warriors flew into view. They were a formidable sight, all dark and menacing with sheer determination on their faces, of what you could see through their battle gear. All flew in a protective manner around the one who had their precious cargo tucked safely in his clawed hand up against the base of his neck. She was hunched up that small, she virtually disappeared, all they could see was the tip of her head, thanks to her wealth of black hair that stood out against his light scales. They landed gracefully near them, and Khrysalia hurried forward, took the woman into her arms and ushered her over near the stones, away from everyone before quickly laying the pregnant fey onto the ground. She just stared at them with nothing but sheer pain in her eyes. Not even fear was evident. What the hell had been done to her with her not even having a hint of fear sparked inside of her?

"Please help me. End my misery," she cried, cobalt blue eyes full of agony. Bite wounds adorned her neck and some even marked her arms and legs. Deep lacerations from claws raked down her arms and across her thighs, making the wounds pucker with redness. Some even had crusts of green/yellow from infection. New bruises were forming over sick yellow and brown ones on her wrists and ankles from being held in places against her will. A harsh red welt stretched across her throat, as if someone had placed something there tightly, which was more than likely a hand or forearm. Dried blood splashed over her body and some crusted around bite wounds! Across her face to her mouth was a streak of a red welt, as though she'd been gagged to keep from crying out loud. After being placed on the floor, she adamantly refused to lay backwards until Khrysalia pulled her forward and looked behind her. Then she stared in horror as a lycanthrope claw dipped in poison protruded from her spine where it had been deliberately placed. The claw, with only the end of which she could see sticking out of the poor fey's flesh, had black tendrils leaking out of it across her deathly white skin, the poison as fresh as the day it got into her system, with what could only be likened to the scorching heat of a thousand burning suns. Hot sticky blood, still fresh, leaked from her repeatedly raped and brutalised vagina that had parts of the flesh hanging from it from the sheer brutality of what had happened to her. Khrysalia hissed in anger at what she saw. She had had enough. The sooner the guys who did this got their comeuppance would be worth everything she was about to do and sacrifice. And how was she still able to carry the foetus that was inside her with what her body had gone through? A sheer miracle! The worst part, well not completely the worst part considering what had happened, but she had no tears or anything in her eyes. It was as if she'd literally out-cried herself and knew it wouldn't do her any good, so she no longer cried, not even with that claw embedded in her back. Her eyes were completely dry.

"What is it?" Gélio asked, noting the anger on her face.

"She's been raped repeatedly from what I can see. And by the looks of it, by something with what can only be either a spiked cock or something much worse. You poor unfortunate child." She put her palm against the fey's cheek, who cried out in agony. The trouble was, she knew exactly what it was that had done it. Those Rogue Lycanthropes. They'd have no doubt attached 'extensions' onto their cocks to make the raping even worse as it would have no doubt ripped the insides of this poor woman to shreds and made them eager to cause even more damage. It was a wonder she hadn't bled out yet! Or that she had even been able to conceive at all considering the trauma her poor body had gone through.

"Please kill me, end my misery. I'm not a simple fey any more. I'm contaminated."

"What do you mean by that?" Gélio enquired.

"The bite marks you see are full of lycanthrope saliva and whatever else they could find, so at the next full moon I will change over. Bad enough I carry the spawn of one. I do not want to change over into one. So either you kill me, or I shall do it myself," she muttered but it was the absolute sheer determination on her face that made them all realise she was indeed very serious about it.

"We know you are serious. But before you die, would you care to let us take your foetus from you? We wish to make the ultimate weapon to stop the Rogues and Bad Ones."

"What kind of weapon are you talking about? How can you? It's just a foetus, a span of cells." They could tell she was interested; even as her blood was now slowly leaking out of her and bled into the ground, creating a dark stain. Her body temperature leaving her cold and shaking. It wasn't a nice way to go, but at least she was out of that place, surrounded by fierce dragons who would protect her with their last dying breath and her magic as well, as she was completely free of that horrible place and away from the brutality of those bastards.

"Khrysalia, this is your part. It's easier for you to explain." Gélio moved a short distance away from them to give them room to talk. He knew he was intimidating and didn't want to overcrowd the already traumatised fey.

"A whole lot of magic and plenty of sacrifices. There is a catch though," Khrysalia said, drawing the fey's eyes to her own.

"What do you mean by the sacrifices? Also, what is the catch?"

"The weapon, our creation, will not be able to die. Well, it will, but it'll be extremely hard to kill it. It will age as we do; but the body will remain youthful and at its most prime. The other catch is we need a foetus for this to work."

"Then take the one that grows rapidly in my belly."

"Listen to me well on this one. In order for us to remove it with success, you will need to be cut open across your lower stomach, me to reach inside and remove it safely. I will then have to transfer it into the egg stone quickly. I won't be able to stop the bleeding and you will bleed out rather quickly. So, therefore, you will die from that and your last moment will sadly be in pain." Khrysalia stared into the fey's eyes, letting her know she wasn't lying or bullshitting about it.

"Fine, I don't care. Just get this foetus out of me. I'm tired of living as it is anyway," she murmured and Khrysalia could tell she was absolutely set about not caring any more as well. Which was truly a shame.

"Why are you tired of living?"

"I've not long lost my FaeSoul and our child I carried. My family have shunned me because of it, when it was murder for my male and I lost the child from the sheer brutality of what happened to me."

"So you literally have no one here." Khrysalia looked sad and Gélio noticed a single tear of sparkling silver magic streak down her cheek and landed gracefully on the fey's upturned face. He hated how pathetic the fey were if one of their own miscarried — they were either shunned or very rarely given a second chance. Sometimes miscarriage was just a simple force of nature. It was horrible, yes, but sometimes it was just unstoppable, unexplainable and just happened.

"Don't cry for me. Take the foetus. Make your weapon. Let me die knowing that this child's been given a second chance for something worth living for," she whispered, her bloodied and bruised hand rising gently to place it on Khrysalia's face, but it fell quickly, leaving behind a smudge of blood.

"What would you like to call your child then?" Gélio enquired, still amazed that this fey had managed to escape from that hell; even after everything she had gone through. How had she done it?

"I don't want to call it anything. You can name it."

"Why do you not want to name it?"

"Because I will be dead by the time it is born — so it is a waste of time. You can decide on what you want to call it."

"Very well, but before Khrysalia proceeds with what we need to have done, may I enquire as to your name?"

"Why?" She turned those pale eyes to his, the intense blue losing its vivid brightness.

"Because I want to know the name of the fey who sacrificed her life for us."

"Very well. I am called Caliana."

"Caliana. Very well, you shall be remembered and buried with honours bestowed by myself and all of those around you. You shall not be forgotten for what you have gifted us with. Khrysalia, it's all in your court now." He faced the witch.

"Yes, we must begin." She glanced over at Gélio, who nodded and with the ease of long practice, he leapt into the air and within the next twenty minutes he had rounded up everyone who was to be sacrificed, willing or not. More than ready to get this over and done with.

As Gélio flew off, Khrysalia moved Caliana into position next to the stone egg, taking her time to add comfort to the already traumatised woman, even though it clearly hurt her due to her face scrunching up in obvious agony. Once she was settled, Khrysalia moved into her own position and called forth the magic that coursed through her veins. The balls of magic in front of each stone began to hum and shine until it was as if a 100 watt bulb shone through each one. By the time that had happened, Gélio had returned to announce that everything was in order. She turned around and her power coursed through her system and streamed through her fingers to crash into individual orbs that circled around her body before slamming into her body, dissolving into her flesh. Her eyes glazed over, startling white, as she rose off the ground slightly. Staring down at everyone, she threw her hands out and violent blue lightning shot from them and turned to Caliana, who just stared in wonder at her.

"I'm sorry for all of what you endured Caliana, truly I am and know that you shall be avenged for what they did to you. But now it's time to remove the foetus and I'm regretful for this last moment of pain I'm sadly going to give you."

"It's OK." She lifted her head up from where it hung limp to the side and gazed at Khrysalia, her eyes already dulling, as her life bled out. She must have been a stunning woman before she was captured, but now it was evident that she was literally just a shell of the woman she must have been. Horrible way to go. And one she couldn't even comprehend.

"I promise we shall give you the burial you deserve. I'll make sure that Gélio gives you the best service he can." She smiled at the girl who gave a shaky smile back. And Khrysalia could see, underneath all the bruises and marks, she was a very beautiful woman.

"OK. Thank you and good luck." With that, Caliana shut her eyes and held her arms down by her sides, fists clenched tightly. Khrysalia moved towards her and crouched down.

"Sweet dreams Caliana." She placed her hands on Caliana's stomach and frowned when the woman flinched at the small contact.

"Will it hurt?" she whispered, eyes squeezed shut.

"I'm afraid so; I'm so sorry. For everything." With that her powers built up inside of herself until it felt like liquid hot lava was running through her veins and then she sent them careening through Caliana, who screamed out in unadulterated anguish. Khrysalia wasn't at all surprised considering Caliana's skin split open as if a laser had gone across it. She reached inside of her, into the woman's very womb and pulled out the barely fertilised foetus. She was small, four weeks along, so it was at most only seven millimetres long, but thanks to her astounding knowledge, keen eyesight and whatnot, she knew exactly what she was looking for. Just how long had she been in those bastard's company to get over the miscarriage and then get pregnant again? It just didn't bear thinking about. Khrysalia moved away from Caliana who stared down at the blooded mess that was her stomach and womb and then gazed up at Khrysalia, who quickly rushed to the stone egg, inserted the embryo inside and sealed it back up again with her blood and a few whispered words of hauntingly sung magic. She turned back to Caliana, but whilst she was busy sorting out the foetus, she'd died. A small smile on the edge of her lips as though she was welcoming death with opening arms, her hands on either side of that ghastly wound, covered in blood, her sightless eyes locked onto Khrysalia. She turned away as she didn't have time to waste and got right to it. She moved to the edge of the hill again, looked down at everyone and slammed her hands together in front of her. Thick black clouds gathered close together until it was gloomy as night over the land. The only light visible was from the stones that hummed with distinguished magic and from Khrysalia herself. She glided down the side of the hill, past everyone, who tracked her every move until she was at the back and in the middle. Then she called forth the black powerful magic that she seldom used and strolled forward, avoiding eye contact with them all. She was completely devoid of normal speech as she was whispering out the spell needed for it all to work in an ancient language not heard for countless centuries. As she walked past the beings, eyes widened and glowing brightly from the magic that shot through their system, mouths opened and screams high enough to rupture eardrums erupted from their throats and she wasn't at all surprised to be quite honest. It meant that the spell was working, but she still looked behind her to double check and she saw that it was. No time to feel guilty though because she had to save Mystic Being. She couldn't fail and as she watched, their bodies frozen in place, they glowed as the magic coursed through their bodies. At least her teacher, rest her soul, was correct in the spell being the right one to work and giving her the instructions and the words for it to work. Even though it had never been tried before, she had to try it now. A once in a lifetime shot! The creatures' bodies were convulsing and then began to bleed through their very pores. As each lost their precious blood, she carried on until she reached the bottom of the hill, turned around fully and faced them. Due to the spell, their haemoglobin had all melded together into one giant, thick blood line down the middle of the lane where she had walked. Every single being was crashed out on the floor, fighting to live. But it wouldn't work. She threw her hands up into the air and the elements that had crashed into her, leapt out of her skin as a single orb of swirling colour. It soared over the beings, dragging their very last thread of life essence out as it passed them, leaving behind a hollow carcass with sightless eyes wide and mouths open on forever soundless screams. After all the life essences were collected, they moved until they were together in a line, hovering parallel with the blood. Khrysalia moved back up the hill, keeping her eyes completely focused on the stone egg that was glowing and pulsing as though eager for what she was about to give it. She moved to stand in front of it and she noticed that Gélio had removed Caliana's body. As she came to a stop, she threw her hands out ahead of her as a ferocious gust of wind blew around her body, her hair whipping around her body in all directions. Raw power channelling itself through her entire system. The rawest she'd ever felt. Power blazed through her veins, her entire system lighting up from within.

"Nalafarylyrain losmriarn cuhlooyryhú," she yelled into the wind, and the blood and life essences she'd removed from the 'sacrifices' soared up over her head and slammed into the stone egg. The orbs of colours immediately followed suit. As Khrysalia lowered her arms, a single life essence strolled past as if they had all the time in the world and thanks to the powers she had, she clearly saw who it was as if they were in a living, breathing body. It was Caliana who smiled and her cobalt blue eyes finally held peace, none of that terror and grief that occupied them before. All her wounds were gone and she was absolutely stunning. She nodded once, then she walked into the stone egg. The light dimmed down slightly and Khrysalia was able to see inside of it. She produced a slight smile; the foetus was safe in the middle, surrounded by a halo of light, that strangely resembled a pair of hands, as though protecting it from the evilness that resided outside of its safe haven.

"Now what?" a deep voice asked from behind, which made her whirl around, magic swirling in her hands, ready to defend herself.

"Greantere Gélio! Don't make me jump like that. I could have seriously hurt you. It is all done. All that is needed now is that final sacrifice for when the child is born." She extinguished the magic.

"And that will be how long?"

"Of that, I do not know. But I am willing to sacrifice myself for that purpose." As she finished what she was saying, the bulk of the clouds disappeared, giving way to the beautiful night sky lit by thousands of twinkling stars with a few dense clouds. The remainder of the day had passed quickly but it seemed mere minutes. Before they could say anything else, more dragons joined them. If she wasn't so sure in her powers and her self-confidence, she would feel quite threatened being surrounded by these powerhouses.

"My lord, what is happening?" a dragon questioned, dipping her head in respect when he looked at her.

"The egg has been securely added and the sacrifices have been completed. Now we need to wait for the egg to develop into that of a normal baby. Then we shall train them to become our fighter, our saviour."

"Back up everyone!" Khrysalia screamed just as the full moon burst through the clouds and its brilliant rays shone down on the egg. It began to glow along the top and down the sides with an extraordinary display of multi-coloured lights of which shot up into the air in a dazzling display that had everyone that was there watching in awe. Eyes glued to the thing in wonder as the foetus inside matured. It grew and grew until it reached the height of an adult. Khrysalia moved away from it and the unthinkable happened. The egg began to glow with an incandescent silvery white light that was absolutely blinding and made them all cover their eyes, but not before she saw that the egg had erupted into a thousand pieces. However, before the sharp shards reached them, they disintegrated into grains of ash, that bounced off their skin like kisses before soaring into the air and disappearing, thanks to the shallow wind that now whipped around them. Then she had to close her eyes before she completely incinerated her retinas. When the light had finally dimmed down, they all opened their eyes again and after they blinked a fair few times, pretty much everyone again stared in awe. Vast brilliantly-bright colours swirled together in a colourful vortex. The colours diminished and everyone gasped. In front of them, floating in mid-air was a woman. Naked as anything, with her body covered in peachy white skin that looked smooth as silk. A pair of blood-red eyes framed by long black lashes stared at them, unblinking. Large fangs fell from her upper jaw and ended in the middle of her chin, sharp as those of a dragon's. Her hair, jet black, whipped around her in the wind that swirled about her like a cloak. Long legs were perfectly formed of sturdy muscle. Hourglass figure. Broadish-type shoulders. Flawlessly proportioned breasts. She was brilliantly formed. She had graceful hands with long black claws. As she landed, her feet with matching black toenails sunk into the plush grass. The moon created the perfect backdrop to this wondrous creation, coating it in its silken rays. Khrysalia took a step forward, slowly so she didn't cause any alarm. Who knew what this being was wholly capable of? She had many a question zooming through her mind, but the main one; how was it possible she had grown into an adult as quickly as she had? Surely she should have been a baby first and raised that way? Or was it because of the magic? She wished her mentor was here, because then she would have explained it to her, if she had known it, that was. As she stepped forward more, the being's eyes latched onto her and it actually scared her. It was as if it was looking into her very soul. Not much scared her but she could feel the raw dangerous power that it housed within. She was even more powerful than her own self.

"Can you talk?"

"Yes." Her voice was sultry and surrounded her in mystery. Her teeth sunk back up into her jaw, so they appeared normal but with a small pointed edge to them.

"Do you understand what has occurred?"

"Yes. I am a creation that you have made with the sacrifices of four hundred beings. Two hundred of light, two hundred of darkness; just to balance it out right. You need me to help you all with keeping everything in check." Again her eyes were unblinking and it was really eerie as fuck.

"Yes, that is correct."

"But in order for it to be completed, I need to drain someone who is alive as the ultimate sacrifice."

"Yes, and that's me."

"Very well. When?"

"In a few moments. I have just a few things to wrap up here first." No point in mucking around now that she was grown and not a baby. Not like she had family or anything anyway — no one would miss her. And the one being who would, had already passed a few years past.

"Very well." Khrysalia quickly finished up of what she needed done, including getting the promise from Gélio that Caliana be buried properly, of which he said yes.

"OK, let's do this." She put her shoulders back and walked over to the creation.

"Before anything happens, what shall we call you?" Gélio called out.

"I do not care what you call me." She regarded him with absolutely no emotion. She literally showed no fear in facing him when he was an absolute force to be reckoned with, and she just stared at him as though it was nothing. Khrysalia realised why, she was an untold force herself so why would she be scared of him? Or anyone for that matter? Who knew just how vast her powers were?

"Very well, give me a few and I shall come up with a name for you."

"Do what you want. It is time." She turned that devil stare to Khrysalia.

"Very well." She moved her hair to the side, giving the creation a perfect striking place. She shivered as the woman pulled her back to her front. Hands freezing cold, yet softer than anything she'd ever felt in her life. Nails pointed and sharp as daggers and for some reason she noticed they were perfectly manicured although they were not coloured or anything. Khrysalia watched out the corner of her eye as the woman leaned forward

23

into her peripheral vision, fangs gleaming white and slick with a little dash of saliva. She did one last glance over at Gélio.

"Recall what I said, Gélio. Find that note I also left in that sacred place but burn it once you've read it and honour us for Caliana's sacrifice and bury her with the full honours."

"I won't forget, Khrysalia. Sleep well and we thank you for your sacrifice." He bowed his head to her, as did everyone else. It was without a doubt one of the biggest honours you could possibly get! Just then, the woman lifted up slightly and slammed her fangs into the side of Khrysalia's neck, piercing the jugular with ease. Khrysalia hissed in a sharp breath from the pain but it quickly disappeared as a wave of a sensual numbing washed over her and she was damn thankful of that. Before she realised it, the light began to fade in her vision. It seemed to diminish inwards until it was as if she was looking through tunnel vision. The woman turned her around, so that the last thing she saw was the moonlight bathing her homeland in light. Truly spectacular. Her breathing then became harsh and her lungs burned as she was fighting for that precious oxygen that kept her alive. She felt the woman remove her fangs and she fell to the floor in a boneless clump on her back. She opened eyes she didn't even realise she'd shut and right in front of her was the woman, leaning over her so she could look her in the eye.

"I thank you for your sacrifice," she whispered for her ears only, and moved away, eyes unblinking.

"You're welcome," she replied, sucked in a huge breath of crisp cool air, took one last look around the land that was her home, or as much as she could see, and released the breath she held. Her hands fell to either side of her body and just like that, Khrysalia died with a small smile on her face as she finally realised that it had worked and the good would have a chance to finally fight back against the Bad Ones. As her soul left her body, she smiled broadly as she soared up the heavens where she was greeted by her loved ones, including her precious son who had cruelly been taken from her at the tender young age of only two hundred. Without a backward glance, she soared into the clouds and her family's awaiting arms, leaving everything else behind. The woman, looking around, turned back and saw Khrysalia's corpse at her feet with the smile on her face and vacant eyes, wet with unshed tears staring ahead of her. It tipped her head back and roared as loudly as it could. The ground literally shook from the fierceness of it. Hands, paws or whatever was near, threw them over ears so delicate eardrums weren't shattered, but even then it still caused them to wince as it didn't completely block out the noise. When it stopped, it whirled around and stared at them properly and every single one of them shuddered slightly and all of them took an instinctive step back, even Gélio who watched, amazed at this wondrous creation as its eyes changed from that vivacious red to a stunning cobalt blue, the fangs receded and she cloaked herself in a black mist that shimmered into a black dress that clung to her body, pretty much the same as what Khrysalia herself had worn, but it suited this being more. At least now the flesh was covered, not that he didn't think the creature was shy whatsoever.

"I know what to call you now." He smiled, thankful that they were truly saved now and that it had whatever it was that Khrysalia had done, indeed worked.

"And what is that?" it asked. She could tempt anyone to do anything if she put power into that voice and it caused him to shiver and not in the pleasant way either! It wasn't something he was comfortable with. Not the whole listening to her voice, etc, but if she used it to her advantage and made whoever was on the receiving end do her bidding.

"You shall now be called Calista."

The being, with its face, neck and hands still smeared in the blood that it had taken from Khrysalia, that stood out sharply against its flesh, hands held by its sides cackling with powerful magic, smiled.

Not a nice smile either; it was a truly sinister smirk that sent chills cascading through his body and no doubt everyone else's, and its eyes positively glowed!

Calista was born. Their leader, their hero, their invincible salvation.

Chapter One
Twenty-thousand years later

In a rural village, basking in the beautiful warmth of the setting sun, two lone bikers in leathers roared up the tarmac on gorgeous bikes of sizzling power. One was a Kawasaki Ninja Zx-14 in black with three slash marks of brutal red. The other a Harley Davidson VRSCF V-Rod Muscle in black and chrome. Utter taste is what they were, and they purred as a decent, expensive bike should. They pulled up short in front of the old convenience store where a group of teenagers aged thirteen to eighteen hung out lazily on the benches to the left of the building, bass music playing from a phone with an attachable speaker in the middle of them. They eyed the 'outsiders' with curiosity and a hint of weariness. The bigger of the two climbed off of his machine and removed his helmet. This caused the kids to look away quickly as they caught sight of the jagged scars crossing down the left side of his neck that resembled three wicked claw marks and his piercing ice cold blue eyes that took in everything.

"Back in a minute," he muttered to his companion who nodded and removed his own helmet. Placing his helmet on his bike, knowing full well that it wouldn't be stolen, he turned and disappeared into the store, immediately covered in a cool breeze from the air conditioning unit, and he certainly wasn't complaining about that. Shifting his gaze around, it was a typical store. Lino flooring, harsh lighting, shelves over stacked with all sorts. Fridges with stuff that needed to stay cool. He caught movement out the corner of his eye, and turned to the counter where a small eighty-ish man sat on the edge of a stool reading a newspaper and tapping his foot against the floor in time to the soft ballad playing on the radio. His name badge said 'Frank'.

"Can I help ye?" He glanced up and then swiftly sat bolt upright as he got the full attention of the intense blue gaze of the scary man that didn't blink and was built up like a brick shithouse.

"Yes. Any chance you could direct me to where Lexis Blackwood lives?"

"And what will ye be needing our wee Lexis for?" His Scottish brogue was unreasonably thick, but at least he could understand him.

"She's my best friend's sister."

"That then must make ya Raven."

"Yes." He was immediately on edge. What exactly had Lexis told this puny man?

"Oo ee, she's gonna be thrilled that ya 'ere already. Ain't nufink else that wee lass done gone on about."

"What has she told you?" Let's hope it was nothing bad. Not that he was ashamed of what he'd done. He'd done it to protect millions of people after all. Not that they'd realise that, but the fact that he did so that made what he did slightly easier. Not by much, but enough.

"Just that you and Luke were, I mean, is in the army. And she told us funny stories of you three growing on up ta'gether before you went in the army."

"OK, now that you know we mean her no harm or are a threat, can you give me the directions now?"

"Guaranteed. Out here, hook a left, follow the street tae edge of town, hook another left and trail the trees tae tha' end. You can't miss the house. And no need tae worry about contacting Lexis. She'll know you'd be near."

"How?"

"No clue. Just has sumfink tae do wiv' tha woman she live with. Very odd fellow."

"Right. OK then. Thanks." With the snippet of Lexis living with a peculiar woman, he left the shop.

"All OK?" his companion, his best friend of over twenty years, Luke, asked.

"Just peachy." He put his helmet back on and started up his bike. The beast immediately rumbling to life.

"Get directions?"

"Yeah. Follow me." He slammed his visor shut, and sent his bike careening out the parking lot. The kids all finally moved when the men left and a few of the older ones ran inside to make sure old boy Frank was OK, so it was obvious they thought he would have caused harm to the old boy, not that they would. They weren't like that even though they knew that they were intimidating. Following Frank's directions, the men easily flowed through the town, passing bog-standard freshly-painted houses with rich green, well-kept lawns. Many of which had families laughing and enjoying themselves in their front gardens with their neighbours, but they all stopped and stared as the bikes roared past. Many wondering who the strangers were, but they got their answer when the bikes reached the end of the road and turned left. Many of the adults glanced wearily at each other, wondering who the men were and gossiping between each other before all talking stopped and they ushered their kids in their homes just as a tall, beautiful woman in leather, on foot, walked down the street towards them. They didn't trust her at all and weren't taking the time to get to know her either. She had the aura of a very dangerous person and they didn't want their families and friends near a person like that. Or receive her intense stare that downright scared them, their big burly men included. A tall man accompanied her, equally as menacing and stared ahead with cold blue eyes. Dressed in black leather, he was a formidable sight. The men on their bikes, completely oblivious of the duo who were slowly trailing behind them, reached the end of the buildings and thick-trunked trees lined the road. Thick and full of bright healthy green leaves, trunks a deep tarnished brown. Bushes kept neat and tidy lined the tarmac and stood proud around and in between the trees. Sending their bikes soaring down the road, the shrubbery suddenly stopped and a huge brick wall was ahead. It looked strong and unbreakable. They pulled their bikes to a stop just as they reached the formidable black wrought iron gothic gates that stood gleaming in the dusk. As they pulled up close, they noticed that the gates held not a single fleck of rust. New maybe? It certainly set off the deep redness of the wall bricks. Looking above them, a sign of iron in the skilled workmanship of swirling letter was: You'll Never Walk Alone. Again removing their helmets, along with their heavy rucksacks, they glanced at each other quick then took in the monstrosity ahead.

The long driveway itself was bumpy and cracked in places that really needed to be fixed. Dead-looking trees stuck out of the ground at off angles. Moss and fungus and other sorts hung from the dead branches, the tips of which tickled the weird mist that seem to crawl around the floor, as though a child might run their fingers through grass. Gravestones of all shapes and sizes jutted out of the fog as though playing hide and seek with you. Chunks missing out of them as well as moss growing up the sides of them and across the top, making them eerily tilt to the side. Thick, oozing slime-covered concreted stairs which led the way up onto a porch, which seemed to run around the property too. Thick stone pillars held up the balcony which ran the front of the house and around the side. The bottom floor held windows every now and then, although they were covered in a fine sheen of dirt and cobwebs. The main door stood back into the shadows as though not wanting to be seen. The wood of it was that dark. There weren't even windows along the top of the door either. It was just one solid piece of sturdy wood. Along the second story of the creepy place, wood was chipped off the window ledges, stones were missing chunks too. Black paint peeled off in places along the balcony's railing. A tall turret stood tall and proud near the rear of the house with a black slated roof. Some of these slates were missing. Some had large cracks in, with smaller ones diving off of them, like little veins. Windows ran up the length of the turret. These were also dark and murky. Both men took all this in with sheer exhaustion, weary from their long journey. Flying in from America was a nightmare. Flights had been delayed due to bad weather. Airport staff had complained about the weight of the bikes and how much space they'd take up in the cargo bay. They were on a private jet for fuck's sake. It was enough to give someone a migraine. The only reason they didn't lash out in anger was so Luke could see his baby sister Lexis, who he hadn't seen in just over five years due to missions for the Army Elite group they were in. But he never failed to send her money every month and he'd paid for her to go to university and made sure she had enough money to live comfortably as well as pay for her housing accommodation. Pretty much all of his wages but enough that he had a small amount for himself. But that was his dedication to her after all. He wanted her to get a better education than he himself got, so he didn't complain whatsoever in paying for her.

"Are you sure this is the right house?" he asked Luke, who pulled a sheet of paper out of his pocket and checked the address from a plaque bolted into the wall next to the gates. But all it gave was the house number. Nothing else that would help them.

"Yeah, this is it. It doesn't actually belong to my sister. She's just living here whilst she studies at university for her third year."

"So who actually owns it?"

"A woman she met in the bar about seventeen months ago. Well, according to her letter anyway, Lexis told me that she had met this woman in the bar, just after she was kicked out from the house she was staying at because of her ex-boyfriend. He was sleeping with the landlady. This apparently caused 'distress' in his 'sexual performance' with the new girl, so she kicked her out. That was where this new one picked her up and now lets Lexis live for nothing. Well, as long as she helps with the housework and keeping the garden sorted, then that's it."

"Sounds like a good deal if you ask me. But geez, couldn't the house be a little not so scary? And so, oh I don't know, a more friendly sort of thing?" Luke just laughed at the disgruntled look on his friend's face. As the man didn't show emotion very often, it was nice to realise he was still human after all. But for him to show emotion to viewing the house was crazy, considering the amount of shit they'd seen over the years. But at least he knew his friend was still capable of showing emotion; it had seemed like forever since the last time he had seen anything flicker on his face.

"YOU'RE HERE!" A high-pitched scream rented out through the air. Both men turned to face the house just as the gates swung effortlessly open and the front door bounced from being thrown open wide and they watched with smiles on their faces as Lexis made an appearance. She was about six feet in height. Tiny compared to them both. With thick gorgeous brunette and gold-streaked wavy hair that fell to the middle of her back. Rich hazel eyes sparkled with happiness, and were outlined in black eyeliner. She hadn't really changed, apart from growing more beautiful and filling out in a way that really was purely woman. Luke got off his bike and opened his arms wide.

"Hey, baby sister." He laughed as she literally left the ground and launched herself at him, squealing happily at seeing her brother, his own hazel eyes bright with laughter. They hugged each other tightly for a couple of moments before he finally set her down, which Raven understood as they hadn't seen her in what seemed like forever. Lexis moved away and turned to Raven.

"Hey, trouble." He grinned, his ice blue eyes warming slightly as he looked at the girl who was the sister he never had.

"Hey, Raven." She hugged him tight for a moment and kissed his cheek before stepping back. Her skinny jeans hugged her hips and cupped legs that were muscular. Her black T-shirt cupped her waist and that perfectly. She'd grown up to be an amazingly gorgeous woman, which he'd known because she'd been an astoundingly beautiful child. What he liked was she said fuck all about his scars and didn't even stare at them. In fact, she stared him right in the eye. Which made him love her just that little extra more, if that was possible.

"How was your journey?" she asked.

"Long," they both answered, and it was. It was now five in the afternoon. Growing dark and they had been up for over twenty-four hours. They would start to get really grouchy if they didn't sleep soon. Sure they were used to it with their job, but now they were on vacation, it wasn't worth the hassle.

"Bless you both. And my God, you guys have grown some, haven't you? I feel so small next to you." She laughed. Raven wasn't surprised, he himself stood at six feet eight whilst Luke was at six feet three.

30

"Erm, Lexis, are you sure you live here? You sure this isn't another one of your jokes?" Luke asked.

"No, I honestly do live here. This is how Calista is. How she lives. Not that I mind. She's great." Lexis smiled happily. Both men gulped and looked back at the house.

"You should see your faces. Come on, it isn't that bad. Anyway, let's go in before people start asking questions, I so have not got the time to answer." Lexis laughed, then turned her gaze to Raven, face all serious.

"What happened to your neck?" She had clearly just noticed his scars.

"War." He was uncomfortable talking about them and luckily she didn't press any more.

"That's horrible! Sorry that it happened to you." Raven smiled at her in thanks as she clearly realised just how uncomfortable he was from her asking, and they got off their bikes and pushed them up to the house. Leaving them out the front, they watched as Lexis pulled a small device out of her pocket and clicked a button. The gates swung shut silently, sealing them in. Shaking their heads, the men turned and followed the woman up the stairs and into the house. They were shocked by what they saw. Standing in the doorway, to their right was a staircase of sleek black stained wood, and black wrought iron bars, leading up to a dark upper floor, bars twisting upwards. The entire stairway twisted slightly, like walking around a bend sort of. To their left, a dark panelled door led to what had to be a living area. To the right past the staircase, led another door, presumably leading to a kitchen as well as access to the garden area. All the walls were panelled in a gorgeous stained oak. Old-fashioned oil lamps hung on the walls, all lit too. An ancient fireplace was placed directly opposite the front door. This was too blazing with life. Logs soaking up the flames almost greedily, feeding the blaze at the same time. Two gargoyles sat either side of the hearth, wings spread wide as if to take flight. Legs bent too, as though just about to lift off, aiding the wings. Veins threaded through them, making them appear real. Body bent slightly, face detailed to perfection. Mouths hung open, dagger-like teeth showing in a sickening grin. Eyes beady and look as if they follow your every move. Bat-like ears stuck out either side of the head, open wide, as though listening to everything that was going on around them. Razor-sharp claws clutched the inch-thick slab it sat on. Back knees bent slightly for leverage in take-off. Both these gargoyles, of course, were the exact same. The floor was made up of huge black slate tiles. To your right, behind the door, in which the men had now closed at Lexis's urging, was a massive clear-stained, dark-timbered cabinet. Photos were held in gothic picture frames, each with a lit candle next to it. A couple fake black and red roses lay here and there, and some miniature gargoyles along the bottom.

"Is this Calista?" Raven asked, pointing to a picture of a woman next to Lexis. They couldn't really tell what she looked like; she was facing sideways, hair obscuring her face, but one thing was for sure, she towered over Lexis and it was clearly obvious she was all woman.

"Yes, that's her. Come on. Let's go into the living room. Calista will be here shortly." The men turned to follow her into the living area.

"How long you been here now, then?" Raven asked.

"Nearly two years if I remember correctly, but it does feel as if I've been here forever. I do what I want, when I want. As long as I don't venture into the black garage or Calista's bedroom. This, of course, is fair enough as everywhere else I'm allowed." She smiled impishly at them.

"Seem to really like it here, then." Luke smiled at his baby sister.

"Oh yes, very much so. When Calista had heard what Leanne had done, kicking me out that is, just because Jason wasn't 'performing'," and yes she did do the air quotes as she said this, "right because I was in the building, Calista went round there and I've never seen two people get so scared in my life. Their faces literally lost all colour. White as sheets, almost like she'd threatened them or something and they knew she wasn't bluffing. And they literally pissed themselves. Oh, it was a thing of absolute beauty, it really was. Plus, she's not a small woman either." Grabbing their rucksacks, she put them just inside the living room door out of the way.

"You sure she said it's all right for us to bunk here? It isn't a problem to get a hotel," Luke asked.

"Of course it's all right. Same rules apply to you two though. The places are strictly off limits. And plus, the hotel in the village isn't all that nice. Also, I want you both here with me." They nodded as they knew she was talking about it from experience and suddenly a loud barking noise came from up above which was then followed by the deafening pounding of footsteps. Lexis disappeared out the room and just as abruptly a squeal of laughter erupted from just outside the door. Both men ran to see what it was, and a beast of a dog was happily wagging its tail as fast as it could and slapping its tongue against Lexis's cheek, paws pressed to her shoulders, effectively pinning her to the floor.

"Ahh! Blodox. Get off me, you brute!" she laughed and the dog complied. He got off her and that was when he noticed the men. Tail stopped wagging, ears went flat; he moved in front of Lexis in a protective gesture and bared his teeth, big fuckers that they were, hackles raised too.

"Blodox, down. They're staying with us." And just like that, the dog went back to being all friendly. But still stuck close to Lexis and keeping a suspicious eye on them.

"Guys, meet Calista's mound of fluff and teeth, Blodox. But he's more mine than hers. He's my shadow ninety-nine percent of the time."

"Jesus, what breed of dog is he? He's huge!" Luke stood there with his eyes wide as saucers as he took in the dog's size and bulk.

"He's a Tibetan Mastiff. He was a gift to Calista from her best friend, Draylan. Blodox's also about one hundred and twenty-five pounds of soft," she answered calmly. She strolled back into the living area, the dog right by her side.

"Erm, looks like he's attached himself to you," Luke laughed. Raven grinned too. It wasn't unusual, from when she was a small child, all animals loved Lexis. It was like they knew she wouldn't dare hurt them. She even got upset if she saw a moth and brushed its wings gently, and if it fell off or something, she was upset for the rest of the day. God forbid she actually killed one. Plus, looking at the dog, he reckoned it was only soft around her. Anyone else? Not so much. That was when Raven got a good look at the room. It was magnificent. Through the living room door, you come across a dark, yet surprisingly powerful interior. The entire house was dark, eerie, spooky and completely unnatural. Walls were painted black and dark purple. Beams were blemished dark. Huge floor to ceiling French doors led outside. Couldn't distinguish what was out there though, it was way too dark. The remaining daylight in which the men had arrived in, had now completely departed and they hadn't even realised it. Flanked on either side were windows covered in black netting and held on either side were deep, rich purple curtains that grazed the floor. Large window seats are covered in black upholstery, with soft purple cushions. Large glass and ebony wood cabinets rested against the back wall. Inside were framed photos of a baby Blodox. Photos of Lexis with her friends and even one of her and Calista, even if was only a side view of the woman. Miniature gargoyles and dragons dotted the cabinet. Although on the bottom shelf in its own place, dead centre, with a spotlight was a shark tooth necklace. The teeth on it looked deadly sharp and was it real? No wonder it was in a glass container. Raven turned away from the cabinet and looked elsewhere. A black nine seater couch curled up in the centre of the room, which already occupied Luke and Lexis, whilst Blodox sat at her feet with his head on her leg, eyes closed as she scratched his ear, faced a gorgeous fireplace. Ragged old stone with black streaks running through it. A thick beam ran along the top, buried half an inch or so into the stone. Black candles stood proud atop it. The hearth was roaring with life, letting out a nice cosy feeling. To the right of the couch, hanging on the wall, was a forty-eight inch TV. Complete with a DVD player. In the middle of the floor, sat a coffee table in the shape of a coffin with a glass top and underneath it was decorated with skulls and bones. Small black mats sat on the top for drinks, etc. Old-fashioned gothic candle holders held their places on the walls, each holding a black candle. Above the fireplace, Raven's attention took root. It was a huge oil painting of an absolutely stunning woman, smiling wickedly. She was standing on a dock in a long flowing black dress, which left her shoulders and arms unadorned, with her silky midnight black hair down and flowing about her. Eyes bright like they were glowing. Lips a stark red against the whiteness of her teeth and against the pale alabaster of her skin. Trees blew in the background. A huge full moon hung bright in the inky black sky. As well as thousands of twinkling stars. The moon's rays were bearing down on her, throwing her shadow to the sinister dark wood deck. A creeping fog was starting to twist its way around her, giving off a mysterious yet utterly dangerous aura, was the added feature.

"Gorgeous, isn't she?" Lexis's voice suddenly cut through Raven's thoughts and looked around at her.

"What? Oh yeah, she is," he muttered. He figured it must be someone of great importance to Calista to have that portrait hanging above the fireplace. He made his way to the couch and sat down. The fire's heat almost immediately seeping through to his cold bones. He sighed and relaxed back, sinking into the surprisingly soft cushions.

"So what troubles did you two have getting here?" Lexis asked.

"Well, for a start, the airport staff wouldn't allow our bikes to be placed on the aircraft. Complaining they were too heavy and would restrict people waiting to go on holiday to allow their luggage onto the plane. Then there was the actual fact the plane we had to get was a private jet. With only Raven and I getting on it!" Luke explained. Frustration evident.

"Then we had to wait around for two poxy hours, with nothing to do. People pushing and shoving each other. Kids crying or screaming. Adults shouting at them. Put it this way, sugar, it's enough to give anyone a migraine!" Raven muttered absently.

"Was it really that bad?" she asked, sympathy in her eyes.

"Oh yeah. It was a definite pain in the ass." Lexis laughed at the disgruntled look on her brother's face.

"Oh, before I forget, would you two like anything to eat or drink?"

"Sandwich and a drink would be nice," Raven grumbled from his spot. Lexis glanced his way.

"Let me guess, white bread, with little butter but enough to know it's there. Cheese cut thinly with a small chunk of cucumber on the side?"

"You still remember, huh sugar?" He used the affectionate term for her and her only. She beamed at him and left, knowing already what her brother liked.

"Damn, can you really believe she can live here for nothing, apart from general housekeeping and helping keep the garden under control?" Luke said. Raven turned his head to look at his best friend of twenty years.

"Yeah, it's kind of hard to believe. But then again, Lexis looks happy. The happiest I've seen her in a long time. I know we heard when she was with that slimeball ex of hers that she was never this happy. Must have been good for her to get rid of him." Luke nodded his agreement. They also quickly took off their leathers, revealing their jeans and plain T-shirts underneath. No point in keeping the leathers on when it was warm inside. They folded them up and put them in their bags before heading back to the spots that they had occupied.

"It is a nice place though. I kind of like it," Luke murmured, leaning back into the couch. Sinking into the cushions with a soft sigh himself.

"Same here. But then again, anything can be better than our apartment that is barely functional, and even more so than the base, where we spend ninety-nine percent of our time."

"Geez, put it that way, shows how much of a non-social life we have. Not to mention sexual encounters."

"Yeah, I know. It sucks. But at the end of the day, better out fighting for those we fight for, than be stuck in a desk job and all that crap." Raven laughed.

"What's so funny?" Lexis asked, walking in, carrying two plates piled with food. She handed one to Luke and then the other to Raven. He looked down at his plate. Sure enough his sandwich was how he liked it. As well as that, she had given him a galaxy bar, and a packet of ready salted flavoured crisps. His favourite! He glanced over at his friend and saw he had a sandwich filled with cheese, cucumber, lettuce, tomato. And a not so healthy slab of butter on the bread and two dairy milk eight-chunk chocolate bar and two packets of cheese and onion crisps.

35

"Greedy SOB." Raven grinned at his buddy.

"I don't care. I'm on vacation. I'm allowed to be." They dug in, only then noticing Lexis had disappeared out of the room again. Raven lifted an eyebrow in question and Luke just shrugged. As clueless as he was. Lexis returned then, carrying two glasses on a tray like a waitress would and talking on her mobile too.

"Yeah, sure Calista. Your glass is on the side. It's filled up. Yeah OK. See you soon." She disconnected the call and closed the phone, before putting it in her pocket. Then handed the men their drinks.

"Place them on the mats on the coffee table please. If Calista sees glass ring marks she goes mental." Lexis shuddered as though remembering something. They did as they were told.

"So when will we meet this Calista?" At that, Blodox ran out of the room to where a banging noise came from within the house.

"In about a minute or so. This is a good thing you two finished your sandwiches. Can talk better then."

"Talk better?" Raven asked, placing his empty plate on the floor by his feet.

"Yes, talk better. In other words, not with your mouth full," She replied, curling her feet under her. Luke sarcastically saluted her which made her laugh.

Calista walked through the door of her home and paused in the hallway outside her living area. She could hear Lexis talking to two people. Must be her brother and his friend she had been on about the past couple of days when she found out they were coming to see her. And coming all the way from America too. Quite a journey. She'd look in on them soon, as she really wanted a drink first. Before she did, she pointed to her companion and then up the stairs, knowing he'd get her message which he did and disappeared up the stairs. When he was out of sight, she walked past the doorway of the living area, instinctively keeping to the shadows and strolled into her kitchen she had lovingly put together with the aid of her kind of best friend, Draylan. Oh the laugh that had been. Him trying to do it without instructions and her with them. She so loved proving him wrong. She laughed silently to herself from remembering it. She whistled softly for Blodox and he immediately came running out of the living room to join her. She pushed open her kitchen door, ushered her dog in and followed. Her kitchen was how she wanted it. All done by her own hand apart from obvious appliances, of course. Walking in the door, you come across black marble counters. Black painted cupboards, lots of cabinets, lined the walls. A top-of-the-range cooker stood tall and proud, sleek dark blue. Which was against a sheer backdrop of black and grey tiles. Drawers and lower cupboards were too filled with appliances that were needed in a kitchen, as well as stocked full of food. A top-of-the-range sink, with extendable hose, sat proud. Stark white and silver brightness against the purple walls and dark marble. A black door sat to the right, housing a chest freezer, upright freezer and an upright fridge. And a state-of-the-art washing and tumble dryer. Just past them sat another door which led to a huge garden, which was bricked off around two acres. The main kitchen area and pantry were tiled flooring, black slate. Calista loved every bit of it. And sure enough, just as Lexis had said, her glass was on the counter, on a piece of kitchen roll, filled nearly to the top. Calista picked it up and downed it in one huge gulp. Placing the glass into the sink, she rinsed it out and placed it on the draining board. Once that was done, she reached into a massive box that rested on the side, opened it and pulled out a freshly cooked stack of ribs. She handed it to Blodox who immediately ran into the main hallway, up the stairs and into his big bed with it. Out the way for a good few hours or so to devour his treat. Shaking her head at the loveable animal, she moved towards the living area, made herself appear invisible, and then looked in on her guests. One man, whom Lexis had called Luke, was, by the looks of him, around six feet and three, maybe four. Judging by the length of his legs. He had shocking hazel eyes that looked to sparkle with merriment. The same as his sister's did. He had brown hair cut short, military style obviously. She could tell by the scars and such on his arms and hands that he wasn't scared to brawl when he needed to. Handy when staying at her place she supposed. He also smelt the smell of a human. This, to Calista, was like a mild strawberry scent. Not overpowering but enough to know it was there. She turned to look at the other man, the one Lexis called Raven. So this was the infamous Raven Calhoun, was it? He certainly piped Calista's interest. This was unusual to say the least. He was human! Same smell as Luke, although he smelt of something different; dangerous and very mysterious. He sat comfortably on her couch, but also with an edginess that would make him leap into action in a matter of seconds. Again, judging by the length of his legs, which she noticed were hugged by black jeans, he had to stand at about six feet eight. His top half was covered in a nice long-sleeved black shirt, which was moulded to him like a glove. A low collar left a tantalizing view of healthy peachy pink flesh, and then she saw it. Peeking out of his top, she saw ragged scars marring the side of his throat as though something with a nasty jagged blade had taken a swipe at him. He had ice-blue eyes with a black outline leaking into the colour that lay fringed by thick black lashes, along with military short black hair. A man of secrets he was. Scars covered his hands. She did wonder as to what other scars he had hidden under his clothes. Knowing full well that everything on her was invisible to the human eyes, she pulled her mobile out of her pocket and unlocked the screen. She used to have one that was a standard flip, but Lexis had told her it was out-dated and old school and had bought her this new one. Good thing she knew how to use it as easily within minutes. She texted Lexis:

I see you, but you can't see me! Invisibleness works wonders, don't you think?

Just to let Lexis know she was actually here and watching, she added a smiley face on the end. Knowing full well the kid would get it.

Raven looked up as Lexis's phone started going off. She laughed at what it said, and put it away.

"What's so funny?" Luke asked his sister, setting his drink back on the table.

"Calista just texted saying she can see us, but we can't see her." The girl laughed again. Raven looked out of the windows but was only greeted by stark blackness and his reflection staring back at him in the glass. No hope whatsoever of catching a glimpse of anyone outside.

"So when are we going to meet this woman who took you in brat?" Raven smiled at Lexis as she giggled. Knowing full well why he called her brat. That was when he caught something out of the corner of his eye, and turned his full attention to what it was and for the life of him actually forgot to breathe. Standing in the doorway was an absolutely gorgeous woman. She had vivid cobalt-blue eyes fringed by black lashes and outlined in black eyeliner with dark purple eyeshadow. She had hair that fanned around her face and went to the middle of her back, falling in lush black waves with the underside a vivid blue. She currently wore a black corset with a halter type strap to keep it in place, topped off with a pair of skin-tight leather trousers. Her feet lay encased in black chained calf length New Rocks that added another inch to her height. Raven guessed she had to stand at least six feet four in bare feet. Her hands lay relaxed at her sides, pointed nails painted black. Although the thing he noticed was she had scars on her arms and hands, so she was battle-worn too? Nice. Good to know.

"Calista!" Lexis said, finally catching sight of the woman at the door.

Ah, so this was the infamous Calista, Raven thought to himself, aiming a quick glance at the painting then back at the woman. She was hell of a lot more beautiful in person than in that painting. The painter just hadn't done her justice, although it was very close. Lexis flung herself at the woman, wrapped her arms around her neck and hugged her for dear life. Calista hugged the girl back, well, holding her up that was, and all the while her eyes darting back and forth between himself and Luke, not so much as a hint of emotion played across her features. Like she didn't know how to take them so kept her expression neutral, which he could understand. Lexis finally crawled off the woman and looked at the men. Calista literally towered over Lexis's six foot frame, making the girl appear small; even though she was considered tall for a woman. Raven looked at her and noticed her arms were now crossed under her full breasts, pushing them up a little bit more.

"And these two are who?" Her voice carried across the silent room. It was one that could compel anyone if she so much as tried, or so Raven thought anyway.

"Calista, this is my brother Luke and his best friend Raven. Guys, this is Calista." Lexis introduced them. She moved away from the woman.

"Be right back, I'm going to get a drink. You guys want anything?" Lexis started out of the room.

"Nah, I'm good," both men said at the same time.

"I'll wait. And before I forget, there is a surprise upstairs for you." Calista said, making her way to the spot which Lexis had occupied, directly opposite the men.

"A surprise?" The girl squealed happily and shot out of the room like the hounds of hell were after her.

"Can I ask something?" Raven said, drawing Calista's gaze.

"What do you want to know?"

"What made you take Lexis in? Not that me and Luke aren't grateful, but we want to know why. Lexis never said in her letters to us." He held her gaze.

"Because I was in the pub waiting for an informant where she was working, she was waitressing and looked really sad. After we got talking a bit, I decided to offer her my place to live."

"And might we ask what you did to her ex and the woman he was sleeping with? Lexis said you went with her to get her remaining things and that you scared them," Luke said, a grin tugging at his lips.

"And what did she tell you?" Calista turned her gaze to Luke's, never as so much as blinking. But Raven noticed that he shrank back a little from the intenseness of that stare. Which wasn't like him at all to back down, but he could see why. She was actually quite intimidating.

"Just that you turned up, looked at them and they turned deathly pale and she said you must have said something to them because they pissed themselves but she couldn't hear as she wasn't near you at the time," he answered honestly.

"Then it is a good thing she didn't hear me. She truly would have blanched at the images which the words I said would conjure up in her imagination. She hasn't got the stomach for it."

"Well, we know that. She never has had the stomach for nasty things," Raven muttered. Calista snapped her gaze to his, like fire ice they were. Beautiful colour, but cold all the same.

"And so I pray tell you two are the ones with the stomachs then, are you?"

"Yeah. We've had extreme training and with the purpose of being able to stomach near enough anything," Raven answered.

"Yes, if you say so. So you mean to tell me you can handle watching children being mauled apart by a pride of starving lions, seen as nothing more than a meal? Or a village ransacked by a herd of elephants that are in a frenzy? Where anything in the way is stomped on and not a care in the world for it? And there is not a thing you can do about it? Or serial killers slashing through victims with no emotion and you aren't allowed to interfere because it isn't in your jurisdiction? Or watching men rape innocent children and beating up defenceless women and you can't do anything about it because again, you have to wait for the cops to turn up?" she said, not once raising her voice, but her tone was enough to know she'd seen it first-hand. Their faces blanched at that. The colour completely draining away. Raven realised then that they weren't talking to an ordinary civ. Military perhaps? If so, what part was she in? Elite like them? Marine? Or perhaps one of those special ops that no one knew about? SAS? That was when an excited scream erupted through the house.

"What the hell was that?" Raven asked, sitting up to attention.

"That was Lexis. She must have found her surprise." Calista said. No emotion whatsoever evident in her voice, or even in her features. It was as though she was made of stone, she was that unemotional.

"That was my baby sister?" Luke said, getting ready to get off the couch and to go see what had caused his sister to scream.

"Yes it was. And as I said before it must be because she found her surprise." At that, Lexis walked in. Followed by a man who had to stand at around six feet three. He had black hair, blue eyes that screamed out that bedroom look women apparently liked. Broad chest, wide shoulders, thickly-muscled arms, legs and thighs. Flat stomach. Drifting his eyes over the guy, Raven noticed he was holding Lexis's hand. His sun-stained skin enveloped hers. But Raven noticed he held her hand as though folding a precious rare and delicate flower. Well, in truth, that was how he saw Lexis. She was like his sister, the one he never had. Whereas he saw her as rare, beautiful, utterly enchanting, all bundled up into one. That was when Luke must have noticed the guy holding his baby sister's hand too. He jumped up off the couch, glared at the guy and demanded in an utterly calm voice, which meant he was truly angry, "What is the meaning of this? You just got out of a relationship!"

"Luke, it was nearly two years ago I got out of that relationship. I've moved on. He's moved on. Big deal. Is it a crime to move on with my life? Heck, I'm so god damn happy right now, don't you bloody think of ruining it for me! It's not like I'm a fucking virgin for God's sake!" Lexis screamed back, her voice surprisingly loud and powerful for such a little thing. The man moved then. His arm swept over Lexis's shoulder and pulled her into his embrace. Her face buried against his chest. And still the guy's blue eyes didn't so much as blink. His face an unreadable mask. Body taut, as though he would fight for Lexis. Which Raven thought was rather sweet in a weird kind of way. Not that he wouldn't fight for Lexis either. He loved the woman.

"Well obviously not when you were with that slime bag! I'm just looking out for you, sis." And that was when he moved to rip his sister out the arms of her new boyfriend, or whoever the hell he was. Raven jumped to his feet to grab hold of his friend when before he had even realised what was happening, Calista had Luke pinned to the floor and Lexis was standing right where she was, although now she was facing forward instead of her back to them.

"Get the hell off of me!" Luke grumbled from the floor. Trying to dislodge Calista from sitting on his chest, but he wasn't able to budge her even a tiny bit! Just how strong was she that she could hold him as though a small child and not even look like she was struggling?

"I think not. Not until you've calmed down. And just for your information, don't try and buck me off, it won't work. I'm heck of a lot stronger than you." She stared down at him, almost like she was daring him to try it.

"Calista, let him up please," Lexis whispered. And sure enough, the woman got off him in one graceful move, much like a ballerina but stayed between the siblings. Which Raven admitted to himself was a damn shame, he'd had such a lovely view down her top. He was the first to admit it, he was all man and probably openly stared but fuck it, it'd been so long since he'd looked at a woman, let alone thought of even touching one, it was a miracle he wasn't drooling.

"Don't even think about it, Luke. As much as I've grown fond of Lexis these past months, I will not and I repeat, not, hesitate to kill you."

"Is she fucking serious? "Luke demanded to his sister.

"Yes she is. Calista doesn't lie or bullshit," a very masculine voice said from behind them all. Everyone turned at that remark, all apart from Calista who stood glaring at Luke still. The man standing there had to stand at least six feet six. He stared at them all from a pair of glacier ice-blue eyes. He had shoulder length hair that was as black as sin. Built like a brick shithouse too. What with a wide chest, broad shoulders and muscles clung to his arms, legs and thighs like a second skin. He was dressed in black biker jeans, a black shirt, with a thick leather jacket hung from his shoulders to his waist and his feet lay covered in steel toe-cap boots. If Raven didn't know any better, he'd have thought he was a biker!

"Draylan!" Lexis cried, and the man actually smiled at her. He pulled her to him and gave her a huge hug.

"How's my favourite little human?" Raven and Luke quickly looked at each other as to wonder why he called her little human.

"I'm absolutely fine. Oh, this is my brother by the way. Luke, and that's his best friend Raven." Draylan looked over at them and nodded, and they returned the nod.

"What are you doing here Draylan? You're supposed to be in Mystic Being," Calista interrupted.

"I know I'm meant to be, but I came here to get you and Tairen."

"What? Why? I've just got here," Tairen said, talking for the first time. His voice deep and husky. At least they now knew his name as well.

"I know that. Think I'd let you run around without me knowing it?"

"Very funny, uncle. Now why?" Tairen let go of Lexis's hand and moved to sit on the couch. Luke moved over closer to Raven, who just sat back down where he was before.

"There has been some trouble and some children have gone missing. So we need Calista to go and find them. And you're needed to do some work from their houses for security detail as they don't want it happening again. They specifically asked for you to work on it," he answered.

"Which kids?" Calista asked, pushing Lexis in front of her so the girl would sit down. Draylan too sat before answering.

"Henry and Melissa's. Christie and Mark. Chrysanthea and Nathan. Nichola and Niall."

"Oh no. All those kids are lovely!" Lexis cried.

"How do you know?" Luke asked.

"Because I'd visited them not so long ago with Calista for a few weeks. They truly are adorable," she murmured in reply.

"How long ago did they go missing?" Calista asked, pulling a pen and paper out of a drawer under her coffee table and handing it to Tairen, who wrote down the children's names and other bits of information that would be of help to Calista.

"Four days ago," Draylan answered. Calista's eyes snapped to his, even though no emotion showed. Raven thought it was an amazing feat that she showed absolutely nothing at all. Even in her eyes, which by only years of practice could you conceal emotion as simply and as quickly as she did. Although what surprised him most was that she appeared no older than twenty-four-ish.

"Remember, it takes me a full day to get here from Mystic Being," Draylan reminded her.

"Yes, I do know that." She turned to face Lexis, who was leaning into Tairen's side and watching what he wrote down.

"Lexis?"

"Yes?" She turned her huge hazels to Calista's cold ones.

"Are you back at university this week or next?"

"No. As we're at the start of July, I go back on the fourth September, why?"

"We're leaving tomorrow. Draylan, Tairen and I. Do you want to come with us?"

"What about Raven and Luke? I can't leave them behind, they did just get here."

"Talk to them about Mystic Being. Tairen will stay here with you to help answer their questions. Tonight though, they will have to share the second bedroom."

"OK, I will do. And why share?"

43

"Because Draylan is in the blue room. Obviously, I will be in my room and Tairen is in with you. And no arguments on the sleeping arrangements." Her sharp gaze went to Luke when she said that, then she turned her attention back to Lexis.

"OK, no problem. What time do we leave tomorrow?"

"You'll be up, washed, dressed and ready to leave by eight a.m. sharp. If I was you, I'd pack tonight."

"OK. Done deal. I'll pack a week's worth of clothes. I don't need to take many as I've loads at the second home. After that, I have to come back here to study and all that crap for university," Lexis said, sitting up straighter on the couch instead of slouching.

"Erm, not to be rude and butt in, but what exactly is it we need to know about Mystic Being?" Raven asked, turning his full attention to Calista.

"That is for Lexis to decide if she wishes to tell you. But know this; it is because she really does trust you. I've trusted her with this secret and I expect you to do the same, for her sake and everyone else's lives it involves. But know this, if you tell anyone, I will hunt you down. There is nowhere on this planet you can hide from me. And that is a fact, not something to say because of my pride," Calista answered.

"That skilled are you?" Luke just had to get that in.

"I know I am. I've had a lot of time on my hands to perfect my skills. Once Lexis explains everything, you will realise I'm not the woman you would want as an enemy." With that, she rose off the couch and walked out of the room. Vanishing from sight as silently as she'd appeared.

"Look, I'm not going to be as blunt as Calista, quite frankly that is just how she is. Calista is only looking out for everyone at Mystic Being. She is a very dangerous woman when needed to be. A ruthless killing machine. No emotions, like a robot. But at the moment, well since she has known Lexis, we've actually seen her smile and laugh so much more than what she usually does. Whereas before, you'd be lucky to even get a response out of her half the time. But anyway, listen to what Lexis and Tairen have to say and not what you want to hear. It'll only be easier," Draylan announced.

"Are you sure?" Raven asked, having no idea what this whole thing was about.

"Yes, I'm sure. Trust me; it'll be a lot better once you understand." With that, Draylan too left the room. Disappearing into the shadows that tried to eat into the living room and consume it. Raven and Luke then turned their attention to Lexis and Tairen.

"Lexis, I'm going to be blunt, what is Mystic Being? And what did Calista mean by once you explain, everything will be easier, and that we will understand?" Raven asked, drawing her attention.

"No butting in whilst I explain, no matter how crazy I sound, OK?"

"OK." Luke said. Raven nodded his agreement.

"OK, well everyone has heard of vampires, werewolves, witches, demons, etc. And that is basically what Mystic Being is. It's a place for mythological beings to go. A haven for them. Very few humans have stepped foot there. It is exceedingly rare. Many beings there have never left in their entire life. It is just the same there like it is here; good, the bad and the damn right ugly. This in general means there are the good areas, the bad ones. But for the ugly, in Mystic Being that is a place where no one ever steps foot."

"Why is that?" Luke asked kind of interested now, although Raven was truly fascinated. He had a secret fascination with things that were mythological and all that. More unusual, more he liked it.

"Because Wendigo's live there," Tairen said.

"What the hell is a Wendigo?" Raven looked perplexed, he'd never heard of one before.

"A Wendigo is a mythological creature appearing in the mythology of the Algonquian people. But of course, they are not mythological. They are real. They are also a cannibalistic spirit into which humans could transform. Or which could possess humans. The simplest factor of describing a Wendigo is that they are malevolent, cannibalistic, supernatural beings. They were also said to be giants. Much taller than that of humans, or so it is said. There is a legend going around saying that when they eat someone, they grow larger, in proportion to the meal it has just eaten. So that it can't ever be full," Tairen replied.

"So basically, drawing it into one big fucking circle, you're telling us they are cannibals." Luke announced, cracking his fingers.

"That I am. Hence, why they are in an area that no one goes. Well, only one person has gone through their land and come out alive."

"And who is that?" Raven asked. Thoroughly interested that someone could walk through where these 'monsters' were and live to tell the tale. He also would have loved to know how they did it.

"Well, the only known person is Calista. She went in after a couple came up to her to get their little girl back. Calista managed to, but the girl was sadly dead, although no one knows how she died because it wasn't from Wendigos. We suspect it was from magic of some sort, or maybe even an accelerated heart rate which caused her brain to overdo it and shut down. Calista though, was unmarked but was splattered in black blood. Like someone had lobbed loads over her. But the thing was, it didn't seem to faze her, not a single bit," he replied.

"Covered in blood. Whose blood?"

"Wendigos." Lexis answered. Luke looked at her then.

"You mean to tell me you live with a woman who came out of God knows where, covered in blood, which apparently belonged to 'Wendigos'. The cannibalistic myths? Excuse me for saying this but it sounds damn stupid if you ask me."

"Yeah well, would you like proof?" Lexis snapped.

"And how exactly will you get proof?" Luke snapped right back. The siblings got in each other's faces then. Both had hands clenched at their sides. Lexis not backing down at all against her older and taller brother, whereas before she wouldn't have so much as raised her voice at him. Tairen and Raven stepped in. Raven pulled Luke back, whilst Tairen pulled Lexis back. Raven, of course, was proud of her; she had finally found her claws, although he didn't admit that to his best friend. Not with the temper he was in at the moment.

"Calm down, Luke," Raven murmured in his ear.

"Well, how will you get proof vampires and all that actually exist?" Luke snapped, completely ignoring Raven. Lexis leaned back into the safety of Tairen's arms.

"Do you really want to find out? You'll probably lose your temper again," she murmured.

"Yes I want to find out so tell me!" Luke demanded.

"Very well. The reason I know they all exist and what we've just told you is factual is because for one, Calista is one of them, although she's unique unto herself. But Draylan and Tairen are," she answered, looking her brother straight in the eye when she said it. So it was obvious she was telling the truth.

"Do fucking what?" Luke shrugged his best friend off.

"It's true Luke. Deal with it. I love Tairen and he loves me. Don't spoil this for me," she whispered, her hair falling over her face as she looked down at the floor. Tears falling elegantly to splash against the wood flooring.

"Lexis, go on to bed sweetheart. I'll have a word with Raven and Luke. If you can summon Draylan down for me, I'd appreciate it please," Tairen said, rubbing his hand up and down her back.

"OK, but please be gentle. They're not used to the idea of it. They might not be able to wrap their minds around it as quickly and as simply as what I did. And I'll send Draylan down, even if he will grunt at me for disturbing him." She grinned at that last part and tiptoed up for a kiss from Tairen. Who quite happily obliged her, even though Luke's growl didn't faze the man/vampire. Raven watched as Lexis looked at her brother actually quite sadly and him with a small smile, before she turned on her heel and disappeared into the awaiting shadows.

"Sit down. I'm going to be bluntly honest on this one and so will Draylan once he gets here," Tairen said, sitting down on the couch himself. Raven and Luke sat back down too.

"So what did Calista do to these Wendigos?" Raven asked, motioning to his friend to keep it quiet.

"When she was asked by Draylan, all she did was hand him a sword that had been strapped to her back. It was stained black by the Wendigo's blood. No one knew how many she had murdered or how many were left. But they weren't happy. All we know is that one ran out of the woods straight at Calista. She passed the deceased girl over to Draylan, yanked his sword off of his belt and slaughtered this Wendigo like no tomorrow. I'll be honest with you men; I would rather have Calista on my side than be on her enemy's side. She is a brutal killing machine. All the time she gets all her missions complete without any problems," Tairen said, resting his big hands on his thighs whilst leaning back on the couch.

"What have you told them?" Draylan said, walking into the room. His upper body was bare, thick corded muscle clung to him like a second skin. The men could really see his strength and such now, not that he was small to begin with anyway.

"Ah, just explaining to them about the Wendigos and what Calista did. And what she's like. The brutal killing machine," he answered. Draylan took a seat next to Tairen.

"And if that isn't the fact. Anyway, what Tairen just said is true, if Calista classes you as a friend, she guards you with her very life. It isn't as bad as what it sounds like, trust me. We've been friends a long time so I should know. Now any questions you want us to answer?"

"How vicious can the Wendigos get?" Raven wanted to know.

"I'll be honest. They're one of the nastiest we have at Mystic Being. They won't hesitate to throw you to the ground and rip into your flesh," Tairen answered.

"And then?" Raven seriously wanted to know, better to know and steer clear of in his opinion.

"Well, they'll rip off your arms and legs whilst you're still conscious and not hesitate to gnaw on it right in front of you. They are a vicious breed and can only be stopped by either decapitation, or a kill shot that renders them in half."

"So it is true about them being cannibals, then?" Raven said.

"Yes, it is true. And I would avoid them at all costs if I were you. You yourself can be changed into one by something as simple as a scratch that draws enough blood, and a bite which transfers their saliva into your system."

"Is it a gruelling process?"

"Yes, it is said to have untold pain that erupts from the inside of your stomach and spreads like wild fire. Your skin feels like it is peeling off, slow inch by slow inch. Your throat becomes inflamed too, so you can't talk or scream."

"And you mean to tell me, you take my little sister to this place? Where fucking cannibals live?" Luke fumed. He was so angry, he visibly shook.

"Yes. And for your information, she is always entirely safe," Draylan said.

"And how the hell am I meant to know that?"

"Because when she is not in our company, she is with an armed guard. We have soldiers there trained by none other than Calista herself in order to protect Lexis no matter what the cost is. No matter what Calista says, she does care for Lexis. You can tell that by the way she acts with the girl." Draylan looked at them and waited for their reaction.

"So let us get this straight, Calista is fond of Lexis. Trained a series of soldiers in order to protect her when she's at Mystic Being. She's safe one hundred percent and you two are vampires?" Raven enquired.

"Yes," Tairen said for the first time since his uncle had walked into the room.

"But how? I mean sure, they must exist, or existed a long time ago for someone to start saying there was something human looking with fangs wandering around and that at night, for it to become world renowned and such. How is it that vampires actually began?"

"I'm not totally sure to be quite honest. Calista knows it more than me. As she knows everyone's legend and how they 'began', etc."

"OK. Fair enough," Raven said.

"Right, any more questions?" Draylan asked. Raven and Luke shook their heads no.

"OK then. Let's head upstairs. It's easier for all of us to go bed now. And tomorrow, I'm pretty sure you'll have more questions to ask us. But until then, sleep."

"Sounds like a good idea," Raven acknowledged and they followed Draylan and Tairen out of the living area and up the stairs. Once they had reached the upper landing, Raven turned back and noticed the candles and such were still lit.

"Erm, Draylan, who will turn the lights out?" Draylan walked over to him and snapped his fingers and the lights immediately went out.

"Like that." Grinning at the look of wonder that was plastered on Raven's face, he turned back and led the way down the hallway slightly until he approached a door. Tairen pushed it open and motioned for the guys to go inside.

"This is your room. Mine and Lexis's is the next one down on this side. Draylan is in between but on the other side. Calista's is obviously the bedroom furthest down the hallway. The door right at the bottom. Can't miss it. Now we'll see you in the morning. We're off to bed. Good night." And with that, he ushered the men inside and closed the door. Raven watched as the door shut and turned as he heard Luke whistle low. He then noticed the room itself. The bed was the main masterpiece. Rich mahogany wood made up the queen-sized frame. It soared up to the ceiling and had blood-red drapes dangling from it; held into place in four corners from upside down hands. Two pillows graced either side of the bed leaning against a robust headboard. Covered in blood-red cases. Duvet was covered in a blood-red cover. Mattress looked full and lusciously comfortable. Looking away from that bed, Raven noticed the walls were mahogany panels. Wrought iron candle holders held their place, each holding black candles. The ceiling was thin panels of bronze. Shimmering slightly from the candles that glowed softly.

The bed was placed underneath a wall wardrobe. Varnished clear oak. The bedroom was masculine and warm. For some untold reason, Raven was greatly impressed. Exactly how he liked rooms. Dark colours with rich woods. He wandered into the bedroom more and sunk down onto the bed, dipping into the softness. He noticed a gloomy aged stone fireplace sat next to the door. Opposite the bed and it was absolutely stunning. He turned his head as he heard a door open and noticed Luke had found an en suite, done in pale blues and gold's. It was a stark contrast to the bedroom. But it was very nice. They quickly took off of their boots and such. Before Raven considered getting into bed properly, he put the lights out. The room fell into absolute darkness.

"Geez, it's been a long time since we fell asleep in a room this dark," Luke murmured. And they quickly scrambled into the bed, sinking into the plush softness.

"True that. It makes a nice change. Anyway, best get some sleep, we've had a long and stressful day."

"For sure. Night man."

"Night." And with that, the men fell into sleep almost immediately thanks to years of army training.

Further down the hallway, in the secluded confines of her bedroom, Calista stood at her bedroom window, overlooking the rolling backyard. She listened intently for sounds around her home. Everyone was in their beds, all on the verge or sound asleep. As should she, but for some untold reason, she just couldn't sleep. Not that it wasn't new to her. She'd sleep when she got back home to Mystic Being. Sure, she had this place in Scotland, but it wasn't home. At Mystic Being, she didn't have to hide who and what she was. Here she did. She sighed and moved to her bed. She flicked her hand and a candle flared to life. She leant over to her bedside table and pulled a thin book and pencil towards her. She soon lost herself into the confines of her drawings. She drew graveyards with spindly trees dotted here and there. Stuff like that. Untold areas from home. As well as some of the mythological beings there. Before she knew it, three or so hours had passed, and a knock at her door brought her head up, a quick glance at the clock and she saw it was now four a.m! She willed her door open and Lexis stood there in her pyjamas, hands anxiously twisting and turning in front of her.

"What is it, Lexis?" She closed the book and placed it and the pencil on the bedside table.

"I can't sleep. For some reason, every time I close my eyes, I see blood," she whispered, looking very much like a terrified child.

"Come here." Calista patted the bed next to her and Lexis didn't hesitate. She bounded across the room quickly and sat next to her.

"Can you explain to me what it is?"

"Did you and Tairen have a talk about you turning?"

"Yes. But he said for when I am ready. Not for when he wants. Why?"

"That is why you are dreaming of blood. This is going to sound weird, but it's your brain telling you that it is ready for your turn. And that it won't cut out or anything. You'll still be Lexis. Brainy extraordinaire and super softy. Now, all we have to do is wait for your heart to agree that you want to change."

"So all the blood dreaming is because my brain knows I'll change over eventually. And that I just have to wait for my heart to get into the change?" It sounded complicated and surely it was meant to be the other way around, but that was for fairy tales, not real life.

"Exactly that."

"OK. That definitely puts my mind at rest as to the whole why of it."

"Good. Now if I were you, I'd head back to bed. Up again in two hours to leave at eight."

"OK, I will. Thank you, Calista." She hugged her.

"Welcome. Now, good night."

"Good night." And with that Lexis left, closing the door quietly behind her. Calista shook her head at how fast she left and looked outside. The sky was slowly losing the pitch blackness as a new day began. She snuggled down into her duvet and watched the sky lighten. Before she knew it, her eyelids began to become heavy weights. The next thing the blackness of sleep pulled at her, drawing her in swiftly and relentlessly quick. But it wasn't as if she fought it; not in the slightest. She fell sound asleep with the rays of dawn lashing through her window, the warm light caressing her through the duvet.

Chapter Two

Calista awoke bright eyed and immediately aware of her surroundings considering she'd only had two hours sleep. She pushed her duvet aside and quickly made a beeline for her bathroom. Her bladder was screaming at her to empty. She swiftly used the facilities, washed her hands, and brushed her teeth. And looked at the state of the person staring back at her in the mirror. A quick pull of a brush through her hair and it was goodbye messy bed hair and hello glossy black locks that she tucked behind her ears. She snapped her fingers and watched as make-up appeared on her face. Black eyeliner around the edges and dark blue eyeshadow topped it all off. Dark blue and black lipstick adorned her lips. She then watched as her hair braided itself — two single braids down the side of her head, keeping it out of her face, but swept back with the rest to hang in a high ponytail. Simple and practical. She wasn't all for the fancy hairstyles and shit. She walked back into her bedroom and rummaged through her wardrobe. She pulled out black leather trousers and a black plain tank top. Along with a black lace bra and lace panties. She changed out of her pyjama shorts and top and put on the clean clothes, which clung to her like a second skin. And then looked around for a pair of socks as Lexis was forever sneaking a pair to wear. She found some in the back of her drawer and pulled them on too. Then she pulled on her New Rocks with the big buckles and chains and it also had a slight heel. Ridiculously comfortable that they were and damn right sexy. She swiftly packed a bag of her essentials and headed out of her bedroom. Candles and such all disappeared so as not to cause a fire whilst she was away. Only the bare essentials remained. Like the bed with the covers and pillows stripped bare and placed neatly on bare mattress. Quite efficient if she did say so herself. She took one last look at her bedroom to make sure everything was as it was meant to be and then shut the door behind her. Not looking back. She walked down the hallway and stopped outside Tairen and Lexis's bedroom door. She knocked quietly and a scant moment later it opened, revealing Lexis all sleepy eyed and as she looked past her slightly into the dark mahogany, black and red bedroom, noticed Tairen all sleepy eyed too sitting up slightly in the bed.

"Come on. Up, we're leaving in one hour. Pack everything you need. Leave nothing behind. Everything but the bare essentials I want you to take downstairs and I'll get rid of them." She didn't wait for a reply; she just turned and walked down the hall a little bit and not bothering to knock she just walked straight in, shutting the door behind her. Draylan was flat out in the middle of his bed, on his stomach, head slightly hidden under a pillow and duvet casually wrapped around his hips. She placed her bag down near the door and walked over to the bed. She leaned over him and then breathed slightly into his ear and his eyes shot open. He grabbed her then pinned her to the bed underneath him, knife at her throat, all within at least five seconds flat. It really didn't bother her that he was naked either, she'd seen him naked many times before and doubted it would be the last.

"Very good. Slowly getting there," she smirked as his eyes focused more.

"For fuck's sake, Calista! I could have fucking hurt you! You know not to sneak up on me when I'm asleep!" He moved off her, threw the knife to the other side of the bed and walked bare arse naked to a chest of drawers. She laughed as he pulled on some boxers. He was really unselfconscious about his nakedness, but for her 'modesty' he covered up.

"And where would the fun be in that? You'll get sloppy if I don't do something to train those instincts of yours. Can't forget how many times it has saved your life thanks to my 'sneaking up on you'."

"Yeah, whatever." He then pulled on jeans and a muscle shirt. Followed by socks and combats. Calista climbed off the bed and walked over to the door.

"We leave in one hour. So pack what you brought with you amongst the few remaining bits that were already here. Candles, etc., bring downstairs for me to get rid of," she said and disappeared out of the door.

"You're such an arsehole," he called out.

"Thank you." She peaked back in and smirked. Then disappeared again. She then moved to Luke and Raven's door and walked in. Both men were instantly awake, sat up in bed and had their guns pointed at her chest.

"Going to shoot?" She smirked at them.

"Shit." Both men cursed and lowered their weapons.

"Time for you to get up for we leave in exactly one hour and as I've said to everyone else, pack what you brought and the candles, etc., bring downstairs with you." She then left as quickly as she could. She refused to let seeing Raven's chest in that tight T-shirt affect her. Why the fuck it did, she didn't bloody know. And headed downstairs, but not before giving

Blodox an affectionate scratch behind his ear as he looked at her all sleepy eyed from his bed at the top of the stairs. She was in the kitchen when Lexis and Tairen drifted in about twenty minutes later, arms full.

"We first ones down?" Tairen asked, placing the candles he had brought down onto the counter.

"Yes you are." She looked up from the food she was cooking and pushed the candles together more and swept them to the side. She then dished the food up, pushing the two plates of a full English breakfast towards the couple.

"Yum! Thanks Calista." Lexis took the plate and moved to the table, then absently dug in with relish, whereas Tairen took his time. She was cooking again when Draylan, Raven and Luke strolled in two minutes later. Arms laden with candles and other things that they had removed from their rooms as she had told them to.

"Where do you want these?" Draylan asked, and she absently pointed to where the others were sitting on the counter. They placed them down where they were instructed and practically drooled at the rich aroma of grub that was sizzling in the frying pans. Three plates waiting on the side, along with a knife and fork. Calista flipped some bacon bits around in the pan with a flick of her wrist. She then dished the food out; and the men helped themselves after she said they could have it. Three moans soon erupted from the men's throats as the food assaulted their taste buds and slid down to empty stomachs. Calista shook her head at them and cleaned up the cooking materials she had used.

"Aren't you going to make yourself something?" Raven's voice echoed through the kitchen.

"No. I don't eat what you do," she replied, and disappeared into the room off to the side of the kitchen.

"What does she eat?" Raven looked at Lexis.

"She drinks blood, Raven. She doesn't eat. Doesn't consume food at all. The only time she does is when we're out in public here so it doesn't appear weird when we're in a restaurant and I'm the only one eating," she replied, and downed a good half of her fresh orange juice that Calista had prepared for her.

"But doesn't that leave a horrible taste in your mouth?" Luke wondered.

"No. It doesn't. After a while of having nothing but that to live on, you soon get used to the coppery taste. Not all blood tastes coppery though," Calista said, coming back into the kitchen.

"What do you mean?" Raven asked as Draylan gathered their empty plates and cutlery together and took them to the sink to wash them but Calista waved him away to do it herself.

"From what I mean, say I was to drink your blood, it'd have a mild strawberry smell to it, but it's very bland. Vampire's blood is rich, full of substance; no smell to it. Dragon's blood is raw, powerful and exotic — smells of rich magic. And others all have their own magic and such to it." She replied, scrubbing the plates clean.

"Oh right," Raven murmured. Calista looked over at him, and noticed the puzzled look in his eyes.

"You did ask," she nonchalantly replied, just as Lexis got up and quickly left the room, her phone ringing in her hand.

"True. So I have to ask, how long was it for Lexis to get used to the idea of everything that you can do. Like the whole blood drinking, and magic?" Luke asked, looking at Calista as she finished the last of the dishes and emptied the sink of the dirty water.

"It was roughly a week or so before she managed to comprehend that I did actually drink blood. The magic, she thought it was some trick that I did but when I explained it all to her, she took it all in good faith. Although, all in all before it finally did manage to sink in properly, had to have been about six weeks. The thing that amazed me the most, was she was like, 'Oh, where can I learn to do something like that?' I remember her eyes sparkling with humour when she asked, but at the same time, she was deadly serious."

"She can learn to do what you did last night?" Raven was utterly amazed!

"Yes. But as she knows, she won't be able to do it unless she changes over." She watched Raven and Luke's reaction for this.

"Change over?"

"You know exactly what I mean by changeover. She knows the consequences of it also."

"You mean in order to do what you do she has to become a vampire? And what consequences?" Raven asked, turning more in his chair to face Calista as she moved around the counter to lean against the bar near them.

"Yes. In order to do it, she has to become a vampire. And the consequences are the risks involved. She knows all about it. What this entails and everything. Draylan and I had a talk with her about it. The ball is in her court. We will not force her to do it. It's one hundred percent her that makes the final decision."

"What are one of the consequences involved in it?"

"If she lives through the transition, in roughly thirty or so years, she will have to fake her death. But luckily for her, as she is so young, we'd probably be able to push it to until she's about fifty-five to sixty. As with the surgery and such you can get today, by that time people wouldn't blink an eyelash at it. But as I said, it's completely up to her if she wishes to do this."

"Oh. Any cases of it failing? Of those that couldn't handle it?"

"Yes; a select few."

"What happened to them?" Raven enquired.

"Look, I won't lie to you, some died. The rest made it through but turned rogue a few months later. Got addicted to the blood, and drained those they caught completely dry."

"And you want my sister to go through this?" Luke's voice went low and quiet, a show of the building anger inside of him.

"It's her decision. And I can assure you now, she won't go rogue," Draylan said.

"How do you know that?" Luke snapped.

"Because no matter how hard it'll be to change over, Calista won't let her go rogue."

"And how is that possible?" Raven looked at Luke's furious gaze to Calista's dead one. Clearly fascinated she could still keep emotions out of her expression, as though it was as simple as breathing. Even her voice was expressively dead.

"Because believe it or not, as Draylan said last night, I actually do care for Lexis. She won't go rogue. Even if she does change over, she won't have it in her to kill. She's too soft hearted for that. Majority of the time, changing over does not change the person."

"But what about those ones that went rogue?"

"I had nothing to do with changing them over. The 'bad ones' in Mystic Being did. Just because over there it's all mythological people you don't realise that in reality it is very much the same here as it is there. The good, the bad and the damn right ugly." She repeated what Lexis had said earlier.

"Oh right." They all went quiet then as Lexis walked back in.

"Who was calling you at this time of the morning?" Luke asked, looking at Lexis with an affectionate smile on his face.

"Just a friend from university who is always up this early to study. Plus, he has an exam soon and needed my help on a couple questions that I know the answer to," she replied and sat down on Tairen's lap and wrapped her arms around his neck.

"Oh right. Fair enough."

"So, what made you cook this morning, Calista, if you don't eat? We'd have cooked for ourselves," Raven said, drawing the woman's cold gaze.

"Ah, she has a weakness for cooking for everyone. She likes looking after people." Lexis replied before Calista could answer. Raven looked at her and noticed she had a huge smile on her face, eyes dancing with mischief.

"Not all the time. Only for small little urchin's like yourself that refuse to budge like an extra limb," Calista said, her eyes holding a faint hint of humour.

"Ah, but you still secretly like cooking, and don't deny it, you do. God help anyone that has cooked in your kitchen and didn't clean up after themselves." Lexis's eyes practically twinkled with cheekiness. Calista huffed at her and moved to the sink to wash up a cup that no one had realised she'd placed on the counter. Raven caught the glimpse of something red wash out of the cup before disappearing into the sink out of sight. Calista looked back at them all quickly and noticed Luke and Lexis were bickering to each other. Just as normal siblings were prone to do. She looked at Raven and caught the look of amusement on his face as he watched them. She delved into his mind and caught a glimpse of the memory that was running through his subconsciousness. She shared the memory with him, knowing full well he wouldn't be able to tell she was rummaging around his mind. She turned away to hide the sudden grin that tugged at her lips. Running through her own mind, thanks to the connection she'd just done with Raven to see what he was smiling about, she saw a very young Lexis, who had to be around about eight or nine, being chased around her parent's garden by Luke as she laughed her head off. Eyes sparkling as Luke ran for her, covered in orange juice. She watched them as though watching through Raven's eyes. The siblings' parents laughing beside him, the entire family content with each other, as well as having pulled Raven into their close-knit family like one of their own. Calista pulled back out of his memory as she felt his gaze was on her. She looked over at him and he looked away.

"What are you thinking, Raven?" Draylan asked, drawing the man's attention.

"What?"

"You have a secret smile on your face, like you're remembering something," Lexis said, smiling.

"Oh. I was just remembering a time when Luke and I, before we went into the army, were around your parents' house and he was chasing you

57

around the garden because you'd deliberately spilt orange juice over him because he ignored you, and you had to have been around about eight or nine at the time."

"I remember that!" Luke said, he too smiling from the memory. "That was when Lexis was screaming in pretend fear as I was chasing her. Screaming to mum and dad that if I caught her, I was going to tickle her to death." He grinned at his sister. She just smiled back cheekily.

"OK, enough of happy memory sharing. Go grab your things; we leave in five minutes," Calista said, and left the room. Everyone followed behind her. Knowing it wasn't wise to argue, but all still smiling at the memory they just shared.

Raven walked out of the kitchen behind everyone else, and headed to the stairs. He noticed Calista, who had gotten up the stairs quicker than he thought was possible, was bent slightly at the waist giving Blodox a rub between his ears. The dog, going by its loved-up expression, adored the scratch. Although, Raven was more interested in staring at Calista's arse than paying attention to the beast. They all headed up the stairs. He watched as Calista stood up straight again and turned around to face them.

"What car are we going in?" Draylan asked, giving Blodox a quick affectionate pat on his huge head. Lexis pushed Draylan out of the way and wrapped her arms around Blodox, giving him a hug. Then she darted off down the corridor with the dog happily trailing after her.

"Land Rover. I sold the Series 5 BMW Convertible." Calista's voice brought Raven back to watching them, and not watching Lexis be the big kid she was.

"WHAT!? I loved that car!" Draylan protested, shock clearly evident in his expression.

"So? It's not like I really drove it much. Was collecting dust in the garage more than I was driving it. So I sold it. Hefty profit too."

"How much?" Draylan asked, walking beside her until they reached the room he had the night before. Raven really wanted to know too. Convertibles alone weren't cheap. He knew that. Saw enough of them at the base!

"More than enough." He knew she was stubborn, but come on. She had to tell.

"Please tell me, Calista. You have to! It isn't like me to beg for anything. Plus, it was my car anyway." Draylan actually pouted at her. Wait a minute; she'd sold his car? Ouch. He'd kill anyone that did that to his car; well, motorbike actually as he didn't own a car.

"I sold it for £120,000."

"That's a hell of a lot of money!" Luke exclaimed.

"Yes, it is. It deserved it too. Considering the amount of things I'd added to it. I think the guy I sold it to was greatly pleased." She turned around and strolled back down the stairs, clearly not wanting to talk to them anymore, and obviously didn't want to get her things from her bedroom either.

"What was done to it?" Raven asked Draylan.

"Cherry bomb exhaust; bulletproof body and glass. It was sleek perfection. Even the roof was bulletproof! It was every man's dream. The engine roared with life. The seats hand-stitched Italian leather of the finest quality."

"Oh, sounds friggin' awesome! What colour was it?" Raven nodded at what Luke said.

"Rich midnight black. But if the sun catches it just right, it's a deep profound red. I saw it once it was completed whilst I was over here visiting for a while. You see, when Calista gets a project underway, she gets so damn secretive at times, and that's pretty crazy! So if you try and sneak a peek at whatever she's working on, and spots you, prepare for the ultimate arse kicking, literally. As for the seats, already told you they were hand-stitched Italian leather, but if you pushed a button, the seats gave out massages and heated up during the winter. Absolute heaven," he replied, looking downright miserable now that he realised the car was now in someone else's possession. Raven was literally amazed. This stunningly gorgeous woman had transformed a Series 5 BMW Convertible into something astounding. All for something as simple as a project? That was incomprehensible.

"Anyway, grab your stuff and let's go. Calista won't hang around." Tairen said, pushing his uncle into his bedroom then going to join Lexis in theirs. Raven and Luke quickly gathered their things that they'd left on the bed. All it consisted of was their rucksacks. Pitiful, but alas, that was it. They then headed back into the hallway and downstairs, following Lexis who had just walked into the kitchen, who was also still being followed by Blodox. They wandered into the kitchen and noticed Lexis was walking through the door in which Calista had gone through earlier. Going through the door himself, he noticed it housed state-of-the-art washing machine and tumble dryer, two freezers and a large fridge. He also noticed the entire decor matched the kitchen. Ahead of him and Luke was another door which Lexis promptly opened and rich sunshine spilled in. They walked outside and that was when they got their first real glimpse of the garden, as last night was way too dark for them to see anything. Thick trees with large olive green leaves bristled in the early morning breeze. Bushes of different greens adorned by plush big red roses cuddled together. Grass, thick and green, reached for the sky, but also begged you to run over it in bare feet to feel the spiky blades stroke the soles of your feet like a tickling caress. It went back as far as the eye could see and it was simply amazing. But probably took a lot of work to keep it in tip-top shape. His phone went off then.

"Tell Calista I'll be along as quick as I can. I can't ignore this," he said to Luke who just nodded. He quickly ran back into the kitchen and took the dreaded call from the withheld number he knew would be his boss and who would no doubt demand for him and Luke to return to base. There was no other explanation as to why he called. The only time he called was when he wanted them back or to send them into unknown places!

"Calista!" She looked behind her from standing in the garden as everyone piled out of the house and looked at Luke as he called for her.

"What?"

"Raven said he'll be along as quick as he can. Someone just called him. No idea what about though. He said that he shouldn't be too long. But whoever it was, I could tell Raven wasn't amused at getting the call, that's for sure."

"OK. Thanks for telling me. You all wait here; I'll be back in a minute." She knew it was that bastard boss of his and Raven's. He would no doubt try and get them back into work when she knew they'd been ordered to have a vacation because they were getting way to damn good at their job. Not that she thought it was a bad thing — take out the bad guys. Why were people complaining? They were effectively looking after them and ridding the world of horrible people. She walked back into the house and thanks to her extreme hearing, she could hear every word Raven was saying, as well as what the person on the other side was saying also.

"But sir, Luke and I have active duty removal. General Wilson told us to take at least two months off." She looked into the kitchen and noticed he looked bone weary, almost as if he was fed up of his boss. Thank God he wasn't hers, or he'd be long dead, literally! She didn't take orders well. Good thing she was her own boss.

"I do not care what General Wilson said; I order you both back here. You are to be sent out over to Afghanistan immediately. And I will not take no for an answer, private!" the 'boss' on the other end of the phone said. His voice was stupidly annoying and that was when Raven caught sight of her, only because she let him know she was there.

"Nothing I can do. Lexis is going to be so disappointed," he mouthed to her. And she felt the unhappiness of upsetting Lexis roll out of him in waves and crash over her like a tidal wave smashing against rocks of a cliff. She shook her head and held out her hand for the phone, which he didn't even hesitate to give her. She too refused to allow Lexis to be upset because of a cantankerous old man on the phone who thought he ruled everyone. News flash to him, he didn't.

"RAVEN CALHOUN, YOU ANSWER ME RIGHT NOW!" She heard the shrill tone of his boss screech through the phone, and damn, talk about grate on your nerves which was saying something.

"Do not take that tone with me!" she snapped.

"Who the hell is this? I was talking to Elite Special Agent Calhoun."

"Yes, well tough shit. You have to talk to me now."

"And who the hell are you?"

"I am Raven's girlfriend. So therefore I should warn you, do not take that tone in which you gave to him with me." Her voice was deadly calm.

"Since when did Calhoun have a girlfriend?"

"Since ages ago. Not everything in his life you army bunch know about."

"Is that so, and you think you know everything there is to know about him?"

"Well, I know more than what you think I know," she snapped, her patience wearing thin. She hated small-minded, bully-type men. She looked at Raven and he was just sitting there looking at her, gobsmacked. If his jaw was any lower, it'd be scraping the floor. She put her finger under his chin and shut his mouth for him.

"Go on then. Tell me what you know about him," Raven's boss said.

"I take it you have his file in front of you, to double check what I am telling you is correct."

"That is true. So please, do tell." His sarcasm was obvious, even over the phone! But she could hear the soft click, click of a mouse so obviously he was just pulling it up now. Liar!

"OK then. He has ice-blue eyes. Black hair which is cut military short for obvious reasons. He stands at six feet eight in bare feet. Fights dirty when he needs to but otherwise doesn't bother at all. He can pack a mean punch in which when he hits you accurately, you know it. He left home at fifteen and never looked back once. He doesn't get on with his family members at all. Black sheep you might say. The main members are his mother, father and little brother. Reasons I'm sure you might know but we won't go into that."

"Carry on." Could the bastard's tone be anymore sarcastic?

"He likes women who can take care of themselves and not rely completely on men to fight their battles for them. Also, he prefers women who have meat on them and ones that are not stick thin. Many people avoid him like the plague, like they know something dangerous lies just below the surface and just the smallest thing could set it off. He also happens to enjoy riding his Kawasaki Ninja Zx-14, because he likes the rush of adrenaline and the sense of freedom."

"And anything else you want to add to that list?" The bastard was really taking the piss now. He was annoying her something chronic and honestly that was never a good thing. She just really wanted to reach through the phone and punch shit out of him. Or even go hunt him down, but she restrained herself. She had more important things to deal with. Plus, she knew one punch from her and she'd literally cave his head in. This would of course kill him instantly and even though he was human and she'd break his skull easily, it would at least satisfy her at the time. She, at times, itched for a good fight, but no one would fight against her. Sucked at times. Well, here they didn't — at home they tried, but failed.

"Well what do you want to know?" she asked.

"Parents' names and ages — same with the brother. What made him join the army? Does he have any illnesses and were they treated? Favourite animal etc."

"Rebecca and Daniel. Forty-six and fifty. Brother is called Richard and he's twenty-four. He joined the army with Luke because he wanted something positive with his life and he also wanted to save lives of people in danger. He doesn't have any illnesses which if that were the case, they weren't treated. Unless you count the cold he had when he was on leave for a break, but that was treated with some simple antibiotics. His favourite animal is a tiger. But he also likes wolves, lions, bears, etc. Anything dangerous really."

"All true. Now why did you take the phone off him?"

"Of course they're all true. I'm his girlfriend, we hold nothing back from each other. And I took the phone off him to tell you he is on leave from the general himself. He doesn't need to listen to you. Plus, Raven and Luke can't come back; we've booked a month's holiday together. So therefore, you will have to find someone else to send to whatever hell hole you have planned for them. Do not call him again." With that, she snapped the phone shut, cutting off the communication before the irritating man could say anything else.

"I can't believe you know all that about me," Raven murmured. Leaning against the counter, he ran his hands over his face and through his short hair.

"I know a lot of things. It can honestly be surprising at times. Well, to others anyway, with what I know and what I can find out about certain individuals. It scares people," she replied. Light that illuminated the hallway suddenly disappeared. She watched Raven's eyes flair wide as saucers.

"What?" she asked, although she already had a pretty good idea what it was that had caused his eyes to go that wide.

"How did you do that?" he murmured.

"Didn't the guys explain it to you last night?"

"Bits."

"Like what?"

"Well, that it was a hell of a lot better to have you on our side than as an enemy. You're utterly ruthless and couldn't give a shit what happens. You're exceedingly dangerous. You're blunt. You think it's better to tell the truth than live with a lie. And that you're also unbelievably strong."

"Anything else?"

"That you are also unique unto yourself. But that you also have the vampire equivalent of bloodlust coursing through your system."

"That's right."

"Care to actually explain that bit to me?" he asked.

"In Mystic Being, a long time ago, there was a massive gathering of beasts, etc., that wanted to create the ultimate weapon so if anyone stepped out of place, they would have a means to destroy it."

"How did it happen?" He butted in; she could tell he really wanted to know. She sighed and moved to sit on a stool next to him.

"They found a nymph fey that had recently found out she was pregnant, but was about to terminate the pregnancy thanks to a witch willing to do it for a price of course. They had managed to persuade her to give them the foetus so they could create this weapon. She agreed. They took the foetus out of her; and I have no idea how they did it as I wasn't around then. They all gathered on Dragon Hill, as that had the best spot for sunlight and such. Well anyway, they gathered around, loads of different creatures, like dragons, fairies, angels, griffins, mermaids, unicorns, vampires, etc. two hundred of good and two hundred of bad. The main ones in which would transfer their powers into this foetus would of course die but they were willing to sacrifice themselves to save the rest of them. Of course, there were a few that didn't want to die and turned their backs on everyone, becoming rogue and creating havoc whenever and however they could."

"Seriously? Why would they do that?"

"Because they thought no matter where you go, there had to be a balance of good and evil or some bullshit like that. But let me get back to explaining to you. The ones who had turned their backs didn't watch what happened so of course they didn't know how it all went down. The ones sacrificing themselves spent the remaining twenty-four hours with their families in order to say goodbye. Twenty-four hours went by and they had already transferred the foetus into this massive egg, which would be better described as a massive boulder, but of course wasn't. The beings all then threw their powers and very essence into the foetus. Of course, some of the ones who had sacrificed themselves were evil but it had to be done."

"Then what?"

"They wouldn't know the outcome until the thing transformed into a baby and it was born. But they didn't actually have to wait long; upon nightfall the egg glowed like a halogen light. They all watched, transfixed as the foetus inside grew before their very eyes. They thought they would have to train the baby up until it reached adulthood; but they were proven wrong. The foetus actually didn't stop growing in the egg until it reached the height of an adult. The others had of course moved back, just in case something happened. According to legend, it was a good thing they did too. The egg erupted into a thousand pieces. Shards flying, but before they hit anyone and caused damage from how fast they went, they disintegrated into grains of sand."

"That's incredible!" Raven was amazed that something this technical and such was out there and that the government or whoever sorted that kind of crap out didn't even know about it! Including the mythological beings, etc. How the hell didn't they know this all existed?

"Yes, I'm sure it is. Well once they were able to see again, as when the egg erupted, the light that came from it was absolutely blinding, all that could be seen was white. Then once they could see, colours began to twirl and erupt together. Moulding together, like an artist would mix their paints is the best way to describe it to you. Everyone moved back; light burst from the figure, and then drifted downwards to land solidly, yet with absolute silence on its feet. And that was when everyone got to look at their 'creation'."

"What was it like?"

"It was of a woman, who had blood red eyes, large fangs that fell from her upper jaw and tips that ended at the middle of her chin, sharp as a razor blade and as thick and scarier than a lion's. Hair was a wild mass of black that swirled around her like a cloak. Her skin appeared to be scaled, as that of a dragon but was a pink flesh shade but actually shimmered a pale peach colour in the sunlight; which they said made the Fruit Fey's crave peaches."

"What else was she like?" She knew he was completely fascinated, that much was evident in his facial expression and wide eyes and the fact he held onto every word she said as well as sitting on the edge of his stool.

"Well, obviously she was naked. Long legs that were made of sturdy muscle and covered in silky smooth unblemished skin. Trim waist. Broadish shoulders. Flawlessly proportioned breasts. Her eyes had then changed from that blood red, to a vivid cobalt blue. Her teeth had shrunk back to a normal size but were still slightly pointy at the ends where the fangs were. She looked like a normal woman, but with a very dangerous aura around her." Calista watched him as the information she gave him sunk in.

"So who was the woman?"

"Are you really ready for that answer, Raven Calhoun?" She watched, not blinking as he gulped slightly and she had a strange urge to follow that motion with her tongue.

"Yes?" He eventually stammered out. She knew he wasn't ready; she could smell the uncertainty clinging to him like a second skin. But then she noticed his eyes were entirely focused on her lips.

"Raven!" She snapped her fingers in front of his face.

"What?" he said, shock evident on his face when he realised he'd been caught ogling her lips. She shook her head helplessly at him.

"Right, come on. We're to leave now." She stood up and together they walked back outside. Shutting the door behind them, she strolled down the pathway in front of everyone who was waiting patiently. And she noticed he didn't enquire as to who that woman was.

Raven got over his shock again of the size of the garden and quickly caught up with the others just as they stopped just to the side of a black-stained building. He watched as Calista placed her hand on a panel that if he didn't know better, would easily have been mistaken for a brick. He watched as part of a brick just above the panel moved as though on a slider and a needle shot out. Everyone watched as Calista took it into her hand and then inserted it into the crease of her elbow.

"Welcome, Calista." A robotic voice came from somewhere as the building's, which actually turned out to be the garage Lexis had mentioned to them last night, thick main door opened. Raven caught the width of the door and it had to have been a good solid inch thick. Then he watched as she disappeared into the dark interior, the dark shadows swallowing her up greedily.

"Where the hell did she disappear to?" Luke asked, looking inside but unable to see anything. In answer to his question, a rich rumbling roar of an engine came out of the inky blackness, making Luke leap backwards. And then a sleek muscled beast of a Land Rover pulled out into the morning light. Side and back windows were tinted dark. The front window was also slightly tinted. It was muscle black with sleek silver alloys, and handles. It was awesome! Raven immediately loved it. Calista got out the driver's side and Draylan climbed in. She then disappeared, quicker than they could blink. It was as though she had never been there and honestly it was freaky as shit but wicked cool!

"OK, where did she go?" Raven asked, looking around.

"Most likely to get our luggage and Blodox," Lexis answered and clambered into the back of the vehicle. Tairen got into the front with Draylan, leaving Raven and Luke to accompany either side of Lexis in the back. They climbed in just as Calista and Blodox made an appearance. They both reached the vehicle a scant few moments later, that was when Raven noticed she carried all their luggage, like a couple of feathers and not loads of clothes and other gear. She placed them into the boot and he watched, transfixed as she muttered something under her breath and they shrunk to three-quarters of the original size! She then motioned for Blodox to climb aboard and he did, without complaint and settled down immediately with plenty of space. She shut the boot and walked around to the driver's side. Draylan put the window down so he could hear her talk.

"I want you to go right now. I'll meet you at Glasgow Airport." With that she turned and walked away, whilst Draylan kicked the vehicle into gear and squealed away. Tyres spinning, trying to get friction to move and left marks on the concrete floor. He didn't so much as question why she told him to go right now instead of wait. Raven and Luke quickly glanced back just as they saw Calista lock into a fight with a guy that was ridiculously large. He towered over Calista but it seemed she didn't care. Flames flew into Calista's hands, the blue matching her vivid eye colour, and she lobbed them at this guy who rapidly dived out the way and that was all they saw because the Land Rover barrelled around the corner and sped down the street.

"Hey Tairen, what the hell was that Calista was just against? Didn't really get a good look apart from it is undiplomatically large," Luke asked before Raven could. Tairen turned to some extent in his chair and looked at them.

"It was a demon. It was most likely sent from the Demon King Kharge as he's had a nasty reason apparently for wanting to kill her," he explained.

"What reason is that?" Raven asked.

"She killed his wife, who had run havoc on everyone; killing and eating anyone she grabbed. Be it either man, woman or child. Or even animal. She was a horrendously vicious cannibal," Lexis replied, and settled back into the seat between him and Luke.

"Well, I don't blame Calista for doing that. Any other particular reason?"

"She's killed loads of his henchmen without a single flicker of remorse. She's slaughtered an army without any help."

"Surely the army got in some good hits?" Luke asked.

"Yeah, they got in a couple good hits but not many. She had a very high kill streak that day. Draylan, how many roughly was it?" Tairen asked his uncle.

"The recorded death of the enemy was nine hundred soldiers. They were armed with knives, swords and machetes, not to mention their sheer brutality, strength and speed. She was armed with only a knife and her own sheer speed and deadly accuracy." Draylan said, keeping his attention firmly on the road.

"A knife? Are you serious?"

"Well, it was more of a machete than a knife." Tairen said and turned back around properly in his chair. Raven was astounded! She'd taken on an army, which was armed to the teeth, with just a machete? That was simply amazing, idiotic but amazing all the same. They all sat quietly thinking about different things and about twenty minutes later Tairen's phone went off, indicating he had a text. Raven noted then that they had reached the airport. They parked the car, climbed out and suddenly Lexis took off running. Raven noticed Calista was there, standing next to a plain-looking man. Tairen pulled their bags from the boot and as he did, they went back to their normal size, handed them to their rightful owners and clipped Blodox's lead on. They gathered their bags and then followed Draylan over to Calista. When they reached her, he handed her the car keys. Calista didn't put them in her pocket, she handed them to the kid next to her. He was a simple looking lad. Black hair. Brown eyes. Lanky; not yet grown into his body.

"Guys, meet Daniel. He's at the same university as me," Lexis said and promptly burst out in laughter as Blodox plopped his butt on her foot and refused to budge until she paid him attention as well.

"Hey, Daniel," they all said.

"So you take care of this motor, you got that Daniel?" Calista said, looking the kid clean in the eyes.

"I promise." He couldn't quite look her in the eye, but Raven could understand why. Her vivid cobalt blue eyes seemed to stare into your very soul and made you wish to tell her every deepest, darkest secret that you had. No matter what they were. Even Draylan wouldn't look her completely square in the face. And even he noticed Draylan wasn't one to not look you in the eye. Must show just how dangerous she really was if no one could.

"Good, considering how much dear old dad paid for it. It would be a shame to have to explain to him that you ruined it before you had it for long."

"Y-yes it would," he stammered slightly. Calista nodded and turned back to the building. Lexis said goodbye to Daniel, who quickly said goodbye back then made a beeline for his new vehicle. They all then moved quickly to catch up with Calista, Blodox's lead flapping between his side and Lexis's leg. They rushed through the doors and into the main airport. Raven noticed Calista then. She had just disappeared through some double doors marked PRIVATE!

"Where the hell did she go?" Luke asked, scanning the crowd. Before anyone could answer, two security guards walked over to them.

"Any of you Draylan Stone?"

"That's me," Draylan said.

"OK, follow us please. All of you." The men turned and walked away. They grabbed their belongings from around their feet and rushed off after the men. Stumbling through the doors, they were led down a long winding corridor to a lone door at the very end. One of the men opened it up using a key card and motioned them through. They did and there, standing on the other side of the room, was Calista. Looking every inch her deadly self.

"Right, let's go." She took Blodox off Lexis and opened another door near her. Walking through, Raven realised it led straight onto the tarmac, which must have been why she took Blodox. Draylan was the last to walk out and turned to the guards. He noticed their attention was squarely on Calista, or more accurately, her arse.

"Gorgeous isn't she?" Draylan laughed at the perplexed expressions on the faces of the men.

"Exquisite."

"Absolutely glorious." He shook his head and shut the door behind him, shutting off their view of Calista. He understood their reaction though, Calista was a gorgeous woman, but she didn't see it for herself. This was rare, as she saw herself as just simple and that was one of the things he liked best about her. He walked over to the plane that everyone else had gotten onto and climbed aboard just as it roared to life, the steady hum only slightly vibrating the floor, other than that, inside the actual plane was silence.

"Everything all right?" Raven asked, meeting him at the door.

"Sure thing. Security guards got a little distracted."

"Let me guess, watching Calista?"

"Yeah. Saying that, you know she actually has no idea how gorgeous she actually is?" Draylan looked at Raven carefully to see his reaction.

"Are you serious?" He was quite amazed; the kid knew how to hide his reactions well.

"I'm serious. She honestly has no idea. She just thinks she's simple."

"Damn." With that, Raven turned around and noticed the luxuriousness of the plane. Lavish thick black carpet. Deep-seated chairs made of this black silk-type material, and as the sun shone on them through the doorway, they glowed a pearlescent red, and they spun around on the spot. They were big enough that they could curl their legs up underneath them and still have plenty of room. At the back of the plane, divided by sleek thick floor length black curtains, was a row of single beds, six in total. Three on either side, all had black skull bedding. Each with a gap in between just wide enough for a table with a black lamp on and the obvious gap to walk down the sides, apart from the back ones, only one side was accessible due to the other side being flush against the wall. Thick black curtains actually hung over the windows. If this didn't prove Calista had money, Raven didn't know what would. They all claimed a seat apart from Calista, who emerged from the cockpit, Blodox by her side.

"Blodox, bed." Calista pointed at the massive dog bed near the door of the cockpit and he immediately obeyed. He settled down in it and began to happily chew on the ridiculously thick bone that was awaiting him there.

"What are those chairs made of?" Luke enquired, staring straight at them.

"High quality silk infused with magic," Draylan murmured and sat down.

"Right, we are on this plane until we hit Melbourne in Australia. Refuel, stretch legs, eat, then get back on here and carry on until Launceston, Tasmania," Calista explained by way of greeting.

"Exactly how long will it take us?" Lexis asked, stretching out on one of the thick overstuffed couches and dragging a laptop across her legs.

"In total, roughly thirty-two hours if not a little longer with the stop and whatnot."

"Oh shit. I just remembered. Raven and I left our bikes at the front of your house!" Luke said, looking quite frantic. Those bikes were damn expensive.

"The bikes are not there. They are with us." Calista turned her unemotional gaze to Luke's.

"What do you mean, they're with us?"

"Exactly that. They're in the cargo along with my Night Demon."

"You brought Night Demon?" Lexis cried out excitedly.

"Sure did." Calista actually smiled at her and Raven thought she looked even more stunning, which was actually kind of hard to beat. Well, he thought so anyway.

"Then how did you get Raven and Luke's bikes here if you have Night Demon?" Draylan asked.

"Do you really need to ask me that?" She smirked at him.

"Didn't think," he replied and grinned back.

"Who is Night Demon?" Raven asked.

"It's Calista's trike."

"And what's so special about it?" Luke looked bewildered.

"Because it's a beast of a motor. You'll see it when we get to Tasmania if she shows you it." Tairen said, speaking for the first time since their little conversation in the car when they had left Calista's.

"Why not tell us about it now?" Raven asked.

"Because we are sadistic bastards. Not as much as Calista, mind you." Tairen grinned at him then turned back to the others, "But we all like to keep up on the suspense. And no point in asking Lexis, she won't tell you anything."

"Fuck you very much, Tairen. I am not a sadistic bastard. I am The Sadistic Bitch. Get it right." Calista grinned in what could be called anything but a smile.

"Sorry Your Royal Highness." He grinned at her.

"I am definitely not that, kiddo. OK, we're getting out of here." She turned and went back into the cockpit and shut the door swiftly behind her. A scant few moments later, the plane began to move, and soon they were air born.

"So tell me, why can't we ask Lexis?" Raven looked at Draylan as he asked the question.

"Because Calista will know, plus Lexis won't break the confident oath of loyalty and trust she has with her," he answered back quite simply. Raven untied his boot laces and kicked off his combats, wiggling his toes in his socks. He didn't wear his combat boots if he didn't have to. And why not get comfy when it was to be a long journey? *Better be comfy than not*, he thought to himself.

"How will she know?"

"Because she is unique unto herself and can also read minds. Didn't we mention that last night?" Tairen got his answer when Raven and Luke shook their head, no.

"Right, well obviously you two now know Calista can do that," Draylan said.

"What else can she do?" Luke asked.

"Near enough anything," Lexis answered, clearly listening to their conversation. She put her now shut-down laptop off her lap, put it on the seat next to her and joined them, plopping herself down onto Tairen's lap instead of the empty seat next to him. From the angle she was sitting, she had Luke and Raven in clear view. And it was obvious that Tairen didn't mind in the slightest that she used him as a seat by the way his arms wrapped lovingly around her waist.

"Give us a few pointers then, so we know what you are dragging us into." Luke smiled at Lexis.

"OK." she agreed, and then turned to face the cockpit which Raven thought was slightly weird. If she was talking to them, why was she facing that way? More so when the door was shut?

"Hey Calista, I'm hungry. Fancy giving me some food?" she called out. Suddenly a table appeared in the space between the chairs they all occupied, followed by plates, cutlery and it was entirely loaded with food. Sandwiches, crisps, drinks, chocolate. Even hot food like pork, roast chicken and such. It was such a vast selection. Raven looked at Luke and by the look on his best friend's face, he was clearly gobsmacked the same as he was. Not to mention the tantalising aromas that assailed their senses and caused their mouths to fill up with saliva threatening to overspill out of their mouths.

"Pretty cool isn't it?" Lexis grinned, leaned forward and snatched up a packet of crisps. One of the many that lay on the table. Everyone else then started helping themselves. Raven noticed that Tairen didn't move Lexis when he grabbed something to eat. To be fair, he asked her what she wanted majority of the time. Then they ended up sharing the brunt of it between them. This was a feat and half if you asked him, considering if Lexis hadn't changed all that much from when she was younger, she rarely shared food. But then he also happened to notice Lexis had most of the food near her — some things never changed.

"So come on, what else?" Raven asked, digging into a still hot beef sandwich that made his taste buds burst to life and sighed happily.

"She can disappear and reappear at will. She's practically bulletproof. It's ridiculously hard to kill her. She is also severely vicious," Lexis absently said, biting into a cheese sandwich.

"How malicious?"

"Severely. She wouldn't hesitate to do something to you if you pissed her off or hurt one of those closest to her," she replied once she'd finished her mouthful.

"Like what?" Luke asked, around a mouthful of chips.

"First of all, don't talk with your mouthful. And second, she'd torture you."

"Yes Mum. And torture?" Luke stammered, after he'd finished his mouthful.

"Only if you severely pissed her off or abused her friendship, or hurt someone close to her; like a friend or those she classes as family."

"What means of torture does she have or use?"

"Acid dripped onto you slowly so it lasts for hours, as it only burns the surface of your skin. Nine inch clout nails down the eye of your penis. Flesh of your penis cut off and then seared back into place, and many others." She stopped there as they all had cupped themselves, apart from Tairen. Only because she occupied his lap. All their faces had lost colour, even Draylan's, and he was used to it!

"Are you fucking serious?" Luke breathed out.

"I'm perfectly serious. That's only her baby tortures. At least you know not to piss her off now." Lexis absentmindedly ate a biscuit, the crunching noise filling the stark silence. Raven looked at the others and from the paleness of their faces, he figured his was the exact same. Even Draylan's was pale, but shouldn't he be used to what she did? But as her best friend, Raven kind of guessed he'd seen her do worse than that. But what had him shocked was the fact Lexis had said it all with a straight face, so therefore he knew she was deadly serious. After Lexis had finished her biscuit, Raven watched as she got off Tairen's lap and walked over to the cockpit. They all caught a quick glimpse of Calista at the controls, but she wasn't watching what she was doing; she was playing a game on a laptop! But she'd turned to look over her shoulder as the door had opened. It swung shut behind Lexis, giving the women privacy. Raven sighed slightly and then knew it would indeed be a long flight, and decided to get comfortable in the chair his butt was currently occupying. He took his eyes off the cockpit door and looked back at the guys. And then watched as the food on the table in front of them began to disappear until it was an empty surface. In the centre lay a single pack of playing cards.

"Calista knows me so well," Draylan laughed when he saw them. And then the game began.

Chapter Three
Melbourne, Australia. Some Twenty-seven hours later

Calista stretched her muscles as she guided the plane to the runway at Melbourne Airport. She checked her laptop, looked at the cameras she had installed in the back of the aircraft and noticed all of her 'companions' had fallen asleep curled up under the thick duvets on the beds. Blodox himself was sound asleep in his bed, sprawled on his back, feet twitching. She wasn't surprised they had all gone to sleep. It was a long flight and as she'd installed the beds, why not put them to use instead of sitting cramped in a chair? She powered down the laptop, then radioed into the main control centre that she was clear to land. They confirmed it. Ten minutes later she had landed, parked up and had everything turned off, the engine hissing as it slowed to a standstill and began cooling after the long flight. She packed her laptop away and then stood up. She again stretched and damn it felt good to sort her muscles out from being in pretty much the same position for a ridiculous amount of time. She looked at the clock and doing a quick calculation, she'd been up roughly thirty-one hours or so. Nothing unusual. She'd gone longer. She emerged from the cockpit. Furthermore, as silently as a ghost, she glided over the carpet to the back where everyone was asleep. She leaned against the wall that jutted out slightly, (she'd had it done that way so if the need came for it, you could draw the big blackout curtain across to aid you in privacy if you wanted to sleep and everyone else was still awake) and crossed her arms over her chest, waiting for them to realise she was there. Their subconscious would realise it. A few moments passed and then Draylan made the first signs of stirring awake. His breathing changed. Became heavier, not the light, controlled way it did when he was sound asleep. He rolled over onto his back and blinked his eyes open sleepily. A slight movement out of the corner of his eye made him turn his head, instantly wide awake. He noticed it was Calista watching him.

"Been watching and waiting long?" He stretched to ease the kink of sleepiness from his muscles.

"Couple of minutes. Could have killed you a heck of a lot of ways before you even realised I was here."

"Well if you're here, who's flying the plane?" Raven asked, sitting up in the bed he was occupying. The duvet falling to his waist. His chest corded with muscle, hidden underneath that black T-shirt. The scar that caught her attention was the one that ran down the side of his neck on the left side, it was more prominent now she was closer to him. Calista schooled her features so no one would know how much it actually affected her knowing someone had cut into this masculine, gorgeous man. His eyes were sleep glazed too, but a couple of blinks later and it disappeared.

"You should realise we are no longer flying. We're in Melbourne. All of you have slept for roughly twenty hours. This might be why you feel much better than you did before." She turned her gaze to Lexis, who was still out for the count. The men all climbed out of their beds and after each had disappeared into the bathroom at the back of the plane to relieve their bladders, gathered their belongings together. The majority of them lay haphazardly all over the floor, just like any other man really who was in a hurry to clamber into bed. She walked over to Lexis, saw that the lass had the decency to put her jeans and jumper folded on the small shelf the bedside table had and crouched down beside the bed. She whispered something, knowing the others wouldn't hear and Lexis woke up.

"Mm hello Calista." She nonchantly stretched and looked around. The men had walked back over to the chairs and were munching on some snacks that she had made appear before she woke them. Because, as she knew Draylan when he woke up, he was always hungry, so she figured the others would be too.

"I take it we've landed in Melbourne, then? As we're not flying anymore," Lexis pointed out.

"That's right, going to refuel. Let you all stretch your legs, grab something to eat maybe and then we'll carry on to the outskirts of Cradle Mountain." Calista stood up, drew the thick curtain across as she knew Lexis would want privacy to change, and then quickly left the plane. Lexis grudgingly got up, ransacked the small storage compartment that Calista kept clean clothes in, changed her top as hers was all sticky from sleeping and sweating slightly, as well as the fact, she'd been in it since they'd left Scotland. Changing her bra and underwear, she then shrugged into a blank tank top and a red T-shirt over it with cut sleeves and Rock Rebel slashed across the chest with skulls. She put on clean black ripped jeans and her trusty airwalks before she gathered her dirty things together, placed them on the bed, grabbed her purse, shoved it into her skull handbag then joined the men. Once finished eating, they all left the plane. Tairen snapped

Blodox's lead to his collar and led the dog from the aircraft. And that was when Raven saw Calista talking to some men. They all approached them and the men next to Calista abruptly stopped talking and looked at them.

Poxy lawyer-type phonies. Raven thought to himself. You'd think he'd hate lawyers, if you guessed that, you got it right. He hated lawyers with a passion. Ever since dear old Mum and Dad had tried suing him for 'damaging their house'. How could he have managed that when he had been six thousand or so miles away? He'd been proven innocent and had even been shown on camera surveillance training at the time of the incident. His parent's lawyers had tried with all their might to take him down. 'Troubled soul that he was and it was clearly a body double'. Such shit.

"So you guys have no problem in spending roughly about an hour or so inside whilst I get the plane refuelled?" Calista's voice pulled Raven from his thoughts. He noticed the lawyer-dressed men had left.

"No, we don't mind waiting. What about Blodox?" Lexis said, scratching the dog's ear.

"I've had permission for him to be allowed in the building as long as he stays on the lead, that he behaves himself and that he also doesn't relieve himself inside."

"OK, cool. We'll be in one of the cafes once you're finished." Lexis took the lead off Tairen and they all turned to walk away when Calista cleared her throat. Lexis looked back to her and she saw she held out her own personal credit card.

"Use this Lexis. I'm not having you spend the money that you need for university." Lexis took the black card from her, knowing it wouldn't do her any good to argue.

"But I can spend some at Mystic Being, surely?"

"Yes, but for now, spend mine. You know money has no real value to me."

"Thanks, Calista." With that, Lexis turned around again and went to the men, but before they went inside, Blodox decided it was his time and sniffed at a couple trees near them before relieving himself up one before wandering back over to them. Extendable leads were a wondrous thing.

"What was that all about?" Luke asked.

"She didn't want me to spend my money that I have to use for university, so she gave me her card."

"What colour?" Draylan asked, catching the last of what she said.

"Black. Why?"

"Geez, that card has the big money on it," he said and Raven actually realised then they'd reached a cafe and Tairen had carefully chosen a table in a select darkened corner, aiding them with a bit of privacy. Blodox's thick padded feet making quick soundless work walking over to Tairen. None of them spoke as they settled into their seats, Lexis quickly kissed Tairen before sliding into a chair next to him.

"So explain to us, how does that card have the big money?" Raven asked, pulling a menu to him.

"Exactly as I said, it has the big money on it."

"How much we talking about?" Luke took the menu Raven held out to him, with nodded thanks.

"Roughly, I'd say about twenty-four billion. Give or take."

"Holy fuck, how she earn that much money?" Raven was severely surprised, the woman was quite simply loaded and yet all she did was hung around in places? How did that work out? Considering him and Luke scrimped and scraped to live. And even then they had meagre money left over to buy necessary things, if they needed it that was.

"She earned it by doing things not very many people would and she was paid the big bucks. Not very many people know about her. I'll be honest with you two; Calista and I have seen you before," Draylan said. And before Raven could ask how, a waitress walked over to take their order. Once completed, had given Blodox an affectionate scratch behind his ear, she disappeared to place their order, Draylan looked back at Raven.

"Go on, I know you want to ask me how."

"What things does she do that not very many people would? And how have you and Calista seen me and Luke before?" Even Lexis was paying attention; obviously she didn't know that Draylan and Calista had seen them before either.

"You heard about that escapade of where top of the range military equipment had been taken as well as very important people?" Luke and Raven nodded. Everyone in the armed forces had heard about that.

"OK, well military personnel, the best that they had, which I'm also guessing was your group, couldn't even get close to get a hold of them or the stolen things. So, the big, big bosses called in Calista — we're talking parliament head bosses here. Both of us had turned up, we passed you two whilst you were in your group training of hand-to-hand combat or something, although everyone had stopped to see who we were. You wouldn't have remembered Calista. She had a long, black cloak on and the hood concealed her face entirely. Plus, due to her height, everyone thought she was a male who just wanted to keep their identity secret."

"I remember now. We were training on the tactical court, keeping up with our hand-to-hand fighting, when the big guys came along. Both you and Calista wore long cloaks, it had us wondering who you were. Only we could see your face but not hers," Luke explained just as the waitress returned with their food and drinks. Each thanked her and quite simply dug in with relish. The meal was hot and blissfully wonderful. The waitress had even brought over a small bowl of offcuts for Blodox, which was nice of her.

"Yes, that was us. It was where the officer in charge of everyone had turned around and asked what they were looking at."

"That's right. What happened next?" Raven asked, and then shoved some sausage into his mouth but snuck another piece to Blodox who happily accepted it.

"We went into the guy's office — of course he had no idea what she could do. He had had only contact through me. He didn't even know what she looked like or that she was even female. I only told him I knew the perfect person for the job. He told us what happened and she didn't show any emotion or anything whatsoever. Vintage Calista basically. The Sarge thought it was pretty cool how calm and such she was, even though he couldn't see her face. I knew no different, to me Calista never showed emotion when on a job, or very rarely even when she wasn't." Draylan paused to take a sip of his coke. "Once explained what had happened and what they needed us for, me and Calista left. We got into a private aircraft they had loaned us and we disappeared. The following day I had radioed in that the weapons had been taken off them safely as well as the missing people. I was bringing them back. The Sarge had asked if I was with Calista, even though we didn't tell him her name, they only identified her as the person in black. I explained I was told to bring them back on my own, so I did. No questions asked. We had only just arrived back when I received a call from Calista." He took another sip of his drink.

"What did the call from Calista say?" Lexis asked. Clearly she was interested too.

"That she was uninjured, and everything had been taken care of."

"How did she take care of everything?" Tairen placed his now empty cup on the table, looking directly at his uncle. Clearly he didn't know either.

"Calista style. Get in her way — she'll remove you."

"Remove as in?" Raven absorbed everything Draylan was telling him. Everything about Calista fascinated him. Was amazing the things Lexis, Draylan and Tairen had told him and Luke.

"Remove as in kill you. Simple as that," he quite calmly said, as though it was the simplest thing in the world. Both men were flabbergasted.

"And she took everyone out, got back the military weapons and the missing people, all without an injury?" Luke remarked, shock quite evident on his face.

"She told us over the phone she had no injuries, but when I met up with her again, she actually confessed to being shot over fifty times. Majority of which landed a place in her back. She also had had cuts and bruises marring her face, chest, arms and legs," he confessed.

"How come I've never seen any scars on her?" Lexis asked, and she'd know, considering she lived with the woman.

"Because she healed herself. The only scar she couldn't heal is the one that is crossing diagonally across her stomach."

"Erm, then what about when Luke and I were at the house and I saw scars and such marring her arms?" Raven enquired.

"It's Calista. You can never know with her. It was probably her way of showing that she could look after Lexis if the need arose and that you didn't have to worry about her not being able to do the job. But then again, only Calista can answer that question."

"Back to the scars, why can't she heal the one across her stomach?" Luke asked.

"Because she had them not long after her birth. Someone tried killing her which clearly failed."

"Evidently, considering I'm still here." Calista's voice jarred them all. They all turned quickly to glance at her. They each had the grace to actually be embarrassed to be caught talking about her.

"We didn't hear you approach. Should have said something. We'd have ordered you a drink or perhaps some food," Tairen said, looking at Calista.

"What I need to eat and drink can't be found here. You know that Tairen," she replied, and absently patted Blodox who had begun nudging her hand for a scratch.

"So you being here, does that mean the plane's now refuelled and ready to go?" Raven announced, drawing Calista's intense gaze to his.

"Yes, so when ready let's go. I don't want to waste any more time. Sooner we leave the better actually."

"Well, we've all finished. Just have to wait for Lexis to pay the bill. And has it really been an hour already?" Luke remarked.

"Actually, it's been an hour and a half. But I would have come and got you all sooner if the plane hadn't taken so long to refuel." Lexis stood up then and the women walked away to go pay for everything. Tairen's eyes were glued to Lexis and Raven had turned slightly to watch Calista.

"Careful, Raven." Draylan's voice seeped into Raven's mind and he sadly dragged his gaze from Calista's arse and looked at Draylan.

"What?"

"Watching Calista like that. If you did that in Mystic Being, you'd be targeted and many people would talk and think you are a couple. Many of which would be shocked about that. No one has seen Calista engross herself into a relationship before. And you'd no doubt be targeted to use as bait."

"So in other words, they think her to be a virgin?" Luke asked, letting the men know he was listening. Not that he could really help it considering they were all seated close together.

"Many do, yes." Draylan took a sip of his beverage; he clearly didn't need to rush to finish like the others did with theirs.

"Do you?" Raven muttered.

"Honestly, I think she isn't. Can't be her age and be a virgin. But saying that, I couldn't give a fuck. She's my best friend. That isn't something I wish to even think about." Draylan visibly shuddered.

"How old is she?" Luke asked, clearly not bothered about asking a woman's age.

"How old do you think she is?" Tairen said, but he wasn't looking at them, he still had his hawk-sharp gaze on Lexis.

"About twenty-five I'd say," he replied. Before Draylan could say anything, Tairen leapt out of his chair and took off. The three men followed, knowing something must be wrong for Tairen to move that fast. Blodox quickly managed to keep up with them, bearing in mind his size! But what happened next actually surprised both Draylan and Tairen.

Calista and Lexis strolled away from the men to go pay the bill and they quickly reached the queue that led up to the tills. Luckily, only four people were ahead of them.

"I really am sorry for all of us talking about you, Calista. I should have realised my brother and Raven would have asked questions." Lexis actually looked upset about it all.

"Don't worry about it. I honestly don't mind. Kind of gathered they would have questions about the woman whom you live with." She reassured her with a quick hug, even if it usually was against her nature but she knew it would reassure Lexis. They reached the tills and Calista watched as Lexis paid for everything, thanked the young guy behind the counter and they left.

"Can I get some chocolate and such for the journey?" Lexis asked.

"Sure. You're the one who's going to be eating it all."

"Don't you wish you could?" Lexis looked up at her, hazel eyes wide and surprisingly innocent considering the amount of shit and such she'd seen since living with her.

"I can eat normal food and drinks like you. I just don't choose to." she replied truthfully.

"I don't know what I'd do without chocolate." Lexis laughed and grabbed a couple of big bars from the shelf as Calista actually smiled slightly at the girl's antics. It was as if chocolate was the most sacred thing in the universe, Lexis held the stuff tight against her chest. Calista watched amused as Lexis picked out loads of other edible things, lobbing them carelessly into the basket Calista had seen lying on the floor and had grabbed. Thankfully money wasn't an issue with her, so Lexis could spend as much as she pleased. They carried it back to the counter and again, had to wait in a queue. A man stumbled into Lexis then, almost knocking her clean over and if it wasn't for Calista's quick reflexes and grabbing her, she'd have gone straight into the side cabinet that housed wine and other small glass bottles of alcohol.

"Oh watch it. I'm standing here," she said, steady on her feet once again and Calista let her go.

"No, you watch where you're going. Immature little bitch." Before Calista or Lexis could say anything to that, the men were suddenly there.

"What did you call my sister?" Luke gritted out from between clenched teeth.

"An immature little bitch. Should watch where she's going," the guy said. Either completely stupid, on something or just didn't give a shit; the guy must not have been fazed by the feral look that had leapt into Luke's eyes. Tairen pulled Lexis to him, wrapping his arms around her protectively, and Draylan held back Blodox, quietly trying to calm the dog who was baring his teeth in a protective manner and hackles raised.

"Are you all right?" he asked, checking her over.

"I'm fine. He just knocked me. Then blamed me for being in the way. I'm in the queue, for God's sake!" she cried out. Tairen turned glacial eyes to the man but before he could do anything, Luke grabbed the man and practically hauled him outside and no one stopped him. Not even the security officers that were dotted around here and there. Might have had something to do with the feral look on his face. It was one of the rare times Raven had seen Luke let his rage get the better of him.

"What will he do?" Lexis asked Raven, who knew her brother better than anyone, as they had never kept anything from each other. But she'd never seen that side of him. And it quite frankly scared her!

"Most likely beat him up a bit. Leave him in a dumpster or something," Raven nonchalantly replied.

"Are you serious?"

"Lexis, it's your turn to pay now." Calista gently turned the girl around and pushed her forward slightly. Lexis paid for everything whilst they waited and she quickly re-joined them. She handed Calista back the card but she just shook her head no.

"Why don't you want it? It's yours."

"No pockets," she said. Lexis left it at that. There really was no point in arguing with her. But where did it come from if she had no pockets? But then she realised, it was Calista. She most likely made it appear out of thin air. They all followed Calista back to the plane in silence. Upon boarding, Lexis turned slightly on the steps and looked at her.

"Where is Luke?"

"I'll go get him." She turned around and a scant few minutes later strolled into the main building. She let her 'abilities' take flight. Every sound disappeared; every scent vanished until she pinpointed Luke's location. He was in one of the men's toilets washing the blood off his hands. She followed her nose to where he was. She turned a corner and the toilets lay directly ahead. She stopped outside the main door and leaned back against the wall next to it. An elderly man walked up to her, heading for the toilet.

"Waiting for anyone, sweetie?"

"I sure am. Can you tell Luke Blackwood that Calista is waiting for him?"

"Of course I can. I'd be honoured to help a lovely young lady like you." He disappeared into the toilet then. Calista smiled slightly, well it was really just the slight corner of her mouth turned upwards, everyone misjudged her on how old she was. She was old enough to be that guy's great, great, great, great, great, great grandmother. Along with a few couple more hundred greats thrown in. Geez, when she thought about it that way, she was damn bloody ancient! And then she noticed that the little man hadn't been disgruntled by her height either. Amazing. Considering she towered over him. Then again, he was most likely used to people taller than him, plus she'd noticed loads of women were quite tall, not as tall as her mind, but tall, kind of the same height as Lexis who was six foot, or just a hint taller. Luke walked out then.

"What you doing waiting? You know I would have come back to the shop."

"Everyone is on the plane, you wouldn't have found us there," she explained, pushing up from her slouched position against the wall.

"Ah right, so that explains why you were waiting then," he muttered, running a hand through his hair.

"That it would. So tell me, what happened to that guy you so kindly took outside?"

"Punched him in the face a couple times, told him he should be more respectful then dumped his sorry ass in a dumpster," he answered honestly.

"Nice one. Might explain the whole washing the blood off of your hands."

"How did you know that?" he asked, as he opened a door for her.

"Because I can smell the stuff."

"Seriously?"

"Yes."

"Can I ask, what does blood smell like to you? To me, it smells coppery."

"To me, it smells of mild strawberries."

"But wouldn't it all smell the same?" Luke again opened another door, this one leading out onto the tarmac and awaiting planes.

"Yes and no. I can tell the guy you just beat up was addicted to smoking which had given him ischaemia. And he also had peripheral vascular disease, which is why he was so wobbly. He was also addicted to alcohol, which explained his sunken face, hollowed cheeks, nasty attitude and why he quite frankly stank."

"Oh right. What is ischaemia and peripheral vascular disease?" He'd actually never heard of them. Raven was the one who paid attention to that sort of stuff, as apparently it was handy to know things for suspects, etc. He was the one for poisons, etc., as that was his speciality in the army.

"Ischaemia is lack of oxygen to the bloodstream due to furring up of the arteries. And peripheral vascular disease is the narrowing of leg arteries," she said, and he realised they'd reached the plane then. Calista pushed Luke ahead of her, just as security reached them. One dark haired, the other blond.

"Calista?" one of them called out.

"Yeah?" She turned around to face them. She had to look down slightly, being that extra bit taller than them. Must have been a bit discouraging, probably not used to a woman being taller than them.

"You've been given clearance for take-off."

"How much time have I got? And why didn't you radio me to tell me?"

"Apparently they tried, but you weren't answering. Then they saw you walking across the platform, and sent us to quickly rush and tell you as we were already down here," the dark haired one answered.

"Oh right, how much time have I got to leave?"

"After the next plane lands which will be in about five minutes or so." Blonde replied.

"OK, roger that. I'll get us out of here quick as I can." The plane roared to life behind her and she rushed up the stairs. She closed the heavy duty door, sealed it shut and looked up to find everyone looking at her.

"No trouble finding Luke, then?" Tairen asked, pulling Lexis closer for a cuddle on the couch. Obviously she didn't mind, because she actually snuggled closer to him. If he had a zip in his side, she'd have unzipped him and climbed inside, they were cuddled that close. Draylan walked out of the cockpit with a nod to her and claimed a chair.

"Nope, no trouble at all," she nonchalantly replied.

"How did you find him? It was packed," Raven asked, kicking his shoes off and stretching his feet. All of a sudden they were hurting, it was actually quite bizarre.

"Magic," she said.

"Fancy being slightly more specific?" He grinned at her, his eyes practically glowing.

"Now what would the fun in that be?"

"Least give us a hint or something?" The other three stayed out of the conversation. They knew quite a bit about Calista's 'magic'.

"You asked for it." She grabbed an empty bowl off the table and placed it in Luke's hands.

"What can you see in it?" Her voice changed slightly. More captivating. Wayyyyy more seductive, but could tell that magic and power coursed through her system.

"Nothing. It's empty," he replied, looking at her.

"No it isn't. Look again." And he did. And there, in the middle of the bowl lay salt crystals. The crystals then moved. They began to harden and solidified together, creating a shape. Raven and Luke leaned closer to get a better look. Calista put her hands together and placed them about four inches above the bowl. The salt crystals then floated upwards, straight into Calista's palms. She closed her hands and looked at the guys.

"Place your hands on mine. Both of you." The guys did. Both were completely transfixed that they didn't need telling twice as well as they were quite surprised that her hands were as soft as they were. Well, on the tops anyway, she didn't let them feel the underside.

"Tell me your favourite colour."

"Black," they both absently replied.

"Why does that not surprise me?" A warm glow began shining out of her hands and it lit their faces up. Raven glanced up and watched as the glow also made Calista's eyes practically gleam eerily. She also wasn't watching her hands, she was looking at him.

"Watch Raven," she whispered and placed a feather-light kiss to his lips and then Luke's and he could have sworn something of his passed from her to him, but he had no idea what; just that he felt less, well energised. The glow pulsed brighter causing the guys to look down where their hands covered Calista's, and when the glow disappeared, she pulled hers free of theirs. She opened her hands and there lying side by side, were two black-handled knives. Blade about as long as a buck knife, but this was exquisitely carved. Both had a tiny black crow carved into the top of the blade, with barbed wire wrapped around it. She handed one to Raven and the other to Luke. Then she turned around, walked into the cockpit and shut the door, all without a backwards glance to them.

"Ok, what just happened?" Luke muttered, turning in the chair and looking at his baby sister.

"Which bit?"

"All of it?"

"OK. The salt crystals hardened to create the blade and handle of your knife. When you placed your hands on her, she essentially took a part of your very essence and put it into the blade."

"So what was the feather-light kiss?" Raven looked at his knife, fascinated by it.

"She breathed a part of you into her, which she transferred into the blade as so only you can use it and if anyone else tries, it'll fall back into harmless salt crystals. People can hold it, but can never use it for violence or anything," Lexis answered.

"How do you know that?" Raven looked up to glance at her.

"Taking off now," Calista's voice called out from the speakers embedded in the walls. And sure enough they did. Everyone waited until they were safely up in the air and once they became level again, they carried on talking.

"The reason I know that is because she made me one. Beautifully lustrous and elegant. Handle was pink and purple twisted glass with a pale black blade which shimmered pink glitter. Someone snatched it off me and tried stabbing me with it, but it turned back into the harmless salt crystals. And don't worry; the guy got a serious beating off Skyri for it, who actually nearly died from it. Well he did die eventually, once Calista had finished with him," she said, when she could see her brother was about to interfere.

"Who the bloody hell is Skyri?" Luke fumed.

"One of the most dangerous beings you'll ever encounter."

"Really, how dangerous?"

"As in, he wouldn't hesitate to rip your head off for looking at him funny. He also wouldn't show how dangerous he actually is; because he can hide behind an easy going, carefree persona but in reality, he can be as deadly as me and Tairen," Draylan said.

"But not as deadly as Calista?" Raven asked.

"No one is as deadly as Calista," Tairen snorted and his uncle looked at him.

"What you snort for?"

"You. Of course, no one is more deadly than Calista," he remarked.

"Well, we obviously know that. These two have seriously no idea just how dangerous she really is," Draylan retorted.

"Back to the blade, what's with the black crow and barbed wire?" Raven enquired.

"It's Calista's mark. Feel privileged that it's on your blade. I've only known her to give it to me, Lexis, Draylan and three others," Tairen said. Raven considered this whilst he put his blade down on the table then looked out of the window and saw vast open oceans. They were moving at an alarming rate. An unusual calmness wafted over him. He had a month away from the army. No harassment, no nothing. Then he remembered about Draylan mentioning something about a scar Calista was unable to get rid of. He left them all bickering playfully with each other and headed to the cockpit. He tapped on the door and at Calista's barked, "What?" he opened the door and walked in.

Calista was peacefully sitting in the soundproof cockpit, watching the swirling turbulent sea pass by underneath her with the occasional sighting of sharks, whales and dolphins breaching the surface, when a knock at the door disturbed her.

"What?" she barked out. Turning in the chair to see who it was that disturbed her, it didn't surprise her whatsoever when she realised it was Raven.

"What do you want, Raven?" She glared at him. He walked in and shut the door behind him to give them solitude.

"I was thinking back to something Draylan mentioned earlier and I'm just going to be blunt with you as that's what Lexis said you preferred and such, but yet how is it you're all powerful and such but yet the scar that resides on your skin diagonally across your stomach you can't heal. Why is that?"

"I will only say this once. The reason I can't heal it is because I suffered that wound a couple of days after I was born and obviously wasn't in the full capacity of my powers then. Maybe people have wondered how I survived it but I did. Once I had gained my full strength and power, I hunted down the guy who had done it and I quite frankly say he wished he never had done what he did," she answered honestly.

"Can I see the scar?" She motioned for him to sit down in the co-pilot's chair, the one she never had anyone in whilst she was flying. Raven did as she said. She waited until he was sitting and facing her. Then she lifted her top up until it reached the undersides of her breasts. She didn't look down; she knew what it looked like, so instead she watched Raven's expression.

"How did you ever survive?" he whispered. He was transfixed by it. It was huge! Curling from the side of her left breast to twist across her stomach to end on her right hip. Had to be about an inch or so thick. But the edges weren't smooth, they were jagged. As though the person who had inflicted the wound had wanted it to seriously hurt and be a nightmarish way to kill someone painfully.

"I survived by sheer bloody stubbornness," she answered, pulling her top back into place.

"You're quite simply amazing, you know that, right?" he said, and leaned forward, placing his lips against hers. He stared into her amazing eyes and stayed positively still. Knowing full well if he moved, he'd go up in flames! Then she did the most unexpected thing, she kissed him back! Tilting his head slightly to the side, he grabbed her hands and placed them around his neck and then closed his eyes, but not before he smugly noticed she'd closed hers first. Thick black lashes, dark crescents against her porcelain smooth skin. He sneaked his tongue out to touch her lips and when she opened up for him, it was all he could do to suppress the groan that tried climbing up his throat. He thrust his tongue inside the moist cavern of her mouth. Her flavour hit him in the head like a forty-five-year-old bottle of Jack Daniels! Their tongues duelled. A knock at the cockpit door broke them apart, she pushed Raven back into his chair more, and then glanced at his jeans where a very noticeable bulge was evident.

"Hey, what can I say? You bring out the animal in me." He laughed when he noticed where her gaze had gone. But then he looked down and blushed a little when he realised that the bulge was massive — biggest he'd ever been! And all they'd done was kiss. He didn't want to think what it'd be like if they went past just kissing. Flames maybe?

"Face forward. You'll thank me for it later." Raven did as she said just as she barked out what. The door opened and Lexis walked in. Raven glanced down slightly, and resisted the urge to sigh with relief that his erection had deflated back to normal as soon as the door had opened and he saw it was her.

"Can I have a private word?" she asked. Raven didn't bother answering; he just got up and walked out, but not before stopping to look at Lexis.

"You OK bub?" he asked.

"I'm fine. Why?"

"Just look a little pale. Get a drink once finished with Calista, yeah?" When she nodded, he gave her a quick hug and then left the women alone, shutting the door behind him.

"What's wrong, Lexis? And no lying," Calista said. Lexis sat down in the chair that Raven had just occupied.

"I'm scared, Cali," she whispered, looking down at the floor. Calista leant forward and put her hand gently underneath Lexis's chin and lifted the girls head up so she could look her in the eye.

"What's wrong?"

"You must know by touching me?"

"Yes, but you need to tell me. To actually understand in what is going on with you," she gently replied.

"I'm pregnant. I just took a pregnancy test as I was feeling sick," she explained.

"And have you told Tairen?"

"No, not yet. I'm really scared. What about university? I can't raise a baby and focus on that too." She broke down, big tears falling down her cheeks. Calista pulled Lexis into her lap. The girl wrapped her arms around her and quite frankly cried her heart out.

"Lexis, I've got an idea about how you can do university and look after a baby." Lexis lifted her head up and looked at her, hazel eyes glossy and cheeks wet from tears.

"What is that then?"

"Well, first tell Tairen that he's going to be a daddy. And second, I'll help you. And so will loads of others. You must remember, you're surrounded by people who love you."

"Do you love me?"

"Like the annoying kid sister I've never had. Tried not to, but you worked your cheeky self into my ice cavern." She smiled slightly as Lexis burst out with laughter.

"Your heart isn't an ice cavern," she giggled.

"Of course it is, but it'll be our secret that you worked your way in first."

"OK." She smiled.

"Now go tell Tairen." She gently pushed Lexis up and to the door.

"Can I tell him in here? Just in case he doesn't take it well?" Lexis actually looked petrified.

"Of course you can. Go get him." Calista faced the right way again and clicked a series of buttons before autopilot came on. A moment or so went past and then she heard Lexis and Tairen coming. Lexis led Tairen into the cockpit and Calista motioned for him to take a seat. He did without question.

"So what's up? You never call me into the cockpit," he asked.

"Lexis wants to tell you something." Tairen turned to look at her.

"What is it, baby?"

"I know we've only been together for about ten months now, and don't get me wrong, these have been some of the best ten months of my life but I have to tell you this." She paused to glance worriedly at Calista who just nodded her head like everything would be all right. She turned back to Tairen, eyes downcast and cleared her throat. "I'm pregnant and you're going to be a daddy," she blurted out. She glanced up at Tairen and was surprised by the look on his face. He was grinning so wide, his cheek muscles must hurt. His eyes were also lit up with unadulterated glee. He looked at Calista.

"I'm going to be a daddy!" he said excitedly.

"Yes, you are," she replied. She watched as Tairen leapt out of his chair and swung Lexis up in his arms.

"We're going to have our own little family, Lexis!" he whispered, hugging her close. Lexis looked over his shoulder at Calista and smiled as brightly as a 100 watt bulb. She squirmed out of Tairen's arms, just looked at him and he simply nodded as though they'd had a conversation and not simply looked at each other, and then Lexis turned to look at Calista.

"Calista, would you do us the honour of being our child's godmother when they eventually come screaming into the world?"

"Of course, I would be honoured. Now go tell the others. We'll be landing within the hour or so."

"Of course. Also, have you got any idea in how far along I am?"

"You're six weeks or so along. Now out." With that, she turned away knowing they'd get the hint and leave. She felt someone lightly kiss her cheek and from the smell of fresh lavender, she knew it was Lexis. Tairen knew not to touch her. A minute later, she heard Raven and Draylan congratulate the obviously deliriously happy couple, and then Luke voiced his. She knew Draylan would sort him out so she tuned everyone out. She put a CD on. One she had personally installed herself. Music suddenly blasted out of the speakers that were embedded into the cockpit's walls. One of her favourite songs came on and she absently turned the volume up. Five Finger Death Punch – Bad Company blared out of the speakers, followed by a contented sigh from Calista.

Chapter Four
Two Hours Later

Calista turned the music off as the island of Tasmania came into view. She flew over the gorgeous island topped with vast mountains and watched as thick lush trees bristled in the wind, leaves on flimsy yet strong branches looked like they were waving at you. Birds soared in the sky, majority freefalling into the treetops in vast magical colours. She finally saw what she was looking for. A small private runway situated not all that far from Cradle Mountain itself. Moving the plane expertly into position, she pulled into line with the runway that lay just ahead, which also happened to be situated about one hundred and seventy-five miles away from Wineglass Bay, her destination, and would take her about four hours to get there via car. Walking would take fifty-six hours. Fuck right off with that one, she'd sooner have her labia tickled with a feather! And she soooo wasn't into that shit!

"We're about to land, you lot. I suggest you buckle up — going to be a bit of a bumpy ride." She clicked off the mic after making that announcement. Sure enough it was bumpy thanks to the jaggedness of the track, but nothing she couldn't handle. She pulled the aircraft to a skilled stop.

"Welcome, Calista." She was greeted via radio by a woman's voice.

"Thanks Jah'nea. Be down in a minute."

"How many accompany you?"

"Including me, six. And Blodox, of course," she replied.

"Roger that. See you in a minute." Jah'nea radioed off. Calista reattached the radio mic to its rightful place and stood up. She stretched the kinks out of her muscles then made her way into the back to the others. She shut the cockpit door, pocketed the aircraft keys and looked at everyone who still had a death grip on the arms of their chairs.

"You can unbuckle yourselves now you know. We have landed."

"Please tell me that it's the only major jumpy part we have to go over," Luke remarked, unbuckling himself as did everyone else. They all stretched to relieve muscles tensed from the flight. Blodox head-butted her leg. She absently stroked his ear.

"For now, yes," she answered.

"So, you mean there will be bumpier aeroplane rides?" Raven practically grimaced.

"Not in aeroplanes, no. I mean by walking."

"How much walking we talking about?" Raven turned his intense stare to Calista's own.

"It's two miles to Wineglass Bay," she said bluntly, no point in pussy footing around the truth.

"Great. Just like in the army. Only we're not hauling along 100 –110 pound backpacks," Luke commented sardonically.

"Pack all your gear. Anything left behind, Jah'nea keeps," Calista said, ignoring Luke's remark. She turned away, grabbed Blodox's things and not bothering to wait around to see if they gathered their things or not, whistled for the dog who immediately appeared at her side and they left the plane side by side. As they did, a fresh gust of wind hit them in the face and both breathed in deeply before letting it out in a contented sigh. A lovely cocoa-skinned woman greeted her at the bottom of the stairs.

"Hello, Jah'nea," Calista said in greeting. Jah'nea was indeed lovely. Real down to earth. Any more laid back and she'd be horizontal. But annoy her or hurt her family, she was one female which you did not mess with. Calista had known her since before she was a fertilized egg in her mother's womb, actually before her mother's, mother's, mother's, mother was a fertilized egg. Thinking of it that way made her feel damn old. Shaking herself mentally, she stared at the woman in front of her. Jah'nea had rich chocolate brown eyes that beheld friendliness, awareness and keen intelligence. She had shoulder-length black hair which also strangely held copper highlights. She wasn't drop-dead gorgeous, but she was a natural beauty. She also had a heart of gold. She stood at around five feet seven. Today she wore a simple black cloth dress that suited her perfectly. And complimented her slightly rounded belly.

"Was the flight all right?"

"Piece of cake. How's the pregnancy coming along?" she answered, and handed her Blodox's bed.

"Lovely to hear. Good thanks, only a little nausea this time and hello Blodox." She laughed, knowing full well nothing got past Calista's attention. The sound one of complete joy as Blodox head-butted her leg, one not wanting to be left unnoticed. She gave the dog a loving scratch, which he quite happily accepted and leaned into her hand for more.

"So who's that?" she indicated with a nod towards the plane. Calista glanced back.

"You know Draylan, Tairen and Lexis already. The other two are Lexis's brother, Luke, and his best friend, Raven," she explained just as everyone got to the bottom of the stairs and said hello to Jah'nea, which the woman returned, all politeness and shit. They all then followed her through the forest for about fifteen minutes when they came across a hut that was more like a bungalow or four, which was raised a good eighteen feet in the air on stilts the thickness of tree trunks. They walked under the structure, to the back where a huge tree sat on its own in the centre. Jah'nea walked over to it and pressed her hand to the bark. There was a slight pop and a section of the wood moved out and to the side, only to reveal a staircase swirling upwards. Blodox barked happily and bounded up the stairs. Jah'nea followed. Calista looked back at the others and motioned for them to follow. They did. They had just reached the stairs when a very feral growl radiated from the surrounding bush, which made Calista whirled around and glare into the direction the noise had come from.

"Markus, I swear, fuck off with that shit," she called out.

"Erm, who is Markus?" Raven asked, right by Calista's ear.

"A fucked up wereleopard who needs his brain sorted."

"How so?" His voice was reasonably calm considering she'd just told him that Markus was a were leopard.

"Because I'm going to skin his sorry hide."

"But then Jah'nea would be greatly unhappy you killed her husband and father to her kids," Draylan idly pointed out, making Raven aware he was there with them — she already knew he had stayed. Calista stayed looking ahead, when the men noticed a thickly-muscled leopard stood watching them from intense yellow glowing orbs for eyes surrounded by thick plush black fur.

"I take it that's Markus," Raven muttered to Draylan.

"Got that right," he replied, just as Markus took off to them. And that was when Raven got a look at the raw power of Calista. One minute she was standing in front of him and the next she was dashing across the forest floor as a jaguar! Although he had to admit, she was gorgeous as a jaguar. Luscious black rich thick fur covered a muscled yet streamlined body. Talk about a shock to the system. He glanced quickly at Draylan to see what he thought but it was impossible to tell what the man was thinking. His face was an unreadable, unemotional mask.

"Draylan, can I ask you something?"

"Sure." Draylan looked at him, the sound of the leopard and jaguar play fighting as background noise.

"Any other surprises like that I should be aware of if I am to be with you and Calista at Mystic Being?"

"Of that I can guarantee. Don't be surprised if she had to change or something. There is nothing she can't change into but each is with a finesse that is purely Calista." Silence suddenly filled the air, causing both men to quickly turn around as to why only Markus was there, breathing in and out quickly whilst he was looking around. Calista was nowhere to be seen. As if she'd never been. Markus flashed back to human form and Raven got a good look at the man. He stood at around six feet four, so same height as Luke, built quite a bit too. Vivid liquid brown eyes held keen intelligence and were on constant alert. Black hair cut short. Skin a warm hazelnut chocolate brown colour. He wore black cloth trousers and a dark brown cloth T-shirt. His feet were bare though, as Jah'nea's had been, Raven thought absently.

"Where did Calista go?" Draylan said in way of greeting. Markus just grinned at him as he walked over, pearly white teeth a stark contrast to his skin tone. Strangely, it suited him.

"And hello to you too Draylan. And Calista ran off into the shrubbery when an arrow made itself friendly with her shoulder," he announced.

"Did you catch a look at the assailant?"

"Only a quick glimpse. Mesmerising gold eyes. Golden marbleised skin," Markus replied.

"OK. Now why would a Marbilian be away from Mystic Being and hit Calista with an arrow? When it obviously takes more than that to wound her," Draylan wondered.

"Could he have been given an order? Or perhaps paid?" Raven asked, drawing the men's gazes to his. And, what the hell was a Marbilian anyway? He'd never heard of it. Another thing to ask later.

"He might have been paid. Or even threatened if he didn't complete the task. It is one thing we will take into consideration. Good thinking Raven," Draylan said. Markus suddenly whirled around and Draylan and Raven looked to what had caused him to turn quickly. Coming towards them from the bush was the Marbilian. Thick oozing blood which was the same colour as his skin slid from various wounds. Some deep, others shallow. Raven had to look twice, as on closer inspection it seemed his skin was melting from his very bones. He had perhaps reached halfway to them when Calista made an appearance. She was bleeding from various wounds but yet she looked as though she could take on the entire world. Raven still thought she looked fantastic. Did anything make this woman appear less unattractive? Clearly fucking not. They watched as Calista ran to the guy, who had turned with his fingernails sharp and serrated like knives, poised for a strike but then he charged at her. They clashed together like massive boulders, loud and very dangerous if caught in the middle of them. He watched, fascinated as she laid into the guy. He got in a few punches here and there that must have stung like a sorry son of a bitch due to what he was and the size of him as well, as jagged claw marks down her face, neck and arms, but yet Calista never so much as blinked, or made a strangled noise of pain! Just how bloody tough was she? What did it take to get her to make a noise, or maybe even give in? Had she ever given in? He highly doubted it. The fluidness of Calista was astounding. She moved like a ballerina, a dangerous ballerina, but one anyway. All fluid limbs but the punches she threw were nothing gentle, judging by the resounding thud as each hit landed a place. Punches, kicks and such were traded between the two. The Marbilian swung at Calista and a blade had appeared in his hand. She did a wide roundhouse kick that caught the blade and sent it flying out of her opponents hand and careening towards Draylan, Markus and Raven, where it landed with a solid thwack above their heads. The guys looked up and saw it was buried to the hilt, and it was still slightly vibrating. They all gulped at the thought of something like that hitting any part of them. Calista was severely pissed right now, so she made short work of the Marbilian. She ripped his arms off, ignoring the high pain-filled screams erupting from it, then tripped him up and proceeded to do the same thing to his legs. But he didn't bleed to death. Oh no, she stopped him from bleeding clean out. Another neat trick of hers. But one barely used and not very many people knew about it either.

"Who sent you?" she fumed, getting right in the guy's face. Suddenly it drew dark, almost as black as night, eerily so considering it was eleven a.m., according to Raven's watch anyway.

"Draylan, what's happening?" Calista heard Lexis call out. Apparently, the darkness and the screams from the Marbilian had caused concern and now they'd come to investigate.

"Calista got shot by a Marbilian and now she's pissed off," he explained, knowing the kid would get it. Calista looked back at the half dead guy at her feet. The only light was from the eerie glow of her eyes that was really bright, like a 100 watt bulb, along with the torch that Jah'nea always kept lit. No wonder they couldn't really see anything, maybe just Calista's eyes and everything the light touched.

"Now tell me who fucking sent you!" The ground literally rumbled from the fierceness of Calista's now booming voice, and sent everyone else stumbling!

"Thank God we have reinforced magical glass windows; they'd have broken by now," Markus joked and for it got a punch off Jah'nea even though she held their thirteen month old son, of which made Markus shut up instantly. He clearly knew when to keep his mouth shut around his mate and it just made his son grin at him and cuddle closer to his mother. The kid obviously knew who was in charge.

"Look guys, the Marbilian is talking." Lexis said and they all turned back to pay attention.

"It was Kharge. He said if I didn't then he would kill my family. I only have my little boy left. Kharge killed my pregnant wife to show he wasn't bluffing." You could tell that had destroyed a part of him by the tone of his voice. When Marbilians found their fated Marbalina, they stayed with them for life.

"And now you expect me to let you live?"

"Yes, I told you who sent me and why he did. I don't want to leave my son an orphan. He's only seven." The Marbilian choked slightly.

"I shall let you live. But you must send a message to Kharge for me."

"What is it? And how am I meant to give him it if I have no arms and legs?" he pointed out. Calista held her hands out and his limbs flew towards her. She aligned them perfectly with the gaps in which she had removed them.

"Brano breano xvarm vrailium," she whispered and a piercing blue-white light shone from her fingers. It attached itself to the limbs and she quickly cast a glance to the others and noticed that everyone was transfixed. Apart from Draylan, which was understandable, he'd seen it before. Once, mind you, but he'd seen it, and only because it had been done to his vicious and cold-hearted older brother who had gone rogue, which caused Calista to hunt him down, brutalising him because he and a friend had tortured Draylan, so she'd done so much more to them, before they had finally succumbed into death's open arms. To this day, she knew he never spoke of it. Not even his niece and nephew knew the extent of what was done to him, they only knew he'd been held captive by his brother and viciously assaulted for four weeks before she'd gotten word about it all and went to his rescue. She turned her gaze back to the Marbilian and the limbs all began reattaching themselves right in front of her gaze. It wouldn't hurt, just got a warm tingling sensation. Once completed, the light disappeared. And the man, well Marbilian, was once again whole.

"Now in answer to your question, tell Kharge to expect me, and anyone he sends after me shall go back to him in pieces," she said and the Marbilian leapt to his feet.

"Thank you for allowing me to live, Calista. If you ever walk through Marbilian lands, ask for Glinther."

"I take it that is you?"

"Yes. Thank you again, Calista. I shall return directly to Mystic Being, give Kharge your message and then I shall return to my boy, Glithero." With that, he turned and disappeared into the surrounding forest. Calista turned to face everyone but due to the sky being overrun by thick black clouds, the only way for them to see her was due to her luminous eyes and the few fire torches that Jah'nea had just lit. A rich rippling roar floated out of the darkness then.

"Everyone get inside and upstairs now!" Calista ordered as she sprinted to them. They all ran up the stairs and as Raven closed the door, he saw her shift into a humungous leopard, bigger than she was when she was play-fighting with Markus. The last thing he saw was Calista sink her wickedly sharp claws into the shoulders of a man who had appeared near to where they had stood only seconds before, and razor-sharp teeth sink either side of the person's face and pull back flesh and muscle trapped behind her canines — blood dripped down her face. Sheer bloodbath already and then the door shut, blocking out anything else. Raven turned around and bolted up the stairs until he reached the part to get off and walked into Jah'nea and Markus' living area. The home was very jungle based but also had a rich overstuffed couch and two chairs. No television, just a radio that was turned off. Rugs adorned the floor in plush dark brown. It seemed to suit the obviously happy couple and their child but Raven couldn't live like that. It'd send him crazy. He noticed a few candles were in the middle of everyone where they were huddled in a small circle at the couch. He walked over to where Lexis was sitting and plopped down next to her. The sounds of the battle going on underneath them loud and stupidly scary.

"How many were there? Did anyone see?" Jah'nea asked, trying to keep her son quiet and calm, so they wouldn't draw attention to the fact they were sitting there, effectively sitting ducks if those who battled against Calista managed to get through her and the door. Sure Luke and him could fight but could they hold their own against shifters?

"Roughly fifteen I counted quickly," Raven announced, dragging himself from that thought.

"Calista will be all right, won't she?" Jah'nea said, cradling her now sleeping son snugly against her chest. Clearly, he had more interest in sleeping and snuggling against his mother's breast than what was going on around him. Smart kid.

"Probably have a few wounds, but she'll be fine," Draylan said. Lexis hugged close to Luke who put his arm around her, as Tairen was missing.

"Where's Tairen?" Raven asked as he noticed that he wasn't there.

"He's with Markus getting supplies," she replied, cuddling her brother close, who happily returned the cuddle with both arms wrapped around her, securing her safety in the protection of his arms. And Raven knew for a fact if anyone tried to harm her, Luke would kill them with no hesitation. Plus, he probably liked the fact he could cuddle his sister close again after so long apart, as they'd always been very close.

"Supplies for what?"

"For Calista."

"Thought you said she'll have a few scratches and that's it? Or do you think she'll be wounded much?" Raven wondered.

"Not really. It's the ones she's fighting I feel sorry for," Draylan said, stretching out in the chair he had claimed. Suddenly gun shots could be heard, then a god awful scream erupted through the darkness, making them all jump slightly.

"Who the hell was that?" Jah'nea asked, trying to shush her child up as he'd woken up from that horrendous noise. Blodox huddled at her side, his head on her knee.

"No idea. I couldn't tell you if it was Calista or not as I've never heard her scream before," Draylan admitted, and they all realised if it had indeed been Calista who had screamed, someone must have caused serious damage to her. Tairen and Markus returned then, overloaded with bandages, gauze, cast makers, etc. They placed them all on the table after asking Jah'nea where to put them. Tairen walked over to Lexis, unclamped her hands from where they dug into Luke's ribs, hauled her up into his arms and promptly sat down with her on his lap. Raven noticed with a small smile on his face that Luke breathed a huge sigh of relief at being able to breathe again properly, his sister must have had one mean tight grip and clearly if she didn't want to let go, she didn't. Tairen sat with one arm around his woman as she cuddled him close, fear evident in her eyes and by the way she nervously nibbled her lip. But it was obvious she was worried about Calista, all of them were. They all looked outside and unfortunately it was still dark, which was still weird. The noise was loud and that made you want to sneakily watch but they weren't stupid and refused to go downstairs just in case they got targeted. Suddenly, intense sunshine shone into the room, blinding them temporarily with the sharp brightness and all of the horrid noises stopped. All they could hear was their breathing and the distant animals that called the forest home, speaking to each other in avid distress.

"Think we should go check on Calista?" Lexis asked, breaking the silence. In answer, Draylan stood up and walked to the tree stairs. Everyone else followed. Jah'nea put her son down in the pen that was just for him, out of danger and trouble, then promptly followed. Luckily the kid found his toys and occupied himself, blanking the adults. Jah'nea ordered Blodox to stay and the dog lay down next to the boy. Content to stay and guard him. They all raced down the stairs and waited for Markus to activate the door to open. Once he did, they all rushed outside. But they soon pulled up short. Bodies lay all over the floor, many missing parts and some even had vast chunks missing out of them. Blood, guts and other things soaked the ground. Weapons lay forgotten and blood-coated. It was a huge bloody slaughter!

"Calista!" Lexis screamed suddenly and raced ahead. Raven watched as she fell to her knees next to a body that was coated in horrendous colours of blood and weird bright splashes of what appeared to be guts. Everyone quickly followed whilst Lexis pulled a tissue out her pocket and tried wiping the blood from the body's face. Raven realised it could be Calista, or so he thought anyway, as it was hard to see what the features were behind all that gore. All that resembled Calista was the black hair and the obvious form of the female body.

"Calista, open your god damn eyes!" Lexis was hysterical. Frantically scrubbing at the face, trying to clear the blood but it just made it worse, not to mention half the face was ripped open.

"Why are you cleaning that dead person?" a very familiar voice called from behind them, which promptly caused them to whirl around quickly and Calista was leaning against a tree, luminous blood covering her like a second skin in places, but she acted as though it was never there and just stared at them with absolutely no emotion on her face. She was exactly as she'd been described, a killing machine. Lexis jumped up and dived at her, wrapping her arms and legs around Calista and refused to let her go. Clearly the blood didn't bother her, she was just glad to see her friend alive still. It didn't affect Calista either that the woman was hanging onto her like a second limb or that she carried her as though she was a feather. She walked to the group just as a guttural screech ruptured through the air. Calista grabbed a hold of Lexis' waist and lobbed her straight at Tairen, who luckily caught the startled woman. She turned around and took the knife off of Draylan that was held in his hand and leaned into a battle stance as old as time. A black-haired beast of a man crashed out of the edge of the forest and charged at Calista with obvious intent to kill. It was plain in his crazed green eyes. He was also decked out completely in black, so he blended in well. When he got within range, Calista leapt onto him, catching him by surprise. But it didn't last long; he pulled a knife from somewhere and drew it sharply down Calista's back as they toppled to the floor. Blood welled and poured out of her, but yet not a sound sprung from her throat. She grabbed the blade and slammed it into the guy's gut. She dragged the blade upwards whilst he still grunted from it going into him the first time. Slicing the guy open without a second thought, she killed him quickly. Then pulled the knife out and threw it away, leaving it to embed itself into a tree trunk. They watched, fascinated as the blood stopped and her back healed itself up, leaving behind unblemished skin. Then she whirled around and they all noticed her eyes. They'd changed from the gorgeous cobalt blue to an intense red and they were focused on them all intently, almost as if she was contemplating draining them dry. Draylan walked over to her and whispered something in her ear. She absently nodded, turned and disappeared into the forest, which seemed to welcome her like one of its own. Draylan walked back to the group, knowing she'd be OK.

"Is she all right?" Lexis asked, shaking slightly.

"She'll be fine. I'm going back to her in a minute. Jah'nea, can they all stay in yours whilst I deal with Calista?" He looked at her and she simply nodded, looking around at the sheer carnage that lay underneath her home with wide eyes.

"What do you mean, deal with Calista?" Raven asked.

"Exactly that. Didn't you notice her eyes had changed colour?"

"Yeah, I noticed. Why is that?"

"Means she's lost quite a bit of blood and now she's starving. Which is why she went into the forest."

"To feed you mean?" Luke said.

"Yes."

"And that's why you want us to go up into Jah'nea and Markus's," Lexis pointed out. Clearly clicking on with what would happen should Calista get her hands on any of them.

"Yes, I don't want her feeding on any of you."

"Why what would happen?" Raven requested.

"She'd dry you clean out and she'd go through all three of you without a second thought."

"Of our blood?" Luke visibly lost all colour in his face at the prospect of that.

"Yes. Didn't Lexis explain to you that she often drinks blood? More so when injured?" Tairen said.

"No, you just did. Lexis only told us Calista drank blood, but not how often or more so when injured. Or she might have, just wasn't really listening," Raven admitted. They all regarded him calmly. He seemed to be taking it all in his stride pretty darn well and not freaking out.

"Well at least you know now," Jah'nea said.

"True. At least we know," Luke murmured. A rustling, stick-breaking, bush-moving noise drew their attention. A few deer burst from the surrounding forest ahead and charged at them.

"Do not move, they'll go around us," Tairen said. They all stayed perfectly still at the tree stairs and the obviously terrified animals did indeed run past. Draylan, thanks to his enhanced vampire vision, noticed blood spots marked some of the fur on a couple of the adult's necks. At a few collective gasps, Draylan turned around. Calista stood watching them, blood-red eyes locked onto their every movement. Her head was tilted to the side slightly and her mouth twisted up in a sinister smirk that was coated in blood. It also ran in rivulets down her throat, soaked into her tank top and stood out brilliantly against her creamy skin. The bushes hid her from the waist down but he knew she was still dressed.

"Everyone upstairs now!" Draylan shouted just as Calista leaned down, picked up something and lobbed it at them. Everyone luckily had moved, apart from Draylan. They stood on the stairs but not moving any further as the thing Calista had lobbed landed at his feet in a sickening thud. They all looked back and those not used to things like it gagged, which was all of them. Draylan finally tore his gaze from Calista and looked down at his feet. The thing that she had lobbed was a carcass. Fresh one but still a carcass. It was a big healthy stag. Or at least it was until Calista had got her hands on it. Now it was staring ahead, eyes glazed over with death, mouth open in a forever silent bleat, with its throat ripped clean open and drained of its sacred blood. It was opened that much, Draylan could see its oesophagus. And because she'd drained it dry, its body had shrunk into itself, outlining every single bone and small lumps which were the internal organs. Lovely. It seemed Calista had chosen to kill and drain this animal rather than go for one of them. Lucky she did, as none of them would have stood a chance. If she was this quick and deadly, they'd have all been drained and dead in a matter of minutes and all would have been without a chance of getting away — she was just too quick. He looked back up at his best friend and she was standing right in front of him with only the stag separating them. He hadn't even heard her move. Her red eyes unblinking and focused entirely on him.

"Still need blood?" he whispered, knowing not to talk loudly as her hearing was even more acutely sensitive than normal. Always was when like this — lucky enough it was rare.

"Yes," she replied, voice raspy.

"From me? Or you are hunting again?" He always helped her out, as she did him.

"Hunt again. I could take too much from you." Even when she was ravenous, she was decent. Well, to those on her side. If you weren't, then it was an entirely different ball game. But he noticed her voice had taken on a rasp as if she had no saliva in her mouth.

"OK, we'll be upstairs waiting." He turned to leave. She reached out and grabbed his arm, her hand cold to the touch but he didn't remove it.

"No. Meet me at Wineglass Bay. To the place we have to go to get home. And whilst I remember, tell Luke and Raven not to worry about their bikes, I'll bring them."

"How would you bring two powerful Kawasaki Ninja motorbikes?" he asked.

"Simple. Use a little bit of magic, shrink them and make them pocket-sized. And no need to worry, they will quite simply work as they do now when I make them bigger again," she replied. It must have looked kind of freaky having a conversation with her covered in blood and eyes glowing with hunger. Draylan must have noticed her attention wasn't entirely on him and looked over his shoulder. By his curse, she gathered he had noticed everyone watching them.

"Draylan, take them to Wineglass Bay. I will meet you there," she said.

"Are you sure? Don't mind waiting for you," he replied.

"I'm sure. I'm big enough to look after myself and walk to the lake."

"I know, just thought I'd be nice." He grinned at her, she returned it even though she had blood-caked fangs which were very prominent. Not to mention the rest of the blood that coated her.

"Your fangs are showing," he pointed out. She removed her hand from his arm then as it must have been tempting her, feeling his blood coursing through his veins underneath her hand and there was nothing she could do about it.

"Because I'm hungry still," she simply responded.

"Well go and eat then, you silly woman. You're no good to me hungry." Draylan stepped around the carcass and draped his arm across her shoulders, bringing her to his side for a hug which she actually returned. It was rare to get a hug from her, as she never let anyone get close enough. So when he received them, he treasured them always.

"OK. I shouldn't be too long." With that, she shrugged his arm off her and disappeared back into the woodland, melding in easily as if she was one with the forest. She walked deep enough into the shrubbery so that they wouldn't see her and turned around. Draylan had his back to her, talking to the group who were listening to his every word. Her gaze for some untold reason drifted to Raven. She still couldn't believe he'd kissed her. And she'd kissed him back! She shook herself to get rid of unwanted memories and turned her back to them. Using her unusual 'abilities', she let them loose, scanning for an animal she could take down to replenish her hunger. She stopped scanning at about one hundred feet ahead of her. It was a pack of wild hogs. They'd do until she reached home. She crept forward, silent as a ghost. Disturbing nothing around or underneath her. The predator and killer she naturally was. She reached the edge of the clearing the hogs occupied and using a freeze spell, froze them where they stood. She made quick work of taking enough blood from each adult, leaving the babies. Even she wasn't that sadistic. Also, it was so as not to cause permanent damage. She quickly finished and stepped back into the surrounding shrubbery. Then she unfroze them. And they obliviously went about their business as though nothing had happened. She walked back to Jah'nea's, but made a detour to the plane. She pulled the keys to the machine from her pocket. By some untold miracle they'd actually stayed in her pocket, considering everything she'd done, and then unlocked the aircraft. She walked into the cockpit and flipped a switch that opened up the cargo bay. She walked back outside and to the rear of the plane and the ramp was down so she walked inside. Only Raven and Luke's bikes, plus her Night Demon occupied the vast space. And even then, they were at the head of the plane, strapped into place so they wouldn't topple over and get damaged. She made short work of untying them and whispered a metal-shrinking spell an old witch friend had told her about a couple of weeks before she'd been brutally murdered for her small amount of knowledge. But it was handy to have it at times.

"Veraneo varno crastamern metal aler shrinkern." The magical words flew from Calista's mouth simply and easily. The bikes were suddenly cocooned in a silver-type light, sparkling and sizzling with power. Only to be described as a child's version of twinkling magic or fairy dust. The bikes then began to shrink. They shrank and contorted until they became tiny metal orbs that sat idly in her palm. She placed them in her pocket and left the cargo hold. Clambering back up the stairs into the aircraft, she quickly put everything in the plane back into its rightful place. She double checked she had everything and noticed Lexis had left a pair of black raven feather earrings on the table next to the bed she had occupied not that long ago. She pocketed them, knowing full well the girl would miss them if she didn't have them. Considering they were the first gift Calista had given her. She locked the plane up and made her way back to Jah'nea's. When she reached the tree stairs, she heard the baby crying. Instead of taking the stairs, she simply vanished and reappeared in the living area. She could hear the adults fluffing around in the kitchen, the smell of cooking food rich in the air. She walked over to baby Samuel, who was crying his little heart out. Before she reached him, she made the blood that coated her disappear as so to not make the baby more distraught than he already clearly was.

"Hey little Samuel, you hush that noise." She picked him up and immediately he fell quiet as he became transfixed with the fingers she waggled in front of his face. Jah'nea came flying out of the kitchen, holding a soaking, half-rinsed out baby bottle in her hand to find out why her baby had stopped crying whilst she prepared his bottle.

"Oh Calista; I didn't realize you'd stopped by. Thought you had left with Draylan and everyone else," she said, once she'd caught her breath from panicking.

"No, not yet. I came by to give you the plane keys."

"Oh yes, of course." Jah'nea hung the keys Calista had lobbed at her on a key hook next to the tree stairs and well out of the way of a very grabby baby. She sat down on the couch and absently bounced a giggling Samuel on her knee. Blodox lay sound asleep in his bed by an open fire, completely content right where he was with the heat keeping him warm, which was a good thing considering he was staying here. It was too dangerous in Mystic Being for him. And he fitted in much better with Jah'nea and her family. He was ridiculously protective of Samuel, which is what they needed for where they lived, at least until the kid hit puberty and his inner leopard emerged. And thank God the dog was kept in here when she was battling those bastard creatures that had been sent to kill her. She didn't want to have to bury the dog, not when he still had years to go. Plus he was a good companion for Samuel to grow up with, much better than herself when she didn't know if she'd return home the same day.

"Go finish his bottle, Jah'nea. I'll leave afterwards." Jah'nea nodded, knowing her son was in safe hands. Calista stopped bouncing Samuel and watched the baby watch her. She ran her hand over her mouth, and felt some of the dried blood; obviously all of it hadn't come away. She quickly scrubbed her hand over the blood and it disappeared. Samuel laughed and reached his chubby hands to her. She made magic flow through her hand, glistening like glitter but it also looked like a rainbow. Samuel was transfixed. Not surprising, mostly anything transfixed him. Even a simple spider walking across the floor or wall held his complete attention. He reached out to touch it and giggled as it washed over his hands. Jah'nea and Markus walked out of the kitchen then and strolled over to them.

"I didn't know you could do that," Jah'nea said, taking Samuel away from her to give him his bottle. Samuel protested until he saw his bottle, then greedily snatched it from his mother and began to chug the warm milk down. Calista stopped the magic flowing as though someone had put a light out.

"Calista, could you help me bring that stag up here you killed earlier? Saves it going to waste," Markus asked, drawing her attention to him.

"Sure. No problem. Got enough space for it?"

"No, we kind of need you to help with that," Jah'nea said not looking at them, but keeping an eye on her still milk-guzzling son.

"That'll be no problem. Come on then Markus. Let's go grab the stag before some other animal grabs it." They both left then. They walked downstairs and outside and luckily enough the stag was still there. But so were the other bodies of the people Calista had killed. She snapped her fingers and all the bodies disintegrated until all that was left was piles of ashes, but they soon blew away with the wind — even the weapons disappeared too.

"Handy to have," Markus muttered.

"You have no idea." Calista shrugged as she knelt down next to the carcass. She placed her hands on the now cold flesh, one against the shoulder blade near where she'd bitten, the other on the hip and a narrow red line appeared, running up against the fur in a straight line from her hand.

"Where the hell did that line come from?" Markus murmured.

"Sh. Let me concentrate." She raised her hands slightly and the line continued down and around the body. She stood up and the lines of the animals began to seep into the skin. Cutting through the flesh and such like a laser. She's carried on until the body lay in three separate pieces.

"That's seriously fucking incredible! Never seen that done before." Markus was marvelled!

"Which part do you want?" Calista asked, looking at him.

"Middle. Can't do anything with the end. And the head, Jah'nea wouldn't want it. So we might as well leave it for the animals," he replied and she nodded. Understandable, as the middle was the most succulent richest part, plus it was the biggest there. She then let out a spine chilling screech which caused Markus to stab his finger in his ear to stop the ringing.

"Thanks for the warning," he grunted and she just smirked at him. And less than a minute later, a Tasmanian Devil made an appearance. Ravenously hungry by looks of it too, what with the wide eyes and drooling mouth.

"Back off a bit, Markus. Let him have the spare meat and then we'll take the rest up to Jah'nea." Markus nodded and stepped back. The little black beast was the real deal. He wouldn't argue with it for sure; and considering he was a wereleopard, that was saying something. But he also trusted Calista and he watched as the dangerous animal approached her as though they had known each other for years. Guess it could smell the alpha predator that she was. Calista ruffled the fur at the base of the neck of the Tasmanian Devil as it eyed up the carcass in front of it. She leaned forward slightly, grabbed the back end and handed it to the beast. He looked at her as though in permission and she nodded. He closed his ridiculously sharp teeth around as much of it as it could and looked at her for a couple of seconds, then took off. The stag's legs flying behind the animal to disappear into the woodland. She lobbed the head away, knowing another animal would eventually find it and enjoy it, because it was the law of the jungle. Kill or be killed. She grabbed what was left and hiked it over her shoulder.

"Let's go. We'll find room in your kitchen for it." Together they walked upstairs again. Once they had, Calista walked into the kitchen and through a doorway which led to their storage room. She placed the slab of meat onto the side and opened up the huge chest freezer. Thanks to her abilities, Jah'nea and Markus had a full working kitchen and all the electrical things that are found in one. She pulled out ready-made meals and put them in the old butler sink they used to defrost things. She then grabbed the stag meat and placed it inside then put everything back that she'd removed, shrinking some so there was plenty of room.

"All done?" Jah'nea asked, standing in the doorway.

"Yes. I've shrunk some of the meals you've prepared, but when you want to use them, just pull them out and they'll return back to normal size," she replied.

"OK, thank you. And I take it this means you'll be leaving now, then?"

"You know I have to. Some kids are missing, got to go and find them. I'm their only hope of being reunited with the parents again."

"So how long before I see you again?"

"No idea. You'll see Lexis, Tairen, Raven and Luke again in a couple of weeks as Lexis has to go back to Scotland because of university. And Tairen will be with her as she's carrying his baby."

"I know. They told me. I'm so happy for them. They deserve the happiness of creating a family and I know they'll be fantastic parents."

"Yes," she said and left the room.

"Shall I let Mama and Papa know you popped through?" Jah'nea asked, following her. Her parents, whom Calista had known since before they were even a twinkle in their own parents' eyes, liked hearing about how she was whenever she passed through.

"Sure, if you want to." The women walked into the living room. Markus was sprawled on the couch, a bouncy happy Samuel on his stomach, who let out a huge burp and giggled then proceeded to place his wet hands on his father's face.

"I take it this means you're off then?" Markus asked and placed Samuel on the floor, next to his toys that would occupy the child.

"Yes. Got to go catch up with them lot," she replied.

"Well, thanks for bringing up the stag and putting it in the chest freezer for us. As well as stopping by to say hello, obviously." He grinned at her.

"You're welcome. And obviously I had to stop by; you're looking after the plane for a few weeks until Lexis and the lads return to Scotland," she replied bluntly. Markus didn't take offence, he knew she was blunt and didn't pussyfoot around either. Had for as long as he could remember, actually even his own parents had said for as long as they could remember she'd always been that way.

"I take it by lads you mean Luke and Raven?"

"Yes. I doubt they'd last a while in Mystic Being without someone always watching over them," she said.

"Ah right, OK. Well until next time, then." He held out his hand and she shook it. Jah'nea refused to shake her hand; she grabbed her for a hug. Calista obviously didn't return it, she never did. She wasn't one for doing that. When Jah'nea let her go, Calista gave them a nod and turned to leave without a backward glance, but not before she gave Blodox an affectionate scratch before he headed over to the boy and curled up next to him on the floor. She knew it would be a long while before she saw the affectionate beast again. Once she had reached the bottom of the stairs, she turned and instinctively headed in the direction of Wineglass Bay. She sighed happily as rich, powerful magic coursed through her system and before anyone could so much as blink she was a sleek, gorgeous black panther. She took off running. Streamlined body and heavy duty paws with razor sharp claws quickly ate up the ground. She darted around trees and flew over bushes. Animals flew in all directions to avoid contact with the powerful animal that ran through their forest. Within half an hour, she finally began slowing down. During the run, she reached deep within her and sent out a magical probe to the Carriers that would take them to Mystic Being.

How may I be of assistance? The static connection buzzed in her mind, she was the only one able to do this so far from the lake.

It is I, Calista. I need a ride into Mystic Being.

How many accompany you? The male on the other end asked.

Six.

OK. I'll send a Carrier with enough room. How far out are you?

Ten minutes, if that. They're going by craft here.

Roger that, they'll leave now to get to you just as you arrive at the destination. Is there any particular Carrier Driver you require?

That's what she liked about the Carriers, they didn't beat around the bush. *Samatoontes will do.*

Very well. He will be en route in a moment. Welcome home, Calista. And with that, the connection was severed. Saved her doing it she supposed. Not to mention they knew what she was like and knew that she would take no offence that they had disconnected from her instead of waiting for her to do it. About one hundred feet ahead of her, she could hear the others. What had taken her a half hour of flat out running had taken the others an hour or so of walking. She flashed back to human form and casually strolled through the surrounding forest, finding peace and solitude from it before she quickly approached everyone. As she drew nearer, she could hear their conversation.

Chapter Five

"So how long before Calista catches up?" Raven asked Draylan, who was making them walk quickly over the rough terrain, as though in a hurry to get to wherever they were heading.

"Not long actually. She can move a heck of a lot faster than we are at the moment. Just ask Lexis," he replied, motioning to Lexis who trailed along behind them, a small smile on her face and gazing up at the animals that ran along the treetops calling and talking to each other and pretty much ignoring them.

"How could my baby sister know?" Luke enquired.

"Because she lives with Calista, so she knows how fast she can walk," Tairen said.

"OK. And you mean to tell us, even with the speed we're walking at the moment, Calista actually walks faster?" Raven couldn't quite believe it as they were walking pretty damn fast. He knew that, because he was starting to feel the strain on his leg muscles. And he thought the army training was gruelling? This was actually worse in some bizarre way. Probably because it was just his legs he was using, whereas in the army, it was everything plus the additional weight that he'd have on his back. Plus his backpack was lighter than he was used to, as he only had clothes in it this time as well as Converse plus his toothbrush and toothpaste.

"Yes Raven, that is exactly what I am saying," Draylan said, looking at him.

"That's fucking crazy!" Luke laughed.

"Hey, Lexis?" Raven called back. When there was no answer, everybody glanced back, but she was nowhere to be seen. She'd up and vanished. They all looked ahead again and she was in front of them.

"Geez woman! Answer next time, would you?" Luke said, snagging his sister to him in a hug.

"Sorry," she replied, returning the embrace.

"How did you actually get ahead of us?" Draylan asked, looking perplexed.

"By me," a voice said behind them, causing them to twirl around again and Calista was standing there looking all calm and collected.

"OK, that's weird. How come it had taken us just over an hour to walk a mile and a bit and yet you're already here? We left before you. You shouldn't even be here with us right now!" Luke said.

"Because I'm a heck of a lot quicker than you are." She just looked at him.

"As we know that's true, but do you fancy finding us a quicker way to Wineglass Bay? My legs are killing me from the uneven floor," Lexis asked, rolling her shoulders to move muscles being weighed down by her backpack and also looking seriously small surrounded by them all.

"Sure." She snapped her fingers and a floating cart appeared. Draylan and Tairen climbed aboard, knowing full well it was safe. Calista lifted Lexis in next, as it was just too high for her to get in on her own, whereas Luke and Raven were slightly more hesitant.

"Come on guys, it's perfectly safe," Lexis smiled at them. Both guys took a deep breath and approached slowly. They looked inside and the floor was covered in mounds of cushions. They hopped inside and sank into the immensely soft pads. Raven sat next to Draylan, Luke next to Tairen and Lexis claimed the centre, so she could see them all and once they'd gotten comfortable, they each let out a happy sigh at being off their feet and the weight of their bags not holding them down any longer.

"Aren't you getting in, Calista?" Raven asked, drawing her entire gaze to his.

"No," was all she said and the cart began to move. It slowly began to increase in speed until they had to be doing a good 40 mph. Trees actually bent and twisted to get out of the way, before snapping back into place as though they'd never moved. It was as if they were made of rubber by the fluidity of the way they moved, it was incredible. Raven looked around and Calista was steadily keeping pace with then, running side by side with the cart. A huge fallen tree blocked their path ahead and before he could ask how they would get over it, the cart rose up to sail effortlessly over it. They all glanced back to find out how Calista would get over it when they saw her jump strenuously over it. She landed flawlessly and carried on, never once breaking her stride. Raven turned to look at Luke.

"Did you see that?" Luke mouthed with clear astonishment on his face. Raven nodded. He felt exactly how Luke looked. And then he heard it, snapping his attention forward. The sound of animals and water slightly ahead of them. The cart began to slow to a stop and once it did, Calista ushered them out of it. Once they did and all their belongings were out of it, the cart up and vanished. Like it had never even existed.

"What now?" Raven asked, stretching slightly before putting his own backpack on, the familiar weight nothing new to him, so didn't really bother him anymore. The only downside was the blasted heat. It was like a sauna. Who knew that Tasmania could be this bloody hot? Then again, it didn't help with the thousands of trees that occupied the island, keeping the heat ground level. No wonder majority of the animals occupied the tree tops.

"Follow and remember to say nothing, just let her do all the talking," Draylan replied, and they all proceeded to follow Calista, who walked out through some trees and Raven and Luke got their first real look at Wineglass Bay, along with the refreshing wash of a succulent breeze that whipped around them. It made a definite change to what they were used to. And, oh God, did that breeze feel like heaven!

The high sun sent rays of roasting hot light down to glisten enticingly on the lake but you couldn't look too long as it was blinding. Grass on every side rich, healthy, thick and green. Massive boulders lay here and there in dusky greys. Further back, it was surrounded by luscious trees with thick trunks and leaves of a stunning, tantalizing green in different shades that melded perfectly together. Mountains adorned by trees dotted here and there, tall and proud, each taller than the other, as though in a race to see who would reach the sky first. Plants in wild colours called the place home. It was gorgeous and utterly peaceful. A rarity in the harsh world outside of this place. But Raven knew that if he was given the choice of somewhere to live, this would be the place. Solitude away from everyone and everything, his idea of heaven. Animals also called to each other and birds of bright beautiful colours flew about above their heads. They followed Calista as she made her way closer to the Bay. The closer they got, the calm almost perfectly still water began to ripple. Then a boat appeared, rising up as though on a huge lift. Raven immediately recognised the machine. It was a sleek 1998 Playcraft thirty feet pontoon in lush silver. But it was unlike any other he'd seen before; this one had a huge glass dome over it. The water running off of it quickly as the boat strolled up towards them and hit the bank with solid black wheels. They watched as it parked itself and the glass dome opened up. What shocked Raven the most was the person that got out of it. He was blue! Shone like marble, but was see through and all his insides moved like water! Another Marbilian maybe?

"Calista, darling!" His voice was inexplicably deep, unnatural. Very bassy. But then again, so was he with the blue skin! He wandered over to them in a steady gate that left deep indentations in the sand with each step he took. Heavy fucker maybe? His eyes flicking to each of them before returning to Calista. They were so weird; it was as if they were water themselves.

"Hello, Samatoontes," she replied, looking it directly in the eyes, but he averted his gaze to her left ear.

"Just you lot today, yes?"

"Yes."

"Right. Let's get you all loaded up into the boat before we get spotted." They all followed, but Raven rapidly tapped Tairen on the shoulder.

"What is he?" he asked when the man had turned to look at him.

"Water demon," he replied. So no go on the Marbilian.

"Oh right. Dangerous?"

"Raven. All demons are dangerous. In fact, everyone you will likely encounter will be dangerous in their own way."

"Good to know. Handy to know actually. And could have sworn he was a Marbilian, considering the one we had seen back at Jah'nea's."

"Well, he's actually half and half. He's a hybrid. Usually cool, calm and collected. Quick to laughter and such but if pushed too far, he is one you don't want to be on the receiving end of." They caught up with the others just as they were about to climb into the pontoon. They clambered inside and the water demon climbed behind the wheel and from the weight of him, the boat sank deeper into the water until it was a crazy inch or so from falling in! They claimed a seat as Samatoontes started the machine which grumbled to life. The huge glass dome rose back up and over; sealing them in and keeping water out.

"So how long are you back for?" Samatoontes asked, steering the pontoon expertly towards the centre of the lake, as if he'd done it a thousand times before.

"I have no idea. However long it takes. But Lexis, Tairen, Raven and Luke are coming back in about two to four weeks' time," Calista replied.

"Coming back?"

"To go back to Scotland."

"Oh yes. I remember little Lexis telling me about her work at university. What year you in now?" he enquired, glancing over at Lexis.

"My last year; the one with all the major exams. But I'm also nervous about if I'll pass or not," she replied, which was understandable as it was a hard course she was on.

"Ah, you'll be fine. Smart little one you are. You'll pass with flying colours." He smiled at her.

"Glad you think so." She smiled back.

"What courses are you taking again?"

"Mythology, Symbology and Ancient History," she replied.

"Well sugar," the way he pronounced the endearment was shuga, exactly as a Cajun would, "you'll be fine. You got Calista, Tairen, Draylan and these two to help you should you need it." He grinned, teeth jagged like a shark's. How exactly did a water demon sound like a Cajun was all that was going through Raven's mind, but he quickly squelched the thought as it would only annoy him if he didn't work it out.

"Thanks, Samatoontes," Lexis smiled back at him. Raven was amazed. This demon had complete and utter faith in her for her courses and he probably didn't even know her all that well, but alas that was the charm she had on everyone; they all loved her. They reached the middle of the lake then and Samatoontes pressed a couple of buttons, which caused them to start sinking. The water rushing over them almost hypnotically.

"Strap yourselves in," Lexis said, knowing full well what would happen next. And everyone did, even Calista, so Raven knew it was serious and pulled the seat belt around him, realising it was exactly the same as race car drivers had in their cars. Over the shoulders and across the lap to lock in one big buckle in the middle of their stomach but this had a symbol of a raven and crow interlocked with glowing eyes. He'd never seen that before, definitely a question to ask later if he remembered. After they had buckled themselves in, a box rose from the centre of the floor. They watched as Lexis shoved her luggage in from the opening at the top, and they quickly followed what she did. Once all their luggage was inside and a lid had appeared, locking it all into place, Samatoontes spun the wheel with an expert flick of his wrist, tipping them onto the boat's nose and proceeded to drive them to the bottom of the lake. That explained the belts as they all jutted to the side, but thanks to the way the seats were and how they were buckled in, they didn't move too much. As they approached, Raven had to wonder if they had a suicide streak in them and glanced over at Calista but she was looking out the glass dome at the animals that called the water of Wineglass Bay home. He looked at everyone else but they seemed bored, apart from Luke who was looking around and wondering what the hell was going on. They drew much closer to the bottom of the lake; the only light was from the miniature lights next to the chairs, but it was enough to see each other. He looked out of the front and noticed all the slate at the bottom was perfect. All apart from a crack that ran the length of one huge part of a slate block, and he noticed they were headed right for it. He looked at Samatoontes and the demon had his bloody eyes closed! Closed for fuck's sake! But then the demon began to chant something. Magic popped and fizzled on the air that currently resided inside their little glass dome and a beautiful pale blue entwined around and actually through them. Raven and Luke looked at each other, then to the front of the boat as a bright light appeared in that crack and watched in utter amazement as it grew and they sailed through it with no problem. Once completely through, he glanced back and watched as it shrank back down; to never exist. Just a black void.

Utterly amazing, Raven thought to himself. They glided through a dark tunnel that had bright bursts of light in different shades of colours that rebounded back before hitting them, and Raven noticed it was from miniature dragons. The light was fire and when it rebounded, washed back over the miniature dragons like a lover's caress, which they seemed to absorb into their skin. They soon burst out of the end, straight into nothing. And then they fell, everyone holding onto their belts for their lives apart from Calista who just looked bored. Luckily it wasn't far and they landed on yet more water and Raven got his first look at Mystic Being. Houses made of old stone with thatched roofs sat in clumps of all different shapes and sizes, with rickety wooden fences around them like front gardens. Shops called attention and held centre stage directly in front of them. Massive trees stood tall and proud, trunks absolutely colossal! Bigger than Raven had ever seen before. Also, huge snowy mountains hung in the background and looked absolutely freezing, but they couldn't see what lay beyond that, it was that big! They then pulled up to a dock and the glass dome just up and disappeared. Millions of sounds and luscious smells assailed them. But all fresh and untainted from the millions of cars and such that roamed their world. Here it was like it was back before cars and such were invented and honestly, it was heaven. Well, it was to him anyway. Calista unbuckled herself and clambered out after they'd all gotten out themselves. She walked into a small hut and they heard a high-pitched scream erupted from inside. A purple-skinned female ran out of the hut; naked as the day she was born. Rich Cadbury's chocolate purple hair flew behind her. And she was also shiny, so clearly she was up to that naughty stuff that caused a sweat. Must have been going at it furiously from how shiny she was. Luke covered Lexis's eyes and laughed when she slapped them away and stuck her tongue out at him.

"Talina put some clothes on, you bloody hussy!" Calista called, leaning back out of the hut door.

"NO! It's better being naked!" the woman screeched. Calista sighed and the next thing that the guys knew, the naked one was no longer naked.

She screamed again at being clothed but didn't remove them, as she knew Calista would do something. And she quickly disappeared into the town and out of their sight.

"Who was that?" Raven asked.

"Talina. The sex fey. Ones you have to be careful with," Draylan replied.

"Why? What's wrong with that?" Luke asked.

"Because they can be violent."

"Nothing we can't handle," Luke replied, rather smugly.

"Sex feys are violent, Luke. They'd crush you like a bug," Lexis said, looking at him.

"How violent?"

"As in they wouldn't hesitate to rip open your stomach and dance around in your entrails and actually cackle with laughter if you don't please them." Tairen said, just as Calista walked out of the hut, trailed by a man that made her look about as a tall as one of the trees. Might have something to do with the guy being a dwarf. They were talking a bit though. But no one knew what about.

"Lexis, I'm off. Tell Calista I'll get the payment when she's ready," Samatoontes said, drawing everyone's attention to the fact he was actually still there with them.

"Sure thing, sweetie. Will you take us all back when we need to go?"

"If you would like me to," he replied.

"Who is the other deliverer?" Draylan asked.

"Zamaranthine," he said. It was pronounced Zamar-an-thine.

"We'd rather have you thanks, Samatoontes." Tairen smiled slightly at the demon.

"Thank you. You know how to call for me once you are ready to go back." He nodded respectively to them and wandered into the lake, well really occan, until it closed over his head and he disappeared from sight. They all turned to look back at Calista and Lexis realised it would actually grow dark within the hour, which was a very dangerous time to be out. Calista finished talking with the dwarf and he scampered away. They quickly walked over to her. She handed Lexis a key, made from black marble.

"I want you all to stay at my place tonight. No arguments either. I'll be back later." With that, she up and disappeared. And none of them blinked, already used to her disappearing on them.

"Come on, guys. Let's go." With that, they walked through the town and Raven noticed people no, a different array of vastly-coloured things of all shapes and sizes, not to mention styles, looking out of windows or stopping what they were doing to stare at them as they walked past. They approached a tree-lined road leading up a hill, the leaves bright and vastly coloured, including some that were dark. The sky that shone down on them shone a dusky red, yellow and pink. When they reached the top, Raven and Luke got a look at the residence which Calista called home.

"Erm, am I the only one who, well, you know, sees a resemblance here?" Luke enquired.

"Sure do, Luke," Lexis said and it was true. The house in front of them was the exact duplication of the one in Scotland.

"How come they're the same?" Raven wondered aloud.

"Because the one in Scotland was designed after this one. This is the one Calista actually hand-built herself," Draylan answered as they followed Lexis up the stairs and inside. And Draylan was right, it was the exact same. Right down to the last detail. It was astounding. Apart from that fact that this one looked like it had a new coat of paint on it and everything was pristine, as well as the surrounding ground around it, including freshly cut grass. They all strolled into the living area. The only thing that was different, that Raven actually noted, was the oil painting above the fireplace that was absolutely huge. Instead of it being Calista standing on a dock at night, it was of her standing in the bright sunshine facing forward in a black leather corselet bustier with black buckles up the front, knives strapped to her with strong Velcro, legs encased in black leather trousers and her feet were encased in black New Rocks on a rolling green hill. The scariest thing was, she had a big ass sword balanced over her shoulder coated in blood and a long-handled battle axe held in her other hand, hanging precariously at her side. Her eyes, highlighted by black eyeliner and sharp silver eyeshadow, burned with a sheer intensity and a sinister blood-red-lipped smile on her face! She was mythical and utterly dangerous. And standing behind her, staring straight ahead with blood coating their mouth, stood a black dragon with a gleam in their vibrant green eyes, wings spread wide in a display of raw power. Claws digging into the ground, blooded as well. It was truly a masterpiece. They all sat down on the couch, each and every one of them exhausted even though they'd slept loads on the aeroplane to get here. But then again, jet lag was an absolute bitch.

"So where do you think Calista's gone?" Raven asked, sinking back onto the couch to try and get warm as the house was freezing. Lexis leaned forward at the fireplace and pulled a box of matches off the fireplace mantel and lit one. They watched as she threw it in, and the logs immediately flared with life. Only the flames weren't red/yellow, they were an electric blue, but they immediately threw off heat, so it was very much appreciated.

"Calista is most likely seeing Skyri. Or Rayne, or heck, maybe even Nikki," Draylan drawled out casually.

"Who the hell are Skyri, Rayne and Nikki?" Luke asked.

"Skyri is a badass motherfucker, dangerous as fuck. Also happens to be a werewolf. So he has the added benefits of having strong, heightened senses, etc. I told you about him earlier. Rayne is a mystifying beauty. Vicious as anything, wouldn't hesitate to rip your throat out. Also happens to be Tairen's twin sister, and Draylan's niece. Nikki is a beauty, intelligent, cunning and can fight ruthlessly when provoked," Lexis answered her brother, sitting back down next to Tairen who swung his arm around her shoulders as if it was the most natural thing in the world. And by the looks of it, it was.

"Oh right," Luke replied slowly. Raven glanced outside and realised it had already grown dark in the minimal time they'd walked up that hill and into the house.

"So what do we do until Calista gets back?" Raven murmured.

"We'll go out onto the back deck; I want you guys to see something." Lexis said and grabbed his and Luke's hands and tugged them to their feet. They followed her out of the French doors and onto the back deck. The view that greeted them was astounding! Directly ahead, scattered miles around, were mountains in the distance covered in shockingly bright white snow that gleamed like firelights. To the right lay more mountains and vast trees. To the left sat the town and houses. Along with the beach, docks and immeasurable open ocean that was a crystalline blue and shone beautifully under the moonlight. Then Raven noticed a huge bonfire had been started and music was playing and people, well creatures really of all different types were dancing and having a merry time. Their laughter carried up to them. Must be nice to be so carefree and not have to worry about anything. Live in bliss. They watched silently for a good twenty minutes before they heard the front door open and close. Lexis left them to find out who or what it was. The guys didn't so much as move. They were completely at ease, calm. Raven watched in stunned fascination at the different ways they danced. Exotic, wild and graceful all mingled together. Some of which was like the waltz, tango, etc. But each one was with grace, like they'd been doing it for years. Lexis reappeared a moment later with a grin on her face.

"Come on, guys. Calista's got dinner!" She disappeared inside again. They all eagerly ran inside and headed for the kitchen, where the ripe smell of fresh food erupted and assailed their senses which made them all groan happily. They walked into the kitchen and hot steaming food lay spread out on the counter, awaiting plates and cutlery next to it all. They began helping themselves when Raven noticed that Calista was nowhere to be seen. He glanced around and noticed that the kitchen also had another requirement that the one in Scotland didn't have. As he watched Lexis push the door open, he'd noticed inside was something he didn't expect. A luscious mahogany table that could effortlessly seat twelve people and still have plenty of elbow room. The seats around the table were the same wood as the table, with black seats that looked really comfortable. The table had blood red mats on it and thick red candles in black gothic holders. Behind the table was a gorgeous fireplace. Rich mahogany made up the mantle, grey stone the rest, again, roaring blue flames. They all grabbed their plates and followed Lexis into the room. They claimed a seat and dug in with relish. Not one of them talking until all the food had disappeared and their stomachs were happily full.

"So any idea on the plans tomorrow?" Raven asked, leaning back in his chair and feeling bloated.

"You'll have to ask Calista. She's out back," Lexis replied. They all took their empty plates back into the kitchen and waited whilst Tairen placed them all in the dishwasher. Even with magic and such floating around this place like air, they still had all the electrical equipment and such like they did on 'Normal Earth'. It was crazy to think they had simple things like a dishwasher. Once completed, they all trailed after Draylan outside. Due to it being pitch black, they had trouble spotting Calista. Who, thanks to always wearing black, quite easily blended in with her surroundings.

"What do you lot want?" Calista's voice called out from the surrounding darkness.

"Come to ask you something," Draylan said, eyes darting around trying to find out where she was. But it proved impossible; she was just too good at blending in with her surroundings even with his brilliant vampire night vision.

"And what, pray tell, is it you want to ask me?"

"Just what it is we are doing tomorrow?" Lexis asked and that was when Calista unexpectedly stepped into the moon's rays, which seemed to caress her like a lover's kiss. And it was almost as if she was one with the night which if you thought about it, she was.

"Go meet up with Skyri and Rayne. Then me and Skyri will go and see the missing children's parents, process the scene and then work out from there what needs to be done next." Her cobalt eyes flashed brightly. She walked up onto the deck with them. Raven thought she looked amazing! Other worldly too. She seemed right at home here. As if Mystic Being was made for her.

"Why can't we all go?" Lexis asked.

"Because you and Tairen are going to show Raven and Luke around the town. Buy things. Introduce them to everyone maybe. I don't care what. And Draylan, I'm sure you'll want to get back home for a while." Calista leaned against the railing. The music in the town square was still going strong. Quite simply crazy. Loud bands erupted through the night then, and brilliant flashes of fire decorated the sky in luminous colours. Some even coming 'alive' as creatures which made a noise then disappeared. Lexis absently glanced at her watch, and as she had already put it to the time Mystic Being was at, she realised it was now eight p.m! During that small trip through the tunnel, they'd gone forward eight hours! Then a crazy thought zipped through her mind. Calista had been up over forty-eight hours and yet she still looked completely sharp-eyed as though she'd slept as much as they had. She felt something watching her and looked up. Calista's unblinking eyes were staring at her.

"What?"

"Do you agree to showing your brother and Raven around with Tairen?"

"Yes. It'd be nice. What time would we expect you back at?"

"I'll let you know. And now, everyone to bed. Busy day tomorrow."

"Can't I watch the display a little longer?" Lexis batted her big hazels at her.

"From your bedroom window." That was all she would allow. Lexis nodded and walked inside, all without an argument!

"Why isn't she allowed to watch the fireworks from here?" Luke asked, moving to the side to allow Draylan to head inside.

"Because some very dangerous things lurk out here in the darkness. Ones that wouldn't hesitate to kidnap her; abuse her and then kill her," Calista said, all matter-of-factly.

"Good to know," Luke muttered and walked inside, all without a backward glance so clearly, he wasn't quite used to that avid bluntness, and Raven looked at her.

"What time are we up tomorrow?"

"If you're not up by nine a.m., I'll get you up," she replied, and suddenly she stiffened.

"What is it?" In answer, she turned around, and embedded in her right shoulder was an arrow. It was buried a good solid inch or so in. Certainly would hurt when it was be removed. Must really suck for her as that was two arrows in less than twenty-four hours.

"Get in the house, Raven." Draylan's deep voice made him spin around. The man stood in the doorway, looking dark and menacing. A humungous double-bladed axe swung over his shoulder, he held it as though it weighed about as much as a small bag of sugar. Raven didn't need telling twice. As soon as the man had made enough room in the doorway that was big enough for him to squeeze through, he did and Draylan quickly shut the door behind him.

"What's going on?" Luke asked, making his presence known. Raven looked at him and noticed Lexis and Tairen were also there.

"Calista got shot in the shoulder with an arrow again. Next thing I know, Draylan is at the doorway with this massive double-bladed axe. Then I got told to get in here, so here I am," he replied, and looked back outside. The other three moved closer to get a better look outside too. Raven noticed Draylan had removed the arrow and held it in his hand. The shocking part, the arrow was twin bladed! The main arrow head, which was ridiculously sharp with dangerously sharp razor blades buried into the wood about two inches down. It was meant for brutal pain when pulled out, yet Calista looked like she just hadn't had an arrow ripped from her flesh. He also noted that the fireworks had stopped going off too.

"What happened to the fireworks?"

"The town stopped them. Plus, the music and the bonfire when lightning erupted through the sky from here. That is how we also realised something had happened," Tairen explained, talking more than he had since they had actually arrived at Mystic Being.

"Lightning?"

"Must have been when your back was turned. When it's here sometimes there is no noise with it; just blinding light," Lexis explained. They absently watched as Calista leaned forward, nose dangerously close to the arrow blades and inhaled. Her eyes flared brilliantly bright, so much so that they actually lit up Draylan's unreadable face when she straightened and looked at him. She said something, he nodded in reply and she disappeared into the darkness. Draylan walked back inside, arrow still clutched in his hand, axe strapped to his back. Calista didn't need it to enact revenge.

"Where did she go?" Lexis whimpered. She knew it was Calista's profession, but she still hated her going out and fighting.

"To kill the son of a bitch who shot her."

"Was it tipped in anything?" Tairen asked, taking a hold of Lexis's hand.

"Yes, it was dipped in Belladonna."

"But that had no effect on Calista." Raven didn't understand. Belladonna was a very dangerous and lethal poison. How that didn't affect her was crazy! But then again, he wasn't really surprised, not with what he'd seen so far anyway.

"Hold on, did you say Belladonna?" Lexis said.

"Yeah, why?" Draylan looked at her, ice-blue eyes unblinking.

"What are the symptoms if anyone, other than Calista got it into their system?" She actually stepped back slightly, away from Draylan and the arrow.

"Many symptoms include dilated pupils, sensitivity to light, blurred vision, tachycardia, loss of balance, staggering, headache, rash, flushing, severely dry mouth and throat, slurred speech, urinary retention, constipation, confusion, hallucinations, delirium, and convulsions, etc. Why?" Luke said before anyone else could.

"Don't you think it's slightly weird, everyone knows that things like that don't affect Calista but yet they use it? Knowing full well that we are here? Well, me, you and Tairen as no one was sure if I was going to bring Raven and Luke with me. Wouldn't it affect you and Tairen? As I know it'd affect me without a doubt." Lexis looked at the arrow that was currently dripping that deadly poison on the floor.

"I honestly don't know if it would or could affect me and Tairen, we never have found out. We never have had to. But you're right, it would definitely affect you three," he replied, just as a high-pitched scream ruptured through the darkness.

"What the fuck was that?" Luke demanded, automatically stepping closer to Lexis.

"Most likely it was the one that shot Calista," Draylan nonchantly replied. Raven glanced outside and could, unfortunately see nothing. He looked back to the others.

"Well anyway, whilst we wait, we might as well grab a drink or something." Luke headed for the kitchen, clearly intent on making good on what he said.

"I'll meet you all there. I'll run this up to Calista's bedroom so she can get rid of it herself." Draylan left, using his vampire speed to zoom up the stairs. They all wandered into the kitchen and waited whilst Lexis filled the kettle up.

"So how long before Calista gets back?" Luke asked, just before Raven could.

"No idea. Depends on how many she had to fight and what kind of damage she wants to do first," Tairen replied, grabbing some orange juice from the fridge. They all dropped into silence then, lost to their own thoughts. A minute later and Draylan walked inside, just as the kettle went off.

"Typical you to walk in just as the kettle's finished boiling," Lexis smiled.

"I am known for my excellent timing." He laughed and winked at her.

"Want tea or coffee?"

"Tea please."

"OK. How do you have it?"

"Wet." He grinned at her.

"Har fucking har, how do you have it?" She smiled at him.

"Milk. No sugar. As I'm sweet enough."

"Right, keep on telling yourself that. What about you two?" She looked at Raven and Luke.

"Coffee, white, no sugar please," they both replied. Lexis set about making the drinks and Raven noted she didn't ask Tairen. Might be because he was drinking orange juice. She placed their steaming drinks in front of them. About five minutes later, they each must have drunk at least half and were bantering between themselves when they suddenly heard the French doors in the living room crash open, slamming against the walls. Drinks abandoned, they all ran into the living area, the doors held open in a fierce wind that rattled through the room, crashing over them in a rush, sending hair all over the place and clothes billowing out as air rushed through them. The double-bladed axe was just inside the door, laying on the floor, caked in blood as though it was flung there in a bid to rid the occupant of their weapon. Raven heard Lexis gasp and whipped his head to the side to face her, following her line of sight. Calista stood on the decking, blood covered her, soaking into her clothes and splattered across her arms and hands. She looked at them and her eyes were the coldest Raven had ever seen. Cold and utterly emotionless. The eyes of a trained killer. She just stared at them and blood was also smeared darkly across one cheek, parts of her hair and dripped from her mouth. It wasn't the normal coloured blood, it was an array of bright colours that stood out brightly against her flesh.

"Who was it that shot you?" Lexis asked, leaning into Tairen's side.

"Rookies. Learner demons." Her voice was husky. She scrubbed her arm across her mouth, smearing the blood across her face more as well as adding extra to her arm.

"Know who sent them?" Tairen enquired.

"Yes, it was Kharge."

"Got to ask, but how do you know it was this Kharge guy?" Raven remarked, drawing that icy gaze to his.

"Because Kharge is a brutal bastard and brands his soldiers."

"Brands them? Do you mean like cattle?" Luke asked.

"Yes." What the hell had she faced out there? Some parts of the blood were red — was it hers?

"What's his brand mark?"

"Dagger with a K in the middle of the blade."

"Lovely." Luke remarked sarcastically.

"So he actually sent rookies after you? Not really so bright is he?" Lexis said.

"They most probably volunteered to show how loyal they were to Kharge," Draylan murmured.

"I wouldn't be surprised. Now everyone off to bed. It's late." Calista said and picked up the battle axe. The drying blood on the handle cracked under her palm, the sound loud in the sudden quietness of the room. All of them took the hint, she didn't want to talk and everyone left, apart from Raven who just carried on looking at her.

"What?" She glared at him.

"Glad you didn't get seriously injured," he said and then practically ran from the room as though the hounds of hell themselves were chasing him. Most likely embarrassed to have admitted that. Calista shook her head and was glad they couldn't see the extent of her injuries. Knives had laid open her skin, some having actual contact inside her! She strolled into the kitchen and noticed all the cups had been left sitting on the side, half full. She put the axe down and quickly rinsed them all out and put them on the draining board, all by hand and not with her magic. She needed something to do to calm down. She walked to the fridge and pulled out a blood bag. She ripped it open and guzzled it down. Then did the same with another five bags before she heard someone heading towards her. She knew before they even entered it was Raven. That man really needed to get over his fascination with her.

"What do you want, Raven?" She didn't turn around, she just grabbed another bag.

"How did you know it was me?"

"Because I'm clever like that," she retorted and then turned around. How he was dressed completely caught her off guard. He only had on his jeans and a very tight T-shirt that really didn't leave much to the imagination. She even absently noted he was barefoot. She noticed that he had long sleeves on, in this heat? Was he covering up something? She noticed he had turned away and was rummaging through Lexis's sweetie cupboard. His arse was solid muscle that actually begged a woman to grab, and knowing Raven, he most probably had. Then why did thinking that make her want to maim someone badly and then kill them when she was good and ready? She shook her head to clear it and slammed the bag to her mouth, which instantly began filling with blood that slid down her throat, it was the quickest way to her system and she really couldn't be bothered with the whole 'make sure it's in a mug' this time. Classy was her middle name.

"Did you hear what I said, Calista?" He turned around and when he noticed the bag, he actually had the grace to appear sheepish. Once the bag had eventually emptied, she gathered the other empty ones and put them in the bin.

"And in answer to your question, no I didn't hear what you said," she replied. But not that she'd openly admit that she was thinking about him. He didn't answer, just walked up to her.

"You have blood on you."

"Well, thanks for that observation. And here I thought my clothes and skin were just getting hard for no apparent reason," she sarcastically snorted.

"No, I mean fresh blood. On your lower lip." Not giving her a chance to remove it, he placed his lips on hers. No other part of him touched her. When she, not him, stepped closer, he wrapped his arms around her surprisingly soft body and hauled her closer. He watched as her eyelids fluttered shut, he closed his and deepened the kiss more. He thrust his tongue into her mouth and tasted the coppery tinge of the blood she had consumed, as well as the rich honey of her. He wanted to gobble her up and keep her for himself, as he didn't want to share. He didn't share well. She suddenly pulled back, much too soon for his liking. He quickly glanced down. Arousal — pretty fucking obvious. Blood transfer: zilch. That was when he heard someone nearing the kitchen. And what do you know, his erection deflated quicker than a needle to a balloon. He grabbed the sweets from where he had dropped them and looked at Calista who was now casually leaning against the counter cradling a blood bag in her hand and was half way through another when the door opened and he glanced over and saw it was Luke.

"OK, you two look slightly awkward," he remarked, helping himself to a glass of water.

"We're fine, Luke. Raven was trying to work out what injuries I had received earlier," Calista said before Raven could think of a remark.

"And they were?"

"Nothing you need to worry about. I've had and dealt with much worse." And wasn't that the god's honest truth! With that, she left to go and take a very much needed shower. Luke turned to Raven as soon as the door swung shut behind her.

"So, go on, how was it?"

"I have no idea what you're on about."

"Bullshit. You can't lie to me Raven. I'm your best friend, have been for over twenty years. We've been though shit loads. Plus your lips are all puffy," he pointed out, a sly grin on his face.

"Fine, it was out of this fucking world! I've never been so turned on in my life," Raven grinned.

"You, my friend have got it bad. But I hope you tell her sooner rather than later. You never know, you two could end up forming a relationship."

"Thanks, man. But I reckon it's too soon to tell her how I feel. Plus we actually have no idea how she'll react. And what possible relationship could we have? She's lived for thousands of years, I'm human. My lifespan is a mere blink compared to hers," Raven said, and left the kitchen with Luke following behind. And thinking on what he said, kind of depressing wasn't it? He was a mere blink to her lifespan. When he died, would she think of him? Shaking his head slightly, he didn't want to dwell on that.

"I'm sure something will work out. You never know what can happen." Raven had no answer to that, turned out the kitchen light and the light from the living area they'd left on and they quickly headed upstairs but pulled up short as they noticed Calista talking to Draylan, who slouched against the door jam in black sweatpants and a tank top to his bedroom whilst she was still covered in blood.

"We'll see what the parents say tomorrow. Then go through the scenes and we'll take it from there," Calista said and Draylan reluctantly nodded.

"Hey, guys." He looked at them.

"Hey," they replied. Calista stared at them with her unblinking eyes.

"Tomorrow, we'll all head into town and you two, Lexis and Tairen can do as you please. Draylan, you'll head back to your place and collect the gear we spoke about. And bring it back here." She didn't wait for a reply, just headed to her bedroom and disappeared inside. All without a backward glance.

"Excuse Miss Blunt there, but she has a good reason for you to head to bed now. I'd get a decent sleep in, as knowing Lexis, she'll exhaust you tomorrow. If not up by nine, you'll receive a wake-up call," Draylan said, and stepped back into his bedroom and closed the door after he respectively nodded his head at them. They shrugged their broad shoulders and headed into the room that was temporarily theirs. Luke flipped the switch and lights flared brilliantly to life. The hallways lights clicked off, like someone had flipped a switch but Raven knew with every ounce of his fibre that it was Calista's magic. And no doubt every single light that he hadn't put out before coming to bed would have gone out as well. He looked back into the bedroom and took a step back. Luke stood dangerously close to him. Hazel eyes unblinking and holding complete and utter concern in them.

"What?" But he already knew the answer to that.

"You've quite simply got it bad. You really need to tell Calista how you actually feel. You can't keep it hidden from her much longer. Even I can see you've fallen for her lock, stock and barrel."

"And how is it that you think I have these feelings for Calista?" He crossed his arms over his chest.

"It is obvious, Raven. Even more considering that you two were playing tonsil tennis earlier in the kitchen." Luke lay down on his side of the bed, fully clothed still.

"Yeah, but it's way too soon! Heck, it's not like we spent a lot of time in her company. How could I have feelings so quickly and this intense?" He sighed and flopped down onto the bed, making Luke bounce.

"It just happens man. Just have to deal with it. As my dad believed and continuously told me and Lexis before he died, *'Never hide your feelings for someone. Because one day, it could be the biggest regret of your life.'* He has a point, but I won't force you into anything for your feelings to Calista. Just know I'm behind you one hundred percent no matter what happens between you both. I mean, she's beautiful, you're not bad looking, not that I swing that way as you know and it's about time that I saw you happy, more so after what happened before. It makes a nice change and I like seeing you happy."

"Thanks, man. I'll keep that in mind. I'll figure out what I'll do tomorrow. Let's crash now, I'm still knackered from the journey here."

"Sounds like a plan and you're not the only one." They unenthusiastically climbed off the bed and stripped down to their boxers. Well, Luke did. Raven kept his top on. Luke was one of the very few who knew what Raven looked like under the clothes, considering he'd been there when a lot of his injuries had happened. But he was more comfortable in a top anyway and he went to flip the light switch and waited whilst Luke pulled the heavy-duty curtains closed. When Luke was back near the bed, he flipped the switch. Once the room had plummeted into darkness, thanks to the fact there was no street lights or whatnot here and that virtually everything in this land was candles, oil or magic based. Apart from basic things in the house that was, or if Calista used her magic and got the house kitted out with electricity, gas, water, etc. It was freakishly dark that Raven couldn't see his hand a mere centimetre in front of his face, stumbled blindly to the bed and found it. Well, his shin did. And he cursed, big time. Which was followed by Luke's very amused chuckle.

"Fuck off, arsehole."

"Sorry. Night man." He knew that Luke knew he didn't mean it harshly. They were always like it. Well, when they could bicker that was. Sad life really thinking about it that way, not allowed to bicker at work. But then again, their job wasn't exactly ordinary and any sort of bickering could literally mean death if they weren't paying attention. Hence, why they were so damn good at their job.

"Yeah, night." He collapsed into the bed. They both snuggled down under the thick duvet and allowed sleep to claim them. Dragging them into the void of absolute nothingness and just forgot the world around them until they had to eventually wake up again.

Chapter Six

Calista rolled over in bed, waking into alertness pretty much instantaneously. Thanks to no alarms and that she had heavy-duty thick velvet curtains hanging over the windows, she had no idea as to what the time was. But due to the fact she knew loads of wacky shit, she knew the sun was just beginning its rise into the sky, so it was around six a.m. She stretched, loving the feel of her muscles stretching heavenly and bones cracking, and then she climbed out of bed. She slightly ached as her injuries healed inside from yesterday's fight but it was nothing a blistering hot shower wouldn't cure. She stumbled into her bathroom, pushed a button on the wall to turn on the spotlights that hung above the mirror, and a few along the ceiling, she flipped the shower on and now her bladder decided to wake up and was screaming at her to empty it. Using the facilities quickly and once the bathroom filled with hot luscious steam, she got into the shower. Thanks to her habit of sleeping naked, she just walked in and the water cascaded over her flesh in hot steamy intervals. Making her sigh in happiness. Nothing beat a good shower. As she lathered her hair, then washed her body, she heard knocking at her bedroom door. She willed open the door and heard Draylan's deep voice calling out to her.

"In here, Draylan," she called out. She quickly ducked back under the spray and rinsed the stuff out of her hair and the suds off her body. She brushed the water off her face and looked at the doorway that Draylan now filled. Looking at him, you'd have thought that the big guy would have looked her right in the eye, but nope, not him, he looked just to the left of her even though he was unconcerned about her being naked. It wasn't the first time he'd seen her bare flesh. Doubtful it would be the last either. It was more than that, it was a hell of a lot of respect and a little fear that caused him to not look her directly in the eye.

"What do you want?" she asked.

"When are you meeting Skyri?"

"Two and half hours," she replied, turned the shower off, climbed out and wrapped a huge fluffy towel around her. Thank God for the miracles of magic and the creations on 'normal Earth' she'd brought home with her.

She did so love a fresh fluffy towel. Like she was being wrapped up in a cloud. One of the few little luxuries she enjoyed.

"OK. Where are you meeting him?"

"Town, when I leave you lot." He turned sideways so she could slip past and into the bedroom.

"OK. You know that Luke and Raven will no doubt shit themselves if they get a chance to feel the raw dangerous power that actually radiates from that man, You know that, right?"

"Yeah, I know."

"Do you regret bringing them?" And wasn't that the million-dollar question!

"Yes. But I only did it for our Lexis. I know for a fact, they're going to get in my bloody way which I really don't fucking need." She sighed and from her chest of drawers pulled out jeans and a tank top. She chucked them onto her bed just as a knock sounded on her bedroom door; the one Draylan had shut behind him for aided privacy. She walked over and yanked it open. It was Lexis.

"What's up, sweetie?" Draylan asked, standing up straight from his slouched position on the bathroom doorframe.

"Personal matter. Woman things."

"Say no more. I'll be back later." He left them then, pulling the door closed behind him. Calista shook her head, dropped her towel and proceeded to get dressed. She looked over at Lexis as she wiggled into a bra. The kid sat on the end of the bed looking at her feet as she dug her toes into the plush carpet.

"What's wrong, munchkin?" She sat her own butt down.

"How can I stop having morning sickness? Because it's really annoying me. Only they lied, its morning, noon and bloody night," Lexis sighed.

"I can always do a spell to which can prevent you from having the sickness."

"But?" There was always a but involved.

"You'll have to have Tairen change you over. As instead of the sickness, you will need to drink from him every couple of days until the baby is born." She pulled the jeans and tank top on.

"Can I bring Tairen in here for a minute and you tell him?"

"Why me?"

"Because you are blunt fucking honest and he'll also listen to you as you're his badass aunt who won't hesitate to kick his butt if he needs it.

Because he'll probably be like, 'oh no, you'd be much better off having sickness.' Shouldn't it be my choice?" Lexis pulled a face. Calista rolled her eyes at Lexis's dramatics and of her deepening her voice to try and get it as deep as Tairen's, but she failed. Big time.

"Go and get your vampire. If he refuses, I'll kick his ass." Lexis snorted with laughter, just as she had intended. Lexis left to go and find her man. She waited until the kid had left before she reached under her mattress and pulled out her black blade, aptly named Cutthroat. She pulled Cutthroat's protective covering out of her bedside table, placed the black blade inside and attached it to her thigh. As it was on the outside of her jeans, it was within easy reach if she needed it quickly. She moved to stand at her stained black oak, with a fire opal decorated mirrored vanity Lexis had specially made for her a while ago. She snapped her fingers and black eyeliner painted itself on her upper eyelids and white on the lower lid, making the intense cobalt blue stand out more than it already did. Blood red matte lipstick clung to her lips, which just begged to be kissed. Skin flawless with a hint of foundation and blush that accentuated her cheekbones. She was quite simply a badass who owned the rock chick look. She pulled her hair up into a high ponytail and tied it off with a simple hairband and wrapped a black leather strap around it. By then she heard Lexis coming back with Tairen, who was asking her questions but she refused to answer. This clearly frustrated him, she could smell it on him. They entered the room, only because the door was open in invitation. They headed over to the bed after Calista pointed to it before they could ask where to sit.

"Right Tairen, I'm just going to be blunt here. You know Lexis is having sickness and she's come to me to see if I could help her with it. But there is a catch."

"What's the catch?" he asked sceptically, looking at Lexis.

"You will have to turn her. And she'll have to drink from you every couple of days," she answered.

"Is this what you want, baby?" he asked Lexis.

"Yes," she whispered.

"What will happen to the baby whilst she's changing?" Tairen asked Calista, looking at her whilst she finished getting ready. Well, collecting her weapons that is.

"Your son will be fine. Just be fully vampire, not half."

"We're having a boy?" Lexis positively grinned at knowing the sex of her baby.

"No. I just called your daughter a boy for shits and giggles," she sarcastically remarked.

"We're having a boy!" Lexis cried excitedly and threw herself at Tairen.

"I heard, Lexis." He laughed and grinned so wide, his cheeks had to hurt.

"Can we get back to the matter at hand?" Calista interrupted.

"What? Oh yeah." Tairen pulled back from Lexis until he could see her face.

"Are you positive this is what you want?" he asked again.

"Yes. I already told you, eternity or nothing for me."

"OK. Calista, we'll need your help. Lexis clearly won't know what to do, and I've never turned anyone."

"Wouldn't you want your uncle to help?"

"I've already asked him about helping when Lexis gets turned. He said you'd be better off helping as Lexis would grow ridiculously hot and she'd strip. Is that true?"

"It is actually. So yes, I can understand why Draylan suggested I'd be better off helping. Lexis, we'll change you tonight. That will give you enough time to tell and convince your brother and his best friend. I'll bring Skyri back tonight to act as muscle and guard the door as I know Luke will come running when he hears your screams."

"Screams?" The colour drained from Lexis's face.

"Well, you didn't honestly expect me to let you think that it's all fine and dandy?"

"Well, no. But surely you'll help me through it?"

"Obviously I'll help. But enough of this now, downstairs and eat. But make sure the lads are awake." They nodded and left without argument. With a quick check she had what she wanted, she left her bedroom, closed the door behind her and Calista trailed behind them but carried on when they stopped at the bedroom that her brother and Raven were behind. She wandered into the kitchen and placed her axe on the floor, handle leaning against the wall. Blade gleaming brilliant in the kitchen light. Ever-present sword placed next to it as well, that also gleamed as well. Draylan looked up from where he was rinsing out his cup.

"Everything OK with little Lexis?"

"Yes." She nodded her thanks as he handed her a glass of blood in a freezer-cold glass. As the glass was perched against her blood-red lips, the door opened and everyone else strolled in. The lads looked like they hadn't slept very well, but she mentally shrugged. Not her problem. Lexis headed for the fridge and pulled out bacon, eggs, cheese, tomatoes and milk. She then expertly began chopping the ingredients and prepared to make omelettes for everyone but Calista. Around twenty minutes later with everyone talking and happily eating, Calista absently glanced at the clock Lexis was adamant to have in the house and noticed the time was nearly nine a.m. Time had already flown by this morning and she really needed to get a move on. Everyone was easily bantering amongst themselves, like it was an everyday occurrence, so she slipped away. She returned about five minutes later and Draylan stood at the sink cleaning up everyone's mess. Raven and Luke sat at the table, no doubt already told by Lexis to stay where they were. Draylan knew she didn't like a messy kitchen and Lexis stood next to him waiting to dry the things, and Tairen was then next in line, no doubt to put the stuff away. But due to the amount of washing up, she whispered a quick spell and the remaining cutlery and everything else cleaned themselves and vanished. Even the sink was sparkling clean and dry. Everyone turned to look at her, eyes wide open.

"What?" she asked, tightening the thick leather belt around her hips which now held her four feet sword.

"How the hell did you do that? And what's with the friggin' sword?" Luke asked, motioning to the sword, along with the axe that lay casually against the wall. So utterly dangerous and yet it suited her perfectly, like it was a limb or something.

"I can do that by magic. I've done bigger stuff than that, all of that was amateur stuff. And the blades are a part of me, hence why they are here," she replied and swung said axe up and behind her to secure it across her back. The weight was so familiar and welcome, her back actually felt naked without it when she was out. It was obvious it was well used, the handle was very well worn.

"Right, anyway, let's go. I have to meet Skyri and then go to the kidnapped children's houses and process the scenes," she said and then walked away. They all quickly followed and damn she was fast! By the time they got halfway across the extravagantly spacious hallway, she was already at the huge black-stained oak door, leaning casually against it, holding it open and allowing rich, vibrant sunlight to pour in and stream across the sleek black slate that also looked like it was sparkling with small gold threads. Black sunglasses concealed her cobalt blue eyes and she looked utterly menacing. Even more than usual, thanks to those gloriously dangerous weapons. Lifting a hand, and using a black painted dagger-pointed fingernail, pulled the glasses slightly down her nose until she could regard them with her flashing eerie and bright eyes. Looking at them, it was as though she saw into their very soul.

"Take your time," she sarcastically said.

"OK, we will." Lexis laughed as she stretched the words out and slowed her walk to that of a snail's pace.

"Move your ass now, Lexis Edana Ammalia Ileana Blackwood!" Calista stood up from her slouch and stalked to Lexis, who squealed.

"I only thought it used to be Mum and Dad that used your full name when you were in trouble." Luke laughed as Lexis hid behind Tairen, using him as a shield, and stuck her tongue out at Calista, who in turn shut the door behind her then grinned at Lexis, who let out a startled yelp and rubbed her bottom.

"No fair!"

"It is in this world." They all shook their heads at the show and headed off to town. Calista pushed her sunglasses back up her nose and followed them until they reached the town which was bustling with activity. Luckily, going downhill was hell of a lot easier than going up. That dangerously sharp axe and sword glinted in the sunlight and must weigh a heck of a lot, but Calista carried it like it was feather light. They stopped in the middle of town where a sleek well-crafted statue held centre stage. It was of a tall, cobalt blue-eyed, black-haired beauty, but the hair actually moved to twirl around the body in the calm breeze. She also had a raven with black onyx eyes with lightning streaks of blue, and a crow with pearlescent blue eyes with lightning streaks of black. Both were coated in a body of black feathers perched on a shoulder each with their faces turned to the side. The beaks held a glass ball that swirled with an array of vibrant colours that drew the eye. A battle axe was strapped across her back and a bloodied sword was pointing downwards in a relaxed position from her clenched fist. The thing that shocked Raven was that it was an amazing masterpiece, as if a hell of a lot of detail had gone into everything. And another thing, the eyes on the statue shone with an inner blue light. Freaky and yet it was a clear tribute to Calista. A sharp crystal clear whistle cut through the air then, drawing their attention.

"SKYRI!" Lexis screamed and ran for a brute of a man who was walking towards them. That was when Luke and Raven got their first close up look of Skyri. The guy was an absolute animal! He had massively thick arms that bulged with inner strength. A barrel chest. Thick shoulders. Hands like shovels. Flat stomach. Huge thighs and calves. Shaggy brown hair lay haphazardly on his head, bangs dangling in his eccentric green eyes. High cheekbones, slightly crooked nose from being broken a couple of times. He was dressed in black jeans and a grey tank top that left very little to the imagination that this man looked after himself. Raw power radiated from him. Harsh scars covered his arms and hands, which just showed he lived a dangerous life but could clearly hold his own. No emotion showed in his features until he saw Lexis and then he beamed what could only be called a shit-eating grin.

"Hey, Lexis," he replied. Voice unnaturally deep but yet seemed to suit him perfectly. He wrapped his arms around her and engulfed her in a huge bear hug that made her appear so small, vulnerable and utterly feminine standing in front of him.

"Guess what, Skyri?" She pulled back slightly and grinned at him.

"What?"

"I'm pregnant!"

"Congratulations! Does this mean our Tairen actually does know how to use it?" He grinned at Tairen.

"Hey! I resent that!" Tairen shouted out.

"Of course he knows how to use it. Very well, in fact. There you go babe, ego all better?" She grinned at her man who just snorted in reply. Skyri put her down and she settled herself back next to her man.

"Anyway, now that you've restored Tairen's ego, does this mean no training? Or carry on until you can't anymore?"

"We can carry on until I clearly can't, obviously. But we won't be able to do any of the real aggressive stuff that we usually do," she replied.

"OK fair enough. All right, guys." He nodded at the others.

"How you doing Skyri?" Draylan asked.

"Been good. Healed exceptionally well thanks to some herbal plant thing Calista has. And you'll never guess, I actually saw Nikki in town a couple of days ago."

"Seriously? But she avoids the town at all costs usually. She stays on Suicide Mountain," Tairen said, casually draping his arm across Lexis's shoulders.

"Must have needed supplies or something then for her to venture down here."

"Yeah, that was probably the only reason. Was she near the house?" Draylan asked.

"Nope, just wandering through town with a black bag."

"Supplies then," Lexis remarked.

"Erm question, why is it called Suicide Mountain?" Luke asked, drawing Skyri's intensely bright burning gaze to his.

"It's called Suicide Mountain for a reason. Rough terrain. Gail force winds. Hailstones the size of golf balls and bigger. Things stick out of the ground, which, if you don't pay attention to, will trip you up. Cut limbs off entirely before you even realised. Or worse, kill you outright. Quicker than you can say fuck me sideways. Unless it's calm weather around it and then it's even worse as you've no idea where any traps or anything are as it's perfectly still and nothing is given away." Raven gulped a little. Most unaccountably suited its namesake then. And this Nikki person lived there. Crazy!

"Enough chit chat. Skyri, you and I are off to the kidnapped children's homes so we can talk to the parents and I can go through the scenes and such etc. The rest of you can do what the fuck you like. Be back later." Calista said and pushed Skyri sideways. He grinned at her and walked away, the man quickly followed. Two very dangerous people they were. And clearly at ease with being in each other's company as they strolled away in silence.

"So that's the infamous Skyri?" Raven asked, turning to look at Lexis.

"Yes. He's one dangerous individual that I'd hate to have as my enemy. But as a friend he's fiercely loyal and ridiculously protective."

"So how close is he to Calista?"

"They're best friends. Have been for longer than we've all been alive for. Or as close as she'd allow to a best friend anyway," she replied, and then let out a high-pitched squeal of obvious happiness.

"What the bloody hell was that for?" Luke glared at her, putting his finger in his ear to stop the ringing. Lexis didn't answer, just bolted away from them. Charging towards a centaur. A real, honest to God, mother fucking gargantuan centaur! The thing had the masculine perfection of a stallion's rear end, a shire horse no doubt by the bloody size of it. The human part of it was bulky. Block solid fucking muscle. Skin was a tarnished bronze, fur a deep tarnished black. Hair a haphazard mess of black. Laughing hazel eyes, well, from what Raven could make out anyway. He could tell though, he was a pretty boy, erm man. He watched as Lexis literally launched herself up into the centaur's arms. He caught her in his arms and hugged her like she was made of the finest porcelain and she dangled a good two feet in the air. Raven looked at Tairen, whose eyes were glued to Lexis.

"What's the whole deal of him being like that with Lexis?" Tairen looked at him.

"Because Lexis saved his wife when she went into labour early. He's eternally grateful for that," he replied casually.

"What? But Lexis knows nothing of that," Luke explained, joining in the conversation. Draylan didn't say anything, just walked away, no doubt going to collect the things Calista had asked for and leaving Tairen to answer their questions.

"Ah, but Luke, she did it real successfully. She went in and did everything without a moment's hesitation. You should be severely proud of her. She's more grown up than you realise." Tairen said, drawing the men's eyes to his.

"Trust me, I am immensely proud of her and I know she's grown up," he admitted, albeit a tad sadly about it and they all watched as Lexis walked back to them, clutching something in her palm.

"What you got there?" Tairen asked.

"Ceasor gave me it." She opened her hand and lying there, same size as her palm, was a red diamond.

"Is that a real diamond?" Raven enquired.

"Yes."

"Why would he give you one?"

"Because it's the highest honour you can give someone here. Calista has an underground impenetrable vault full of them in vast colours, shapes and sizes. As well as all sorts of other expensive metals including gold, silver, etc."

"That doesn't actually surprise me." Luke grinned at Lexis and she grinned back.

Calista and Skyri headed away from them all and sauntered in the direction of the first kidnapped victim's house.

"So, who are those guys with our Lexis?" Skyri enquired.

"Luke, the short one is Lexis's brother and Raven is his best friend of something like twenty years," she replied, not really paying attention.

"How they taking to being here?"

"Confused. Awed by it all."

"Like Lexis was then?"

"Kind of, at least she understood it quicker than them." Skyri didn't answer, as they'd reached the first house. It was a pert house. Unpretentious. With a front porch and a white picket-fenced front garden.

Just like the other homes here on the outskirts of the town. Kid's toys lay scattered across the otherwise immaculately kept lawn with the short grass, tidy flower beds ripe with life. Skyri opened the gate and let Calista in first, then shut it behind him. Calista quickly scanned the surrounding area out of sheer habit, adjusted her axe and sword then waited as Skyri knocked at the front door. Not even thirty seconds later, it was opened to reveal a male Elvin Fairy. He had neat brown hair and starburst bright brown eyes that were large. He was classically handsome, tall at around six feet two or three. He was quite simply how Elvin Fairy males looked.

"Oh, thank God it's you, Calista. We had heard of your return but had no idea of when you'd turn up." His voice was deep, but not too deep.

"Yes, well, I had things to do first. Now, how about you let me in, get what I need, leave, go to the other homes and then let me go bring your daughter and the other children home?" she said in her usual straightforwardness. Virtually everyone was used to her bluntness. She had, after all, always been like it.

"Oh yes, sorry." He moved to the side and bid them entry into his family's home. They walked through the adequately clean house and led them into the living room. It was light, airy and smelt of wood smoke and vanilla. Light wood furniture called the place home. An Elvin Fairy woman sat on the pale light brown couch-like furniture. She had long gold shimmering hair. Pale skin but she had the beauty of the Elvin women. Eyes were a lake-blue crystal, swimming in unshed tears. Her features were classical and sophisticated. She was clutching a bright pink ballerina bunny rabbit teddy to her chest. When she noticed Calista and Skyri, she quickly bounced to her feet and hurried over to them. Calista held her hand up and she stopped. Calista refused to let anyone touch her, not even Lexis unless they were alone and even that was rare. Luckily the kid knew it, so used her hugs on Tairen now.

"Thank you for coming as quickly as you did, Calista," she acknowledged with a graceful bow that majority of people did to her. Like she was fucking royalty or something like that instead of the mercilessly, cold-hearted stone cold assassin who lived to kill. Literally. And loved every minute of it.

"Yes. OK. Now, as blunt as I am, how was it that your youngest daughter was taken, yet the eldest two weren't?" She already knew the answer, but wanted to hear it from them. She absently crossed her arms and looked severely intimidating, which wasn't surprising, considering she had her battle axe strapped across her back and sword attached to her hip and an assortment of knives strapped to her body as well. Plus her piercing cobalt blue eyes that were unblinking and righteously scary. Plus, they were highlighted in eyeliner, so that made them stand out even more.

"The eldest two were at my mother's, Naomi wasn't feeling well having just come from being sick. Melissa and I were cleaning up from having dinner, when Naomi came in complaining of a bad stomach ache. Melissa told her to go back to bed and that once she'd finished washing up, she'd be right up with some medicine. Naomi didn't argue, just went to bed. It was unusual, and showed how ill she was. Naomi always usually argues about going to bed, we think it was just a typical six-year-old." Henry ran a hand through his hair, and sat down on the couch, "Melissa finished washing up, I told her I'd finish up, she went to Naomi but a minute later, she came back down screaming that Naomi had been kidnapped." He ran a shaky hand over his face, clearly distraught.

"How do you know that? Could she have been in the toilet?" Calista noticed Skyri said absolutely nothing, just stood there looking all menacing, like usual.

"Because this note was on her bed," Melissa murmured, she reached into her pocket and withdrew a piece of old parchment, which she immediately handed to Calista, who glanced down at it.

As you can see, I've taken your daughter, amongst others. Of course, you shall send for that deadly assassin, Calista. Just tell her Kharge the All Powerful has your child. If you want her back, then Calista, yes I know you'll be reading this, bring yourself to Fire Stoke Mountain. But the children won't be easy to get to, oh no. They'll be placed in, shall we say, cages that you need to use that brain of yours to master, but until then, bye for now. Murderous plots don't think for themselves after all.

Kharge:

the ALL powerful.

"Fucking bastard," she said and handed the note to Skyri. She didn't bother acknowledging that the couple sucked their breath in between their teeth at her foul language.

"What exactly did he mean by cages which you'll need to use your brain with?" Melissa asked. Typical Elvin Fairy! Majority of them were oblivious to the known dangers in the real work and kind of lived in a fantasy bubble. That was one of the things Calista hated about them.

"Exactly that. So in order to get Naomi and the other children back, Kharge will have, with no uncertainty set up a series of traps and puzzles that Calista would need to overcome," Skyri replied matter-of-factly and in his own usual bluntness.

"Can you show us the bedroom?" Skyri also asked before they could comment on what Calista had just said, the swearing that was.

"Yes, of course," Henry replied just as two kids ran into the living area.

"Is Naomi back?" panted the girl, who was the spitting image of her mother. Calista noticed her eyes were the same lake crystal blue but mixed with starburst brown. She would quite simply be a heartbreaker when she grew up.

"No Eliana, she isn't. But Calista here will help get her back for us," Melissa said. The alive or dead bit left unsaid. Both kids swung around to look at her. As she'd already taken in what the girl looked like, she did the same to the boy. All wrapped up into one big sum, he was the spitting image of his dad, just with his mother's eyes.

"Hello," they murmured.

"Hello," she replied. She wasn't a complete monster, she did have manners. *Sometimes*.

"So is it true what Mum says? That you'll help get Naomi back?" Eliana asked.

"I won't help. I *will* get her back."

"Right, if you'd follow me, Calista," Henry intervened and led them upstairs. They reached Naomi's bedroom and Henry pushed the door open. It was a typical six-year-old girl's bedroom — pink, pink and even more pink. Calista walked in and closed the door behind her, shutting Henry and Skyri in the hallway. She heard Henry gasp in astonishment, but Skyri was used to it by now and heard him lean against the wall to wait for her. She placed her back against the door, hands spread, palms out slightly in front of her, fingers pointed to the floor. She closed her eyes and evened out her breathing.

"Svern remendiando zvrch calandvazo," she whispered and the room went black. And then things that happened in the past replayed themselves. She quickly shifted through what was up to a week old, until she found the scene she was looking for, that had happened five days past...

Little Naomi put her hands against her bedroom door, and used the strength she didn't have to open it and quickly shut it after scrambling inside. It took her effort, it was literally just a normal door but because she wasn't well, it felt as though it was made of solid steel. She was ridiculously sick, pale, clammy, cold yet hot to the touch. And she felt downright irritable which wasn't like her at all so she knew she definitely wasn't feeling well. She slowly approached her bed, her feet felt heavy like someone had tied weights down to them and she collapsed bonelessly on top of it. It took energy she had stored for an emergency to move, so she figured she'd wait until her mum came up to help her. She knew her mum would just move her gently and then tuck her into bed and give her that strawberry-flavoured medicine that would help her sleep and she'd get better within a few days. A moment later she heard her bedroom door open but she didn't as so much as move thinking it was her mum, plus she just didn't have the energy. But then she smelt raw, disgusting unsophisticated sweat. She immediately knew it wasn't her parents. Mum smelt of ripe peaches and magic whereas Dad smelt of raw magic, the norm for Elvin Fairy males. She reached deep inside her and was about to scream when a massive hand flipped her over onto her back and clamped itself over her mouth and pretty much her entire face. She lifted wide, terrified eyes upwards, peeking through spread fingers and locked onto sickeningly yellow eyes. It was a Dark Demon. It blew this pale blue glitter powder in her face and she suddenly found she could no longer move. She was wholly and completely paralysed. She watched helplessly as he tied her up and slung her over his shoulder, all the while she was helpless to fight back, let alone scream out for her parents. As he climbed out of her window, the last thing she saw was her bedroom window ledge before her eyes and then the world went black and she happily slipped into the warm embrace of unconsciousness. And she was pain free as well.

Calista made the memoir disappear and the room returned to normal. She had obviously left out the part of Melissa making an appearance to find her daughter missing. She pulled the door open and immediately Henry snapped to attention from looking at his hands that he was rubbing together and Skyri stood up straight from leaning against the wall.

"What did you find out?" Skyri asked.

"Naomi is ill. She unquestionably wasn't joking about this one. And it was a Dark Demon with sickenly yellow eyes. Only a few have actually been seen, so shouldn't be that hard to identify if I see him again." She looked at Henry then. "Anyway, he used Glitter Paralysis to momentarily control your daughter. He tied her up, slung her over his shoulder, clambered out the window and disappeared into the night. Just as his feet had hit the floor, Melissa walked in, screamed and came straight to you," she replied and walked off downstairs.

"Is she always that blunt?" Henry asked Skyri, who had just shut Naomi's door.

"Yes. Always," he replied and motioned Henry to go back downstairs. They did, go downstairs that is. Calista had just relayed to Melissa, Jake and Eliana what she had already told Henry and Skyri.

"So, what is to happen now?" Eliana asked, tears clearly evident in her eyes.

"I have to go to the other houses where the children, who were also kidnapped, live. Then go back to mine. Pack a few essentials and then leave for Fire Mountain and bring them all back home," she replied. No point in lying to the kid. She'd have to learn eventually that it did no good lying.

"Thank you for helping find Naomi," Melissa said. Calista snapped her cold eyes to Melissa's sad ones.

"I will not help 'in finding Naomi'. I will find and bring her home." Calista wasn't bragging, she just knew she'd have no problem in finding the chit. It was the getting them out and back home that would create a slight problem. She didn't need help, she'd find them on her own.

"Sorry. I did not mean to offend you."

"Keep your apology. You know how to repay me once I return with your daughter. For now, I must take my leave." With that she did actually leave.

"Erm, Skyri?" Henry called out, just as the man was about to follow his best friend.

"Yeah?" he asked, turning slightly.

"What is it exactly Calista wishes for in return?"

"Money," he answered instantly.

"How much?"

"Half a million should do it nicely. But maybe wait until Calista returns to make the payment. And perhaps to make a deal with her so you don't have to pay it all in one go and panic that you don't have it. I'm sure Calista will allow instalments of it, to find what suits you best. Now, I must leave and go to the other homes with her. I bid you goodbye for now." And he too left without so much as a backward glance. Knowing full well they wouldn't argue with the price of payment, not when their daughter's life was on the line.

Chapter Seven
Later that morning at Fire Mountain

Kharge grinned sickeningly as his demons placed the children he'd had kidnapped at his feet. They were filthy, stinking and no doubt hungry. But he actually didn't give a shit, sadistic bastard that he was.

"So you reckon that Calista will come here for you?" he asked, leaning forward to pick up his skull cup full of blood. He looked to the children and they all looked at him with a silent plea — none answered his question which he knew they wouldn't. Fear paralysed their vocal cords. He took a mouthful of the still warm blood and stared at the children. The main door into his hall slammed open and his eighteen-year-old daughter, Scorcha, came in. She was his image, just more feminine. Thick black hair with brilliant red underneath that accentuated her ruby red eyes. Today, he noticed with pride, she wore black jeans and a tank top with Fire Bitch in blazing red writing on it. So very much like her mother used to be. He wondered if his dear wife had still lived, would she and Scorcha be as close as what he and she were? And would he and her be as happy as they were in the beginning? Now that he thought on it, even though he had loved her, they had grown distant. She'd taken other males into her bed, whereas he had been faithful to her. But once he'd found out she'd taken other men, he'd killed them and banished her to another room. They were civil around Scorcha though, even though she'd been only six at the time.

"Hello, Father," she said as she drew nearer. She didn't so much as acknowledge the children.

"What brings you here?" he enquired. Usually during the day she was sleeping, well until at least early afternoon as she preferred the night. So very much like her mother did. And himself actually.

"I need a new plaything. That demon you got me isn't very entertaining. Usually just cries and pisses himself when I walk into the room," she huffed.

"You know where the prisoners are kept," he replied and her eyes locked on him.

"How about one of them?" She pointed to the kids, who had recoiled in stark terror backwards, as far as their chains would allow them. Clearly they'd heard of her brutality of her 'playthings'. Well, apart from one, he just glared at them and hugged the small sick one to his chest. Someone had spirit; he'd give them that. Too bad he planned on breaking it, but oh how much fun it would be to see how much he had before he broke.

"No. They're my bargaining chip to Calista." Scorcha hissed at Calista's name being mentioned. Not that he blamed her. She had taken away Scorcha's mother, because she'd gone on a killing rampage and killed about one hundred men, women and children before Calista had lobbed off her head. What was so wrong with a little killing now and again?

"Well, OK then. Can I get a hit in?" Ever so bloodthirsty, his Scorcha was.

"Of course you can."

"Awesome. Anyway, what's for dinner? I'm like, actually starving!" She glared at him. Only she could get away with looking at him like that and not have him retaliate.

"Go ask cook. She'll tell you." He watched, amused as Scorcha practically ran from the room. She was like her mother in that way, when she was hungry, you knew about it! And it didn't matter as to what time of the day it was either. His amusement quickly deserted him when one of his watchers walked in, weary and obviously scared by the slow, careful way he was walking.

"Your sire…" he said, and quickly bent at the knee in a bow.

"What is it?"

"Calista has returned to Mystic Being. She's currently going around to the children's homes."

"And what about all those sent after her?" He knew what had happened to them, due to the fact that the Marbilian he had sent had been left to live, but Calista had told him to personally deliver a message to him. The Marbilian had barely made it out alive from Kharge's temper exploding. He definitely wasn't using that Marbilian again to do a job.

"Killed." The demon outright refused to meet his gaze.

"And what is there to know also?"

"Our source has told us that once she has gathered all her information and collected her things that she'll need, she'll be on her way over here. And apparently, she's quite pissed off." He visibly shook, no doubt thinking Kharge would do something to him. Scorcha came back then, munching on a hunk of meat. Voracious little carnivore that she was.

"Leave us," she snapped and the demon didn't need telling twice. He up and disappeared.

"You see Lviana around?" Lviana was Scorcha's long-time friend. Both had caused immense trouble when they had been younger but he was thankful his daughter had a friend, even if said friend spent a lot of time with her thighs spread. Had ever since she had become of age and realised she loved sex.

"No. Have you tried her room?"

"Actually, no. Bloody tart could be busy for all we know and I really do not need that image imprinted onto my brain." She practically shuddered.

"Well, knock then," he replied and cast a glance to the children. All were still wide eyed apart from the littlest, hers were closed and that one who was stubborn, a shifter by the smell of him, stared back at him in defiance with what can only be described as burning hatred in his red-rimmed black eyes. He was going to have fun breaking that out of him. He needed a new slave boy. The smallest was also deathly pale, which meant she was very sick. It just made him wonder at just how much longer she would last for before she succumbed to the awaiting arms of death. Not that it would bother him in the slightest if she died. Just a mere inconvenience. Dare he go and take another child or just wait for Calista to turn up for these ones? The latter won.

"Yeah, true. See you later." She left. Kharge clicked his fingers and two brute demons stepped forward.

"Take them back to the cell. Feed them too. No good to us dead as bargaining chips to Calista." They nodded, gathered up the kids quickly and left. If they ate, they ate. If not, not his problem. Kharge stood, stretched, downed the last of his blood, the cup quickly taken by a slave and walked to the part of his home that was his own private quarters. Strolling through the living area to the back, he flung open his bedroom door and in his room stood Lviana and Scorcha, who'd clearly only arrived. Now why wait to see him in his bedroom instead of the living area?

"What do you two want?" He leaned against his black stone fireplace.

"Can we take the buggy out and go to Fire River? And don't worry, guards will go with us," Lviana said, looking him clean in the eye. The shit really had no sense in being scared.

"Yeah, sure," he replied and Scorcha let out a joyous whoop and ran out of the room, whereas Lviana took her time. He knew Scorcha would be safe — his men knew better than to let her be injured.

144

"Thanks for letting us go Kharge," she murmured as she passed him. His hand struck out, caught her around her throat and slammed her against the stone wall.

"If anything happens to Scorcha, be warned Lviana. I will take it out on you."

"Understood." Kharge saw arousal flare in her yellow/orange eyes. He drew in a breath and sure enough, the scent of her arousal hit him. He let her go even though he knew if he so much as wanted, she'd accept him in her bed and she wouldn't complain, no matter how rough he'd get.

"Get out of here, Lviana." She did. He shook his head and closed the door the chit had left open. He flipped the massive deadbolt across and made sure everything was secure and shut tight, stripped to his bare skin and crawled into his huge black bed. His cook would send someone to his room once the food was all prepared. He sighed and closed his eyes. A small, stress-free power nap wouldn't do any harm. It was hard work being evil after all.

Calista cracked her neck as she and Skyri left the house they had just visited and luckily enough, it was the last one. She gazed up into the sky and guessed it had to be at least seven in the evening from the way the moon hung in the sky. Took longer than she had originally thought, but not to worry as she was used to the long hours.

"Where to now?" Skyri asked, letting out a jaw-cracking yawn.

"Back to mine," she replied. He nodded and together they made their way back to hers. Walking through the town it was eerily quiet. But then again, many of the children would be tucked up in their beds now, sleeping soundly and dreaming the dreams of innocents whilst their parents relaxed.

"It's rare it being this quiet, there are usually those rebellious teens out," Skyri pointed out.

"That is true. But since the kidnappings, they're all being cautious as they now realise that it could have easily been them." Calista looked up the hill that alone housed her home and saw lights illuminated in some of the windows.

"So this means that they're now scared?"

"Half the reason. Also shows that they're learning that much more dangerous things lurk in the darkness that'd most likely use them as a tooth pick."

"Well duh, you do roam the streets." Skyri laughed as he dodged a punch from her. He laughed even more when she just shook her head helplessly at him. Thankfully she was used to his humour. They finally reached the top of the hill when Skyri pulled Calista to a stop.

"What?" she asked.

"Am I staying here tonight or best to go home?"

"Crash if you want. I don't care." And she didn't. He actually stayed over more than he was at his own place so it was as if he bloody lived with her. Obviously it didn't bother her, because if it did, he wouldn't be around as much as he was. Before he could reply, the front door burst open and Luke stormed out with Lexis chasing after him.

"Luke! Wait!" she cried, but he blanked her and carried on walking past them and down towards town.

"Care to explain, Lexis?" Skyri asked, drawing the kid's tearful gaze.

"He practically went ballistic because I told him I'm changing over." She sniffed and glanced down the hill to her brother, who was stomp-walking away.

"Skyri, go and bring him back. Tell him it's her choice," Calista said and he nodded, then left to bring back Luke. Calista turned Lexis around and directed her into the house. As they walked in, they could hear muffled shouting. But with Calista's hearing she could hear word for word as if she was in the room herself. She threw the living room door open and immediately the shouting stopped. Directly ahead of her, Tairen and Raven were right in each other's faces, but had turned their heads to look at her. At least she knew Raven wasn't afraid to get into someone's face, even if the other one could rip his head off with one well-placed swipe with his hand. But then she reckoned with the size of Raven, it wouldn't be easy to take him down. She threw her hands out and sent the men flying in opposite directions, not stopping until their backs were against the walls.

"Now everyone calm the fuck down and care to fucking tell me what this is all about," Calista hissed, drawing everyone's attention.

"Raven and Luke are against Lexis changing over. It's her fucking choice!" Tairen snapped, his fangs sharp and very evidently sticking into his lower lip, eyes blazing with red hot anger. It was very rare Calista saw this side of him, she was more used to seeing his uncle angry than him as he was usually so very calm. Well, until Lexis and his family were threatened then he became the monster she and her uncle had trained him to be. Well, she trained him to protect himself; but he soon had proved that he was more than capable of handling himself.

"And why is that?" She turned her glacial cold gaze to Raven.

"Perhaps if you'd already fucking listened to me. I don't care if she changes over, as long as it's what Lexis wants, then I couldn't actually give a shit! All I want for Lexis is to be happy!" Raven said, ice-blue eyes spitting fire. The first main emotion she'd seen in his eyes apart from lust. She noticed his body was coiled like a spring and she was certain if she let him go from where she had him pinned against the wall, he'd go off like a rocket and destruction would no doubt be done. And if anything was so much as scratched in her home, she'd take it out on them, consequences be damned.

"And what about Luke?"

"He doesn't want her to go through the pain we were told comes with it." He finally looked at her.

"Right, and I suppose you both lost your tempers before Lexis could tell you that I'll be helping and that I'll absorb the sheer brunt of the pain? No? I can tell from that look on your face Raven. Perhaps next time, listen to her completely before jumping to severe conclusions." Calista then left the room and a minute later, the men crashed to the floor in a heap of limbs. They staggered to their feet and they looked over at Lexis, who was silently crying with tear tracks lying against her cheeks.

"Sorry for jumping to conclusions and that like I did, Lexis. You know it's because I don't want you hurt. You're my family and I can't even think of you being hurt, let alone see it," Raven said in way of apology.

"It's OK. You're my family too and I love you dearly, but you have to admit, you really should have let me finish before you and Luke began shouting like you did."

"I know. I really am sorry." He walked over and pulled her to him for a hug. When they broke apart, Tairen walked over and pulled her to him for a hug also.

"I really am sorry too. For shouting and such like I did. I love you babe," he said and kissed her quickly.

"I love you too," she replied, just as Skyri walked in.

"Hey! What about me?" he replied, fluttering his lashes at her. Lexis laughed and hugged him before he wiped away the tears and the streaks on her face.

"You know I love you too, Skyri. Even if you do make me black and blue." She grinned at him.

"Erm, black and blue?" Raven asked, clearly perplexed.

"Black and blue as in bruises, Raven. As Skyri's teaching me how to defend myself. Even though rogue that he is; can be quite unfair at times."

147

"Oh, please. I'm not tough on you at all. Tairen has suffered more from me than you have."

"Only because you know if you really did hurt me Calista would hand you your hide in a box, tied neatly in a bow with your intestines." She grinned at him cheekily.

"For sure." He laughed.

"Anyway, I take it this means you got Luke back?" Tairen asked.

"Yeah, but Calista's having a word with him out front."

"About what?"

"About Lexis going through the change. He was just afraid and he's upset about the way he lashed out. He doesn't want you to go through the pain of it. Calista is reassuring him that she'll be there through the entire thing," Skyri replied, looking at Lexis as he said this.

"Where are they?" she asked.

"I already told you, out front." The front door opened then and Calista and Luke walked in. Both wore unreadable expressions. Calista stood in the middle of Raven and Skyri as Luke walked up to Lexis.

"Can I have a private word please?" he asked. She nodded and they walked off, no doubt for obviously a private conversation. Calista would block it out, as otherwise she'd be able to hear them word for word. She'd respect their privacy, she knew Lexis would appreciate it.

"Resolve your issues?" she asked Tairen and Raven.

"Yes. He was just concerned for Lexis," Tairen explained.

"Well, that's all right then." She looked to the kitchen door the siblings had disappeared through.

"What are you looking at the door for?" Skyri asked, but she didn't reply. Just held her fingers up on one hand and counted down and as she reached one, Lexis and Luke walked through the door. Obviously they'd had the world's quickest conversation, or Luke had just wanted to say sorry privately. Knowing him, it was the latter. She smirked at Skyri, who just rolled his eyes, clearly used to her antics.

"Everything sorted?" Tairen enquired.

"Yeah." Lexis smiled and moved to her man, who draped his arm across her shoulders as though it was the simplest and easiest thing in the world, and by looks of it, it was considering how often he did it. Draylan walked into the house then carrying a few large boxes balanced on top of each other. He handed Calista a small red/black box that she opened up without hesitation. Lying inside on silk red velvet lay a sleek silver-bladed knife with a black oak handle with small indentations sticking out for grip.

The blade had a jagged edge that criss-crossed like the teeth of a shark. Swirling patterns adorned the silver, in a language of long ages past. It was the language of the first mythological beings. No one could talk the language now; but due to Calista's 'unusual birth', she could.

"What do they say?" Lexis asked, looking at the masterpiece.

"It means stronger than expected. Beautiful assassin," she replied. She pulled the blade out of the box and Calista handed it, handle first, to Lexis.

"Oh my, it's as light as a feather," she remarked, and ran her finger lightly over the blade and it left a slither cut on her flesh. She hissed from the shock, Calista took Lexis's hand into her own, and using her 'powers' healed the cut quickly and Lexis smiled gratefully at Calista. Then she handed it over to Raven so he could see. Calista dropped the hand and looked at Draylan as he nudged her. She took the boxes off him, and held them like they weighed nothing at all.

"This everything I ask for?"

"Yes, including a few extra rounds of ammunition and blades," he replied, and rolled his shoulders to loosen them from the weight that had held them down. Damn boxes were fucking heavy.

"Excellent," she remarked and again up and disappeared.

"OK. That would take some serious getting used to," Luke said with a sly grin.

"Don't you know it! It actually took me six to eight months before I got used to it," Lexis grinned.

"Did it really take you that long?" Raven asked, and handed the blade to Skyri.

"Yes, it did. But now it's just a way of life for Calista and me," she replied.

"Tairen?" a voice called out. They all whirled around to face what had called out to Tairen and what stood in the entranceway gobsmacked the lads. A lone figure stood in the doorway, they couldn't really make out features and such because there wasn't a lot of light in the vast hallway and it was pitch black outside. So that fucked them up trying to see who it was. But by the lenient voice, they could tell it was a woman.

"Rayne? What are you doing here?" Tairen asked and walked over to the thing blocking the doorway and drew it into his arms quickly for a hug.

"Who's Rayne?" Raven whispered to Lexis.

"Tairen's sister," she replied.

"Didn't know he had a sister!"

"Yeah. They're actually twins and are really close. Just be warned, she's blunt as anything but she's a gem." They both looked back and Raven got his first look at her as she stepped forward into the light. She was a mystifying beauty. She had unusual turquoise eyes, with pupils split like a cat's but they also seemed to see into your very soul, kind of like Calista's did, and they were highlighted with black eyeliner and blue eyeshadow. She had curly hair that fell in a thick wave of white blonde silk with the roots and part of the top accentuated with ice blue, to the middle of her back. She wore black jeans that looked like she'd been poured into them and a black tank top with the saying Bite Me on it with a vampire mouth that was slanted in a corner, kind of like a smirk. Boots with chains covered her feet, New Rocks if he wasn't mistaken. Ears were pierced with scaffolding bars as well as studs of silver skulls. Sensual full lips were painted red and pierced in the middle. Hands were graceful and had long black nails and she wore fingerless biker gloves with studs. She had a leather-studded jacket slung over her shoulder that she'd hooked around one finger. Biker chick eat your heart out. Raven thought all she needed now was a motorbike and she'd be set. She was tall, around six feet one. She was the light to Tairen's dark and it actually suited them both. Raven watched as Tairen said something to her and she nodded, a slight smile on her face and then she caught sight of Skyri. Her face went into an unreadable mask and her eyes practically hardened. Handing her jacket to her brother, who hung it on a hook by the door, she walked up to Skyri, swung her arm back, clenched her fist and hit him square across his jaw. And this was all before he could stop her; it was over in a matter of seconds. And even Raven could admit that it was an impressive right hook. Girl had some mighty power and strength behind her.

"Fuck you!" she snarled.

"That an invite?" he grinned and she actually punched him again. This time though, the laughter left his features, his eyes hardened and his body tensed up and then he began to change, right in front of everyone. Raven noticed Lexis had moved to stand behind the solid wall that was Tairen and Draylan. Raven looked back at Skyri and quite simply froze. Skyri had transformed into a seven and a half foot tall monster! Fur in rich black covered him. His face had contorted into a deadly muzzle with a highly sensitive nose and snout that held dangerous sharp, pearl white teeth that practically glistened. His eyes were a sizzling bright green still. Sickenly hazardous claws hung from his hands. Legs were thick and muscular, pretty much the same as when he was in his human form, only these were longer and his feet were long and tipped in claws. Wolf paws! But then Raven noticed Rayne didn't so much as flinch — she held her ground.

"Do not hit me again, Rayne." His voice was unnaturally deep.

"Or else what?" The woman just would not back down. Was that a trait her uncle had taught her or was she just naturally stubborn? Or was it both?

"Or else I'll kick your sorry fucking arse!" he growled.

"Ha! I'm not scared of you." She actually lifted a hand and studied her nails; like she didn't actually give a shit that Skyri was a domineering male. Raven and Luke carefully worked their way over to the men and Lexis, but in a way in which didn't call attention to themselves. All the good that did them; Skyri and Rayne were completely oblivious to everyone else.

"Erm, how dangerous can Skyri be when he's like this?" Luke asked, keeping a wary eye on the lycan.

"Very," Tairen said.

"Why did Rayne punch him?" Raven enquired.

"No doubt because he teased her again. Both are seriously mad about each other, but think the other person has no feelings for them," Draylan replied.

"But surely they realise they have feelings for each other? Everyone can tell. Even I can and I don't even know them," Luke pointed out.

"We know that." Draylan looked back to his niece and Skyri, who were still arguing and completely blanking everyone else and Raven noticed that his hands were clenched and his muscles taut as if ready to leap into action to protect his niece at any cost.

"Does it bother you that your niece is interested in a lycanthrope like Skyri?" Raven asked.

"No; it actually doesn't. Besides, at the end of the day, she's old enough to make her own decisions, lest they are right or wrong, and I'll back her one hundred percent." he answered truthfully. Raven looked back at the arguing duo and noticed something slim and shiny in Rayne's hand. He opened his mouth to say something but Rayne had already stabbed Skyri in the shoulder with what he realised was a blade she'd had on her. Skyri, still in that form, dived for Rayne, but she'd already moved and she had chosen to head in their direction. They all leapt out of the way before she ploughed into them and Skyri flew past. With the speed of his inner wolf, he quickly caught up and grabbed Rayne, forcing her to a stop. She took another swing at him, but he caught her hand. He flung her up onto his shoulder, despite her screaming, kicking her legs and bashing his back with her fists. Nothing was working to make him put her down though. Then he transformed back into his human self as easy as breathing.

"What is going on?" Calista's voice could be heard clearly over Rayne's colourful screaming. They all looked to the upper landing and Calista stood there and to Raven, she never looked better. She began walking down the stairs and looked at Skyri, who had a smirk on his face.

"Nothing. Just going to throw Rayne into the ocean for a cooling off," he replied in answer to her question, looking just past her left eye.

"And what did she do to deserve this?" She stopped at the bottom, next to Lexis.

"She stabbed me."

"Ah, but did it not heal when you shifted?"

"So, still hurt like a motherfucker."

"Of course it would bloody hurt. It is an object going through your skin and muscle after all. Anyway, now isn't the time to fling Rayne into the ocean; put her down. It is time." Calista waited whilst Skyri put the vampire down, grumbling as he did though. Rayne wisely kept her gob shut and moved to stand next to her brother, clearly knowing Calista would indeed kick her arse if she uttered a single sound. It was obviously one thing to provoke Skyri but an entirely different kettle of fish to piss of Calista.

"Time?" Luke asked, looking at Calista.

"Time for Lexis to be changed over. You will wait down here, all of you. And no arguments, Tairen. I don't need the hassle. Skyri, you'll help. Afterwards, I'll send Skyri down to get you when it is completed." She didn't wait for a reply, just ushered Lexis upstairs, who glanced behind her and smiled slightly at them all, but panic and fear were evident in her eyes.

"OK, that was weird. Why couldn't she hug us bye?" Luke enquired, looking up the stairs as his sister disappeared round the corner.

"Because it'll just prolong the turning. Lexis will be fine. Calista won't let anything happen to her," Tairen replied. But he didn't look at them, he too was watching where Lexis had disappeared.

"How do you know that?" Raven asked as Draylan ushered them all into the living room, even though he had to physically push Tairen to get him to move. They all plonked down on the couches and then proceeded to wait out the agony of waiting for Lexis to change over from human into vampire. Rayne leant against the fireplace though, the blade she'd stabbed Skyri with in her hand now clean from blood... erm, how? And she used it to pick under her nails with. Raven's question remained unanswered.

Chapter Eight

"Which room are we going in?" Lexis asked, voice trembling.

"Tower," Calista replied. Lexis had never actually been in the tower room before. Heck, she didn't even know how to get to it and God forbid she'd actually tried! But what lay ahead? She knew she'd have to be strapped down and that Calista would take the brunt of the pain that she knew would come with it. And honestly, she was very thankful for that! She followed Calista into her bedroom. Lexis watched, amazed as Calista walked over to the fireplace and pushed the mantel. It shuddered slightly, and a huge crack appeared right through the middle. Then it groaned, and opened up to reveal a staircase but it only consisted of four to six steps. Lexis jumped slightly when a hand landed on her shoulder. She glanced back and breathed a sigh of relief when she saw it was Skyri, but his face was expressionless.

"Come on, Lexis. Sooner we start the better," the woman said and pulled her onto the steps. Skyri quickly followed and the fireplace rumbled shut behind them, shutting them into blackness and Lexis reached behind her and grabbed Skyri's hand, who squeezed back gently in encouragement and gave her a small amount of courage. She knew as long as she had these two with her she'd be safe. Lights soon appeared, the walls glowing with fluorescent lights. The stairs moved, travelling upwards. They carried on for about twenty seconds and then Lexis noticed a door appear before them. Calista pushed it open and walked in. Lexis and Skyri quickly followed but couldn't see much, just the silhouette of Calista as she flicked her wrist and lights flared to life on the walls. Lexis blinked abruptly to get her eyes to adjust to the sudden brightness in the room. Lexis stepped into the room and glanced around. A double wrought iron bed, naked apart from the mattress, lay against the side wall. All of the walls were black that gleamed in the light. Opposite the door were two large windows covered in a thick, black curtain. A claw-footed bathtub lay in a corner, a pull-out screen next to it to aid in a bit of privacy. What shocked Lexis the most, against the wall with the door, was a steel table. Like the ones they use in hospitals, only this was covered in a black sheet and was on wheels.

"Actually, Skyri, do me a favour. Go bring all of them up here. It'll be a lot easier on Lexis to have familiar faces around her," Calista announced as she motioned Lexis over to the bed. Lexis looked back but the door was swinging shut as Skyri was nowhere to be seen.

"What do I have to do?" she asked, sinking down onto the mattress.

"First of all, remove all makeup. You'll thank me later." She threw a pack of make-up removal wipes to her and Lexis hurriedly removed it all, which luckily was only basic make-up, no contouring or shit.

"Better?" she asked when she had removed it all. Calista put the used wipes into the bin and threw the pack by the window.

"Much."

"OK, now what?"

"I'm going to need you to strip down to your underwear."

"Why?" she asked, even though she complied. She knew not to argue but no harm in asking.

"Because your clothes will constrict you. They'll rub against your skin and feel itchy and they'll annoy the hell out of you and basically you'll want to rip them off."

"But wouldn't my bra and underwear annoy me also?" She placed her jeans and top on the floor next to the bed as there was nowhere else to actually put them. She lay down on the mattress as Calista had motioned her to do. She watched as the woman, her best friend who knew literally everything about her, placed rope restraints around her ankles and wrists, as so she was spread-eagled. Not in the middle of the bed as she would have thought but slightly over to the side, as if giving enough room for someone else to lay down next to her. Plus they were tight enough that she couldn't move, but not enough to cut off vital blood circulation.

"It'll be a mild annoyance but you'll soon pay no attention to that and deal with what else is going to happen. As well as the fact that I don't think you'd want your brother and Raven to see your 'goodies', do you?" she replied when she'd made sure that the shackles were secure. Lexis shook her head and then the door opened. The guys all walked in and they quickly hurried over to where she lay, all modesty leaving her mind, she wasn't exactly shy. Hadn't been for years. She knew she had a great body with lush curves, so what was there to hide? Zilch. Plus, her man liked her curves considering how often he told her. Tairen leaned down and kissed her.

"It's going to be all right, beautiful. I love you." he whispered.

"I love you too." She smiled gently up at him. He moved to the side and allowed Luke and Raven to each kiss her cheek and whisper that they loved her which she said back, because she did. They were her brothers. Raven might not be blood related, but he was damn sure her brother, and if anyone argued with her, she'd rip their head off.

"I want you to sit down now guys and I want you to promise me something," Calista asked, looking up from what she was doing. They did as they were told, sitting with their backs against the wall as there weren't any chairs to sit on.

"What do you want us to promise?" Raven said.

"I want you to promise that no matter what happens, you will not interfere with what I am about to do, or try to help Lexis either." She walked over to the metal table and Lexis strained slightly to see on it and for what Calista was doing but for the life of her, she couldn't bloody see! So she just put her head back down, no point in giving herself a neck ache when it really wasn't worth the hassle.

"OK, we promise. But what happens if we do interfere?" Luke asked and Lexis noticed the colour had drained out of his face slightly. Just what was on that table to make her brother's face drain of colour?

"You'll annoy the hell out of me and break my concentration on helping Lexis through the pain." Draylan snorted at that and everyone looked at him.

"What?" She looked over at him as well.

"What you snort for?" Tairen looked at his uncle with an eyebrow raised.

"Because she's bullshitting, and well, Calista, you know it!"

"So? Just don't want anyone getting in the way. Most definitely if they realise what's going on," she replied. She pulled a knife up from the table and turned to face Lexis, whose own face drained of colour as the size of the blade in Calista's hand was fucking massive! Carver's knife that it was. Or maybe it was even a butcher's blade! Either way, it was fucking scary and gleamed wickedly in the low lighting from the candles she'd placed precariously around the room. Couldn't she have chosen a smaller knife?

"What is that for?" she murmured. Calista didn't answer, just walked over and lay down next to her, settling down on her side, her right arm high above them, hand out of Lexis's sight.

"Look at me, Lexis." She looked into Lexis's eyes and for the life of her, she just couldn't turn away. Everything began to fade away until only the succulent cobalt blue of Calista's eyes could be seen. Tunnel vision, eat your heart out! Which she was thankful for at this precise moment in time. Calista's left hand drew small swirling patterns over her belly, it wasn't ticklish though, it felt warm and created a calming sensation that washed over her. When she was limp with no tension in her body, she felt a small tug on her wrist as if someone had pulled the rope slightly. Then something warm, yet sticky ran down her arm, into her armpit then down on the mattress. She managed to break eye contact and gazed up at her arm, and pressed against her wrist was the blade Calista had picked up earlier. And the thing that was running down her was her own blood! How the hell hadn't she felt the blade rip open her flesh? Unless that was what the tug was? Panic started to set in as she looked at how deep the blade had gone and she snapped her gaze back to Calista's and knew the woman wouldn't let anything happen to her. What happened to there being pain? She knew there should be pain considering she'd seen that bastard blade in her arm! She didn't feel anything except calm and a small wave of sleepiness that was creeping up on her and then noticed the slight strain of tension around Calista's mouth and around her eyes. She was holding it all back for her. Everything, so she didn't feel a thing, just warmth. She didn't have to take it all! But Lexis couldn't utter a single word, her lips even though she could move them, no sound emerged. Not even a whimper. It was as though she had absolutely no control over herself but was completely aware of everything and it was fucking scary! Had this also been how those poor children had felt? She was petrified but she trusted Calista and blinking, as that was all she could do at the moment, stayed looking at Calista's eyes as the woman stared right back, a small tilt of her mouth to reassure her, until blackness began to creep in around the edges of her tunnel vision. Before slipping unconscious from the blood loss, she could have sworn she felt lips softer than the inside of a rose press lightly against her cheek. But she could say this, Calista never moved. She stayed through it all. What a great friend she thought and finally succumbed to the blackness that was calling her, now she was blissfully unaware and she was grateful!

Calista watched as Lexis slipped into unconsciousness, eyes drifting shut and her body going completely limp. Blood had pooled around them, but she didn't dare move for another minute or so until she was absolutely positive Lexis was completely out. Pulling the blooded knife from the woman's now limp wrist, she climbed off the bed. She quickly checked vital signs and the beat underneath her fingers was faint but strong. It was good. She looked over to the lads and noticed Rayne had joined them, obviously not wanting to wait downstairs. She watched as they all stared wide-eyed at Lexis and saw the blood that was pooled around her, a trail drying on her skin. They couldn't see before because Calista had been in the way, but now that she had moved, they saw it clearly. Not bothering to judge their reaction, she walked to the other side of the bed, her back to the windows and she leant over Lexis, tilted the woman's head back slightly, opened her mouth, placed the blade over her wrist and slashed.

"Jesus fucking Christ." She heard Luke mutter in horror, but she ignored him. She made sure a healthy slash of her blood went into Lexis's mouth, then ran her fingers against her throat, getting her to swallow. Once she was satisfied enough blood had gone into her system, she swiped her tongue across the wound, clearing up the blood. It was already healing over, in a matter of minutes it would completely disappear. Because Lexis was already on her back, it was easier to get that first vital bit of blood into her system. Calista wiped the blood from the knife on her leg, put it back on the rack as she would clean it properly later and looked at Draylan and Tairen.

"What?" they both murmured.

"In those boxes you brought for me Draylan, is also a vast amount of blood. Bring it over with a pair of scissors so you can easily cut it instead of using your teeth. And it will be quick, easier and cleaner to get it down Lexis's throat." She motioned to the boxes she'd brought up earlier and they quickly ran over and did as they were asked and with arms full of as many as they could carry, ushered them over to the bed and placed them around Lexis to grab easily for when they needed them. Rayne stayed slouched against the door casually but Calista knew she would leap into action in a matter of seconds. Luke and Raven still hadn't taken their gazes off Lexis, but thankfully they hadn't jumped in to 'help'. Calista shuffled Lexis over until she was in the centre of the mattress with room beside her should they need to gain control, which they most likely would have to.

"Skyri, I'm going to need you over here. Rayne, you too." They quickly crossed the room and Calista motioned for them to stand at Lexis's feet.

"Do you want us to help?" Luke asked.

"No. I want you to stay where you are. Because once Lexis is wholly changed over, she'll be very hungry when she opens those pretty eyes of hers." Calista applied more rope to cover Lexis. Only this time it went across her stomach, chest and upper legs, virtually pinning the woman to the mattress with the knots underneath the bed so she couldn't be tempted to untie them. Knowing Calista's knots, she'd be there a while even if she managed. But for a safety measure, she whispered a spell that wouldn't allow anything to damage/tamper with it. Well, this one was until she left the room.

"How hungry?" Raven murmured, drawing Calista's gaze.

"As in, she'd drain you completely dry of your blood in a matter of seconds if she was free."

"Oh." The last bit of colour drained from his face. Calista picked up a blood bag, moved to the right side of the bed as Draylan and Tairen had taken up the left side, leant over the mattress to Lexis's mouth.

"Ready?" she asked. Everyone nodded. She tipped Lexis's head back again, ripped open a corner of the bag using her fingernail, opened her mouth and tipped it down her throat. She moved to the wrist she had pierced with the knife, leaned forward and ran her tongue slightly over the puncture mark, sealing it shut so the blood she would pour into Lexis wouldn't come back out again from the wound. She then poured another six bags, one straight after the other down Lexis's throat. And only then did the woman begin to gain colour in her skin again, which was a relief. It meant her body was accepting the change. Calista put the empty bags in a small bin near the door, and then she heard Lexis begin to shiver, the bed rattling slightly.

"Rayne, open the window for me, she will need it when the flush begins." Rayne didn't need telling twice, just opened the two windows as far as they would go and a fresh ocean-scented breeze swept through the room as if it had been waiting to caress them.

"What's happening?" Luke asked.

"She's converting. You're lucky you're even in here. Calista and I didn't want you here. But we let you, for Lexis. Because of how much she loves you two. Plus, she didn't want you worrying downstairs," Skyri said and placed his hands on Lexis's leg, which had started to thrash around. Even with his massive form, Calista could see he was starting to strain. New vampires were always ridiculously strong.

"She didn't want us worrying? Are you fucking serious? We're worrying right fucking now!" Luke fumed, jumping up from the floor. Raven grabbed him and held him so he wouldn't get in the way. It was rare seeing him lose his temper, but he could understand as to why, it was his sister after all. And thankfully, he could hold him back, considering he was the stronger of the two. He didn't like that she was in pain either, his little sister of his heart, but he had to remain strong, if not for himself, but for Luke and for Lexis as well.

"Calm yourself. If you think about it, at least with us here we can actually see what is happening and not what we'd only be able to hear," he hissed into his ear. Luke nodded and kept his gaze on his baby sister. Calista looked at Lexis, approached the bed and lifted an eyelid up. Eyes had rolled back into the skull. She let go and bent to pick another blood bag up. Suddenly Lexis bent backwards, pulling those thick ropes taunt across her skin, threw her head back and let out a god awful scream, one that was laced with untold agony. Conversions sucked on the best of days. Like liquid lava running through your system. Dropping the bag on the bed, Calista placed her hands on Lexis's stomach and immediately the woman stopped screaming and her body lowered back to the mattress. Everyone watched, eyes wide in fascination and awe, as Lexis's two canines lengthened into pearlescent white fangs. Without looking back, Calista held her other hand out and Draylan handed her an opened bag of blood. Calista expertly climbed onto Lexis and sat on her lower stomach, pushing the woman fully into the mattress and sticky blood. There was no chance she was bucking her off, which everyone was grateful for. But just in case, Calista locked her knees against the girl's ribcage.

"Draylan, grab her head and hold her still." Draylan leaned forward and did as he was told. Calista used one hand to keep the woman's jaw open and poured the blood straight down her throat. The bag quickly emptied and Calista looked at Tairen.

"She's in the final stages, hence the screaming, I kind of sped it up a bit. Don't want her moaning as it takes effect over the span of something like twelve hours. When she wakes, she'll be hungry and very hormonal! Skyri, Rayne, Draylan you'll all head downstairs, taking Raven and Luke with you."

"Why can't I stay with Lexis?" Luke asked, looking at his sister who was still flat underneath Calista and outright shivering. Not from the pain, but from the amount of cold blood that was now coursing through her system as well as the wind that strolled through the room and brushed over them like a lover's caress. Obviously he hadn't heard what she'd just said.

"Because she'll be very hormonal. And that can only mean one thing in what she'll want," Skyri answered before Calista could.

"Are you saying what I think you are?" He paled.

"Yes. When she wakes up, your little sister will want blood and hard, hot sex. Well, want isn't the word I'd use; more like she'll crave it which is why Tairen will remain behind. Don't really think you want to offer up your blood and cock to your sister," Calista remarked with her usual bluntness and climbed off Lexis, who lay limp and unresponsive on the bed but with just that slight shiver now coursing through her body. She looked over at them and saw both of them shaking their heads hard. She heard a sharp hiss behind her and spun around and she was greeted with Lexis looking at her. Eyes were no longer that lovely hazel colour, but a sizzling blood red. The stark hunger that resided in them very much noticeable. She was no longer the quiet, human Lexis. This was the blood-craving, sex-wanting vampire Lexis. Dangerous. Unpredictable. Lethal. As all newly-turned vampires were. *Tairen was in for a treat* she thought to herself. No sense in saying that out aloud.

"Everyone leave but Tairen. I'll be down in a couple of minutes or so." Calista waited whilst they all disappeared out of the room with thankfully no complaint and looked at Lexis.

"Tairen, strip." Calista kept her gaze on Lexis, who in return watched her, although she was tugging at her restraints. Luckily she couldn't break eye contact thanks to a silent spell that Calista had conjured up. She also whispered a spell that would hold Lexis in place until she left the room. She untied the ropes and removed the shackles. She then quickly stripped Lexis out of her bra and panties with scissors and threw the scraps over her shoulder. And made the blood on the mattress disappear without a trace. Lexis growled in her throat, like a rabid animal and fought to move from where she was immobile.

"Are you sure she won't mind you doing that?" Tairen asked looking at the discarded underwear. Lexis continued to glare at Calista, whilst she ran her tongue over her fangs. Calista looked over to Tairen and almost laughed. The man was actually blushing and was of course very much naked but had his top over his privates.

"Oh please, Tairen, as if you need to be embarrassed. I've seen a lot worse than you standing there naked."

"I know but still, you're like my aunt. No you are my aunt, my family. And that's what makes it somewhat, no actually, majorly uncomfortable."

"Well, that's understandable. But I will warn you, once I leave this room, Lexis will be free to move and she will attack you. And don't worry even in raging blood lust, she won't hurt you. She loves you too damn much."

"OK. Thanks for the warning," he replied and looked at his woman. He noticed her skin was that smooth curvaceous form from before that he absolutely loved. Well, she also had a bit of a tan now that would never fade. Calista walked up to him and placed the syringe full of blood in his hand.

"What's this?"

"Blood with a knockout drug in it. Give it to Lexis when everything else is over and it'll make her sleep, so her body can continue to transform properly."

"OK, I will do."

"I'll return later to make sure you're both all right. And I'll bring along extra blood too." Calista headed to the door and pulled it open.

"Thank you, Calista. One thing though?"

"What?" She looked back at him.

"Make sure it's just you please. I don't want Raven or Luke seeing Lexis at the end of however we end up. Plus, how is the baby?"

"Your son is fine. He's completely changed over into a vampire now and before you ask, he'll be a healthy baby when he's born and Lexis will be fine too as long as she keeps up with the blood drinking."

"Thank you."

"Spare pillows and duvet are in the small chest under the bed, your side. You will need them afterwards but don't worry about closing the window, you will be thankful afterwards."

"OK, and again, thank you. Also, when do I give her the syringe?" he replied

"As I just said, after everything is done. So basically, when she's finally calmed down from the blood lust, shoot that into a main artery and she'll slip into slumber, along with her bloodlust and horniness being sated, OK?"

"OK, thank you. Just wanted to double check," he murmured, put the syringe on the floor so it was within easy reach, plus there was no bedside tables and walked her to the door, ever the gentleman.

"See you later." Calista smiled slightly as she then listened to what she could hear as she closed the door completely behind her, breaking the spell that kept Lexis bed bound. It was a God almighty thump that shook slightly through the door as Lexis dived on Tairen, sending him crashing into the door and demanded him to hurry up. Calista actually did smile then and knew Tairen would look after her in very single possible way he could. That was all she was interested in. That he'd be able to help her and that she'd recover from this ordeal that her body had just gone through but knowing Lexis, as she was a fighter, she'd recover in leaps and bounds and pick up the tell-tale signs of hunger and such easily enough. Not to forget she'd soon realise she was no weakling and learn to hone her body into the weapon it could become, if she wanted, but Calista doubted she would. Lexis wasn't a fighter, she was a lover. But she would realise that she'd be stronger, faster and could take a hell of a lot if push came to shove. She absently waited whilst the stairs spiralled downwards and once at the bottom, she walked out into her bedroom. A lone candle sat on her bedside table, lit, the candle's flame fighting against the shadows that surrounded it. Draylan must have left it for her. She walked into her en suite, shut the door and turned the shower on. She was sore, but mostly it was tiredness from helping Lexis through the change. She'd taken virtually all the pain and thanks to her sheer stubbornness, she didn't let the others know just how bad it actually was. She was glad she'd taken it, otherwise there was no way Lexis would have been able to survive it; her brain would have short-circuited and she'd have died and that was a big no go. Yes, she knew how to bring back the dead but that didn't mean she wanted to use it. But for Lexis? Damn right, within a frickin' heartbeat! She quickly used the facilities, stripped and hopped into the shower to wash away the blood that had gotten onto her that she had literally not noticed. The hot water slid heavenly on and down her body, easing away the tightness of her muscles from the strain of helping Lexis through her change and making sure she didn't miscarry her child. That was one of the risks of changing someone if they were pregnant — ninety-nine percent of the time they miscarried during the changeover. Not this time though, she was adamant to save their child. She reached out from her cocoon of heat and pulled a bottle of the 2in1 shampoo and conditioner to her. She was going to have a lazy shower, she couldn't be bothered doing first the shampoo, and then the conditioner. Fuck that. She wanted a quick shower, change and crawl into bed and try and get a decent sleep for once.

"Calista?" Skyri's voice could be heard coming from her bedroom. She willed the door open and Skyri soon filled the entrance way.

"What do you want?" she asked, not bothering to hide her nakedness. It wasn't the first time he'd seen her naked and highly doubtful it would be the last. Plus, it wasn't as if she was shy. Far from it actually. She didn't have a single shy bone in her body! Never had, most likely never bloody would.

"Raven and Luke want to know how Lexis is. They asked me to come and check," he replied, again looking slightly past her left eye.

"I'll be down in a couple of minutes then let them know," she replied and ducked back under the water. Once she was clean from hair crap and soap, turning the water off, she got out, wrapped a black fluffy towel around herself, and strolled into her bedroom.

"So why didn't they come to find out themselves?" Muttering to herself, she quickly dried herself and snapped her fingers and immediately she was dressed in black jogging bottoms, tank top and the other essentials of course. Hair damp, she slung it up into a ponytail. She guided Skyri out her bedroom, shut the door behind them and they strolled quiet as mice downstairs. Question obviously unanswered and so much for her bloody early night. Oh well, she would make due, as she always did.

"So, do you honestly believe Lexis will be all right now?" Raven asked, drawing Draylan's attention.

"She'll be fine. Calista won't let anything happen to her. Because believe it or not, Calista does actually care for Lexis."

"Oh right. Got to ask though, when Lexis was changing over, I thought that there was meant to be a lot of agony? But with Lexis there wasn't." He actually looked perplexed.

"That's because Calista absorbed majority, if not all of the pain when she placed her hand on Lexis's stomach earlier," Rayne said, actually talking since they had come back downstairs.

"I had wondered about that. About how Lexis started screaming, Calista touched her stomach and then Lexis didn't so much as twitch when Calista cut into her wrist. How did she do that?" Luke enquired, but before anyone could answer, his stomach let out a huge growl.

"Sounds like you're hungry," Draylan smiled.

"I guess I am. Now that I think about it, I actually haven't eaten anything today, well since before we arrived," he admitted.

"Come on, then. Let's go scrounge out some food from the kitchen." Draylan led them into the kitchen and Raven sank onto one of the bar stools, followed quickly by Luke. The vampire rummaged through the cupboards and fridge, whilst they all happily waited for him to make something.

"And in answer to your question, it's Calista. She has her own way of doing things. Plus, she sped up the change, hence why we had to shove so much blood down Lexis' throat, to catch up with it. And we've already said Calista can take hell of a lot of pain and not mutter a single sound whilst it's happening." They heard someone walking towards the kitchen then and the door opened not even thirty seconds later, and Skyri and Calista walked in. Calista blanked them all as she walked to the fridge. He turned his gaze to Skyri and noticed he actually looked tired. He glanced back to Calista and blinked. She was looking right at him as she drank from a dark bottle.

"So how did it go?" Luke asked, obviously he'd waited long enough, eager to find out about his sister.

"She's fine. Lexis changed over completely without a problem," Skyri answered and grabbed a blue coloured bottle from mid-air that Calista had thrown to him before getting another blood bottle for herself, at least that was what he was sure it was.

"So where are Lexis and Tairen?" Luke nodded his thanks to Draylan as he handed him cooked luscious smelling food, then looked behind him at the kitchen door, as if expecting his sister and her boyfriend to walk in at any moment.

"We'd already told you what will happen once she had changed over. Raging hormones and dangerous hunger," Calista said and rinsed her bottle out.

"I remember you telling us," Raven announced, drawing Calista's attention.

"Oh yeah. Guess I had a momentary brain slip," Luke shrugged.

"Yes. But no need to worry about them, we have more important things to worry about." She walked out of the room then, all without a backward glance.

"What's more important than knowing my baby sister is fine?" Luke demanded.

"The missing children. As Calista pointed out, Lexis is fine," Skyri said, standing near the doorway.

"Well, I suppose so. But you can see where I am coming from."

"Actually, not really. As I'm not close to my family," he admitted. Raven thought that was odd. Weren't lycanthropes like normal wolves that craved being in a pack. The closeness of being in a tight-knit community? Now that he thought about it looking at the people around him, he realised that this was Skyri's pack. As wacky as they all happened to be, but it was family for him. And who was he to judge considering his own fucked up family? The ones who couldn't tolerate anything to do with him. Then he realised, actually Luke and Lexis were his family. Simple as that. Wouldn't change it for anything. So he knew exactly where the man was coming from. He then climbed off his stool and didn't stick around to hear whatever else they said; he went in search of the woman who completely fascinated him. He found her in the living room, staring out the patio window, arms crossed over her chest. The only reason he'd actually noticed her was because of the light from the burning fireplace. Even though the curtains were open to allow in light, it was as if the clouds had deliberately hid the moon.

"What do you want, Raven?" Her voice echoed through the chilling darkness.

"How did you know I was here?"

"The way you walk, you are slightly heavier on your right side." She didn't even turn around as she replied. He walked up and stood beside her. He looked at her and paused. Her eyes had gone a silvery white/blue colour. He looked outside to try and see what she was looking at, but for the life of him, he couldn't see jack shit. Just blackness. He looked back at her and stepped to the side in alarm. She was looking right at him. That unnerving silvery white/blue colour had disappeared and her original cobalt blue was back, but they were unblinking and seemed to see right through him. It was quite unnerving.

"How did your eyes change so quickly? And what the fuck was that silvery white/blue colour for?" He actually trembled! Him, who laughed in the faces of terrorists and walked away, yet he actually fucking trembled under the intense stare of this absolutely stunningly beautiful woman, who faced danger head on and didn't back down. Protected her friends, as he didn't know if she actually had family, but he knew she'd fight with her life for them. And honestly, that amazed him. He was the same, but his family was Luke and Lexis.

"My eyes change to all colours, Raven. I've always been able to do it. And as for the silvery white/blue is, how can I put this? You know how snakes can seek out their prey by using this heat sensing ability?" Raven nodded. Calista turned to fully look at him.

"Well my eyes change when I'm hunting or seeking anyone, they change to that silvery white/blue. I don't know why, they just do."

"So you mean to tell me, that your eyes can seek out thermal images, the same in which snakes' heightened senses can?"

"Yes, exactly that."

"Are there any others who can do that?" His legs were suddenly jelly so he sat down, before he actually made a fool of himself and fell down. Plus how cool was that if he could have that ability. God his job would be so much easier if he could do that!

"No. I'm the only one. And hello, Luke." Raven glanced over his shoulder quickly and sure enough his best friend stood in the doorway.

"We had wondered where you had disappeared to. You've been gone nearly half an hour," he murmured and walked into the room. Followed by everyone else. Rayne had a raw bloodied meat sandwich in her hand, which she handed to Calista.

"Don't want you going hungry. One bottle won't do you for long." Calista nodded and began eating but Raven paid little attention to that. He'd been gone from the kitchen for nearly half an hour? But it had hardly seemed that long. Just how long had he stood at the living room doorway ogling Calista for?

"Twenty minutes." Said the woman's voice through his thoughts which caused him to look up and blush. Had she been reading his mind or had he said them out loud?

I read your mind. Her voice echoed through his brain like a silky caress.

So you can hear what I am thinking? Can Skyri, Draylan or Rayne?

No, only I can. OK, slightly weird having a conversation without actually talking. Thank God he was sitting down already!

"Twenty minutes what?" Luke asked.

"Nothing," she replied before taking a bite of her sandwich.

"OK, and I guess this means Lexis is now a fully-fledged vampire?" Luke asked Calista, drawing her gaze.

"Yes," she said. Everyone quickly sat down as if she'd say something. But she didn't. She just stayed where she was with her mouth shut, staring at Luke, who was sitting on the edge of his seat, looking at her. Well at her nose. Unable to look her quite in the eyes and that was saying something; he always looked people square in the face.

"Got to ask, who's the oldest and youngest?" The words flew out of Luke's mouth, and he slapped his hands over his gob. Colour quickly flooded into his cheeks. Skyri roared with laughter and even the corner of Rayne's mouth lifted a little. Even Draylan was smirking slightly.

"Nothing wrong with being honest and blunt Luke. Honestly be as blunt as you like," Draylan said.

"OK, but it isn't something to ask."

"And as Draylan already said, don't worry about it. Anyway, Calista you want to answer, or shall I?" Skyri smirked at his best friend, who just shot him an irritated look. She turned her gaze to Luke

"I'm old, but nowhere near the oldest. And as of now, the youngest out of us is Lexis. But in the whole of Mystic Being, technically the youngest is a baby born ten minutes ago."

"How old are you?" The remark about how she knew a baby had been born ten minutes ago left unquestioned as they all knew she knew freaky shit.

"Just so you know, Mystic Being has been here long before cavemen in your Earth, so therefore I'm roughly twenty thousand years old, give or take."

"Sorry to say this but damn, you're old," Luke said. Raven sat there stunned. The woman he was madly in lust, even a hint of love with was twenty thousand years old? The bit that annoyed him, not the age, but the fact that countless thousands of men had touched her body, kissed her luscious lips, been inside her, made her throw her head back and scream out in heart thumping pleasure was enough to make him want to severely contemplate stone cold murder on the men who'd been with her. And he didn't actually give a shit about the consequences either. He knew he shouldn't think of that but honestly, it ripped through his mind like a hurricane. He looked up and Calista was staring straight at him. He didn't say anything, just left the room. Not even stopping when his best friend called him. He walked through the kitchen and outside, coming to a stop on the decking. He leant against the railing and ran his hands over his face.

"Raven." He lowered his hands and there she was. The woman he wanted to do stone cold murder for.

"What do you want, Calista?"

"Why did you suddenly leave?" She pulled the door shut behind her, giving them more privacy.

"Can't you just read my mind and find out that way?"

"No. Because you're angry, a barrier of sorts is shielding your thoughts."

"But surely that wouldn't stop you?"

"With everyone else no. But with you, for some reason it's harder to get in," she admitted.

"Oh, right."

"Yeah. So want to tell me why you left so quickly?"

"Stone cold murder."

"Excuse me?"

"You heard me, Calista. Stone cold murder."

"And why murder? Stone cold murder for what instance?"

"Doesn't matter, it's a stupid fucking reason." He turned around and actually gave her his back. But he was that angry, he just quite frankly didn't give a shit.

"Well, I do know it all started once I told you and Luke how old I am. Angry energy filled the air, waves of it coming off you."

"Yeah, well it happens." He actually flinched when he felt her hand on his upper arm. She made him turn around and he just looked at her. Looking right into her eyes.

"Tell me," she whispered, voice washing over him like a thousand butterfly kisses.

"Fine, I want to murder all those lucky bastards who touched you. Kissed you. Got to feel your hands on their bare flesh. Feel your naked, soft willing flesh beneath theirs. Heard your screams and moans of pleasure," he snapped and walked off. He wandered down the grass hill, lit only by the rich, beautiful three quarter moon now that the clouds had dispersed. It also shone through the trees, creating shadows that danced together and created fantastical pictures. He stopped about half way and then dropped to the floor. But even that took energy to stay upright so he just went boneless and flopped backwards, throwing an arm over his eyes. He knew it was wrong to snap at Calista like he had, but he couldn't have helped it.

"You'll get cold laying on the grass." He looked up and sighed. Would she just let him beat himself up mentally alone?

"At least it's an ideal punishment for me."

"Don't be so silly." She sat down next to him, wrapping her arms around her legs and placed her chin on her knees.

"You know, you look nowhere near as intimidating as you do when standing and staring at people," he said as he sat up.

"Yeah, but you know I'd spring into action quicker than you could blink." She wasn't bragging, just stating a fact, he knew that. She was nothing if not blunt and factual. A trait he admired in her.

"Yeah, I know. So why don't you leave me to sit here alone and go back to the house, in the warm?"

"Concerned for me, Raven?" She turned her head and looked at him with those gorgeous blues and he swore his heart actually missed a beat. Stupid fucking organ. Couldn't it just beat to pump blood around his system and not hurt when he thought of her not in his life anymore? Could one die from heartbreak?

"Not like you really need to ask that question," he snorted.

"True, as I know you're a little in lust with me as well."

"Maybe even a little in love, I'm afraid." He looked out beyond the trees at the bottom of the rolling hill to the wide open ocean that lay tantalisingly in the distance, not looking at her. A look of pure helplessness on his face.

"Raven, is that why you stormed out earlier?"

"Yes, I know I shouldn't have, but I really couldn't have helped it even if I'd tried."

"OK, but I should warn you, you really don't want to be even a little bit in love with me."

"Why not?" She moved and knelt in front of him. She placed her hands on either side of his face, making him have no choice but to look at her.

"Because it would drive you nuts watching the day to day danger I go through. As well as I could and do disappear for months at a time. All without anyone having a clue as to where I can be."

"But surely it'd be nice to realise someone loves you?"

"Maybe one day," she replied.

"Surely you've thought about it?"

"Not really. I don't dwell on what I can't have. I'm an assassin, I don't deserve anything else. Actually, I don't know anything else, so why dwell on something you've never had?" She leant forward a tiny bit and to stop him from asking any more questions, she placed her lips to his. A groan, he couldn't have stopped even if he had tried, rumbled from his chest. He grabbed her and deepened the kiss. Her lips were exactly as he remembered. Soft and succulent.

"I wondered how long it would take you," Luke's voice broke them apart, as much as Raven hated it.

"Fuck off, Luke," he actually growled. He looked back at Calista and sighed as she gracefully stood up. He looked at his best friend and glared, which only resorted in Luke's grin to kick up another notch.

"What do you want, Luke?" Calista asked, her voice and expression blank, as if she'd sealed off the entire lot of her emotions.

"Came to find you both."

"Why?" Raven stood up and knew he wouldn't be able to kiss Calista again, but he could wish that he could. She suddenly up and vanished. Quicker than you could blink and all without a word.

"Now where did she go?" Raven asked, looking around.

"Probably to check on Lexis and Tairen," Skyri announced, making his presence known, but he was closer to the house than what they were.

"Oh," he said. How the fuck did they not notice Skyri? Did he always move around so quietly? Or was it a trait for all wolves? Thank God this lycan was on the good guy's side — he'd hate to have him sneak up on him and do something. That would make for a really bad day!

"Anyway, come on. It's late and we're all up early to say goodbye to Calista." They followed Skyri back to the house. It happened to be eerily quiet, apart from the fires which gently cackled in their stone pits.

"Will I be able to see Lexis tonight?" Luke asked as Skyri shut the door and locked it.

"You'll have to ask Calista once she gets back," the lycan replied and they strolled into the living area.

Calista quickly vanished from standing with Raven and Luke and solidified in her bedroom. She impatiently waited for her fireplace to open and again waited until the tower door appeared. She listened quietly for noise the other side, but heard nothing.

"Coming in," she called out and opened the door. The rich fragrance of sex and blood drifted over her, which made her wrinkle her nose. She walked in and sprawled haphazardly on the bed, was an exhausted Tairen and his 'blanket' was an equally shattered Lexis. Her face was mashed against his chest, dried blood at his neck where she hadn't cleaned it up properly. In his hand was the now empty syringe of blood and it dangled over the edge of the bed, out of harm's way.

"Time to wake up sprogs." She kicked the bed, hard enough to rouse Tairen. Lexis slumbered on which wasn't actually all that surprising. Tairen blinked as the light played havoc on his sensitive eyes. But it was only candles burning so that helped slightly. His eyes began to regain focus and saw Calista standing at the bottom of the bed looking at him. He looked down at himself and noticed Lexis, luckily the way she was splattered across him, covered private parts. He dropped the syringe, where it clattered to the floor and ran his hands over his eyes to wake himself up more.

"How you feeling?" His 'aunt's' voice made him look at her.

"Tired. Sore. No energy," he replied, voice slightly slurry.

"Well, that is to be expected. Now I'm going to move Lexis and try to get her awake enough to get some more blood into her. Plus, you need blood too. And Luke wants to see his sister; I think more so he can reassure himself that she's fine."

"OK. But not long as we really need to sleep. And so do you to start fresh tomorrow."

"Trust me, Tairen. I can still start fresh tomorrow even without a decent sleep. God knows I've done it enough times over my life." She reached over and grabbed the syringe, capped the end and threw it on the table nearby, just so he wouldn't accidently stand on it.

"You know, even though I've known you all my life, I actually have no idea how old you are. Uncle Draylan refuses to tell me or Rayne."

"Twenty thousand years old, give or take." She looked at him with an unreadable expression.

"Geez, you must have seen fucking loads!" His eyes were shockingly wide as he looked at her.

"Yes. Now get ready to pull on some boxers because I'm going to move Lexis now."

"Wait! Where are my clean boxers I brought up?" He looked around, but couldn't see much from the position he was in.

"On the floor next to you," she replied.

"Thanks and ready when you are." He prepared himself and Calista placed her hands around Lexis. She looked at Tairen, who nodded and she stood upright, pulling the slumbering woman with her. Tairen lunged to the floor and quickly pulled his boxers on. Calista held a very naked and flaccid Lexis until he was sitting up in bed again. She put Lexis back on the bed and made her sit up against the headboard she'd made appear. Well, she wasn't completely sitting up, she slumped. Standing back, she snapped her fingers, and pyjama shorts and tank top covered up Lexis's nakedness.

"Thank you for covering her. I think a duvet will be too heavy against her sensitive skin, not to mention as constricting," Tairen said and stretched out his tired, sore muscles. Bones cracking and a sigh left his mouth at how good it felt.

"Not a problem. Lexis, time to wake up." She lightly shook the woman and she sluggishly opened her eyes. Due to now being a vampire, her eyes were a vivacious hazel. The flecks of green quite bright but yet stunningly beautiful. They'd look even more dazzling when highlighted in cycliner.

"Oh hello, Calista." She smiled and stretched leisurely.

"How you feeling, kiddo?"

"Hungry, but also tired and blissfully sore." She laughed full heartedly and Calista shook her head. She turned to the table that housed her instruments. She leaned over it, and pushed a section of the wall. It went in slightly and then popped out and opened. Inside laid a dozen or so haemoglobin bags. She pulled some out and turned to the couple on the bed. She handed them to Lexis along with a pair of scissors to open them. So she wouldn't have to use her fangs which would still be very sensitive for a few more hours and it'd hurt.

"Luke wants to see you Lexis," Calista sat on the bottom of the bed.

"Ok. I know he must be worried. Also, how is the baby?" She quickly drained a blood bag.

"He's fine. Went through the change with no problem whatsoever."

"So he's a fully-fledged vampire like his daddy and now me?" She handed an open blood bag to Tairen, who kissed her cheek in thanks.

"Yes. Now I'll go grab your brother and bring him up here. Then you two get some more blood then head to bed. Draylan wants everyone up early to apparently see me off." Calista rolled her eyes at that and headed to the door.

"Why so early? What time do you plan to head off at?" Lexis's voice stopped her.

"Six to seven-ish, which leaves you about seven hours sleep once Luke has been up."

"It's midnight already?"

"Nearly. From when we started at eight p.m., you were in transition for an hour that I obviously helped along so it wasn't a twelve- hour changeover. Then from nine p.m. to about now, Tairen was taking care of you."

"Is Skyri going with you this time?" Tairen asked and then tipped a bag of blood down his throat.

"No. I'm going on my own." Before Lexis and Tairen could say anything else, she closed the door behind her. Once she'd reached her bedroom, she heard voices coming from down the corridor in one of the bedrooms. She stopped outside the bedroom she could hear the voices from and bluntly listened to the conversation. She knew it was between Raven and Luke, there was no mistaking their voices. She held her hand up against the door and thanks to her super amazing power and shit, she created a 'window' so she could look in and they'd be none the wiser.

"I can't believe you kissed Calista! Always thought she'd sooner rip your head off than actually let you kiss her!" Luke remarked and chucked his jeans onto a chair, his hoodie quickly followed.

"Well, showed you wrong didn't it" Raven grinned at his best friend.

"Would you do it again?" Luke was point blank serious. His eyes full of intent.

"Within a heartbeat," he admitted.

"Man, you have it bad."

"I know I do. I've never actually thought I could feel this way about anyone," Raven sighed.

"Lust can do that to you, my friend."

"Honestly man, I think it's more than that. And I reckon Calista knows it too. Actually, I know she does, because she isn't stupid." Calista had heard enough. Collapsing the 'window', she knocked on the door. It quickly opened and Raven stood looking at her.

"Yes?"

"Not you. Luke. Lexis is awake. Figured you'd want to see her before you go to sleep." She looked past Raven and noticed Luke had sprung off the bed and was quickly pulling his jeans on as he was just in his T-shirt and boxers.

"What about Raven?" Luke asked, coming up behind his best friend.

"Only you. It's to put your mind at ease. You can reassure Raven when you get back."

"I suppose so. Don't mind do you Raven?"

"Nope. I'll grab a shower whilst I wait. And Calista is right; it'll reassure you to see her for yourself."

"OK then. Ready?" He looked at Calista.

"Let's go." She turned and walked in the direction of her bedroom. Not bothering to wait for Luke, she knew he'd catch up. She opened her door, stepped to the side and Luke sauntered past. She looked back down the hallway and Raven was what can only be described as, intently watching her. He quickly disappeared into the bedroom and she turned back and led the man up the stairs to the tower room his sister and brother-in-law occupied. As they neared the door, she smelt raw anxiety fill the air. She looked at Luke.

"It'll be all right you know."

"But what if it's changed her?" He turned worried eyes to her.

"It hasn't. She's still your baby sister. Being turned doesn't change the person in how they were on the inside. Outside appearance is the same as well apart from she now gets fangs when she's hungry or shows high emotion and she won't age. Her skin will stay smooth and beautiful for the rest of her life. The perks of being a vampire I suppose," she reassured him and opened the door that had appeared. She quickly ushered him through and shut the door. Luckily the couple had found the box holding the pillows and duvet and had them over themselves as Luke rushed forward and embraced Lexis, who just managed to get a blood bag out the way, in a huge bear hug. But before he could get a proper hold or her return it, Calista ripped him away and shoved a fresh blood bag under Lexis's nose. Luckily, the duvet hadn't slipped off her, showing her assets to her brother, which would have been slightly awkward for them.

"What you do that for?"

"Newly turned vampire plus hot fresh blood pulsing through your veins. Put it together." She knew when he had, because his eyes widened and his mouth made a small 'o'. Lexis quickly drained the bag and looked at Calista.

"Why can't I hug him?" She actually looked like she was about to cry, in fact tears welled up in her eyes.

"It's because you're newly turned, babe," Tairen said, handing her a new bag once she'd drained the other one.

"I don't understand."

"Newly turned vampires have very little control over blood lust. It's why we usually keep them isolated for the first twenty-four hours. Once the twenty-four hours are up, you actually start having much better control over it. It will take you a while to get used to it but once controlled, you will have no problem hugging Luke or anyone for that matter," Calista announced and handed the couple another blood bag each. Tairen would need to keep replenished as well as he'd given a lot of blood to Lexis.

"So no hugging Luke or anyone for an entire twenty-four hours?"

"That is what I said."

"What about Tairen?"

"You can hug and kiss Tairen without a problem. Your body is already used to his blood so it's satisfied. But don't hug your brother or Raven, you'll drain them dry in a matter of seconds and there would be nothing they could do to stop you considering you're a lot stronger than them. Not being sexist or anything, it's a vampire thing, you get the increased strength, speed, etc., that Tairen also has. Draylan and Skyri will be notified and will help keep an eye on you. As will Tairen, of course. And you'd have a hard time getting your fangs into me, you'd be knocked out quicker than you can say, 'puny vampire'."

"Good, because I really don't want to murder or injure anyone," she murmured and intertwined her fingers with Tairen's before she let out a huge jaw-cracking yawn. Tairen handed Calista the empty bags and she put them in the bin.

"This is good. Now, get some sleep. Your body is still getting used to the drastic change. We'll see you in the morning." She pushed Luke to the door.

"See you soon, Lexis. Love you." He looked over his shoulder at her.

"I love you too," she replied and spooned herself against her man, who wrapped himself around her, cuddling her close.

"Oh, and before I forget, come tomorrow morning when you awaken, you'll be able to hug everyone again. Consider it a transitioning gift." Calista ushered Luke onto the steps and shut the door behind her before they could reply and the last thing she saw was the couple settling down for sleep, exhaustion clear on their features still but Lexis with a slightly stunned look on her face then a God almighty shit-eating grin as Calista's words sunk in and then she saw no more. They didn't talk as they travelled downwards and quickly walked through the master bedroom a moment later before Luke looked at Calista.

"At least I know she's well now," he said.

"Yes, so no need to worry any more about wondering if she'll pull through or not."

"Yeah, true. I'll head back to the bedroom and reassure Raven. Thanks for letting me see her."

"You're welcome. I'll see you in the morning with everyone else."

"Yeah. See you later." And he left. Thankfully shutting her door behind him then hurried down the corridor to the room he and Raven were sharing. Calista shook her head and changed into some pyjamas. Well, more like pyjama bottoms and left her tank top on she'd changed into from her shower. She crawled into her bed, willed the lights off and stared out of her bedroom window. About ten minutes later, someone knocked at her bedroom door. Very rarely a moment's peace for her, good thing she was used to it now. She willed her door open and a huge shadow filled the doorway.

"Can I come in?" Skyri's voice called out.

"Sure. What's up?" She sat up a bit in bed and looked at him. One of the very few beings that she actually called friend.

"Is it still all right to crash in here with you? Everyone's gone to bed."

"Sure. Not a problem. Even Draylan's crashed?" She watched as Skyri shed his clothes but kept his boxers on that Lexis had gotten him last Christmas. Human holidays didn't usually, if ever, happen here but Lexis was adamant about it, so they indulged her, and every single person who knew her, including those in the village, spoiled her rotten. She smirked slightly at what she saw. Mr Modest he apparently was, more like bullshit. He was no more shy than she was, so must be for her 'modesty' or some shit. He shut the door, further blocking the light from the hallway. From the moonlight, he made his way to the bed and clambered in. Calista threw the duvet corner over as he neared, making it easier for him to get in.

"In answer to your question, even Draylan is out for the count, snoring actually. And cheers for letting me crash in here. To be honest, it'd be creepy sharing a bed with Draylan. Done it once before, never again. I'd sooner sleep on the floor than share with him again," he replied as he climbed in and drew the lightweight cover over himself.

"Not a problem. And that's comprehensible. Anyway, I'll see you once we get up in about seven or so hours."

"Night," he mumbled as he rolled over, giving her his back and she soon heard his breathing deepen and even out as it never took him long to fall asleep. She couldn't help but wonder why he hadn't crashed in with Rayne, but then again she wouldn't have let him. When she stayed here, she always had a bed to herself. And it was hardly the first time she and Skyri had shared a bed anyway, so it didn't bother her. She then calmed her breathing down and deep listened. Draylan and Rayne were indeed out for the count. So were Luke and Raven. Tairen and Lexis themselves were also sound asleep. Clearly it hadn't taken everyone long to go to sleep which wasn't surprising considering the day they'd had. She sighed and snuggled down into the bed more. Drawing her duvet up to her chin, she looked back outside and glanced at the moon that hung brilliantly in the night sky, adorned by hundreds of twinkling stars. She smiled slightly at the sense of peace that washed over her. She threw her hand out and the thick curtains swept across the window, effectively blocking out the light. Once the room plunged into total darkness, she closed her eyes. Body relaxed for the first time since leaving Scotland and coming back to her beloved Mystic Being. She always slept better here than anywhere else, maybe because this was her home. Other places just happened to be places to stay. Here she didn't have to pretend to be someone she wasn't or be careful of her strength or other things she could do. Heaven. Within moments, sleep washed over her, pulling her into the black abyss. She fell asleep with a secret smile on her lips.

Chapter Nine

Raven woke up to the sound of harsh wind slamming against the house. He absently glanced at his watch and quickly scrambled out the bed. It was bloody half six! Calista would be leaving at any moment and he would actually like to see her before she went and left for God knows how long. He listened intently as best he could to his surroundings, but due to that fucking wind, could only hear Luke's deep even breathing. How the hell Luke slept through him rushing off the bed, he didn't know. Usually he woke up from the sudden shift in the mattress, must have been more tired than he realised. He quickly rushed into the bathroom as his bladder woke up and screamed at him to empty it. Once finished, he washed his hands and splashed cold water onto his face to wake him up more. It drained the remains of sleep away. He brushed his teeth quickly as well as after a quick check with his tongue — they felt rough and disgusting. He walked out of the bathroom and Luke groggily stumbled past him, closing the door shut behind him for aided privacy. Raven shook his head a little and absently thought that even though they were in the army, Luke hated early mornings. But then again, majority of their work did actually involve nights. Shoving that thought away, he quickly grabbed his backpack, pulled out clean boxers and changed his dirty ones for the clean ones. Then pulled a plain black long-sleeved T-shirt over his head — it didn't leave much to the imagination that he was physically fit. He then pulled on jeans which were quickly followed by socks and combat boots that were comfortable. Luke stumbled out of the bathroom then and looked around for his own backpack.

"You see my backpack?" he asked, his voice gruff.

"Your side of the bed which is where you put it last night," he replied as he shoved his dirty clothes inside his own pack, after making sure a certain small compact pot was tucked into the bottom inside another bag. Only Luke knew about it and what it was used for.

"Oh right, thanks." Luke quickly found his pack and changed like it was just below freezing and his clean clothes had built in heaters. Ever dramatic was his best friend.

"So any idea as to what is happening today?"

"No idea whatsoever. We'll have to ask Lexis." Raven turned as a knock interrupted them. He pulled the door open and Skyri stood on the other side, intimidating as anything, dressed completely in black! The man was built, but was it steroids, plain working out, magic or just how he was naturally built? He figured it was any of those but definitely not steroids.

"Yeah?"

"Time to come downstairs. Calista's leaving in a matter of minutes."

"OK." They quickly followed Skyri downstairs and headed for the living area when Lexis's voice washed over them.

"Aren't you hot in that?" They walked in and Raven instantaneously sought out Calista. He found her. She was dressed entirely in black. Hair up in a high ponytail. Black, thick-soled combat boots covered her feet. But what shocked him the most, over the top of a simple black T-shirt, was what looked like a protective chest piece or bullet-proof vest. It had straps of tough Velcro, to hold it in place and many, many knives of various shapes and sizes, instead of pockets.

"No. I rarely do." She answered Lexis's question.

"But do you normally carry so much added weight? Surely it must tire you out?" Lexis asked and that was when Raven noticed the weapons. She had knives strapped to her leather-clad thighs. A large battle axe was strapped to her back. Aided with a sword. Black eyeliner highlighted her eyes. Lips a dark blood red. She had no other make-up on, yet she looked exotic and immeasurably dangerous. Major turn on for him. And damn she suited the assassin look perfectly as well.

"No, Lexis. It doesn't tire me out. Yes, I do carry the extra weight as weapons aren't exactly light you know." Calista actually looked amused.

"Well if that's the case, surely someone is going with you as you said Skyri is staying here this time."

"Concerned for me, Lexis?"

"Yes." She didn't hesitate to reply. Raven noticed what Lexis wore then. Black shorts just noticeable from the hem of a baggy T-shirt that must belong to Tairen as it drowned her. Practical and comfortable. Along with airwalk trainers. Her hair was put in a high ponytail and she had on minimal make-up.

"I'm not going on my own. Nikki is coming too. And Lexis, you should know that I've been carrying weapons since I was born, I'm used to it. It barely registers that I'm carrying them now."

"Who is Nikki?" Luke enquired.

"She's a fallen vampire angel. One of the most dangerous women, and lives alone. Never been seen with a companion, unless it's Calista, me or Skyri." Draylan said and then passed Calista a syringe full of strange black liquid.

"Guys, I'm heading off. Need to go make the final touches at my new place. Calista, I'll see you when you get back, OK?" Rayne said, drawing attention. Raven admitted to himself that he forgot she was there, she was so quiet. But then he realised she had just come down the stairs, so had still been upstairs, hence why he'd forgotten she was there.

"Yeah, no problem. We'll work on that blade balance in the blacksmith hut when I get back too," Calista replied and Rayne nodded before she left without a backward glance, disappearing into the already bright morning sun before shutting the door behind her.

"So how dangerous is this Nikki?" Raven asked, moving into the living room more, instead of standing in the hallway like a piece of furniture.

"As in she'd sooner rip your stomach open, pull your intestines out, dance in them and laugh her head off whilst she does. And then maybe pour acid into your wound, just for extra shits and giggles," Draylan remarked.

"Sounds erm, lovely." Raven appeared like the mental image didn't affect him, but inside he was being sick. Obviously with his job he'd seen some pretty fucked in the head shit, but that was just a bit too much. God, the agony the people must have gone through for this Nikki's sick entertainment. He mentally shook those thoughts away and focused back to everyone talking.

It isn't as bad as you make it out to be. Calista's voice whispered through his mind. He snapped his gaze to hers but she wasn't looking at him, she was looking at Lexis.

That's what you think. It's gross. Pouring acid into someone's wounds. It's fucked up.

That is how we are. Nikki and I didn't earn our reputations by being gentle. Besides, would you rather do that, or have someone do it to you? In order to survive, you have to be ruthless at times. She did actually have a point there.

I know. Still doesn't mean I have to like it.

I understand. And just like that, she disappeared out of his mind and for some untold reason, he felt like it was as though he was missing an important piece of his being.

"What was that black stuff in the syringe?" Lexis's voice brought him back to the conversation.

"It's an oil-based liquid we found not long ago. Not far from here in fact. Skyri and I will sort out what it is and the components involved," Draylan answered.

"Can I have a look at it?" Luke asked and Calista handed him the syringe. Raven watched as his best friend took the syringe carefully and studied the liquid, even so much as holding it to his nose but quickly pulled back as if it stank. He looked over at Raven.

"I take it you know what it is." He already knew that answer, could see that clearly on Luke's face. The excitement in his eyes, the science nerd was in force now!

"Oh yes. When we were in Tasmania, do you remember that grossly sick oily substance we stumbled across at that underground lab we infiltrated and the scientists we had with us told us to keep away from it?"

"Hazily, that's your department, but what about it?"

"This is the same. Only more liquid than solid." He looked at Calista, "You know what this means right?"

"No. So enlighten us." She didn't so much as blink at them.

"It means thanks to this syringe its relatively harmless. But once squirted out or whatnot, it isn't and that's bad for us considering the hazardous chemicals used to create it," he explained and handed the concoction back to Calista, who put a cap on the end and put it into a safe that was designed to look like a drawer, which only she knew the combination to.

"And how do you know that it's not oil, but a concoction of dangerous chemicals?" Draylan asked.

"Because in the army, in a handpicked group of elite soldiers, the very same me and Raven are in, actually tested it. Well, not personally. Our commanding officer and high-tailed scientists did."

"And just who did you test it on to find out what it did?" Tairen asked, just as a knock sounded on the front door.

"I'll get it!" Lexis flew off the couch and disappeared into the hallway and out of sight, as though the knocking at the door had been a lifeline. Clearly she didn't want to hear how they'd found out it rotted your insides. Saying that, she never could handle hearing stuff like that. She was the sensitive one. More about laughter than horror she was. But surely she would be able to hear it with her new vampire hearing? But then who was he to judge if she wanted to plead at not hearing anything.

"You were saying?" Draylan asked, drawing attention back to the conversation.

"Oh right, yeah. Anyway, we know it boils your insides because our big bosses tested it. Well, their scientists did. They tested it on some dangerous terrorists, or TANGOs as we call them. Ones that were on death row as well, and our bosses said, 'just helping them along a bit'. They had apparently screamed for twenty minutes to half hour before their brains couldn't handle anymore and basically shut down on them, knocking them clean out. I also know it can burn through your flesh as they tested that as well. A few drops here and there on their skin."

"Do you have any idea what these dangerous chemicals mixed into it are?" Draylan's cold eyes held keen interest.

"No, I actually don't. All I know is that it has Fluoroantimonic acid included."

"Fluoroantimonic acid?" a slightly accented female's voice called out. Drawing their attention to the doorway, Raven heard Luke suck his breath in slightly. Standing just slightly behind and to the left of Lexis, was an astoundingly beautiful woman. In his opinion not as beautiful as Calista, but she was a close second. Her eyes were eerie though and seemed to see into his very soul. They were a deep shade of purple with a black outer ring with black eyeliner that made them stand out more. She had a small pert nose with a small silver ring through the left nostril and a luscious mouth that was cherry red, with snake bite piercings. Bright purple and black hair in long dreaded weaves, with a long side fringe dyed black and purple zebra style. Pure silver earrings covered both ears in a stunning swirl with blood red rubies which curled around the top, down the helix to secure itself through the lobe. She wore a dark purple corset-type top with black lace and a tiny purple tartan skirt. Black boots with a chunky heel and chains covered her feet. But what shocked Raven the most, was the fact she had wings. Huge black ones that were folded elegantly at her back. And each individual feather was outlined in glistening silver. Truly spectacular and no doubt ridiculously strong. She also had tattoos! Left thigh had a flaming skeleton holding a cigar between his teeth and the Dead Man's Hand deck of cards in his hand. Right calf had a black and grey skull with a branch underneath, sidewalk with a walkway and just under the skull was a swing with a girl on it. A chest piece consisted of a red skull with fangs and sunken eye sockets, topped off with black and grey flowers. Her left upper inner arm had skull and crossbones. Left forearm had a black and grey owl with a skull body and a brightly coloured death moth in the centre. Right forearm had a big kiss mark with miniature skull and bones through it. He guessed she stood at around six feet two.

"Yes, Fluoroantimonic acid. It's more systematically known as fluorium hexafluorositibantide and fluorium hexafluoridacantimonate. It's an inorganic compound with the chemical formula H2FSbF6," Luke said, obviously getting over his shock at seeing this woman.

"What can it do?" Lexis asked with a perplexed expression on her face and even Raven was impressed. He knew that Luke had a deep fascination with science, but just how far did this fascination go? A lot by the looks of it if he was able to just rattle off the scientific formulation with no hesitation whatsoever. He had never paid much attention before, just enough that he was able to do his job.

"It is an ionic liquid created by reacting hydrogen fluoride with antimony pentafluoride in stoichiometrically equivalent amounts."

"In a term that we'll understand," Tairen said, smiling.

"Sorry, I can get carried away a little and forget I'm not talking to other people who understand the scientific terms. It's basically 10^{16}, which are 10 quadrillion times stronger than one hundred percent sulphuric acid. And of course everyone knows not to mess around with sulphuric acid. Even at a fairly dilute concentration, it's about ten times more acidic than the contents that reside in your stomach. You most certainly do not want to spill it on your skin. But majority of people learnt not to muck around with Fluoroantimonic acid. Well, those who know what it is and where it exists, etc. And they shouldn't, based on the silvery-white antimony with a pH of -31.3, it's 100,000 billion, billion, billion times more potent than stomach acid. So therefore, it makes its rambunctious cousin, sulphuric acid, look as gentle as a vanilla milkshake with whipped cream and a cherry on top. You couldn't pick up a bottle of it because after it ate through the bottle, it would literally dissolve your hand."

"OK, fair enough but it pretty much begs a simple question: how is that stuff stored?" Lexis asked, clearly amazed at what her brother was telling her, even if she didn't understand properly.

"Easy if you know what it is, its polytetrafluoroethylene."

"What the hell is that?" Raven asked. Why, oh why did he have to use scientific words? He looked around to everyone else and noticed that they all had a look of sheer wonder on their face, apart from Calista who had zero expression. And Luke was smiling, even the angel looked slightly impressed if you classed the slightly raised eyebrow and lip as impressed.

"It's more commonly known as Teflon. Thanks to its carbon-fluorine bonds — the strongest single bond in organic chemistry — is not only unreactive, hydrophobic and 'non-stick' but it's also immune to a host of corrosive super acids."

"Since when did you get all scientific?" Lexis asked, outright amazement clear on her face as well as in her voice.

"Have been for ages, I need to for my job. Plus I like science believe it or not."

"What about you? Are you all scientific too?" Draylan asked, turning to look at Raven.

"Nah, don't be silly. I'm just the hired muscle and the one who they send in when it's the dirty work. Luke is the brains' behind it all. Need it sorted with science or a tactical plan constructed, then he's your man."

"Are you sure?" the angel asked, turning that weird gaze to his.

"Oh, I'm sure. I'm more of a punch or shoot first, ask questions after type of guy." Which was just how he liked it.

"I just bet you are," she smirked.

"And how would you know that?" Luke said.

"Luke! Be nice," Lexis snapped, eyes flashing.

"Worry not, Lexis. I've dealt with much worse things than your brother's temper." She put her arm around Lexis's shoulders and gave her a hug which Lexis returned without hesitation.

"Still, doesn't give him an excuse to be an arsehole though, Nikki." Raven looked amazed; this was the ruthlessly dangerous Nikki, the Fallen Vampire Angel? Saying that, there was a dangerous aura around her. So he wouldn't actually put it behind her to be utterly ruthless and such if she had to be. And now the whole wings thing made sense too.

"True. But alas it has already happened."

"Who actually are you?" Luke asked, still obviously not registering that it was Nikki.

"I'm Nikki. The Fallen Vampire Angel extraordinaire." Those eerie eyes unblinking. Raven looked at Calista, and paused. Her eyes were glazed over like a corpse, but obviously she wasn't dead, she was very much alive as she was still breathing.

"Erm, what's with Calista?" His question brought everyone's head round.

"Nothing, she's just having an out of body experience," Skyri said.

"Out of body experience?" He looked at Nikki.

"The easiest way to describe it is that her 'soul' has left her. She can do this at will. She can leave her body behind and actually attack those she's after. Quite unusual and I believe she's the only one that can do it."

"Thanks for that, Nikki." They all snapped their gazes to Calista and she was very much 'alive'. Those ice-cold merciless eyes watched them.

"You're welcome," she said sarcastically and actually had the audacity to grin, showing brilliantly bright even white teeth, but on one of her fangs was a small skull-shaped diamond. Strange yet suited her.

"Yeah fucking yeah, now come on, we'll go sort out what other weapons we will need to take with us." She actually pushed Nikki out of the door. She ushered her into the hallway and pushed a slab. And as though on a spring, part of it sprung out and to the side, revealing a pitch black tunnel.

"What do you want guys?" She didn't so much as turn around.

"See what type of weapons and such you have and if they're the same as ours back home," Luke said, clearly nosey. Raven also.

"Trust me; they're totally different to what you have at home." She didn't bother explaining, just followed Nikki. She travelled along the well-known path leading to 'The Room of Mass Destruction' as Lexis had labelled it when she had first brought the woman here. She also knew the guys were following her, she could hear them stumbling due to the avid pitch blackness, but she could see as though it was daylight. Nikki did it on pure instinct considering how often she was down here. She absently waited for the guys to get closer to her and reached out, her hands connecting with their chests.

"I hope to God that's you, Calista. I'm not a fan of the whole touching thing," Raven said, and she could tell he wasn't lying. She'd smell it otherwise.

"Luke, carry on walking ahead. I want a private word with Raven."

"Sure. Just carry on ahead?"

"Yes. You'll eventually see the light near the end." Luke snorted at that but went on ahead. Calista waited until he was out of earshot and looked back at Raven. She snapped her fingers and a pair of lights flared to life on the wall between them. Raven jumped back a little from the burst of light that suddenly illuminated the blackness and seared his retinas.

"So what do you want to talk to me about? As there wouldn't be any other reason as to why you'd stop us and tell Luke to carry on walking ahead."

"What did you mean by you're not a fan of the whole touching thing? Because if I remember correctly, it was you pulling me forward for a kiss."

"I know that," he snapped. "Look, I only let a select few actually touch me. It was because of something that happened to me in my past."

"Care to elaborate on that a bit? I still won't think any less of you, just so you know." She watched as he leaned against the wall, well more like flopped. She waited as he gathered his thoughts together.

"Are you sure you won't think anything less of me?"

"I did just say that. And I don't say anything I don't mean."

"Good to know." He fell silent. A good five minutes or so passed before he actually looked at her again. She could see the thoughts rushing about his mind, making her wonder as to where he would start.

"Well, you know how I had left home permanently at fifteen to sixteen, never looked back and such?"

"Yes."

"No one knows the full extent of why I did." Calista actually did. She'd already rummaged through his memories. She had that done the first night she'd met him. Even if it had been an unusual challenge to do so, but she'd managed.

"And care to tell me?" She knew it would help him to talk about it. Even the military hadn't gotten it out of him. No matter how much those bastards had pressured him. She felt rather than heard him sigh.

"My parents abused me. Not sexually, but mentally and physically and even more so when my brother came along. My bedroom consisted of a single bed with ratty old pillows and shaggy old duvet with no cover. No sheet. A single wardrobe held what little clothes I had. No carpet covered the floor. I wasn't allowed slippers or anything like that. I had my brother's hand-me-down socks, which used to have a lot of holes in. Shoes literally used to fall apart. I got bullied a lot because of it but my parents didn't care. They didn't go to parents' evenings or anything like that. If they got called to the school and the teachers had anything good to say, my parents used to be like, 'oh we don't need to know what he's like. If he's in trouble, then obviously he'd be sorted out but grades and good behaviour, we don't need to know about that.' They never did care. I used to get a punch or a slap when we left. In the public eye, they were sophisticated, graceful and all that shit but it was all a farce. So there you have it, I'm the poster child for patheticness." He didn't look at her, refused to. Just stared straight ahead.

"Whatever makes you think that? You overcame that abuse. You've made something positive of your life now, Raven. So, don't you *ever* think you're pathetic!" Calista said, and walked away. The flames dimmed down to a soft glow. She strode down the corridor and walked into the room at the end. Nikki was slouched against part of the wall that was bare, her wings curled around her slightly, a knife in her hands running the tip underneath her wickedly sharp blood red nails. Luke was rummaging through a collection of knives.

"What's this one called?" He pulled out a wicked looking blade with rough cut edges.

"Sinister," Nikki replied after she'd glanced up.

"Who made these incredible weapons?"

"I did, Luke," Calista said, making her presence known. She watched as he whirled around and the blade dropped to the floor from his loose grip. But it didn't hit the floor, it paused mid fall, rose up and went back into the box it was from. It was comical watching as Luke's eyes went wide.

"OK, how?"

"Sheer magic," Nikki replied, who had just moved away from the wall. Calista shook her head and began pulling an assortment of weapons out of their designated places. She tossed a black blade to Nikki who caught it expertly and put it into a case and attached it to her arm. She then pulled out a single vial. It was clear, with a crystal blue powder inside.

"What's that?" Luke asked, as she put it in her pocket.

"Glitter dust."

"And that is what exactly?"

"It makes your victim paralysed. Doesn't matter how strong you are, how much magic and such you have, it will paralyse you for a good hour or so. You can't scream or anything. Just lay there and are helpless to do anything."

"Sounds really nasty stuff."

"That's how it works in this world. Sometimes it's kill or be killed."

"Survival of the fittest," he murmured. Calista nodded her agreement. She then continued to sort through her weapons. She handed some to Nikki and tied two machete-type knives in a diagonal arch across her chest. Once they were all loaded up with their arsenal, they left the room. Nikki in front, Luke in the middle and Calista pulling up the rear. Thanks to hers and Nikki's eyes, they saw the tunnel perfectly clear, but Luke's useless human eyes worked crap. He was virtually blind but that didn't stop him from marching on ahead in determination. They reached the halfway park where two single torches were still burning from earlier and Nikki stopped, which of course promptly made Luke collide into her from the sudden stop but he quickly stepped back with an apology.

"What's wrong?" He then saw what. Calista looked around them both and also saw what had made Nikki stop. Between the two flames, a single punch mark dented the wall. Surrounded by fresh blood that dripped and

186

cracked plaster. She didn't need to smell in order to realise who done it. Only one person could have done it. Raven. Clearly he'd gone back up to the house to try and calm down.

"Come on, keep on moving." She nodded and then carried on forward. Calista nudged Luke and he moved forward. Once they were near the start of the tunnel, the light from the half-way-ish point disappeared. Walking back out into the main house, they could hear everyone talking in the kitchen, so they made a detour for there. Walking into the kitchen, Calista wasn't surprised when she saw Skyri leaning against the counter, bickering playfully with Lexis, who returned it open heartedly. Tairen was sitting at the table, going over the map of the entire huge island that was of Mystic Being with Draylan.

"Where's Raven, Lexis?" Luke asked, swinging a chair out and plopping down into it.

"Wasn't he with you?" Silence erupted through the room, as everyone turned to look at Luke.

"No. He stopped to speak to Calista, then she came down to us, and he didn't. We walked back, and he was nowhere to be seen," he answered, and looked at Calista, but instead caught the backend of her as she walked out the door, her weapons left against the wall, well the big ones anyway, her knifes were still attached to her. She strolled through the house and out the front door, and then sniffed slightly. She turned her head to the left a little. Sitting in the shadows, blending almost perfectly in, was Raven. He had his eyes shut, head resting back against the house, one leg bent at the knee with his arm resting on it, the other dangling down the side of the porch. He wasn't relaxed by any means, she could see his muscles all tense, like a bullet waiting to be shot out of the barrel of a gun. She moved towards him, and knelt in his line of vision. Before so much as blinking, Raven's eyes snapped open and he lunged forward, about to tackle her to the floor, but she moved quicker than him and ended up pinning him to the floor instead. She noticed his eyes had changed to a much brighter blue. More vibrant. Shockingly bright. She stared at him and he stared back. Her hands held his wrists pinned to the floor by his shoulders. His hands locked around her wrists as though ready to change their positions as soon as she let up, not that she would. She also knew for a fact if he managed to get her on her back and she looked to the side of her, she'd have had a shadow from that bright light of Raven's gaze. Surely human eyes didn't glow? No, she knew for a fact they didn't, so why did his? Was it part of the vampire gene she found that ran through his system?

"What's going on with you?" she whispered.

"It happens when he loses his temper. This is what I was telling you earlier. This is also why he hates to lose control. It's taken him as long as I've known him to control majority of it, but he's been known to have a few hiccups now and again." Luke's voice brought her head up and Raven head-butted her. For all the good that didn't do. "It varies on what brought on this bout of anger. The last one lasted that two days you were told about." She nodded and looked back at Raven.

"Luke, can you leave us alone for a bit? I'm going to bring him back from this bout of anger."

"How? No one else has been able to before. Not even me lately, I've just waited with him until he's ready to come back to his calm self again."

"You don't need to know how, I just will." She waited until she heard the door shut, not once taking her gaze off of Raven, who held her gaze back. Even when he didn't know her, he refused to look away. He always looked her in the eye. It actually made a nice change.

"What's going on with you?" she repeated from earlier. But Raven didn't comment, just growled at her.

"Fine, we'll do it the hard way." She stared at him, her eyes unblinking. Then she mentally drilled into his brain, not the least bit gentle in doing so, but because he was under the influence of anger, he didn't so much as let out a peep of being hurt. The memories that assailed her were phenomenal. All from his childhood. No wonder he was pissed off. The things his 'parents' had done to him was unforgivable. They weren't parents, they were monsters and that was saying something considering where she was from, and what she was dealt with daily. But how they treated his younger brother was not fair at all, they should have treated him the exact same, considering he was the older sibling. The worst one that got to her, was where they threw him into a cupboard, no older than six. All because he'd tried playing with his baby brother, who was running around the dining room table squealing in delight as the father chased him. He'd only wanted to be a part of their family; but because he was 'different', they effectively caused him to be the black sheep of the family and that was harsh. And the biggest thing she noticed? Raven looked nothing like his parents apart from the blue eyes although theirs were all dark, his were ice cold. He was dark haired, they were all blonde. She'd look into it more when she didn't have to go rescue the kids. She hauled herself out of his memories and looked at him, his eyes still hard and staring at her.

"Let it go Raven. They can't hurt you anymore. No one can. Not unless you let them," she whispered, and then did the only thing she could think of. She kissed him. She also put a cloaking spell around them, making them invisible to the naked eye. She soon felt him begin to kiss her back. His hands left their ridged state and curled around her wrists loosely. Soon he took over the kiss. But she pulled back before it got over heated. She looked down into his eyes and saw the hardness had all but disappeared, as had that bright intense blue. They were back to their normal, non-glow human self.

"Hi," he whispered.

"Hi yourself. How are you feeling?"

"Pretty good considering the view." He grinned. She shook her head at him and moved away. Nice to know he was back to his charming self again, so she knew he was OK.

"I didn't hurt anyone did I?" His voice made her look at him over her shoulder.

"No. You just made a hole in the wall and you've sat out here until I managed to calm you down."

"Thank God for that."

"Does your temper get that bad?"

"Sometimes. I have managed to rein it in a hell of a lot, but I still worry for those around me when it slips through my hands and it's unleashed."

"Well that just shows that you're a caring human for those around you. Although I must tell you, you sure do pack a punch when you headbutt."

"Who did I headbutt?" He looked downright concerned then.

"Me, because I had you pinned to the floor from where you tried to tackle me as I spoke to you when you were sitting on the porch."

"Oh God, I'm so sorry."

"Don't worry about it. It'll take a lot more than that to hurt me."

"I know but that still isn't the point. I'm sorry I headbutted you," he answered honestly. She nodded acceptance of his apology and he followed her back into the house where everyone stood waiting.

"You OK now, man?" Luke asked, walking up to his friend and checking him to reassure himself.

"Yeah; I'm fine," he replied.

"Right, now we're all hunky dory again, Nikki, it's time to go." Calista said and put her weapons back into their rightful place as Nikki handed them one by one. Once she'd checked they were secured properly, she waited whilst Nikki strapped on a few blades herself then the two highly dangerous assassins strolled out the front door, leaving everyone behind them and carried on all without a backward glance.

Chapter Ten

Lexis stood at the front door, watching her best friend and Nikki head off on the quest of bringing back the children. She always hated when Calista went away on missions like this, but knew she couldn't stop her as Calista had been doing it for a good twenty thousand years now though so it was obvious she was ridiculously good at her job, but she still worried. She was a natural worrier, she just couldn't help it. When the women finally disappeared from view, she shut the door softly and sagged against it. She could hear everyone in the kitchen laughing between themselves when she heard the smash of a glass followed by someone curse. And her new sensitively highly acute senses smelt blood which made her eyes flare and fangs elongate, she was a newly turned vampire after all. Little control over it at the moment. She flat out ran into the kitchen, bursting through the door that caused it to bounce off of the wall and would have launched herself at the person who'd cut themselves if Tairen hadn't caught her tightly, and held her against his chest. She saw it was Luke and visibly cringed, then her eyes caught sight of the blood that dripped onto the floor and she was instantly transfixed, her gaze unblinking. Draylan moved quickly and shoved an opened bag of blood under her nose, which she promptly emptied in a hurry. She went through five bags before she regained enough control over herself.

"This is fucking ridiculous," she muttered and leant back against her man's chest.

"Don't forget, you were only changed over last night. It's all still very new to you," Luke said, smiling gently at her as Draylan handed him a plaster.

"Still sucks."

"True, but you are a stubborn bugger, so you'll gain control over it reasonably quickly," Raven said and handed Luke another plaster as one didn't quite cover the cut mark.

"Least you think so. Draylan, can I have another blood bag please?" She turned her brilliantly bright gaze to him, he nodded and rummaged through the fridge for another bag. He quickly located one and handed it to her. She smiled her thanks, ripped the corner off and quickly drained it.

"Don't forget, Calista said something about as a gift, you'd be able to hug people." Tairen reminded her.

"Yes, but for when?"

"Why don't you try now?" Tairen encouraged her and took the empty bag from her hand. So she shrugged and hugged Luke, and absolutely zilch happened. It was as it was before she'd changed over. She hugged him tightly for a few moments more before turning back to Tairen for the remaining blood bag which she quickly drained.

"I can hug you!" she squealed in happiness when she had finished her bag of blood.

"Maybe that was what caused the 'gift' to kick in? Once you'd had that blood?" Tairen said before handing her another one, which also got drained quickly.

"Could that have been what triggered it? The first blood bag of the day?"

"Very well could be, babe. But at least now you know that you can hug people and not be tempted to suck their neck." Tairen laughed as Lexis playfully slapped his stomach.

"So what are the plans for today?" Luke asked, putting the used kitchen roll and such in the bin.

"Go town. See some sights. Maybe even head down to the beach for a bit." Lexis replied, handing her brother the empty blood bags so he could put them in the bin.

"Sounds a plan. But we don't have any money," Luke remarked.

"Sure you do. Calista left you some money which you can use whilst you're here," Tairen said, before he disappeared out of the kitchen. He returned a moment later with four brown bags. He handed everyone one, apart from Draylan, who had his own money. They all reached inside and pulled out silver coins of different sizes and with different pictures on.

"What are these?" Raven said, looking over the unusual coins.

"Currency," Lexis replied.

"This is unlike anything I've seen before. What do these pictures mean? And the sizes valuate the different price right?" Luke looked at some of the coins in his own hand.

"Crow is £2. Dragon's wing is £1. Werewolf claw is 50p. Vampire fang is 20p. Thunder bolt is 10p. The others are just plain 5, 2 and 1ps which you can see as they just have a number on them."

"How will we remember?" Raven said.

"Turn the coin over, it has the worth engraved into it. And you'll soon remember what is what. Lexis soon picked it up." Tairen handed over his bag of money to Lexis, not that he needed it, he had his own which was now theirs but he still handed it over. She didn't complain, just added them together. The lads turned some over and it was true, numbers sat embedded in the back.

"Come on, let's go," Lexis said, shoved her money in her backpack and practically ran out of the door.

"Don't forget your towel for the beach," Draylan called out, which made Lexis dart to the left, pull open a door and grab said towel, and shove it in her backpack.

"Happy now, Dad?" she drawled. Draylan nodded and threw his arm around her shoulders, giving her an affectionate hug. As they all left and started down the hill towards town, the wind started to pick up, causing the rich smell of the ocean to rush over them, followed by the sounds of people laughing and enjoying themselves down below. It had to be no later than ten a.m., but it was already alive with people. They finally reached the town and a boy, who had to be no older than five, with peachy pink skin and wide pearl pink eyes, screamed at the top of his lungs and charged at Lexis. She swung him up into her arms and gave him a cuddle. He started babbling a mile a minute, but Lexis caught the drift of it.

"Connor, you know that's naughty. So why do it? You're all that your mum has. Stop being an imp and behave when she says, OK?"

"But, Miss Lexis, it wasn't only me," the kid grumbled.

"Doesn't matter. If you know that it's wrong, don't do it. Show the others how to be good."

"Like you are?"

"Yes." She smiled and put him back on the floor.

"OK. I will do that!" He puffed his little chest up in pride and she poked him, causing him to let the breath out and he squealed with laughter as she tickled him.

"Connor, come along," his mother called out.

"Bye." He hurried off and took hold of his mother's hand. She smiled over at their group and together they walked off, again the kid talking a mile a minute, but all the while his mother smiled down at him.

"So what's that kid then?" Raven enquired, looking around, noticing all the different creatures of vast colours, sizes and heights.

"He's a fruit fey."

"Fruit fey?" He turned his gaze to her.

"They're completely enamoured with fruit. They grow all the fruit around here, well on the Fey Island which is a five minute boat ride from here. Acres of it. Then they all handpick it and sell it. The most expensive bit of fruit is strawberries," Lexis replied, looking through a window close to her.

"How much are they?"

"£10 for a box."

"And how many are in a box?"

"You know the boxes we have back on 'normal Earth'?" She turned to look at him and he nodded.

"Well, three of those boxes are equivalent to a box here."

"That's a bit expensive, isn't it?"

"No. Not when they're rare and the fruit feys only plant them once a year."

"What's the cheapest?" Luke asked.

"Oranges."

"And they're how much?"

"20p each. And they are big, soft and full of flavour. They are very moreish," she replied, then disappeared into a shop without a backward glance.

"Now what's she found?" Raven followed her into the shop and stopped up short. It was a clothes shop, with a thick aroma of incense burning. Walls painted warm red, stained, well-worn wooden flooring. Windows letting in a lot of light. Clothes of all shapes, sizes as well as prices were everywhere. Including bags, jewellery. Make-up and shoes. For men and for women. It was warm and inviting, no wonder Lexis came in here. He felt someone nudge him and looked down and Lexis was standing right next to him.

"What do you think of this?" She held up a black leather-looking dress against herself, making it end about mid-thigh.

"I reckon it'd look really nice on you." He had no clue on the fashion of women but guessed he said the right thing as she smiled at him. Fangs evident. But then he did a proper look at the dress she held and indeed it would suit her.

"Trixie, how much?" She turned to the sales assistant, who quickly rushed round the counter and over to them, flip-flops slapping against the floor as she hurried over. She wore a pale pink tank top and denim shorts; hair was sun-streaked blonde, powder blue eyes. Skin was a light blue. She was quite thin. And that made her unavailable in Raven's book. He didn't do thin women. He liked them when there was something to cuddle; not a sack of bones. Yes, that was his personal preference, and that was what he'd stick to. The only thing big about her was the boobs that seemed ready to topple her over at any given moment. Besides, she didn't have a smidge on Calista. Well, to him anyway.

"Oh girl, I have the nicest pair of heels for that dress. You'd kill to have them!" Trixie said and dashed to the back of the shop.

"So what's she?" Raven nodded in Trixie's direction.

"She's a water nymph."

"Water nymph?"

"Born in the water. Adores the stuff," she replied, just as Trixie strolled back over.

"OK, here you go." She handed Lexis a pair of black velvet high heels that were more strap than anything else, but again, would go perfect with the dress.

"How much for both?"

"£40."

"Cool." The women walked over to the counter to exchange the money and put the stuff into a bag. Once done, Lexis walked over to Raven who was rummaging through some T-shirts. All black and some had a skull on the front with dripping fangs. Others had sayings, and some were plain.

"Why don't you buy one?"

"Yeah, OK." He took his size off the rack in the plain ones and took it to Trixie.

"That's £4 then please," she said as she totalled it on the till then bagged it. Lexis came over just in case he needed the help.

"And you need help why?" Trixie's powder-blue eyes unblinking looked at him but quickly averted her gaze to the side of his head when his own cold gaze looked at her. She probably realised just how big he was. She barely came up to his waist.

"Trixie, be nice. He's human. So not from around here," Lexis butted in.

"You mean like you, baby doll?"

"I'm not human anymore." She opened her mouth and her fangs slid down with ease before they snapped back up into place. She already had it down to pat, she was a fast learner and Tairen had taught her how to control the movement just that morning.

"Oh girl, check you out! About time that hunky vampire of yours got around to turning you!" Trixie grinned and dashed around for a hug then promptly took the money from Raven that he held out to her.

"Tairen didn't turn me, Calista did."

"No way! When did it happen?"

"Last night."

"Girl, and you can already hug people? And have control over your fangs?" Trixie stared, amazed at her.

"Gift from Calista. She knows I'm a hugger. And you know me, quick learner." The women shared a grin.

"No friggin' way! I knew Calista had power but damn, I had no idea she could change you over as well! That's like, wicked cool!" Lexis laughed and high fived her.

"Oh, got anything in for Tairen that I ordered?"

"I think so, give me a minute and I'll go check." They watched as she dashed out the back and whilst they waited, Lexis showed Raven some of the necklaces and such that were for sale. He definitely liked the stainless steel skull bracelet. Hearing the patter of flip-flopped feet, he looked over at the door where Trixie had disappeared just as she made an appearance, carrying a small box. She handed it to Lexis who opened it up. Inside was a gorgeous sterling silver watch with skulls and it had engraving etched into it. Was a gorgeous work of art and even he admitted that it was well worth the money.

"Thank you. How much?"

£1,400. As it's the limited edition one we saw in the catalogue and personalised as you asked for." Lexis paid with no problem whatsoever. Raven noticed she used Calista's black card. They might be in the land of magic, but he noticed Calista had brought over the payment methods and such of 'normal Earth'. Not to mention electricity etc. What else did they have? He did notice though that they had no cars and such. So walk everywhere? Watching as Lexis packed her package away so Tairen couldn't find it, they said their goodbye's and walked out. Raven blinked from the brightness of the sun. It seemed so much brighter here than where they lived. Could be because they were closer to the sun in some weird way? Or because there was no towering buildings etc?

"Now what you buy?" Tairen huffed playfully at Lexis.

"Nice black dress and heels." He noticed she didn't say anything about what she had gotten him.

"And that robbed us how much?"

"£40 for both."

"That isn't bad." He smiled and took the bag off her and everyone noticed she didn't object so it was obvious that he did it quite often. And luckily, he didn't look inside it either otherwise he'd see the gift.

"So where now?" Luke asked.

"Beach? See how good your water skills are?" Lexis grinned cheekily at him.

"Better than last time we were at the beach." Raven grinned at that, considering the last time they'd been at the beach together, Lexis had dived on Luke and dunked him under the waves.

"We shall see," she taunted and they walked down to the beach front. Strolling onto the surprisingly cool sand, despite the blistering sun, it was already half full. Children running around squealing with laughter and genuine happiness. Parents keeping an eye on them. Just like a typical beach, only this was with mythical creatures. The group all headed further along the beach, and sank down to a space that was a little distance from all the families and they had plenty of elbow room. Also, it was so they could talk without people overhearing. Raven and Luke put down the big rug so they could all sit on it. Tairen put in some stumps at the corners to keep it in place. Draylan put down a decent sized picnic basket and sat down, and everyone else followed suit.

"So, what was it like?" Luke asked out of the blue.

"What was what like?" Lexis looked over at her brother, whilst Draylan handed her a sandwich from a basket of food he'd gotten whilst she was in the shop with Raven.

"Changing over."

"Scary. No pain though." She took a chunk out the sandwich and moaned. Peanut butter and jam. Yum.

"I thought pain was involved?"

"It usually is with pain. Hell of a lot. But Calista took it away for her," Draylan answered as she had her mouth full of food.

"But it looked like nothing was wrong with her." Raven pointed out, and shoved the last bit of his own sandwich into his mouth.

"Calista is able to absorb a hell of a lot of pain. I've never once heard her cry out in agony."

"Really?" Luke enquired.

"Certainly, and I've known her a long time." Before anyone could comment, a football came to a stop next to them and a boy with little horns atop his head and a dark complexion came bustling over. Lexis handed him it.

"Thanks, Lexis." He grinned, showing teeth, pointed like a shark's and ran back to his friends.

"Do all the kids know you?" Raven asked, taking a sip of his drink.

"Pretty much. It's because when I'm here, I spend a lot of time on the beach. So the kids have gotten to know me pretty well, as have their parents," she replied, just as a nineteen-month-old came scrambling over, a huge beaming smile plastered on his chubby face, giving everyone a glimpse of baby fangs. Eyes a wood brown already showing keen intelligence. Lexis laughed as the kid threw himself at her and cuddled him close.

"Hi Skrack." She smiled at the boy's dad who wasn't far behind his son.

"Hey. You know he does that every time he sees you."

"What, smile?"

"And runs for you like it's the end of the world or some shit. How you been anyway kiddo?"

"Good, I went through the change." She smiled at him.

"You mean, you're no longer human?"

"Exactly that. I'm now vampire. As is the baby."

"You mean Tairen actually knows how to use it?"

"Fuck off, Skrack." Tairen glared at the man, who just grinned.

"Of course he does." Lexis handed him his son back and laughed at the disgruntled look on Tairen's face.

"So who's these two?" He nodded towards Luke and Raven as he settled his son into his arms more comfortably, even though the kid was wiggling wanting to get down and run around.

"This is Luke, who's my brother. And Raven, his best friend and might as well be my second brother." She grinned at Raven when she said that and he grinned back. She wasn't fibbing, he pretty much should be her second brother considering how close they all were to each other.

"Oh, the military guys you told me about. And another brother to boss you around, or is that just my luck with my brothers?"

"Not the only one. I get bossed around by them both. Well I did, can hold my own now." She grinned cheekily and Skrack laughed.

"Cool, well welcome to Mystic Being. Now I'd better go and feed this trouble maker or I'll never hear the end of it. Catch you all later." He turned and walked away, his son laughing as he playfully slapped his father's cheek, and then waved at them all, which they did back, causing the boy to laugh happily before he was passed to his mother, who cuddled him close. They turned away as she began to breastfeed him, her husband's arm around her shoulders as they disappeared into the crowd. Raven noticed no one blinked at the mother feeding her child, which was nice, as he'd seen a lot of women slated for it. What was actually wrong with wanting to feed their child? Even if it did come from their breast? Heck, that was all there was before bottles were invented! Shaking his head, he turned back to the company he was with.

"So what's he?" Raven asked.

"He's a wood nymph. They live in the trees. They cause the leaves to change colour. Trees and flowers to grow etc."

"What's with the sharp teeth then?"

"To gnaw on bark. They eat it and causes the tree to make new bark."

"That's so weird; but I suppose someone has to have the job." Luke laughed as Lexis playfully thumped him. Then he leapt to his feet, motioned for her to stand up, which she did, then he swung her up into his arms and ran to the sea, dumping her into the cold waves, laughing as he did so. She came up spluttering and dived on him with incredible speed, taking him down from surprise. Draylan, Tairen and Raven howled with laughter as the siblings play fought for the upper hand. Lexis easily holding her own against her boisterous big brother. Both with huge beaming smiles on their faces and each taunting the other about who was the better sibling. It was just as they were back when they were younger and it was a lovely sight to see. It was as if all their troubles and such couldn't reach them here, and that was pretty damn good for him. His life back on 'normal Earth' was getting too much for him now. All the killings and such were really starting to take their toll on him. It was crap. Luckily Luke and him only had a few months left of their service, he was surprised they'd been allowed this vacation considering they were coming to the end of their service. He wasn't complaining though, it was just what they needed. But when they went back and finished, then it was time to search for a new job. Doing what, he didn't know. Something in construction maybe? Or private security? Bodyguard? He reckoned he'd go nuts sitting behind a desk all day. Or maybe him and Luke could move here with Lexis when she had her baby? Could that work? If so, would they get a job here even though they were so vastly different to everyone else? Snapping from his thoughts, he watched the siblings continue to harass each other, both soaking wet from dunking each other, a smile on his face, along with Tairen and Draylan as they lounged in the sun.

Later That Day

Calista jumped over a fallen trunk that lay in her path and Nikki flew over it before landing without a sound and carried on walking.

"So, the humans. Why are they here?" Nikki asked, the first they'd spoken since leaving that morning.

"Lexis. She hasn't seen her brother in like, five years or so."

"Why ever not?"

"Because of him being in the army. He gets very little time off. I suppose the good thing is he sends money to Lexis every month without fail. And a shit ton of letters they exchange back and forth."

"Well, at least that's something I suppose. So when are they going back?"

"Two or three weeks, when Lexis goes back. They have a few days or so, with her in Scotland, then they go back to their job, and Lexis goes back to university."

"How is she doing with it? I know from before she was starting and stupidly nervous."

"That was two years ago, Nikki. She's in her last year."

"Fucking hell. Where's the time gone?" Nikki wove around a tree that was in her way and nearly bumped into a little boy who was bawling his eyes out, but making no sound. Shivering from fear, as it was evident in his eyes which were as wide as saucers and the colour of storm grey as he stared at her.

"What's wrong, kid?" She knelt down before him, folding her wings back so as not to appear threatening. Not that it really worked, she was intimidating just looking at her.

"My m-m-mother's boyfriend tried k-k-killing me," he stammered, and bit down on his knuckle to keep from making a noise.

"Why did he try and do that?" Calista too knelt before the boy.

"Because I said no to doing something, as I was putting cream on the cut he put on my sister's back when she didn't stop crying."

"And what did your mother do?"

"Laughed and after he nearly killed me, she dragged him off to her bed," he cried. Fat tears finally rolled down his face. Clearly he couldn't keep them in anymore, which was understandable from what he'd gone through so far. But they were silent tears.

"Nikki, take him home to Lexis. Tell her I've appointed her as guardian. No one will argue with me on that decision. Then get his sister from his home and take her there too. But take Draylan with you and Skyri, just in case the parents start some shit. I know you can look after yourself, but it won't hurt to have them two with you, considering you'd have to contend with them as well as keep an eye out on the kids." Nikki nodded and stood back up again. She knew not to argue and could see the logical side of it all considering the size of the two men, so that would help in her favour as well. Not to mention if it went to shit-creek, they'd easily dispose of the adults and keep the kids out of harm's way.

"Who is Lexis?" the kid asked.

"First of all, what's your name?"

"I don't have a name. My mother never gave me one. She just calls me it."

"And your father?" Calista asked.

"He died before I was born, or so mother said."

"Well, how does Alexzander sound?"

"What does that name mean?"

"Defender of mankind," Nikki said.

"I like that. But I'm only four. I'm no defender." At least the tears had stopped and his eyes seemed to harden with purpose. Maybe because he now realised he was getting out of the bad situation he was in?

"You can grow up learning how to fight and defend yourself. Plus, you've been looking after your sister, so you're already starting to defend those who can't look after themselves," Calista said and also stood up, towering immensely over the boy.

"What about my sister?"

"She can learn the basics. Not as brutal as the men's but it'll be enough that she won't be laughed at for throwing a punch." Calista had respect for the kid — he was more concerned for his sister than himself.

"What name will she have? She's the same as me, just called girl or it times two. And we won't be a charity case. I'll pay for our keep from the money I'll earn." Raw determination shone brilliantly from his eyes. His skin was a peachy colour with the overtone of a light grey tinge to it which stood out against the dirtiness of his clothing. Which consisted of one piece of clothing that looked to be a hand-me-down from at least five different people and had holes throughout. She could just make out he had underwear on as well; but they were threadbare and the edging was prominent against the cloth. How could his parents let him dress like this? Disgusting.

"Call her Jinx. And if Lexis asks what that means, tell her it's Latin, meaning Spell. And you won't earn money for a while yet. You need to train first. Until then, you can strike up a deal with Lexis and Tairen. They'll be your legal guardians."

"Why can't it be you?" He stood up as high as his little height would allow, which was to Calista's kneecaps, but she could appreciate the effort and determination.

"Because I won't be around a lot to train you. Lexis and Tairen will be. They'll show you the right and wrong. They'll educate you too, because you'll go to 'normal Earth' with them and they'll raise you there and you'll be taught how to blend in with the humans. Learn basic survival skills. Everything you'll need to know until you're old enough to move back here permanently and learn the fighting skills. I will warn you, it will not be easy. It will be brutal. You will learn the hard way, as does everyone else. No mercy given, no matter how much you would want it."

"But how can I do that? I'm nothing." He gestured to his body, but she saw the spark of enthusiasm in his gaze, as well as the flare of hope in realising he could learn to defend himself, and not be a punch bag for anyone ever again.

"You'll be taught magic, skills. Everything to survive. But betray us, I'll tell you now, you'll be hunted down and eliminated."

"Eliminated?"

"Destroyed. Killed," Nikki said. No point in lying.

"OK, so when can I start?" The kid didn't so much as blink at what she said.

"As soon as you're settled in. So in about a week or so. Nikki, take him back. I'll carry on. I shall see you when I get back. If anyone asks, well it's obvious why I sent you back." And with that, Calista turned and walked away. Not once looking back. She heard Nikki hustle the kid ahead, and looked over her shoulder. The kid was next to Nikki, asking questions on weapons and the best battle strategies. It was almost enough to make her smile. The kid looked tiny compared to her but Calista knew, given time, he would grow into a strapping male who would be a force to be reckoned with, of that she wouldn't have any doubt. Waiting until they'd disappeared into the dense forestry, she turned back around and walked away. And then it clicked as to what he was, he was Shadow Fae. But why was he cast out? Shadows were supposedly as tight-knit as you could get. One of which to enquire about no doubt. Shoving that thought to the back of her mind, she focused on her task ahead. Calista wound through the trees, trekking further away from everyone and going deeper into the forest. She wound past bushes, stepped on leaves, plants and tiny bones left from animal kills. She had to have walked a good nine miles on her own when she stumbled across an old abandoned log cabin. Plants clung to the wood precariously and without a care in the world. Dense, vibrant flowers made it home. She walked up to the door and pushed. Fucker was stuck. So she leant back on her heels then threw her weight forward, slamming her fist into the wood about an inch above the small wooden handle. It groaned in protest. She heard metal crack and punched again, until the dead bolt inside had been beaten clean off. Fuck, she loved being strong! The door swung open on rusted hinges woven together with tree sap. Strong but not strong enough. She walked inside and sneezed. The place was coated in a good inch thick of dust, and weeds had knocked the window out and crawled in. She began circling her hands, and the dust started to swirl together until it was a giant dust sphere. She kept up the hand spinning until she was outside, and threw her hands out. Therefore, scattering the dust to the wind which had just slightly picked up. She headed back to the weed-covered window and ripped the weeds away. Glass stuck out in precarious positions, waiting patiently for someone to crawl through the window so they could rip them to shreds. Calista wasn't that stupid. She spent precious time plucking the glass free and by the time she'd removed it all, dusk had swept overhead creating fantastical shadows and mind tricks. Remembering the old glass spell she'd been taught from an elderly witch, she held her palm up in the middle of the hole. As she murmured the spell, glass formed underneath her palm to spread outwards until it filled the gap. It was of the one-way type that the police used, no one could look in but she'd have no trouble looking out. How she liked it. She walked back inside and shut the door behind her, and leant her axe and sword against the wall. She turned around and thanks to the dust having been removed, she saw old writing etched into the walls. Dragon language. It was an old protection spell. Rarely used now and that was an understatement, as the dragons kept to themselves. She ran her hand gently over it when the walls began to move, like it was breathing. The symbols, instead of being hollowed out, filled in with a blue that was shimmering, like dragon scales in the sunlight. She stepped back and pressed her back to the door. The symbols left the wood and crashed into each other in the middle of the room. A blinding flash came out of nowhere, and in its place was the head and neck of a dragon, one with which she was very familiar. Gélio. Lord of Dragons. Fierce Warrior. One of the top five Dragon Lords. Even like this his head and neck was huge and dominated the room.

"Leave now before you regret being in this place. You are not welcome." His voice was booming.

"Oh, lay off, Gélio. It's only me." She stepped away from the door.

"And since when do you come to this cabin? It's got to have been a good fifty years since you've last been here." His eyes were that vibrant, luminous gorgeous green that seemed to stare through her and were so familiar they was nice to see.

"I have to go to Fire Mountain. Seven children have been taken from their homes by Kharge."

"Whatever for?"

"To get to me. He knows I'll come for them. And no doubt to use for his own gain."

"That bastard. Make him pay, Calista. I know those children do not deserve it. Will you be passing Dragon Hill on your way through?"

"Yes. I think it's about time I saw you again —" She stopped talking as she heard branches snap outside. She snapped her head to the side and moved quietly and stealthily to the window and looked out. She could feel Gélio's gaze follow her. But he kept quiet; he knew what she was like. In the moonlight that shone brightly from the huge moon, she saw the outline of a man. Not just any man. Raven. What the fuck was he following her for? How did he manage to move through the forest and not be attacked?

"Gélio, we will talk when I see you." He nodded and disappeared. No questions asked. The symbols on the wall lost their vibrancy and went back to simple hollowed-out etchings. She threw open the door when he had gone and the man she really didn't need following her was stepping out through the forest into the clearing.

"What the fuck are you doing here? You shouldn't have followed; you should be back there safe with everyone." She wasn't known for pleasantries.

"I know. But I had this, what can only be called a gut-feeling, that something really bad will happen."

"And you thought you'd tell me this. Raven, it's pretty much fucking guaranteed something will happen on these missions. But I've had twenty thousand years to deal with this sort of shit. Go back."

"I can't. Something was following me. I'm positive of it." He suddenly stumbled forward, a look of absolute shock on his face. She walked out into the moonlight from the hideaway of the shadows.

"What followed you?" And then she got her answer. A lycanthrope stood slightly behind Raven, one of his hands hidden behind Raven. No doubt its thick, curling claws were digging into his back. The beasts unblinking rage red eyes stared right at her, a sinister smile on his face. Then a female emerged from the woodland on the male's left hand side, fully turned. Her glowing blue eyes holding keen interest for wanting blood spilled. Clearly this duo were Rogues. Calista didn't say anything, just stepped forward more and then the female charged at her. Razor sharp claws and killer teeth snapped at her but Calista dodged them. She reared her fist back and slammed it into the female's face, shattering some teeth on impact, but not before cutting her knuckles in the process — the bitch's teeth were sharp. The male roared and threw Raven, who smashed back first into a tree, fell to the floor, smacking his skull off of a rock and slumped unconscious in a boneless heap. Then he charged into the fight and slammed his own fist into Calista's face. She snapped her head back and the male's fist sailed past her and hit his woman, who again howled in pain.

"Chrystophe, slaughter her!" the female yelled at the male, blood pouring out her mouth. He turned to her and charged, caught her around the waist and slammed her into the floor, dirt and debris flying up around them. He rained blow after blow down onto her face, but she didn't so much as flinch. She returned the punches. She did so love a dirty fight; it got her blood racing through her system ridiculously fast, and she loved it! Then she caught movement out the corner of her eye. Chrystophe's mate was heading towards Raven, who still hadn't moved. He must really have hit that tree hard. Then she remembered he was human, he wasn't used to being slammed into trees and such like she was. Or being hit with such force either. Then the scent of blood reached her nostrils and she saw a trickle of plasma leave his nose. She had to end this fight quickly and sort out Raven before others strolled into the area attracted to the scent of blood. She struck out at the male and her fist shattered his eye socket, which promptly caused him to howl in rage and pain. But Calista didn't waste time. When his upper body was in plain view and unprotected, she struck out again. Her fist slammed into his chest, shot through ribs and curled around his heart. She pulled backwards and a sickenly suction noise followed. Blood gushed all over her face and chest, but she didn't care. She ripped the male's heart from his chest and flung it away. He looked down with evident shock. She grinned in a sickening smile.

"Fuck," he cursed and slumped forward, one hundred percent deadweight on top of Calista, sending them careening back to the floor. She wiggled a little bit and got her arms partly free. Putting her hands against the chest of the body, she hurled the corpse off her. It went flying overhead and landed with a solid thump on the dirt floor. Dust particles flew up in the air before floating back to settle on the floor. Then she jumped to her feet and charged at the female, but quickly came to a stop. The woman had Raven's unconscious form in her arms, with the ease of strength known for a lycanthrope, and a bone knife at his throat. She knew from experience that those fucking bone knives were sharp as fuck. Plus this one was also coated in dried blood of all colours. Who else had they killed?

"Back off or I'll slit his throat," she growled and then noticed Chrystophe lying dead on the floor, a massive hole in his chest and a look of pure shock on his face.

"Chrystophe!" she whimpered. Then her blood eyes hardened and she sneered, her remaining teeth lengthening those that of a wolf. Calista narrowed her eyes and the knife disintegrated into dust. The woman howled and threw Raven to the floor, thus making him bang his head again but Calista wasn't paying attention to that. She had a crazed lycan female charging at her again. But she made quick work of her, as all playing and such was off. Calista quickly made short work of the woman, and gave her the same fate her male had. Heart ripped from her chest. But the female got in a good blow, dragging her long jagged claws down the side of Calista's face and through her lips, cutting deep, blood instantly pouring out. But Calista didn't cry out from the pain, she'd had a lot worse. It was more of an annoyance than anything else. The female on top of her finally toppled forward, dead as a doornail, her weight annoying Calista so she chucked her, making the female come to a stop on top of Chrystophe's corpse with a sickening splat. She jumped to her feet and brought forth lightning in her palms. She quickly incinerated the bodies as well as the hearts that lay discarded where she had dropped them. The smell of burning flesh was disgustingly horrendous but it was necessary. When the bodies were nothing but ash, Calista walked over to Raven and bent to pick his unconscious form up. Lifting him with ease thanks to her incredible strength, she walked back into the cabin. There was no furniture so she conjured up a decent sized double mattress topped with thick, plush furs that would keep him warm. She then placed him down into them and covered him with a spare one. She walked back from the unconscious man, who even out of it, to her was still drastically handsome, which confused the hell out of her. She never thought of stuff like that. Turning his head, she inspected his injury. A five centimetre cut scraped along his hair line and made his hair sticky with blood. She made short work of repairing the damage, cleaned him up before standing up straight and quickly glanced outside and she saw the wind had picked up and the ashes were forever scattered. She made sure the door was firmly shut and a simple, yet powerful spell would keep anyone out. Thanks to a regulator spell, the temperature in the cabin stayed the same. Warm. Not too hot or too cold. Perfect. She blacked the window out, conjured up a small lit candle, and then moved to sit in the shadows waiting for Raven to wake up, her facial wound completely forgotten.

Chapter Eleven

Nikki walked through the woodland with Alexzander who asked her questions about what Lexis and Tairen were like, exactly like a curious child would be once he realised she wouldn't hit him for asking questions, no matter what they were. She might be an assassin but hurting kids was a no go with her.

"They'll smother you in love and cuddles. They'll teach you how to look after yourself. Gift you with amazing memories that will make you smile whenever times are tough. They'll show you what it is like to be part of a family," she answered honestly.

"That's all I want for my sister. For myself, I don't care."

"Surely you must?"

"Not at all. I might only be four but I have since learned that there is harshness in this world. More so than love. Love is fake and we shouldn't chase it." He quoted that as if he had been taught it from birth. His mother sounded a right bitch and that was saying something considering who her parents had been. Moving at a relatively quick pace, the kid managed to keep up which impressed her. And what else surprised her? She wasn't annoyed by his questions either. She glanced upwards to see how far the sun had moved across the sky.

"Nikki?" She looked back down to Alexzander but couldn't see him. She gazed around her and he was to her left about ten steps away, kneeling down and looking at something in the dirt.

"What is it?"

"What is this?" He looked back over his shoulder at her and motioned her over. She gazed down at what he was pointing at and saw fresh marks. Lycanthrope by the looks of it. Some of which were that fresh, the ground around the corners hadn't yet dried. The tracks were headed away from them, so she didn't really pay all that much attention.

"By looks of it, it is lycanthrope."

"What is that?"

"Werewolf."

"Oh, dogs then?"

"Don't ever call them dogs to their faces. They'd rip your head from your shoulders. Who told you to call them that?"

"Mother's boyfriend. Said they're worth nothing, only as decoration."

"Well definitely don't say that to their face. Besides, one of my best friends is a werewolf. You'll meet him soon."

"OK. What are they like?" He stood back up, put the leaves and such back where they were that he had moved and together they started walking again.

"What? Lycanthropes?"

"Yes. I've never seen them before."

"They look like a normal man, only big built with eccentrically bright eyes. They're very strong, highly dangerous and very brutal when in a fight. You do not want to get caught between a male and his mate. They will literally fight until death." She wasn't going to lie to him.

"Fair enough. How much further?" Nikki glanced down at him and he was walking with his back straight, hands relaxed down by his sides, soldier worthy right there. And he spoke incredibly well for a four-year-old, which she was quite impressed about.

"Nearly there." They walked another ten minutes or so in silence and it wasn't the awkward silence either. Nikki was perfectly comfortable with the child and that kind of freaked her out, she was no good with kids, of any bloody kind apart from animals. Animals were easy. Reaching the outskirts of the hill that Calista's house resided on, Warriors Lane as the townsfolk had dubbed it, she stopped and Alexzander did as well. They were still hidden by the surrounding forestry so that helped as she really didn't want to have to explain to the town's people as to why she had a kid with her. She knelt before him and put her hands on his shoulders, pushing him gently into some bushes so he would become hidden until she come back.

"I need for you to wait here for me. I'm just going to go and get Skyri and Draylan and then you can show us where you lived with your mum, OK? And we'll go and get your sister and you can begin your life with us crazy bunch of misfits."

"OK. Just promise me something?"

"What's that?"

"That you will come back for me." He stared her right in the eye as he said that and she could see he meant it from the bottom of his soul.

"I promise I will come back for you. Now settle back and don't make a noise. I will be as quick as I can." She stood up and he scurried back a tiny bit more, the bushes falling back into place and shielding him from view. If you didn't know he was there, you'd never have seen him. Perfect. She turned, walked away and emerged out of the forest. Stretching her wings wide, she leapt into the sky and it took all of a minute to reach Calista's house. She landed gracefully on the front porch and strolled into the house. Following the sound of voices, she headed to the living room. Everyone was there apart from Raven. So he had found his balls and followed Calista had he? Well, that would be the ultimate test for him and for her as well. Her friend deserved to find happiness finally. God knows she deserved it. Standing in the doorway, she saw Lexis was up and currently sucking on a blood bag and her eyes were twinkling in merriment as she stared at her brother who was grinning at her.

"Hey, Nikki," Tairen called out, letting everyone know she was there.

"How you feeling, kiddo?" she asked Lexis as the woman pulled the bag from her mouth.

"All good here. Still a little tired but I'm good. I'll be fine after I've had a good night's sleep."

"Good to hear." And she was happy that about, honestly.

"So what you doing here, Nikki? Thought you were with Calista?"

"I was with her, but we stumbled into a bit of a problem. So Skyri and Draylan I need you to come with me." She looked over at the vampire and werewolf who lounged lazily in an oversized armchair each.

"Why us? Can't you deal with it?" Draylan asked.

"Yeah, I can but not when a four-month-old is at risk." Both men snapped to attention then.

"And where is this child? Why are they at risk?" Skyri looked about ready to snap someone's head off already, which was good for her. Saved her doing so and she'd just done her nails as well.

"Shadow Fae territory. They're being abused." That was all she said before the men jumped to their feet and stormed over to her.

"OK, let's go." If she managed to get Alexzander to tell her where the houses were, then she could leave him behind but she knew he'd want to be there when they rescued his sister. She could already tell he was protective as hell which wasn't a bad thing in this world.

"Hold on a minute. Lexis, I'm going to need you to make sure we've got milk and all that shit in. Guaranteed the kid will be hungry. I'm going to bring her brother as well, he's four. OK, I'll be honest. He's outside in the woodland waiting now."

"What the hell is he doing outside on his own at four?" Lexis demanded which was exactly what Nikki wanted. She could tell she would be a fierce and protective momma.

"I left him hidden in some shrubs as I didn't want to bring him in here without knowing what I'd find. I'm not that heartless."

"I'm not saying you are, Nikki. I'm just concerned for a four-year-old."

"Which is also what I want to tell you. You and Tairen will become their adoptive parents. Calista already said she trusts you with them and obviously she'll give you money to help. So take advantage of that fact. Use her black card."

"Oh, don't you worry I will. Now please go and get those children and bring them back here." Nikki bowed her head slightly in respect and left, the two men quickly following her. They strolled out of the house and she directed them into the forest. Once they'd walked in a little way, she stopped and so did they, looking around for the kid she knew they wouldn't be able to see unless he wanted them to. She could tell he would be one of the few who'd actually use the shadows and shrubbery to his advantage and she would make damn sure that he'd hone that skill in perfectly, even if it meant her and Calista training him themselves.

"Alexzander, come on out," she called and a moment later, the boy appeared without a sound.

"How did you manage to do that?" Draylan asked him, drawing the boy's gaze.

"Did what, sir?" Nikki could sense that he was nervous but he refused to back down.

"You don't have to call me sir. My name is Draylan."

"Is this the man who you told me about Nikki?" he asked her, his face unreadable.

"Yes. This one is the werewolf and that one is the vampire." She motioned to each individually so the kid knew who was who.

"So you're to help me get my sister?" She was impressed as the kid openly asked Skyri that question, considering the majority of adults, let alone kids, couldn't look him in the face but this kid did.

"Yes. And are you really only four years old?"

"Yes. Why?"

"You just speak so well for a four-year-old is all."

"Don't other four-year-olds talk like me?"

"Not as well, no. Speech is just starting to properly kick in by then."

"Oh. I didn't know that." The kid shrugged.

"So how did you manage to hide so well?" Draylan asked again.

"No idea. Done it long as I can remember," he answered honestly and looked back at Nikki.

"Come on, we can't dally around any longer, let's go and get your sister before night descends over us." She turned around and took off. Alexzander walked by her side, the males behind her. The big intimidating fuckers that she trusted to have her back.

"Where are we heading?" Draylan asked.

"Do you know Shadow Fae territory?" Alexzander asked, not looking back.

"Yes. Desolate place. A world of shadows as many have called it," Skyri replied.

"Yes. We're heading there. Mother lives on the outskirts. She's a shaoàluray so they keep her on the outskirts away from everyone. Not that it bothers her. Lots of men visit, so she is happy."

"How do you know that word?" Nikki demanded. That was a word that a child should not hear, let alone say! And for his mother to openly admit it in front of him? Disgusting!

"Mother describes herself as it. She has a, erm, something in her tone of voice when she says it."

"Do you mean pride?" Skyri asked.

"Yes, that's it!"

"Guys, sh. Hide, someone is coming." They all dived into bushes either side of them, the thick foliage easily covering over them, Alexzander huddled next to her, as quiet as anything. The only way she knew he was there, apart from where she had watched him sit next to her was the fact his hand touched her leg. Other than that, she wouldn't have known he was there. And they hid just in time as well as four willowy type, brown skinned men broke through the forest, swaying from drink from a flask they passed around. They were disgusting. Three of them rubbed their crotches and laughed as the other tripped over a log. Sweat-soaked hair clung to their scalp. Half their teeth were missing and lips were chapped. Shadow-grey skin was clammy and uncared for so was all chipped and scaly looking. An equally disgusting woman trailed along with them, itching her own crotch before one of them swung her up into his arms and kissed her. He laughed as she grabbed his crotch in a blatant way to show she wanted it and not caring who saw. They ripped their clothes off and Nikki turned Alexzander to face her so he didn't have to see anything as they stumbled through the bush slightly ahead of their position. The kid didn't complain, and thanks to years of not showing anything, didn't jump when he suddenly reached out and ran his hand lightly over some of her wing feathers. Instead, she watched as they tumbled to the floor, the male slamming into the woman as she moaned. Another sank to his knees at her head and whipped his dick out, which she took into her mouth. The other two whacked theirs out and began playing with themselves whilst she laughed and revelled in their attention, even so much as letting them rub their dicks over her chest and she ran her hands all over them. One of them laid down and wiggled underneath her before slamming his dick into her ass, which caused her to bow her back and moan around the dick in her gob. Disgusting slut. They all slipped away, as silent as they dared to be. Even if they'd made noise, she doubted it would have stopped the sex fest going on. As they made a wide diversion around those having sex, and made sure they were quite a distance from them, she put her hand on Alexzander's shoulder. She looked down at the boy as he looked up at her. As she looked at him, she noticed that what had gone on behind them hadn't fazed him whatsoever. Just what the hell had the kid seen in his short four years of life? Either way, once he went into Lexis and Tairen's care, he'd have the best upbringing the couple could give them, of that she had no doubt. Not to forget, he would be hopelessly spoiled, not just by Lexis and Tairen, but all of their dysfunctional family.

"How much further to your house?"

"A little further ahead it splits in two ways. I don't know what direction you call it but I do know the way to go." She noticed he didn't so much as say anything about what had happened back there, but she was sure, thanks to his mother, he'd already seen enough. More so than any child should ever see.

"OK, let's go." She let out a low whistle and the men soon joined them again as they had split up to avoid detection until it was safe enough to team up again. She motioned for Alexzander to take the lead and the boy did. They walked another five or so minutes before coming up to the divide exactly as Alexzander had said was ahead. She followed as he took a right and they walked in silence as she took a look at their surroundings. Cottages that could easily houses four to six beings quickly turned to shamble cottages that would be lucky to house two people comfortably. Until they came across one situated with its back against the shrubbery. Windows were filthy as if they'd not been washed in years. Scum, moss and other coloured fungi bracketed the door, walls and floor around what she'd called a shack.

"This way." He then cautiously proceeded to lead them just inside the forest, away from the others and keeping out of sight, heading towards his 'home'. Waiting until Alexzander walked slightly ahead of them, Nikki pulled the men to the side.

"Can you believe he bloody lives here? Why doesn't his mother want what is best for her kids?"

"Unfortunately, a shaoàluray has no concern for children or anything apart from getting her fix of sex. It's kind of like a person who is addicted to drugs, or alcohol or whatever, all they are fixated on is getting that fix," Draylan muttered.

"I know that but damn, you'd think she'd want to provide better for her kids."

"Nikki, can you hear that?" Alexzander's whisper shot to them and she hurried forward to him. When she got to him, she knelt before him and then she heard it. A child crying and a woman laughing.

"Who is that? Do you know?" she asked him.

"Crying is my sister. Laughing is my mother. It won't be long before she grows weary of the cries and the slaps begin." He said this as if it was an everyday occurrence. She motioned Draylan and Skyri closer and together they quickly devised the plan on how to rescue the child, just as the main door opened and a male strode out, quickly disappearing up to the decent cottages and out of sight.

"OK, Alexzander, you will be with me. Draylan, you and Skyri distract the mother and whoever else happens to be in the place, if there is anyone there. I do not care if that means rid them of this world. Our top priority is to remove these kids safely and take them back to Lexis and Tairen. Alexzander, do you by any chance have any other clothes or anything you wish to take with you?"

"No. I was not gifted with anything but the clothes I have on my back."

"Well, we shall soon remedy that. Now let's go." The men split from them and tore across the ground to come up to the front of the shack whilst Nikki and Alexzander went to the window as there was no back door. She waited with baited breath in the shadows with the child clutched up tight against her leg, his entire body shaking. She wrapped a wing around him, covering him in the silky soft feathers, acting as a shield. He looked up at her and for the first time since she and Calista had bumped into him, she saw absolute terror in his eyes. Nikki waited with baited breath as she heard Draylan and Skyri flirt their way into the shack, which didn't take all that long and the door shut before she moved. If she knew the men, they knew when to lay on the charm, and she had yet to see it fail. Alexzander stayed glued to her side but she didn't complain, at least she knew where he was. She looked through the window and saw the men talking to what had to be Alexzander's mother. She was dressed in rags, the top clinging to her dirty skin loosely, like it didn't fit her properly. Bottom half was covered in what looked like a giant handkerchief haphazardly tied so that it would be easy to remove. Her hair was the custom shadow Grey but looked black thanks to the amount of dirt in it. Nikki looked closer and saw the woman had leaves, fucking leaves, in her hair! She was a thin woman, with hardly any meat on her. She was what people referred to as an ironing board. She was completely flat! Nikki had never liked the extra pounds she carried, and no matter how hard she trained to get rid of them, if she so much as looked at food, she gained it right back. Clearly it was her burden to carry them, so she might as well get used to the little fuckers being there. Snapping herself back to attention, she noted that Alexzander's mother was barefoot, toenails long since chipped and disgusting. Had she never heard of a pedicure? Or at least sort them out and file them so they were at least OK to present to the world? Disgusting, uneducated, dirty woman. She looked around and was revolted by what she saw. A double bed with a thin mattress was in one corner separated by a ripped sheet that was hung up. Opposite, again sealed by a tattered sheet, was a mattress that was half missing on the floor with what she thought was a blanket but could been mistaken for a piece of cloth with holes. Next to it was the other half of the mattress with clumps of moss-covered mud around the edges to create a barrier of sorts and, in the middle of it was a baby girl who at the moment was sound asleep, but she was only in a cloth nappy with a faint blue tinge to her skin, which wasn't normal at all. The thing that got to her the most? The fact that this was where the kids had to live. She looked over at the men and caught Draylan motioning her to look at the baby so she did again. Using her enhanced vision, her eyesight zoomed in and looking above the sleeping child's head, lay a skeleton. A child-sized skeleton lay with a layer of dust with a crack on the skull just above the eye socket.

"Wait here. Do not follow me," she ordered Alexzander who nodded and crouched down low. And then she snapped. Storming round the side of the building, wings snapping with agitation, she kicked the door open which resulted in it bouncing off the wall and causing the baby to wake up in a screaming fit. The mother turned wide, half-glazed eyes to the doorway where Nikki stood with her eyes blazing and mouth slightly open, lip raised in a snarl with her fangs long and gleaming to sink into flesh and drain this sorry being of her blood. She stormed in and picked the child up and handed her over to Draylan, who rushed outside with her, most likely to try and warm her up.

"How fucking dare you be a mother! That child is freezing cold! I'm surprised she fell asleep. How fucking dare you!"

"She is not cold. She would have let me know," the mother stammered.

"Lies. She was too cold to make a fucking sound until now! And I don't give a fuck! It is your duty as a mother to care for your child or children! You do not let them suffer. They are to be at the top of your list. NOT WHEN YOU CAN GET FUCKING LAID!" She screamed at her and the windows erupted and a dirty, food-stained bowl shattered on the table, sending shards everywhere.

"If I do not get laid, I do not get paid so I can't give them food!" the woman replied, holding her hands up defensively in front of her chest like she was afraid someone was going to attack her.

"Then go out and get a job like everyone fucking else does instead of spreading your thighs for anyone and everyone!"

"Juliana, do not answer her anymore," a male voice called from behind them. Nikki whirled around and saw a male had Alexzander by the scruff of his neck, nails digging into the skin so he couldn't run away. But the kid didn't cry out from the pain of it so just how used to it was he? Then she took in the male. He was the same height as Skyri, but very thin and scraggly. If he had looked after himself, he could probably give a good fight, but he wasn't, so it would be easy for them. He also had dull grey, slightly glazed eyes with ratty and unkempt grey hair as well as sickly pale grey skin. His clothes were disgusting as well, but obviously he didn't give a shit either. He stunk as well of old sweat and sathreàthaine which resulted in them becoming high and was very, very addictive. Pretty much like 'normal Earths' drugs, only this was so much worse and made you gaunt in the face and body within six months to a year of using it. And by the looks of this guy, it wouldn't be long before he went down that track. Could that also be another reason as to why Juliana sold herself? To fund his habit?

"Milako." Juliana, as they had now learned was her name, breathed in relief that he was there and then she noticed the boy.

"So you came back then," she snarled at him, and Nikki narrowed her eyes. It was as if another person had completely taken her over or she just hated her children that much. Nikki glanced outside the window and noticed the little bit in Draylan's arms was starting to kick up a fuss from being cold so he leaned through the window, grabbed a baby carrier that looked pretty new, albeit dusty from being on the table, shook it and then tucked her into it and tied her up against his chest under his tank top so she could absorb his body heat, and all you could see was the tip of her head. She quickly settled, which Nikki was thankful for. She was most likely grateful for being warm. And no doubt could hear the steady beat of Draylan's heart so that must have been a plus as well. She'd heard from the village that was what parents did to comfort their babies. Draylan again disappeared from the view of the window.

"Do not talk to him like that!" Nikki snapped.

"You do not talk to her like that!" Milakọ snapped back and then released the child, pushing him forwards so he stumbled but luckily he quickly caught his footing. And he didn't move, because he knew if he so much as did he'd get the wrath of the male on him.

"I will talk to her however I fucking like. You and no one else can order me about who I talk to or how I fucking talk to them!" She turned her furious gaze to him. And clearly that was the wrong thing to say as the male charged at her. She braced herself for impact but it never happened. The male went sideways instead and out through the wall. She glanced to her left and smiled in an evil way. Skyri had partially shifted so his face had elongated into that horrendously powerful muzzle that had the bite force and strength stronger than that of a crocodile or even a hippo! His hands held huge claws that could render a body in half with a well-placed strike.

"Milakọ!" Juliana screamed and went to move outside but Nikki blocked her by throwing out her wings.

"I don't think so." But Juliana tried again so Nikki backhanded her, the resounded slap loud in the quiet space. Juliana stumbled before toppling to her arse. But she didn't stop, in fact she just rolled onto her hands and knees, then tried crawling to Milakọ. Her cheek bright red from the impact of Nikki's hand.

"She just won't learn. Alexzander, look away." She motioned for the boy to turn around but he just shook his head no.

"Very well." She'd given the boy warning and then turned to Juliana who had just crawled past her. She grabbed the woman's ankle and with one hand threw the woman backwards. She stalked towards her and Juliana frantically looked around for a weapon or something. Nikki watched as she lunged across the room to the table, pulled a knife out from underneath a cracked plate and held it up defensively.

"Stay away from me! Take the children! I don't fucking care! I just want Milakọ!" Nikki looked over at Alexzander and the men. Draylan had an unreadable expression on his face as he watched her and Skyri from the doorway, who was watching Milako who was slowly stumbling to his feet, a dazed look on his face. Alexzander had stark fear in his eyes but he didn't so much as make a peep, nor did he move apart from going to the wall that was behind him and out of the reach of everyone. Nikki turned her head back to Juliana.

"Now care to explain why you'd rather take that piece of scum over your kids?" She barely managed to keep from locking her hands around the throat of the idiotic woman.

"I never wanted children! And Milako gives me what they can't!"

"That's ridiculous! They're your children. Created by you and their father, grown in your womb and you brought them into this world. A child is a lifelong commitment!" Draylan butted in.

"I NEVER WANTED THEM! I WILL KILL YOU, YOU LITTLE RAT BASTARD! JUST LIKE ME AND MILAKO DID TO YOUR FATHER!" Juliana screamed and charged at Alexzander with the knife with the obvious intent to end his young life. Nikki grabbed her wrist before she could take any more than a few steps and snapped it with ease, resulting in Juliana crying out in pain and cradling her hand to her chest. Nikki had had enough. She threw the blade away where it hit the wall and fell to the floor in a clatter. Turning fully to face Juliana, the woman was no longer the afraid woman. Before her was a woman with cold, dead eyes who obviously cared for naught but herself. Nikki decided to test what she'd do and let Juliana past who did without a moment's hesitation.

"What are you doing, Nikki?" Skyri asked, his voice even more gravelly thanks to talking with a muzzle.

"Having some fun." She grinned sadistically and Skyri snorted. They all then moved out of the building towards the couple just as Juliana got to Milako who took a couple more wobbly steps before managing to stand straight. Juliana stood next to him, a sneer on her face as she openly glared hot hatred at Alexzander. Nikki stood in the middle and just slightly in front of the men.

"Nikki, we've got company." Draylan motioned with the tilt of his head to their right and sure enough they did. It was a group of Shadow Fae made up of men, women and some teenage children. They must have been drawn out of their homes by the noise. But Nikki wasn't worried, if they wanted to watch, then they could. It wouldn't deter her from what she was about to do.

"Let them watch. Draylan, you protect the kids at all costs. Skyri, you've got the male," she said as she braced herself to combat the female who had a new blade clasped in her palm that her male must have given her.

"Oh yeah!" he grinned, the wolf's teeth gleaming with saliva. As one, they stalked towards the couple. They traded places to easily grab who they were after and as they neared, Milako reached down below his trouser leg and pulled out a fucking machete! How the fuck did he have that stashed? But then she saw the tight band that would have held it in place, which answered that question.

"Be careful. And I want him dead."

"How dead?" Skyri grinned at her.

"Deader than dead! He beat those children!" She knew was the right thing to say to Skyri as all emotion went out of his face and he became the fearless killer she knew him to be. A child being physically abused was one of the worst things someone could do where he was concerned, along with rape, mental abuse and outright murder. Nikki watched Juliana for tell-tale signs of muscles tightening as if to sprint away or whatnot but she saw none of this. In fact, the woman just openly stared at her. She threw her wings out in a wide display, showing off the beautiful feathers before bringing them in hard behind her and charged Juliana. She slammed into Juliana hard, sending them careening to the floor but Nikki had done this thousands of times and she easily become the victor as she landed on Juliana's chest, effectively pinning the woman to the floor. Grabbing her wrists, she slammed the one holding the blade into the floor over and over again, making her loosen her grip on the knife. When she was able to, she threw the knife out of reach. It helped that her other wrist was broken, so it was useless.

"I told you I was going to kill you." She smiled, her fangs very prominent. Juliana tried her best to fight but it was of little use, it wouldn't work, Nikki was a lot stronger than many realised. She suddenly heard Milako scream and turned her head to look. She saw Skyri had the man pinned to the floor, had his claws sunk into the man's shoulder joints and was slowly working his way deeper. And Milako was trying his best to fight him off but having two hundred and eighty pounds of werewolf perched on your chest and trying to shift him wouldn't be easy. Well, Skyri was more around the three hundred and twenty pounds mark when in full werewolf mode. Made a badass partner in the field. She made Juliana turn her head and used her forearm against her cheek to keep her watching and they watched as Skyri literally ripped Milako's arms from their sockets and threw them away.

"Hey, Draylan," she called out to the man guarding the kids.

"What?"

"Good thing has come from this, at least he's 'armless now." Ha fucking ha, she had made a funny!

"Really Nikki?" Draylan grinned at her and she grinned back. He knew what her warped sense of humour was like. Getting back to business, she deliberately made Juliana, by keeping her face sideways with her forearm, watch as Skyri skinned Milako slowly and painfully. The man's agonized screams erupting up to the sky.

"Milako!" Juliana screamed and Nikki just laughed. Skyri threw his head back and howled. The fierce howl shook the ground and Nikki caught a glimpse of Alexzander watching him with a small tilt of his head, along with the baby now watching with a small smile on her face and her steel-grey eyes trained on Skyri. Which was weird for a baby to do surely? Weren't they meant to be crying in fear at hearing a howl like that? Or at least hiding their faces and covering their ears at what was going on in front of them. Either which way, Nikki realised that they'd settle in with their misfit family perfectly. Then she realised Draylan must have turned the child whilst her and Skyri were busy so she could see what was around her. She turned her attention back to Juliana who bucked and somehow she got one of her long legs to wrap around one of Nikki's wings and pull backwards, causing Nikki to go backwards or else she'd lose feathers and that was a no fucking go! Nikki went with the pull back and rolled backwards into a kneel. Juliana scrambled to her feet and turned as if to go and help Milako. Nikki refused to let that happen and dived at the woman, knocking her back to the floor. Sudden silence crept over them then and both women turned their head to look at the men.

"You know, you could have made it worse for him." Nikki shook her head as she looked at the now blooded mess that was once Milako. His torso was ripped open, revealing a grey/black ribcage and all his internal organs were black apart from a small mass that was attached to the ribcage. It was a vibrant blue which meant the man had been sick and wouldn't have lasted much longer. All Shadow Fae's had internal workings much like a human's but theirs was more advanced with the whole digestion thing or some shit, she couldn't remember what Calista had once told her about it all. Well, apart from the heart, it was twice the size of a human's. And it was also the fact of they were black and not pink.

"I know, but he wouldn't stop screaming," Skyri replied and with a well-placed strike, detached Milakǫ's head from his shoulders, it stopped just short of Juliana's face. Nikki flipped the woman back over until she was on her back, arms trapped against her sides and kept there by Nikki's knees.

"NOOOOO!" she again screamed. Nikki decided enough was enough. She sat backwards and threw her fist into Juliana's belly, breaking skin, muscle and such until her fist was inside the woman. Juliana threw her head back and screamed in agony as Nikki clenched her fist around the woman's womb and pulled backwards, pulling everything with her, until it left the woman's body with a sickening squishy noise. Rearing back, she held the woman's baby-making kit and threw it away. Blood coated her hand which she licked, because hello, vampire, but spat the blood away. The woman was plagued with sickness and instead of healthy fresh blood, hers tasted as though she was riddled with a poison of some sort and it was bloody disgusting. There went that potential meal. Sucked but she would wait until she got home.

"Now you won't be able to make any more children and abuse them as you did those two! Juliana Satraangra, by myself Nikki, Vampire Angel Extraordinaire and official right hand of Calista, I hereby sentence you to death for the untold abuse of your children. The unlawfulness of causing your children to starve from your own selfishness to not provide for them. For the failure of putting your own selfish needs above those of your son and daughter. For the failure of the other child who's skeleton still resides in your property which was murdered no doubt by your lover whom Skyri has now eradicated from this world. As well as the murder of the father of your children. It is now your turn to join him in hell." And with that, she placed her hands on either side of Juliana's head and ripped it from her body. She then proceeded to literally rip the woman to shreds, her long nails and brute strength making easy work of the woman's flesh, peeling it from her body in ribbons and throwing it left and right. Eventually throwing the last handful to the side, she leant backwards and screamed to the sky as power surged through her. Her fangs long and prominent, gleamed from a coating of saliva. Quickly closing her mouth, she opened eyes she didn't realise she had closed and got to her feet. Blood coated her hands, legs and some of her torso and also her face. Giving her a sinister look, not that she needed the help. She shrugged and didn't think anything of it. She'd had worse. Hazard of the job she guessed. She moved away from the skeletal mess and using an ancient spell that Calista had once taught her, caused the bodies to catch fire. Saved massively on the clean-up duty. Not saying a word to anyone, she walked back into the shack and gently picked up the fragile skeleton of the child. Even though she had blood on her hands and it transferred over to the bones, she didn't stop. Carrying the fragile load back outside, she walked to the edge of the forest, knelt on the grass and placed the remains beside her. Then she began carving out the earth using her fingers and her sharp talons that had yet to recede from her anger.

"Here Nikki." She turned her head and saw Alexzander standing there with a small spade in his hands. She took the spade from the child but then she noticed the other injuries the poor child at her side had suffered at the hands of its mother and Milakọ. Broken arms, broken legs. Fractured ribs. Hips that looked like they'd been dislocated and put back in place again, by an untrained hand no less. The poor child. She wanted to kill them all over again.

"Thank you." She then dug a hole about sixty centimetres long and forty centimetres wide, put the spade down and then placed the bones inside and using her hands instead of the spade, put the dirt back on top. Alexzander knelt beside her and helped. His little hands sinking into the dirt and helped cover his sibling. Once they had finished, Nikki knelt back on her heels and wiped her forehead with her forearm before looking at the boy next to her.

"Alexzander, why did Juliana never bury the child?"

"I don't know. I asked once, got beaten for it. She told me that it was to remind me that should I ever overstep my bounds, then Milakọ would do to me what he did to that baby."

"How did they die?" she said they as she didn't know what sex the baby had been.

"I remember she had these big beautiful blue eyes framed with long black lashes and wispy black hair that stuck out in all directions. One day she must have been starving, her tummy was swollen. He beat her black and blue first because she cried her eyes out for her mother to nourish her. I remember that he laughed as she screamed in pain and using his hands, broke her legs and arms with a horrible crunch noise before reaching for this box thing he had on the table and hit her over the head with it. She went very still and quiet after that," he replied, absolutely no emotion in his voice or face. Imagine a small boy having to witness his sister being murdered right in front of him. It was absolutely disgusting. And too afraid to say anything lest it happened to him.

"What happened to you?" She wished she could bring back those from the dead but she wasn't that skilled. She'd love to kill Juliana all over again.

"I was held back by Juliana. She hit me every time I made a sound. I learned quickly to keep quiet or even show that I was in pain," he muttered. She noticed he called her Juliana and not mother. Already he was distancing himself from being known as her son, which to be fair, wasn't a bad thing.

"OK. Well that will not happen ever again for you. If it does, I'll kill them myself, OK?" She made that vow there and then. Alexzander looked at her and for the first time in no doubt a very long time, smiled. As in, truly smiled. It lit up his entire face and even through the dirt that caked part of his skin, it was amazing to see. Knowing she was the reason to cause it made something inside of her ache a little. It also turned him into a truly handsome child, who she knew would one day grow into a very handsome man. Women would have to watch out.

"What injuries did they give you?"

"Broke my hand. And erm, he erm..." She looked at his hand and noticed one was deformed slightly, no doubt from the break not being set right.

"He what? Don't worry, he can't hurt you anymore."

"He used his thingy on me." He gestured to his neither regions.

"He raped you?" She was gobsmacked.

"Yes. Said every time he looked at me, he saw my father. Said it was to make a man out of me," he whispered and lowered his head to look at the floor.

"Never again will I, or your new family allow anyone to hurt you. I wish he was still alive, I'd kill him myself." She was fuming. That man had dared rape an innocent child? All because the boy looked like his father? What the actual fuck?

"I believe you," he muttered and looked at her before he stepped forward and laid his head on her shoulder. She wrapped her arms around him and he shook from the violent emotions running through him. She used her wings to shield him from everyone's view to allow him privacy. A few minutes passed as she just held him until he calmed down and brushed the silent tears from his face. She noticed he didn't so much as blink at the crap coating her, even if some had also rubbed off on him slightly.

"Nikki, can I ask you something?" He pulled back so he could look her in the eye.

"Of course."

"Please don't tell anyone what I just said."

"You have my word." And she was one who never backed from her word.

"Thank you." He smiled at her and she reached out and brushed a tear away.

"You're welcome. I shall always keep it between just us."

"OK. So now what do we do?" he asked as Nikki clambered back to her feet and took the boy's hand, he locked his against hers as if to never let go. She snapped her wings back out of the way.

"Let's get you back to your new home but before we do, we'll stop in town and get you some clothes and food." Nodding easily, Alexzander fell into step with her. Reaching the men, Nikki noticed that Skyri had changed back into his normal self. And Draylan was trying his best to settle a now irritated little girl.

"Pass her to me, Draylan. I'll try and settle her." Alexzander let go of Nikki's hand and held his hands out for the baby. Draylan didn't hesitate, just untied the girl from in front of him and handed her over. Alexzander, even though he was just four years old, expertly tied the child to his own chest, but with her facing outwards so she could view the world around them. Linking his hands against her belly to hold her close he smiled up at them all before he whispered to the girl to be quiet. And amazingly, she did and curled her fingers around his own. She quickly dosed off. Obviously trusting those around her to keep her safe. That they would all do without hesitation, even at the expense of their own lives, because let's face it, that's what their family did for each other and these kids were part of their ragtag group now.

"What is her name again?" Skyri asked.

"Jinx," Nikki said and they moved off. They quickly walked away from where they were, headed over to where the crowd was, who all backed up slightly when they neared and Nikki realised her and Skyri were still coated in blood but she really did not give a fuck.

"We're taking the children. No one is to stop us or else they will become exactly as that shaoàluray Juliana and her plaything Milako have ended up," Nikki said, refusing to take any shit from anyone. No one refused them as they walked past, not so much as a whisper as if they knew they were all on a hair trigger. Getting to the edge of the forest, Nikki noticed Alexzander looked back over his shoulder at what had once been his home before facing forward and striding on with steely determination. And it was then, she was proud of him. She knew he'd be a fighter and definitely fit in well with their oddball family perfectly. Together, in silence, they strolled through the forest until they reached the town where Calista and all of them resided. Alexzander stopped up short as he saw parents laughing together, children running around screaming in laughter chasing each other or being chased by parents who were laughing with them. Teenagers being teenagers clumped together in large groups of friends talking about anything and everything. Kids stood not far away kicking a ball between them. Nikki looked at him and watched as emotions played over his face. Obviously he had never seen how children were meant to act. He would soon get to know what it was like to be a normal child. Nikki began the trek towards Calista's home, followed by everyone else. They didn't so much as utter a single word until they got outside the main door to the building.

"Are you sure that Lexis and Tairen will take care of us?" Alexzander asked, drawing the gaze of the three adults.

"Just you wait and see."

"Oh, OK. Can someone take Jinx by any chance? My shoulders are sore."

"Pass her here." Draylan took the now awake child and cradled her against his chest. The other two were grateful for this as he was the only one to have experience of having kids around considering he raised Tairen and Rayne. When Nikki had comforted Alexzander, that was the first time she had ever done that, so she was thankful she had obviously done it right.

"What happened to getting us clothes first, Nikki?" Alexzander's small voice reached her ears.

"I feel it would be easier for Lexis and Tairen to give you clothes considering they're your parents now. And honestly, I'd have no idea on what I should or shouldn't get." Nikki opened the front door and walked in first, just to ease the boy's mind that he had nothing to fear and noticed he didn't question her as to why they didn't stop. He quickly followed as did Skyri and Draylan. Taking them towards the living room, she walked in and caught sight of Lexis and Luke curled up in the armchairs chatting away whilst Tairen was nowhere to be seen. She stepped foot into the room a bit and Lexis immediately turned her head to look at her and jumped to her feet.

"You're back! That was quick. We weren't expecting you back until at least this evening. Did it go OK? Are the children safe? You didn't get hurt did you?" Lexis hurried over, the last question asked due to the blood no doubt.

"I'm fine. The men are fine. The kids are as well. No need to worry, Mum." Nikki smirked.

"Oh, shush you. You know I'm a worrier." Lexis grinned and quickly hugged Nikki, who returned the gesture, but made sure no blood transferred onto her.

"Good to know you can hug again and not rip our throat outs."

"Gift from Calista. Of which I am truly grateful for."

"Which isn't a bad thing then. Anyway, this is Alexzander." Nikki pulled the boy into the living room so Lexis could get a look at him.

"Hi." She smiled at him.

"Hi," he replied and then looked down at his feet, only now becoming shy.

"Alexzander, this is Lexis. She's to be your new mum now. And Lexis, this little one is Jinx," Draylan said, coming into the room with a bouncing child against his chest, before handing her over to Lexis.

"Well aren't you a beautiful little one." Lexis laughed as Jinx gum grinned at her.

"So what have you got with you? Clothes? Shoes?" Lexis turned to ask Alexzander and Nikki noticed he looked back up at her to reply. Had that been beaten into him as well? To always look into the face of the person talking to you so as to not appear rude?

"What are shoes?"

Lexis looked at him as he asked that simple question. How did the child not know what shoes were? She gave a quick glance at his feet and saw that he was barefoot and he was incredibly filthy! Leaves and sticks clung to his disgusting, hard clothes that had more holes than anything else. His toenails and fingernails were long and caked in dirt. He had well and truly been neglected which was ghastly. How could someone do such a thing to a child? Two for that matter as she regarded Jinx who was equally just as dirty.

"They cover your feet to protect them. Like this." She pointed to her feet and Alexzander followed her gaze and made a small 'o' with his mouth.

"OK, first things first, what happened out there?" Lexis turned her gaze to Nikki.

"The mother and stepfather are no more. Everyone else in the village didn't so much as stop us. The kids are now one hundred percent completely yours and Tairen's, exactly as Calista had said."

"OK. Understandable. Then let us go down to the town and we shall sort you kids out with everything you need to make a fresh start. I refuse to let you be in those rags any longer than necessary." She turned back into the living room properly and grabbed her skull head bag from where it was on the floor that had her purse and such inside.

"Luke, meet your new niece and nephew. Me and Tairen have adopted them." She smiled at her brother as he stared at her.

"Tad filthy aren't they?"

"Yes. But we're going to town to get them clean clothes and such. Everything that kids will need to be clean. They're like this because their mother was a terrible person and obviously didn't care about her children, which is horrible. So I'll love them enough to last a millennia," she said with steely conviction which no one doubted at all.

"The reason we're like this is because she was a shaoàluray," Alexzander explained.

"Alexzander! I told you to never repeat that word again!" Nikki snapped out.

"Sorry. But she was." He looked down at his feet then and Nikki watched as Lexis put her hand under his chin to make him look at her.

"We know honey, but we don't want you using that word, OK?" He nodded and she smiled at him. And that was when Nikki knew Calista had made the right decision in Lexis and Tairen adopting the kids.

"What is a shaoàluray? Did I say it right?" Luke asked, standing up and stretching.

"You did and a shaoàluray is what you would call a prostitute," Nikki answered.

"Oh lovely."

"OK, before this gets anymore weird, let us get these children cleaned up and such. I will not tolerate them being like this anymore," Lexis butted in. She was disgusted by the filth on the kids. As soon as new clothes and accessories were brought, they were marching back up here and she was going to get them clean from the shower, into fresh clothes, food in their stomachs and smother them in love and hugs. And let them know they were in good hands for the remainder of their lives, or for as long as she lived anyway.

"What's going on?" A voice from behind caused her to twirl with the baby cradled against her and she beamed a huge smile as she saw her male.

"Tairen, this is Jinx and Alexzander."

"Shadow Faes. Tad far from home aren't they?" He stepped more into the room and regarded them with his beautiful blue eyes.

"Their mother was a shaoàluray, Tairen. Nikki, Skyri and Draylan killed them and brought the kids to us. Calista said we are to raise them as if they are our own," Lexis explained before handing him the baby.

"How do you know she was a shaoàluray?" He cradled the baby in one of his hands and held her against his chest, as if it was the most natural thing in the world.

"I told her," Alexzander piped up.

"And how old are you?"

"I'm four. And Jinx is four months," he replied. They were so young, it was heartbreaking.

"Then you should not know that word. Even adults dare not utter it."

"I know. Aunt Nikki told me so. But it is what Juliana was."

"Juliana?" Tairen turned questioning eyes to Nikki who had no emotion on her face, like a mask, after hearing Alexzander call her his aunt.

"His mother."

"She is of no mother to me. Lexis is my new mother," Alexzander said, standing as high as his little self would allow and Lexis's heart swelled with pride.

"Well, at least that's settled, but it still doesn't tell me who Juliana exactly is, apart from being the woman who birthed these kids and that she was a shaoàluray."

"She was a waste of a woman who was more interested in laying on her back with her thighs spread than care for her children. No one else interfered either when we took the children away. Although I'm sure they wouldn't have considering they watched me and Skyri kill Juliana and her floozy with ease. So they knew that if they interfered, we'd kill them as well," Nikki replied.

"OK, so what are we going to do now?" Tairen bounced Jinx in his arms, making the baby giggle.

"We need to get them clothes. Then we'll bring them back here, shower, etc., before they put the clean clothes on. Then we'll go from there," Lexis replied, holding her hand out for Alexzander, who just stared at it.

"Do you not want to hold her hand?" Draylan asked.

"Hold hands?" The boy turned his head to look at Draylan.

"Like this." Tairen showed him what he meant and took a hold of Lexis's hand, locking their fingers together.

"Why do you do that?"

"People do. It's something people have always done. Adults do it with people they love. Parents do it with their kids to keep them safe as well as to feel loved." Lexis replied.

"Oh, OK." He reached out with his little hand and grasped her own, locking his fingers with hers, copying how Tairen had done it. Lexis refused to admit what that did to her. She didn't want to scare him. Although she was sure he'd be doing it often with her, not that she would complain in the slightest. She looked at Nikki and the blood on her.

"You are not leaving this house until you've got rid of that blood on you!" Lexis glared at her. No way was she making the kids' first shopping experience one where their aunt and uncles were covered in blood, no chance whatsoever!

"Oh please, it isn't the first time I've gone out covered in blood."

"And I'm sure it won't be the last. But I am not having my children get their first shopping experience with their aunt and one of their uncles in blood. No thank you. No way. Get washed!" She actually stamped her foot and Nikki laughed.

"Yeah, we can tell you'll be a great mother." Nikki whispered a removal spell that Calista had taught her and the blood disappeared, even from Skyri himself.

"You called us your children," a small voice said from beside her and she looked down at Alexzander as he stood looking at her with a perplexed expression on his face. She took Jinx from Tairen before answering Alexzander.

"Well you are my children. From now on until the very end of time, you and Jinx are my children who I will love and cherish no matter what. And anyone disagrees with that, I'll kill them myself," she promised and the ache she'd felt earlier, disappeared, as though it had never been. Instead a fierce protectiveness towards them made itself home inside her. One she knew would never leave until her last dying breath, of which she was most certain. Sided right alongside love.

"OK," he whispered, and a single tear escaped to run down his cheek. She knelt down in front of him and wiped it away.

"No more tears unless in happiness, OK?"

"I promise." He wiped under his eyes before anymore fell and smiled, which was copied by Jinx herself, although she was too young to understand what they were smiling about.

"Good boy. Now come on, let's go and get you some new clothes. I refuse to let you be dressed in that horrendous thing for a moment longer." She led him out the living room, followed by everyone else. One hand kept Jinx locked on her hip, which luckily the little girl didn't mind, she was content to cuddle and carry on sucking her fist. As they wandered down to the town, Alexzander's hand locked with hers every single step of the way and she wasn't complaining one single bit, but then she noticed he had Tairen's hand as well. As if they were a simple family out for a stroll. Lots of people stopped to stare at the children but Lexis paid them no need. She had no need of what they were to say, she had a goal in mind and it was as simple as that. To dress her children! And if anyone wanted to say anything, then she'd show them she was no human anymore, but a hard shot vampire who was as fierce as a dragon protecting their own. And she'd rip anyone to shreds if they disagreed with her or if they so much as muttered anything bad about her babies. And she knew Tairen would defend them with his very life as well. Luke walked just behind her, along with Nikki and the men.

"You can all wait out here if you want. I shouldn't be too long." Lexis started to steer Alexzander towards a shop, when Draylan stopped her short.

"How about we meet you back at the house later? That way you can get the kids whatever it is they need, then we'll come back tonight for dinner and whatever else we'll do."

"OK, yeah. Sounds a plan."

"I'm going to go meet up with Rayne and scope out her new place. I'll meet you back at the house later, OK babe?" Tairen said, before handing over Calista's black card that she had all access to.

"Sounds good to me. That way, Luke can help me with the kids." She grinned at her brother as he groaned playfully. She swapped Jinx from hip to hip to relieve some pressure, kid might be skinny but deadweight was heavy on the hip bones and the sooner she got a buggy, the better for the child and for her. And she noticed Alexzander also swapped sides so he could continue to hold her hand.

"See you later."

"Indeed you will. Give Rayne my best and we'll come visit soon with the children." Tairen nodded and gave her a quick kiss before he left to go to Rayne's along with Draylan.

"See you tonight." Nikki bowed her head respectfully, leapt into the air in a display of pure muscle control, spread her beautiful wings and soared off.

"I'll pop by either later or tomorrow, OK kiddo?" Skyri smiled at her.

"No problem. Thanks for the help today."

"Of course." Skyri then walked off without a backwards glance.

"That is control and half that is," Luke said, watching Nikki disappear.

"Yep. Now come on, let's get you kids sorted." She directed them into a shop, shutting the door behind her and reached over for a basket, but Luke beat her to it.

"I'll hold it, As that way you can grab whatever you need, and don't have to worry about struggling with it. More so, as you have the kids attached to you like an extra limb." He grinned at her and she was definitely not one to complain about that. She would take any help she could get. They quickly filled the basket with all sorts of things for Jinx and Luke disappeared to grab another basket they could load with things for Alexzander. She hugged Jinx to her as the baby suckled her own fist happily and looked at Alexzander who was staring at an outfit just in front of him.

"What's wrong honey?" she asked him.

"Can we get this one for her?" He took the one he was on about off the shelf. It was tiny black and pink tights, a frilly skull tutu and a black vest-type top with short sleeves decorated with bright pink skulls. Lexis knew without a doubt that Tairen would also approve of that.

"Sure. Put it in the basket." She smiled at him as he eagerly did so.

"Lexis?" a voice called out and she turned slightly.

"Nixie! How are you honey?" She smiled at the woman in front of her as she walked over.

"Tired. Hungry. Sweaty. Usual mum stuff," she grinned. She was a lovely, naturally attractive woman with beautiful wild silk grey hair with blue and purple woven in through the strands, sparkling blue eyes and a gorgeous tanned figure. She also had piercings and tattoos. Her make-up accentuated her features beautifully. She was currently in a stunning mid-thigh length black dress with a pentagram halter front which suited her perfectly. Made her legs seem a mile long and her feet were encased in a pair of black Iron Fist doll shoes. She was one of the nicest people Lexis knew and she also happened to be Fey Royalty and when she sang, you listened. She had the soulful voice down to pat! But God forbid anyone if her temper got out, she had one that made you shut up and listen or there was consequences. And luckily, she didn't let her temper out often, plus everyone whom she ruled over, loved her. She had the calming effect over them that way. Also, Lexis classed her as a very good friend. One of the very first ones she had made here in Mystic Being.

"How is the little one?"

"Beautiful as ever! Looks exactly like her dad but has my personality."

"Poor kid," Lexis laughed, as Nixie nodded in agreement.

"What did you call her?"

"Turaya."

"Oh, that's a lovely name. What's it mean again?"

"Star. Which of course suits her perfectly as she is our little star."

"Aw. That's adorable."

"I'm sure we won't think that when she's a toddler and screaming the house down. So who's the kids?"

"Lexis and Tairen are our new parents," Alexzander butted in, curling his arm around Lexis's leg in kind of a protective manner. She knew without a doubt that boy would grow to be exactly like Tairen. A damn good man.

"So, you've adopted them, huh?" Nixie smiled.

"Yep. And we'll be even busier soon. I'm growing one in the oven, so to speak."

"Oh girl. Congrats! I'm so happy for you!" Lexis moved Jinx slightly as she was started to slip.

"Thank you. I wouldn't change anything for the world," she grinned.

"Don't blame you. Oh, hello." Lexis looked at who she said hello to and it was Luke.

"Nixie, this is my brother Luke. Luke, this is Nixie."

"Hey." He smiled at her then looked down at Alexzander.

"Come on, kiddo. Let's go hunt through the lads' section whilst the women talk."

"Oh. no need. I really must go. Don't want Valentine to start worrying that I'm out for so long. Not while I've left him with the newborn anyway," Nixie said and Lexis realised she had a bag full of baby clothes. Well baby silks and such, which was to be expected from Fey Royalty, not that you'd realise it looking at Nixie at the moment.

"When I finish university and come back here, we'll have to meet up for a good long chat and maybe do a girls' evening or something, OK?"

"Now that sounds a good idea. But for now, I must bid you all goodbye." And with that she turned and walked out of the shop, quickly disappearing out of view. Lexis took no offence, it was the way she was. Plus, she had loads of bags so guaranteed she wanted to get back home to her Royal Drooliness.

"So who was she?" Luke asked, drawing her attention.

"Nixie, Fey Royalty. Her husband is Valentine, or Val as those close can call him."

"So it's just Valentine for everyone else?"

"Not really, Val is more known as the Fey King so that therefore makes Nixie the queen, so it's usually Majesty or My Lady. So everyone is known to call him King or Royal Highness instead of his actual name apart from those allowed."

"But I saw no jewels or anything on her…"

"She doesn't wear them if she doesn't need to. Usually only wears them when she hosts a party or she has to put her foot down in a court room. When I come back, and if you so wish, you and Raven can come back with me and I'll take you to the castle and you'll see her in all her jewels and whatnot. She makes them look great! Plus, I might persuade her to host a party again, those are always fun." She began dumping boys' things into the empty basket Luke had got but it didn't take all that long to fill it up. She would just have to make a bigger trip when Tairen was with them. For now, this would do them, at least for a couple of days anyway. Walking around the store, grabbing other essentials, like nappies, milk, etc., she noticed Alexzander was keeping very close to either her or Luke, but she wasn't complaining. At least that way she knew where he was.

"Lexis, don't forget a buggy," Luke reminded her just as she switched hips with Jinx who had dropped off into sleep again.

"Oh, thanks for reminding me. I'd have no doubt forgotten. Let's go see what we can find." Moving to the section of buggies and whatnot, she tried squeezing through but it was ridiculous with holding the baby as well.

"Pass her here. Then you and Alexzander can go and hunt for one." Lexis didn't complain and handed the child over to Luke who cuddled her against his chest with absolute ease, one arm locked under her bum and the other around her back to keep her against his chest. How did he know how to hold a child? Shoving the thought to the back of her head and mentally taking note of asking him later, she quickly scouted through the variety of buggies and swiftly found one that would do her the world of good. It was a double buggy. One in front of the other. It would be very helpful once her son was born but for now she'd be able to put Jinx in it as well as Alexzander as he was small for his age and it would help his legs, at least for a little bit. Luckily it was at the edge and she pulled it over to Luke.

"Nice choice." And it was. It was black and decorated with small white skulls and the thick wheels had 3D skulls printed on it. Perfect for her and Tairen as well as the kids. Before moving, she noticed the umbrellas for the buggy and grabbed two white ones. The white ones would help against the heat of the sun, repelling some of it off of the kids.

"Thanks. OK that's everything I need to get for now. If I forget anything, I'll pop back later or get Tairen to." Grabbing everything together, they shuffled to the till and the assistant quickly totalled everything up. Whilst Lexis paid for it all, Luke took the kids and everything outside. She thanked the clerk then hurried outside and had to blink at the light adjustment. Inside was cool, calm and not bright. Outside it was bright and like a furnace in the afternoon. She quickly pulled Jinx from Luke as the child woke up groggily and started to kick up a fuss. No doubt from being so warm, not that she blamed her. Now that the sun had hit just past its peak, it was hot as hell and disgustingly uncomfortable. She pulled the child's dirty clothes from her so she was just in her nappy, which thankfully was only marked by a pee so that could wait a few more moments. Throwing the disgusting clothes into a bin, she handed her back to Luke before she set the buggy up which luckily was just folded up. She put Jinx in the top part and plugged in the white umbrella that would shield her from the sun's unrelenting rays. She looked at Alexzander and saw he was starting to sweat and struggle in the heat as well, not that he said anything about it though.

"Do you want to sit in the front of the buggy? Save you walking in this heat?" she asked him and he nodded, wiping his forehead to catch the sweat that dripped. She quickly unclipped the front bar and he climbed in. She didn't bother clipping the bar back as she knew he wouldn't try and jump out, so she put it in the small basket underneath. She also noticed his feet were red and a little swollen from walking on the hot floor. She mentally told herself off for that, she should have gotten Luke to carry him instead of walking, but not once did he mutter his feet were hurting but from now on, she would have it no more. And then she smelt it. Fresh succulent ice-cream. Snapping her head up, she saw Michael's Store who did the best, thickest and creamiest ice-cream ever! Well, in her opinion anyway, everyone else could shove it.

"Wait here a moment." Luke nodded so she scrambled over to the shack, brought herself, Luke and Alexzander an ice-cream each and Jinx a baby bottle of cold milk. Paying for everything and thanking the clerk, she hurried back to them and noticed Luke had set up the other umbrella so it shielded Alexzander and the boy was just sat in a pair of the clean underwear she'd brought him.

"Where are his dirty clothes?" she asked, handing over the ice-cream.

"In the bin. It was literally just an old pillowcase. Filthy underwear so I got him to change into the clean ones before stripping off that horrendous thing."

"Thanks. Here Alexzander." She handed him the ice-cream and he just looked perplexed at her.

"What is it?"

"Ice-cream. Lick it. Like Uncle Luke is." She watched as he took a small lick and a look of sheer bliss crossed his features before he started to gobble it up. And then she knew he'd be an ice-cream fiend, just like she herself was.

"Slow down, sport. You'll get a brain freeze," Luke laughed.

"A what?"

"It is when something very cold touches the center of the palate, or the roof of your mouth. The cold temperature can set off certain nerves that control how much blood flows to your head. The nerves respond by causing the blood vessels in the head to swell up. This quick swelling of the blood vessels is what causes your head to pound and hurt. Some people call this a "brain freeze," even though nothing is really happening in the brain — it's all in the blood vessels of the head. And it can hurt a lot if you're not expecting it, so just go slowly, OK?" Lexis was awed; her brother really was a total geek! Just like her!

"OK." And sure enough he did. Lexis handed her melting ice-cream to Luke to finish, she wasn't in the mood for it. She handed the milk bottle to Jinx who greedily sucked on the nipple and sighed in happiness as the coldness from the milk took away some of the heat her little body was producing as well as taking away the ache of hunger too, because Lexis knew without a doubt she wouldn't have been fed today so far, which really annoyed her.

"Right, let us get away from here and back up to the house. We'll unpack everything and then get the kids washed and into proper clean clothes. I refuse to allow them to be dirty for much longer." The fierce momma in her was coming out in storm. Luke nodded in agreement, grabbed the bags of clothes and followed her as she pushed the kids back up the hill to Calista's. She began to struggle slightly about half way up so Luke took the buggy off her and she took some of the bags from him, the heavier ones he wouldn't let her take, just put them up his arms a little and carried on. Together they made it up the hill and into the house. Going into the living room where she dumped the bags, Alexzander jumped out of the buggy whilst Luke pulled out Jinx before putting the buggy at the back of

234

the living area out of the way. Lexis quickly turned a dial on the wall and swift cool air began to circulate the house. Thank God Calista had thought to install an air-con system as the heat here was horrendous at times. They had to get Brynafa (winter) out of the way first, and then the nasty Halynakn arrived. They knew it as Halynakn, but on 'normal Earth', it was known as summer. Here though, some days the temperature got as high as 110 celsius or 230 fahrenheit, if not higher. In other words, fucking hot, and you avoided leaving the shadows, lest you burn badly.

"Luke, can you take Alexzander upstairs for a shower. I'll sort Jinx out."

"No problem. Come on, kiddo. You're about to become marvelled." Alexzander looked at Lexis and she smiled at him.

"Go on, it'll be all right. You can trust your uncle." That must have been all he needed as he followed Luke out the room. She placed Jinx on the couch perched upright in the corner and rummaged through the bags looking for some clothes for the children. A quick glance at the clock showed it was already four p.m. Majority of it the day had already flown by. Guess that happened when she was busy trying to provide for her children. She glanced upwards as she heard the front door go and then her man filled the entryway.

"Hey, beautiful."

"Hey, handsome man." She grinned as she stood upright and he looped an arm around her waist and kissed her senseless to which they heard laughter. Turning their heads as one to the couch, Jinx was beaming a gummy grin and clapped her hands together.

"Hello, sweet princess," Tairen said, swooping the baby up into his arms and was rewarded by her slapping her hands against his cheeks and beaming that gummy grin at him.

"I think someone likes you," Lexis laughed and continued rummaging through the bags.

"The feeling is entirely mutual. Where's Alexzander?"

"Luke took him upstairs for a shower whilst I sort out some clothes for them then bath Jinx."

"How will you bath her?"

"Kitchen sink I was thinking. She's small enough for that which is handy."

"When will you introduce her to the shower or bath?" He looked over at her.

"I'm thinking when she's a year old or so for the shower. Bath next time, as I'll get in it with her."

"Sounds a good idea." She smiled and took Jinx from Tairen. Heading towards the kitchen, she filled the sink up a little with warm water, stripped Jinx's nappy from her and placed the squealing baby into it. She immediately slapped her hands in the water, laughing in merriment and causing them to laugh along with her. Quickly washing the child, who soon realised she loved the feel of the water running over her, so it was easy to bath her, Tairen held his hands out with a fluffy towel and Lexis handed a freshly scrubbed, lavender smelling Jinx over to him. Rinsing out the sink, filth travelled down the plug hole. Lexis looked at Tairen as he cuddled the baby who let out a wide yawn.

"This is disgusting." She swished more water around before dumping the dirty nappy into the bin.

"Sure is. Luckily she won't ever be like that again."

"Not through neglect anyway."

"Definitely not through neglect. Being normal kids, yes."

"Guaranteed, and I wouldn't be surprised if you're there with them making mud pies and all sorts." She laughed, strolling back into the living room and was greeted by Luke and a squeaky clean Alexzander who was wrapped in a towel that covered him from his chin to his feet. His hair clung to his scalp and brushed his shoulders and it was a dark black. She'd get him a haircut in a few days or so. She doubted he'd ever had it cut or brushed properly.

"How do you feel now?" she asked him.

"Good. Can I go back in it?" She laughed and looked at Luke, who was grinning.

"Enjoy it, did he?"

"Sure did. He loved it. Wasn't so keen on the shampoo and whatnot but once he realised what it was for, he soon got the hang of it. After the first wash, I brushed his hair out whilst he was still in it, so the water helped to detangle it slightly, then washed it all over again. To say it was filthy was an understatement, but at least it is now knot free. Although he does need a haircut."

"Oh, that's good." She then sorted out a pair of pyjamas and trainer socks for him as they weren't going out anymore so no need for proper clothes. She passed the clothes to Luke and he helped Alexzander get dressed whilst she dried and dressed Jinx as Tairen had left the room for a moment. She looked up as she heard a gasp and smiled as Alexzander ran his hands over his new clothes.

"How do they feel on you?" she asked before putting Jinx's leg into the right part of her lightweight pyjama bottoms. She wasn't going to put her in a sleep suit, she'd be too warm.

"Amazing. Best thing ever!"

"OK, kiddo. Sit on the floor a minute." Luke held up the pair of socks and Alexzander did as he was told. Luke quickly put them on him and he literally squealed in excitement and wiggled his toes. Lexis laughed as she watched Alexzander be a true child. Maybe for the first time since ever.

"What's that squealing noise?" Tairen asked and walked into the living room carrying a small bag.

"Me!" Alexander laughed and wiggled his toes again. Lexis finally managed to get a wiggly Jinx into her pyjamas properly along with a clean nappy and put her on the floor where she immediately giggled at the feel of the rug beneath her head, rolled over and ran her face over it, causing everyone to laugh, which prompted her to grin at them all. She was very active for a four month old, but Lexis wasn't complaining. It meant she was healthy, considering the start she had had to life. She gazed at Alexzander and whilst he looked relatively healthy, she was going to get the local doctor to give him a check over, just in case. She looked at Tairen who sat down next to her with a small bag in his hand.

"What's in the bag?"

"Something for the kids and for us as well." He pulled out two rolled documents and handed them to her. She opened them and they were official adoption papers stating that she and Tairen were now the legally adoptive parents of Alexzander and Jinx. As well as passports for the kids, all that was missing was photos of them, but that wouldn't be too hard to get a photo of them for it and she noticed they had her last name due to Tairen not having one, as it wasn't a thing here. At least until they married officially when Calista got back, then it would all be official and she couldn't wait!

"How did you get these so fast?"

"I didn't. Nikki did. I saw her in town as I was heading back here. She handed me the bag, said you're welcome and took off."

"Well remind me to thank her big time."

"What's that?" She looked up from the papers and right in front of her was Alexzander looking at the paperwork then back at her. He reached up and wiped away a tear she didn't realise she'd shed.

"These are the proof that me and Tairen are now your parents." She smiled at him.

"Really?"

"Yes, honey. You are now officially mine and Tairen's children. And I promise you from right now until the end of time, we will love and cherish you both."

"Can I hug you?" he asked.

"Honey, any time you want a hug, you can have one, no matter how big you are." Lexis handed the documents back to Tairen, opened her arms wide and Alexzander launched himself against her, curling his little arms around her belly and held on. She looked up as she heard a baby giggle and saw Luke had got down onto the floor, leant back slightly against the couch, pulled Jinx up onto his stomach and was bouncing her slightly, a broad grin on both their faces as they stared at each other. Lexis knew he'd accepted them as well and was pretty sure that Luke would spoil his new niece and nephew. Alexzander soon let her go and climbed into Tairen's arms to hug his new dad. Tairen wrapped his big arms around the boy and hugged him back, swamping the small boy but the kid didn't mind, in fact just snuggled closer. Was obvious he knew he was evidently going to be cherished, loved and well protected and if the guess was as good as hers, she reckoned Alexzander and Jinx would be kids who would soak up as many hugs as they could possibly get. Lexis stood up, stretched and walked out of the room but not before looking back at the scene behind her. This was her family. Well some of it. And she made a promise to herself. That she would not let the kids down so long as she had breath in her body and she was sure Tairen was the same. Smiling, she turned around and disappeared out of the room to grab a quick shower, change into something a bit more comfortable then she'd prepare a feast for everyone. It was one of the things she was good at. Feeding her family.

Chapter Twelve

Raven awoke to a ferocious pounding in his skull. Opening his eyes blearily, he quickly shut them again as sunlight from outside seared his retinas as it streaked across his face. That explained why his face felt warm. Rolling to his side, he felt rich thick furs beneath him. Furs? Thought he was in the woods? So shouldn't he be on leaves and such? He tried again to open his eyes and because he'd turned over and moved, the light wasn't so bad. Blinking, once he'd adjusted to the light, he rolled back over and he could just make out a figure sitting in the shadows. Then his memory came swarming back. He'd gone in search of Calista, thinking he'd help her along with finding the children, when he'd been caught by two werewolves his gut told him were bad news. They'd finally found Calista. They said something to her and the next thing he knew he was flying through the air, crashed into a tree, everything went dark and then he woke up. What the hell had happened when he was out? How long had he actually been out for?

"Is that you, Calista?" He couldn't see most of the person, just the lower part of legs and the bottom of feet encased in boots. Then intense, vibrant blue eyes shone out the darkness like spotlights.

"Yes, it's me." She moved forward a little bit, so her face was in the light.

"Holy fuck, what happened to your face?" He knew his eyes were wide as saucers but he couldn't help it, that wound was ghastly and how the hell wasn't she screaming in agony? Anyone he knew if they had suffered a wound like that, they'd be screaming as loud as they possibly could.

"Werewolf bitch got a good shot in with her claws." She shrugged like it was no big deal.

"That must hurt like fuck. Why didn't you heal yourself?" he demanded.

"Because I had far more concerns saving your ass from being made into werewolf kebab." She blinked. That was the only reaction she gave. But then he watched, fascinated as her face literally began to knit itself together again until it was perfect unblemished skin. How the bloody hell did she do it so casually? And why hadn't she done it when he was out? Or better yet, why wasn't she screaming in bloody agony?

"What happened after I was knocked out?" He sat up, and the furs bunched around his waist. His T-shirt clung to him from sweat and heat. Other debris hung from him too. It was a blow to his ego that he'd been knocked out so easily. But then he remembered that in this world, nothing was what it seemed. Still a blow to his ego, but not as much now.

"I killed the lycanthropes and then brought you in here. You've been unconscious for roughly ten hours."

"Why didn't you just leave me then and carry on?"

"Because you can't be left alone in this world as you'd be eaten alive by things that would literally eat you whole. Well, after they played with you a bit as they'd probably never encountered something like you before."

"Because I'm human?"

"Yes. And because you're not of this world, so it would be fascinating to them," she replied. He rolled his shoulders and groaned from the pain that shot through them. How hard had he hit that tree? What damage had been done to him?

"Why won't my brain comprehend it?"

"Your brain isn't equipped to deal with that. It can handle knowledge from your Earth, but here? No. We've realised that with Lexis. Yes, you might have seen a lot more than her, due to your age and what you do for a living, but here she has more knowledge than you."

"Can she deal with it?"

"Barely, she couldn't comprehend most of the stuff she had seen so I did a memory swipe."

"Memory swipe?"

"I cleared her memory of what she'd seen. She knew exactly what I was doing."

"How did she know what you were doing?"

"She asked me to do it."

"Oh. Well that's one way she knew I suppose. How do you do it?" He struggled to his feet. His legs were quivering but he really needed to empty his bladder as it had just unpleasantly informed him.

"Is there a toilet around here?"

"Through that door behind you, shower too." He stumbled through the doorway and sure enough, there was a fully functioning decent-sized bathroom. So out of place for the log cabin, but he quickly realised that was magic for you, or at least Calista's magic that is. He rapidly emptied his bladder and turned the shower on. Rich thick steam quickly filled the small bathroom up; he stripped out of his clothes, leaving them where they ended up and stepped under the sharp spray of hot water. He sighed happily as the water rushed over him, sending the dirt that caked him like a second skin off and down the drain. He ran his hands over his face, wiping the water away and looked around for shampoo. There wasn't anything. No shampoo, conditioner, soap. Complete zilch. It was completely bare.

"Erm, Calista. There is no shampoo or anything in here," he called out and a scant few seconds later, the door flew open. He whirled around so his back was to her and he was standing there in all his fierce glory. Luckily because he'd turned around, she didn't see anything. But he did look back at her over his shoulder.

"What?"

"There is no shampoo in here to wash my hair," he pointed out lamely. She didn't say anything, just held her hand out and a bottle appeared. Zero fragrance. Even that was strict military as that was all that they used as well.

"Why no fragrance?" He took the bottle from her and squirted some into his palm. Then he remembered he was stark bollock naked. And his cock decided that was the opportune time to start to rise. Thank fucking God he had his back to her!

"Fragrance leads to things smelling you out. No fragrance gives them something harder to track," she said matter-of-factly and left, closing the door swiftly behind her which caused a cold draft to waft over him. He quickly finished in the shower and got out. A single towel sat on the side, next to the sink. He wrapped it around his waist and was startled a little bit. It was warm as if it had been sat on a radiator instead of the side. He shrugged thinking Calista was responsible for it, grabbed his dirty clothes and walked back into the main cabin. Calista stood looking out of the window, although looking at what, he had no idea.

"By any chance are there any clean clothes around here? I can't go out in these dirty, ripped ones." Calista turned around and he noticed she didn't so much as look at any part of him apart from his face. Did he even attract her? He wondered if he did. Did anyone attract her?

"Yes, they're on the furs." He turned his head and sure enough, there was. Everything was in black, even the bootlaces, just how he liked it. He grabbed the stuff and was about to head into the bathroom to change, but the door leading outside opened and shut behind him. He whirled around and glancing through the window, saw Calista outside in the bright sunshine staring into the woodland, her back to him with the sun highlighting her

241

hair and body. He quickly dropped the towel, letting it pool at his feet, and pulled on the clothes. No boxers, but he didn't care. Wouldn't be the first time he'd gone commando and doubtful it would be the last either. Socks covered his feet, comfortable boots slipping on over the top. He tightened the laces military style; and double looped them again so they wouldn't come undone easily. Nice and tight. Good. The clothes fitted faultlessly as well. How did she do that? He hadn't told her his size. But he wasn't asking how. He threw the towel into the bathroom, careless of where it landed and followed her outside, but not before throwing on a long sleeved top that hugged his body and left little to the imagination that he looked after himself.

"What are we looking for?" he asked, stepping up next to her.

"You see these two tracks. Something or someone was here last night whilst you were unconscious and I wasn't in my 'form'."

"Any idea what it was?" He completely avoided asking what she meant by not in her 'form'.

"It looks like lycan." The print was approximately the size of a polar bear's, but with longer and deeper claw indentations.

"It looks?"

"It's hard to tell. These are longer, deeper claw marks, so it could either be a really big lycanthrope, or a demon. But as I said, it's two tracks so might even be both."

"But would lycanthropes and demons work together?"

"Not usually, but they have been known to form uneasy truces for a while."

"Why are the tracks here then?"

"They took the bodies of the two I killed yesterday. I don't know why they didn't attack. Might have been because the cabin is concealed a lot, and it was black inside. Whoever they were, they weren't very bright. They didn't check inside the cabin and even if they did they wouldn't have seen anything. And if they'd looked, they'd have seen that the window had been cleared from weeds and such but it was mucky." She knelt down and he did too and ran his hand over the prints.

"What's with the dried edging? I thought all the ground was hard?"

"They were heavy, but with the added deadweight of the corpses, pressed down into the dirt more, breaking through to the soft, pliable mud underneath. This explains the dried-out edging. It's from the soft mud hardening against the heat of the morning sun's rays, even aided by last night's moon." He stood up and stretched his legs from their bent position.

"What now?" He liked the fact she knew what she was on about. Made a change from other women on 'normal Earth', the groupies as Luke called them, thinking that they knew everything, but didn't know jack shit. He liked that Calista didn't brag or anything. Just was straight to the point. She didn't pretend to know things, or act cocky. She was, well Calista.

"Well as you can't head back now, people will know you're here with me, you might as well tag along. We'll head up on Suicide Mountain, collect a few things, head to Dragon Hill, through the swamp and on to Fire Mountain. Get the kids and come back."

"Simple as that?" He grinned at her.

"Nothing is as simple as it sounds." He stood watching the sunlight shine on her, making her eyes positively glow.

"How long do you think it'll take in all?"

"Roughly a week or so. It really all depends on how much ground we cover when we move, because we can move during the night as well if it's safe enough. Don't worry, you'll be back in plenty of time for when Lexis takes you and Luke home. By the way, did you tell them you were coming to help, or did you just leave?"

"Left a note."

"Very macho." Raven laughed, he couldn't help it. It rolled out from his stomach, a deep gut-wrenching laugh, which was one of the best kinds. Once he'd controlled himself, he saw Calista was just staring at him with a weird expression on her face.

"What?"

"Nothing, come on." He didn't know what else to say to that, just followed her into the forest. Raven glanced over his shoulder at the cabin, and froze. He turned around to face it properly and his eyes widened. The weeds that had been taken away were growing back avidly. The window caved in from the pressure of the vines, shattering it again.

"Why did it do that?" He turned to Calista, who very quickly put her hand over his mouth, and motioned him to be quiet. His ears strained to hear something, but all he could hear was the animals and wind rustling through the vegetation. He shrugged his shoulders in a 'what is it' gesture and she shook her head and pushed him back into a tree, her back against his front, her arm twisted up and over to keep her hand on his mouth. Then he heard it; boisterous laughter. Then the leaves rattled and a horde of demons broke through. All in an array of different, wildly bright-coloured skins. Huge horns adorned their heads in all different sizes and in different directions, razor claws on their hands and feet. The biggest ones had what resembled hogs, very much dead in their arms, the heads flopping with each movement whilst the things cackled and grunted with each other. They stopped and Raven didn't move. How didn't they see them? But yeah, he didn't as much as twitch, just in case. Neither did Calista. She was a frozen mass. Under different circumstances he'd prefer her soft and willing underneath him. He mentally shook himself to clear those thoughts before a certain part of his anatomy stirred. The demons ripped one of the hogs apart right in front of them and ate its flesh right off the bone, with the blood spraying in all directions, including over them. Lovely! Cheers for that one mate! He had been clean. Not so much now. Typical! The demons howled with laughter as blood and slivers of meat dripped from their mouths, along with bones they spat out. Once the animal had been devoured, they moved on, clearly going home, wherever that was. Raven and Calista waited a good five minutes before they so much as moved and Raven felt a weird caress wash over his skin that caused goosebumps as the woman he crushed over glided away, literally as soundless as a ghost.

"How didn't they see us?" he asked, wiping blood from his face.

"Cloaking spell. If they'd have caught us, we'd have been exactly as that hog was. Lunch." That explained the weird sensation just then.

"Oh." Not much more he could really say to that. They took off into the woods and didn't talk again for a few miles. He knew not to talk. Not with Calista's eyes forever moving and her ears twitching as though listening to all the sounds around them. As if someone might jump out at them at any given moment. After a few miles, a bitter wind started howling through the trees, making Raven shiver. But he didn't ask to slow down or go a different way. Chills ran over his skin though. It was weird, as the sun was shining through the trees. They walked through a crop of pearlescent white trees that glinted in the light. One minute it was green and lush, the next that white sickly colour. Even the ground had no signs of life — all the plants were dead, wilted and horrible looking. They stopped at the edge of a desolate wasteland. This had to have been about a mile thick before it touched the bottom of a mountain that caused Raven to tilt his head back onto his shoulders to look up. In all its avid glory sat Suicide Mountain, coated in pristine white snow. Naked trees with spindly branches that looked like gnarled fingers dotted here and there. Twinkling cobwebs hung from them, glistening in the sunlight. That explained the cold wind he felt. He followed Calista as she began heading towards it.

Few hours later

Calista climbed up the mountainside without a care in the world. This side of the mountain housed very little that'd attack or maim her or Raven so that helped. She looked over her shoulder and stopped. Raven was a short distance back and his skin was pale with a slight blue tinge to it.

"Why didn't you say you were cold? You'll get hypothermia and then you'll be no good to me," she called down to him.

"I didn't want to slow you down," he shouted back and stumbled slightly. Then she realised exactly why he hadn't said anything. Stubborn, just like her. Men and their massive ego didn't help as well. She shook her head and waited for him to reach her. When he did, she saw clearly just how cold he was. The blue in his skin was becoming more vibrant. His lips were starting to chap badly. He also shook slightly as well. But not once did it slow him down. A real trooper. She knew she should have warned him of the harsh coldness of the mountain, but she realised he wouldn't have listened to her at all but would have said just carry on. She sighed and rubbed her hands together, then placed them on his cheeks. He moaned happily as the warmth from her flowed into him. She stayed that way until the colour had returned back to his skin and his lips weren't chapped anymore. Personal radiator she was.

"You really should have said something. If you got hypothermia, you're definitely no good to me for help or anything," she repeated.

"Yeah, I realise that now. Any chance of a jumper or something?" She immediately stepped back and a thick fleece and coat covered him. Along with thermals under his jeans and fur lined his boots. A thick wool scarf covered half his face. Even a fur hat topped the outfit. That'd keep him warm. She turned around, not waiting for his 'Thank you', and carried on. About halfway up, a branch snapped and she froze. Raven quickly slammed into her back, because obviously he was watching where he stood and not completely what was in front of him. She didn't so much as move a muscle. He quickly regained his footing and realised something was wrong and he too froze. Something was definitely wrong. Calista saw something shine out of the corner of her eye and turned her head slightly. There, not far ahead of them was a creature that regarded them intently. Ice Marbilian maybe? As the body was a crystal-clear marble. The internal organs blue. Bones were a white/blue. Blood a sparkling pale indigo colour that rushed around the body in plain view, even though it was slightly eerie. The eyes were a different story, white as snow and locked firmly onto them!

"What is it?" Raven whispered.

"Ice Marbilian. I'll distract it and you run to the top of the mountain. Do not stop to look back or try to help me." She then moved away from him and sure enough the creature followed her every movement but then she caught sight of a female version of it rise out of the snow not all that far from them. Small, with the obvious bits that made it female. This one hissed at them and crystal sharp teeth shone in the gleaming sunlight. The female charged at them and Calista didn't waste any time, just lashed out catching the thing in the stomach with her foot, sending it backwards. So much for this side of the mountain holding less possibilities of something/one trying to kill them. Just her bloody luck it had to be today of all days that these wanted to scour this side for food or whatever. She battered the female backwards, well aware the huge male was now charging towards her. Clearly more intent on protecting its female than in killing Raven. That was the loyalty in Marbilians. Threaten their loved ones, they went for you. No matter if they were ice, fire, water, earth or whatnot. She twisted into a mid-air flip when the female caught her across the face and sent her flying. She landed on her feet and brought out the knife she kept in her boot. She shot her fist out and threw the blade into the female's cold beating heart. The short resistance of blue bones giving way until the blade slammed home into the muscle that kept the body alive. The creature let out a howl that sounded as though an ice glacier was breaking apart just as Calista was tackled into the snow by the male. She lashed out, catching the male in the face. Atlantic-cold blood rushed over her, but it didn't slow her down. She slashed as much as she was able to and got in as many hits as possible. They rolled in the snow and Calista landed on top. She reached down, ignoring the male as he dug his steely sharp claws into her love handles. She didn't flinch; just put her hands around his throat, sunk her own talons in and promptly ripped his head off. She didn't take time to gloat; just dropped the head and tore off across the snow to the female, who was trying to crawl away, whimpering. Sinking her hands into the woman's crystal-clear hair that shone in a lilac hue when the sunlight hit it, she pulled the female back, making plasma gush out of them both, saturating the snow in a bold slash of colour.

"It's over for you now," she whispered and looked up when branches snapped. Raven stood up ahead, staring at her. No emotion in his face whatsoever. He just calmly watched her going about her killing business as if he'd been with her for years! And somehow, that made something inside her melt a little. She quickly averted her eyes back to the woman trapped underneath her who started to claw at her arm to make her let go. She curled her spare hand around the woman's throat and rich hot heat cascaded out of it. The female screamed in agony and dug claw-like nails into Calista's wrist to try and move her as the heat began to literally melt her skin. The smell of burning marbled flesh strong and nasty but Calista held on until the head finally toppled to the side to land in the snow. She climbed off and left the corpses where they were, knowing because they didn't have the heat of the blood rushing around their systems, the bodies would melt into the ground where they lay, becoming part of the land. She climbed the rest of the mountain and stood next to Raven, who didn't say anything to her, just turned around. Blood coated her, but both didn't seem to notice. Or if he did, he didn't say anything about it. Once she stood on the top of the mountain, the view that greeted her never failed to bring a sense of calm about her.

Chapter Thirteen

The view was astounding. It wasn't just one mountain like everyone thought, but a collection of six miniature ones! But because they sat pretty much overlapping each other, it appeared as though they were one and all were covered in snow. They sat in a circle all strong looking and appeared to be totally invincible. Towards the bottom, a good half mile up the sides of the mountains, sat snow covered trees, looking frail and delicate, beautifully twinkling in the sunlight that beamed down on them. It seemed as though they were protecting something. And sure enough, in the middle sat an incredibly clear blue lake. Clearer than any he'd ever seen before. It was breathtaking. But what was even more weird, a large old oak log cabin atop a thick platform floated in the centre of it. Just floated. Not on stilts or anything; at least nothing that he could make out anyway.

"Who lives there?" Raven asked, and stumbled down the hill after her.

"Nikki." Calista stepped onto a platform that was slightly sticking out and grabbed Raven, hauling him onto the platform too.

"Sit down. You don't want to be standing up for this." He sat down with no questions asked. Calista sat down too and the platform moved out of the mountain and headed straight for the cabin. A few moments later they descended onto the deck next to the cabin, and Calista got off the platform, followed by Raven. They walked along the old wood that seemed ready to break at any moment and strolled up onto the porch that wrapped itself around the cabin. Opening the front door, she walked inside. Light poured in through the windows, washing over the wooden floor that was smooth yet well-worn in places. Walls were old oak panels that strangely suited the place and were accentuated by old-fashioned oil lamps dotted here and there. The main area was taken up by what would be the main entertainment centre. This held two huge couches that you'd quite literally sink in. A spacious black-stoned open fire that was cold at the moment held centre stage flanked by two gargoyle statues. Between the couches sat a gargoyle-based glass-topped coffee table that had a dragon candle holder on top with a black candle. Along the wall the fireplace was on as well as the wall furthest from the door, sat bookshelves from floor to ceiling. And every single shelf had books on them, all different sizes and colours. Shelves bowed from the weight of them, even books lay on their sides on top of others. You couldn't fit any more on if you tried. It was every bibliophile's wet dream! A large black marbled kitchen sat to the left, holding all of the necessities. Further along, it was a dead end from what he could see as no lights were on.

"Is this it?" Raven asked, gazing around and caught Calista leaning her own small arsenal against the wall.

"No. The bedrooms and bathroom veer off to the right. Which is why it looks like a dead end just there."

"Oh, right. How many bedrooms this place hold?"

"Three." It was definitely bigger than you thought from looking at it outside; but alas, that was what happened when you were in a world run with magic.

"That's not bad. So why are we here?"

"Because one of the bedrooms happens to be an arsenal of weapons. And considering I left some of mine in the cabin back there, I can't really go back and get them. Waste of the journey."

"Understandable. How long will we be here for?" He gazed out of the window and saw dusk was already settling in quick. Where the hell had the day gone? But then again, all that walking they'd done soon added up the hours of the day, he just never realised it. Must have been because of the comfortable silence they'd been in, so it didn't really register.

"Tonight. We'll leave just before dawn. You pick the couch you want."

"What about you?"

"Don't worry about me; just pick the couch you'll be sleeping on."

"Why not pick a bedroom?"

"They are just bare. No furniture or anything in them. Apart from Nikki's and I don't think she'd appreciate anyone sleeping in her bed." And she walked off down the corridor. Thinking back to what she had just said, if this was Nikki's place, why wasn't there any other place to sleep? But then again, as he'd met her, she seemed the type to be a loner. Much like himself and Luke. Although they had each other's company. Shrugging, he picked the one furthest from the fireplace and then hunted through what was the kitchen. Everything was neat as a pin, exactly the same as the rest of the place. Was Nikki some sort of neat freak? Then he opened cupboards and drawers and saw that the vast majority of them were empty. Most things were scarce. A couple of sets of knives and forks. Some plates. Cooking utensils, etc. Didn't she have money? Or maybe this was all she needed. He left the kitchen and strolled down the now lit corridor to where he heard a grinding noise. He saw one of the doors open, and soon filled the space. Even these walls had oak panelling and black flooring. The old-fashioned oil lamps from the main part of the house decorated these walls as well. The window was covered in black velvet floor-length curtains that were held open by a silk dark purple ribbon. Calista was bent over an old-fashioned grind wheel which was turning rapidly from her foot as she pushed on a pedal. She held a huge double-sided battle axe against it, sharpening the blades. She expertly welded it. But soon it was sharp enough to her liking, as she ran it over her thumb and sliced through the skin almost straight away. She turned her head and looked straight at him as he walked into the room, his shoes making a small noise against the wood flooring. He didn't stop until he had reached her side and took her hand into his, thumb sticking up. He wiped his own across it and the blood smeared but underneath was neat, uncut skin as though she hadn't just cut herself.

"How?" he whispered.

"Good genes?"

"Was that a joke?" He smiled at her.

"No." He laughed at the instantaneous rejection. He couldn't help it. He noticed she turned away, but caught the smile that lifted her mouth. It was a proper smile almost. Not just a small tilt of the lips. She picked up a small throwing knife. The blade didn't gleam at all. Obviously blunt.

"Can I try?" He nodded to the stone wheel.

"Sure." She stepped to the side and handed him the weapon. He stood where she was, one foot placed on the pedal that was just a slight rise in the flooring. She showed him how to hold the blade against the stone at an angle; enough to sharpen, but not enough to destroy the weapon.

"Now you need to push down on the pedal. Not a lot though, the more you press, the faster the wheel turns. Push it and I'll tell you when it's fast enough." He did as she said, and once the stone had picked up enough speed, she pushed his hands down until the blade hit stone. Small sparks started to fly around his hands, but they didn't hurt when they landed on his skin, they just disappeared. Calista stepped away a little bit and he was left to do it on his own. It wasn't as easy as she made it look. He had to grind the knife to the side to get the whole blade. But it was fun. Well, to him it was anyway. It was totally different to what he was used to. But it was as though he was back in the olden days, mid-14th century, as a blacksmith. Did they feel pride in the work they did? It also had a strange calming sensation to it, everything that was going on, disappeared. Once he thought it was sharp enough, he lifted his foot from the pedal, the machine slowing down to a stop. The blade gleamed nicely in the sunlight steaming through the window that Calista had uncovered.

"Do you reckon this is sharp enough?" he asked and turned to look at her. All that was present was her legs and butt. The rest of her was buried inside a huge upright chest thing. She stood up quickly and looked at him.

"There is some testing stuff next to you. Put the knife onto it and slide downwards, if a cut appears, it's sharp enough." And she returned to rummaging in her box, clearly dismissing him. He turned to look at the table, and sure enough, there was this parchment-type stuff on the table next to an assortment of other tools. He put the knife to it, and dragged it downwards. And a simple cut appeared in it.

"There is a cut," he called out, and nearly jumped out of his skin when a hand appeared next to his arm to grasp the blade. Not the handle. The actual blade! Blood soon dropped onto the table. He pulled the knife away and whirled around and came very close to Calista. Closer than he ever had before, even when they'd kissed. And he saw her eyes weren't just that fantastic cobalt blue. They had a smoky green ring around the outside and around the pupil. They were stunning. Why hadn't he noticed that before?

"It's sharp enough. It'll do." She took it from him and stepped away. She cleaned the blade of her blood and placed in it a protective sheath, then handed it right back and he took it.

"And why the sheath?"

"So, you don't accidentally cut yourself. Some of the places we'll have to go through, if blood is smelt, they'll hunt you down and not stop until they find you. And because you're human, your blood has a different smell to it so it'll be tantalising to them and they'll want to know what the source is."

"Understandable." She turned away and he held the now covered blade in his own hand, fingers curled instinctively around it. She returned to rummaging through that huge box when she pulled out another black-handled axe. But it was a small throwing one with a gold blade. Bloody gold! And about half the size of the one that usually lay across her shoulder blades. Still looked like a dangerous motherfucker even though it was gold.

"Sharpen this for me, please," she asked and held it out, blade to the floor, her head still hidden. He laughed silently and did as she asked, not asking questions as to why and at least he knew she had manners. Thank God for that at least. He quickly sharpened it, straightened from his hunched position then tested the sharpness against the block. It sliced clean through, cleaving the thing nearly in half. Was it meant to do that?

"Erm, Calista…" He looked over his shoulder, his voice must have portrayed his unease because she shot upright and turned her sharp gaze to his.

"What?"

"It sliced right through. Nearly cleaved the block in half. Is it meant to do that? I didn't sharpen it that much either." She walked over and he saw the look of recognition in her face as her gaze landed on the dangerous weapon.

"Yes. Because it's Flamyon. Made from the fire pits of Anghel Mountain from warrior angels. Nikki took it when she was banished from Anghel Island." He turned to fully look at her.

"Banished?"

"Banished."

"Why?"

"Uncontrollable. Wasn't at all like the other angels. She was all for vengeance. Merciless. Never hesitated to jump into a fight then talk it out afterwards. Then it didn't help she got bitten by a vampire and nearly had her throat ripped out."

"So she's literally one of a kind."

"She is now. Her older sister had gotten chomped too. Turned her downright malevolent; must have kick-started something inside of her that was just below the surface. The power and the rush she had from it went to her head."

"Had?"

"Yes. Had. Lyia was sent to what is the equivalent of prison for angels."

"Oh. That must have hurt Nikki to realise her sister was now forever locked away."

"Actually, no. Lyia was forever trying to prove to everyone that Nikki was an abomination."

"Abomination, how?"

"She's been the only one to ever have black and silver wings as well as different coloured eyes. Everyone else is gold, bronze and silver."

"How did Nikki end up with black and silver? Do you know?"

"Turned out her own mother, Sharlyr, tried using Whytches Syrum. This is a poison to angels. She tried injecting it straight into her womb to kill Nikki, but it obviously backfired and Nikki is the only known angel to have a resistance against it. It is why her wings are the colour they are. Same as her eyes. Angels have eyes the same colour as their wings, and

252

sometimes their skin is the same too. Well, it's more of a shimmer as they all have pale skin, but it's a shimmer of gold, silver or bronze flecks. When she was born, her mother again tried to kill her using the syrum, but it affected her instead because she was still suckling Nikki."

"How so? And Nikki has purple eyes not black and silver, is that a trait of it?" Raven leaned against the table next to him, clearly wanting to know how it all worked.

"That we are aware of for Nikki. I've never really looked into it to be honest. And Sharlyr started by losing her mind. That's what it does. It slowly started to affect her and when Nikki was around about five years old, the other angels had finally deemed Sharlyr too deranged and dangerous to live. So I got called in. Told the situation and Sharlyr was brought in to the High Angel Council. She was wrapped in Angyloi, chains made of a substance that looks like silver but it isn't, is used to restrain literally any angel. Immovable angel guards held Sharlyr to her knees wrapped in this stuff. It wasn't pleasant. Sharlyr was a complete mess. Wings were in shambles. Chunks were missing. Feathers missing in places, which made it pretty much impossible for her to fly. Her clothes were literally scraps. She'd also scribbled nonsense into her skin, some of which were so fresh, they still leaked blood."

"Couldn't they clean her up a bit?"

"No point. She was going to die. But I can understand why they should have. She reeked."

"Why is that?" He waited whilst Calista leant against a huge device thing, ankles and arms crossed.

"Nikki was there. She was bruised and battered. Half her face was literally one giant bruise with a very prominent black eye. She was also dressed in scraps but it didn't seem to bother her. Even at five years old, she showed no emotion on her face. Her eyes were hardened. It turns out, just before the mother was caught, she'd had one of her 'episodes' and had taken it out on Nikki as she was the only one in the place at the time. But even though young and small, Nikki had managed to get in some shots back. I remember seeing Sharlyr had a bust lip; one eye was swollen and she had small teeth like indentations in her shoulder. Once Sharlyr was held in the room, on her knees like a piece of trash, they questioned her, even asked Nikki questions. I don't know the exact questions asked but it was obvious they had the answers they wanted, because they had deemed Sharlyr guilty. Then I was summoned into the hall from a room I was waiting in."

"Must have been quite an entrance if you had been called in to be executioner."

"Not really. I was dressed all in black. I had my axe across my back, and two throwing knives held in cases across my chest and my sword at my hip, which is my usual attire as I'm sure you've noticed. But I also had a slightly different version of their axe with me. Mine was mixed with their blood and fire. Which is what Flamyon is kind of, but I had tweaked it a little bit, so it was much more dangerous than their usual blade."

"That doesn't surprise me. What happened next?"

"Sharlyr saw me and screamed in absolute fright. Then she was begging me to not kill her. Let her live. She would try and get better. Lock her up but don't kill her and let her live for her children. This I couldn't allow. Not with everything that she had done."

"Why didn't you lock her away?"

"Because angels can live past millennia. She wasn't that old in angel standards. Sharlyr was roughly four hundred years old when she died."

"So, she was about three hundred and ninety-five years old when she had Nikki?"

"That's the thing with angels, they can't conceive very well. Eighty percent of the pregnancies are still-born. Or some have slight differences which they can't stand. Shall we say, they're quite snobbish. Also that is why angel children should be cherished because they're all the more rare, no matter if they're born different."

"What happened next?"

"I took my Flamyon into my hand and approached her. I stood next to her and looked at the High Council. Asked what would happen with the child. They answered they'd put her in the care of a family of elder angels until she was of age to live on her own. I guess you could say they didn't like the answer I gave back to that statement."

"What makes you say that?"

"Because I told them I'd take Nikki with me and she'd return when of age. They didn't argue."

"I wonder why," he sarcastically said.

"Anyway, after that, a few angels began herding Nikki out of the room, but she was screaming no, she had to stay. I said if the child wanted to stay, we should let her. So they didn't object, just stood either side of her and waited, they knew better than to argue with me. I looked at Nikki and asked if she had anything to say to the woman who brought her into this world. The one who was now muttering in a bunch of gibberish in a high crazed voice and clawing her arms. Nikki had walked over, stood facing Sharlyr and in a voice that was clear, crisp and unemotional, denounced Sharlyr as her mother. Called her a womb donor and even that was too good for her. I remember Nikki had looked at me then, nodded once and walked away back to where she had stood before. Even after Sharlyr screamed for her to stop and listen to her mother. But the kid didn't. Good for her I say."

"Don't actually blame her. That's pretty damn harsh, what her mother did in the first place. It wasn't Nikki's fault she was conceived."

"Yes. Well, I then pulled Flamyon out of its case, and the blade hissed and spat as though it was alive. I held it to Sharlyr's face and stared into the woman's wide eyes. 'You are forever deleted from this here planet, universe and everyone who knew you will forget.' I remember saying that to her; then clicked a button on Flamyon's handle. The blade shot out towards her throat, separated and clasped around as though a collar. Sharlyr screamed as the white-hot heat of it cut through her skin until her head became unattached from her neck, balancing precariously on the blade that had sealed shut again. After that, well, I threw Sharlyr's head to the High Council where it bounced at their feet and they only had to dispose of the body, no blood as the heat of the blade had cauterised the wound, I nodded once and walked away, But not before stopping at the colossal, high gold and white marbled doors and motioning for Nikki to follow. She quickly caught up as the guards who held her let her go without hesitation so she could be with me and I knew the Angel Elders wouldn't say anything to me taking her from them."

"What happened to her father? Couldn't he have raised her?"

"No. He had died when she was about one. He was a warrior and had been set up by jealous angels under his command who had banded together and got him killed. When it had been found out what had happened, they were executed. Again, by me. After I had ripped their memories out and they'd begged and pleaded for forgiveness."

"How bad was it when you ripped their memories from them?" He shifted slightly before getting comfortable again. He wasn't really a talker but talking with Calista was so easy. As if he'd known her for years.

"Bad. They bled from their eyes, ears and mouth. Not that I cared. They soon realised that they'd die so they tried to fight. I took them all down within minutes. Never to hurt anyone again. Before the last one died, I found out where they'd left Nikki's father's body, which was recovered and he was given a warriors funeral."

"Suppose that was a good thing then, considering how he'd died. How long did Nikki stay with you?"

"She stayed with me until she was eighteen. So thirteen years she stayed in my home and was under my protection and care. I taught her how to fight and how to defend herself. Trust very little and how to keep people away so they couldn't grow attached to you."

"How long ago was this?"

"It has to have been a good eleven thousand years or so ago now. Yes I know that is mind boggling for you but alas, that is life here."

"You've really known her for eleven thousand years? That's a long time to know someone. And I thought my friendship with Luke was a long time."

"We've not always seen each other. It was once five hundred years before we saw each other again. She stayed here; I was on 'normal Earth'."

"Oh right. That must have been amazing to see the planet change and such over so many years." He got a faraway look on his face, as though trying to picture it in his mind's eye.

"Yes, it was. But I had more important things to deal with than take awe at the world changing around me. I wasn't, and still am not, a patient person. But if the time calls for it, I can wait a very long time."

"So what happened when you returned home?" They left the weapons room and headed back to the main living area, both sinking down onto a couch each.

"You do know this is the most I've spoken in a long, long time." She stared at him with unblinking eyes.

"Really?"

"Yes. I guess I just find it easy to talk to you." She shrugged. He grinned. He couldn't help it. She snorted at the grin, which just cracked it up a higher notch.

"Anyway, you say you raised Nikki until she was eighteen. Didn't see her for a long time."

"Yes, that's right."

"What were you doing that you didn't see the child you'd raised for nearly five hundred years?"

"I was on 'normal Earth', and other places. On a mission to remove and destroy some beings from here. Once I'd returned, everyone was saying Suicide Mountain was a no-go zone. It was a hazard. Those who went didn't return. When I'd asked why, they said a fallen vampire angel with black and silver wings was killing anyone who stepped foot near the top of the mountain. That is if you made it past all the traps and such that were set out up the sides. I didn't bother waiting around then, I headed straight for it. When I eventually got to the top, I saw the same view as you did earlier. Only, there was no cabin and no trees. Not to mention that the lake wasn't the size it was then either."

"Then what happened?"

"I saw Nikki flying towards me. Hatred bright in her eyes. Mouth wide open with fangs dripping in saliva with an earth shattering scream. Nails stretched out ready to take me down. Wings flapping hard to give her speed. She slammed into me and I didn't move, she just rebounded off of me. I remember she blinked a fair few times, and stood frozen to the spot."

"That must have been a bit of a shock when she rebounded off of you."

"Just a fair bit; she asked who I was and when I told her, she broke down into great wracking sobs."

"What? Nikki had cried?" He was shocked beyond belief. Tough nut Nikki had cried? Blimey.

"Yes. She'd been told I'd left her for good. And I had also died. So it was as if she literally had no one left in this world. She said it was as if she was forever deemed to live an outcast and completely alone."

"What happened after she'd finished crying?"

"Believe it or not, I hugged her. That was really all I could do. But from then on, she's was as she was back at the house when you met her. We know where we stand with each other. As good as a friendship as I'd allow. And we're both comfortable with that."

"Understandable." He smiled, but then let out a jaw-cracking yawn. Calista stood up, disappeared down the hallway and reappeared a moment later with a towel and handed it to Raven.

"Bathroom is the first door you come to in the hallway. You might want to brush your teeth and such. There is a new toothbrush and toothpaste plus a new razor still in its packet in there for you to use."

"OK. Thanks." He walked away and quickly used the facilities, barely taking notice of the lavish black topped marble sink and side but he did however take a little extra in the huge walk-in shower with its wide array of showerheads. He eventually emerged from the bathroom, washed, shaved and fresh breath. It was a godsend to be clean again. He noticed Calista had moved the couches so they were both facing each other and at an angle from the hearth, he chose one and sat down on it. The coffee table had moved as well, just slightly further down between the couches. Then Calista walked into the spacious yet snug room carrying some duvets and pillows. She handed him two pillows and a thick duvet. It'd certainly keep him warm.

"So why is it we've stopped here? It has just turned seven p.m." he asked, looking at his watch that had been forwarded to the right time, thanks to Lexis and a quick glance outside of where the sun was setting, creating beautiful colours in the sky.

"We won't travel these mountains in the dark. It is perpetual suicide."

"Well, it explains the name."

"Exactly. Also, have to make a pit stop in Dragon Land. I have to see the leader."

"Who's that?"

"His name is Gélio. He's a considerably large boy. If I remember properly, he stands at about seventy feet high and fifty feet long."

"That's a big boy for sure!"

"Yeah. Just don't say that to his face. Gélio is old, very old."

"How old we talking about?"

"Bear in mind, dragons can live for a very long time and Gélio is about forty thousand years old."

"Damn that is old. He must have seen a hell of a lot in his time."

"Yes. You can tell. He's got nasty scars and age old wisdom in his eyes."

"So why have you got to see him?" Raven wiggled more on the couch, getting comfortable and yanked the duvet up to his chest.

"He asked me to."

"Any idea what it could be about?"

"None, as Gélio wasn't forthcoming about it and he'll only say stuff to you face to face, as he doesn't trust messengers apart from sending a message saying that he requests an audience with you."

"Nothing wrong with that."

"No, there isn't." She turned slightly and pointed to the fireplace and a spark of hot heat shot into it, instantaneously igniting the wood that voraciously consumed the fire almost thankfully. Snapping her fingers, the oil lamps quenched their light. She stood up and drew the long thick drapes closed over the windows, blocking all the light out. This plunged the room into darkness apart from the light emanating from the fireplace, but it was almost a warm, almost homely type atmosphere. Apart from the wood crackling, there was no other sound around them and Calista dropped onto the couch and drew the duvet up and over her to rest it just under her chin.

"So why we going to sleep so early?"

"Because I want us to leave before dawn. The sooner we're out of here and on our way the better."

"Fair enough. So Lexis told me and Luke that you're able to go a long time without sleep. Is that right?"

"Yes, it is."

"How long?" He turned onto his side so he could look at her.

"The longest was three weeks, four days, thirteen hours and thirty-five seconds." She didn't look at him, just continued to gaze at the ceiling.

"Damn, that is a long time."

"You tend to not sleep when you're being tortured."

"You were tortured?"

"It does happen once in a very long time. It didn't bother me, to be honest."

"It didn't bother you?" He couldn't keep the disbelief out of his voice, even if he tried.

"No. Because I got the information I was after. And they died and hurt a lot more than I had." Raven was astounded. She made it sound as if it was an everyday thing.

"What information was it?"

"Just information. Sleep now." She rolled onto her side, turning her back to him. Clearing dismissing him. He sighed and turned his back to her also. Was he so wise to have followed? Or was he just fooling himself into thinking something would happen between them? Did love do that to a man? Make him foolish? He didn't have any previous experience; he'd never been in love before. Before his brain started thinking more, he closed his eyes and fell into the land of sleep, the sound of crackling wood the only sound that could be heard.

Chapter Fourteen

"Do you think Raven's OK out there?" Lexis asked, cuddling closer to her man as the fire crackled, giving both light and warmth to the four people gathered in the living area.

"He'll be fine. I doubt Calista would let anything happen to him," Luke said and took a huge bite out of his sandwich.

"How can you be eating at a time like this?" she snapped. "Your best friend is out there in that bleak, treacherous wildness. Not a clue what is around the corner, and it's all for Calista?"

"First of all, I'm hungry. And have more faith in the man. He'll find her, if he hasn't already. He has this eerie ability in finding people really quickly and efficiently. Plus, I doubt Calista would let anything or anyone hurt him. She's not a total bitch."

"I wouldn't be so sure about that. I've seen Calista in one of her 'bitch' moods," Nikki said, her wings semi-curled around her as she sat leaning against the couch end closest to the fire. The silver in them sparkling a tantalizing colour and creating fantastical colours up the wall behind her. Lexis thought it was beautiful. And she was the only angel she knew who could create colours using her wings.

"Why would he even go after her anyway?" she enquired, looking at her brother.

"Love."

"Love? As in love with Calista?" Her eyes went as wide as saucers at that. It was true that you learned something new every day.

"Yep. Love for Calista. He's been practically smitten since he first saw her. That whole love at first sight balooha." Luke smirked at her and she wanted to slap it off his face. Love was a fantastic thing. Love at first is what had happened to her and Tairen, well more so Tairen. She hadn't noticed him until she'd been there a week, but the love had soon claimed her as well. And she definitely wouldn't change it for anything. But she knew, one day her brother would fall in love and she couldn't wait to see it claim him as well.

"He's going to be on a wild ride trying to get her," her man answered, shifting on the couch and she realised her elbow had dug into his ribs.

"Sorry," she mumbled and he just flashed her his cheeky grin, which pretty much meant she was going to get it when they were alone. But damn if that didn't thrill her!

"How so?" Her brother's voice jarred them.

"Use that brain of yours, Luke. Calista doesn't let anyone close to her. Heck, I've just managed to slide under that tough skin of hers." There was no chance in hell she'd admit that Calista had told her she'd slid deeper; that was between them and no one else.

"But I thought you were close?" Genuine puzzlement on his face, and Lexis couldn't help but smile.

"As close as anyone can actually get to her. Heck, Nikki how long you known her for?"

"A good eleven thousand years, give or take a few."

"And how close are you to her?"

"A smidge ahead of you I think."

"So clearly it means she has trust issues," Luke said, scoffing the last of his food.

"Pretty much," Tairen laughed.

"So what happens if you start pissing her off?"

"Go on love, you tell him." Tairen nudged her gently which made her roll her eyes.

"One caution. If you carry on, she will kick your ass so hard, just looking at a chair will make you cry," she said, as though she'd said it a thousand times before. Lexis looked at Nikki who just grinned in a warped way and then bit into a BBQ chicken thigh that she had cooked earlier.

"Wipe that grin off your face. You know Calista has a short fuse. I just hope Raven knows what he's getting himself into." She turned worried eyes to look out of the window at the dark sky which hugged the huge luminescent moon. Backed up by slashing rain, fierce lightning and ground-shaking thunder.

"He has to learn the hard way. You know Raven, he doesn't do anything the easy way," Luke said.

"Even in the army?" She turned to look back at him, she wasn't that ignorant.

"More so then but he's also one hell of a soldier. And even our commanders have said that."

"I remember you telling me in a few of your letters. Did he really dress up as a terrorist?"

"We call them Tangos and yes, he sure did. He just casually walked past their guards, who didn't so much as blink at him, went down these tunnels and planted a few bombs along the way. All without a single incident."

"How did he manage it? Raven is far from those type of people and still is human. Plus he's not exactly small in height either." Lexis was astonished. Terrorists weren't exactly trustworthy and for him to get into their camp and plant bombs along the way, completely unheard of!

"Face paint."

"You serious?" Tairen sounded like he didn't believe him whatsoever. Before they could say anything else, Jinx let out a God almighty cry from upstairs and Tairen got up and raced to go get her, using that notorious vampire speed. He just as suddenly appeared again with her cradled against his shoulder, braced securely in the crook of his arm, sucking furiously on her dummy and clutching his top with one of her tiny hands. And Alexzander was in his other arm, rubbing his eyes and trying to stay upright before he toppled over in sleep. Tairen put him down and he walked over to Lexis. Her man disappeared out of the room with Jinx.

"Come here baby." Lexis held her arms out for him and he eagerly climbed into them. She drew a blanket around him and cuddled him close, rocking him slightly and not even a minute later, he fell back to sleep. She looked over at Tairen as he walked back in the room and saw Jinx was guzzling down a bottle of milk. That explained why she had woken up.

"Wonder what caused Alexzander to wake up as well?" Luke said, drawing Lexis's gaze.

"No idea. Maybe from what happened to him before. It could take a little while before he gets used to sleeping anywhere else and realising nothing is going to hurt him here. Or that Alexzander doesn't have to wake up every time she cries."

"True. OK, where were we?"

"Talking about Raven and the camp," Nikki reminded him.

"Thanks. But yeah, I'm deadly serious. He darkened his face and neck, added a few scars here and there. Put in contacts to change his eye colour to a muddy brown and that was pretty much it. He didn't have to change his hair colour as it's already dark. He had done it without our general's authorisation though. They'd argued about it for a good half hour and God knows our man didn't back down. When the general firmly put his foot down, Raven did it anyway. He'd gotten ready and waltzed past the general's office and flipped him the bird." The pride in her brother's voice was obvious. And they all suddenly burst out laughing as Jinx let out a loud belch as Tairen winded her before she grinned at them all before rubbing her eyes. Tairen cleaned up the little bit of dribble she did, checked her nappy was dry, laid back in a slouch on the couch and cradled his daughter against his chest, gently rubbing her back in circular motions, which must have been the trick as Jinx closed her eyes and drifted off to sleep again. Lexis smiled as she watched the way her man was with their baby.

"How do you know he did?" Nikki asked, drawing the couple's attention away from the kids.

"I was in the tent. The general wanted me to keep an eye on our 'devil'. By the time we got outside, he'd gotten on a motorbike, which we'd taken a few days before, and driven off. He made a wide trip around to their camp, making it appear as though he wasn't coming from our own camp. We waited a trifling six hours before he returned, which had to have been around four to five a.m. at this point. Once he did, the general grabbed him, but quickly let go, as he remembered the last person who'd grabbed Raven had gotten his hand and nose broken very quickly."

"How did that happen?" Tairen enquired, clearly enjoying the tale but then so was she and Nikki, although the other woman wouldn't admit it, she just stared at them.

"One of the guys in our group was being a bastard and had heard about what would happen if you grabbed Raven, so decided to be the big I Am and grabbed him. Before anyone could stop it, Raven whirled around, punched the guy in the face, tripped him and stamped on his hand as hard as he could, pretty much effectively breaking the bones and making it completely useless."

"What happened next?" Ah Nikki, Miss Blood Thirsty, as always.

"We jumped in. I pulled Raven away; the others got the guy on the floor. The general called Raven into his office and must have grilled him for a solid hour and not once did he talk. Finally, the general gave in, not easily done but it happened. And Raven sauntered out, his face completely expressionless. Body language unreadable. He walked past all of us without a single glance and disappeared into the tent me and him shared. Nothing else happened after that until the middle of the night the following day."

"What happened?" Lexis wiggled a little, but was still enthralled in the story.

"Have to wait until I get back from the toilet. Need to go point percy at the porcelain!" He darted from the room really quickly.

"Point percy at the porcelain?" Tairen turned a puzzled look at Lexis.

"Go for a pee."

"Oh right. So anyway, do you believe him?" Tairen asked.

"Yes. Luke's never been able to lie. Even as a young kid."

"Must have helped your parents then," Nikki laughed.

"Not really. We didn't lie to our parents. We were all close."

"If close, why did Luke run off and join the military?"

"I honestly don't know. He has never has told me his reasons why. No matter how many times I asked him, he refused to tell me. All I know was at sixteen, he and Raven left for a long weekend camping trip, which they did often. They came back late Monday evening and I was already tucked up in bed asleep. That morning after they'd returned, at breakfast, Luke informed us that he and Raven were enlisting into the army. To say we were shocked was an understatement. But to say one thing about my brother, he's very stubborn and wouldn't be talked out of it. Even Raven couldn't be talked out of joining and he's more stubborn than my brother, and that is saying something. But we could understand why with Raven, it seemed he wanted to prove to himself more than anything what he was capable of."

"How long after they announced that did they officially join?"

"He told us in June. They officially joined in September. I'd not long turned eleven. So we never have found out why. Besides, a few years later, just after my fourteenth birthday, Mum and Dad died in a massive car crash. Luke, who had changed a lot by then, more muscle, more serious, the guy he is now actually, came back for the funeral with Raven and thanks to the money he'd saved up, we found a cheap place for me to rent so I could live there which was just down the road from his military barracks and a ten minute walk from the school I was at. And we sold our parent's house while he was back as well because it was too much for me to live there on my own, so the money from that helped too, well to feed me and such. Majority of it has gone into a savers bank account for emergencies."

"But then you didn't see him again for a few years." It wasn't a question, just a fact. Lexis nodded anyway and moved Alexzander so he was next to her, wrapped in the blanket and head on a cushion, deadweight kid was making her arm go to sleep. But he looked like her own little angel so she wasn't complaining but he'd be more comfortable laying on the couch instead of on her. She noticed he wiggled his foot back until it rested against her thigh and he smiled in his sleep. And damn if that didn't make her heart melt.

"OK. I'm back. Where were we?" Luke strolled in and carefully sank down into the couch, careful not to jar his nephew.

"You got to the part where Raven went into the tent you two shared and that nothing happened until the middle of the night," Nikki reminded him.

"Oh yeah. Well, in the middle of the night, once we were all sound asleep, Raven snuck out of the camp. That man can be ridiculously quiet when he needs to be, like you won't know he's actually behind you until it's too late quiet. We all got woken up by a massive explosion. We all raced out of our tents, in our sleep gear, to find out what the hell had happened and we saw the general standing next to someone. We stopped up short when we realised it was Raven. He had the ring leader we were after on his knees, with hands tied behind him and gagged just in front of Raven, and the general was talking to him. That was when we heard a gunshot. Just one. We heard the general shout for a medic as he grabbed Raven's arm but the man pushed him away, turned around and let out this terrible roar that no doubt came not just from his chest, but his stomach. And I shit you not, it was the scariest thing I have ever heard come from a man. It was as if it wasn't human at all!"

"He was shot?" Tairen asked.

"Yes. But it didn't seem to register. Once he finished that roar, which I repeat was scary as fuck, he dove head first into the few Tango's who had survived the bomb blasts. I have no idea how he killed them, but in a matter of minutes all we had was deathly silence. I remember I ran up to the general, who had a clear view of everything, expecting the worse. But as I looked, Raven was still standing. He was also surrounded by the dead Tango's and coated in their blood and it dripped off his hands and splashed all up his face. Honestly, I think he killed them with his bare hands. He nodded at us once and walked off. He was a stone cold merciless killing machine. It was if the blood didn't register to him. Even the general had lost colour in his face as he had had a clear view of what Raven had done."

"Where did he go?"

"He went and cleaned himself up." He sighed. "After that, he was back in our tent. I went to see him and the injuries he had — I couldn't help the gasp that slipped."

"That bad?" Lexis moved and leant over to her brother, taking his scarred, callused hand into her soft, dainty one.

"How he didn't seek a medic we will never know. I knew he was stubborn but this is an understatement. He was sowing his own wounds shut! Well the ones he could reach anyway. And as far as I knew, he didn't even have any painkillers to help either. I remember when I saw him, he had a pair of pliers embedded into his stomach — he was digging out a bullet. He had no emotion or anything on his face. It was as if he was completely devoid of emotions and was a robot or something."

"Like a true solider," Tairen muttered.

"But surely even a true solider knows when to accept help?" Luke turned his piercing gaze to Tairen's.

"Yes, but he has his pride. Maybe it was just easier to sow his own wounds than rely on a medic."

"But it isn't right, have to learn when to give in now and again. I guess Raven just doesn't know when to give in."

"And that is why he's perfect for Calista," Nikki said, standing up and stretching her wings out before snapping them back close to her back again.

"And why is that?" Lexis asked the fallen angel.

"Because he happens to be stubborn and doesn't give in easy. This is exactly what Calista needs. Look, I've never *ever* seen her with a guy. Not one who is willing to actually fight for her. Or want her in any way other than for her help. Or unless it is Draylan and Skyri working with her." Nikki left the room after that statement.

"Is she serious?" Luke asked.

"Yes. I'm afraid she is. I, too, have never seen Calista with a guy. Perhaps she's right; Raven will be a good accomplice or more for Calista." Lexis smiled at her brother.

"I guess so. I'm more worried for Raven than Calista." He smiled back.

"And why would you be worried for him?" Tairen asked.

"Because, hello! Have you perceived the power that woman welds? Raven is literally nothing compared to her."

"But that's the good thing. Haven't you noticed that Raven has his own inner strength?" Tairen said, sitting forward on the couch as much as he could with Jinx attached to him. Lexis nodded her own agreement and quickly darted her gaze to the clock which sat centre stage above the fireplace. It was just past ten p.m. The time had flown by and they hadn't even realised.

"Yes, I have noticed. Will that be enough?"

"It might be the only way he can get through to her. He has the inner strength which will attract her. If she didn't want him with her, she'd have sent him back by now. And trust me, she'd know how to do it."

"But doesn't she work alone?"

"Yes."

"Then why would she let Raven stay with her?"

"She might have found out he has something to prove in himself. Maybe it's his steel determination. Maybe even his determination to get things done and not waste time. We won't know until she gets back and we ask," Tairen replied and let out a jaw-cracking yawn.

"Do you think if we, or more so, I set out to find him, I'd find him?" Luke enquired.

"No. They'd have covered a vast distance by now. You'd have no chance," Lexis answered and stood up.

"Why wouldn't I?"

"Because there are a lot of things out there in which wouldn't hesitate to kill you. Simple as that. And besides, Calista would have covered her tracks by now because if she doesn't want to be followed, she won't be."

"Oh, that's understandable. I take it it's bed time?"

"Yes. I'm getting really sleepy. And it's best we go to bed as guaranteed these little munchkins will have us up early." She smiled as she took Jinx from Tairen's chest, cuddling the warm baby to her and he picked up Alexzander who curled up in his dad's arms.

"OK," he agreed.

"Good night, Luke. We'll see you in the morning."

"OK. Good night." Lexis took a hold of Tairen's hand and together, the couple walked out of the room. Destination: their bed.

Luke smiled slightly as he watched his sister walk out. He couldn't call her his baby sister; she'd long since grown up. And that actually depressed him. He wanted his tiny, eleven-year-old sister back, who'd pull pranks on him when he didn't expect it and squeal with delight as the cold sea washed over her toes when they took family outings to the seafront. But now she had grown up hell of a lot, was in a strong relationship and not to mention pregnant. Plus she was now a mother to two fantastic kids. She'd make a fantastic mother to them and be as fiercely loyal and loving as their own mother had been to them. That was without question. Then it sank in, oh man, he was an uncle! And he knew without a doubt, he'd be highly protective of them as well, just as he was for Lexis. He waited until Lexis and Tairen had disappeared completely out of earshot. Thanks to that bloody ultra-sensitive hearing vampires were known for, he had to wait until they'd shut the door to their soundproof bedroom, thanks to some powerful magic by none other than Calista herself. Just how great were her powers? And what powerful being had given birth to her? Was it all hereditary? If so, did any beings like her still live or was she the last?

Questions of all sorts bounced around his brain at rapid speed. By the time he thought of one, another jumped up and claimed its place virtually instantly. But the main question which kept on making an appearance was:

Was Raven OK?

All he wanted to know was if his best friend was alive or dead. He glanced at the clock and realised he had been staring into the fire for almost an hour! He clambered stiffly to his feet and stretched. Sighing happily as he loosened up. Creeping to the living room door, he stuck his head out and strained his hearing. Complete silence met him. Lexis and Tairen were no doubt cuddled up sound asleep in their bed. His niece and nephew asleep in their own beds again. And Nikki had disappeared to God only knows where. He walked over to the huge patio doors and crept outside. Well, once he'd opened the door just enough to squeeze through. The cold air immediately hit him, causing him to shudder slightly. He kept to the shadows just like Raven had shown him numerous times to remain virtually invisible unless looked for properly. Once he'd reached the porch edge, he sank down with his back against the house and knees drawn to his chest, staring out over the vast view that was ahead of him. The sky gloriously clear and twinkling with millions of stars. He must have sat like that for a good old while before he heard a slight shuffling of feet to his right. He glanced over and couldn't help the smile that easily came to his face when he saw who it was.

"Come here. You'll freeze, you numpty." He held his arm out and Lexis snuggled up close into his side, soaking up his warmth eagerly. Luckily she'd got out of wanting to rip into his jugular so cuddling was no problem anymore and for that he was thankful. He missed cuddles with her.

"What are you doing out here?"

"Thinking."

"Wondering about Raven?" She tilted her head back against his arm and looked at him. He couldn't look at her, instead gazing out across the distance to the ocean that glimmered in the moonlight.

"Yes."

"One worded answers solve a whole lot of nothing." She nudged him.

"You've been hanging around that philosopher uncle of your man's." He nudged her back.

"Most of what he says does make sense."

"This is true. I take it he's the calm, reasonable one between him and Calista?"

"You're changing the subject. Thought we were talking about Raven?"

"We are; but don't mean I'm not curious about everyone and everything here."

"Good point. Tomorrow, want me to see if we can find a Scryer?"

"What the hell is a Scryer?"

"They can locate pretty much anyone on the island. I only know of one that resides around near here. Well, Nikki does. I can ask her to look for him."

"Him?"

"Him. His name is Scrynelavr."

"That's undoubtedly different." He grinned at her.

"Yes it is. I call him Scry for short, so much easier." She grinned back.

"So he'd be able to find Raven?"

"He might. Depends on how lucid he is at the time."

"He crazy or something?"

"Yes." The voice of that answer had them both turning their heads to the patio doors.

"How is he crazy?" Luke asked, just as Nikki stepped into the moonlight which, in his opinion, caressed her porcelain perfect skin and stroked her wings like a lover. Was he falling to the same fate as Raven? Actually feeling something for Nikki? He hoped not. They were so unalike it was crazy. For a start she was an angel and he was just a lowly human. She was beyond gorgeous and he was, well him.

"He just is. He rambles to himself. His mouth is virtually non-existent. He has no eyes; just fur going up and over but he has prominent deep eye sockets."

"And what is so special about being a Scryer?"

"It isn't a good job, because you become mad. They can literally see inside of you; right down to your very soul even though they have no eyes. Never let them touch you. They can, quite frankly put, rip your deepest, darkest secrets out and get all giddy when they find out what they are."

"That doesn't sound that bad."

"They can also take on the appearance of what you are wearing. What you wear, they wear. It's all part of their glamour. They're fucked up beings." Nikki moved closer to them and jumped up onto the railing, instantly curling her bare feet around the bars.

"OK. That's slightly weird."

"Slightly?" Lexis turned her head to look at him like he was crazy and he could comprehend why.

"Come on. Look at what you've thrown at me and Raven in the past forty-eight hours or so. Something like that, piece of piss, we can handle it. What we can't handle is Calista. I wouldn't even want to!" He shuddered and Lexis pushed him jokingly.

"No, you wouldn't. But I'm sure Raven wouldn't give up the opportunity." She laughed, then let out a jaw-cracking yawn.

"Bed. Go on. I'll see you when we wake up tomorrow." He nudged her a bit, thus proving his point he wanted her inside.

"I think you mean today," Nikki said, leaning back against a support.

"Tomorrow. Today. Whenever we wake up. I'll see you then."

"Yeah, OK. Night, big brother." She gave him a quick hug before clambering to her feet.

"Good night, little sister."

"Good night, Nikki."

"Sweet dreams, little one." He waited for her to go inside before turning back to face the gorgeous woman in front of him.

"How bad is it out there? And don't lie."

"I don't lie. And bad doesn't comprehend it. It's a vicious world out there. Kill or be killed."

"Pretty much as it is on 'normal Earth' then."

"But surely not everywhere you go?"

"Actually, when you think about it, no. Some places are good, no violence or anything."

"And where do these places exist?"

"I'm actually not sure. I know it existed when mine and Lexis's parents were alive. Our house was full of happiness and love."

"At least you know something like that does exist." She turned her gaze away and right before his eyes, they hardened and her entire body stiffened.

"What is it?" He was immediately alert, but knew to stay in the shadows.

"Shadow fairy. And an annoying one at that."

"Shadow fairy?"

"That's right, human. Shadow fairy." He snapped his gaze to the right, saw nothing there then looked down and standing in front of him on the deck, no taller than ten centimetres tall, was a fairy. Its skin was velvet black, with grey hair slicked back into a sophisticated ponytail tied with magic. He was naked, apart from a tiny black leaf with silver veins held by shadow magic against his groin and buttocks. He was lean, with tiny defined muscles over his body. Wings were a dusky grey colour, blending perfectly against his skin.

Fairy in his prime. Luke laughed in his head, not daring to, out loud.

"Shae, what do you want?" Nikki asked, watching as the fairy fluttered up onto her bent knee to look her in the eyes.

"I have news for you!" His voice was actually quite deep for one so small.

"What news?"

"Lyia has escaped." The fairy actually jumped from her knee and hid behind Luke as a ferocious look appeared on Nikki's face that was haunting and unquestionably frightening. Even Luke was hesitant to make a move in case it made her wrath turn onto him and at that moment he could see why she was said to be undoubtedly dangerous and ruthless! But in all honestly, it made him quite hot watching her.

"Since when?" Her voice was hard and clipped.

"As of one hour ago. I tried locating Calista. But I could not."

"She's off saving some kids; you won't find her. How did you find out?"

"As you know, I'm a sneaky fella and you asked me to fly by numerous times to Anghel Prison to make sure Lyia was still in her hole. Well this time, guards were dead. A Flamyon was missing and her cell was literally caved in. I dug through, and there was nothing there. So I immediately flew to tell you."

"OK. Hunt around and see if you can find her. I know this is a big place, but I trust you, Shae."

"OK. I'll come back when I find something." He flew off into the shadows, easily disappearing from their sight.

"Who is Lyia?" Luke asked, causing her to look back at him.

"My older sister. Crazy as anything. Took after our mother."

"And she escaped?"

"Yes. From Anghel Prison. She has been there for a long, long time."

"How long?"

"Near enough my whole life."

"That's a long time. How long ago was she sentenced?"

"Since I was five years old."

"And you're how old?"

"About eleven thousand years old or so."

"Oh. Must have seen hell of a lot then." He didn't even blink at how old she was.

"Too much at times." He watched as she twisted her head away; the moonshine caressing her skin. It made the image sear itself permanently into his subconscious, not that he minded.

"So what happens now that Lyia has escaped?"

"We'll have to wait until Calista is back. She's the only one who has the means of stopping her. Once I know, I'll go hunt down Lyia and rid her from this world." She turned steel hardened eyes back to him.

"As in kill her." It wasn't a question, just a statement of fact.

"Yes; exactly that." He didn't flinch or anything. He knew Nikki was an assassin for hire. It was her profession to rid this world of horrendous people. As was his job on 'normal Earth'. So, who was he to judge that? Only he wasn't called an assassin; he was a member of the elite group of men trained specifically to deal with the killers normal Military Personal couldn't. Wait, no that did make him an assassin, because his small elite group had to do the jobs no other fucker could. Damn it did! So he definitely wasn't one to judge.

"Look, if I were you, I'd go to bed. It's almost half past twelve and no doubt Lexis will have you up early tomorrow morning for a day out down to the beach so she can show off her big brother."

"Yeah. That wouldn't surprise me with her. So night." He stood up, stretched his muscles from sitting so long and headed back into the house, silently closing the door behind him before realising she hadn't replied to him.

Nikki waited for him to go back into the house and heaved a sigh. That was a decent male there. Surely there was a lady back home for him? No surely not, otherwise he'd have brought her along with him. And besides; Lexis had told her a while ago that he was single. Had been for as long as she could remember, which was a waste of a male if you asked her. Then a thought went through her mind; exactly how many woman had gotten a taste of him? His kisses, etc? She shook her head of unwanted images and a murderous rage that swept through her system quicker than a hiccup and seemed to make her blood boil from the thought, and went soaring up into the night sky. When at a reasonable height, she looked back at the window that she automatically knew was the room Luke was in and noticed he was looking through the curtains, watching her. She wasn't surprised. He gave a curt nod and disappeared. Her heart did an odd flip, but she ignored it, refusing to examine why it did that. Turning around, she zoomed away into the avid darkness to clear her mind. Well, she hoped that helped. She didn't need a complication of thinking of a future with a man. Even a human like Luke. No matter how scrumptious he was. She couldn't let herself get attached. No matter what happened. It would only end in disaster and downright heartache. But she wasn't sure if it would be just him or would it be her as well? Either way, she'd been on her own since forever and she had no idea how to deal with relationships. Sure, she saw people in them every day but it was foreign to her. She shook her head to clear her thoughts and shot up into the sky, up into the clouds, disappearing from view.

Chapter Fifteen

Calista woke up to the moonlight still flowing through the window she'd uncovered sometime in the night. It washed into the living area, stroking her face. She glanced over at Raven who was still out for the count. One arm thrown over his eyes to block out the light and his other hanging precariously over the side, knuckles grazing the floor. She threw her blanket off her and on the balls of her feet, dashed down the corridor to the toilet, as her bladder took that as an opportunity to wake up. As she came back out, bladder finally emptied and her teeth brushed, she absently untied her hair from the ponytail, gave it a quick brush and put it back up, out of the way and no hindrance to her then. She walked into the weapons room and loaded up. She placed Flamyon back into its case and hid it away. No good someone finding it who shouldn't. Once she'd collected everything she needed, she gathered a few weapons for Raven. No point in him being unarmed, she was good, but it would still help for him to be armed as well. Walking back into the living area, Raven was still out for the count on the couch, the blanket now curled around his waist. Leaving his chest covered in that long sleeved top that really didn't leave much to the imagination. Which she had to admit to herself, was a very nice chest indeed. He had muscle adorning his biceps which bulged from their bent position. His stomach was rock hard and he must have smuggled paint rollers under them. His shoulders were broad and defined. She turned away before she did something that she would regret. She didn't want to cause Raven's 'obsession' with her to grow. Considering once this mission was over, he'd go back to 'normal Earth' and she would go back to protecting Mystic Being and all its residents. Doing what she did best. What she was 'born' to do. Sometimes it sucked, but it was all she knew.

"What time is it?" Raven's sleep husky voice stirred something inside her but she beat it back before it could rear its head more and rotated to face him. He was blinking his stunning blues, getting rid of the sleep that had sealed them shut.

"Time to get up. We leave in ten."

"OK. Give me five." He threw the blanket off him, that tight like a second skin, long-sleeved top and jeans giving her a healthy view of muscled calves, thighs and the most perfect arse ever that was showcased tightly when he bent slightly, grabbed his bag and disappeared into the bathroom.

"That man should be illegal," she muttered to herself and then stopped up short. Had she really bloody said that? And out loud no less! She needed to watch what she said, and no more gawking at Raven. She put everything back how they had originally found it, the blankets and pillows she put back into the storage. Looking around making sure she'd covered everything and seeing she had, she pulled a small map out of her pocket. Gazing at it, she quickly worked out the best route for her and Raven to take to get to first Dragon Hill, then on until the Fire Mountain. She heard the bathroom door open then, and turned her head to the side just as Raven came around the corner and headed towards her; clean black jeans and long-sleeved top now covered him. Along with his steel-toed boots, done up military style: tight. And he'd freshly shaved as well! God he was yummy. She mentally slapped herself then! No more thinking of that. She shoved the map back into her pocket.

"Ready?"

"Yeah, I am." She nodded and they headed to the front door.

"What's with the long sleeved tops by the way? You'll roast out here in them."

"I'll survive." Not really an answer but his problem.

"Before I forget, the weapons on the couch you were on, grab them." He quickly grabbed them, stashing them away on his body with years of practice and they walked out the door.

"Does this have an adjustable strap?" She turned to look at him as he held a protected knife in his hand.

"No." She took it from him, and held it against his thigh, refusing to think of the hard muscle under her fingertips. The strap lengthened of its own accord and sank around his thigh, tight to him without cutting off blood supply to his lower leg. It was sturdy and wouldn't be lost. Magic, wonder of the world.

"How does that feel?"

"It's fine." She stood up and was close to him, so he did what she *didn't* want him to do. He kissed her. And damn it, if her insides didn't get all excited! She pulled back before it got out of control.

"You really have to stop doing that."

"Can't help the fact you're just so kissable." And he grinned at her, looking utterly boyish. She rolled her eyes and shut the door behind them.

They strolled to the floating platform and when they reached it , Calista sat down and Raven followed suit, just in time as it began to move. They really couldn't afford to topple off. First off, it'd just really annoy Calista. Second, the fall would kill Raven. If the creatures that called the lake home didn't get him first. They waited until it reached the top of the mountain, and they clambered off. The wood sunk down into the snow, seeming to melt right through it and it formed over again, concealing it, leaving behind flawless unblemished whiteness. They quickly raced down the mountain, Raven quickly keeping up with her by walking in her footsteps. She didn't want to waste time on the mountain; lots of things hung out there at night. And she couldn't afford to defend Raven when she had kids to save. At the bottom of the mountain, as quietly as they could, they moved into the dense forest. Walking into deeper ground, they found that the natural light didn't really aid them, Instead it just seemed to peek through the dense leaves and thick branches that dominated the tree tops. Many of the leaves were the size, if not bigger than a standard dinner plate. In other words, bloody huge! Night creatures of weird and wonderful shapes howled and yapped amongst the tops. Occasional debris rained down on them, but it wasn't harmful. It was just leaves and small twigs.

"What are those things?"

"What things?"

"The creatures playing above us." She glanced up and a small smile actually tugged at her lips.

"They are called Grycans."

"What the hell are Grycans?"

"Small gremlin-type animals that scavenge on rotting flesh."

"Then why hide in tree tops?"

"Easier to move without being gnawed on themselves. Once they find rotting flesh, they drag it back up into the trees and have a loud feast."

"Loud feast?"

"They chatter loudly and make sloppy noises when they rip the flesh off the bones."

"Lovely." She really couldn't miss the sarcasm in his voice at that, even as he hesitantly gazed upwards and watched as he watched them watching him with their glowing yellow eyes.

"Think yourself lucky you don't hear what else they do."

"Which is?"

"Using the bones, they hit them against the trees and howl along. Their own version of music, basically. But some sound sloppy from the blood and such still attached."

"Oh joy." She rolled her eyes and they continued onwards, not bothering anymore with the Grycans. Strolling through the forest, they walked in what Calista was not used to when with someone… comfortable silence. But then again, she was rarely with someone anyway. Ninety-nine percent of the jobs she was given she was on her own. It was a very select few that she had either Skyri, Draylan or Nikki with her. They walked along quietly for a good hour with no disturbances or anything. Weaving in and out of the trees and brushing though prickly bushes.

"Motherfucker." She turned her head to Raven as he swore. He was shaking his hand.

"What's wrong?"

"I don't know. Something bit me." He held his hand out, and sure enough he had a miniature circular bite mark in the fleshy part of his thumb and first finger.

"God damn fleshers," she mumbled and stepped around him, motioning for him to be quiet. She placed her hand against his spine and felt him stiffen. She knelt down behind him, and sure enough, clinging to the back of his jeans, to the inside of his knee grinning at her, was a flesher. It looked like a cross between a leech and a fairy. The body of a leech, wings, arms and legs of a fairy. Its face held a circular mouth with icky, long serrated teeth. Rows of the fucking things. It had no eyes, but it had a highly sensitive sense of smell to be able to scent the plasma coursing through its 'host's' body. It made it easy for it to find where the blood was closest to the surface of the skin in order for it to feed. Most of the time you didn't feel it feeding on you, but somehow Raven had. They didn't touch her, must be because of all the different blood types she had coursing through her system, not to mention even they weren't stupid enough to bite her. It was about half an inch if that in size, so not fully grown. Fully grown fleshers stood no taller than three to four inches tall. She pulled it off his leg where it had dropped when he shook his hand, before it dug through his jeans with those sharp teeth to his flesh below, and held it between her fingers. She walked back in front of him and showed him. His face scrunched up and she barely blocked a grin.

"So that's what a flesher looks like."

"Yes. It's rarely seen because it's so small, plus this is only a baby one. And they mostly stick to the dense forestry."

"So why attack me?"

"You're the only human it has encountered in its life. As I told you before, your blood smells of mild strawberries and it likely had no idea what you were, so sampled you. But instead realised your skin isn't as tough as many of ours are, so ended up taking a chunk of flesh from you."

"Skin isn't as tough as yours?"

"Mine is ten times tougher than yours."

"Oh, right. I get you now." She let the flesher go, and it sat gallantly on a leaf, its mouth wide open, sitting silently waiting for its next host to come along. They also weren't the most intelligent of creatures either. In fact, they were quite stupid. They headed off and she glanced at Raven's hand and saw it was still bleeding. Not good in a world where cannibals and blood suckers lived. She took a hold of it, instantly making him stop.

"What?"

"Your hand is bleeding. We need to stop it."

"How are we going to do that? We have no supplies for that sort of thing."

"Trust me." She held it in front of her, brushed her thumb over the wound and whispered a small healing spell. She soon let it go but he didn't drop it, kept it where it was. She watched his expression, it was of awe as he watched his skin knit itself back together and the blood disappeared, appearing to sink back into his body. It was something she'd done a million times before, but to her own body. Once all the blood had disappeared, Raven shook his hand.

"OK now?"

"Yeah. Thank you. Even the small pain is gone."

"Small pain?"

"According to doctors at the Military Base Luke and I are at, they told me I have the start of arthritis in my hand which is what caused the mild pain I had; but I let very few people know it hurt, otherwise they'd use it against me. This is the best it's felt in a long time."

"Why would they use it against you?"

"Because there was a mole in the group and they were trying to figure out who it was. If they'd known that, they'd have used it against me. Sign of weakness and all that. As we're all meant to be one hundred percent." She was surprised he admitted this to her. Clearly he trusted her. Why though? She was one of those you did not trust; she'd use anything against you if you betrayed her. Obviously he was willing to take that chance with her.

278

"Why admit this to me?" She just looked at him.

"I don't know. This, shall we say, instinct or gut feeling I have, tells me I can trust you."

"Are you sure you're not part vampire or something?"

"Now I've seen your world, I honestly don't know."

"Tell you what, as we're heading into territory where they'd use any weakness against you, we'll discuss this later yeah?"

"OK. What territory are we in?"

"Just keep your gun ahead of you and not slung down your back." He slung it ahead of him, taking the familiar weight into his hands, just like old times.

"You didn't answer my question."

"We're heading into the Marbilian villages. They won't know what you are and won't trust you, even though you're with me. Just keep your gun with you. They're a pesky lot, but don't worry about their colours. Marbilians are all in different shapes, sizes and colours. Also, if they get too cocky, load the gun and put it in their face, prove that you won't take no crap from them or else they'll walk all over you and laugh whilst they do it."

"Good to know," he muttered and followed her over smoothed out tracks in the mud. But it had sprinkles of glitter, dust and such attached to it. Was that meant to be like that? God, this world was so confusing with all its different things! Calista strode through the forest like she had been here a thousand times before; which knowing her, she had been. She'd been all over this island, including the underwater world that the Water Marbilians called home. Strolling through the dense forestry, Raven realised he could see things a lot easier and glanced upwards. Dawn had crept in and now it was growing lighter by the second. Quick glance at his watch and it showed it was seven a.m. They moved together, stepping over twigs and other things that really didn't need to be studied close to find out what it was. Walking roughly two hundred yards, they began hearing adults talking and kids screaming with laughter. Calista motioned for Raven to walk beside her; if they saw him behind her, they'd think she was protecting him. They emerged into the very edge of the huge camp. Everything quickly turned to a standstill. Children ran back to their parents, staring at them with huge eyes, wide with curiosity but with fear too. They knew exactly who she was. Parents held morning dishes of food whilst other adults held washing, brooms, all sorts to start their day. They walked further into the camp, her face an unreadable mask.

"Where is Glinther?" she asked an obviously pregnant gold Marbilian.

"He should be in the big bark hut over there." She pointed with a gold finger then disappeared back inside her tiny one. They headed for the hut that stood out from the rest, almost like a guardian of the camp. She could hear talking inside and banged on the wooden door that was tied together with dried-out tree sap. Raven stood next to her, staring at the door, refusing to look at everyone behind him. The door opened and Calista merely arched an eyebrow at the sight of the kid in front of her. He stood as tall as her hip, but he had a fierce glower on his face, until he realised who he was looking at. And that glower immediately vanished and he bowed his head respectfully at her.

"Miss Calista. Are you here for Father?" He had a right to ask, as she usually only made appearances when she had to rid something from this world.

"Yes. Is he here?"

"No. He went out." At that, he flew out of the doorway as if he was pushed, barely missed bouncing into Calista, and a slimy green Marbilian walked out.

"Don't stand around boy. Get back to bloody work."

"I don't have to!" he screamed then promptly ran off.

"Where is Glinther?" She turned her gaze to the slimeball, who had the decency to shrink back in fear.

"He's in one of the mines."

"Fine. Come on, Raven." She turned and walked away. Arrogant shit, they always thought they were better than everyone else. They weren't.

"So what is his job?"

"He's of dirt."

"Dirt?"

"Yes, dirt. When the green Marbilians die, their bodies literally crack open and their blood flows into the dirt, thus creating life. And their body breaks down as well, sinking into the ground."

"So you're saying, all around us, it has been created by these Marbilians who've died?"

"Not all of it. Some. Now shh." She turned away and right in front of them, this dark Marbilian male threw his fist out, connecting with a small yellow/green skinned child's face.

"Don't you ever ask that again!" he hollered, and drew back his fist to hit them again. But before he could, Calista grabbed hold of his fist, having moved faster than their eyes could track.

Raven watched as she moved faster than any of them could track. One moment she was with him, the next she had that brute's fist in her hand before he could hit the kid another time. He looked around and noticed everyone had stopped to watch. Even children peeked out from behind their elder's legs they hid behind.

"You know damn well better than to hit a child." Calista's voice was low. Major pissed off. That just made Raven hot. Even better than her being angry? Angry sex! He should be so bloody lucky. Even nice, long sex with her would be fucking amazing. Why did she have to be off limits? He mentally shook himself and got back with the program. He agreed that a child shouldn't be hit. They should be cherished and surrounded by laughter, love and a sense of security.

"He deserved it!" he stammered.

"Why did he deserve it?"

"He stole from us! If he's hungry, he should go and ask somewhere else."

"Where's your parents, kid?" She turned those brilliant eyes of hers to the frightened kid who couldn't talk from stark terror, so Raven stepped forward and crouched in front of him, drawing the kid's scared eyes to his own.

"Where are your parents?" he asked gently, even smiling gently.

"Dead," he whispered. Luminous yellow eyes stared at the ground as he wiped the yellow blood from his face, smearing it down the side of his hand and across his cheek.

"Since when?"

"A while now," an adult said, causing Raven to look up at them.

"I want him to answer, not you." Then he turned his gaze back to the kid who now stared at him. Fuck him, but those eyes were bright. And yet, he could see a very keen intelligence in them.

"A-a while now."

"And how long is a while?"

"Forty-five days," he mumbled and tears sprang into his eyes, but they didn't fall. Tough willed obviously.

"From what?"

"Kharge." He looked back at Calista who nodded once at him.

"And who is that guy to you?"

"My mother's brother." Any more venom in that sentence and Raven would be dead. Raven turned to face the Marbilian.

281

"What's your name?"

"Grethòr."

"OK, we'll get to the bottom of this and get you fed, OK kid?" He nodded and Raven got back to his feet before turning to face the uncle.

"Why won't you feed a member of your own family?"

"It has nothing to do with you, vermin!" the thing sneered at him and that was the turning point for Raven. He walked up to the male and quite simply punched him in the face, breaking his nose virtually instantly. It hurt his hand but he wouldn't show the bastard that it did, not when he got the satisfaction of hurting him.

"You fucking bastard!" It leapt at him and Raven brought his gun up, shoving it in the thing's chest, stopping it dead. Clearly it knew what damage the gun would cause from a point blank range shot. And Raven wasn't one to toot his own horn, but he was a damn good shot at a long distance, up close and personal? He definitely wouldn't miss but he'd cause a lot of damage first.

"I am, yes. But no need to spread the word around, people will figure that out for themselves. Now, if I were you, I'd feed the kid. He's your nephew. When Calista and I return from our trip, and I find out you haven't fed or looked after the kid, I'll come back and quite simply blow your fucking head off." He didn't raise his voice, but the message was clear as the male's eyes widened. And with that, he walked off, all without a backward glance. He strode through the trees, but was suddenly pulled to a stop. And sure enough, Calista walked around to stand in front of him.

"Want to tell me what that was all about?"

"I don't like kids being bullied or picked on just because their parents died and another family member doesn't want the burden of caring for them. Someone had to stand up to him, and it doesn't have to be you all the time."

"I've dealt with a lot worse than a stupid Marbilian like that."

"I gathered that. But doesn't mean on this trip I'll stand back and let you do all the fighting. If I know how to do something, it's fighting. If I go down, I go down. Least I went down doing what I do best."

"And what if the one you are fighting has a leverage over you?"

"Such as?"

"Strength. Height. Ability to move faster than your eyes can track. Teleportation. All sorts."

"I'd still give it my best shot."

"A true warrior you are." He looked at her, really looked.

"Yeah, and if I'm that much of a warrior, then why was I sent to the worst places on 'normal Earth'? Laughed at by women and men! Only Luke and Lexis treated me as an equal."

"Is this what it is all about? Proving your worth?"

"No. Yes. Oh, I don't fucking know!" He turned and slammed his fist into a tree, the bark groaning and splitting. The pain that radiated up his arm felt good, so he did it again. Before he could hit a third time, he was spun around and pinned to the tree.

"Do you really think hitting that tree will bloody help? Look, you're one of the fiercest ones I know and that is really saying something. Don't put yourself down. Everyone else that laughed at you and such? They're just jealous of the fact you're more of a man than them and have done something in your life other than being a brown nose by sucking up to someone's arse. So don't fucking listen to them anymore, OK, just do your own thing and fuck what they think." With that, he watched her walk off and he sank to the floor. Could that be what he'd been doing? Trying to get into everyone's good books for being a damn good soldier, or as Calista said, warrior. He heard something coming towards him and drew his gun up, but soon relaxed as Calista walked through the bushes just in front of him. How long had he been sitting there? Glancing up at the sky, he realised it hadn't been long.

"Come on. We're heading into the mines."

"Erm, mines?"

"Yes. We need to see Glinther. We need a place to crash for tonight. I would carry on, but it's the start of Brynyfa. So nights come in quick here. It'll be dark by five p.m."

"What the hell of Brynyfa?"

"You would call it winter."

"Oh, right." He stood up and followed her into the forest. They walked about one hundred yards, and heard deep voices. They broke through the shrubbery and Raven wondered why she didn't stop to see who was out there. Then he comprehended it was a large collection of massive Marbilians. All in an array of vast sparkling colours. They soon stopped talking when one had stiffened, and they turned as one giant unit to face them.

"What do you want, Calista?" a bright green one asked.

"Glinther."

"He's down in the mine still. You and your human will have to go down and get him." How did they know he was human? He'd really have to ask Calista that when they were alone. Maybe all of the beings here had heightened senses so they could smell it on him. Or had word gone out that he was with her? Or had they heard it from the village? Either way, it was damn annoying.

"Fine." And he oddly noted she didn't correct them in calling him her human. That shouldn't have sent a tingle of happiness tingling through his system but it did. They walked across the ground to holes in the floor. They seemed to go slightly diagonal, with stairs for easy leverage in getting down.

"Raven, you wait here with the men. I won't be long. And you lot leave Raven alone, or you'll have me to deal with, if he doesn't blow your head off first." And with that, she disappeared.

Chapter Sixteen

"So what does Calista want with Glinther?" a huge silver Marbilian asked, his eyes glistening in the sunlight and Raven turned to look at the one who had spoken.

"And what is it to do with you?" He outright refused to bow down to them, not after what Calista had said. That made him feel good and no one was taking that from him! No matter who or what they fucking were.

"We're just wondering. We never see her around here unless she's hunting something or wanting information. And even when hunting, it's exceedingly rare to spot her until it's too late. Let alone her being with someone."

"I don't know what she wants with him. Only I know it has something to do with night time that's going to start creeping in real soon."

"It is?"

"Yes, Brynyfa is drawing close as well."

"How do you know Brynyfa is near and what it even is?"

"Calista," a gold one muttered in answer for him. They all turned to look at him.

"Has she gone into the mines yet?"

"Yes. She also left strict instructions as she headed down into them."

"What were they?" a smallish Marbilian asked, no doubt a teenager just starting to learn the job.

"Leave the human alone."

"Why would she care about what happens to you?" They turned suspicious eyes to him.

"Haven't got a clue," he admitted. Did she honestly believe he couldn't take care of himself? Sure these bastards were huge, but didn't mean he wouldn't go down without a fight. He hadn't earned his reputation as a stone-cold fighter and a hard arse motherfucker because he was a pussy. He'd sooner deal with someone with his fists than talk; which is why Luke did the interrogation ninety-nine percent of the time. Raven was just the brute force and honestly? He was quite happy with that.

"Are you shagging her?" a huge green Marbilian asked, but before Raven could reply, a slim hand with long black nails shot through the dirt beneath the guy's feet, curled around an ankle and wrenched him down through the ground. He let out a startled scream as he disappeared before it sealed shut over his head as if it had never moved. It had also eerily looked like Calista's hand. Then he was thinking who the fuck could it have been? They were the only humanoid type ones around, so obviously it was her and it damn sure wasn't him, considering he was above ground and he undoubtedly didn't have feminine black nailed hands.

"What the fuck?" They all moved, eyes frantically scanning the floor in case it happened to them. All so wary of one woman. It was almost enough to make Raven laugh. He wasn't scared of her, was very much infatuated instead.

"Clearly she didn't like him asking that question." Raven's lip curled up slightly, by no means was it a smile. His eyes stayed the same bitter cool. And the ground rumbled beneath their feet almost as if in a warning. But just as suddenly it stopped. He looked around and noticed everyone was keeping a wary eye out, most gazes on the floor, so he slouched against a tree a little bit from them, crossed his ankles and shut his eyes. Thank you military for training him how to fall asleep almost instantly, no matter where he was. He sure did need it now even though he'd slept like a log in the cabin. He held the gun to his chest, finger on the trigger. He might appear relaxed, but he could spring into action quicker than they thought a human could move. He wasn't going to let them know, unless absolute necessary.

Calista dragged the guy down through the ground until he landed on the floor some one hundred feet below her hovering form, sending a fume of dust up as he bounced to a stop.

"What's going on?!" he stammered, He looked around and his gaze landed on Glinther who was leaning back against the wall staring at him, arms crossed over his thick, solid chest.

"You said the wrong thing to that human," Glinther replied, not moving.

"Do not repeat what you said." Calista drifted down to the floor, looking ready for murder.

"I only asked a simple question." She stared at him as he watched her cautiously.

"When it refers to me and I can hear you, then do you not think it'd be wise to hold your tongue?" Marbilians were so full of shit. Only Glinther seemed to have any brains.

"I didn't know you could hear us."

"You should realise by now I have exceptional hearing. And you know better than asking questions like that. And the answer is no, he is not sleeping with me."

"It was just a joke!" he cried, but she paid him no attention, just looked away to Glinther.

"What?" the Marbilian asked.

"Put him to work. Before I kill him for his inability to keep his mouth shut; or I'd just do what I did to you only I'd string up the pieces." At that, Glinther blanched and hauled the male to his feet as though he was a small child.

"Down to the bottom of the shaft there, I need a few more loads of rock. I'll send down a few others to help, along with some pick axes. Don't argue, you're here for a wage exactly like the rest of us. I've seen you slouch against the wall and let the others do the job and once you heard I was on my way around to check process, you got to work. So from now on, you'll be watched carefully and when you don't think we are watching, we will be." He pushed the male in the direction he wanted him to go to, then turned to face Calista.

"You know everyone is going to ask what you did to me."

"Then just tell them. It's not like you're suffering anymore."

"This is true."

"Precisely. Now, as I asked before I heard that untimely question, is there a spare hut in which Raven and I can spend the night?"

"There should be. Once I've got all down here sorted, we can head back and I'll make sure there is a spare one and it's habitable."

"Very well. How long roughly? As Brynyfa is closing in on us, so the days will be becoming a lot shorter."

"But I thought you travelled best during the night?"

"On my own yes. But because I have a human with me, I need to take extra precaution."

"Why?"

"Because one stray hit from something with immense power will kill him pretty much instantly. I don't need the bloody hassle."

"Hassle from what?"

"Lexis. Raven is Lexis's brother's best friend."

"And God forbid, that woman gets angry. She has a mean old temper on her." He didn't mean it harshly, they all liked Lexis but they'd seen her once in a very rare rage and when that had happened, even Calista had raised an eyebrow at the woman.

"Don't we bloody know it."

"Does her brother know she has a fierce temper on her?"

"No. He still thinks she's the quiet, shy kid he left behind when he went to the army to provide money for her."

"Oh, right. Least she had money and someone to care for her." They all knew her parents had died when she was a child.

"Yes. Anyway, I'll send more of the lads down here and I'll wait for you above ground. Don't disturb me, I'll be against a tree with my eyes shut. Throw a small stone near my foot and I'll wake up."

"OK." And with that, she took the sloping stairs back above ground. She walked out into midday light. She'd been below ground for two hours! And considering the travelling she and Raven had done, the hours zoomed past them at a rapid rate. Taking a step onto the land above ground, she looked around. Most of the Marbilians were sitting on the ground, eating their food. She walked over to them and as they saw her, they leapt to their feet.

"After you've finished eating, need as many of you as possible to head down into the mines to help that waste of space Veraos."

"To do what?" the only teenager out of the lot of them asked, his metallic eyes on her forehead — even he had heard to not look her in the eyes.

"You'll have to ask Glinther." And with that she strolled away, looking around for Raven. She spotted him leaning against a tree, eyes shut. Even from the distance they were, she could see his chest rising and falling easily. He was asleep. She soon dropped down beside him, her own back against a thick, sturdy tree. Raven opened one eye, saw it was her and promptly closed it again, all without moving a single muscle. Impressive.

"Calista?" She looked up and it was that kid.

"What?"

"Is it true we heard you're going to go rescue kids that Kharge has taken?"

"That's right."

"But I thought you worked alone?"

"I usually do."

"Then why is he with you?" He motioned to Raven, who carried on slumbering. Or so the kid thought. Raven was awake; just pretending to be asleep still. He'd been awake since she'd sat down next to him.

"Personal reasons. I'd go head back to them lot now if I were you. You're going to get real busy soon."

"Will you still be here when we finish? I know its cowardice, but I don't like walking back to camp with all these lot."

"Why?"

"Because they're brutish. Think it's hilarious to play pranks on me when I'm not paying attention."

"Well, I'm staying for a while. And it isn't cowardice; you're just fed up of their jokes. This is understandable, they're meant to be the adults. Now go back to work." The kid nodded and darted off.

"Like how you avoided his question on us," Raven mumbled from beside her.

"Yeah, well it isn't anyone's business if we're sleeping together or why you're with me." She turned her head to look at him and he lifted his own and stared at her. Was he really the only one not scared of her? It made a nice change. But one she wasn't willing to closely examine.

"And are we?"

"We've slept in the same room twice now. But I really doubt that's the kind of sleeping together they were on about."

"They're on about the other kind." It wasn't a question, but she still heard his heartbeat speed up. Almost as if he liked that idea and she had no doubt he did.

"Let them think all they want. We know the truth."

"Yeah. So what's going to occur now?"

"Wait for Glinther to finish in the mines, which will take a couple of hours. Then everyone will be heading back to the camp and we'll get a hut for us to sleep in for the night. Then we'll leave tomorrow and travel as much as we can."

"So what do we do whilst we wait?"

"Sleep. And before we know it time will have passed and we can head back to the camp."

"Why is it called a camp? Camp is with tents."

"It's what they call it. They don't like calling it a village."

"Fair enough then." She didn't comment and laid her head back. Closing her eyes, therefore dismissing everyone around her. She heard Raven shuffle, and glanced at him out the corner of her eye. He'd also laid his head back, eyes shut, arms crossed over that immaculate chest. Gun in between them both. Two killers ready to pounce at any given second. His backpack between his thighs. After that thought, she settled in for sleep.

An hour and a half later

Calista woke up to an uneasy feeling. She looked around and no one was around, apart from Raven who still slumbered next to her. So because there was no one around, they must all be hacking away in the mines. Then Marbilians let out high-pitched, half-crazed screams and dust shot up from the main hole into the mines. She leapt to her feet, nudged Raven who bolted awake and took off at a run to where the teenager crawled out of one of the smaller holes, spluttering up dust that he'd inhaled in between gulping in a lungful of air.

"What happened?" Calista hauled him to his feet.

"Veraos got angry with something Glinther asked him to do and hacked away supports we'd put up, so the mine collapsed and they're still trapped. You have to save them!"

"What caused him to be angry?"

"Glinther asked him to move over to another part of the mine, which was only a short distance next to him and he just flipped. Shoved me out the way as I was talking to Glinther about what he needed done with a cart of stones we'd moved and next thing I know, I hear a massive snap which must have been his axe slamming into one of the supports. Then all I know is the mine began collapsing in on itself. Glinther caught me under my arms, threw me to the small hole I crawled out of so I could get you for help."

"OK. Raven, you keep the kid with you. I'm going into the mine." And with that, she disappeared into the swirling dust that still hadn't settled. Heading downwards, she swept her hand out in front of her and the dust sunk to the floor. The rubble that greeted her was astounding. She couldn't really see anyone, the occasional arm, hand, foot or leg. Even parts of torsos and that was only due to their bright colours.

"Hello!" she called out. Muffled calls came back at her from all directions. She soon made quick work of pulling people out of rubble; leaving them in the large floor space that somehow was left untouched. But she also used her powerful magic to keep the place from collapsing in on itself and crushing them all to death. Well them, not her. It would just hurt! She made a quick headcount and realised she still had Glinther and Veraos to find.

"Anyone seen Glinther and Veraos?"

"They were in the main mine part. Where Glinther had asked Veraos to go," a pale Marbilian coughed and pointed down a way in which was partially blocked. She stood at the start of the beginning of the walkway, the area blocked off by the rocks. She threw her hands out and power surged through her. Rocks obliterated into themselves, freeing the way. She held one hand up and sent a horde of magic into the ceiling to keep it from collapsing as the rocks disappeared. A huge bulk of the rubble then disappeared, leaving behind a solid wall made up of a collection of different beautiful stones and jewels, Glinther and Veraos calling for help from behind it. Bending down and grabbing under this ridiculously large rock right in front of the wall, she stood, picking the stone up as though it was as light as feathers. She carried it back into the main part of the mine and dumped it. Ignoring the shocked gazes of everyone else, she ran back to where she had been. She dug through more of the wall of rocks and such until she finally saw Veraos's arm, his usual vibrant shine dull and sickly. She didn't want to use magic, just in case it caused more harm than good to the two trapped behind so she resorted to her phenomenal strength.

"Veraos?" she called out and the arm moved slightly. She grabbed onto it with both hands and pulled, yanking the man out of his pile of rubble. A nasty gash ran down the length of his side and across his thigh, thus spilling his gold blood all over her. He began whimpering as he saw it, clearly the pain starting to kick in once he realised the magnitude of his injuries. She pulled him to his feet, and carried him out into the main area. She laid him on the floor, placed one hand on his side and the other on his thigh. Using her unique powers, she called his blood that had washed out onto the chamber floor and onto herself and it came slithering along in a trail a cm or so above the floor and leaked back into Veraos's body, causing him to sigh happily as it sunk back into him. Which wasn't surprising; it would feel like warm water washing over his body. Once she was certain he would be fine, she went back into the chamber, stood as still as possible in the centre and let her senses fly. She soon located Glinther. He was further back in the rubble than Veraos was, but that wouldn't stop her. She dug even more into the rocks, throwing them this way and that behind her, not looking where they landed. Soon she saw Glinther. Well, part of his head.

"I'm going to get you out of here," she whispered near him, and shoved her hand through rock, sailing through the other side; she felt something cold and grabbed it. Pulling backwards, it was Glinther's hand she'd grasped. She rocked back on her heels and pulled him with her. Well, his arm anyway. She used this to her advantage, she continued moving backwards, her grip on the Marbilian solid until finally he sailed free from the rocks. He had deep gashes over his body and one of his legs was missing. It wasn't a cut that had been created from the rocks, but from a bloody axe! Veraos. No doubt about it. She laid his body on the floor, and shoved her hand back into the space he had occupied, the rocks threatening to cave in on themselves. She finally found the leg and pulled it out, just in time. As the rocks tumbled down and sealed the gap up, she turned away and placed Glinther's leg where it was meant to be. She then proceeded to heal the wounds. She did the same mumbo jumbo that she had for Veraos's blood and she watched as it seeped from the wall and slashed across the floor and over Glinther, to where it sunk into his skin causing him to sigh even though he was unconscious. Then she concentrated on reattaching his missing limb, and that was no easy feat with a Marbilian. They didn't have the nerves and such everyone else did. It was literally just marble with muscle in between. Hence, why they were highly sought after to help with the war, because of their brute strength. She made quick work of bringing him around and once he was stable enough and on his feet, they left the chamber. Walking out into the main part, she saw Veraos was sitting up but still acting like a big girl's blouse, cradling his arm that had scrapes on it from where rocks had caught him.

"Oh, quit your blabbering. You're no worse than a newborn babe," she snapped and disappeared topside. She looked around and found Raven leaning against a tree whilst the kid was sitting on a low hanging branch, swinging his legs and they were chatting as if they'd know each other for years, it was a nice sight. The kid saw her emerging and jumped down and together they walked over.

"Everyone safe?"

"Yes, they're starting to come up now." And sure enough everyone was soon out. And that was when the kid let loose on Veraos. He jumped on him, and due to the element of surprise, floored the much larger man. He started throwing his fists, connecting solidly. Blood soon began to leak from Veraos's face. Not that it stopped the kid but soon Glinther stepped in and hauled the boy off and despite the man's own injuries, he easily removed the kid.

"What the hell are you doing boy?" he growled, catching a hold of him when he again launched his small body at Veraos, who was now back on his feet, but he was ready this time.

"He caused the mine to collapse! If it wasn't for the fact I'm small enough, and quick, I would also have been trapped. What if Calista hadn't of been here? What if I had to go back to the village and bring back help? By that time, you all could have died. Explain to me how I could have possible explained that to your wives and children!"

"Kid, calm down. It was an accident," Veraos said.

"No, it wasn't! I saw you swing that axe." Everyone looked at him after that announcement.

"Why Veraos?" one of the workers asked, and then promptly coughed up more rock dust.

"I didn't do it!" he muttered. As if that was answer enough.

"Right, enough of all this, we need to head back. Night will be settling in within the next two to three hours," Calista butted in with the finesse of practice.

"Yeah, good idea." The men collected their work gear that hadn't been trapped in the mine, and started heading home. Not as fast as they usually did, but taking their time due to injuries. Once the majority of them had disappeared from view, Calista turned to Veraos.

"You know it wasn't an accident. And if I were you, I'd head into the village and plead for your forgiveness. You'll be lucky to be allowed back into the mines again."

"I have to be allowed. It's my job."

"You don't have a wife or children to pay for Veraos. And I'm sure you'd eventually be able to find some sort of other jobs," Glinther said.

"That isn't the fucking point!" he retorted and if it wasn't for Calista standing in the way, she was pretty sure he'd have lashed out at Glinther again.

"Go home." He clearly had the brains to not argue with her, just whirled around and stormed off.

"Well, that was fun. What's next?" Raven sarcastically said; drawing her gaze to his to find that he had an amused expression on his face. Then again, so did the kid actually.

"Did you really need to say that?"

"Yes. Yes I did." He grinned and she rolled her eyes, and took off back to camp.

"Why did you say that?" She heard the kid ask.

"Because I can." She heard the confidence and laughter in Raven's voice and was so tempted to smack him for it; but she knew if she did then that would cause people to talk as to why she would let that simple remark get to her. And she really couldn't be bothered with that shit. They all fell into silence and soon emerged into the camp. An old woman let out a frantic squeal and dived on the kid, who couldn't really say much as his face was mashed up against her chest. Calista left them to hug it out, following Glinther to his hut with Raven hot on her tail. They walked inside, and it didn't house much. The living quarters held a largish wooden frame, with slats of wood stuffed with fallen leaves and moss for padding which was clearly what they sat on. Walls were mud entwined with glittering magic. Kitchen was sparse; a divider was made of dense mud with thick bamboo sticks sticking out the ends by a scant few centimetres. It was enough to hurt if you didn't pay attention to where you were walking. Sleeping quarters sat at the back of the hut, both were made up of moss and covered in tarps. A small walkway past that was where they hung what few clothes they possessed. Very little, but it was all they had. As well as the fact that they didn't require much, they were happy majority of the time living off the land and being simple, content Marbilians.

"What makes you so sure Veraos was the one who made that mine collapse?" Glinther asked over his shoulder whilst rummaging through some things hidden from view.

"Grebynar told me he had seen Veraos take a pick axe and swing for the posts," Raven said.

"The kid admitted that to you?" Glinther turned to look at him.

"Yes. Figured he could trust me."

"Fair enough then. So he admitted it to you and then told us, but the question is why would Veraos do that? We were all part of a team."

"Guess he was fed up of you being in charge," Calista muttered and moved to the window, looking out into the camp and watched as people scuttled about doing their own thing. If he didn't mention his leg being axed off, she wasn't going to say anything about it.

"But it was a nomination. It wasn't my fault he wasn't accepted."

"We know that. But sometimes people don't take it as well as others," Raven replied.

"Look, we don't have time to worry over why he did what he did. Where is the spare hut?" Calista said. But didn't look back at them, continued to watch the campers.

"Outside; turn left, it's the last one on the right, set into the woods."

"Come on, Raven."

"Thanks, Glinther," the male said as he followed her outside. They headed in the direction Glinther had told them and five minutes later found the hut. And sure enough it was secluded from the others. Half in and half out of the forest. Exactly as she liked it. They strolled through the door, and it was set out the exact same as Glinther's. Apart from the beds; they were on slightly raised stilts, just enough space to slide her axe and swords under.

"How long are we staying here for?" Raven slapped the raised straw platform that was their seat, and bugs of all sizes and colours ran out whilst squealing their distress but they paid no attention to that. She took note that Raven didn't so much as blink at the different bugs as they disappeared from sight. Calista refocused and soon cast a spell that sent every other single unwanted thing in the hut scattering for their lives. Mounds of bright and dark bugs scurried from crevices and holes and ran outside. Not to mention followed by a ball of dust that had meshed together.

"Until morning. I know it was before dawn we woke up; but if I were you, I'd sleep now. Tomorrow there will be no rest, not for a long time."

"Why?"

"Because we need to get to Dragon Hill as soon as possible."

"How long will it take us to get there?"

"Most of the day; and then we have to get through the gates."

"Gates?"

"Huge mystical bone gates guard entry way into the Hill. Behind them are guards literally all the time. You'll see what I mean once we get there."

"OK. So any chance of some food?"

"Oh, you wily human. Hungry?" She smirked at him and he stalked right up to her and got in her face. Ever the one to not back down and damn if that didn't impress her. Not that she'd openly admit it to anyone though.

"Yes."

"And what makes you so sure I'll feed you?"

"I'm useful to you. You also like the fact I'm here with you and that I don't back down easily. Plus, if Lexis got wind of the way you treat me, then she'd be worse on you than your enemies and well you know it."

"Sure. I can also make you disappear quicker than you can say fuck me sideways." She stared at him. She wasn't one to back down either. Actually, she never had, or would. But she had to give the man credit, he didn't back down from her either. And that made a nice change.

"Yeah, but she's made an impression on you so you know you won't."

"How the hell have you figured me out already?"

"It's a skill I have. I can analyse anyone and figure them out within minutes of meeting them."

"Never heard of humans being able to do that."

"I've done it ever since I was a kid so it's pretty much like second nature to me now." He turned away from her and leant against the ledge that framed a window, clearly not wanting to talk about it.

"Are you really sure you're fully human?"

"Has there ever been an instance of people from here having intercourse with humans and producing offspring?" She leant against the wall next to him.

"Not to my recollection, no. But we can also bring it up with the Dragon Lords."

"How would they know?"

"They'd find a way to see what else is coursing through your veins. Just be warned, do not let a boy called Murfy touch you."

"Why?"

"He can see into your memories, worst fears and such and use them against you."

"But if he's a boy, how can he know what to do?"

"He's also six thousand years old. He has the height, mental state and temperament of a four-year-old. Only Gélio, his dragon mate Nyhkohl, and I are immune."

"Good to know. So will this Gélio be able to let me know if I'm wholly human or if I'm something else?"

"He very well should be able to. Now, come on, everyone is gathering around for the big feast."

"Big feast?" He turned sharp eyes to her, a confused expression on his face.

"Everyone gathers around every second or third night in front of a huge bonfire, cooking meats and such. And just have a good time basically."

"Like a huge BBQ."

"Exactly. Let's go. You are hungry after all." Raven clearly didn't complain, he all but ran out of the door. She wasn't surprised, considering they both heard his stomach growl with the anticipation of food. She followed at a more pleasurable pace and shut the door behind her. All his stuff was in there; her weapons still clung to her back and hip. There was no way in hell she was leaving them behind.

"Raven!" He turned his head at his name being called and Grebynar motioned him over to where he stood with the woman from earlier who was no doubt his grandmother and a large burly green Marbilian male who protectively had his arm around the woman.

"Hey, Grebynar." He high fived the kid, who let out a laugh and introduced him to his grandparents.

"So you're the human who managed to calm down my grandson?" the male asked.

"Just about. He's quite stubborn."

"Is it true, what he said? That Veraos was the culprit?"

"Afraid so."

"What the hell is his problem?"

"I think it was because he was fed up of Glinther being in charge and wanted to take over." Raven glanced over his shoulder and found Calista almost immediately. She was now sitting on a large rock, grinding a sand stone against her axe, sharpening the already impossibly sharp blade.

"What's going on between you two?" the male asked, clearly having followed his line of sight.

"Lurvvvvv." Grebynar laughed and ducked as Raven went to swat the side of his head.

"I seriously doubt that. Calista has never, ever been with someone. Not for as long as I've known her anyway," the woman said, her voice soft. This was weird considering what she actually was.

"How long have you known her?" Raven looked at her straight in the eyes, no point in not. He looked Calista in the eyes and why would it be any different from anyone else?

"Since before I was a mere twinkle in my mother's eyes."

"That's a long time," Grebynar said. Not being cheeky, just stating fact.

"Yes, it is. So I know what I am on about. I've never, ever seen her with a male. Apart from Skyri or/and Draylan. But that's because ninety-nine percent of the time, they work on cases together. Everyone knows its strict business and professionalism between them." He turned at a startled scream and saw that a woman had collided with the blade that hung precariously across Calista's lap. What was she even doing that close? But he took one look at Calista's face and saw she had already dismissed the woman as others flocked around her to bandage up the wound that she'd caused herself. In fact, Calista just grabbed a piece of rag and wiped the blood off the weapon before carrying on with what she was doing.

"So how come you're actually here then? I've never heard of a human in Mystic Being," Grebynar's granddad asked, which made Raven turn back to look at him.

"My best friend, Luke, his sister is the woman who often visits with Calista from 'normal Earth'. Luke and I haven't seen Lexis in around about five years, and we had to have a well needed rest. So, we came to see her, and one thing led to another and we're here now," he answered. He wasn't going to go into full detail about it. He wasn't that crazy. Sometimes, it was best to give as little information out as possible. Besides, he didn't really know them. Even those he did know he kept at arm's length. And with Luke, he kept him at wrist length, the only one to ever get close enough.

"No more talking of this boring stuff, let's go eat," Grebynar butted in and pushed his laughing elder over to a place so they could join in with the food and music. Clearly it was the same here as in 'normal Earth' — growing lads loved to eat!

"That boy really has no idea of the dangers lurking in this forest," the male muttered, watching his grandson and wife laugh together as they piled plates high with food of all colours and bickered between themselves.

"I think he's getting the idea," Raven looked at the burly male.

"What makes you say that?"

"You should have seen him at the mines. He had a wild-eyed, crazy look. He was ready to do damage but I stepped in and managed to calm him down. Has he always had a short temper?"

"No, never. The voice of reason. He was always the calm one."

"Not now he doesn't. He's growing up, and his temper is getting quite short. If he doesn't learn to control it now, he won't when he's older and that could be dangerous."

"Yeah, you're right, that wouldn't be good at all." They both turned as someone shouted out more food was ready. Typical men they were. When either food or sex were concerned, everything else didn't matter, and because sex wasn't available, they settled for filling their stomachs. They quickly grabbed as much food as their hands would allow, took a place on the floor and promptly starting filling their mouths with sweet, deliciously hot food before entertaining Raven with untold stories of Grebynar growing up and the mischief he caused with his unruly friends.

Before everyone realised it, due to the fun and laughter that had taken place, the night had flown by and everyone should very well head to bed as the sun had long since set. Torches had been lit and placed precariously around the camp. But the main light was from the huge bonfire which still blazed brilliantly. As Calista stood up, she sent a spell to the fire sending it roaring into the air in a fierce blaze, which got everyone to quickly turned their attention to her.

"To bed." That was all she said before tiny Marbilian children let out yawns and sleepily rubbed eyes whilst complaining of not being sleepy. Teenagers grumbled but knew not to argue and parents gathered their children for a well-deserved rest. She bade everyone goodnight, and they all left to head into their own little homes, all without proper argument.

Leaving her to extinguish the fires of which she did with minimal effort. A single sweep of her hand and the lights winked out and once the lights had gone out, the whole place plunged into avid darkness. An entirely different world met their eyes. She watched Raven as he looked around. All around them, everything began to glow softly with a warm inner light. The moonlight was rich and powerful as it shone through the treetops to caress their skin like a lover's touch. Huts soon had lights extinguished as families settled in for sleep. Without another word, she turned and headed to the hut she would be sharing with Raven, who was one step behind her, knowing to keep his distance from her weapons least he be cut in half. They quickly reached their temporary sleeping quarters and rushed inside. She put her hand out and fire shot from her fingers to glide along the floor, stopping in different places until they all had a spot, then grew bigger, moulding into lit candles. The duo quickly got prepared for sleep, not at all thinking of modesty or what have you and once ready, Calista made two single chunky mattresses appear. With a heavy-duty duvet and plush pillows. Raven didn't utter a word, just crawled into one and swiftly fell into a deep sleep. Calista extinguished the candles' warm light, put a protection spell around the hut that would keep anyone out, placed a thick blanket over the window, fundamentally blocking out all light from trekking in from the outside world. She felt her eyes change, making the darkness fade until all objects inside were a darker shade of black. Thus making it a lot easier for her to navigate around without banging into anything. She moved over to her mattress, took her weapons off that she'd forgotten still rode her body, placing them all on the floor within easy reach of her and climbed into bed. Pulling the duvet up to her chin, she rolled onto her side, facing Raven. She still didn't trust anyone behind her back. Twenty thousand years of sleeping on her own, it wasn't something you could overcome in the blink of an eye. Before she knew it, sleep crept in swiftly and claimed her. Not that she complained.

Chapter Seventeen

Noises outside woke Raven from his deep, comfortable sleep. He blinked a few times and sat up. Candles gleamed in warm brightness, creating fantastical shadows up the walls that looked like they were dancing. Looking around, he didn't see Calista but before he could call for her, the door opened and she strolled in; a bowl of steaming hot food in her hand which she held out to him, along with a spoon.

"Eat, as I'm not sure when you'll be able to eat again." He didn't argue, just dug in. The food looked like porridge, tasted like porridge but was lime green.

"What is this?" He shoved another load into his mouth. The heat soaking into his body, instantly warming him up and the aftertaste was amazing as well. It was crisp hot apple, like you'd find in a hot apple pie!

"Gleynaryoneamarnytyme."

"What the hell is that?" He didn't even want to comprehend trying to pronounce it.

"You're more known to call it porridge."

"Porridge isn't green," he pointed out.

"Ah, that's because there is an ingredient added which makes it that colour."

"Nothing bad is it?"

"No."

"What is it?" He looked up, but she'd already turned away. He noticed she was dressed too. Which was a shame; he'd have loved to have seen her flesh again like last night. Even if it was only a quick peek, but it was enough for him to know she was perfect. Peachy white skin that begged him to touch it. Ample curves in all the right places. A generous arse! He mentally shook his head before his thoughts turned naughty and finished off the food.

"It's proteins from plants which are actually good for the body. Don't ask what, I have no idea. I didn't pay attention to that."

"What, schooled were you?" He shoved more of the food into his mouth, thankful for the hot and surprisingly delicious meal.

"No. I already knew things. You'll soon realise that. Anyway, we need to go. We've got a lot to accomplish in the short time we've got. But you also learn along the way." She left, all without a backward glance. He looked down to his food and realised it was all gone and then he felt all warm inside. Was that the secret ingredient? A warming agent or something? Either which way, he was grateful and so was his belly at being full. He put the bowl on the bed next to him, and proceeded to get dressed. Only, he couldn't find his things. He walked to the door and peeked outside. Calista was nowhere in sight, but then he couldn't really see in the dark. He shut the door and looked around. Soon found his bag; it was at the back of the hut, nestled on a table next to Calista's axe. Why the hell had she left her axe? But then again, she was just as deadly without it, and he knew she'd be back. Putting on fresh clothes, he put the old ones in his bag. Just as he was tucking the last of his items inside, the door opened, just a slight whisper of wind but it was enough to catch his ears. He glanced over his shoulder and leapt out the way. Just in the nick of time. An almighty axe went crashing into the table, embedding itself a good inch or so deep into the wood! It even sliced through the handle of Calista's own weapon. Ooh, she was going to be so pissed off when she found out.

"What the fuck!" he stammered out, watching the crazed thing in front of him as it tried to free the blade from the table. It was grotesque. Huge gnarly black horns covered its black, bald head. Serrated teeth held home in a mouth that was lipless. A black serpentine tongue darting out now and again. Body was big. It must have stood at least seven feet tall, but due to the height of the hut, it had to bend over slightly. Legs were muscular and all that brawn and height was held up on feet which strangely reminded Raven of velociraptor's feet, which also included the huge claws that dug into the floor that he knew would easily gut a man with ease with a well-placed strike. He moved away, hoping he'd reach the now closed door, but then had to duck again as the beast's thick claws on the end of an exceedingly long arm lashed around and caught his cheek. Hot, blistering pain seared over his face, but he refused to cower. He darted to the side as the beast swung the axe that he'd finally managed to get free when it realised that Raven didn't go down screaming from the pain. That was when the door exploded inwards. The shards flying at the thing. Raven, luckily was out of firing range. Damn good thing he moved when he had otherwise he'd be a porcupine with the shards of wood stuck in him. He glanced over at the beast and darted to the side again just as the axe embedded itself into the wall he was just standing in front of. Did the thing ever quit? He was suddenly grabbed by the back of his shirt and hurled outside. He landed on his arse and that was when Calista strolled past, and disappeared inside. He turned around slightly on the floor and Marbilians of all shapes, sizes and colours were peering out of their homes at the commotion, only to quickly dart back inside as a high-pitched, horrified scream erupted from inside the hut. Raven clambered to his feet and felt something wet hit his hand. Glancing down, he saw it was blood. Oh right, he had a face wound. Looking around for something to put against his face, he couldn't find anything. No way was he using a bloody leaf! And God knows there were enough of them around. Ignoring the wound, he peeked inside but couldn't see anything. But he heard screeches and hard thuds of flesh hitting flesh. He moved back from the entryway in just the nick of time. The beast flew out, skin hanging from it in places. Sickly, slightly translucent yellow blood leaked from wounds. Some of the claws were missing, as were some of its teeth. Calista stepped out of the darkness, ripe fury rippling off her which made her eyes glow in shocking brightness. Her face was emotionless. Blood coated her in a filmy yellow that had already dried slightly in places. She also had a few wounds herself from where the creature had tried to defend itself. She lashed out against the beast, and it cried out as a large slash opened it up. What fell out made Raven gawk. It was a friggin' heart that was at least four times the size of a human's and with a good nine chambers in it! The lungs on either side were even bigger! It was also a gross lemon yellow with horrendous green veins running through it. The organs gushed to the floor in a sickly splat. The beast howled and bent over, trying to push its organs back inside but failed miserably. They were too sloppy and slipped through its claws. It toppled backwards onto its ass, a stunned expression on its face.

"Failed?" It said in a coarse voice that gyrated through Raven's bones like nails down a chalkboard.

"Unsuccessful," Calista said, magic burning in her hands. Creating a beautiful rich cerulean flame that she sent flying at the beast. Its screams ripping through the air, as the rich smell of burning flesh soared upwards along with the flames. She turned back to Raven and her eyes latched on to his face, or more aptly his wound.

"What happened?"

"He hit me. And I think some of it might have been from some of the shards off the door that came hurtling in as you kicked it open." He didn't sound angry. Just stating fact.

"OK. Want it gone?"

"Yeah." He didn't move as she put her hand on the wound. It hurt as it was raw and itchy from dirt and debris from where he had landed on the floor. Warmth swept inside of him and the irritation and such vanished as she moved her hand away.

"All gone?" He nodded and she disappeared back inside the hut and he followed. But due to his useless human eyes he couldn't see fuck all in front of him. A hand on his chest pushed him backwards and he complied. Calista walked out of the darkness, her weapons back in their rightful places on her. Looking very much like the vicious, beautifully dangerous assassin she was.

"What happened to the axe handle?"

"It's back in place," she said, handing him his weapons and backpack.

"I take it we are leaving now then?"

"Yes. As I said yesterday, we have a long way to go yet before we arrive at Fire Mountain so we need to get moving as much as possible. More miles we cover the better."

"Understandable. Who knows we are leaving?" He shrugged his backpack into place and followed her, the moonlight aiding his travels.

"Glinther knows. He didn't have much choice when I went banging on his door."

"Must have been a nice wakeup call for him," he snickered and fell into pace besides her, his long legs easily keeping up with her own lengthy legged stride.

"Wouldn't care if it wasn't," she muttered and they strode into the dense forest, leaving the camps behind them just as the first rays of dawn crept over the sky. Why the hell did the nights and such seem to fly by here? Or was it because they'd slept so much that the time had passed much quicker? Either way, it was shit.

Midday

Calista sauntered through the shrubberies and walked into a huge private enclosure of bushes that had enormous multi-coloured roses in it, as well as the trees which also had the plants climbing up the thick trunks. Brilliant flashes of ultraviolet purples, reds, greens, yellows, cobalt blues and different shades of sun orange. Beautiful colours that tried to outshine each other. Stunning vast quantities of them scattered around. But it was only those types of flowers and nothing else. The ground was pretty much untouched by creatures apart from thick moss and other typical forestry coating the wonky floor. There were occasional disturbances of jutting roots that also blended in with the floor because of the moss covering it, but you could make it out, due to the fact they were bumpy and sticking out at weird angles. She strode through with Raven hot on her trail, and the moss and such actually parted so they touched dirt not moss. Roots sunk back into the ground to avoid being touched. They walked through, and about halfway, she caught the sound of wings fluttering. She stopped and looked around, her eyes scanning the area. She soon found the source. Tiny little Pooka's were pirouetting in and out of the flowers, creating magic in making the flowers bloom. Downside, they were extremely poisonous. Both the Pooka's and flowers.

"What you stop for?" Raven's voice jarred her, causing her to turn her head and look at him.

"Do not touch the roses or the things inside them. They're poisonous and will kill you quicker than you can say *fuck me sideways*."

"Look, fairies!" Raven pointed out, finally just catching sight of them. And of course that was the wrong thing to say. All of them froze and turned to look at them, each 'fairy' having a mask of fury riding its face, eyes blazing.

"We is not fairies! We is Pooka's!" a brilliantly bright leaf-green one said, fluttering out of the rose it was sitting in and flew right up into Raven's face. Its angry little face all squished up.

"Back off." Calista placed her hand between them and the Pooka flew backwards so as not to make contact with Calista's palm.

"We means you no harm, Miss Calista. But this inferior being must realise we is Pooka's, not silly pesky fairies." Its voice was high and pitched, almost as bad as nails grating down a blackboard.

"Good, now back away from the human." She didn't so much as blink.

"Human? Whats is a human?" A vibrant pink one flew up towards them, wings beating furiously to reach its destination in record time.

"That is a human." She pointed to Raven.

"Cans I touch it?" She reached out, pink claws curling eagerly.

"No, off limits!"

"Buts humans are myths. I wants to see if its reals."

"You can see him standing right in front of you so obviously he is real." She rolled her eyes at Raven and he barely kept the smile off his face.

"One touch?"

"No."

"Yes, Miss Calista." Utmost disappointment spread over her features and the two Pooka's flew back to their flowers, effectively leaving them alone.

"Bloody things," she muttered.

"Miss Calista, mights you have the Pooka's Cheeries?" a lavender one called out.

"Not with me, Pook. Next time."

"Okays." The tiny Pooka flew off.

"What are Pooka's Cheeries?" Raven asked, turning her gaze to his.

"Pooka's Cheeries are small balls. You're more to think of them as marbles. But inside, they're full of poison that only Pooka's can eat. Hence why they're called Pooka's Cheeries."

"Why though? Does it make them joyful?"

"Very. It's like an aphrodisiac for them." She put her hand on his shoulder, turned him around and pushed him ahead of her, not wanting to stay here any longer, she had the kids to rescue after all.

Chapter Eighteen

Clearing the woods that housed the Pooka's and their deadly flowers, Raven and Calista strode forward with purpose. It wasn't every day you got to walk miles and miles through uninterrupted woodland and it made a nice change from the haggard dry desert or the concrete cities he was used to. They strode through thick shrubbery, not a word spoken between them. But he was fine with the silence. It suited him. He wasn't a big talker anyway. They must have walked a good mile or so, it was hard to tell as they were zigzagging, but they soon came across bushes soaked with red.

"What are these?" He turned his head to look at Calista, who stepped forward and ran her hand on some of the leaves, and they parted on a whisper. Like they were thanking her magically for stroking them. Like a caress maybe?

"They're Carraeach Someraos."

"And that means?"

"Bush that bleeds." He burst out laughing. He couldn't help it and it was the fact she'd said it with such a straight face.

"Who came up with that?" he asked through bouts of laughter, before finally gaining controlling of himself again.

"I don't know. Someone stupid obviously. But it's effective. Don't touch it."

"Why, what happens?" He immediately sobered up.

"It sucks majority of the blood out of your system; leaving you a virtually hollowed-out carcass."

"But I don't see any bodies around from that happening." He looked around, and there was fuck all.

"That's because the Carraeaos's eat them."

"The what?"

"Carraeaos's eat them. They're little blood demons that are sitting under the leaves waiting on unsuspecting prey. Once caught in the thorns of these plants, you're dead. No ifs, no buts. You're dead. End of. Then it's dinner time for them."

"But you touched them."

"Immune." She grinned in an evil way at him and he rolled his eyes but swiftly followed her through them. Just as they'd passed them, the massive things snapped back into place. Rustling as though in irritation. Clearly angered at not having nourishment. But then he watched as this deer-type creature that was bioluminescent green with black hooves and swirling green eyes strode into the plants and let out a bleated scream as the bushes swarmed it. The blood quickly drained from the creature, its eyes rolled back in its head and it toppled to the floor, dead. He saw small black bodies scramble down the plants and attack the carcass in merriment, literally crawling under the skin and ripping through the flesh and bone, devouring it. Turning back the way they came, he saw Calista was a small distance ahead so rushed to catch up. Once he'd caught up, they strolled through another small collection of normal, safe bushes. They burst out the other side and the forestry stopped. Just stopped. Like it had been intentionally set in that way. Just ahead of them was a lusciously thick grass-covered hill that the pair went over. At the top sat a cluster of rich, vibrantly thick trunked healthy trees with huge leaves soaring and upturned to the blazing overhead sun soaking in its rays. Bushes curled around the bottom of the trunks, with beautiful exotic flowers blooming in full. Walking through them, rich exotic smells assailed their senses, that Raven had the suspicion that if he bottled those fragrances, woman in 'Normal Earth' would pay literally thousands of pounds to get it. And here he was getting it for free, lucky bastard he was. Soon the shrubbery cleared, leaving a blank dirt floor about twenty feet wide which stretched each way as far as the eye could see. Directly opposite them, Raven's eyes widened. Two huge opalescent gates stood tall and proud, each crafted with bones that sizzled in the light from burnished magic and the sun's hot rays. Two pillars of ten feet thick, solid marble kept the gates upright and in place and stood at least sixty feet high. The skulls of two dragons sat on top of them, mouths semi open showing the gleaming teeth that sparkled in the light, eyes completely blank, staring straight ahead at nothing. Behind the gates sat two guardian dragons. Both as still as statues and in full battle gear. Bone helmets adorned their already scared, tough skulls. Muzzle and a small section of their necks remained free for help in a battle. Both had luminous blood red eyes which gleamed fiercely from the hollow shadows of their helmets. Huge wings lay folded back securely against their muscular, battle-honed bodies. Thick legs supported their weight with ease. Chunky claws a horrendous eight inches long. Past the terrifying beasts, the floor was just dirt. All life cleared away from innumerable feet and other things travelling over it from countless millennia. He followed her to the gate, the sense of being watched beating down on his back. The feel of a thousand eyes watching his every move. They stopped before the gates and the dragons moved to block entryway; side by side. Unmoveable. They towered over him and Calista. Easily reaching a good twenty-five to thirty feet high each and an impressive fifteen to twenty feet long.

"Leave. This is a private sanctum only," one said, its voice deep and gravelly and it stared at them with intense red eyes.

"No. I'm here to see Gélio."

"And why would Gélio want to see you?" Its eyes narrowed as it looked down at them.

"Because I'm entitled to see him. More so when he asks me to come here personally."

"Name?"

"Calista."

"Oh, shit. Sorry, Miss Calista. We did indeed get informed by Gélio himself that we were to expect you. Who is that with you?"

"His name is Raven. Personal as to why he is with me. Just let me through before Gélio gets anymore impatient." She threw her hands out and the magic hissed and recoiled. Great serpentine looking tendrils of the stuff. Recoiling up and over the wall that stood next to the marble pillars. The gates burst open, swinging soundlessly as though welcoming them. The two dragons stepped back into their place, allowing them passageway. Walking past, Raven kept his gaze forward, not wanting to draw attention to himself. Winding past them, the gates slid shut, effectively sealing them in. He braved a look over his shoulder, but the dragons paid him no attention whatsoever. He faced forward again and they made a sharp right turn. The walls were extravagantly tall, which shielded you from the harsh rays of the vibrant sunlight, so fire was placed strategically in small holes in the walls along the way, about every two feet or so. It was roughly two hundred feet high and one hundred and fifty feet wide. Clearly wide enough for two dragons to walk side by side, if they didn't mind brushing up against each other now and again. They must have walked a good one hundred feet, made another sharp right turn but the walls ahead were no longer smooth. These had deep gashes marring the stone. Evidently, they were claw marks, as if something huge had tried to escape. The walls held huge holes, sealed with ridiculously powerful magic; even Raven could feel the vibrant hum of it. But what they housed freaked him out. Psychotic dragons. All wearing the equivalent of a dragon straight jacket. In which were bones from dead dragons entwined with magic placed over their back and down their sides, sealing their wings firmly against their sides. Claws were in a translucent liquid. A desharpener, if you could call it that. Mystical locks wrapped around their legs, like chains but of smoke, essentially keeping them in place and clearly making escape totally impossible. The smoke disappeared into the rock, so they wouldn't break it off. A single smoke ring dangled beneath the cells, each with a name to identify who was who, but not written in English. Dragon language maybe? Raven looked around and there had to be dozens of these cells, each full. And he noticed each one was looking at him and Calista, eyes crazed, mouths open in gruesome grins dripping with saliva. A huge gold and bronze dragon sat locked up to their left, head tilted to the side, gaze fixated on them. Crazy eyes taking on a sickening gleam, like it was hungry for their flesh and it was disgusting.

"Calista, back so soon," it hissed loudly at them, its forked tongue glided over its lips in a sinister grin. She blanked him. Raven knew to keep quiet, so said nothing. The dragon danced from side to side, more of a sway as it opened its giant jaws and sniggered like a maniac as its eyes gleamed with total neurosis as it watched them. Calista put her hand on Raven's shoulder and ushered him forward and he had no choice but to obey. About two hundred yards down, the cells had finally stopped and they made a sharp left turn. The walls were once again solid, but had many deep indentations. Almost as if something had tried to escape and had failed. Ragged marks scored the floor too, some as deep as two to three feet! Raven kept his gaze half on the floor, half ahead so not to stumble in the gouges that in some places were longer that he bloody was and deep enough that he could hide in it and not be seen easily. The floor soon glided upwards. He felt rich swirling air hit his face and looked up properly, just as the walls stopped. Ahead of them, in wide vibrant hues of green, were rolling hills as far as the eye could see intermingled with trees and bushes with huge fluorescent flowers. Decorated with vast shapes, sizes and vast stunningly bright colours that glistened in the sunlight, were dragons. Lots of them. All in groups. Laughing, joking and just soaking up the sun's rays, or just laughing as baby dragons bounced around with each other. Raven looked at Calista and she looked at him.

"What?"

"So this is Dragon Hill then."

"Yes. But don't let the laughter and such fool you. They'd sooner eat you than pay attention to what you have to say. They don't trust anyone but dragons and even then some of them are jittery. With the exemption of the Dragon Lords."

"Dragon Lords?"

"Up there on that big hill. See the pillars?" He followed to where she was pointing and to the west of their position, seated high above everyone else, which would give them a full view of everything that was under their rule, were the Dragon Lords. He couldn't really make them out, but the pillars were colossal gothic masterpieces of white that glowed passionately in the light. And of course their huge forms in flashes of colour, but that was all he could make out although he wasn't going to try, it'd just give him a headache from straining and to be fair, he really couldn't be bothered dealing with that shit right now. All he knew was guaranteed was that they'd be big mother fuckers!

"Come on. Let's get this over with." He followed her down a wide staircase, well, slope really. Didn't have steps. Once they reached the ground floor, every single dragon stopped what they were doing and turned to face them and Raven had never felt so tiny in his life. Or uncertain. He dared a quick glance to Calista and she didn't seem fazed at all. In fact she started walking forward. The silence was deafening but he knew they were curious as to why they were on their land. So he took all emotion off his face, buried the uncertainty plus everything else deep like he was so good at doing and followed Calista.

Calista refused to be intimidated by their stares and moved forward. Why should she? When she knew, and so did they, that she could kill them quicker than they could her? God, she loved being powerful. Her long legs quickly ate up ground and she noticed Raven managed to keep up easily enough with her. They moved past vast groups of dragons, many of which moved babies out of line of fire, shielding their children from view. What did she want with the whelps anyhow? She had sufficient troubles and such of her own. But that is also what they told their children if they misbehaved. That Calista would come and get them. Quickly eating up the distance between them and the Dragon Lords, it still took at least half an hour to cross to them. And by that time, the sun was setting to their east, a beautiful collection of colours that shone brilliantly on the open ocean and small scattered islands that was the view. And vibrant colours streamed across the sky. Drawing to a halt, magic pulsed under her feet. Raven bounced into her but quickly regained his footing.

"Don't say a word. Let me do all of the talking, OK?"

"Most unquestionably. You know who we're dealing with here; I haven't got a bloody inkling."

"Of course." She glanced at him over her shoulder and saw the slight grin on his face, probably trying to impress her using big fancy words. So why the fuck was it working? Rolling her eyes, she moved forward and didn't stop again until she stood in front of the Dragon Lords. Now that they were closer, Raven could see what the pillars were. They were indeed huge gothic masterpieces of stark white marble laced over with webs that glowed avidly in an array of all colours, literally pulsing with intensity, but you could see that from afar. Closer, it was breathtakingly beautiful. Entwined magic that took on the impression of a dragon glided around and through the marble. As if it was that that kept it all in place. Between each pillar that was a good five feet wide and two feet thick, was a single seat. Seven of them in total. And atop those seated comfortably, were seven magnificent dragons. All of which had serious expressions on their faces and of which were no doubt highly dangerous. Hence, why they were Dragon Lords. In the heart of their semi-circle, in a pit that was five feet wide, ten feet long and six feet deep were boisterous burning flames of green, blue, red and yellow white which were creating menacing shadows behind the lords, as well as making their eyes and expressions even more sinister than they already were. The lords were on one side, they stood on the other, but he wasn't complaining, he was warm from the flames, so he was happy. He'd leave Calista to the talking as he wholeheartedly stood on what he said before. She knew what was what and he didn't have a bloody clue. And he'd only talk when directly spoken to.

"Calista." The biggest, badest motherfucker there looked at her.

"Gélio." She looked him directly in the eyes. They knew she wasn't one to look away, no matter who she was looking at. But for Gélio, she respected him, she didn't respect the others. And she knew there and then that she'd annoyed them; she hadn't put 'Lord' in front of his name. Fuck 'em! She wasn't here to play games. But she was the only one who was able to get away with it, considering they knew her wrath as she'd previously killed a lord when he had gone rogue against them all, no one else had been able to stop him, and she'd been called in. It had taken her less than a day to find and eradicate him from the world. Gélio stared at her through beautiful liquidescent emerald green eyes that seemed to see right through her. He was huge! Jet black in colour. Thick battle-scarred velveteen green spines with black veins carved their way sharply down his spine and tail. Chunks and scales were missing from his big, muscle-clad body —

obviously he was a dirty fighter. He was the tallest and most dangerous dragon to ever live. Standing at a monstrous seventy feet high, and a scary fifty feet long, he was a sight to behold. And one whom you did not fuck with. He was the Big Dragon Lord. Supreme ruler above all else. And because he'd held his place for so long, it was pretty obvious he'd seen and done a lot in that time and could definitely stand his own.

"Why are you here, Calista?" a crimson dragon enquired; her aurora borealis-coloured eyes unblinking.

"To speak to Gélio. Preferably alone."

"And what is that creature behind you?" Bearing in mind she'd never left Mystic Being in all her life, it was obvious why she was curious about who and what Raven was.

"Human. Stays with me."

"Human? That's supposed to be naught but urban legend." Her scales rattled in irritation, much like a rattlesnake's.

"Clearly not. Considering one is standing directly in front of you."

"Does it talk?"

"Lyvia, that is enough questions for today. All of you, leave us," Gélio said, his voice holding no room for argument. They all turned and walked away, not once looking back.

Chapter Nineteen

Once the dragons had left, Raven released the breath he didn't realise he was holding. No wonder his chest had begun to hurt. And he'd thought that it had only been nerves. Clearly bloody not. On the virtually silent exhale, Calista moved her head slightly and turned that beautiful gaze on him.

"Big, huh?"

"I know you warned me, but it's still mad enough at how big they actually are. My brain is having a hard time believing that they are real and not really a figment of my imagination."

"I can hear you, you do realise that?" That deep baritone voice rippled over Raven, sending a stream of goosebumps coursing down his spine and not the good kind either. Raven quit looking at Calista, not that he particularly wanted to and looked up and up, straight into those liquid green pools of Gélio's eyes. His eyes seemed to stare right through him, and that freaked him out. He nodded; he didn't trust himself to say anything. He also knew when to keep his trap shut.

"You know why we're here, Gélio." Calista smoothly took over the attention from the big beast.

"The children."

"Yes. We are going to need you to allow us into the crypt."

"You yes. Him no."

"Why not?" Raven asked.

"Because it is a sacred place. All of our records are in there."

"I promise to not touch. And records?"

"Records of every being to ever live. The Crypters are the ones who keep it in check and up to date."

"What are Crypters?" He turned a questioning gaze to Calista.

"Historians of Mystic Being."

"Oh. I still promise not to touch anything."

"I forbid it," Gélio said, his voice stern, leaving no room for an argument.

"Lay off, Gélio. He won't touch shit. I need one thing and we'll leave. I know exactly where it is in the crypt, so don't worry." Well, it was pretty clear Calista wasn't afraid of Gélio.

"What exactly is it you are after?"

"Blade." Just that one word and Gélio raised himself to his full height and that was even more fucking scary than when he was slouched.

"You can't be serious? The Crypters won't allow you to remove the blade."

"They can't stop me. They have no way of stopping me and you know it."

"What's this blade you're on about?" Raven enquired.

"Blade of Souls."

"What the hell is that?"

"It's a blade made of glass with souls of people it's killed inside."

"Oh, so why do you need it?"

"It'll look good with my collection," she sarcastically retorted.

"I'm serious. What is so special about this blade?"

"It'll temporarily stop the Lava Lady so I can get inside Fire Mountain. Not to mention if you actually stumble across spirits, the blade will protect you. It's the only weapon to be known to hurt a spirit."

"Isn't there another way in?"

"Should be, yes."

"There are numerous passageways into the mountain. It's finding them and getting in without being caught that's the problem," Gélio said, his huge head swinging up to gaze behind them as a thunderous noise hurtled towards them. Raven and Calista looked behind them as so they could see what was making all the racket. What it was couldn't have shocked Raven more, well actually, that was surprising, considering they were standing on Dragon Hill. Bounding towards them was a curvaceous lady dragon with scales a striking shade of fuchsia. Eyes were a shimmering magenta. Large spines danced down her back and tail in shimmering black. Massive striking white teeth lined the thick muzzle, shielding a pink tongue. As she drew nearer, Gélio glanced at them and rolled the one eye facing them then turned to face the female. The female wedged herself next to Gélio, looking very much the part of the Dragon Lord's Lady.

"Now why wasn't I informed that Calista was here?" Its voice was quite high pitched for such a huge creature. Luckily it was also quite pleasing to the ears.

"Because you were too busy somewhere no doubt dancing and singing as usual," Gélio said.

"You love it so don't be such a grouch, Father Time. Calista dear, how are you?" Raven looked at Calista and saw she was smirking a little. Who was this dragon anyway?

"I'm fine, Nyhkohl. I see you haven't changed."

"Clearly not. Someone has to keep Father Time here on his toes." She grinned, her teeth gleaming as she knocked her shoulder playfully into Gélio's side, which of course sounded like a thunder drum. But Raven caught a flash of movement behind them and watched as her tail entwined itself with his, the colour standing out brilliantly against the darkness of his. Clearly she was of great importance to him if he allowed her to do this and not be worried what creatures around them thought.

"And who is this with you? Since when do you have a companion?"

"This is Raven. Remember little Lexis?"

"Sweetest little human I ever did meet. What about her?"

"Raven is her brother's best friend. Refuses to let me go rescue some kidnapped children on my own. Deems it 'too dangerous'." And yes, she did do the air quotes with her fingers.

"Clearly you underestimate Calista's power." Nyhkohl looked at him, her eyes no longer twinkling in merriment but with stone cold zero emotion. And he realised there and then, she might dance and sing as Gélio had said, but she was, as he saw now, clearly in avid control of the playful side and her ruthless commanding side with an ease that still astounded him.

"No, I do not underestimate her. But it can't hurt for me to tag along." He didn't back down.

"And why would you want to tag along? You're nothing but a human. Completely defenceless against pretty much most, if not everything, in this world."

"I can fight, I'm not that helpless," he said. He didn't care that he could be crushed by her foot, he wouldn't back down easily. He never had and never would.

"Nyhkohl, he has the temper and strength of a vampire," Calista butted in.

"But he's human, how is that possible?" Both dragons looked at him then in avid curiosity and Raven turned his gaze to Calista as what she said registered.

"Wait a minute; temper and strength of a vampire?"

"Yes. When I got told about how you found people and the strength in which you muster from it, I dived into your mind as deep as I could go and realised you possess the power and strength of a vampire. But I couldn't muster up enough power in that thirty seconds I scanned you to dive into your past to when you were conceived to find out if your parents had the gene of it."

"You can do that?"

"Yes, I can. Quite easily. I've done it a hell of a lot over my many years. So if I'm able to get enough time for it, then I can dive into your mind and find out what I need and we can get the answers which we need to find out just why you have the strength and temper of the average vampire."

"And how much time will you need to do that?"

"Properly or quickly?"

"Both?"

"Properly can be up to an hour of my mind merged with yours. Quickly, ten minutes, but it will hurt like an absolute motherfucker."

"Erm, do I get to choose?"

"Yes."

"Then properly it is. I don't want it to hurt like a motherfucker."

"And why not?" Nyhkohl asked, drawing both their attention.

"Because if it causes me agony and we get attacked, I'm vulnerable. I don't underestimate the fact that Calista can defend both my arse and hers; but it still would suck!"

"This is very true. The male's pride is such a fragile thing." Nyhkohl laughed and danced away from Gélio as he playfully nipped at her.

"Right, all seriousness aside; I'm going to the crypt and you can't stop me, Gélio. I need that blade. Not to use, but what's inside," Calista said.

"Which blade would that be?" Nyhkohl asked, all laughter leaving her features and becoming the Dragon Lord's High Lady. Deadly and dangerous he didn't doubt her to be.

"The Blade of Souls." Raven looked back and forth between them, then pointedly stared at Nyhkohl as her features literally solidified right before him and her eyes became a glacial magenta.

"Why?" Her voice was hard edged and even Gélio turned to look at her in shock. Clearly it was very rare to see her like this.

"I need it for what is inside. I don't want the souls."

"Calista, you more than anyone else know how dangerous it'll be to open that up."

"Why will it be dangerous?" Raven looked at Calista; he knew she wouldn't lie to him.

"Because the souls that reside in the blade, if they somehow managed to get out, would create utter havoc. More so now than when they were actually alive and resided in bodies. And I really don't have the time to go around recollecting them to put them back."

"Then what exactly is it you need if not the blade?" Raven was slowly losing track of this conversation.

"There is a gem situated inside, just before the souls. I need that."

"Why?"

"I'll explain more when we're in the crypt. We're getting unwanted attention." Gélio and Nyhkohl turned to follow Calista's line of sight as she wasn't paying attention to them and a smile of pure joy lit up Nyhkohl's face.

"Who's that?" Raven nudged Calista in the side.

"That's Murfy. He's Nyhkohl and Gélio's adopted boy. Don't in any means let him touch you or you touch him."

"Why? He looks harmless." And he didn't look scary or whatnot at all. He had to be about the height of a four-year-old. He had the giddy happy-go-lucky laugh of a child without a care in the world. His hair was a gleaming black that glistened in the fading sunlight with hues of vibrant red. As the boy grew closer, Raven could make out his rosy-cheeked complexion and his tantalising green and yellow eyes that literally sparkled in merriment as he dived onto Nyhkohl's face and hugged her as he giggled in happiness.

"He's what we call a Scryer. This means he can dive into your deepest and most private thoughts. He can access your deepest fears, wishes, dreams, etc. When he finds out, he tells either Nyhkohl or Gélio. Luckily, what he sees, he can't remember."

"Does he access your thoughts?"

"No. I'm what's more known as an anti-Scryer."

"What the hell is that?"

"It means she can't be read at all." He turned his head back around to look at Gélio as the dragon looked at him.

"By anyone?"

"Yes, by literally anyone. Which is why she's a powerful ally and best not to be your enemy."

"Now that I can certainly understand." He watched then as Murfy climbed off Nyhkohl's face and padded over to them, pure wonderment on his features as he stared at Raven.

"Calista?" He raised his small arms and she picked him up and that's when the kid started to shake. His eyes rolled back in his head and his small fists clenched at his sides.

"What's wrong with him?" Raven asked, making sure none of him touched the small child.

"It happens now and again. It's a power over-lapse."

"Power over-lapse?"

"Murfy is an extremely powerful Scryer. Sometimes all that power doesn't agree with him."

"But he'll be OK, won't he?" He watched Murfy calm down in a matter of a minute and he sagged in Calista's arms, head on her shoulder trying to catch his breath.

"Yes. He'll be fine."

"Good." He turned away so he didn't see the expressions on their faces.

"Why do you wonder?" Nyhkohl asked, drawing his gaze.

"Don't like seeing kids hurt or anything," he muttered and that was an understatement, which is why he did what he did on 'normal Earth'. And that was when he heard a flapping noise. Glancing skywards, he saw a structure of bones whizzing towards them. He was grabbed by the wrist and pulled into Calista's side. She handed Murfy back to Nyhkohl who tucked him under her wing with a strict command of stay and he noticed the kid didn't so much as argue, just tucked himself deeper into her side.

"What are those things?" Raven asked Calista.

"Skeletal Dragons. Now I need you to be quiet, and follow everything I tell you to, no questions asked or anything, OK?"

"Yeah, sure. Not a problem." She nodded and turned to face Gélio.

"We'll leave you to deal with it."

"Since when do you back down from a fight?"

"Since this isn't my fight. You're Dragon Lord, you protect Dragon Hill." She had him on that one.

"Fine. Go to my left, head down the cliff. The cabin you use is down in its usual place along the stream that eventually merges with the sea. Untouched since the last you used it. Good luck in your quest." He bowed his huge head to them, which they returned.

"And what of the blade?"

"Collect it upon your return," Nyhkohl said.

"Why?"

"Because if Kharge gets a hold of it, then all bets are off."

"She's got a point," Raven pointed out. And before anyone else could say anything, the Skeleton Dragon landed just ahead of them.

"Ah, Gélio, care to stand down as leader and let the rightful one take his place?"

"No chance of that *ever* happening." He turned to face the enemy, blocking them from its sight, which she used as an opportunity to leave and motioned for Raven to keep quiet and to follow her. He followed quietly after Calista. Once they had reached the edge of the cliff, Calista looked back over Raven's shoulder to make sure they weren't being followed, or had gained any unwanted attention. Luckily they hadn't.

"Just follow me and don't make a noise. If they realise there is a cabin down here, they will kill us. No questions asked, and they won't listen to Gélio."

"OK," he muttered. He took a deep breath, looked out over the vast ocean that was amazingly clear with incredible shades of blue and greens intermingled together and not for the first time since he had snuck away and followed Calista he realised he should have stayed behind and waited for her to return. The things he had seen was crazy and quite frankly hard to digest. But he would do as he was trained to do. Move on and deal with it if it arose again. Realising Calista had moved on, he hurried after her. As they strolled down the cliff face thanks to a cutting just wide enough for them to walk side by side comfortably without one of them scraping their arms on the rock face, keeping quiet Raven glanced around, absorbing his surroundings. Which was a force of habit now. He refused to say anything, he didn't want attention brought to them. He walked just behind her, which was easier than beside her considering he was a large bloke, he didn't want anyone near him; not when he realised there were things out there that could bloody well eat him and use his bones as a tooth pick! He was majorly out of his comfort zone, and that was saying something considering what he did for a living. And it quite frankly pissed him off. But that was just his pride maybe? Or because he was realising just how fragile his humanity was? They finally reached the bottom of the stone stairs and rich clean sand greeted them. It was the cleanest he'd ever seen! Which was amazing, considering he'd been to a lot of places all over the world. Well 'Normal Earth'. But then again, this wasn't any ordinary place. Strolling onto it, it crunched under their feet. Walking along the sand that began mixing with a little grass, he glanced up and realised they were keeping close to the cliff side. They rounded the bend just slightly ahead of them and Calista stopped short. Thank God for him paying attention to what he was doing instead of staring at the floor, he didn't collide with her. Glancing past her, his breath left him in a silent rush. In front of them just slightly to the right, hidden partly in shadows and swirling vines of ivy lay a gorgeous log cabin. Even though it was old and clearly well used, it just made it all the more spectacular. He had a secret love of old log cabins. They seemed snug and kind of homely kind of to him. The wood was old and a little bashed here and there. It was made from solid thick trunks from the huge trees interlocking with each other, creating what no doubt was an air-tight cabin. The door blended in perfectly with the rest of it. If he didn't see the slight indentation at the top, he never would have guessed it was the door. Next to the door slightly was an open gap, which he guessed was meant to be a window but it didn't have a pane of glass and the only reason he had seen it was because of the slight gap between some ivy. In front of the cabin, to the side, was a stream of a lush blue. They quickly crossed the sand, waited whilst she opened the door and together they strolled inside. He was shocked by what he saw. It was literally the opposite of the outside. It was that cold inside, Raven could see his breath and goosebumps rode his arms. So weird, considering it was so hot outside. Looking around, there was no furniture or anything, just a big empty space. The wall opposite the door had ragged claw marks down it. Actually, all the walls did. Some as many as six or seven streaks together. What the hell had caused that? Some sort of seven-toed or fingered creature? It was one animal he didn't want to meet that was for sure judging by the deepness and thickness of the grooves. Dust littered the floor, a good inch or so thick and the smell was horrendous. Indicating it hadn't been used in a while.

"We'll stay here tonight," Calista said, rubbing her hands together quickly.

"OK. But what will we sleep on? Or use to warm up?" he enquired. Sure, he was used to harsh conditions, but why sleep in hardship when he had a woman who controlled powerful magic as easily as breathing, and create something comfortable to rest on. He really didn't want to be breathing in dust particles whilst trying to sleep that was for sure. She looked at him and then he heard it. Glancing around, the harsh cackle of magic was in the air. Wind ripped through the cabin then, whistling over the floor and around his body, but it was warm, not cold. He glanced back at her quickly and the magic made her eyes positively glow and her skin cast a healthy sheen but she wasn't paying attention to what she was doing, she was watching him. He watched in awe as the room filled up, until he couldn't see past the end of his nose. And just as quickly as it appeared, it vanished. And he took a step back in sheer wonder. The room had literally transformed. The dust had gone, the smell had been replaced by the rich scent of the ocean that lay just outside this secluded wonder. To their left, a magnificent queen-sized bed draped in plush black silk sheets and huge fluffy pillows called attention near the back of the building. To their right, was a huge fireplace he hadn't noticed before. Next to it was perfectly cut logs to add to the flames when they started to die down. Two high-backed, overstuffed armchairs sat before it, both turned somewhat so the occupants could face each other without getting neck ache and still receive the warm heat from the fire. The walls held old-fashioned gothic holders, each with a burning candle that created fantastical shadows that danced along the floor and walls. The floor was covered in luxurious rugs that he was positive your toes would literally sink into. Even the marks on the walls had vanished. Then he realised one vital thing was missing.

"Erm, Calista... where's the bathroom?" She turned that gorgeous gaze to his again.

"Outside. There is a small fresh water stream that you saw in front of us to the side that bleeds into the ocean. You can go there and use that to freshen up and take care of personal needs."

"Oh, right. OK. Cool. I'll go freshen up, back in a bit." He turned and strolled outside, his bag still slung over his shoulder, full of stuff he'd need. He couldn't wait to freshen up, he felt icky as anything. Not to mention fill up the five water containers he had which should hopefully keep them going on their journey. At least until they got the kids, after that, well they'd figure it out when the time got to it.

Chapter Twenty

She waited until he'd left and the door had closed behind him before she let out the breath she was holding. It rushed out of her mouth and the pressure left her chest. What the bloody hell was wrong with her? She had never, ever reacted this way to a guy before. So what was it about Raven that completely fascinated her? The downside, he was human. So if they did anything, she would have to be very careful. Her strength was legendary after all. The thing that shocked her, was she was ready to lay it all down with him and literally lose control. Not have to hold anything back. And that wasn't like her. Nothing attracted her. She lived day in, day out doing the same shit because that was what she'd been born to do. To protect those who couldn't protect themselves. Then one mental image rushed forward, one she'd actually been thinking about for a while now, not that anyone knew. It was of herself and Raven naked, joined together passionately. She knew instinctively that if it happened, he'd be amazing. He was already astounding at kissing, which she knew first hand. Snapping out of her thoughts, she started up a fire with a simple flick of her wrists, from countless centuries of practice, it was as natural to her as breathing. Then she did something she would never do with anyone else; she moved to the middle of the cabin and faced the wall that only the door and a single window were on. Arms outstretched, she called forth the black magic that coursed through her veins.

"Valerinayrah instrughhu ctashnah." She repeated it twice, magic flaring in her palms. The wall had a film of smoke wash over it, and as it vanished it became a window. She could see out but to look at the cabin, it would literally be the same, no change whatsoever. So of course, Raven would be none the wiser. It was as she had done when she overheard Raven and Luke talking back at the house just after Lexis's change. As it cleared properly, she was greeted by the sight of the fresh water stream that ran through the rocks. It was deep enough that it hid the lower part of the body but not the chest. Not that she was prudish or anything. She didn't have a shy bone in her body. Once the spell had taken hold, everything was in view, as if the 'window' didn't exist. And the breath she had in her lungs exhaled sharply. Raven was waist deep in the stream, the evening sun glistening off his back, catching the water droplets that clung to his skin. She watched, transfixed as he ran his fingers through his hair, his back muscles bunching up together from that simple action. And thanks to that fucking thought which kept on racing through her mind, she wanted nothing more than to run her tongue and hands over him! Her lungs burned for new air but she couldn't seem to catch her breath. And then he turned around and that much-needed breath rushed through her mouth and straight into her lungs, the screaming pressure lifted as though in appreciation. And thanks to her watching Raven, she watched as his head snapped upwards and looked around. No fucking way he had heard her sharp intake. Impossible. His hearing wasn't that advanced. He shrugged, then carried on doing what he was doing and she about managed to keep her tongue in her gob and stopped herself from drooling. His body was gorgeous. Rich, healthy skin coloured by endless hours in the sun stretched taut over rock-hard biceps, shoulders and torso. His stomach had a drooling six pack that she wanted to run her tongue and hands over. His thighs, that she could see through the water, were thick, solid muscle that easily supported his weight. He wasn't like those enthusiasts that you see at shows, etc. He was a normal man who just liked to keep fit and healthy. Well, he'd have to considering what he did for a living as it wouldn't be any good being a slob. It was then she noticed the scars. The main one, it was at least three inches thick and it cut across his body. From his right pectoral about half way across. Almost as if someone had tried cleaving him in half. Much like the one that rode across her stomach. Smaller ones adorned his body thus proving to her he wasn't at all the golden, no troubled man Lexis had told her about. Or maybe that was when she knew him, he'd grown up since then obviously. Or maybe Lexis said that because that was how she wanted to remember him, not some hardened brutal fighter who didn't take shit from anyone and clearly didn't mind getting down and dirty either. Calista narrowed her gaze on Raven, feeling a weird sensation in her lower stomach. It was also one she refused to pay attention to and analyse. And whilst she was mentally beating herself up, Raven had left the stream and now stood in the sunlight fully, water droplets glistening on his skin, and the worst part; they teased her! And her eyes widened at what she was seeing. His legs really were as defined as the rest of him. A light sprinkle of black hair dusted them. His arse was to die for; easily bounce a coin off of it, or better yet, dig her nails in. Then he turned around and she had to catch her jaw before it hit the floor as what she saw shocked her. He was completely bald between his thighs, so she could see everything as clear as day as it wasn't obscured by coarse hair. Even though he wasn't erect, his cock was about the thickness of her wrist, and she knew for a fact that when he got erect he'd be a big one. It was the same golden colour as the rest of him. Was it an all-over tan, or was that his actual skin colour? Whatever it was, he looked yummy enough to eat. And by God did she want to! OK, who was she and what had happened to the level-headed, don't give a shit Calista? It was only a male body. *Raven's body*, that stupid, annoying inner voice of hers muttered, and damn if she didn't agree. As he dried off, she noticed something. How she hadn't noticed them before was beyond her. Raven was tattooed! He had a gorgeous dragon piece on his left thigh that looked as though it would come alive at any moment. A raven bird with a blooded eyeball in its mouth was perched on a collection of skulls on his right thigh. His shoulder blades had skulls with bone mohawks, with sharp tendons sticking out sharply and the mouth open in a scream with dagger sharp teeth dripping in blood. All done in avid colours. Absolutely stunning pieces of art. How did he manage to conceal them? What did he use? And why would you want to cover up that art? How didn't she notice it though? That was the main thought running through her mind. Then she knew how he concealed them. His long-sleeved T-shirts and the jeans. He was a mystery. And she'd get her answer one way or the other, even if it meant burying into his subconsciousness and rummaging around through his memory.

"Valerinayrah instrughhu ctashnah fyrantahrya." She muttered the counter spell and the view of Raven and the surrounding landscape disappeared as the wall became solid again. She mentally shook herself, then made her way to the fireplace and sinking into the soft armchair, the fire's heat soaking into her bones, and she sighed at the warmth. Sitting there in the quiet, she could feel a huge storm brewing, so the sooner the cabin warmed up the better as they'd need to stay warm. Well, Raven would. It would take the temperature to be at least -15 for her to be affected. Hence why it was so easy for her to trudge through the blizzards and not be bothered by it. Clambering to her feet, she changed into a pair of baggyish sweat pants and a tank top. Her feet encased in warm thermal socks. She wandered over to the part of the cabin that was a meagre space, snapping her fingers and in a blinding flash it was taken over by what resembled a kitchen and she reached into a low cupboard and pulled out a small glass tumbler. Reaching into another cupboard, she yanked out a bottle of good old Jack Daniels Whiskey that she put there some hundred or so years ago. Turning around, she opened up a partition in the cabin's wall and thrust the glass out. The chink, chink, chink of falling ice filled the tumbler. She waited until it was about a quarter full, then closed the partition. She soon had it full of the good old Jack Daniels and took a sip, the burn of it travelling down her throat and ended in her stomach. That was one of the things she loved about 'Normal Earth', their different quantities and types of alcohol. Even though it did nothing for her, she liked the taste. It was nowhere near as potent as the things you found here, but hey ho, winners can't be choosers. Taking another swig of her drink, she heard rustling outside and knew Raven was getting close to coming back inside. She headed back to the chairs and sunk down into the cushions. With a simple flick of her wrist and a tiny spell from years of practice, a plush stool appeared in front of her. Swinging her feet up onto it, she sighed happily. Now this was the life. Peace and quiet, a roaring fire and a decent tumbler of JD on the rocks. It was one of the many things she loved about being in this secluded cabin by the sea, no fucker to disturb her and she could almost forget she was one of the very few that stood between good and evil. Thank fuck she wasn't squeamish with the amount she'd seen in her twenty thousand years of life. She really would be fucked if she was! She wiggled her toes whilst she sighed as the fire's heat started to warm up the soles of her feet through her socks and began working its way up her body, relaxing her even more. Nothing beat the tranquil lull of an open roaring fire. The door opened then and a healthy gust of cold ocean air blew inside, causing the flames to wave around but luckily didn't threaten to extinguish them. She looked around the side of the high-backed armchair and saw it was Raven, who had changed into clean clothes and had wet ones dangling from his hand. Glancing up, he looked at her.

"Got anywhere I can hang my clothes? I gave them a quick wash outside." He looked around for somewhere to hang them.

"Lirienedri," she whispered and his clothes became instantly dry.

"Damn, now that is handy!" He grinned as he shoved everything back into his backpack. She just rolled her eyes and turned back around, taking a sip of her drink. The burn of alcohol was a much-needed welcome, it took off the fact she knew what he looked like properly underneath those clothes. Sure, she'd seen him back at the house before they'd left to get here, but that was a quick glimpse, this time it was a full-on stalk/perv. He soon joined her, leaving his bag at the door in case they needed to make a quick getaway. He sank down into the chair and groaned at how good it felt. She noticed he hadn't put his boots back on, just his socks. She watched out of her peripheral vision as he closed his eyes and sighed as the fire's heat sank into his bones and his body relaxed.

"So what time will we be leaving tomorrow?" he asked, not bothering to open his eyes.

"Just after dawn hits. We need to cover as much ground as possible, I'd carry on until I got the kids back home safe, but because I have you with me, we need to make stops."

"So, in other words, I'm a liability?" She heard the anger in his voice and turned her head to look at him.

"Raven, there are things in this world which you can't even begin to comprehend. Many of which would gladly dine on your flesh, whilst you're still alive. I'm just looking out for you. That's all. Plus I don't really think Lexis and Luke would appreciate it if I brought you back to them dead."

"I suppose you have a point there. But I really don't expect you to fight every battle and such for me. I'm a big enough bastard to deal with it myself. If I get too much out of my element then obviously you can help but I am quite capable of dealing with my own battles; I've done it since I was five years old."

"That's the thing, Raven, you are completely out of your element here. I'm the only thing that stands between you and certain death out here in this wildness. I'm not bragging or anything. I know you can take care of yourself, but there are things out here you just won't be able to hold your own against." He didn't say anything else to her then, just continued to stare into the fireplace because he knew she was right. A good half hour passed in what was an actual comfortable silence before she moved. She'd long finished her drink and as she picked the glass up from the floor she glanced over to Raven and very nearly smiled. He had his head on his fist and was sound asleep, feet propped up near hers on the stool she'd made appear. It was clearly obvious he was exhausted from the trek, not to mention everything he had seen and the beings he had encountered. It would be a complete overload. Too much information for his brain to process, but she noticed he was certainly taking it all in stride. She stood up out of the chair and stretched. Muscles screaming and bones cracked from being in one still position for too long. She moved away from the fire and put her empty glass back in the kitchen. Leaning back against the counter, she closed her eyes as she gently massaged her temple as a vicious headache had appeared out of nowhere. She hated the fuckers but she knew it was a sign of she was overtired and had to get much-needed sleep. It was her own fault, as she rushed to get here but because she had to do a pit stop at Jah'nea's because of the plane, not to mention she had everyone else with her, whereas before she could have just disappeared and reappeared at Wineglass Bay within a few seconds, instead of almost thirty hours fucking later! Damn passengers. She couldn't fail those kids. A pair of warm, callused hands suddenly covered hers, forcing her to open her eyes wickedly quick and found herself staring into Raven's, which were full of concern.

"How the hell did you move without me hearing you?" She lowered her hands, forcing him to do the same. It had rarely happened before, so it actually startled her that this human could move that quietly.

"I've always been able to move quietly when I needed to."

"So you thought you'd try it with me?"

"Who better to try it on than the most famous assassin?" He grinned at her.

"Got a point there." She refused to give him the satisfaction of seeing that his grin affected her.

"So what now?" he enquired.

"Get you fed and watered. Then sleep. As it's going to be a long day tomorrow. I'm going to want to at least be half way to the swamp tomorrow."

"How far is the swamp?"

"Around about one hundred and forty miles. And don't worry, I don't expect you to walk the whole way."

"What will I do? Run? Jog?"

"Do you remember that cart thing I made appear in Tasmania to get us to Wineglass Bay that moved with incredible speed and was comfortable for you lot to sit in?"

"Yeah. What about it?"

"I'll sort out a transport kind of like that."

"And what about you?"

"I'll be in it with you, because when we get to the swamp, some parts of it are not just swamp land; parts of it are actually pure acid that no one can survive in. I can, but it'll leave great big, nasty welts on my flesh that'll take a few days or so to heal. And I don't have the time to worry about finding the healing herb I need to get rid of the burns because I have to get those kids back."

"Oh, right." There wasn't really much he could say to that. He walked over to his bag, reached inside, pulled out a bottle and disappeared outside quickly. Rushing to the stream, he put the bottle in, filling it quick and as he headed back in as it was getting damn cold, he took a swig of the ice-cold water. The water was revitalising and the coolest, cleanest he'd ever tasted. If he bottled enough and he took it to 'Normal Earth', he would make an absolute fortune by just how pure it was. He drank about half and recapped it. No point in wasting it, not with the journey they were on. Getting back inside the cabin, he replaced the lid, put it in his bag and let out a jaw-cracking yawn.

"Look, why don't you go and use the bed for some much needed sleep? I'll sleep in the armchair," Calista said, drawing his attention to her.

"Why don't you join me?"

"Because I have never shared a bed with anyone before. Don't particularly want to start it now." He shut the door behind him, effectively shutting the cold out that had crept in with the growing night.

"Ever?" That surprised him. A gorgeous woman like her never having shared a bed? Did that mean just sleeping or was it more than that?

"Only with Skyri, and even then that's if he's at mine late or we're on a mission together, but majority of the time I sleep against the wall."

"Why not now? We're both adults, Calista."

"Because I could become used to you beside me and that would be disastrous."

"How the hell would it be disastrous?"

"Because many people in this world would kill you if they found out we slept in the same bed together. I know we're adults and I know I couldn't actually give an actual fuck what people thought if they did find out, but many would even go to lengths as to kidnap you and torture you for information on me. Try to find out my weaknesses, etc."

"Then why take the armchair if you don't care? I sure as hell don't."

"For your safety."

"My safety? What the hell does my safety have to do with us sharing a god-damn-motherfucking bed for one blasted fucking night?" He got right into her face then. Fuck the pleasantries. He was past caring and he didn't give a fuck what would happen to him for doing it either.

"I'm looking out for you, Raven." She stared right back at him, not backing down. Not that he expected her to. He actually had yet to see her back down from anyone.

"I don't need fucking protecting. I've done it since I was five years old. I've always looked after myself. I don't need you to look after me!!"

"Yes, you do! This world is not like the one you are used to. In yours, there are guns and stuff. Here there is magic so much more powerful than you actually do realise. Beings with strength and powers that can't be comprehended in your world. So don't you dare, not at fucking all say you don't need me to look after you when you know for a fact that I do! I know

328

you can look after yourself, I don't doubt that Raven, but here I'm the Supreme Alpha. You're bottom of the chain."

"Why the bottom of the chain?"

"As I said, it's a, as you say it, dog eat dog world out here. You're at the bottom because you're human. Easy to kill. And not to mention, easier to break."

"I'm tougher than I look."

"I don't doubt that. But you have to take it into consideration there are things here that can literally eat you completely whole in one bite! Or plants that if you so much as brush up against them, the barest skin contact will kill you."

"How?" The anger left him in a sudden rush now that he had the time to contemplate she was right. He really was completely out of his element here. And in some logical part of his stupid male brain, he realised that she was right, he would be kidnapped and tortured for information. In addition to the fact he didn't know anything, it would be for nothing. And when they realised that, he would be killed. Maybe not right away; they might have their fun of torturing him, not killing him until he begged them to do it.

"You really want to know?" She took his wrist in her hand and dragged him over to the bed.

"Yes," he answered as he sank down onto the mattress, sinking into the plushness. It didn't surprise him at all that the bed was comfortable. She did work magic after all. She sat down next to him.

"OK. Well, there are certain plants which we have here that you have back home. But these ones are a hell of a lot worse."

"What ones?"

"We have enormous pitcher plants, skunk cabbage, giant hogweed, wolfs bane and adventurous rosary pea to name some."

"What the hell are those?" He'd never heard of them! And that was saying something, considering in the army, they had a guy in their group who was literally a plant fanatic. He knew everything to do with plants, along with their poisons if they had any which was very useful in the places they went to. And thankfully they had Luke, who was a poison fanatic himself, so put those two together, they'd solve pretty much anything to do with plants and poisons. But he was the first to admit that he did blank them out when they started rabbiting on about it all so that was maybe why he hadn't heard of them.

"Giant Pitcher, formally known as Nepenthes Attenboroughii, is a giant carnivorous plant which secretes a nectar-like substance to lure unsuspecting prey into a pool full of enzymes and acid. Sticky downward ribs make it virtually impossible for anything to escape. They grow in the nitrogen-deficient environments, so therefore get their nutrients from their decaying victims. Here they grow to an astounding ten feet tall or more."

"Sounds charming."

"Yes. Now stop butting in and listen. I'm only going to say this once."

"Sorry," he muttered and turned more on the bed, giving her his full attention.

"We also have Skunk Cabbage, officially known as Lysichiton Americanus. These we have in our swamp, that I had brought over many, *many* years ago. The odour of it is often mistaken for that of an irate skunk, hence the name, until the huge golden or purplish flowers are seen emerging from the leaves. It emits severe calcium oxalate poisoning which results in death. And before you ask, calcium oxalate is an extremely corrosive toxin that burns the flesh and shuts down the vital organs. Here they grow to about four to six feet high."

"Ouch." Raven actually put a hand onto his stomach, as if he could picture it or even feel it.

"We also have Giant Hogweed formally known as Heracleum Mantegazzianum — causes damage by mere skin contact. It can only destroy through co-operation with an extra-terrestrial body; our sun. Which, thanks to it being sunny here pretty much all the time, that's every day that it can destroy. It's photosensitive and oozes a thick sap that coats the skin upon impact, which almost immediately reacts with the sun and starts a chemical reaction which burns through skin and tissues, leading to necrosis and the formation of massive, purple lesions that can last on the body for two years or more. Stands at around six feet seven to fifteen feet five inches tall."

"That's ridiculous." She just looked at him as he butted in and rolled her eyes.

"Now we have Wolfs Bane, more known as Aconitum, which has rich leaves of dark green colouring, with white or blue flowers. It contains large quantities of a poison called pseudaconitine, which is used for hunting. When ingested, an intense burning feeling in the limbs and abdomen is immediately felt. In large doses, death can occur in as little as two to six hours. All parts of the plant consumed are poisonous. Only 20 ml of pseudaconitine is needed to kill someone. Grows here to be around about six feet tall. Then we have Rosary Pea known as Abrus Precatorius. It might sound sweet and downright pious but it's actually the most dangerous plant on your 'Normal Earth' and one of the most dangerous here as well. Grows to roughly twenty to forty feet tall, with flowers that are red to purple in colour. Its seeds, red with black dots on one end, contain a particular lectin known as abrin which when chewed or swallowed, death will follow shortly afterwards. It is one of the most fatal toxins ever. And lots of fey use it to poison their arrows as well as their swords."

"How does it kill you?" he butted in. He couldn't help it, he was completely fascinated and he knew Luke would be also if he was here. He was the scientist of the two, but it didn't mean he wasn't interested in it.

"After the vomiting, fever, nausea, drooling and G.I. dysfunction that's when. But before all that happy-go-lucky shit, you get bizarre hyperexcitability, oedema and fatally convulsive seizures, renal tubular degeneration, bladder and retinal haemorrhage and widespread internal lesions typically develop."

"Sounds like a fun day in the park then," he sarcastically retorted.

"It's not something to laugh about. In your world they're dangerous, here they're positively fatal without a doubt. I've seen many of the creatures here succumb to them but not before complete torture is endured. I've even been known to use them in my favour. It also helps that I'm immune to every single poison and such that is in existence. Not to mention there is no antidote."

"How exactly did you use them?"

"I've thrown victims into them. I've extracted the poisons from the seeds or the plant itself and injected it straight into my victim's veins and laughed in their faces as they screamed."

"Damn, you truly are violent. My type of woman." He grinned at her.

"I'm really not your type of woman."

"Oh, you certainly are. You can trust me on that one."

"And just explain to me how I'm your type of woman?"

"You're a protector. Look after those who can't look after themselves. You defend them with your life. Exactly as I do on 'Normal Earth'."

"Raven, there is an enormous difference between me and you. I'm a creation. You're human."

"Minor technicality."

"No, there isn't Raven. I was born of a stone egg and magic. You were conceived and born from your mother's womb. You had a childhood, even though it was shitty one from what you told me. I was 'born' as I am now. No childhood for me. I was born already with my powers and the ability to kill, and from all those that sacrificed themselves to create me, I have shit loads of memories and spells that are forever engrained into my subconscious."

"What's that actually like? All those memories, spells, etc."

"At times, it's a living hell. Other days, it's downright useful. But majority of the spells in which I have 'accumulated', I've used over and over again, they're pretty much like second nature now."

"Oh, right."

"Exactly. Think yourself lucky you had the chance to grow up, learn things your own way. I know yours was hard, no one's is peachy perfect. I haven't had that privilege. I was born as I am now. I have no childhood memories apart from those who died in order to give me life."

"True." He let out a jaw-cracking yawn then.

"Come on, you need to sleep." She stood up and stretched herself, muscles groaning in protest but damn it felt good.

"No, I don't." He bounced to his feet, grabbed her hand and pulled her to him. Pulling her flush against his chest and before she could stop him or know his intentions, placed his lips on hers and kissed her with a passion she knew was from deep within his very soul.

Chapter Twenty-One

Raven sighed happily as he kissed her. He knew he could *easily* be addicted to her and the funny thing was he really liked that idea. And that was saying something as he never ever thought of being addicted to anyone before. He smiled inside as she began to kiss him back, her nails digging into his biceps and oh, he really didn't care. Turned him on in fact.

"What the hell are you doing to me?" She pulled back and stared at him, her chest rising and falling in rapid succession. It was obvious it affected her as much as him, he was panting like a dog in the midday sun in the middle of a heat wave.

"I think it's pretty obvious."

"Yeah? Care to enlighten me?"

"Well, what was I doing?"

"Kissing me?"

"Nope. I was tongue punching your tonsils." He winked at her and then he got the shock of his life. She threw back her head and roared with laughter. The sound deep and musical with her eyes literally sparkling with merriment and it was the most beautiful sight he ever did see.

"Well, I've certainly never heard of that before," she said when she could finally talk again.

"Care for another demonstration?" He wiggled his eyebrows mischievously at her and then held his breath as he waited for her answer.

"Why another one? And since when do you ask for permission or whatnot? You just help yourself to whatever it is you want."

"Yeah, good point." So he did. He pulled her against him again and lowered his head. Slowly kissing her yummy mouth, which she returned. He pushed her back against the wall and ground his erection against her lower belly. His fingers dug into her waist and hers dug into his shoulders as if they couldn't get any closer to each other.

"I want you," he groaned against her lips.

"Want me how?" She blinked open her eyes she hadn't realised were shut.

"I want my cock buried deep inside you. I want to give you as much pleasure as I possibly can."

"Well, that's definitely blunt and to the point," she grinned.

"What can I say, I'm a blunt kind of guy. Plus, you prefer it." But it was no time for discussion. If he didn't have her naked and underneath him in the next twenty seconds or so, he thought he might actually die from the pain of his erection and those damn fucking blue balls of his! He clamped his lips down on hers, bruising her with his kiss. He picked her up and instantly his blood flowed even more around his groin, as impossible as that seemed. She clamped her legs around his waist, locking them together. He felt the power in her thighs as they clamped on his hips. Not that he was complaining in the least. He took a few steps forward and his knees hit the bedframe. He carried on forward, tipping her onto the mattress.

"Calista, I can't wait; I need to be inside you. I crave it like I need my next breath!" He groaned as those amazing nails of hers dug deeper into his shoulder blades, no doubt leaving indentations. She blinked up at him, those gorgeous eyes of her glazing over with passion. He began to pull her clothes off her, the soft texture of them all surprising him. But he got caught trying to drag her trousers off. She pushed him off, scrambled to her feet and stripped. Slowly. Teasing him like nothing else ever had! Not even the professional strippers Luke and some of the other guys in his unit had organised for his birthday turned him on as much as watching her strip. Then he got a look at her face, she was unsure of what she was doing. He got off the bed and approached her.

"Are you OK?"

"Not really. I have no idea what I am doing," she said, tipping her head forward slightly so he couldn't see her eyes, which was really so unlike her.

"If you're unsure, we can stop. I won't force you to do anything you don't want to." He tipped her chin up so she looked at him. Her eyes were unusually large and bright.

"Really?"

"Really, really. I'm not a monster that forces a woman to do something she doesn't want to."

"That's good to know. And erm, I should be honest."

"About what?" He literally looked puzzled.

"I've never been with a male before."

"So you've only been with females? Because you know, I'm OK with that." He winked at her.

"No!" She laughed, the tension leaving the room as quickly as it had seemed to arrive.

"So what then?"

"I've never been with anyone in that way before." She just watched as it seemed to sink in then because his mouth opened on a silent 'O'.

"Yeah. So I can understand if you want to stop."

"But why are you willing to let me have, what is no doubt the most amazing gift ever?"

"Because as stupid as it sounds, I trust you."

"But you don't trust anyone."

"Yes I do; it's just very, very rare that I give my trust to anyone or anything."

"Well, I'm glad you trust me."

"If I didn't, I wouldn't let you do this to me." OK, so she had a point in that one.

"This is very true. But only if you're one hundred percent sure."

"I'm one hundred percent certain." He pulled her close to him again and kissed her. And then he heard it, her voice, sultry and seductive in his head and he wasn't freaked out by it either. Clearly he was already growing comfortable with her popping into his head at random.

Are you ready?

"For what?" he asked out loud, pulling back slightly. She ran her fingers down his stomach until she cupped his erection snugly against her palm through his trousers. He groaned as she rubbed slightly, the friction immense.

"For us to do this."

"Damn fucking right I am!" He ground himself into her palm. Point fucking obvious.

"Well, that's all right then." She rubbed her hand enticingly against him again as her eyes began to flare with passion. The intense blue light creating a shadow behind his head. She stepped back a little and grinned. Raven flew back across the room to the wall, feet dangling off of the floor. It was as if he was glued in place, when in reality it was Calista's magic. Raven tried wiggling to see what his movement was and it turned out to be zilch, just his eyes moved and mouth opened. Had his vocal cords though. He watched, excitedly, as Calista snapped her fingers and his clothes disappeared, his cock waving like a flag for attention. Such a good thing he was perfectly comfortable in his masculinity that it didn't embarrass him… well OK, maybe a little. But damn, who wouldn't be excited if they had this beautiful woman in front of them. His eyes were glued to Calista, as she slowly but surely stripped out of the rest of her own clothes. She provocatively did a strip tease that professional strippers would be envious of. His breath left him in a whoosh as he realised her breasts lay encased in a gorgeous cobalt blue lace bra that cupped her generously and suited her eye colour perfectly. She quickly pulled her leather trousers off and sent them flying over her head to land somewhere on the floor. Which promptly made him draw in a breath too quickly and it hurt. But fuck that, he didn't care! Her underwear was the same colour as her bra and cupped her lusciously. He actually dribbled and was pretty sure his tongue hung out. Her panties were just a slither of fabric, leaving most of her arse cheeks bare. Her legs were long and built gloriously of well-defined muscle. Her arms graceful and with enough muscle tone to indicate she looked after herself well. Her skin was peachy white and he desperately wanted to run his tongue across her flesh. She turned and faced him. Her scar across her stomach did nothing to stop the raw need that was crawling under the surface for him, waiting for the perfect opportunity to burst free. I mean come on, everyone has scars. Even he had plenty of scars. Eyes about bulged out of his head and she sauntered closer to him, her hands disappearing behind her back. He heard a small click and her bra became loose, she shimmed the bra straps down and sent it slithering to the floor. Her breasts were bared to him and then she shimmied out of her panties, joining them with the bra, in a swirl of blue.

"Holy mother of fucking God, you're perfect!" he whispered. And what shouldn't have shocked him, but did, was that she was completely bald between her thighs too. She smiled and stepped up closer to him, close enough that if he was able to lean forward slightly, he would be able to touch her. Filthy thoughts went zooming through his head of what he wanted to do to her. But he knew to hold his tongue so he didn't scare her away. The thing was, even though she was perfect to him, her smile was the most beautiful thing about her, and he could tell it was genuine and that meant a lot to him.

"I'm not. I'm just me," she replied.

"If I could move, I'd show you just how beautiful you are." And suddenly he found that he could move, so he put it into play. He grabbed her and pulled her into his arms, kissing her passionately. And he smiled to himself when she returned it. Fingernails again digging into the top of his shoulders. As the kiss got more heated, he began to feel something start to trickle down his chest. He pulled back and gasped, as did Calista. She'd pierced his skin on his shoulder and it was blood trickling down him!

"Oh God, I'm sorry!" She immediately moved back, but not before he saw the flare of her nostrils as the scent of the blood assailed her senses as well as her pupils dilating as the smell rushed to her head.

"Calista, its fine. It really is. It's only a small bit of blood. Let me get a tissue and I'll clean it up." He had to blink a few times first because the scent of it was going straight to his head. Why did that always fucking happen?

"Raven, are you OK?" He opened his eyes he didn't realise he had shut and looked at her.

"Yes." His breath was getting faster and faster, until it was as if he was shallow panting.

"No, you're not. What's wrong?" She grabbed a hold of his shoulders to keep his attention on her.

"Get that tissue. It's going to my head." He groaned and placed his hands on either side of his skull as though in pain.

"Has it always been this way for you when blood has been around you?" He noticed she had better control over her senses than what he did.

"No, never. Well not until I got here. I mean I had a strange small particular liking to it; but nothing as bad as what it is like at the moment."

"Hmm, then it seems that the vampire gene in you is stronger now you're here with the mythological ones. Understandable. Rare, but understandable."

"So I definitely have the gene then? And why would it be stronger? God, can't you remove it now?"

"So it appears, considering your reaction. And I'm not entirely sure why, but yes I'll remove it."

"Then why haven't you got a tissue?" He looked at her and then he saw as to why. Her eyes were locked onto the blood still trickling down him.

"Huh? Oh, tissue, yes sorry." She stepped back and was about to turn around when he grabbed her hips.

"Use your mouth," he whispered.

"But I won't be able to stop if I do."

"Yes, you will. I'll remove you."

"You're not strong enough, Raven." He knew she wasn't being harsh, just stating the facts.

"Trust me, I will make you move if I need to." She nodded and stepped forward again.

"OK then." And with that, she placed her mouth onto the wound and sucked, which caused Raven to moan, dig his fingers into her hips and drag her flush up against his body which was another reason for the moan because she was gloriously naked against him and damn it felt perfect. The scariest thing? It felt like home and he'd never felt at home before.

Calista's eyes fluttered shut as she closed her mouth over the wound she had made in Raven's shoulder. A deep groan rumbled from her chest as his blood shot over her taste buds, down her throat and hit her stomach. The taste of him was strong and exotic. It had a hint of strawberry from his human side; but he also had the stronger over flavour of pure magic and raw untapped power that flooded her system. She was afraid he could become addictive and that actually scared her. But for the life of her, she couldn't stop drawing his blood into her system, her hands locked onto his biceps, her grip secure.

"Calista, that's enough." She heard the rumble of Raven's voice right next to her ear and it shot through her to her already throbbing cunt, making it more wet with anticipation. She might be a virgin, but fuck her, she knew what was happening to her body. She was becoming sexually aroused and majorly so at that. And from that, she sucked harder, drawing more of him into her. He was a fucking aphrodisiac! One who she was afraid she could become addicted to very easily.

"Calista." Her name was a groan on his lips. Then she felt pressure on her face and her jaw popped free from his shoulder. Blood stayed on his shoulder a little from where her lips had been pressed, but thankfully it had stopped. It also coated her lips. She drew her gaze back to his and actually leaned back. Raw desire shone back at her; his once dead, ice-blue eyes were now bright and very much alive. She grinned as she realised she'd made him like that and ran her hand across his stomach; fingers rolling over his abs and she smiled even wider when his muscles twitched. Power shot through her as she realised she had him completely at her mercy and she bet everything she had that it didn't happen often. Until another thought crept through her mind. And that fucking thought began to dim everything down, the fire inside of her began to diminish.

"What's wrong?" He curled his fingers under her chin and forced her to look at him as she hadn't realised she'd looked away.

"Nothing."

"Yeah, right. Don't start lying now. Now tell me what just went through that head of yours." He dragged her to the bed and sat her on the edge of it.

"Just realised something."

"Care to tell me what?"

"It's stupid."

"Just tell me." He put his hand under her chin and stopped her from turning away.

"I just realised that I'm not the only one to make you excited."

"That's what's going through your mind?"

"Yes. Like I said, it's stupid. Obviously I know you're not a virgin, but it didn't stop the thought going through my mind."

"And how did it make you feel?"

"Like I wanted to rip their heads off for being able to touch you. To feel your body above theirs with your weight pushing them into the mattress. To feel your cock pounding away in their cunt. Your tongue duelling with theirs and making them moan."

"Not much thought then." He smiled at her and she smiled back a little.

"Not really no. But then again, you got angry earlier when you thought someone had touched me in that way. Well I can assure you, this is the most anyone has seen me apart from when I was 'born'. I mean sure, they've seen me naked, but not, well vulnerable."

"Well, I'm glad you've picked me to see you like this, and I must admit it's one of the best views I've ever seen." He grinned and she actually laughed.

"You reckon?"

"I know so. And just so you know, I've never been this turned on before."

"You're not just saying that?"

"No. I don't say something I don't mean." She smiled at him and leaned forward, kissing him. He eagerly complied and kissed her back, tasting his blood on her lips, which somehow excited him even more, and he wrapped his arms around her waist and hauled her against him. Their bare skin touching and exciting him even more if that was possible. She shifted and pushed him back onto the mattress, their lips still locked together. His cock was a solid mass against her stomach, but that wasn't where she wanted it. She wanted him buried as deep inside her as he could go.

"I want you inside me," she whispered against his lips. Before she realised it, she was on her back and he was hovering above her, a smile that pretty much lit up his face and his cock nudging her between her thighs, causing her to get even wetter! If that was even possible.

"All in good time. I want this to be one you remember."

"I highly doubt I'll forget."

"Oh shush, woman," he laughed as she harrumphed then stopped laughing as his eyes made contact with her breasts. Nipples hard and eager for him. The areola's flushed with rushing blood, begging him to lock his mouth over them and ravish them. So he complied. She sucked in her breath hard as his tongue rasped over her nipple, sending a sensation of unusual tingling down to her womb. She watched, transfixed as he moved from one to the other and back again. All too soon he pulled back, her nipple leaving his mouth on a resounding pop.

"Do you know why you've got nipples?" he asked her.

"Huh?" She looked at him with passion-glazed eyes.

"Nipples. Why they exist."

"Care to explain?"

"Well, boobs would be pointless without them." And just like that, she threw her head back and roared with laughter again. He chuckled with her, and rose above her again so his face was level with her own and damn if she didn't take his breath away. She smiled up at him and he felt like he was the tallest man alive at that moment. Then he got back down to business.

"Still want me inside you?"

"Yes!" She groaned as two of his fingers grazed down her labia. Teasing her like nothing else ever had.

"Well, you're going to have to wait. I've wanted to do this for a while now." And with that, she stared, wide eyed as he opened her legs wider, shoved his shoulders in the way so she couldn't close her legs and stared at her bare wet flesh.

"You're beautiful!" he whispered and lowered his head.

"O-ooh my God," she breathed as his tongue rasped over her slit, creating exciting tremors that ran through her entire body. She yanked her hips back slightly when a ludicrous burst of pleasure shot through her system and she heard Raven chuckle slightly against her.

"What a-are you l-laughing at?" She struggled to catch her breath. This had never happened before!

"That dear, is a small bundle of nerves that are there purely for pleasure, and is what's more commonly known as a clit." He pulled back slightly and breathed a stream of hot air against said swollen, wet clit, causing her to shudder.

"Oh." She watched, transfixed as he leaned back down and continued torturing her with his very skilled tongue and before long an intense pressure built in her lower belly. She stared at him watching her as he pleasured her.

"What's happening to me?" she actually whimpered.

"What?" he breathed against her.

"I've got an intense pressure in my lower belly."

"Good." She could see the smile on his face, so she figured that was a good thing.

"What will happen?"

"Just go with it. Until you can't take anymore, you'll be fine, just let it go." He then set his tongue into overdrive on her and she just about managed to keep her hips on the mattress and completely lost track of what he meant by just let it go. Her fingers dug into the mattress, sinking deep. She locked her elbows so she didn't dig her claws into Raven and cause him pain and then she stopped thinking altogether as the pressure built and built until she literally could take no more. She felt like she was going to explode! And she did. Hard.

"RAVEN!" She screamed his name as she locked her thighs together around his head, keeping him where he was. It was extremely intense, and when it finally stopped, she let her legs drop lifelessly back to the bed. She watched though hooded eyes as he crawled back up her body. His lips and some of his chin glistened from her juices. He ran his hand across both and smiled at her. His face was red from where she'd stopped oxygen getting into his system but it didn't seem to have bothered him in the slightest. She smiled back and he kissed her, their tongues duelling together, tasting herself on his lips. Then she felt something start to stretch her pussy, making her pull back and stare at him.

"It'll be OK. I'll try and not hurt you but I can't promise," he panted slightly. She wiggled slightly to ease the ache between her thighs, causing Raven to moan slightly. She watched, transfixed as his eyes literally burned into her own, the emotion sizzling through them stunned her. It wasn't just passion there. Something much more seemed to be beating to get free. She gasped as he broke through her hymen and kept on tunnelling through her unused passage. She moved back slightly, but he grabbed her hips, his fingers digging in, keeping her in place.

"Don't move. It'll only make it worse. Let your body grow accustomed to having me inside you," he whispered, raining butterfly kisses over her face and with concentrating on that, she eventually noticed the pain had started to disappear and she realised they fit like two jigsaw pieces coming together.

"The pain has gone," she whispered.

"You sure?"

"Yes." She wiggled slightly and a burst of pleasure shot through her, making her eyes widen.

"Your eyes have changed colour," he whispered.

"What colour are they?"

"Black outer ring with lavish purple mixed in with your blue."

"They've never been that colour before. Must be because I'm horny."

"It's beautiful on you." He smiled and she returned it before she wrapped her long legs around his waist, encouraging him to do something as clearly she wasn't interested in talking and gasped as he began to move. So clearly he had gotten the message! As his pubis rubbed against her clit as he moved back inside her, it sent more pleasure shooting through her system.

"I'm sorry, I can't go slow any more. I need to go faster," he groaned into her ear, his slight stubble rubbing against her cheek.

"Then go faster." And oh God, did he ever. He began to ruthlessly pound into her. She locked her ankles together so he wouldn't go anywhere and just held on for the ride. Her claws still dug into the mattress.

Raven couldn't get enough of her. He pounded into her tight cunt over and over again. Her inner muscles gripping his cock with every penetration. It was the best thing ever! And he could die a very happy man now. She felt just as incredible as he thought she would — actually no, she was better! He ground himself against her, his pubic bone rubbing against her clit with every move he made, which made her moan and her legs tighten a little more around his waist. He knelt up on his knees then and moved away slightly, causing her to open her eyes and stare at him with those gorgeous eyes glazed over with passion. Which gave his ego quite a boost!

"What are you doing?"

"You'll see." He grabbed her legs and pulled them over his shoulders and slammed his cock back inside of her, which effectively made him go a lot deeper than before. He ruthlessly pounded into her, as hard as he could. She was moaning and it was music to his ears. He reached between them and flicked his finger across her clit. She bucked beneath him as pleasure shot through her and he just grinned and did it again. With her legs still over his shoulders, he leant forward until his face was level with hers, effectively bending her so he could go even deeper.

"I want you to scream for me." He began going harder and faster. Then did the unthinkable, he bit her, right where her neck joined her shoulder. He bit her hard enough to draw blood, which he greedily sucked down his throat as quickly as he could. Her blood was rich and exotic with ridiculously potent power that flowed through his body. He could easily become addicted to her. He leaned back a little and licked the wound, taking any stray blood with him. As he continued to pound into her, he watched as the wound healed itself and he felt her nails now dig into his shoulders. He turned his attention to her and stared into her eyes, passion giving them a glazed glow. Raven felt her body tightening around his cock and her legs leaned heavily on his shoulders. He threw his hips back and forth harder than before. Supporting his weight on one hand, he put his other between them and found that snug little bud that resided enticingly in between her legs and smiled when he found it was hard and slightly throbbing. He brushed his thumb across it and grinned wider as she bucked against his fingers.

"Raven, please!" She begged and damn if his male ego didn't swell even more then. He would bet everything he had that she didn't say that word often, if hardly ever.

"Please what?"

"Let me fucking come!" she growled, her eyes bright and casting a glow across his features.

"As you wish my love." He noticed she didn't correct him at calling her his love, even though he'd called her it twice now. He pounded harder into her and strummed her clit in rhythm. He felt himself on the verge of orgasm but he refused to finish before her.

"Oh fuck!" she screamed as her body tensed and he felt her orgasm coat his cock in more of that delicious fluid that graced her walls. Holding him inside of her with a killer-tight grip, he couldn't hold back anymore. He moved his hand from between her thighs, braced himself over her and went harder. His balls tightened up against him as his orgasm rushed up his cock and before he could stop it, he burst. His seed shot out of him and fired straight into her womb. He threw his head back and roared her name as he came. When his body finally finished emptying itself, he pulled his cock free with a sweet pop and it hung limply and well used between them. He shuddered as he let her legs fall from his shoulders and rolled to his left so he landed on his back and didn't collapse on top of her. They lay quietly for a while, each just too spent to do anything else. It even took precious energy to talk, so they didn't, but it actually was a comfortable silence. Raven finally mustered up enough energy to slide to the bottom of the bed, as it was against the wall so that was the only way off it and stood on shaking legs, hands gripping the mattress so he didn't fall over. He glanced up at Calista and his chest swelled with male satisfaction. She was sprawled haphazardly across the mattress, her cunt in perfect view for him as her legs were open and she was still glistening from her orgasm. Her nipples hard still and pointing to the ceiling. Her chest rising and falling in harsh breaths still. She was also covered in a silken sheen of sweat as was he.

"Come on, we have to clean up." He lightly tapped her ankle with his hand and was rewarded with her weakly kicking her leg out.

"Just get back into bed, I'll use a spell for us," she grumbled which caused him to laugh and shook his head at her.

"Nope. This calls for a good old-fashioned dunk in the cold stream to cool us down and clean us up. Come on, woman!" he growled mockingly and she glared at him.

"Fine." She huffed and swung her feet over the edge of the bed and slowly sat up, groaning slightly as she did so.

"You OK?" He was instantly there, running his eyes over her very naked body with appreciation as well as concern.

"A little sore, but that's to be expected." She stood up and swayed slightly so he grabbed her upper arms to steady her. She smiled her thanks, then moved so he dropped his hands. They walked to the door and he stared at the sway of her hips and ass that again begged for his hands to run over them. She was gorgeous clothed, but naked? She was breathtaking! The cold breeze that washed over him made him lift his gaze up and saw she'd opened the door, rich moonlight greeting them. Thousands of stars twinkled like diamonds across the black blanket. Strolling outside together, nakedness completely forgotten, they stood side by side soaking up the rays of the gorgeous moon. This was his favourite time in the day and he couldn't think of anything better to look at, apart from the naked woman who currently stood at his side enjoying the peace and quiet.

"This is my favourite time of the day," he muttered and felt her gaze on him.

"Why?"

"Because here I'm not judged by people who can see me. I'm at peace. Vast open ocean in front of me, the moonlight caressing my flesh, the wind stroking me gently as it passes. Peace and quiet."

"Why would you of all people be judged?" she asked, turning to look at him properly.

"Because of the scars on my back, my neck and face. And the one across my stomach. And because I apparently give off a 'dangerous aura'." He actually did the air quotes, causing her lips to lift at the edges. He smiled back at her; when she smiled it seemed that she lit up from within and it was beautiful.

"What scars on your back? And so what that you have scars on your neck and face. To be quite honest, it just shows you've lived a hard life and come out the victor from it. Plus, I kind of like it." At that announcement, her eyes widened, she spun on her heel and walked off, as though she was embarrassed to have admitted that. He quickly hurried after her, grabbed her wrist and spun her around until she was flush up against him.

"What did you mean by that? And you'd have seen the scars on my back when I got off the mattress ten minutes ago."

"I wasn't particularly paying attention to your back, Raven. And I meant that you might have the scars but they're nothing compared to mine. Yours don't distract from the fact you're an incredibly handsome man. In fact they just add to your features. Look, to be quite fair, I'm surprised you don't actually have a woman back home for you."

"I'm about to tell you something I've told no one else. Only Luke knows because he happened to have been there at the time, even though it was about three years or so into our friendship. But I somehow believe I can trust you and I know you won't tell anyone else. There was a woman once and her name was Nyohmi. We met in our last year of high school, so when I was around fifteen to sixteen. I thought we were in love, when in reality she was just using me for a place to stay as she'd been kicked out of her parents' house and I'd already moved out. She had also been cheating on me with a guy round the corner. Apparently I couldn't give her what she wanted."

"And that was?" He turned around so she couldn't see the anguish on his face and sat on a boulder near the stream that they'd unconsciously arrived at. He buried his face into his hands as the memories shot forward at a rush.

"A stable home. A child. A steady income so she could be a stay-at-home mum whilst I was out slaving away at work for enough money to pay the bills and give her money to splash out on 'luxuries that every woman needs'."

"That's ridiculous. How did you know she cheated on you?" He felt her hands on his own and moved them away from his face and saw her standing before him in all her naked glory.

345

"As I was only seventeen at the time, I managed to get a part-time job at a local bar and because it was a quiet Thursday night, they let me go home early. I was working with Luke, he said night as he was staying another hour as he was helping shut up and was getting a lift so I left. I got back to the studio apartment I shared with Nyohmi, walked in because I knew she'd be home and stopped short. She was flung over the kitchen side with her skirt flung around her hips, thong shoved to her feet and was being fucked by the guy from round the corner. She was really into it as she kept on moaning his name and begging him to go harder. All I remember was losing my temper, knocking the guy to the floor and using my fists to, shall we say, pretty his face. A neighbour heard her screaming and called the police. As well he called Luke, who was down as my emergency contact plus the neighbour knew he'd be the only one to calm me down. He arrived just after the police and I was apparently in the corner of the living area watching them all intently. And without any emotion in my features apparently. It was as if I was dead inside. But by the way I was coiled tight, they could see I would lash out at literally a split second's notice."

"What did the police do?" She brushed his cheeks and he realised that tears had leaked. Fucking tears!

"They tried to calm me down whilst paramedics tried to get to the guy to assess just how bad he was. But I wouldn't let them near him. Nyohmi had managed to get behind the police, bawling her eyes out. The whole dramatic flair shit. Luke finally made an appearance, managed to get past the police when he told them who he was and rushed straight towards me. He hunched down in front of me so I'd look him right in the eyes and the git just grinned. And to this day I'll never forget what he said to me." He smiled himself as he remembered that very day.

"What did he say to you?" She sat down on the floor and crossed her legs.

"He told me to not let that spineless waste of space get me down. And that I shouldn't have knocked the poor guy out; it wasn't his fault he was snared by the viper."

"I take it he didn't approve of Nyohmi?"

"No one did. Apparently they all saw her for the user that she was."

"Which I can understand. So what happened next?" He knew what she was trying to do, trying to get it off his chest and out of his system. And he couldn't love her more for that if he tried. Wait... love? Really? Did he really just think that? Did he love her? Yes. Yes he did. And it scared the ever living hell out of him. But at least he realised the love he felt for Calista was nothing to what he had thought he'd felt for Nyohmi. He now realised with Nyohmi it had been lust, not love.

"He finally got to calm me down. But he told everyone to leave and they did, thankfully."

"Even the guy you beat shit out of?"

"Including him. The paramedics got him to the hospital in time otherwise I'd have been done for murder. In cold blood as well, but to be fair I really didn't give a shit."

"What happened with Nyohmi?"

"Last I heard, because Luke did a search, she was in a psychiatric institution."

"Whatever for?" He finally lifted his head properly to look at her. He really didn't understand why he had to tell her all of this, but she was so damn easy to talk to. Like he had known her for years.

"Because of me. She never got over what I did. And she went on a wild, crazy and downright dangerous bender of drugs and alcohol."

"Not a good way to go. Do you blame yourself?"

"Yes."

"Why?"

"Because it was my fault!" He shouted, then immediately regretted shouting at her so he stood up and walked off. She didn't deserve his anger. No one did. He should have more control over himself, for God sake! He hated how quickly his anger surged forward. All that work for restraint seemed to be wearing off and he didn't have the time to book in when he was back 'home'. It barely worked the first time. And he really didn't want to go through all of that hassle again.

"It wasn't your fault!" she hissed from behind him and he then felt her arms come around his waist. He looked down and stared at her peachy white interlocked hands against his own dark tanned stomach. Dark nails curled into claws.

"Please let go," he whispered. But of course she didn't, she just worked her way around him until she stood face to face with him. That moonlight playing gorgeously across her skin and somehow making her even more beautiful.

"Why should I let go?"

"Because it was my fault and I'm disgusting. I don't want that to seep into your beautiful body and contaminate you."

"Raven! Don't you dare talk like that. And why like this all of a sudden? Or are you forgetting what we did twenty minutes ago?"

347

"I could never ever forget that. You gave me the most beautiful gift of all. And I don't know why I'm like this all of a sudden, I guess it's the memories." He shrugged helplessly.

"Well, that's the beauty of memories. You can bury them deep into your subconscious memory and can forget about them. Or if you want, I can completely remove them for you; but before you agree to that, just so you know, it will be permanent. No going back."

"No. Let me keep them. They remind me that not everyone is a complete arsehole."

"If you're sure."

"I've never been more sure. And thank you for giving me the option." He smiled gently at her and kissed her; he couldn't help it. He just needed to. But before they got right into it, he pulled back.

"Come on, let's go get washed then get some sleep. Who knows when we'll be able to get a decent sleep again. At least, for a while."

"Now that sounds like a very good idea." She moved away from him and he quickly followed her to the stream. Now that they weren't standing in front of each other and he was completely absorbed by their conversation, he finally took time to admire her body again. Sleek, perfect skin that was soft to the touch with defined sinewy muscle that showed her strength. Legs a mile long and he smiled as he remembered having them locked around his waist, or better around his head. Shaking away those thoughts before he got too excited again, he dipped his toes into the water and sighed as the surprisingly warm water washed over him. He moved deeper and he saw that parts of it had actually widened, so instead of it being a near crystal clear colour, parts were a deep gorgeous blue.

"Be careful about the dark blue parts." Calista's voice jarred him and he glanced over at her.

"Why?"

"Because they're sink holes. They're that deep, even Gélio can fully submerge himself in it."

"But why use that when the ocean is just over there?" He pointed to his right.

"Sometimes it's nice to have the sweet cool water of a stream wash over you instead of the saltiness of the ocean," she casually replied and he shrugged. She'd have no argument off him on that one. And how did Gélio manage to submerge himself? It didn't look that deep, or wide! But then he shrugged, thinking magic must be involved. They leisurely took their time laying down in the water to let it wash over them and thanks to Calista's magic, they washed their hair with fragrance free shampoo as well as fragrance free body wash; but it was so nice to scrub himself clean he didn't care. Once they'd completed their bath, they casually lay on the soft verge, bodies drying in the light, yet warm breeze, as the stars blazed above them. Raven closed his eyes as pure contentment washed over him. The memories of his past didn't faze him either, and that was a rarity. When the bastard memories decided to surge to the surface he was a miserable fucker for a few days afterwards and he was the first to admit it. But to be honest; they didn't bother him now and he was pretty sure that was because of Calista. Soon the only sounds he could hear was the ocean, their steady breathing and the soft whispers of the wind as it slowly drifted over and around them. It was the kind of quiet and peace he could easily become used too. Downside, he knew he couldn't, because he had to go back to work on 'Normal Earth' and that was the complete bastard part as he really, really didn't want to go back. It was weird; he felt like he belonged here and on 'Normal Earth' he didn't. The wind caressed them lovingly as they lay with their eyes closed, enjoying the quiet and the sounds of the water rushing around them.

"Come on, Raven. Let's head inside before it gets any later." Calista's voice jarred him, causing him to open weary eyes and regard her almost sleepily.

"Can't we just lay here?"

"No, we have to go back inside. Plus there is the comfortable mattress waiting for us." She stood up, gifting him with a wondrous view of her sleek nakedness. He didn't think it would be a sight he'd ever get bored with.

"Oh, all right," he huffed and got to his feet. Quickly they shook off the excess water that clung to them.

"How long were we here for?" he asked.

"At the water? Hour or so."

"Oh, right," he muttered and quickly followed her to the cabin, eyes glued to her arse. Damn she was gorgeous and her arse just begged his hands to run over it. When they finally got into the warm cabin, he watched as she flung out her arm and the fire extinguished itself, causing the room to disappear into darkness.

"You do realise I can't see?" And then he got the shock of his life. A light began to form beside him and as he turned his head, his breath left him in a whoosh. The light was Calista!

"How do you do that?" he asked, staring.

"I don't know. I've always been able to do it if I want to." She shrugged and walked to the bed, leaving him no choice but to follow her.

"Does it hurt?" he enquired, reaching out and touching her arm. It didn't hurt him; she just felt warm.

"No. It doesn't hurt."

"Do you feel anything when it happens?"

"Not really; just slightly warm, as if I'm wrapped up in a big fluffy jumper and jogging bottoms."

"Handy then. Especially if you're out in the world and it's freezing."

"Indeed it is." She sat down on the mattress.

"Can you control just how bright you go?" He was completely flabbergasted. He was surprised he wasn't freaking out right about now. But her glowing was about normal for what he'd seen at the moment!

"Yes, I can. I can control it until it's as if I'm not glowing at all."

"Damn now, that is handy. Wish I could do it."

"Why?"

"It'd be a neat way of being able to keep warm. More so with my job; you never know where you will end up until they tell you."

"Must be hard if you want to go on holiday or something and they've got a job for you to do but you don't know when you'd be deployed."

"This is true. Thank God I've only got six months left."

"What will you do afterwards?"

"I don't know. Get a normal job maybe? I do know with the money I've saved I'll get a better place than the dinky two-bed flat me and Luke share though," he replied as he clambered onto the mattress and lay down. She quickly followed and lay down next to him and dragged the lightweight cover over them, but not before making sure they were completely dry first.

"Does Luke have the same amount of time left as you?"

"Yeah, he does. To be honest with you, both of us can't wait to get out. We're fed up of it now."

"Well let's hope you find something that suits you when you leave then."

"Oh, I hope so. I know it'll be hard for us to get a job. But a job is a job, we won't care what we get."

"This is true, a job is a job."

"Oh I know; don't you worry about that."

"Good."

"Yeah. Even if it's a desk job, at least I know I'll be going home every night instead of the rare once a week or once a month or whatever." He let out a massive yawn then.

"Right, get some sleep. We leave at dawn."

"Roger that; good night Calista."

"Good night Raven." And with that; they both quickly slipped into sleep, both utterly exhausted.

Chapter Twenty-Two

Calista groaned slightly at the harsh morning breeze that streamed through the doorway and over her... Wait, what? Her eyes flashed open, catching sight of a formidable shadow towering over her and she leapt to the right just as the thing moved, highlighting itself from the sunlight and she realised what it was. It was a fire demon. Then she saw its arms slash downwards, embedding his double-bladed axe into the spot which a few seconds ago she had occupied, sinking the humongous weapon deep into the mattress, which luckily jammed it thanks to how hard it had swung down. She landed heavily on Raven who grunted at being woken up in such a rude manner, until he caught a look at the rude reason why. He roared as anger coursed through his system quicker than a bullet leaving a gun barrel, pushed Calista off of him with a quickness that left her wide eyed, mouth hanging open as she collided back first with the wall and dived at the creature whose pearl pink eyes had widened in shock at the roar that left Raven. It dropped the axe it had managed to get free just as Raven had leapt, so it clattered to the floor in a loud bang, which unfortunately brought the demon out of its shocked state, but not before Raven slammed himself into it with surprising force and tackled it to the floor where they landed in a mass of tangled arms and legs. Calista crawled to the edge of the bed, a slight twinge between her legs causing her to pause quickly. It proved she was no longer that lily white virgin she'd been for so long, but she definitely was more sore today than she was last night. Well, a minor hindrance, she'd suffered a lot worse when facing a teething Ghrowlaer and that was pretty bad. Snapping herself out of her thoughts, she watched, utterly impressed with Raven as he slammed the demons head over and over again into the floor, which wasn't easy considering he was just a human, but then she remembered he also had the vampire gene so perhaps that aided him a hell of a lot more than what they had originally thought. She really needed to do the mind meld with him and find out just how deep it went.

"Who the fuck sent you?" he growled into its face, which would have made a Ghrowlaer very proud and that was saying something.

"Kharge. Not that it's anything to do with you, puny human," it hissed back from between tiny jagged teeth coated in black spit and grass green blood.

"How do you kill this sorry piece of shit?" She knew he was talking to her, but yet never took his concentration away from pinkie, maybe because he somehow knew that if he took his concentration from him, it would give the demon those few seconds to change their positions.

"Separate the head from the neck or rip out the heart." She leaned down, gripped the axe handle and stood with it. Even though she was naked, it didn't faze her. She hefted the huge weapon above her head and let her arms drop, swinging the blade downwards, stopping a mere few mms from the creature's throat.

"Tell me why he sent you!" she said, the stone-cold killer that she was unflinching.

"As if I'm going to tell you," he hissed and spat at her. The black spit flew at her but before it could hit her, Raven's hand shot out, caught the flying gunk and smeared it back over the creature's face, effectively burning it in the process. How the hell didn't it burn him? It burned everyone! Well, almost everyone, she was immune to it. But still, it should have burned him!

"Try again. Answer her!" he hissed, shoving his own face as close as possible with the axe being the only thing that kept them apart.

"Do you honestly think he'll make it easy for you to rescue those pathetic children? Really? If you think that, then you're so much more stupid than people realise!" Raven didn't give her time to answer, just lifted the creature's head up and slammed it back down onto the floor with as much brute force as he could muster, putting a massive hole in the floor and splitting the being's head wide open. Blood gushed out around it, coating the floor in that green grass colour. The demon's eyes rolled back in its head as it died. Calista quickly grabbed Raven and hurled him off the body. And just in time as well, for the body began to heat up but the outer shell didn't burn, instead it let out his last breath and died.

"Well, that was interesting," Raven smirked at her and wiped his cheek, leaving behind a trail of the demon's blood.

"What I want to know is why didn't that spit of his burn you? Demon spit always burns."

"I honestly don't know. I really don't." He held his hand out, remains of the spit still there so he quickly wiped them on the demon's clothes and then showed her his hand, it was as if he had never touched it.

"Hm, well that's handy to know. Must mean you are immune to it then. But we'll keep that little tidbit to ourselves for now. Right, let's get rid of this fucker and be on our way. No time to dally." She watched as he walked away, totally appreciating the fact he was stark bullock naked and damn, that man had a tight tush she wanted to sink her nails into again! Then she saw the scar he was on about, it rode from his left hip and curled upwards to the middle of his shoulder blades, about an inch thick and jagged. How hadn't she noticed it before? Then she knew, she had been too busy staring at his butt. She snapped herself to attention and headed outside. She walked a little distance and saw what she was looking for. She quickly strode back to the cabin and saw that Raven was now dressed and was tying his boot laces back up. She didn't bother with the old fashioned way of getting dressed, she was magic baby! Snapping her fingers she clothed herself. Black jeans, tank top and boots. Simple but yet effective. She couldn't be bothered with her usual attire of black leathers. Although, she did take the time to strap her weapons to their rightful place on her body.

"Are you ready?" she asked Raven once she was ready and saw he'd also attached his two knives to his thighs and one to his upper arm. All within easy reach. Gun slung over his shoulder to dangle at his side, but easy to grab and swing up if he needed to shoot. Fingerless gloves covered his hands.

"Yes."

"What's with the gloves?"

"Precaution. And these beauties aren't just gloves."

"What are they?" She stepped closer and took one of his hands into hers. They just looked like normal wool gloves to her.

"They're rigged."

"How?" She dropped his hand.

"Believe it or not; they're my handy work. Gunpowder. Just need a light, a twenty second delay for you to run before they go boom!"

"Very nice."

"You reckon?"

"God yeah. Just because we have magic doesn't mean we can't marvel at the wonders of gunpowder and such that exists," she replied and hauled the demon carcass up onto her shoulders as if it weighed absolutely nothing and ushered him out of the cabin.

"Wait here a moment." She didn't bother waiting for a reply, just walked off down the beach a bit more and came to a cluster of rocks. In the middle was crystal clear water. She threw a rock in and the water immediately began sizzling. Steam rose from it, wicked hot. Much like a sauna. She watched as a small creature seemed to materialise from within and shot right up to balance on the rock ledge.

"Who goes there?" it hissed between jagged teeth. With beady eyes, with the colour sloshing like water, it glared at her before it realised who she was and quickly averted its gaze. Body was small, no bigger than twelve inches or so with three inch long claw-type nails on its fingers and toes for ripping prey apart.

"I meant no disrespect Miss Calista," it murmured. She was the only one they literally feared, as everything else they just saw as prey.

"It's fine. I've brought food for you," she replied, before dumping the carcass into the water. The cannibal water goblin broke into a horrible crooked-toothed grin and dove back into the water. She looked down through the steam and watched as a collection of the goblins began to rip into the carcass but soon she couldn't see anything from the last lot of blood that hadn't burned and the flurry of bodies. Shaking her head, she walked away, back to Raven.

"What was that?" he asked.

"Cannibal water goblin."

"Anymore we'll encounter?"

"Of them, probably. They hang out at the swamp a lot. Anywhere there happens to be huge bodies of water, they'll be there."

"Note to self, avoid the ocean." He grinned as she rolled her eyes.

"They can't survive in the ocean, it's too salty for them. Well, they can go in it but not for long. Not like they can with streams and such. The swamp is even worse. All the dead things that reside there are literally just a massive buffet for them."

"Do they eat everything then?" he asked as she directed him back the way they came when they had arrived yesterday.

"Pretty much. The bones and such they usually crush down into a powder and use, and bear in mind they're ridiculously strong as well. Or they use the bones for decoration."

"Decoration? How?"

"In their homes. Or jewellery. You have to realise, they can break it down and remould it into different shapes and such. Actually, quite brilliant if you get the lucky chance of watching how they do it."

"I take it you know that because you've seen it?"

"Not only seen it, I taught them how to use it in ways that would help them."

"That's incredible."

"Not really. I just have my uses now and again."

"So they're really the clean-up crew of Mystic Being."

"You could say that." He didn't reply as they'd finally reached a small distance from the cabin and again, keeping to the cliff edge, they stopped. Calista drew her hands together and sent a ball of what looked like green fire towards the hut. But it didn't blow it up, instead it splashed over it, with roots and vines curling up and around it. Making it appear as if it had been untouched for countless years. Extraordinary.

Raven turned back to face the way they were set to go, shrugging his backpack into a more comfortable position ready for their journey. Before he'd taken so much as three steps forward, Calista flattened him against the cliff with an arm thrown over his chest and flattened herself just as a massive shadow swept over them. Glancing upwards, any sound he was going to make from the uncomfortable things in his pack digging in his spine vanished. It was a huge fucking gold/bronze dragon! But not full of rich healthy muscle and a strong physique but as if it had been decaying slowly. Chunks of it was missing, globs of it seemed to have melted off like wax from a candle and froze in that way. He could see parts of its ribs and decayed black internal organs that leaked through the bones. Eyes were dead and vacant, staring at nothing. Its snout was crushed in, as if something with great strength had hit it. Causing teeth to jut out at weird angles and its tongue wasn't long like other dragons, it was half the length in the mouth as if it had been torn, albeit brutally, out. Ouch. Its claws were half missing and jagged so it'd hurt hell of a lot if it caught your flesh. The tail was more bone than anything else, with what looked like shards of wood or something sticking out in various places. Its wings were ripped, had burn holes through and had obviously been broken a fair few times from the crooked way the bones were. It flapped them hard as if it struggled to keep its huge form airborne. The part that really got him, was the giant axe that was embedded in its skull! The handle snapped off as much as it could without removing the actual blade. Between its shoulder blades sat a red being that was laughing with sickening yellow teeth holding something in its black clawed hands that gleamed in the early sunlight.

"What the hell is that?" he whispered.

"Which one?" Calista whispered back.

"Both." He dared not take his eyes from the sky, and kept as still as possible so not to draw attention to himself. He wasn't that stupid.

"It's a dead dragon brought back to life by dark, powerful magic by the looks of it. That thing on its back is a fire demon.

"What do we do?"

"You go back to the cabin. I'm going to go help the dragons. If that dragon is being controlled by dark magic, they'll have no luck against it. Not without me. And before you argue, don't. This is what I do for a living. It can't kill me, hurt me yes, kill no. But it can kill you. And if it sees that I am protecting you, then it'll use that against me and to be fair I really don't need the hassle right now."

"I understand. I know I have no chance whatsoever against that thing."

"Good. I will return as soon as possible. No matter what you hear, do not come out!" He didn't argue, just turned around and headed back to the cabin. But quickly stopped short as he saw the vines had indeed grown back quickly as if they had never been disturbed. Then he saw a slight gap and realised it was the door, so rushed forward, pushed them aside and hurried into the cabin, the shrubbery snapping back into place. He turned around when he was inside and looked out from between the thick leaves that he could barely look out of and because of that, he quickly shut the door too, knowing it was of no use trying to look through them.

Calista leapt into action as soon as she heard the cabin door close, signalling that Raven was safely inside. She bolted up the sloping steps to the top of the cliff just as the dripping corpse spat out a gob-full of thick black tar coated in rolling flames. It landed near Gélio's claws as he appeared out of nowhere to dive and land in front of two unprotected fledglings, which was saying something considering his size. She watched as Gélio hid a grimace as the boiling substance splashed onto his scales, burning him. Using that as a leverage to move because everyone had their attention on him, she crouched as low as she could and using a quick burst of energy and speed, dashed across the grassland before diving into the huge collection of Warrior Dragons that backed Gélio. She skidded to a halt next to one of the meanest, most brutal dragons alive, only second to that of Gélio. He was a handsome, towering mass of black muscle that stood a head and half shorter than that of Gélio himself. He had stunning blood-red spines that danced from his high-arched neck, down his spine and ended at the tip of his tail. Some had chunks missing as well as his body housed deep crevices of healed-over claw marks from obvious battles. His wings were folded elegantly against his sides of deep black, flecked through with red. She noticed he had caught sight of her as he winked and lifted the flap of his mouth, giving her a glimpse of his saliva-coated white teeth. He then snapped his blood-red and flame-yellow eyes back to what was going on ahead of them and she did the same. Holding on with one hand so it didn't topple from the wind created by the dragon's wings, regarding them all from the angry green eyes, was a red demon who smiled sickeningly at them, showing off its disgusting yellow, rotting teeth coated in saliva. Its skin flaking off in dribs and drabs. He also had a tarnished blood-stained sword clasped in his hand. Obviously the dead beast below it was being controlled with black heinous magic, but by who, she had no idea. She would find out who it was, hunt them down and rid them of this world. As she regarded the dragon in front of her, she saw globs of the tar that clung to its body gave it a patchy uneven look. Claws were also missing from its feet, leaving dangling decaying flesh in its place. From where its mouth hung open, thanks to her enhanced vision, joy that it was, she would see that its choppers were held in place with corroding black gums that had them collapsing in on themselves and the teeth were pointing in all sorts of angles. You could see the ribcage and the deflated red lungs with black patches that were as long as Calista and a good three feet wide. Not surprising they were so big. They did have to power the dragon when it was alive. Perched in the middle of the lungs, standing out against them was the blackened heart which was easily the size of the half of the lungs. He also had a very noticeable hole that had pretty much his entire left side on show. But it was the chew marks around the edges that drew her attention, it was as if something had taken great delight in eating from it, which also explained where the other organs had gone. But if that was the case, why leave the lungs and heart? Was it because they were covered in the tar? Snapping back to attention, it was obvious the beast had died either near or in the tar pits of Teàrr Mons. Not a very pleasant way to die and it was obvious he had sadly suffered a long time before he had finally succumbed and walked into death's cold eternal grasp. She looked at the group behind her, noticing a pale green female dragon herding the two fledglings away to safety as quietly as possible so not to draw attention to her or them.

"What do you want?" Gélio's booming voice snapped her attention into focus again.

"For us to rule? Please you stupid beast, I do not need to explain what we want," the demon hissed.

"And what makes you so sure that you can defeat us?"

"Like this." It raised its arms and began chanting a spell she knew all too well thanks to ripping it from a Death Whytches' mind. She looked back at the second in command and when he again looked at her she mouthed, *brace yourself*, and he nodded slightly, which meant he understood what she said. As Gélio was about to take a step forward, she placed her hand on his tail and because he was that good, no shock played across his features or even a single twitch of his muscles apart from where her hand was which let her know he recognised it was her. Looking at the demon, she watched as the spell removed the 'cloak' and a solid two hundred or so dead dragons flapped soundlessly on the gentle breeze and each held one to four demons of all factions. Lovely!

"Are we meant to be intimidated?" Gélio actually looked uninterested.

"Well, considering that it looks like you are outnumbered and that you don't have Calista here to help you yes." It chortled with laughter as it brought the dragon down to land on the cliff edge. Calista glanced up at Lagiòcrus, Gélio's second in command, who had walked up beside her, but he stared ahead, eager and ready to do battle. She could tell by the eagerness in his eyes, the tightness of his body, claws dug slightly into the ground. As soon as Gélio made the command, he would no doubt be the first to charge forward. She pulled her axe from behind her and swung it in a circle loosely to flex her wrist so she would have easier advantage for her to kill. And kill as many of those fuckers as she damn well could. The eagerness that coursed through her body to eradicate them from the world was an addictive high she got, so she was very eager to get started.

"So that must mean I am just an illusion then," she retorted and walked forward, drawing all attention to her. They all hissed at her and before they realised it, the bad lot attacked, aided by the black magic for speed and agility.

"Calista, quick!" She bolted up Gélio's leg and settled between two spines just as one of the corpses attacked Gélio, raking its claws just below her foot. She stood up and dived on the corpse, slamming into the demon that resided on its back, sending them both tumbling to the ground, where they landed with a thud but quickly bounced back to their feet. She didn't hesitate and launched herself at the demon whilst he was still dazed. She threw punch after punch that it gave back but it didn't stop her. Before she could gain the upper hand, it shot backwards and lobbed a fire ball at her which she quickly deflected. Before she could retaliate, a giant leg appeared above the demon's head and stomped on it, killing the fiend but also sending an arch of black/red blood over her. This caused her to grimace, which she quickly hid on her features, from the heat of it as it washed over her skin. Not a burn, as she was immune, but the heat was still horrendous.

Nodding her thanks to Lagiòcrus as he wiped his foot against the grass before gearing up for another kill, she soon forgot about her wounds as she called forth the magic. She began to glow and looking around, saw corpses and demons on the floor, taken out but the victors weren't without their own set of injuries. Just as she was about to send her magic out to claim the lives of those still fighting them, she caught movement out of the corner of her eye. Turning her head, it was the last person she expected to see. Raven. Why couldn't he just stay fucking put?

Raven couldn't hold back any longer. He had to do something, he just wasn't one to sit back and watch. There must surely be something he could do. Even if it was to act as a decoy. He quickly left the safety of the cabin, once he had double checked that his weapons were attached to himself in their rightful places. Backpack in hand, he ran outside and climbed the cliff steps, quickly reaching the top, but hid his backpack first, and just as he saw Gélio rip the throat out of a dragon and bite a demon in half, a huge arc of blood followed. Looking around, he caught sight of Calista, glowing as her magic rose inside of her. Before he could say or do anything, her gaze snapped to his. She shook her head no, but he didn't care, he had to do something. Just as he was about to move, he finally saw the wounds on Calista. Burn marks coated her arms, hands, chest and the left side of her face, but she seemed completely oblivious to them. He knew she must be in agony from them but how she managed to not even grimace was a miracle! But then he knew she was stubborn as anything and one hell of a fighter so he knew that wouldn't slow her down. He also saw blood coating her as well, but again, it didn't seem to faze or register she was covered. He moved, but not enough to draw attention to himself. It helped that he kept bent low, and everyone was interested in fighting each other rather than pay attention to the human running. Just as he was half way to Calista, he spotted a black demon creeping up behind her, a battle axe held in the air. He didn't think twice, but bolted flat out across the ground, weaving past creatures. He dived past Calista before tackling into the beast, crashing into it in a solid thump, causing it to stumble back from the force and shock of the impact, which Raven used to his advantage. He knocked the axe away, hooked his foot around its thick ankle and tripped the creature back, sending it crashing to the floor and quickly dived on its chest. Unfortunately, it got over its shock quickly and raked its claws down his sides, leaving blooded furrows in its wake. Raven hissed as hot blazing pain shot through his body but not enough that he couldn't complete his task. He rained heavy blows to the creature's face, feeling and hearing its bones break from the impact of his fists. He caught sight of another demon heading straight for him out the corner of his eye, grabbed his knife that resided in his boot and threw it. Sending it home right between the creature's eyes, killing it pretty much instantaneously. Not one to gloat, he turned his attention back to the arsehole under him, who had started to wiggle, obviously aiming to have the upper hand, which was a big fat no! He whipped out his blade that he kept in the back of his jeans that Calista had given him, and slammed it to the hilt into the side of its neck, sending a lovely spray of blood in the air, coating Raven.

"Smile, chicka!" he growled as he sliced it ear to ear, before climbing off, literally picked up the hulking mass of muscle and sent it barrelling into another as it ran at him. Using the stamina from years of military training and just pure instinct, he cut through at least a dozen before he managed a good thirty-second breather and looked for Calista but he didn't see her until he just happened to glance upwards. She was perched between Gélio's spines welding flame balls she was lobbing at anything which got within reach. When Gélio swooped low to the ground, he watched as Calista vaulted from him to land in the group of the most demons, absolutely kicking arse. Just as he was about to move, he heard the tell-tale sign of someone behind him. He didn't move until the last second as the creature behind drew its weapon. As he heard the scrape of a sword leaving its protective covering, he whirled around with his own black-blood-covered blade and slammed it to the hilt in the beast's neck.

"I don't think so, arsehole." He yanked out the blade and slammed it into its eye socket — blood and eyeball spewed back at him. Lovely. But he didn't let that faze him. He removed the blade and kicked the foul creature back as it toppled to the floor in a crash with a very stunned expression on its face. He didn't wait to see if it was dead, he knew it was, just whirled around for his next fight but was confronted instead by Calista.

"What the hell are you doing?" Her eyes were practically spitting fire at him, but he didn't care, he needed to help, he wasn't one to sit back and do nothing.

"I couldn't just sit around. It was driving me crazy. I had to do something."

"I get that. I really do. But you don't realise just how dangerous everyone here is. One stray hit, they will kill you. One hit and they will cave your chest in."

"I gathered that. But honestly, it won't stop me. The only two I live for are Luke and Lexis. Without them, well, I wouldn't be who I am today or maybe even here."

"Hardly the point, Raven. Now piss off out of the way so I don't have to worry about protecting you and making sure you stay alive!"

"You aren't the boss of me, Calista. If I want to fight I will."

"I will not be the cause of you dying."

"It's my choice!"

"Tough —" before she could say anything else, a blade shot between them, slicing clean through Calista and stopping just short of embedding itself in his own chest. Raven stared, horrified as he looked at the blade and its wicked serrated edging and back up to Calista's face. But she wasn't worried, oh no! She had the look of absolute rage on her features. He glanced behind her and standing there with what could only be classed as a shit-eating grin plastered on its face and a wicked gleam in its bright orange eyes, was one of the demons.

"Move back," she whispered. He didn't need telling twice, just took a huge step backwards. Just that look on her face was enough to stop him from arguing. When he had moved back enough, he watched, completely enthralled as she reached behind her, clasped the hilt securely in her hand, pulled the blade out with a sickening squelching noise as it moved past organs and muscle, before whirling around and lobbed off the demon's head. It all happened in a matter of seconds. Raven was amazed. She didn't even blink as she removed the blade. How the hell did she do that? His insides were cramping up just watching! He watched as her skin knotted itself back together until all that remained was the holes in her tank top. She looked past him then and before he could look over his own shoulder to see what had caught her attention, a huge shadow swept over them. With a small feeling of dread settling into his gut, he tipped his head back and he was greeted with a huge mouthful of teeth, a black tongue and a gob-full of breath that smelled about as pleasant as a thousand rotting corpses left to bake in the midday sun in the middle of a heatwave. Not to mention the oozing saliva that coated the rotting teeth. Looking past them he found he was staring into sightless black eyes. Fucking dragon was huge! The head alone must have been as big as he was tall! He caught sight of a foot moving from the corner of his eye but the next thing he knew, he was suddenly sent flying before crashing to the ground, enough to wind him. But he leapt to his feet and as he regained his footing after sucking in a gob fall of air, whirled around in time to see Calista slam her sword through the dragon's mouth and out the top of its head, taking a lovely coating of brain and black, clotted blood with it. The beast reared back, taking Calista with it, a horrendous howl leaving its throat before it crashed back to the ground, once again forever silenced. She landed back on her feet and glanced back at Raven. He looked at her just as the demon that lounged on the beast's back charged at her and he snapped to attention, then dived at the creature, tackling it to the ground. It threw him off but he quickly regained his feet and they scrambled for its weapon. The demon, thanks to its strength and slightly faster speed, got the weapon first. It swung the huge axe out to the side and took a swipe at Raven's legs. But he jumped so it missed and used the momentum of the wide swing to his advantage. He slammed his fists over and over again into the creature's face, breaking the skin and causing hot sticky black blood to run down its face and coat his hands, but that didn't stop him. He landed a punch square on the jaw and as it bent over, he yanked on its horns, sending it crashing to its knees and then smashed its face into the ground with the momentum of dragging it down. It slammed nose first with a resounding crunch before he grabbed its head, causing it to look up at him whilst on its knees. Before it could do any damage to him, he hooked his foot under the axe handle, flipped it up and caught the handle in his hand. He held the weapon at the creature's throat, cutting it slightly with the sharp blade. Not that he gave a shit but at least it knew he meant business. He looked up at Calista and saw her watching him intently.

"Your turn." He moved to the side a little as she stepped forward and didn't so much as blink as he watched her burrow her hand into the demon's chest and rip the heart from its chamber. The huge black organ nearly overflowed her hand and it made a sickly slurping noise as it continued beating with the last bit of blood rushing through it.

"You bitch," the thing cried as it toppled over. She dropped the heart next to its head.

"I've had enough of this shit," she muttered and Raven felt the untold draw of raw power then. She drew her hands up, fingers curled as magic sparked in between and around her fingers. Thick black clouds rolled across the sky as if someone was dragging them, casting the entire plain in darkness. Thunder rippled through the clouds, loud and demanding. Lightning also lit the atmosphere in bright flashes, dominating the sky. Still Raven pulled Calista's sword out of her scabbard at her waist and circled around her, keeping an eye out for anyone wanting to advance on them both but also watching as the only light was now from Calista herself and the lightning. He glanced around and couldn't see anything apart from the glowing eyes of all the creatures still alive. All the fighting had stopped and everyone was watching them. All that could be heard was heavy breathing, so he stopped circling her and stood slightly to her left and back. A menacing look on his face, no one could doubt which side he was on. If they wanted to go for some, he'd fight to his last dying breath and he reckoned they knew it, considering they'd have no doubt seen him slaughtering demons that had gotten off their own dragons. Wind howled through the land, whipping into them, but it didn't faze them. He spared a glance at Calista just as she threw her hands out and all the evil ones screamed. Not normal screams. No, these ones caused Raven to dangle the sword from his wrist by a strap he saw near the handle and slap his hands over his ears as they were horrendous! High pitched as if someone was dragging their nails down a blackboard or as if someone had grabbed their balls in a tight grip and was squeezing. Not pleasant at all. Or perhaps as if they were being burned from the inside out. There was no telling what Calista was doing to them. The shrieks finally stopped after what seemed like forever, but in reality, was no longer than a minute or two. He removed his hands and gripped the sword again as the clouds dispersed along with the thunder, lightning, and howling wind, and raw overly-bright sunlight cascaded over them in a wash of light and warmth. He rubbed his eyes from the brightness that startled his retinas. When he was finally able to see, he saw that the evil ones were vanquished. Their bodies littered the floor. Mouths gaping wide open in silent screams, eyes wide and sightless. Claws and fingers curled up from agony. Some had died on their stomachs, others had died on their backs or sides. Either which way, it was a victory for them and he was damn glad of that.

"Well, that was certainly one way in aiding us," Gélio said, drawing their attention. Raven blinked as he saw the damage to Gélio's body. He had fresh blood oozing down his left side. Massive claw marks ran down his side, front of his neck and across his mouth. One was also really close to his eye. He was lucky he hadn't been blinded. Chunks were missing from his spines from where he'd been bitten from the dead dragons as well as swiped at with swords or axes, etc. Teeth marks dotted his rib cage, some so deep as to show off his bones. Either way, how he was cool, calm and collected with the amount of injuries he had was a testimony of his brute strength and willpower to not allow anyone to see how weak it was making him.

"Want some help, big guy?" Calista asked him.

"If you'd be so generous." Raven knew she was powerful; I mean, come on, look at what she had just done, but watching her as she healed Gélio was extraordinary and literally a sight to behold. The blood ran *up* his body and disappeared back inside. The wounds healed over until all that was left was a faint scar that you had to properly look for to know it was there. But she completely healed the ones across his face. Even the parts missing from him had regenerated, and the only indication that Gélio felt anything was from the slight contortion on his face and the curl of his lip plus the slight stiffening of his body. When completed, he nodded his thanks.

"Price?"

"On the house this time." He again nodded his thanks then headed for Nyhkohl, who fervently accepted her mate and together they flew off.

"Where are they going?" Raven asked from where he stood.

"He's off to reinstate himself into her good books," Calista replied. Then it clicked as to what she meant. Raven nodded and watched as she moved to the edge of the cliff from where they had come up from where they had stayed at the cabin. He did not want to think of the dragons having make-up sex. That would be disgusting and something he really didn't want to picture.

"Now what do we do?" he called, moving to stand next to her.

"Get rid of the corpses. Get the stone from Blade of Souls. Get the children. Get back safely so they can return to their families and get started on their counselling of what has happened to them," was her simple reply.

"And just how do you plan on getting rid of the corpses? There are a fair few of them," he said as he gestured behind his shoulder.

"Like this." She gave a shrill yet sharp whistle and he looked over to where she pointed. Down on the beach, where he had watched her throw the dead demon from earlier, he realised it was actually an entire rock cluster. It began to bubble, like a jacuzzi, but before he knew it, a tidal wave of small black bodies shot out of the water to land with a solid thump on the sand. It was at least one hundred of the cannibal water goblins, in all size and ugliness. Even female ones, but that was only shown from the lumps that resembled their breasts and a small piece of fabric or whatever it was across them and the centre of their legs. The males only had it across their privates, the rest of their bodies were naked and all gleamed from the water droplets. They glanced around with wide beady black or yellow eyes and they all moved as an even bigger one shot from the rocks and landed on the sand. It had huge beady black eyes and jagged, yellow teeth so big its mouth couldn't shut properly. Claws hung from its hands and feet that curled and looked as dangerous as a velociraptor's! It looked up at them and with a roar that belied its size, charged up the stairs, and the smaller ones followed as well, all eager to follow their leader. When they reached the top, thick globs of saliva left their mouths and dripped to the floor when they saw the scattered mess of dead bodies, claws on hands and toes literally curled in anticipation of what was to come. They looked over at him and Calista.

"Eat?" the big one asked, talking hard because of its teeth.

"Yes, you can, but just the dead ones!" she said and they all cheered and dived on them, using abnormal strength for their size to drag the bodies and literally lobbed them over the side of the cliff so they could eat in private at the edge of their home. Creature comforts obviously. Even teaming together in dragging the ten or so dragon carcasses over the side. What surprised Raven was how they moved them. They literally rolled up in themselves, like little balls and shuffled the beasts along that way. In a way, it was actually quite remarkable to watch, considering they moved everything with an ease that obviously belied their hidden strength from their size. Raven looked around and noticed thankfully that they had not lost any of the good ones. Injured yes, but that could be sorted. Sheer luck was noticeably on their side for this. Once all the bodies of those deceased had been rolled or even kicked over the edge of the cliff, which was a good half hour as the Water Goblins got rid of the lifeless, along with him and Calista helping. The Water Goblins all cheered, eagerness bright in their eyes as they regarded their feast below before looking back at them.

"Thanks," the biggest said, before they all bowed before Calista.

"Oh, do get up," she muttered and they did. Raven moved to stand beside her.

"If you shall need us again and you are near, you know how to contact us," the one in charge replied.

"I do. Now go." Raven didn't so much as move or show any emotion on his face as he watched as they literally turned into crazed animals, snapping, snarling and deep-crazed laughter as they raced down the slope, pushing each other to get the ones ahead of them to move quicker. Some even so much as darting off the side when they were about half way down before they dived into the mass of bodies and began chewing through muscle and fat and crunching on bones as easily as a knife through butter. Excited chatter amongst themselves as they tucked into their buffet. He was surely glad that he wasn't on the receiving end of that as it was disgusting! And he doubted he'd forget the sound of that laughter or the sight of everything for a very long time.

Chapter Twenty-Three

Calista moved away from the cliff edge and headed towards the dragons that remained behind. Lagiòcrus regarded her from one eye; the other sealed shut from a jagged wound.

"Bring your head down here, big guy," Calista said, opening her arms. She knew Raven was keeping a short distance behind her as he watched her like a hawk. She was not going to admit to herself or anyone that it actually made a nice change that someone was watching out for her purely because they wanted to and not because they got paid for it. Draylan, Skyri and Nikki non-withstanding. Lagiòcrus lowered his head without hesitation as it was clear that he trusted her. She placed her hand over the wound and the other on the side of his snout just below another gash. Magic soared out of her hands and caressed his face with a bright blue glow, causing him to hum in contentment. When the light disappeared, Lagiòcrus's eye was healed as was the gash just above the slit of his mouth. All that was left was a very faint scar that you wouldn't know was there unless you looked for it; the same as she had done for Gélio. Calista patted him to let him know that it was done and he stood back up tall again.

"What is payment this time?" he asked.

"On the house," she replied and looked at Raven who hurried over to her side when he realised, she was looking at him as he was scuffing his boot across the floor instead of outright staring at her.

"What?"

"We need to get moving. Sarhsha, I need for you to come with me and Raven back to the cave of keepers so I can get the Blade of Souls." She turned to the Seer dragon, who regarded her from behind Lagiòcrus with wide, white eyes. She was one of the few who had remained uninjured in their fight thanks to Lagiòcrus keeping anything away from her.

"But Calista, you know the dangers of that blade, and God forbid anything escapes from it," she whispered, her voice hollow and scratchy sounding thanks to a serious injury she had received a while ago. Her throat had been slashed by a traitor that Lagiòcrus had killed as it turned out, him and Sarhsha were Dragon Souls. It wasn't unusual that two dragons from different factions become mated but it was extremely rare for a Seer to mate anyone other than another Seer, but as Calista watched, it was pretty obvious that Lagiòcrus and Sarhsha were completely in love with each other, plus not to mention bonded males were downright protective of their loved ones.

"I know that, but I still need the blade. I require the gem that resides in it."

"Whatever for?" Lagiòcrus enquired.

"I will show you once I get it." Majority of the dragons knew that it was dangerous but they didn't actually know just how deadly it was and that was the way she wanted to keep it. Strolling past both Lagiòcrus and Sarhsha, and knowing full well that Raven was close behind her, she headed to the dragon's sleeping quarters. As he walked beside her, she noticed he still had her sword. She held her hand out and he handed it back over without question. She ran her hand over the blade, cleaning it from the blood and returned it back to its scabbard on her back. A few moments later, of them all walking in silence, rolling rich green grass covered hills greeted them. Taking a stroll across the lush greenery, not a word was said between them but not that Calista complained, she preferred the silence. They soon reached an incline where it was nothing but a giant hole that even Gélio could hide in and not be seen. She walked inside, knowing full well the others would follow. Walking about ninety feet ahead, she reached a plain wooden door that was about seven feet high and turned back to Sarhsha.

"Best bet is to wait here until we come back. They'll only moan if you follow us in."

"Of course. I shall see you soon." She bowed her head, turned around and left the cave to patiently wait for them outside, no doubt just happy her mate was still alive. Calista knew for a fact she'd be snuggled up against him whilst they waited for their return.

"I need for you to do me a favour once we are inside." Calista looked at Raven, who looked back at her. Only way he could was due to the blazing torches that resided on either side of the door.

"And what is that?"

"Whatever happens, do not ask to see her 'friend'."

"Why not?"

"Because it isn't, shall we say, normal."

"Have you looked around? Nothing here is normal. At least not to me anyway." He had a point there.

"Don't say I didn't warn you." They both turned as one to the door and Calista knocked. Not even a minute later, it opened soundlessly and they were greeted by a pale, thin woman who had pale white eyes, dead pink lips, her nose had slits in the nostrils and dead white hair hung around her shoulders lifelessly and dull. She also stood all of about four feet eight-ish.

"Can I help you?" Her voice was emotionless and her teeth were black and rotten and tilted in on themselves.

"I need to see Seliana," Calista replied.

"And what do you need to see Lady Seliana for?" The disgust in her voice was evident. Foolish child had no idea who she was dealing with or she obviously just didn't care. After all, slugs, or slaves as they were also known as, were only loyal to their 'owners'.

"None of your business, Worm. Now move!" Because the door was open, Calista barged past, followed quickly by Raven and just in time too, as the woman closed the door with a resounding slam. Striding through the place, Calista glanced about to see what was around her and the entire place was empty apart from just ahead. There was a raised platform on a mound of skulls of all shapes and sizes. Many of which were stained with dried and fresh blood of all colours. The woman who had answered them at the door, scurried past them and clambered onto the steps of the platform when a horrendous crunching noise shot through the room. Looking towards the back of the room where the noise came from, a woman walked through. She shoved something into her mouth as she chewed and swallowed whatever it was, regarding them from the only fantastical thing about her, — her eyes. They were brown but sparkled as if they housed thousands of stars that were surrounded by long lashes. She was a plain thing. Mousy brown hair, slender build. Thin lips and she had a long haphazard scar down the side of her face and cut across the middle of her lips which kind of left them in a permanent sneer. She was dressed in a plain brown floor length dress that covered her arms down to her hands as well. She was the Keeper of the Blade. The one she was here to see.

"Calista, to what do I owe this visit?" Her voice was husky, but not a good husky, as if she'd had major damage done to her vocal cords. Going by her face, it wouldn't have surprised them in the least. Plus, looking at her as her dress moved from her throat, Calista caught sight of a thick scar. Failed attempt at a throat cut maybe? Or was it from torture? Either which way, she didn't give a shit. She was here for one thing and not for pleasantries.

"I need the Blade of Souls."

"Whatever for?"

"I need the stone inside."

"And that is forbidden," its little assistant hissed.

"Worm, I can talk for myself. But she is right, it is forbidden."

"And since when do I go by the rules? Where is the blade?" She headed over to the woman, fed up of her stupid questions and she really needed to get moving.

"I can't divulge that information to you," she hissed and scurried away. But Calista was quicker and grabbed her around her throat, dragging the woman closer to her before putting her face up close, even though she had to pretty much bend in half to do that. Damn woman was a tiny thing, probably no taller than five feet two or three.

"Do not make me repeat myself." She stared and Seliana looked away. As her eyes kept on moving to something behind her in the tell-tale way that something was about to happen, so she glanced over her shoulder to find out what had caught Seliana's attention, and just in the nick of time, as Raven tackled Worm to the floor, hard, yanking an axe out of her hands, that she no doubt wanted to use against Calista. She watched as Raven jerked the woman up slightly and then slammed his fist into the side of Worm's head, causing the thing's head to snap back into the floor with a solid crack and her eyes fluttered closed. Green blood leaked around her from where her head had hit the floor, coating her white hair. Raven climbed off the woman, axe still in his hand, knuckles dripping blood from Worm's face and he towered over Seliana as she stared in fear at him.

"Now if I were you, I'd tell Calista and I where this godforsaken blade is so we can get what we need and move on, then no one else will get hurt."

"And why should I tell you, filthy vermin?" Seliana spat at him. Raven looked at her and she let Seliana go and stepped back, eager to see what Raven would do.

"For a start, vermin is rats. I am not a rat as you can see. Now tell me!" He backed her up to the wall, using his big body and strength for intimidation. His eyes pretty much snapping blue fire.

"No!"

"Fine, then we do this the hard way." He turned to look at her and she just stared back at him, actually quite impressed, not that she'd say anything about that.

"Care to do the mind dive? But make it as painful as possible." She grinned at him sadistically and dove into Seliana's mind, causing the woman to crumble to the floor in a mess of limbs as she let out a bloodcurdling scream. Calista pushed through unwanted memories from the woman until one memory seemed to stick out the most. Her most favourite memory was the fact she repeatedly used Worm for her own sexual needs, including using Worm between her thighs a lot and gyrating herself on the woman's face, which caused her to get off. She'd then put on a strap that had a plastic penis on the end and repeatedly raped Worm, who dared not utter a sound as it was inserted in either her vagina, arse or sometimes her mouth. Then Seliana would gyrate herself against Worm's mouth again until she got off. That was the memory that stuck out the most. Really? Bloody woman! She dug deeper, raking her 'claws' down the insides of her memory wall, causing Seliana to scream again and clasp her hands to her head. Calista soon found what she was looking for. The blade resided in a small room off to their right in a wooden box. Pulling free from Seliana's mind, Calista watched as Seliana lifted her head hesitantly and yellow blood trickled from her nose and corner of her mouth.

"The blade is in the small room to your right, Raven." She motioned to where she meant and he looked over his shoulder and sure enough, there was the door. As he stepped away to go to it, Seliana grabbed on to his ankle.

"NO! You are not allowed to enter there!" she hissed and he kicked her off him, just as he was jumped on from behind by Worm. Fighting her off, he noticed Calista had grabbed Seliana and whirled her around to watch what was about to happen, and no matter how much the woman fought to get free, she didn't have the strength to remove Calista's hold around her neck.

"Do we need her?" Raven asked, throwing Worm off him and she bounced on the floor.

"No." And that was when she saw his inner killer come out. And damn if it didn't impress her. His eyes hardened. His mouth become a thin line and sheer determination was etched all over his body, and it seemed as though his entire body got just a little bit bigger. He turned to face Worm just as she launched herself at him again, a knife in her hand. She watched as Raven easily disarmed her and threw the knife away where it clattered to a stop in some shadows and shoved the woman away again.

"You leave my mistress alone!" Worm screamed, her voice high pitched as froth came from her mouth, her white eyes clotted with burst blood vessels standing out against the redness on her face. She charged at Raven again who waited until she reached him and Calista watched as his arms snapped upwards, grabbed her neck and literally ripped her throat out. Blood spurted in an arc of green. Raven dropped the collection of flesh from his hand and it fell to the floor in a splat. He turned to Calista and he stared

371

at her, unblinking. His breathing was calm and even as if he hadn't just killed a person. She looked at him and felt a sharp blaze of pain in her side. Looking down she saw a blade sticking out of her side, above her left hip. Before she could retaliate, Raven launched himself at Seliana and she actually had to take a step back. His face was downright malicious, his eyes held the absolute promise of murder. He ripped Seliana's arms from their sockets, sending blood spurting and as she leaned forward to sink her teeth into any part of him she could reach, he stepped back out of reach and slammed his fist into her face. She spat teeth out and more yellow blood trickled down her lips and chin. Obviously she was intent on guarding the blade with her very life, but why? What was she hiding? Calista watched as he threw away the arms before he got down and dirty to literally destroying Seliana. She screamed at him and no matter what was happening to her, she was trying to retaliate any which way she could, but it was of little use, he was too quick and way too strong for her. Calista watched as he made short work of killing Seliana. Not that she was complaining. But she was also impressed. She watched as he let out a growl that even Skyri would be impressed by, grabbed Seliana by the throat and pretty much ripped her larynx out, leaving it to dangle in his hand as she toppled over in a boneless heap, blood seeping around her, head slamming off the floor before dead eyes stared at them. He threw her chunk of flesh atop her, moved away and pulled open the door to where they needed to go. She walked next to him and stepped into the room just behind him. She snapped her fingers and light flared in her palm, aiding them in what they needed to see. Stepping further into the room, Calista threw her hand out, sending the light spinning into the room to circle around the walls, thus aiding them better. She stepped forward another step and heard a mighty crunch and looked down. Her foot had gone through a skull. Demon by looks of it with the small horns jutting from the forehead, which showed it was a teenager, just coming into his own. So what was his skull doing here? She looked up as Raven passed her and watched as he headed to the single stand that stood dominant in the centre of the room. It was rich mahogany engraved with dragons and skulls. Beautiful workmanship. Resting on top, was a stunning chest about the size of a jewellery box with 3D roses all up the sides and accentuated by green glass vines. Calista walked up next to Raven and opened the doors. Resting inside on a pillow of onyx black velvet was the Blade of Souls. It was a multi-coloured blade with a glass handle. Inside that handle, was an orb that glowed, casting its own light over their faces. Calista reached inside and pulled it out.

"So that's the Blade of Souls?" Raven asked, drawing her gaze to his.

"Yes."

"Thought it would have been bigger." She rolled her eyes at his grin and flipped open the end of the blade and looked inside.

"Are you serious?" she grumbled as what she was looking for was nowhere to be seen.

"What's wrong?"

"The stone is missing."

"Maybe that could be why Worm and Seliana didn't want you in here? Could they have been in on it?" he asked, looking into the handle himself.

"Might be."

"So if it's missing, why is the orb glowing?"

"Decoy." She reached inside and snagged it out, crushing the ball in her fist and it crumbled to the floor in a sprinkle of dust. She then snapped the lid shut and put it back onto its cushion.

"So what now?"

"We carry on with the mission. I'll let Gélio know about the blade and will deal with it once this mission is over with."

"What was the stone for again?"

"Stops the Lava Lady for a few minutes. Allowing me to get inside Fire Mountain. I'm just going to have to find another way in."

"Are there other ways in?"

"Yes. It'll just take that bit longer to get in though." She stepped back and he waited as she extinguished the lights and then shut the door behind them before they walked back outside. As they walked out of the cave in silence, the heat of the midday sun bore down on the land. Stepping out into it from the shadow of the cave, they both had to blink a couple times so their retinas could adjust to the difference in light. Calista was the first to recover and looked around, quickly catching the attention of Sarhsha, who was on her own at a scented pool.

"Did you get it?" she asked and because they were closer to her, they both could see the scar on the underside of her neck from when she was previously injured, just before Calista had been 'born'. Not the newest one that made her voice sound hollow and scratchy, but the previous one from when she became into her power of a Seer.

"No. Where is Gélio?"

"Let me get him." She took a couple steps and shot up into the air, the wind easily catching her wings allowing her flight. Calista looked at Raven but he was picking at the blood on his hands.

"Want me to get rid of it for you?"

"No thanks. I'm sure it won't be the only lot I'll get on me. We should just focus on what is happening. I can deal with getting clean later." And wasn't that a whole new surprise to her, she knew that men nowadays only wanted to be clean and not covered in different coloured blood, have flesh stuck under their fingernails and other small flaky bits of skin attached to their clothes. She was impressed. Even she had big enough balls to admit that. But she noticed he still had wounds from earlier. Why hadn't he said anything to her? She snapped her fingers and he healed over and he shot her a grateful smile. A huge shadow swept over them along with the sound of huge flapping wings and she glanced up, catching the eye of Gélio as he landed a little distance from them.

"Did you get it?" he asked.

"No. It's missing. She must have sneaked it out and given it to someone."

"Why would Seliana do that? She promised to uphold her oath of protecting the stone."

"Obviously whatever she was given in return was worth it."

"What happened to you in there?" Raven snapped his head up and saw Gélio was looking at him, more pointedly at the grime that clung to him.

"Killed Worm and Seliana."

"Why?" And Calista watched as Raven explained what had happened in the room.

"Well that certainly explains the blood and bits of flesh clinging to you. So what are you to do now?"

"We're going to go and rescue those kids. We need to get going. I don't want them in there with Kharge any longer than they need to be."

"Understood. Good luck on your quest." Gélio bowed his head before launching himself into the sky and disappearing from sight but not before dropping a parcel and Raven's backpack at their feet. Calista leant down and picked it up. Opening it up, she saw that it housed a single vial with a swirling red liquid and some food and water for Raven for whenever he would need it.

"What is it?" Raven glanced at it.

"Dragon's blood. And I'm guessing it's Gélio's." She opened the vial and drained the contents and a surge of untapped raw power rushed through her system. Then she handed the bag to Raven who nodded thanks but put it away in his backpack.

"Wonder why he gave it to you?"

"Probably to give me a boost. Getting blood around here is scarce."

"Really?"

"Of willing hosts, yes." She noticed he didn't say anything to that, just nodded.

"How much power did it give you? As your eyes are glowing a tad more than usual," he remarked.

"A lot. Gélio is one of the oldest alive so his blood is very potent with power and magic. Luckily, no one really knows just how powerful otherwise he'd be mercilessly hunted."

"Not surprised if they'd be after power."

"True. Anyway, let's go. We have a lot of ground to cover as quickly as possible." Calista ushered Raven up the small collection of steps they needed to reach topside and together in silence, walked out of Dragon Hill. Raven glanced over his shoulder and saw Gélio, Nyhkohl and the other lords up on their perch on the highest hill in all of their gleaming colours, talking amongst themselves. Quickly looking around, everyone had resumed what they were doing. As if what had transpired with the demons and dead dragons hadn't happened. But he guessed they were just celebrating the fact that no one had lost their lives, or did things like that happen quite frequently so that any reason to be alive was worth celebrating? He also wondered if people around the island and surrounding land had wondered as to why the sky had gone really dark for a few minutes before the sun made an appearance again. Or where they used to the unnatural phenomenon of Calista and her powers? He took a deep breath and followed Calista to the main gates, ignoring the prisoner dragons as they passed them and went out to finish their quest.

Chapter Twenty-Four

Tairen stood on the patio just outside the main doors from the living room balancing Jinx in the crook of his arm as she guzzled down some cold milk. He smiled as he watched Lexis team up with Alexzander and attack Luke who tickled them, causing the kid to laugh hysterically. He realised this must have been the first proper time the kid had laughed in the four years of his life. Well, there would be plenty more laughter and happiness from the boy if he had anything to say to it. And no doubt his woman would make sure the kid knew love, happiness and belly laughter for the remainder of her days. He watched Lexis laugh as she mucked around with their son. Their son. He would never for the rest of his life get tired of calling Alexzander his son or Jinx his daughter. He also vowed he was going to love them as much as possible for the remainder of his days as well. He would also love them the same as the son that grew in Lexis's womb, and any other children they would be blessed to have. He yawned as he looked down at Jinx who was watching him with her bright eyes, hair sticking up on end from her recent nap even though it was one p.m. But then again, she'd woken at five a.m. and through the baby monitor he had on the bedside table so they could hear her as she was in the adjoining bedroom to theirs, demanded to be fed. Before he or Lexis could get out of bed to tend to their baby, they heard the bedroom door open and Luke began talking to her, which caused Tairen to grab the baby monitor as it had a camera on it, put it on his chest and angled it so that both of them could watch in astonishment.

"Now, little Jinx, how can such a tiny baby make so much noise? You hungry little one?" He smiled as he picked her up and cuddled her in his arms. Jinx looked up at her uncle's face, hers all scrunched up and puffy from crying.

"Now, no more of that crying, you're meant to be all smiley. Let's get you changed, fed and leave your parents to catch up on more sleep so you've got me little one, just as handy as I'm already awake." Luke bounced her slightly and she smiled at him. He grabbed a clean nappy, baby wipes and a clean baby grow before he disappeared out of the room, cuddling his niece. He shut the bedroom door quietly and walked past their door, taking his niece downstairs to go and feed her. Tairen looked at Lexis,

"Now we know he cares. But why was he up at this time?"

"No idea. Maybe worried about Raven? I'll ask him in the morning." She settled back into sleep, curling into his side. He put the baby monitor back and cuddled her close. Knowing they could trust Luke with their daughter, he settled back into sleep until it was time for them to awaken.

Coming out of it, Tairen realised Jinx had stopped feeding so placed her against his shoulder and burped her. She let out an absolute belcher and giggled. He pulled her off his shoulder afterwards and turned her around so her back was to his chest and his arm banded around her and up under her bum so she essentially sat on his wrist so she could watch everyone. He yawned again, which was surprising considering Luke had taken care of the kids, feeding them both and he and Lexis had slept until at least ten a.m. Maybe because they'd had a long and exhausting couple of days and it was now catching up with him? Either way, he was sure they'd all sleep very well tonight. Gazing back to his family, he watched as Lexis walked over to him and took a drink of her ice-cold water that was perched on a small table they'd pulled outside.

"It's so good seeing him smile and laugh." She burst out laughing as Alexzander leapt onto Luke's back and pushed his uncle over, before rolling away so he couldn't get grabbed.

"Me too. Making memories." He smiled at her and watched as she kissed Jinx's cheek.

"Definitely. Have you got to go out to your uncle's today?"

"Nope, I'm all yours. I was, however, thinking of us taking a stroll to the beach."

"Now that sounds a good idea!" She beamed at him, as he knew she would as she adored going to the beach.

"Yeah, and we can get the kids used to the sea as well as I'm pretty sure we'll be there a lot during them growing up."

"What makes you so sure?"

"Because you're their mother and happen to adore the beach, so I have no doubt you'll be there with them a lot."

"True." They laughed together and he watched as she leant her face into Jinx and gave her another kiss on the cheek. This caused the baby to blush then burst out laughing and stretched her arms out, wanting to be cuddled by her mother. Tairen handed her over with no complaint. Lexis cuddled Jinx who sighed in happiness. Then he noticed she had a slightly worried look on her face, like she was over thinking some things.

"What's wrong, love?" Together they sat on the steps leading off the patio.

"Just over thinking some things is all."

"Like what? You're not meant to over think things, babe. Enjoy this time."

"I know I'm meant to enjoy things but I can't help it. I'm just thinking now we have Jinx and Alexzander to care for, as well as before we know it, the little one I'm carrying, how will we cope when you have a two-bedroom house and we can't exactly live here with Calista. It would drive her insane with three children under the age of five under her roof permanently. Not to mention I need to go back to Scotland to finish university before baby is here. Then we need to find our own home and everything."

"Actually, I was going to wait until later for this, but now is as good a time as any to be honest. I don't have that house anymore. Sold it to a single father and his kid. I've spoken to uncle, and he's given me the deed of ownership to that house along the beach you liked."

"The six-bedroomed one with the front porch covered in vines that is just off of the beach and the huge back garden with the brick wall?"

"The very one." He smiled at her.

"Oh my God! But how can we pay the bills, etc? I'll have to find a job here when I move back permanently as soon as I've finished university."

"You don't need to work babe. I brought the house outright from uncle."

"But Tairen, that house is something like half a million because of the size and location."

"I know. You also know what I'm like when money is concerned, if I don't need to buy anything, I won't. Plus, all the money I've collected from working for Calista, Draylan and Skyri I've saved. We don't need to work. We're billionaires, babe."

"What?" She just looked at him with wide eyes.

"Billionaires. Calista showed me how to manage my money and how to get interest and all that shit on it, which I've done as it's in the bank. Put it this way, you know how rich Calista is?"

"Yeah, she's got something stupid like twelve billion or something isn't it?"

"Nope. She's got roughly about twenty-four billion. If you add up everything that is on her black card, along with all the diamonds, emeralds, etc. in her private vaults."

"Holy shit. I didn't actually think she had that much."

"Oh yeah, you soon learn how to accumulate vast amounts of money considering how long she has been alive for. Well anyway, we have about two to three billion in the account I opened for us both yesterday when I was with Rayne. I also changed over the deed at the same time, so we are both on it."

"Are you bullshitting me?"

"No, babe. Completely honest. No need for you to work, if you don't want to. Or you can always open up that day care you wanted to. I'm sure parents around here wouldn't hesitate to let you care for their young whilst they work. Might relieve some tension in some families knowing their babies are safe with you. And it gives you a purpose in helping children with their learning, etc."

"You reckon I could do it?"

"No, babe. I know you can."

"God, I love you."

"I love you, too."

"You know what this means, right?"

"What's that?" He couldn't help but cup her face and run his thumb over the incredible softness of her cheek, before he caught a wayward strand of hair and tucked it back behind her ear.

"This means we're going to officially live together. The next big step in our relationship."

"Damn right. Now we have the perfect house. Our own little family to raise. Plus there is something else I want to do when Calista and Raven return from their mission."

"What's that?"

"I want us to officially wed. In the way of the old."

"Blood bond."

"Exactly that. But also the big wedding you've always wanted. Plus, I don't think everyone here will forgive me if I didn't," he laughed.

"Damn right! But aren't you forgetting something?" Before Tairen could do anything, Jinx let out a massive gas bomb that had both the adults laugh out loud then they groaned as the smell reached them. It definitely wasn't just a fart. Luke looked up at them with Alexzander, before looking at each other then headed to them.

"Pass her here, Lexis. Me and the kid will change her and we'll grab a quick drink as well before we carry on our play fight."

"You won't hear me argue." She laughed as she handed Jinx to her uncle. She wiggled in delight as Luke gave her a quick kiss on the cheek before he and the kids disappeared into the house. Tairen waited until they were out of sight before looking back at the love of his life.

"Now where were we?"

"I think you were going to ask me something."

"Oh, yes." He moved until he was in front of her, kneeling on one knee. "Lexis Blackwood, the lady of my heart. You make me proud every single day I'm with you. I've loved you from the very first time I saw you. You're it for me. You're the air I breathe and the soul that resides inside of me. Would you do me the honour of becoming my wife?" He held his breath.

"Yes. Yes! A thousand times yes!" She threw herself on him and sent him barrelling onto his back on the ground. He laughed as she rained kisses all over his face. He grinned and kissed her back. She finally let him up for air and he sat up with her on his lap facing him. He turned slightly and pulled a small box from his pocket. He opened it up for her and watching her face, he smiled as tears formed as she looked at the ring he'd gotten her. It was sterling silver, as she didn't wear gold, with a huge diamond in the middle, accentuated by four skulls that held it in place. And each skull had diamond eyes that reflected the sunlight. He took it out of the box and slid it onto her finger. It was the perfect fit.

"Beautiful." He smiled at her as his heart was nigh on full to bursting.

"I love it! I love you, Tairen!" She kissed him again but they soon got pulled apart by a small pair of hands. Turning their heads, they looked at Alexzander who stood grinning at them.

"Did you say yes?"

"I sure did, kiddo." Lexis showed Alexzander the ring and he let out a big whoop with a fist pump into the air before wiggling his way between them. They wrapped their arms around their son who sighed in contentment to be between his parents and absorbed their hug.

"So you knew did you, Alexzander?"

"Yeah. He asked Uncle Luke first when I was with him." Lexis smiled at Tairen as she realised he had asked Luke if it was fine to marry her, because he couldn't ask her dad as he was no longer alive. Her man wasn't all about tradition, but that was really sweet.

"Can I ask you something?" Alexzander's small voice brought them out of their happy little bubble. Tairen looked at him.

"Of course you can. You always can."

"Not really something to ask, but I know it's really soon, but I feel like I've been here since like, forever and erm, I don't want to call you Lexis and Tairen anymore." Lexis pulled back more so she could look at both males.

"Then what do you want to call us, honey?" She heard the back door screen open as Luke wandered back out with Jinx, but they didn't turn to face him, just focused purely on their boy. Luke knelt beside them with a now clean Jinx in his arms.

"Go on, kid. Exactly as you said to me when we were in the kitchen. Trust me, they won't hate you for it." Luke smiled reassuringly at the boy, who had a bit of a worried look on his face, who then climbed off them both and stood up, back straight and looked them both square in the face.

"I do not want to call you Lexis and Tairen. I want to call you Mum and Dad because that is who you are to me now." Lexis looked at Tairen as Alexzander said that. Tairen looked back at her. Then they both grinned so wide, their cheeks hurt. Tears built up in her eyes so quickly that everything became a blur, but she leant forward and dragged Alexzander back into her arms.

"Oh baby, of course you can call us that!" Alexzander grinned at them both and they wrapped both their arms around him again. It was now officially Tairen's favourite day. The love of his life had agreed to marry him and Alexzander wanted to call him Dad. Best day ever! He did, however, swipe his thumb under Lexis's eyes to catch the tears that fell, before she wrinkled her nose and used her arm to scrub her face even if the other one stayed wrapped around Alexzander.

"Told you they wouldn't hate you, kiddo." Luke handed Jinx to Lexis so she could cuddle the baby who wanted to join in. They watched as Alexzander threw himself at his uncle in a burst of giggles and the boys again went tumbling to the floor, each trying to get the upper hand in tickling each other. Lexis shook her head at her brother and son and stood up off Tairen's lap. He bounced back to his feet, kissed her cheek before he got her the drink that was sat unforgotten. He took Jinx from her whilst she guzzled it down. Her man was forever thoughtful in that way. She watched as Alexzander accidently stood on Luke's hand and a look of absolute horror covered his features and he quickly dropped his head down to stare at his feet. She watched as his hands clenched and he visibly tensed.

"What you tensing for, kiddo?" Luke asked him.

"I'm waiting for the beating now," he whispered, but Lexis heard it. She gasped at that statement.

"Alexzander, I'm not going to beat you for something that was an accident. Plus, I'm tough skinned, I can handle it. See." He wiggled his fingers in the boy's face which caused him to give a little smile.

"Come here." Luke yanked the boy to him and put an arm around his shoulder. Small tender words were whispered to the boy in his ear that she couldn't quite make out but it must have worked because he turned more in Luke's arms and cuddled him close. Luke smiled and wrapped the boy in his arms before he tickled him. Alexzander burst out laughing and pushed his uncle who went sprawling on his back and then dived on top of him. Back to their play fighting which caused Lexis to smile again, as did Tairen she saw.

"I've got an idea," he said when she'd finished the last part of her drink.

"What's that?"

"First of, how about Luke and Raven become Alexzander's godfathers. And Calista and Nikki become Jinx's godmothers? Even though I'm sure everyone will spoil them no matter what."

"That's a fabulous idea. I know everyone would eagerly agree. And for that we have no doubt. Our kids are going to be spoilt, and not just presents, but love, friendship and pure happiness as well as safety." She smiled at her man.

"Damn right. Also, how about we head to the beach? Get the kids used to the sand and water. Plus, it's a gorgeous day, so what better way than doing it now? Although I'm sure Luke already made sure the kids have the proper swimming attire when you both went shopping yesterday."

"Yeah, we do. I noticed he'd snuck it in when I was paying. I love how quickly he's accepted them though as his niece and nephew."

"Same here. The kids are never going to doubt that they are one hundred percent ours and that we'll always love and cherish them. Although, I am thinking of making sure Jinx isn't allowed to have a boyfriend or even think of boys until she's at least one hundred!" Lexis burst out laughing at the face he pulled.

"Oh please! If she's going to be anything like you, it won't stop her from sneaking out. Yeah, you heard me, I know those stories from Draylan." She laughed at the irritated look on Tairen's face.

"I'll kill him. He wasn't meant to say anything about that!"

"I asked him if there was anything I should worry about with you. He said when we were separate that you'd try everything you could to sneak into my bedroom at night so we wouldn't be apart too long when I was here and that's when it crept up."

"Yeah, OK. I suppose I'll let him off, considering you love him."

"Damn right. He raised you and Rayne to the best of his ability and you turned out fantastic. Not to forget, you'll be a fantastic dad to our babies." She motioned to Jinx who had currently leant over in her arms and was slobbing all over his knuckle whilst her hands were locked around his fingers.

"Good save." He laughed and they turned back to watch Luke and Alexzander mucking around together in the grass. About ten minutes later, she was getting too eager for them to head to the beach, so she made Jinx let go of Tairen's hand, wiped the beads of sweat from her forehead and faced her brother and son who were now sitting on the grass side by side and throwing small stones down the hill to see who could get it the furthest. She could tell Luke was letting Alexzander win, if the giggles and playful shoves were anything to go by.

"Luke, Alexzander. Come on. We're off to the beach. As it's a beautiful day, might as well make the most of it," she called out and watched as her brother and son glanced over at them before getting off their butts and brushed themselves down before walking back to them. Tairen was happy that Luke was so easy with the kids and that he had no problem whatsoever in calling them his niece and nephew. He reckoned that Luke, and Raven for that matter, would become a big part in their kids' lives. Walking into the house with them all, he and Luke went into the kitchen to sort out food to take with them whilst Lexis got the kids ready. Once they had finished, she came into the kitchen to prepare some bottles for Jinx with the aid of Alexzander who was looking smart in his new shorts, so he and Luke left and dashed upstairs to hurry getting changed. Even though it was past midday, it was scorching hot so it called for his black shorts, and he threw a white tank top on as well, but he knew it wouldn't be long before he took it off to soak up the sun's rays. Even though he was a vampire, he could and did soak up the sun often, which was why he was so tanned all the time. It was also one of the things that made him laugh on 'Normal Earth', that they portrayed vampires as creatures of the night. Well, some of it was true. He did need blood to survive, and he had excellent night vision, not to forget the enhanced speed and strength too. But other than that, he could go into the sunshine as often as he so chose. As he exited his and Lexis's bedroom, he pulled up short as Luke was right outside the door, arm raised as if to knock.

"What's up, man?" he asked.

"Sounds a daft question, but got any shorts I can borrow? I didn't think to pack any when me and Raven went to Lexis's as we didn't reckon we'd need any in Scotland."

"Sure man. Any colour in particular?"

"Black or blue will do." He followed Tairen into the bedroom.

"No problem." Tairen walked into their walk-in closet and came back out with a blue set of shorts. Dark blue of course, but blue all the same. He saw Luke was looking at the painting that was hanging on their bedroom wall above their fireplace.

"Beautiful, huh?" he said, walking over and handing the shorts over.

"Thanks. And it's amazing. Who did it?"

"Calista took the photo on a camera Lexis had, then she went to see someone who did it for us." And the craftsmanship was indeed amazing. It was of him and Lexis, standing on the beach next to the candlelit table with their dinner on that he'd set up, and they were facing the camera with a beautiful sunset behind them. He was in a pair of trousers with a crisp white shirt and a leather jacket. Done up all smart and it suited him. He smiled as he watched Luke look at his baby sister, who was quite frankly all grown up and an astoundingly beautiful woman, inside and out. In the painting, Lexis had on a black corset-styled dress that cupped her curves and fell to mid-calf in the front but fell to her feet at the back. Strappy high heels that were a brand called Hades covered her feet, and she had a bouquet of luminous multi-coloured roses clasped in her hands. Her neck was accentuated by a black lace choker with a huge fire opal crystal in the centre. The best part, she had some of her hair down and some threaded through an onyx and diamond tiara he had brought her. Her make-up was perfect with black eyeliner, brown eyeshadow that made her eyes gleam and a beautiful smile on her face that radiated from within and made her eyes twinkle. Lips weren't painted, but glossed over to give them a nice shine.

"It's amazing. When was this done?"

"A few months into our relationship. I'd surprised her on the beach with a dinner, music and lots of laughter. She was the sophistication of grace that night and the best dance partner I've ever had. She literally took the breath out of my lungs when I saw her walk up with Calista. Well, I think she took everyone's breath away." The love in his voice was evident but anyone who knew him, knew that he was utterly and wholeheartedly smitten with her.

"You love her a lot don't you?" Luke asked, a smile on his face.

"With all that I am. I have honestly never been this happy before. She's literally the light to my darkness. I know its soppy; but she's the one for me. She's my Tylaitosk, which means Vampire Soulmate before you ask."

"Certainly a mouthful." Luke grinned at him and they left the bedroom.

"Sure is. But you do know I would literally die for Lexis, right?"

"Of that I have no doubt."

"Good. Because it is true."

"What did you mean also by she took everyone's breath away?"

"I'd paid for people to serve us from the village who were eager to see me settle with her and this was one way of making her happy, that they wanted to see as they all adore her. I had also paid for a live band as well."

"You wanted it to be perfect for her."

"Oh yes, and so long as she's happy, then I know I'm doing it right."

"Indeed, you are, my man. You certainly have my loyalty for that. And I saw that ring on her finger. Rock big enough?"

"Big enough it won't bug her. I know what she's like. And you don't disapprove that I proposed to her whilst you had the kids instead of with you there, considering I did ask you if it was all right first?"

"Nope. I can see you make her happy, and that is all I want for her. Plus, it'd be nice to have another brother that isn't Raven." They both laughed at that, knowing full well just how close him and Raven were, but honestly, it would be nice to have a brother as all he had was Rayne and Draylan. He couldn't exactly call Skyri his brother, he was more of just a very good family friend than anything else.

"True that. The real question is, do you reckon Raven would approve?"

"One hundred percent. He loves her like the sister he never had. When we first met, after a couple months of him always being around mine, all three of us grew close. We were dubbed the three musketeers by my parents. And you know this means that Raven is now your brother too. Me and him might not be related by blood, but he is my brother in every single sense of the meaning of family."

"I totally get it."

"Awesome. Now give me a minute to change and we'll go join them downstairs, as I'm sure Lexis won't want us hanging around any longer than necessary." Luke hurried into his bedroom, yanked his boots and jeans off and changed into the shorts. He also changed into a light blue tank top and put on his black converse he'd had buried in the bottom of his backpack. Leaving the clothes he'd previously had on, on the bed, he hurried back to

Tairen who waited in the hallway, closed the bedroom door and followed the man. They descended the stairs and Lexis walked out of the living room pushing the buggy that the kids already sat in. Alexzander in his own pair of little black shorts, now had a baseball cap to shield his eyes from the sun. The rest of him was bare. Jinx was quite content to lay in just her nappy for now. Smart kid. Tairen smiled at his family. Lexis had also changed as well into a bikini set with a skirt. Blood red, as black would be too much in this heat, at least that would be the excuse she'd use. Feet were in flip flops with her manicured black toe nails. Hair was up in a ponytail so was easier to manage in the heat and she had sunglasses perched atop her head. She was a beautiful woman even without make-up. And her belly had a slight bump to it where their son was safe and just starting to show. She radiated with the inner healthy glow of pregnancy, which he thought suited her perfectly.

"Ready?" she asked as she saw them.

"All good to go." Tairen took the picnic basket off her and motioned her towards the door that Luke had opened. As she moved past Luke, Tairen saw him suck in a breath.

"Since when did you have ink?" he asked. And that was when Tairen realised he'd seen her back piece that started just above her arse and ended slightly below her neck. When she was changing over, they wouldn't have been able to see it, considering Calista had her on her back for it, well, after she'd drained her of her blood. The men couldn't have seen it as her back had been to the windows and afterwards, she'd been on her back through the rest of it all. She pulled her sunglasses down to shield her eyes before answering him.

"About a year now. Stunning isn't it?" She laughed. And it was. It was a huge multi-coloured dragon with its front feet on a skull that was open on a scream.

"God yeah! Where did you get it done?"

"Someone Calista saw in, I think it was Greece. We were over there for a mini break and I said I really wanted a tattoo so we went."

"Kind of a big piece for the first one, don't you think?"

"Nope. Second one." She showed him her inner left ankle where an infinity symbol sat in bright purple with L and R in the middle.

"Check you out, kiddo!" he laughed.

"I know, right. Such a grown up." She laughed with him.

"What's the L and R stand for?"

"Luke and Raven. My brothers for infinity." Luke hugged her quickly for that before he let her go and they walked into the sun. Tairen smiled and shut the door behind them just as Lexis leaned over and opened the white umbrellas on the buggy for the kids.

"So big brother approves, huh?" Lexis grinned at him as they started down the hill.

"Oh yeah. I'll have to join you next time. Well, once the little one is born of course."

"So a brother/sister tattoo maybe?"

"Sounds a plan."

"So what ones have you got? I'm sure you've got some." Both she and Tairen looked at Luke then. Tairen was intrigued. Luke had tattoos as well? He watched as the man rolled his shorts up and on his thighs, facing each other was two skulls, mouths open with bone mohawks and blood dripping from their mouths. He turned, lifted his tank top up and he had a dragon on his back, it was in black and grey and stood clutching a skull in its hand.

"Oh wow. They're incredible." Tairen liked the skull ones the best.

"Thanks."

"Why two skulls the same?" Lexis asked.

"Symbol for me and Raven. We have the same ones. A friend/brother ship sort of thing. Only mine are on my thighs, his are on his shoulder blades."

"Fair enough. But shows how similar we are even though we haven't seen each other for a few years, we both have dragons on our backs." She smiled and he nodded in agreement. Both men then put on their own sunglasses and they fell into a comfortable silence as they moved through the town to the beach. Even the kids were quiet. She checked Jinx who had fallen asleep and Alexzander was looking around in avid curiosity at the different people going about their business. They soon reached the beach and after finding a spot a little away from those who were already there, Luke pulled out the huge picnic blanket they'd packed.

Luke spread it out on the sand and he watched as Tairen knelt down and pushed a small pole into the ground with a hook at the top, kind of like tent pegs that secured the blanket into its spot. He claimed his spot and watched his sister check Jinx and Alexzander sprawled out next to him.

"Luke, can you help me with this please." Lexis's voice got his attention and he saw she was now trying to put a huge umbrella parasol thing into a weighted base that was in the middle but at the back of the blanket. He stood up and did it for her and opened it up, bringing a lovely space of shade for them if being in the direct sun got too much for them. He sat back down in the sun but kicked his shoes off. Looking around, he caught sight of someone out of the corner of his eye that he didn't think he'd see again, well not for a while anyway. Nikki. And she was walking directly at them. He faced her properly then, and his breath caught in his throat as he noticed what she wore. Very fucking little! She had on a bikini in black that encased her breasts lovingly. The scrap between her legs didn't leave much to the imagination. Her hair was tied up in a loose ponytail at the top of her head, and no dreads! She still had the zebra-styled fringe and the purple and black colouring though. She was also make-up free and damn she was a gorgeous woman. He let his eyes travel down her body and stopped at her midriff. Her belly button was pierced. And it had a small hoop through the middle with a small butterfly with skulls dangling from it. Her long legs were smooth and shiny. Well, actually, all of her was as though she had put on moisturiser or that body oil stuff you could get. Feet had flip flops on with small skulls along the straps. As she got closer to them, he noticed something that got him. Her legs and feet were inked as well! Left foot had a 3D scorpion on it and her right foot had script work on it saying *The Definition of Beautiful Does Not Require the Word Skinny* in beautiful slanted writing with miniature skulls around it. Left thigh had a flaming skeleton holding a cigar between his teeth and the Dead Man's Hand deck of cards in his hand. Right calf had a black and grey skull with a branch underneath, sidewalk with a walkway and just under the skull was a swing with a girl on it. And damn if they weren't works of art!

"All right guys," she said as she drew nearer to them.

"Hey, Nikki," Lexis replied and the men just nodded to her.

"Hi Aunt Nikki." Alexzander jumped up from where he'd sat down on the blanket.

"Hey, kiddo. Seems the new happy family life is settling in well with you." She smiled at him and sat down, curling her wings back so they were out of the way.

"Oh yes. And I have you to thank for that!" He launched himself at her and hugged her tightly. Luke watched his nephew hug her, which she returned with a small smile on her face. He quickly moved away again and sat down on his mother's lap and she handed him a small juice box.

"So how come you're in town? And in a bikini no less?" Lexis enquired.

"Because I was planning on having a swim and saw you lot heading down here so I thought I'd join you. Don't mind do you?"

"Of course not. You're always welcome to join us," Tairen replied.

"So how are you liking it here so far?" Luke looked at Nikki as she directed that question at him.

"It's good. Hell of a lot better than where I live. It would be better though if Raven hadn't wandered off to go and join Calista."

"Well, we all know he's got something for her. Maybe this is what they both need."

"What do you mean by that, Nikki?" Tairen asked, before jumping up and pulling Jinx out of the buggy as she let rip a good cry. Clearly she wasn't interested in sleeping any longer.

"Exactly that. He has something for her. I don't know if it is perhaps love, or maybe lust. Either which way, he feels something deeply for her. And it's about time she found some happiness," she replied and then looked at Jinx who was staring at her.

"I think someone wants you to hold them," Lexis teased.

"No way. I don't know how to hold a baby. Nor do I want to find out. Anyway, Lexis, get up, we have a water date." She grinned at Lexis who laughed and made Alexzander stand up as he had decided to use her lap to sit on and not the blanket. He grumbled around his mouthful of sandwich then made a beeline for Luke, who happily accepted him and smiled as his nephew settled into his lap and wrapped his arms around the boy as he continued to eat his food. In such a short time, a day at most, he realised these kids literally meant everything to him. They had wormed their way into his heart and he loved them unconditionally. He knew without a doubt he would do whatever he could to make sure that they always had a smile on their faces and that they'd be able to know that they could always come to him if they needed someone to talk to, someone to love them and someone who would offer advice if they wanted it, or if they just required someone to give them the support they needed. He would lay his life down for the kids, including the one that Lexis was carrying and no doubt any more she'd have in the future. He lifted his head up from looking at Alexzander and smiled as he watched Lexis and Nikki stroll into the water. Then he blinked, Nikki had tattoos on the back of her thighs as well! Underneath her perfect arse was Beautiful Disaster with some swirls. She was beautiful that was for sure. But a disaster? He doubted it. He watched, transfixed as Nikki's wings literally sunk into her skin until her back was perfectly unblemished. The women dived below the waves and he looked around trying to see them until he saw them raise their heads above the surface.

"Can I do that?" Alexzander's voice brought his gaze away from the women.

"Sure you can. We will have to teach you how to swim though."

"Can we do it now?" The kid was pretty much vibrating with excitement as he shoved the last mouthful of his sandwich in his gob. Tairen laughed as he watched his son. Jinx was now content to lay on her back on the blanket, sound asleep as she'd been fed.

"All right, come on then kiddo. Let's start this lesson." Luke clambered to his feet, chucked off his top and trainer socks and Alexzander followed him to the sea. Lexis and Nikki strolled out of the water then and walked up to them.

"Where you two going?" Lexis asked, wiping the water droplets from her head.

"Uncle Luke is going to teach me to swim!" Alexzander bounced around them, laughing.

"Oh really?" She smiled at him.

"Yeah. You never know if it'll help him out later on down the line," Luke replied.

"This is understandable. Plus, it's making memories and if we live here, then guaranteed we're going to be here at the beach a hell of a lot so sooner he can learn to swim, the better."

"Definitely. Nothing wrong with learning to swim. Plus, when confident, he'll be able to chase you and such in the water. Not to forget, memories of fun times." He laughed as Alexzander eagerly agreed.

"Most definitely. Right, come on then, we'll help you as well." Together, they all moved back into the water and began their lesson on helping Alexzander swim. Tairen, content to relax on the blanket with their sleeping daughter snuggled next to his leg and watch his family teach the boy to swim.

Chapter Twenty-Five
The following day at Fire Mountain

Kharge sprawled across his bed haphazardly, glaring at the ceiling whilst palming his shaft. This was one of the times he missed having his wife around, she'd have soon batted his hand away and sorted it out herself. Which obviously he wasn't one to complain about ever. Well, he wasn't until she'd died anyway, now it just sucked. He was used to doing it himself, but he was seriously contemplating looking for a woman to call his own again. He'd been alone for a long time and he was getting damn lonely. Running his hand up and down, he had the biggest case of blue balls going. As he felt the pressure start to build indicating he would soon blow his load, a knock sounded on his door. He had no idea who it was or what they wanted considering everyone, apart from those on guard, should have been in bed sound asleep as it was the very early hours. He sighed as the gentle knocking continued and climbed off of his bed. Whoever was there would soon get an eye full of his rock hard dick and tight balls but he didn't give a shit. He threw open the door and the last person he expected to stand there did. It was Lviana's older half-sister, Braelynn. She was a Nightmare Fire Demon. She mostly kept to herself although she did sit with him sometimes in the evenings, talking about anything and everything, but it was really unusual for her to be at his door. But the times she sat with him and spoke to him, he valued them unconditionally. She was *literally* the only friend he had. And she didn't judge him at all.

"What do you want, Braelynn?" he asked, draping an arm on the edging of his door. He watched as she ran the tip of her tongue over her lips as she gazed as his naked body, more importantly, his dick, before snapping her jet black, red-rimmed eyes back to his face.

"I saw the light on under the door so I knew you were awake and well, Lviana is all talk and no walk, and knows I have no problem in saying something to someone's face. So she asked me to ask you if she and Scorcha are able to go out to the ocean for a swim or something at day break?" That was one of the things he admired about her most, her bluntness and the fact she looked him in the eye as she spoke to him. And because their mountain was close to the ocean, well about a mile or so, he supposed it was OK for them to go.

"I suppose so. As long as they take guards and the fire buggies as well."

"Of course," she replied. As he looked at her, as in properly looked, he noticed she was quite simply gorgeous. Shapely muscled legs that seemed a mile long, plump in all the right places and huge tits that he'd easily be able to hold in his hands. Attractive, razor sharp eyes, thin nose and plump lips that just begged to be kissed. Trapped behind those lips were perfect white teeth with the canines sharper than usual, much like a vampire's but nowhere near as long. The only difference from other demons was she had pale pink skin, thanks to her mother, who was the demi-goddess, Nightmarë, who had been killed by Calista for causing absolute horror to anyone, be it man, woman or child. Calista had absorbed Nightmarë's very essence, so no one could do a resurrection spell, and bring her back. Braelynn's dad had been a fire demon, which was the parent she shared with Lviana. Daddy dearest, had died by Braelynn's own hand, when Lviana was ten. Her hair was a mass of shiny, thick black and red tresses that fell to the middle of her back but also feathered around her face. It begged to curl your fingers in. Horns adorned her head as well, hair weaved around them. Black and sharp as anything but dainty, and a pair that no one wanted to mess with considering they emitted a poison that stripped the flesh from your body and ate you alive when she was truly pissed and in a fighting mood which he had seen only once and that was enough. She was a tall female, standing at he reckoned at six and a half feet-ish. Made a nice change considering all the women around here where five feet seven, or under. Also helped he didn't get a backache from looking at her considering he stood at almost seven feet tall in flat feet.

"OK, I will leave you to your peace. Sorry to disturb you at this hour. Thank you, sir," she remarked, ever polite, but he could tell she hated being polite, but did, as he was her king. She stepped backwards, turned around and began walking off. He now just perceived she had a striking arse, and he was unquestionably an arse man. And the black denim shorts she wore didn't leave much to the imagination that she had a desirable, full-cheeked backside. Her top was a black tank with two red handprints over the breasts. Her feet were bare with black-painted nails.

"Braelynn?" he called out. He knew she'd always had a thing for him, but had never overstepped her bounds, most probably due to it being when his wife was alive, as well as not trying anything because she did actually respect her memory. They'd been close after all, well, so he thought anyway. She stopped at him calling her name.

"Yes?" She looked at him over her shoulder.

"Come here." He knew in that instant, he would have her. His wife was long dead and it was about time he became uncelibate. And damn if she wasn't a desirable female. How he hadn't seen it before, he didn't know. Blind, that was what he had been… Fucking blind! She walked back over to him. He reached out, took her hand and pulled her into his room, shutting his door and slamming the bolt into place. She stood next to him and just stared at him. He knew she had no fear of him and it actually turned him on that she didn't. Even his wife, who had grown men tremble before her, had had some fear of him, but this woman, Braelynn, didn't.

"So what do you want?" she asked.

"I want to ask you a question, but turn around for me." She did as asked, giving him her back. He glanced down as a piercing pain hit him and saw his dick was literally straining to her. Fucking blue steeler! He had thought his erection had gone, clearly not. He moved toward her but didn't touch.

"I want to know why you like me." He was blunt and to the point.

"You want my honest answer?"

"That is why I asked." She looked at him over her shoulder, but didn't turn around.

"Because you don't look at me like I'm a disgrace. Or that I'm a freak of nature because of my skin colour. You look at me and see me. As Braelynn and not as just the Nightmare Fire Demon who is to be avoided at all costs," she replied honestly. He stared at her and lifted a hand up to run it over her cheek. She made no move to stop him. Using his hand on her face, he made her turn around.

"Who has looked at you like you're a disgrace or said anything about your skin colour? I will always see you as Braelynn."

"Everyone."

"Even your sister?"

"My sister is a piece of impractical fucking shit. She is only attentive in gaining anything for herself. She does love Scorcha, but just her. No one else."

"Way to tell the truth."

"I don't see the point in lying. Gets you nowhere. And I mean what I say about Lviana."

"I noticed."

"You know she wants you, right? If she gets you in her bed, it is purely for bragging rights that she bagged the King."

"I did gather as much with her, but that would never happen. And what about you?"

"What about me?"

"Would you brag if you got me?"

"No. What happens behind closed doors is between us. And if people want to make assumptions, let them. But know this, if anyone steps out of line about it, I will kill them, I don't care who it is. Plus, you are King, you are allowed to have whoever you want. Even someone as lowly as me." As he looked in her eyes, he could tell she was totally honest in that.

"Good to know. And you are not lowly whatsoever." He better not hear her say that about herself again, or he'd spank her luscious ass. Actually he'd do that anyway, but that was completely beside the point!

"I suppose so. So am I to go back to my room or do you need me to let the nightmare out for someone?" That was what he usually called her for, well he did before his wife passed. After that, it was usually just for her company in the main hall or for someone to practice knife throwing with. She never missed and he was always impressed.

"No, something else entirely." He didn't give her time to answer, just leaned forward and captured her mouth with his. And something happened he didn't think she was capable of. She turned very responsive. She kissed him back like he was her oxygen. Her fingers crept up the sides of his face and into his hair, just below his horns that had straightened into sharp points with his raw desire. Usually when he jerked off, they stayed curled, but with Braelynn, they flared upright. That was how you knew a demon was truly into it, his horns elongated. She moaned into his mouth as their tongues duelled together. He reached down and literally ripped her clothes from her body. Moving back from her, he admired her body. She was flawless. As he looked at her face, her skin was flushed red with arousal. Plus, he could smell it. He yanked her to him and kissed her again, hands creeping around her body to cup her arse. As he pulled her body up and flush with his, before he could do what he wanted, she pulled back.

"Are you sure? I'm not exactly mating material."

"Seriously? Have you felt the steeler I'm supporting at this moment? And shut up Braelynn. You're gorgeous. Don't you ever doubt it, OK?" He gave her a small smile.

"Yes, sir." And then what else she said registered.

"And what you do mean by not exactly mating material? Sex is normal."

"The first time I had sex, it was forced on me by my father's right hand man whilst he laughed and said it was to be our little secret. No one has come near me since."

"And how old were you? How old are you now, actually? I realise I don't actually know." He did keep her flush against him though, her body was soft and warm, whereas most demons were hard and damn she felt damn good in his arms.

"I was fourteen when it happened. And I'm now one hundred and forty," she replied.

"A babe, barely coming into her womanhood. The fucker! What happened to him?"

"I ripped his dick off after I plagued him with nightmares for a month. Then shoved it down his throat in front of my father and his men. Then I ripped his heart out of his chest, threw it to my father and walked away. Been here ever since."

"Remind me to never piss you off." She smirked at him and he smiled back, "And OK, well I will make this as enjoyable for you as I can. But between me and you only this is. Everyone else, I'm the nasty Fire Demon King got it."

"Yes, sir."

"And stop with the sir! It's Kharge, OK?" She nodded and actually kissed him instead of him kissing her first. He picked her up more and she wrapped her legs around his waist. His cock strained as the heat of her centre brushed over him. He growled as she moved her mouth away from his and kissed his cheek and to his ear which she circled with her tongue. He stumbled to the bed and fell with her into it. He put his arms out to brace his fall so all of his weight didn't crush her. Moving back a little so she stopped tormenting him with that tongue of hers, he ran his hand down her body and to her pussy. He reared back even more as he felt smoothness. He'd actually never been with anyone who was bald there before, even his wife had had hair there, not loads but a light covering. He pushed a finger between her lips and she rolled her hips as he teased her hidden pearl. He tormented her for a few minutes, and watched as her head thrashed over the bedding, hands, no claws, digging into the mattress. She glared at him.

"Kharge, would you fuck me already? I can't take much more!" She actually growled at him and damn if that wasn't a turn on! He rose above her, positioned his shaft against her and slammed into her, tunnelling his way through tight walls that gripped him in a vice-like hold.

"Fuck, you're tight."

"No shit!" She began moving, moaning as he slid in and out of her.

"I can't go slow. This is going to be hard and fast, OK?" He groaned at how good she felt.

"Do it." She bit her lip hard and a drop of blood rose which he leaned over and licked off. Her blood was heavenly! Raw untapped power, the likes of which he had never known before. He grabbed her legs, threw them over his arms at the elbows, pretty much bending her in half and ruthlessly pounded into her. He looked at her and watched, amazed as she literally begged him for more. Soon he felt her inner walls begin to quiver with her growing orgasm and pounded even harder against her, his pelvis rubbing against her clit.

"KHARGE!" She threw her head back and screamed, claws grabbing his horns in a vice grip. He couldn't hold back as her walls gripped him and with a last powerful slam, seated himself as deep as he could go and emptied himself, shooting straight into her womb. Holy shit. It had never been like that for him, not even with Tirana. Finally, able to catch his breath, he pulled his now flaccid member from her body and collapsed next to her, he didn't want to crush her, he was a heavy bastard after all. She lay panting next to him, skin a fine sheen of sweat, not that he was complaining.

"I will leave now," she whispered and went to get up. He grabbed her and pulled her back to him. Pulling her leg over his thighs and arm across his stomach, he held her tight to him.

"Stay here. And Braelynn?"

"Yes?" She gazed up at him.

"You're mine." He stared at her as that sunk in.

"Why me?" she asked with wide eyes.

"Because you're special. You treat me normal, everyone else sees me as King. And you're gorgeous." She properly smiled at him then and his breath left him in a whoosh. When she smiled it literally transformed her. Stunning!

"So does that just mean I'm your mistress or something?"

"No Braelynn, I'm going to make you my queen. I realise now that I should have actually done that a long time ago," he admitted.

"Can I tell you something?" she whispered and actually ducked her head. He lifted her head with two fingers under her chin.

"You can tell me anything."

"I've loved you for as long as I've known you," she confessed.

"Why didn't you say anything?" They'd known each other since she was eighteen-years-old when Tirana had found her wandering the woodlands on her own, half wild and crazed, dressed in simple scraps that covered her private areas. She'd taken her in and taught her basic skills, hygiene and how to eat properly instead of like a crazed animal. It had taken her a year before she had so much as allowed a man within arm's length near her, and her back was always against the wall. It had taken her longer before she'd look anyone in the eye, but as soon as she'd seen him, they'd instantly befriended one another. She'd look him in the eye, she'd talk to him until the wee hours of the morning. It had taken another six months before she'd told him who her parents had been and then they'd worked together. They'd gotten closer than even her and Tirana had been, which had infuriated the woman, considering the amount of arguments they'd had about it. Once she had found her courage and her backbone, she was literally a force to be reckoned with. No one messed with her. And when Scorcha had finally come screaming into the world, she'd devoted her life to making sure the child was kept safe. Of which he was eternally grateful for. Even Scorcha had admitted they had spent copious amounts of time together, just hanging out talking and laughing together.

"Because you were with Tirana. And I didn't want to come between you both. You'd been with her since just before she introduced you to me. I was her friend. I couldn't do that to her."

"And now?"

"Now she's dead. And you, handsome Kharge, are all mine. And so help me, if someone tries to take you now that I have you, I will kill them," she said with deadly conviction in her voice. And he believed it. He still couldn't believe she loved him. And thinking on it, he loved her as well. Most likely always had but had also thought of it as a love of friendship for her because she'd been friends with Tirana and had soon befriended him as well. But he doubted it was that reason now.

"Braelynn?"

"Yes, Kharge?"

"I love you, too. I think I have for a long time but never acknowledged it to myself, until now that is." He actually laughed as she grabbed him and kissed him. His heart felt full now, not that dead and full void he had before. Could she have been what he had been missing? Thinking on it, yes. Yes she was. He moved then and as she turned over with a smile on her face, he spooned her, something that was foreign to him, but he comprehended he could get used to it very quickly as he cuddled her plush body against his. She quickly fell into a deep sleep from their love making, whilst he laid there and listened to her steady breathing. When they awoke, he would let everyone know that she was their new queen and if they didn't like it, then they'd be destroyed. Simple as that. And before sleep took him, he realised that she hadn't told Lviana that it was OK for her and Scorcha to go out in the morning. He shook Braelynn awake.

"Braelynn?"

"Hmmmm?" she murmured sleepily.

"You didn't tell Lviana that they can go out tomorrow," he reminded her.

"Damn it. OK, give me five." She was instantly awake and climbed out of bed, picked her clothes up, but realised they wouldn't fit her anymore considering he'd literally ripped them from her body with excitement, so yanked his shirt on that she saw on the floor. Damn if that didn't make his chest swell with pride that she didn't mind wearing his clothes. She stormed from the bedroom after flicking the lock free and disappeared from view. He stayed where he was. He reckoned the only one who would disagree with him making Braelynn his queen would be Lviana but then it was nothing to do with her. And how would Scorcha take it? That was one thing he hadn't thought of but he realised Scorcha would have to deal with it, he was a grown man who had been celibate for long enough and was entitled to find love and happiness again. Plus, she actually liked Braelynn, had told him of the many times that Braelynn had sat talking with Scorcha about anything and everything. Even the first time that Scorcha had her monthly bleed, she'd raced over to Braelynn to find out what the hell was going on with her body, or so he'd been told. That wasn't exactly something he could talk to Scorcha about. He glanced up as he heard the wisp of cloth and saw it was Braelynn back in the bedroom, taking off his shirt, which she let drop to the floor before shutting the door, flipping the lock back into place. She hurried back to the bed and slipped under the duvet he was now also under completely, curling her back against his front. She pulled his hand around and in front of her, and he clasped her breast in his hand. She rose back up, her butt rubbing enticingly against him but he wouldn't press her into sex again and blew out the two candles that burned on the table next to her, bathing the room into avid darkness.

"Did you tell Lviana?"

"I did. And she also noticed that I wore your shirt."

"She didn't give you any shit did she?"

"She tried; but I soon told her to shut her trap or I'll kill her myself but not before I plague her with nightmares. Then I added fuel to the fire, and told her I'm now her motherfucking queen." He laughed outright at that.

"I bet that went down well." Damn she was a turn on! He loved that she could hold her own.

"About as well as we could have hoped for. Scorcha approved though, she gave me a quick hug and said thanks for making you happy."

"I'm surprised she didn't protest."

"Not when I had your shirt on and considering I smell of you, there is no mistaking where I've been." She laughed with him.

"There is that." He kissed her shoulder and settled into his pillow.

"Good night, Kharge," she whispered, placing her head on his bicep that was just behind her. He didn't complain, just moved his arm a little bit more to make it a tad more comfortable for her. She laced her fingers through his.

"Sleep well, Brae." He smiled as he noticed she didn't tell him off for shortening her name and settled in as sleep claimed him, arms wrapped around his female.

Three Hours Later

Raven awoke from where he and Calista had bedded down for the night. High up in the treetops, out of sight and completely hidden from view, he stretched out along the thick branch he was perched on and glanced up just slightly above him and looked at Calista, but she wasn't asleep or anything. All he saw was the bottom of her feet as she stood on a tall branch and was looking through the thick foliage. He clambered to his feet and swung up to her. Breaking through the forest top, his breath left him in a rush as he took in the wonder of the land. It was just breaking dawn in from their left across the ocean. The water was an array of blue/greens swirling together. The sun, that huge ball of fire glowed hot orange in the low thick clouds that clung to the sky. They watched together as the sun slowly moved higher, the clouds below it a cascade of fiery yellow whilst the ones above looked like a blood bath crushed in with black. Night creatures chortled together as they got ready for their day sleep. Raven turned his head to the right, looked past Calista and saw smoke rising from the middle of the trees as villages awoke to begin their days. The mountains all gleamed in their own way, soaking up the morning rays. Suicide Mountain shone a stark white against the plush greenery. Other mountains rose out of the ground covered in greenery and even from here he could make out the tiniest bit of colour from the different flowers. Turning to look around, he stopped dead as he saw Fire Mountain. It stood away from all the others, jet black rock with rivulets of steaming lava. That was their destination. A whole bucket load of fun. Not. Continuing to look around, he saw other islands dotted just off of the coast, again all covered in plush life. Apart from one that stood a little further from the rest. It was solid white and looked dangerous and uninhabitable for those who were sane, more so than Suicide Mountain, if that was even possible.

"What's that island over there called?" he asked.

"Snow Island," Calista said after following his line of sight to which one he meant.

"Apt name. Anything live there?"

"Yeah. Snow Marbilians. Ghrowlaer's. A type of cattle that live off snow. And a seriously dangerous dragon named Attör you do not want to mess with."

"Why is that?"

"Because he's that dangerous, even Gélio doesn't interact with him unless absolutely necessary."

"Why?"

"Because Attör is a force to be reckoned with. He's pure white. He's that dangerous, his saliva is made up of all kinds of deadly acids. His claws, when fully extended, emit Fluoroantimonic acid and he also happens to be the only dragon in existence known to do this. His spines, when erect, also secrete poison so potent that only 0.01ml will kill an adult dragon, all within a very painful hour. His name actually means poison, which suits him perfectly obviously."

"Fuck, no wonder he's left alone on that island on his own."

"Exactly. Obviously I go and see him now and again, considering I'm the one who put him there."

"Why you?"

"Because I don't react to his poisons. We have no idea why, I just don't. And I put him there because even from a dragoling, he was set in his ways. Avoiding everyone. He came to me for help, so we found Snow Island was only habited by the cattle, etc. that live there now. So that was the best place for him. I taught him everything he knows, including how to use his poisons, etc."

"That's crazy!"

"Yeah, but it worked."

"So how do you know that his poisons don't work with you?"

"We did an experiment to see."

"Whatever for?"

"To pass the time when I was visiting him. It was also a long time ago." She turned away from him then and Raven looked around again. Clearly she was finished with that conversation.

"You know what, this is stunning. I have never seen a sunrise like it," Raven commented and Calista looked back at him.

"Never? Considering what job you do?"

"No, never. On 'Normal Earth', ninety-nine percent of places I go, sunrises and sunsets for that matter are obscured by buildings and other shit. The rare instances I do see any, they're definitely nothing like this, considering we also have streetlights and such. Takes away the beauty of it in my opinion."

"Yeah, I notice that when I'm there. Anyway, come on, let's get a move on. We have quite a distance to cover today and I don't plan on going slow, so I hope you're up for some quick walking."

"How quickly are we walking?" he asked as they clambered down from the top. He snagged his backpack where it was tucked away, shrugged it on and less than thirty seconds later, they clasped the last branch and swung down. He stretched again, and followed Calista as she turned and stared ahead. He wasn't going to say anything about which direction they were going, she knew the way to go.

Midday

Strolling through the forest as quickly as their legs would carry them, Calista kept an observant eye out around and ahead of them. Animals were rustling around and above them, but she ignored it all. Other creatures went around doing their own business. They were no threat to her. She caught Raven out of the corner of her left eye, taking note he was easily keeping up with her, which was impressive as she didn't exactly walk slowly. She then got a tingling feeling on the back of her neck, almost as if something was watching them. She glanced back behind her but saw nothing.

"What is it?" Raven asked.

"I'm not sure. Feels like someone or something is watching us." She turned fully and stared into the bushes. Up ahead was a demon, perfectly hidden in the shadows, but as it raised its gaze, the bright red eyes stared right at her.

"What should we do?" She looked at Raven and noticed he also had caught sight of the demon. Before she could answer, it let out a belly rumbling roar and charged at them, a huge machete clutched tightly in its fist. She braced her feet apart slightly and hands relaxed at her sides. It barrelled out of the shrubs and tackled her to the floor, but she used its momentum to her advantage and carried on rolling, coming out the victor on top. She didn't bother asking who sent him to hunt her down, she just grabbed its head and wrenched it from its neck, killing the beast instantly. She stood up, dumped the head next to the body and wiped her hand over her face, removing the blood that had covered her from the arterial spray. She picked up the machete and handed it to Raven, who took it without question. She glanced up at the sky and saw it was already midday. They must have easily covered a good ten miles with the speed they were walking, which was a good thing. She looked at Raven and he just stood there scanning the surrounding bushes in case anyone else tried to come upon them in surprise. Gun in one hand, the machete in the other.

"What?" he asked, making her realise she had been staring.

"Just looking at you thinking how easily you've already adapted into this world. And that it seems as if you've always been a part of it here instead of being an outsider."

"Is that a good thing or a bad thing?"

"Right now, it's a good thing."

"How come?"

"Because so far all you've shown is that you take no shit. You aren't afraid to stand up for yourself, no matter if they're smaller or a hell of a lot bigger, stronger or faster than yourself. It's quite impressive."

"Is that a compliment from the famous assassin?" he smirked at her.

"Yeah, don't let it go to your head. Now come on, let's get moving. We still have twenty or so miles to cover before nightfall."

"Not to be a downer or anything, but I don't think I'm capable of walking another twenty or so miles by nightfall. It's taken us half the day just to walk ten miles."

"I know. Which is why we will walk a little more, then I'll produce that cart I told you about earlier and we'll get in that to get to the swamp."

"OK, no problem." They again fell into a comfortable silence as they trod through the land. He glanced skyward about an hour later and noticed dark clouds trekked across the sky and the temperature dropped slightly. Which he was thankful for as it was muggy as fuck!

"Reckon it's going to rain?" he asked.

"Yeah. Will help clear this bloody humidity," she replied, before throwing her arm out and he bounced into it.

"What?" He looked around but couldn't see anything that would have caused her to stop like she did.

"Just ahead. A pack of Wendigos are eating."

"So do we go around or above?"

"Around. If we go above, we could startle the animals and they'd know we're there." She looked up at the tree tops to make sure nothing was above them, which luckily at present there wasn't but it didn't mean that nothing would be there later.

"Oh shit! Too late, we've been spotted." He nodded to just ahead of them. They'd stopped eating and regarded them from dead eyes, mouths literally dripping with sticky saliva.

"Do not let them near you. A bite or a simple scratch with saliva in it will turn you." She pulled her blade from behind her back and Raven swung his gun up. Good thing he could shoot with one hand, as the other was currently occupied by the machete. The four Wendigos that were in front of them hissed and broke through the shrubbery. They were tall, at least seven feet. No hair on their scalps. Sunken features. Eyes literally sunk into their skulls with a glazed dead look. Skin was stretched taut over their bodies, accentuating the bones beneath. Clothes were threadbare and hung from their frames. They were disgusting. Saliva dripped from their mouths, dribbling past thin lips and black/yellow teeth. They were, quite frankly, revolting.

"Roger that. How do we kill them?"

"Sword through/removal of the heart. Decapitation. Nothing else works. Chop arms and/or legs off, they keep on coming. All they are interested in is their next kill. But they'll eat you whilst you are still alive," she replied, twirling her swords with fluid wrists.

"Well, I think that would ruin anyone's day. Let's not make it ours." He gripped the handle of the machete he still had. He reckoned his gun would be pretty useless in this fight, so shrugged it off, along with his backpack and dumped them next to the tree he was at. Before Calista could reply, the Wendigos attacked. More than they realised were there in the first place, so there was at least ten to fifteen of the fuckers. Flesh from their victim still dangled from their mouths and some had it in their hands. He darted to the side to draw some in his direction, which thankfully some did. As one got close, he lashed out with the machete and a head went tumbling. Body splattered to the floor and before he could do anything else, four swarmed him. He slashed and hit them with everything he had in him. He dispatched two quickly and swung his head back just as one lashed out with his claws, scarcely missing Raven's face.

"Hell fucking no!" he growled and that familiar faint red haze drifted over his vision, which he sunk into willingly instead of fighting it and he literally ripped them to pieces. Body parts and other horrendous fluids went flying and soon heads rolled. As soon as he realised the danger had passed, the haze disappeared and he got a look at what he had done. Bodies littered the floor. Heads poking out of bushes, along with arms and legs. Clothes were shredded and scattered across the ground. Blood soaked into the ground and surrounding woodland. He looked down at himself and blood with some bits of flesh coated him as well. Black sticky substance. Luckily though he had no bite wounds or scratches. Win! He gazed over at Calista who was bent at the waist.

"You OK?" She stood up and looked at him as he walked back to her.

"Yep. That last one was a fucker to kill." She grabbed her bloodied sword from the floor and took in the state of him.

"No marks or anything, right?"

"Yep, nothing. This is all theirs. So why was that last one a fucker to kill?" He grabbed his backpack, shrugged it on and then picked his gun up, swinging the strap over his shoulder.

"He was bigger than the other fuckers. Bigger they are, longer they've lived, harder to kill." She kicked at a head next to her foot, which rolled away, but left an eye behind.

"Ah gotcha. How big was it?"

"At least ten feet. But as they're always hungry, it finally bent over enough I could lob off the head."

"At least he was considerate enough for that." Raven laughed and they soon left, after grabbing their gear they'd dropped in order to fight easier. As they reached the part where they first spotted the cannibals, they found two bodies. A mother and her small child. Well what they could tell as their stomachs had been ripped open so the Wendigos could get to the soft innards.

"What the hell is a Blue Marbilian doing this far inland?" Calista bent at the knees and put her hand against the mother's forehead. Raven gave her a moment of whatever it was she was doing before she stood back upright.

"Any idea?"

"Yeah. They'd been blindfolded and shoved out here. The mother got a look at who organised it all before she was blinded."

"Who would want to harm her and her child?" Raven looked at the kid and noticed he wasn't pure blue, he was mixed in with green.

"Her fiancé. Because the kid wasn't a true blue. According to the mother's memories, he knew this before he got with her, considering she was two months pregnant when they got together."

"So why murder them?"

"Turns out, he wanted her home and small fortune she'd got from working, she'd saved as well as the small amount from the kid's biological father that he had earned before he died. It had taken her until her son had just turned four, to get it. So basically, he'd killed her to get the money, as well as the home they'd shared."

"And the kid?"

"Killed, purely so he would have no witnesses and because he just didn't like him."

"Tad harsh. What about her family?"

"We will inform them when we get back. Then he can be rightly judged. Here hold this." She held out her sword for him, as her axe was still attached to her back. He took it from her and held the blade resting over his shoulder. Flat side though so as not to slice his flesh, he knew how sharp the fucker was. He watched as she pushed her hand down into the dirt and it began to bubble. The bodies sunk into the ground and once they'd completely disappeared, she removed her hand and the earth settled as though it had never been disturbed. He waited whilst she dusted her hands on her trousers and stood back up again before handing her sword back.

"Neat trick."

"Better than having to actually dig the grave."

"True that! When you did your mind delve thing, ever find out what their names were?"

"Niña and Lucas."

"Rest in peace guys," he murmured, then motioned for Calista to get moving so they could get their journey under way.

Chapter Twenty-Six

Calista strolled through the forest with Raven in a surprisingly comfortable silence. She was actually quite surprised at how easy it was to just walk with him and not talk. Usually when with others, they tried to engage her in conversation but soon gave up when she did nothing more than grunt. Not that they didn't try again a few hours later. As she glanced up at the sky that peeked through the tree tops quickly, she realised they'd made quite good time despite the hindrance that they'd had a while back. She looked over at Raven and saw him picking the blood off of his hands as he walked.

"I can get rid of it if you want?"

"Or any chance of a lake, river or something around here I can dunk myself into?"

"Nope. Unless you want to go swimming in the swamp?"

"Good God, no. OK, work your voodoo magic and clean me up." He grinned at her as he said it and she shook her head. Good to know he hadn't lost his sense of humour. Surprisingly, that was one of the things she actually did like about him, not that she would admit it out loud. She put her hand on his arm and muttered the cleaning spell she knew. Power shot out of her hand and ran through and over him, causing him to shiver. The blood and other bits that clung to him detached themselves and fell to the floor before leaking into the ground. Once he was clean, she removed her hand.

"God, I wish I could do that. You have no idea how handy it would be to do something like that."

"I'm sure I could teach you eventually."

"Really?"

"Well, yeah. I wouldn't have said I'd teach you if I didn't mean it."

"Awesome!" He grinned and she actually chuckled.

"So how long before we get to the swamp?"

"Another mile or so before I have to summon up the cart. Then we'll be there another mile after that."

"Bloody hell, we definitely made good time then. I didn't even realise we'd walked that far."

"True. We have definitely made good time." She wound her way around a bush and stopped short. Raven, who thankfully was paying attention, stopped just before colliding into her back.

"What is it?" he asked, looking around the side of her. She motioned to the floor where small four-toed prints dotted the ground.

"What caused that?"

"Goblins I reckon." And judging by the screech that shot through the air, she guessed right.

"Good or bad?" Raven muttered as he looked around.

"No idea until I see them." Which, luckily, wasn't long, as when she looked ahead, two stood watching her and Raven.

"Calista," the bigger of the two said, dribbling past his two extended bottom canines that strangely looked like upside-down tusks you'd find on an elephant, only obviously nowhere near as big.

"Gzzaker, what are you doing this far from home?"

"Hunting for women," he replied.

"Why not the women near you?"

"Taken. We find some. We go hunt them now. Bye." She watched as Gzzaker and his friend scurried off.

"What did they mean by hunt women?" Raven asked, watching the direction they'd disappeared in.

"They hunt down the women. Then if the woman is impressed by his tusk size and if he charms her, they mate."

"Sounds quite barbaric."

"Oh, it is. Goblin sex is not something you want to be around to witness."

"Sounds like you're talking from experience."

"Oh I am. There is nothing more wrong than seeing the goblins go at it whilst biting, clawing and bleeding each other."

"So a bit of BDSM then?"

"If you want to call it that. But imagine being bitten by those tusks. No ta."

"Yeah, that doesn't bear thinking about." He shuddered and followed again as they wound past bushes. Calista reckoned about an hour later, they'd walked the mile or so they needed because the ground started to get very unsteady and ridiculously soft under foot. Stopping, she threw her hands out and using old power, drew upon the cart that she'd used on 'Normal Earth' for everyone. Raven didn't so much as make a sound as he climbed aboard before she did. They quickly shed their weapons and sank down into the cushions. Once they were seated comfortably, the cart began to move. Zooming over the bushes and around trees, within an hour, she realised they had entered the swamp properly. Trees were bogged and some had even fallen over. Land had now given way to water that was covered over in algae in a sickly green colour. An occasional bush stuck out of the water, leaves slumped with the weight of the algae clinging to it. Looking around, she noticed some alligators swimming around, silent killers waiting for their next prey to get within reach of them. Birds she'd long since brought over from 'Normal Earth' chirped in the trees or some even flew along the top of the water, hoping to catch food. It also happened to be disgustingly hot and a 'dry heat', which was not typical of a swamp, she knew, but God, it was horrible here! It was even worse in the middle of Halynakn! They moved past a couple of storks who were poised silently in the water, watching and waiting for unsuspecting fish to swim past. Ah, nature at its finest. She looked over at Raven, who was watching everything around them, as they moved past.

"Remember what I said about when we get nearer to where we need to go, well let me do the talking. The two dragons we're meeting are not fans of new people and can only just tolerate it when I visit."

"Who are they?" he asked, facing her again.

"Sarucha is the female we're here to see. Her Dragon Soul is Apophis."

"So why do they live in the swamp? Surely they'd want to live on Dragon Hill?"

"Because they're recluses and prefer their own company than being around others."

"Fair enough," he muttered, as they continued deeper into the shrubbery. About ten to twenty minutes later, she spotted a hill of rolling rich grass. Completely out of place considering where they were but it meant they had neared their destination. The cart began to slow as they neared the mound, she shuffled to the edge of her seat and pulled her weapons onto her back again.

"Grab your stuff, we're here." He did as she asked and she noticed he didn't so much as ask how she knew. Which considering the amount of shit he'd seen her do, she guessed this was normal. At the top of the knoll of mud and grass, the cart stopped moving altogether and she disembarked first. She slid slightly into the ground but it wasn't anything unusual considering what was around them. She waited whilst Raven jumped out, backpack once again in place as well as his gun and the machete he'd yet to hand over, not that she cared. He could keep it, not like she didn't have an abundance of them already. Plus, in a weird way, it suited him as well. She made the cart disappear. Yes, they had used the cart to get them to the swamp quicker, but already night was crawling in. That was the thing when the season changed, it got darker a lot quicker, which in her personal opinion was the best time. She was definitely more of a night person than a day lover. She adjusted the strap on her shoulder for her axe and looked at Raven.

"Remember what I said, let me do all the talking and follow in the footsteps where I stand, as you really don't want to be caught in a soft part as you will literally sink quicker than standing on quicksand."

"Lovely. OK so what direction are we going in now?" She motioned for him to follow and headed north east. At least half an hour later, she picked up the faint tell-tale splashing of a heavily bodied creature hitting the water ahead of them. She held her hand up for silence and they strode through the shrubs just in front of them.

Raven looked at Calista as she first walked through the bushes and quickly followed. A quick glance to the sky showed the daylight fighting with the night for dominance but it was obvious night would prevail considering it was that time of the day. How had the day gone so fast? Or was it because he was content in the company of Calista that he just didn't realise the day had flown by? He focused back on what was ahead of him as they moved past the bushes and walked into an open plain of land. Trees had been felled and ripped out. Bushes as well. Grass had been cleared so it was literally just compacted dirt with a few splotches of grass here or there that refused to die. He adjusted the strap on his shoulder for his gun that dangled against his ribcage, and kept the machete in the scabbard Calista had made appear for him so he could wear it over his other shoulder and against his shoulder blade without slicing himself open. He moved to stand side by side with Calista and just about managed to keep from shitting himself. Just slightly ahead of them, nestled between trees and hidden in the shadows, was a dragon. And it was staring right at them. He glanced at Calista and she just looked bored. She took a step forward but he noticed she kept her hands relaxed at her sides.

"Sarucha," she called out.

"Calista." It returned in a raspy voice, as though it hurt to talk. And because he'd already seen the vast wonders of this world thanks to travelling with Calista, he kept the shock off his face as the ground shook and a shadow ahead emerged. Bracing his feet apart slightly to keep himself upright, he watched as a dragon emerged from ahead. Raven gawked at the huge beast. She had to stand at just shy of forty-five feet high he guessed. Her bulk was balanced on four thickly muscled legs with huge feet tipped in dangerously sharp claws the length of carver knives in which would easily render full trees in half with a well-placed swipe. Her mouth was full of razor-sharp gleaming white teeth. Her snout was shorter than the other females he had seen on Dragon Hill. The skull was protected by two massive horns that started from the corners of her beautiful black highlighted coloured eyes, curled back to twist around the top of her head and end in deadly sharp points. Spines cover the rest of her head. Ghastly black scales adorned the rest of her tremendous body. Her back had huge spines set in three rows a couple of inches thick that blended perfectly against her naturally black body. The swamp's dirty water, leaves and other foliage coated her in a filmy texture that shone sickeningly in the sunlight. Her body was a solid mass of muscle and not a single ounce of fat anywhere. Tail muscles that he could see were taut and strong. Her wings were huge and black and were folded tightly against her body when not in use, which was now.

"What colour are those eyes of hers?" Raven whispered.

"They're what is called Ethiopian Welo Opal. One of a kind, which is why she is here mostly. Creatures would kill for her eyes, considering they're literally gems. Worth a million or so for each eye," Calista replied.

"Holy shit. Don't blame her for hiding, then!"

"Exactly."

"Calista, what are you here for?" The dragon stepped more into the fading light and Raven saw what made her sound all raspy. She had a horrendous three-claw scar slashed across her throat, kind of as if someone had tried cleaving her neck open.

"We need a place to stay for the night and considering we were near here, I thought I'd come and ask you."

"Why are you near here?" The ground rumbled as she settled down onto the floor.

"Me and my companion, Raven, are after some kids Kharge has kidnapped from their homes. We're on our way there now. But you know what it is like travelling at night."

"I do. And who is this Raven? What species is he?" She turned those eyes to him and he felt as if she was staring right into his very soul, kind of like Calista's did.

"He's human. Well, that we know of. I've got to do a mind delve and see what is going on."

"Why, if he is human?"

"Because he has the strength, etc. of a vampire. Not to mention I've seen what he is like when blood is around. Pupils dilate, tips of his ears twitch and his nostrils flare."

"Tips of my ears twitch?" He turned with no doubt, a quizzical look on his face.

"Yes. Anyway, that is why I need to do the mind delve."

"If he is supposedly vampire, why has it taken this long to show itself?" Sarucha's voice drew their attention again.

"Might have been because he was raised on 'Normal Earth'. So, if I do the delve, we will know for certain."

"If that is the case, what will happen after that?"

"Nothing at the moment. We carry on to Fire Mountain and rescue the kids. After that, we will figure out what to do about what we find."

"Do you think he's changed over more the longer he has been here?"

"Honestly Sarucha, I have no idea. Although it seems some things have advanced a hell of a lot since he has been here."

"Really? Such as?"

"Quicker to anger. Blood is more tempting, etc." Raven nodded in agreement. There was no point in denying that when it was purely fact.

"Understandable you want to mind delve then. OK, there is the cave just slightly ahead to your left. Use that for the night. I will keep Apophis away and explain that I gave you safe passage through the swamp land at day break."

"Thank you, Sarucha. Will we seen you in the morning?"

"Most likely not. I will be with Apophis until you have left. Until then, good night."

"Good night. And again, thank you." Raven followed in silence as she led the way to the cave they were to stay in for the night. A few moments later, they reached their destination. Standing at the mouth of the cavern, Raven moved inside following Calista as she lit a fireball in the palm of her hand. It was a prodigious size, it could easily house a dragon or two. He waited whilst she sent the fireball to the ground and it ignited into a small fire, kind of like those that are used on camping trips. Looking around, the walls were dark grey with vines of plants crawling up them with beautiful flowers that were open and they let off a delicate scent. The floor was clear of anything. The ceiling, that he could see because of the minimal light, was bare, like a normal cave would be.

"What is that smell?"

"The flowers?" Calista looked over at him.

"Yes. I swear I've smelt it before."

"The purple coloured one is called Blue Lady Hellebore and secretes a lavender smell. And the other white flower is called Moonflower and here it smells of vanilla. No other flowers will bloom in the dark of the cave here."

"Interesting. So how comes they're the only two here?"

"They are the only two I brought over to Sarucha to enjoy in the cave."

"No others?"

"Nope. She didn't want anything too overpowering. Did you notice her snout was considerably shorter than the other dragons we saw?"

"Yeah, I noticed that. How come?"

"You can't say anything about this, but it's because of her mother. She tried using this serum she'd heard of to get rid of the pregnancy. But obviously it didn't work and she gave birth to Sarucha. Well, the egg that she was in. Six weeks later, she was born. Shorter snout and everything. It's highly sensitive. Along with her ears and eyes."

"I promise not to say anything. And damn, that sucks for her. Obviously she hasn't let it stop her from doing anything."

"Nope. In fact, her Dragon Soul Apophis, has the same as her. But his is because of his parents being father and daughter."

"Damn, inbreeding and a half that is!"

"Yes. Definitely. But his father was killed for it, considering he had raped his daughter to get her pregnant."

"Ouch. What happened to his mother?" He sat down on the floor on the sleeping bag she had made appear and quickly took his boots off.

"She died when he was about twenty-five or so. She was in a fight with a male who tried to force himself on her and he slashed her throat."

"Damn, that sucks. What did Apophis do?"

"Killed the male outright. Then moved out here to the swamp and has been here ever since."

"If that is the case, then how did he meet Sarucha?"

"He was summoned by Gélio to Dragon Hill for something, I have no idea what, and he saw Sarucha where she was on the edge of the cliff and the rest is well, history."

"How long have they been together?" He watched as she settled down on the other side of the fire and he watched as the flames washed light over her and made her eyes gleam. Damn, she was gorgeous.

"Bear in mind, everyone who lives here, lives for a very long time, so they've been together about four thousand five hundred years, give or take a few decades."

"Bloody hell! That's a long time to be together."

"Not really, Gélio and Nyhkohl have been together since before the start of his reign and that's been easily thirty thousand years."

"Holy shit! Wait, I remember now, me and Luke were being told that Mystic Being has been around long before humans, etc. on 'Normal Earth', so that doesn't really surprise me. Must be top of his game if he's been in charge that long."

"He's the longest one to reign since the beginning of us here at Mystic Being. He can definitely hold his own in a fight. And ninety-nine percent of the time, it's more squabbles he has to sort out, which he is fine with. Well, it's either him or Nyhkohl who deals with it."

"Definitely." He glanced outside and was surprised it was full blown night. Fuck, it crept up on them quickly. He stretched out, shoulder blades cracking and he released a groan at how good it felt.

"Here." He opened eyes he didn't realise were closed and shot back a little bit. Calista was crouched right in front of him, holding a bowl that was steaming.

"What is it?" He took the bowl off of her.

"Chicken breast with scrambled eggs, cheese and mixed veg." She grinned as she handed him a fork and he dug in with relish.

"Where did you get this from?" he asked after swallowing a mouthful of the delicious food.

"I'm magic. You should know this. Besides, it's full of protein, etc. that you need to keep up your strength and plenty of calories too, which I'm sure you won't mind considering you're on holiday and not on a strict diet with the military."

"God yeah. Load up on the calories and protein. Believe it or not, this is my weakness."

"What is?" She laughed as she moved back to her side of the fire.

"Give me any good, decent food and I'm pretty much putty in your hands." He laughed outright before shovelling more chicken into his mouth. He groaned again at how good it was. Considering it was sprinkled with chinese barbeque seasoning. His absolute favourite.

"Good to know." She laughed again and damn if he didn't enjoy the sound. He watched as she made a bowl appear for herself and they settled into comfortable silence as they filled their stomachs. All too soon, the bowls were empty and they disappeared with a simple swish of her hand. Bottle of water came flying at his head which he caught easily before opening it up and taking a good chug. He was a happy man, food in his belly. Decent place to sleep and a fire to keep him warm. He was simple that way. Not to mention that he had a gorgeous woman to keep him company as well. Sure beat looking at Luke or the others of the military group he was in.

"I thought you couldn't eat food and whatnot?" he asked, looking at her.

"I can, but ninety-nine percent of the time I don't. Easier to live on a liquid diet, more so when I'm out on missions."

"OK, you got that right. Would suck if you had to continuously look for food or drink to keep you going. But if you live on the liquid diet, how do you get it? I'm sure it is a ball ache carrying bags around full of the stuff."

"If I'm fighting, I subdue the victims and drink it straight from the source."

"How?"

"With fangs." She opened her mouth and he blinked, just blinked as her fangs extended to the middle of her chin.

"Holy shit. Lions have nothing on you, do they?"

"Sure they do, they use theirs to shred their prey. Mine are for sinking into flesh and draining them of their blood, if I so choose to. Plus lions, tigers and all that, are broader than mine."

"I meant lengthwise and they look wickedly sharp."

"They are, which is ideal for what I need them for. Also good for tearing into flesh if I need to."

"Have you ever needed to?"

"Oh yeah. Countless times over my existence."

"And when not needed?" She opened her mouth more and he watched as they disappeared back into her gums, until they appeared as normal teeth, albeit still pointed.

"Don't you need them to drink?"

"Nope," she answered before chugging her drink back. He waited until she had finished and watched as she made it disappear.

414

"So when shall we do this mind delve?" He took another mouthful of his water to wash the last of the food down before leaving it at the side next to his backpack.

Chapter Twenty-Seven

Calista looked up from where she was untying her laces as Raven asked her about the mind delve.

"Now?"

"Sure. Sooner we get it done with, sooner we can get to sleep. It sure has been an eventful day." He grinned at that and she couldn't help but laugh at him.

"Yeah, OK. Get comfortable then." She kicked her shoes off, stood up and moved to sit behind him. Legs either side of his waist. She waited whilst he wiggled backwards until his back hit her chest. He crossed his ankles so his feet soaked up the heat from the fire. His arms were relaxed over her legs, palms facing the ceiling.

"Keep your eyes ahead and the images will play as though on a screen, which will kind of remind you of an old-fashioned cinema reel. Only without the noise."

"OK, no problem. What about blinking? Won't that affect it?"

"Nope. So no need to worry about not blinking to see what plays."

"Will it hurt?"

"No. Because I'm taking my time, it won't hurt like it did when we were with Seliana when we got to the Blade of Souls."

"OK. Good. I don't really want to deal with screaming my head off whilst you dive through my brain."

"Shut up, idiot," she chuckled at the sarcasm in his voice. He laid to the side so he could look up at her.

"I'm just saying."

"Yeah, so am I." And because for some untold reason, that she couldn't resist, she kissed him. He growled against her lips and threaded his hand through her hair to deepen the kiss, but all too quickly she pulled back before it escalated.

"No! We have to get this delve out of the way first." She smiled slightly at him as he groaned at her before licking his lips.

"Yeah, fine," he grumbled as he settled back to where he was originally. She smiled when he was back against her chest properly and placed her hands on his face, fingers spread slightly.

"It won't hurt, but it will be as if a warm caress is around you whilst I'm doing this OK?"

"OK." He relaxed, ready to begin. She breathed in deeply before letting it out slowly, closed her eyes and sent her presence into his mind. She washed over it, exactly as she said, like a warm caress, and dived deep. She soared past memories of things that had happened in his lifetime, good, bad and the downright dirty. She saw him when he got accepted into the military and the happiness he felt. Or the time he got the keys to the small apartment near the barracks he and Luke shared. Then it turned horrible. She saw the abuse his parents gave him until he moved out at fifteen. She saw the cold hostile looks they kept on giving him, then they were all loving to his brother. What the hell caused people to do that to their children? If, and it was a big if, she ever had children, she would protect, cherish and love them with every fibre of her being and would easily lay her life down for them. Snapping from her own thoughts, she sank deeper into the subconscious of Raven until, using her unique 'gifts', she went right back until the time he was conceived. This was what she was looking for and let it play out. She didn't know how she could do this, only that she could and some days when it was needed, it was a blessing, the others… well, she kept it stored in the deepest part of her, locked away with all that she could. In an impenetrable steel box, locked in chains and welded shut. Joys of her subconscious maybe? She shook her head slightly and glanced at Raven.

"You ready?"

"Ready as I will ever be," he mumbled and she looked back up at the wall as the image of a woman appeared. And she immediately knew who it was. His mother, Rebecca.

Rebecca sat at a vanity table of rich mahogany, brushing out her damp long blonde hair. Her dark blue eyes twinkled from passion that had yet to die down from her body. A silk dressing gown, done up, but still revealed parts of her pert high breasts, was all that covered her passion-flushed skin. A huge man stood behind her, naked but for a towel draped around his waist. He stood at least six feet seven. Ice-cold blue eyes stared at her whilst his lips were all puffy from her kisses. He had a flush to his cheeks from passion, that she could see above his slight beard. He also had small bite marks on his shoulders. She smiled at him as she turned and put her brush down. He smiled back, revealing shiny white teeth. His canines at the front just slightly longer and pointed; but nothing to cause alarm and think of them as abnormal. She watched as he turned around to put the towel he was using on the edge of the bed, luckily it was the one she had used herself. He had a giant skull with a mohawk, mouth open in a silent scream the length of his back. Blood dripped from fangs in its mouth. Underneath it had Warrior written in his own language, the only reason she knew what it said was because she had asked him when she had first seen it.

"So when will I see you again, Lucian?" she asked, gliding over to him before rubbing herself against him.

"I'm to be out of town for anything from four to six months. But you know me, I'll let you know when I'm back in town and we'll sort out when to meet, OK?" he said in his deep baritone voice, the words coming out like a caress, even though English was his second language or so he said, as he wrapped his arm around her waist, pulling her even tighter to him.

"So I have to wait until you're back before I get to have you again?"

"Oh, no. Let's go now." He leant forward and nibbled his way up her neck before he kissed her. She curled her hands up and around his neck, holding him to her. He put his hands around her waist and threw her onto the bed. Rebecca sighed happily as he crawled up her body, before locking his lips against her throat. She felt a sharp sting as he sucked, before she felt untold pleasure and the intense build-up of an upcoming orgasm surfaced. But that soon extinguished itself as the front door of her home opened.

"Rebecca love, I'm home," a voice called up as the front door shut and she heard the clatter of keys hitting the dish in the hall they kept them in.

"Oh shit! Daniel is home. He wasn't due home for another three hours or so," she whimpered as Lucian licked her neck and then moved away.

"Then our time must end. I shall send word when I return." She watched as he quickly dressed, removing everything of his and disappeared out of the window. She looked around and noticed it was as if he had never been. She dived off of the bed, stripped the sex-sodden bedding, wrapped the damp towel in the middle of it so it wouldn't be found, ripped off her dressing gown, draped it across the stool in front of her vanity and flew into the en suite and turned the shower on.

"I was just stripping the bedding and now I'm just getting a shower, Daniel. I'll not be long then we can sort out dinner." She looked in the bathroom mirror quickly and thankfully, the bite marks that she was sure Lucian had done had disappeared as though they had never been there. She opened the shower door and dived under the water, wet her hair and slathered on some shampoo. She stepped forward as though to reach for soap and looked at the doorway. Her husband stood there staring at her naked flesh in a hungry gaze. She knew he'd make his move and they'd make love in the shower… one of her favourite things to do!

"Well, now that there is the most gorgeous sight I ever did see," he purred as he began stripping away his suit. He was a very attractive man. Tall, muscular but not like a bodybuilder size, lean and sinewy that suited him perfectly. He wasn't gym mad, but he liked to look after himself, which she wasn't one to complain about. He had dark blue eyes framed by thick black lashes. Slicked back blonde hair and he stood at six feet two, perfect for her. He was soon naked and she quickly washed off the shampoo as he joined her. Daniel leaned forward and kissed his wife. She was the best thing to ever happen to him. He pulled her up into his arms and she wrapped her legs around his waist. Because they easily got worked up together, he slammed himself into her. She arched her back as she moaned. He grinned and continued to pound into her, over and over again. They soon erupted together and he helped her finish her shower before he took her back to their bedroom where he could properly love her in their bed, showing her the attention and love she so very much deserved.

Calista fast forwarded from that to twelve weeks later when they found out Rebecca was pregnant with Raven and because she was so good at not jumping when taken unaware, she didn't let Raven know she was surprised when he gripped her thighs on either side of his hips. Until then, he'd held himself completely still and relaxed. Now he was tense. She removed her hands and he turned to rest on his knees between her thighs and looked at her.

"You OK?" she asked.

"Yeah. Just not exactly something I want to see, my parents having sex."

"I can understand that but unfortunately we needed to see. Before that, did you see anything suspicious about that guy your mum was cheating on your dad with?"

"Apart from the fact she actually cheated on him and that the guy's name was Lucian? And that his tattoo matches one of mine? Apart from I have two of them and he has just one? No, what else?"

"He's a vampire. When it looked like he was giving your mum a hickey on her neck, he wasn't. He was feeding. Hence why she had that certain look on her face."

"Oh, OK. So what else do you need to find out?"

"I'm thinking of when they go for the twelve-week scan. And then your birth."

"Oh gross, you mean I have to see me being born, which when I say it like that is absolutely wack."

"If you want to find out why you have the strength, etc. of a vampire, then yes."

"Any idea who he is?"

"Yes, his name is Lucian Cruorem. He's the Vampire King. He's one tough son of a bitch. Deadly as they come but he leaves you alone so long as you leave him and his vampires alone and don't anger him. I've dealt with him a few times over the years."

"So he's still alive? And what does Cruorem mean?"

"Very much so, and Cruorem means blood in Latin."

"What did he need your help with if he's the Vampire King?"

"He had heard rumours that someone was trying to overthrow him. Apparently he was too soft and should instead rule with an iron fist."

"Who was it that was trying to overthrow him?"

"His sister and her husband, who also happened to be a fire demon."

"I take it you stopped them?" He moved a little as he was sitting at a bad angle.

"Very much so. I took out her husband by ripping out his throat. And I took her back to Lucian so he could question her as to why she did it. She just laughed, spat in his face and called him a pathetic waste of space and that she should have killed him when she had the chance."

"What did Lucian do?"

"Ripped her throat out with his teeth then walked away."

"And what about you?"

"What about me?" She stared at him, unblinking.

"What did you get for helping him?"

"Six million. And a couple diamonds, emeralds, rubies etc."

"That was your payment?"

"It's what he agreed to give me should I help find out who it was as quickly as possible."

"How long did it take you to find out it was his sister?"

"Two days."

"Damn, now that is impressive."

"If you've been doing it as long as I have, you pick up a lot of things. Including those around you who are lying or plotting something. I could tell from Charlene that she was plotting something from the amount of time she spent whispering with her husband in the corner of the hall instead of joining everyone for a meal, which made me suspicious. Anyway, come on; let's get on with it then." She settled back down and he turned back the way he was. She placed her hands back on the sides of his head. She sank back into his memories and soon found where she had originally been. She soon fast forwarded to Raven's birth, which she did skip, as she didn't think he'd appreciate seeing himself being born, which would have been a whole lot of weird to watch. She noticed Rebecca was in labour with him for a good seventeen hours though. She snapped to attention as it all began to unfold in front of her and Raven. Hopefully, it would allow them to find out why they were so nasty to Raven.

"Here is your baby Rebecca. He's as healthy as can be considering he was born two weeks late." The nurse handed Rebecca the small blue-wrapped bundle. She held her arms out and the nurse placed the baby into the cradle and she brought the babe to her chest. He had ten perfect toes and ten perfect little fingers as they'd come loose from the blanket. They couldn't see the top part of his head because of the blanket.

"Isn't he perfect, Daniel?" She smiled at her husband.

"Oh yes," he murmured and kissed his wife. Even though she was still sweaty from the gruelling labour, he still thought she was the most beautiful woman to ever live. He lifted the blanket from the babe's head and all emotion left his face. The baby had a full head of jet black hair! Not his or Rebecca's blond. He looked at Rebecca and she noticed as well. She stared at the baby in her arms.

"Can you give us a moment please." He glanced over at the nurse.

"Of course. I'll go and fill out the bit of paperwork I need to record his birth with. I won't be long." They both waited as she disappeared out of the door and that was when the baby let out a high-pitched scream. He grabbed a bottle the nurse had prepared and handed it to Rebecca to feed the kid. As she put the teat in his mouth, he began to voraciously suck. He sat down in the chair that was beside the bed and looked at Rebecca.

"Care to explain why he has black hair and not our blond?" He was proud of himself, he didn't raise his voice, when in reality he wanted to scream at the top of his lungs.

"I, erm, it was a long time ago! We used protection and it was the once. I feel so bad for it, Daniel. Please, please forgive me," Rebecca sobbed, fat tears began to trickle down her cheeks.

"Just the once?"

"Yes. Just the once. I swear. And it will never happen again! I promise you, Daniel. I'd sooner kill myself than betray you again. As soon as it happened, I felt so bad I scrubbed myself raw."

"Fine. But you do realise I will never see that child as my son, right?"

"Yes, I understand. We will still raise him, right?"

"Yes, but only because our parents and other family members know you were pregnant. If they didn't, I'd have said throw him into an orphanage. But as soon as the kid is of age, then he's to be kicked out and I never want to see him again."

"OK. I understand. Does this mean I am forgiven?"

"Yes, Rebecca. But that is only purely for the fact I love you so damn much. Just don't do it again, I wouldn't be able to handle it."

"I won't, I promise." He gave her a quick kiss and they settled into silence as the baby chugged away at the milk, unaware of what was around him or what had just gone on. As Daniel's phone rang, he was about to answer when the nurse walked back in.

"Sorry to intrude, I forgot to ask what the child's name is." Daniel looked at Rebecca.

"You picked the name already, so that's what he shall be called. I need to answer this, it's my mother." He quickly left the room as he answered the call.

Rebecca looked over at the nurse who leant over the table that was next to her, paperwork in hand, pen waiting to sign in what the child was to be called. Before she could answer, the baby finished the bottle and due to not having done it before she didn't know what to do after he had finished.

"Oh, here. He needs winding." The nurse sat the boy up and showed her how to hold him and burp him. All too soon, the kid let out a huge burp and blinked at her with his huge ice-blue eyes. Another thing that was against her and her husband — they both had dark blue eyes. All their family members did, well apart from a few who had brown, green or hazel. But the majority had the dark blue, not ice ones like his.

"Thank you for that. I honestly wouldn't have had any clue whatsoever how to do that."

"Didn't your parents show you?"

"No, I'm the youngest. And I have no nieces or nephews yet. They're to be born next year."

"Ah, that explains it. I am sure that your parents will help you when you show them the little cutie. He's going to be a heartbreaker when he's older." She smiled down at the baby who smiled before he settled down to sleep. He was a contented baby with his belly full, clean nappy and warm.

"If you say so," Rebecca murmured and placed the baby in the small crib that Daniel had brought with him. She was thankful the baby settled quickly into sleep. She just didn't have the energy at the moment to deal with a crying baby.

"OK, so what name will he have?" The nurse again had the pen in hand.

"He'll be called Raven Lucian Calhoun." She replied and tugged the thin hospital blanket up to her chin. She was sore, tired and desperately needed some sleep. Rebecca watched as the nurse jotted it down quickly.

"No problem. Do you want to know what weight he was?"

"Yes please." She was anything if not polite, considering that was how she had been raised.

"Even though he was two weeks late, he weighs a good nine pounds ten ounces. The doctor recons if he had been born on time, he'd have been around the eight to nine pounds mark only."

"Blimey. No wonder I'm so sore," she muttered.

"It's to be expected. Every mother will hurt after delivering a baby. If they don't hurt, they're fibbing." The nurse smiled as she dimmed the lights.

"I'll let you get some rest. Do you want me to send Daniel back in?"

"If he wants to. Tell him I'm asleep so if he wants to go home until tomorrow, he can." She sighed and shut her eyes, sleep quickly rushing in to greet her with open arms.

Calista again pulled out of the memory and Raven turned to look at her.

"So he's known all along that I wasn't his. That certainly explains the hostility against me he has," Raven sighed.

"Yes, but it isn't right. It wasn't as if it was your fault your mother shagged someone else." Raven shrugged at that and moved, his butt was starting to go numb. He stood up, stretched and moved to the cave entrance before leaning his shoulder against the wall, crossing his arms over his chest.

"But surely she shouldn't have been so hostile to me as well?" He jumped slightly as her arms came around his waist to lock at his stomach.

"No, she shouldn't have. But I can't talk for people and how they treat their children. All I know is that you are a credit to yourself and not to them for the way you turned out."

"You say that now, but you didn't know me when I was fifteen or sixteen. I was a right arsehole."

"Everyone is an arsehole at some point in their life. Hell, even me, on more days than I care to count." Raven couldn't help it, at that answer, he burst out with laughter. When he finally controlled himself, he turned around in her arms and hugged her.

"Thanks for making me feel a little better about myself." He grinned at her and she openly returned it, making him treasure it all the more.

"You're welcome. Want to do more mind delving or will that be enough?"

"Nope; that'll do. All I wanted to know was what it was like right at the very beginning. If I'd done something to make them resent me or if they'd always been that way."

"Don't you ever blame yourself, Raven. It's their loss not knowing the great man that you are. Although I'm surprised none of your aunts or uncles did anything to help. Or your grandparents." She stared at him defiantly.

"Nah, they've never liked me either. Barely tolerated me in the house when we used to go and visit. And you know, you keep on talking like that, people might actually think you like me." He grinned at her.

"Maybe I do." She huffed and walked away, leaving him with his mouth hanging open. He charged after her, spun her around and wrapped his arms around him.

"You know, you're the only one then apart from Luke and Lexis that can tolerate my surly arse."

"You don't have a surly arse. I'm worse than you." She then proceeded to shock him, she wrapped her arms around his waist and hugged him back. Two hugs in the matter of two minutes. Damn if he wasn't going to treasure that along with that smile she gave him.

"Careful, people would definitely talk, seeing us like this." He laughed but didn't move away from her.

"Then let them talk, about time I took something, well someone for myself," she muttered against him. Raven smiled so broad, his cheeks hurt. But damn it was a good hurt.

"Is that a declaration that you want to keep me?"

"Keep you? You're not a possession." He let his arms drop back to his sides as she moved back from him.

"I know that, I meant keep me as in relationship keep me."

"I've never been in a relationship before, Raven. I don't know how to be with someone. I've never been with someone who knows me completely," she admitted, looking at the floor. He moved his hand to under her chin and forced her to look at him.

"I'm willing to learn. And who's perfect? Every couple learns how to be with each other."

"I'm not easy to get on with. You know I go on dangerous missions the majority of the time, along with all sorts of other shit."

"So? Is that meant to scare me off? Who followed you out here without a bloody clue to where he was going or what he was getting himself into?"

"You did."

"Exactly. So what do you say? Give me a chance to show you, you deserve to be with someone who will love, cherish and support you in everything?"

"Yeah, maybe. Are you still in lust with me?"

"Lust? You think I'd follow anyone if it was just lust? Calista, you probably won't believe me at the moment, but know this. I don't lust after you, well actually a lot but come on, you're a gorgeous woman, but I've never felt like this about someone before. Never this strong, never this powerful. I am hopelessly and unconditionally in love with you." He stared her right in the eyes as he admitted that. He didn't want her to think he was bullshitting her.

"You love me?" She blinked at him.

"Yep. Wholeheartedly."

"Want to know something?"

"What's that?" He took her hands into his. She didn't have soft hands like he remembered her having on the aeroplane, she had calloused rough hands, as that of one who had to deal with handling weapons and surviving day to day. She was the dangerous assassin he absolutely loved. He honestly wouldn't change a single thing about her. He loved the fact she stood up for herself, had rough hands which showed she had lived and wasn't into the whole soft, manicured hands like others were. And she could get down and dirty and didn't complain about a speck of dust getting on her, which was seriously hot.

"I kind of think I'm a little in love with you as well," she whispered and turned away quickly. When he finally managed to pull his jaw up from the floor, he hurried after her, dragging her to a stop.

"What?"

"I think I'm a little in love with you as well," she repeated, staring at him.

"Just a little?"

"Raven, I have no idea as I've never been in love with anyone before."

"OK, I can understand that. OK, then let me try and help you understand it. How does it feel inside of you thinking I'm going away? Or that I could die on this mission with you?" He watched as she thought about it — he would be patient.

"Honestly? It feels horrible. I get an achy feeling in my chest, kind of as if something is missing. What does it mean?" she asked.

"It means you're not a tiny bit in love with me. You're a whole lotta in love with me."

"Oh."

"It's OK, I can wait, I'm like a slow-growing fungi, I'll grow on you." She snorted at that. "Come on, let's go get some sleep. We're going to need as much as possible over the next few days." He pulled her to the sleeping bags. They changed into clean, comfortable sleeping clothes thanks to a snap of her fingers and they settled in quick. He watched as she extinguished the fire with a wave of her hand, plunging the cave into avid darkness. He laid down in his bag and put his arms behind his head and stared at the ceiling as it came alive.

"Erm, Calista, why is the ceiling glowing?"

"Think of it as glow in the dark algae. It's not poisonous or anything though, it's more of a night light," she said through the darkness and then he jumped as his bag undid itself and zipped itself up with hers as she wiggled down next to him, curling into his side and draping an arm and leg over him.

"What is it from?"

"Vines that come out at night from in the cracks of the ceiling. You can't see them in the daylight."

"Ah right. Anyway, come on now, let us go to sleep. I need my beauty rest. You're OK, you're always gorgeous." She snorted at that.

"I am not. I'm just me."

"And that is one of things I love about you. You have no idea just how gorgeous you are."

"Yeah, yeah. Also I want to do something for you."

"What?" he asked in the surrounding darkness.

"A gift of inner fire."

"Inner fire?"

"Inner fire, like the dragons use. It will come in handy if you need to defend yourself in dire need. But it really is for emergencies only, as it will ignite your entire being. And no one will be able to touch you whilst you're 'lit', as it will literally incinerate them."

"OK, go for it." He waited with baited breath as she placed her hand over his sternum. He knew he could trust her with whatever it was she had in mind. Anything to help him he would appreciate.

"Just breathe. This won't be pleasant for a couple minutes." He breathed out slightly, trying to regulate air in and out when a horrendous pain shot through his sternum. His blood felt alive, like someone had ran acid through his veins. He ground his teeth together to keep from crying out. Hands lay clenched at his sides so as not to hurt her. A few minutes later, she removed her hand and he let out a shaky breath.

"Well, that wasn't exactly pleasant. But how will I be able to use it?"

"Say ignes interiorem lucem."

"What does that mean?"

"Inner fire light."

"OK, that works. So I say it then when I want to use it?"

"Yes."

"And to stop it?"

"You say penetralibus ignem."

"Let me guess, fire out?"

"Yeah. Anyway, we really need to get some sleep now. Good night Raven." He felt her lean up and wondered what she was doing until he felt her lips touch his in a gentle kiss goodnight.

"Good night." He kissed her back before they settled down for sleep. He laid there watching the luminosity of the stars outside the cave entrance, one arm wrapped around Calista as she sunk into a deep sleep, the other still behind his head before he felt his lids start to close and didn't fight it as sleep too claimed him. The last thought to go through his head was that he could easily get used to falling asleep with her locked in his arms and her head resting on his chest. And he noticed how well that they fitted together, side by side, and it all felt right, no — perfect! As he lay there, the last of the pain from the inner fire had extinguished itself, as though it had never been. Oh magic, it truly was a phenomenal thing indeed.

Chapter Twenty-Eight

Lexis woke up the next morning with Jinx screaming down the baby monitor. She got out of bed, after untangling herself from Tairen, slipped on her slippers and walked into Jinx's room. She was wailing a good one, fists flying and everything.

"Now, now, little baby. What has you all sad?" She picked her up but she continued to wail. She shifted her lightweight vest top and got a lovely aroma. She wrinkled her nose and placed the baby on the changing bed. She quickly changed her nappy and Jinx soon settled down from crying but still sniffled. She changed her vest for a clean black one with a baby dragon on it. Adorable little purple socks covered her feet.

"Let's go and get you fed, seeing as you are up now." She carried Jinx out of the bedroom and glanced up from smiling at the baby as the door opposite opened. Alexzander stood there rubbing his eyes, his adorable skeleton onesie twisted around his ankles.

"You OK baby?"

"I thought I heard Jinx crying."

"It's OK, I've got her. She needed changed and I'm going to feed her now. You go on back to bed."

"OK." He didn't argue, just went back into the bedroom. He left the door open though and she watched as he jumped back into the bed, shuffled under the duvet and quickly settled back into sleep, curling his arm around his stuffed tartan teddy bear Tairen had bought earlier, which also happened to be bigger than he was himself at the moment. She smiled slightly at the sight and then scurried downstairs as Jinx started getting upset again. Standing in the kitchen, waiting on her bottle to heat up a little in the microwave, she jiggled the baby against her chest, trying to keep her calm enough so she didn't wake up anyone else. Glancing outside, she saw dawn was breaking across the horizon, creating a vast array of colours across the sky. It was beautiful. Rich oranges, reds and yellows, with the small hints of blue. She hoped it was going to be a gorgeous day, she planned on setting up the swimming pool, sorting out the barbeque and having a good time. The microwave dinged, drawing her from thoughts and she pulled it out, sprinkling it on her wrist, it was the perfect temperature and held it to Jinx's mouth, which she latched onto with a sigh and stared up at her with her striking eyes. Lexis left the kitchen and went into the living room. Fluffing up a cushion, she placed Jinx into it before curling around her, pretty much blocking Jinx between herself and the back of the couch. She rested her arm against her bicep and traced her fingers lightly over Jinx's belly. Before she realised it, Jinx finished her bottle and she quickly burped her before they settled back into the cushion. Jinx fell into a contented sleep with her small fingers curled up in Lexis's palm and Lexis smiled. Before she knew it, she was jolted awake as a blanket covered her. Standing above her was Tairen who smiled at her.

"Hi beautiful. I didn't mean to wake you."

"What's the time?" She quickly glanced at Jinx but she wasn't there.

"Ten a.m. And before you panic, Luke has the kids in the garden. They're sitting on the deck whilst they eat their breakfast." She sat up and rubbed her eyes.

"When did he take her from me?"

"About half an hour ago. He did it as carefully as he could, said he didn't want to wake you up." She moved the blanket off her and stood up. Stomach rumbling, she went into the kitchen and went into the pantry to the red fridge that was set to the side. She pulled out a blood bag, tore off the corner and swallowed it quickly. The pain eased off but she had another just in case. Once that was done, she threw the bags in the trash and looked out of the back door. Luke was perched sideways on the porch, laughing at Alexzander as he raced around the garden whilst he cradled Jinx to his chest. She opened the door and he turned to face her.

"Hey sleepyhead. Sleep all right?"

"I did. Why didn't you wake me when you took Jinx?"

"You must have needed the sleep, I'm used to functioning on five or six hours' sleep in the span of twenty-four hours."

"Why so little?"

"Because of the military. Was ingrained into us from when we first joined, just a habit I just can't seem to break. Doubt I will until I leave permanently."

"How long have you got left?" Tairen asked, coming up to stand next to Lexis and wrapped his arm around her waist.

"Six months. And counting."

"Why counting?"

"Because it's got tedious. As weird as it sounds, I want to find a nine to five job or whatever, settle down, raise a family. You know, normal shit. Whereas now, I've only got you guys and Raven."

"We can understand that. I'm sure you'll find someone." Lexis smiled as Alexzander raced over.

"Did you see how fast I ran?" he grinned as he plopped down on the floor. He was changed into a pair of shorts and a T-shirt with the slogan 'If mum says no, I'll ask my uncle'.

"I sure did. Proud of you, kiddo," Luke laughed.

"Bet I could catch you," Tairen said, stepped forward, which caused Alexzander to squeal in excitement, jump to his feet and dash off laughing. Tairen, walking quickly, pretending to be a growling tickle monster after him. Lexis sat down at her brother's feet.

"I see you picked his clothes for him today."

"I sure did. I'm the proud uncle, I'm allowed." He laughed as she shook her head.

"So, I've been meaning to ask, do you think Raven is OK out there?" She motioned with a tilt of her head to the forest.

"If anyone can survive it, it's Raven. You should see what he is like in the military. He's literally a force to be reckoned with. Hardly anyone wants to deal with him."

"Why?"

"It's kind of weird actually. He has untold strength. He's got an uncanny ability of taking down his targets when needed. One guy learned that the hard way."

"That bad?"

"Oh yeah. Thing is, it was one of the guys on the base. He had not long transferred in and had heard of Raven's 'abilities', was giving it large in the bunk room that he could most likely take him in a fight. At this time, he'd actually never even met Raven, let alone seen him. Everyone was snickering and saying he was talking out of his arse, myself included. He thought he was God's gift and that everyone should bow down to him because of some of the things he had accomplished, which mind you, were pitiful compared to the shit me and Raven had done."

"A right twat he sounds like," she snorted and waited whilst he moved Jinx to the other side of his chest, holding her now with his left arm.

"No doubt about it. It was annoying as anything. He had a whiny voice as well, not to mention his name was Richard. Anyway, he was going on that he could take Raven in a fight, could do literally everything better than he could. Everyone disagreed but he wasn't having any of it. We were all sitting on chairs in a cluster together, it was rec time before we had to sleep. Raven wasn't in the room, he was in the gym, as always during rec time. Lights were dim, as we preferred it that way, rain was pelting down the windows, wind was howling, you know a typical storm, when the main door burst open and Raven walked in. He had on sweat pants and a tank top, which really didn't leave much to the imagination of the fact he's seriously ripped, but not in a bodybuilder type way, he just likes to keep himself fit and healthy. He had his gym bag in his fist and a towel draped across his shoulders. Of course, cocky wasn't having any of it and told him that this room was for elite soldiers, not wannabe gym builders. I told him to shut his trap. He wasn't having any of it and got right up in Raven's face. I told him to back the fuck off before he regretted it. Richard wasn't having any of it."

"What happened next?" She crossed her legs, getting comfortable.

"I saw the dead look cross Raven's face, as in he was completely unreadable. It's a look no one wants to see, trust me on that one. I jumped to my feet and grabbed Richard, which I shouldn't have done as he slugged me one. He turned back to Raven and told him to leave, he was unwanted here. Another guy told him to leave him alone. Richard said he wasn't scared, and he was willing to wait for real competition to get here. I remember Raven looked at me and said, who's the new kid? I told him his name was Richard and he had heard of the infamous Raven and was bragging that he could take him out and everything. Raven had smirked at me before turning back to Richard." Luke smiled at the memory as Lexis dived off of the porch to run after Alexzander as he'd fallen and hurt himself.

Everyone in the unit stopped what they were doing and watched the scene unfold. Raven stood staring down at Richard who had to actually look up considering Raven was a big bastard.

"So, you reckon you can take Raven on, do you?"

"Yeah. He's a snot-nosed punk who doesn't know how to respect his superiors."

"And you happen to be superior, huh?"

"I know I am. I'm the best at hand to hand. Firearms. Pretty much everything they throw at me."

"Right, and you do know how tall he is, right?"

"From what I've heard, he's all of six feet. I'm six feet three. So I already tower over him, not to mention I'm heavier and can throw a punch better."

"OK then. Go to the gym. I'll get Raven and you can go hand to hand with him in the ring. Literally anything goes, no holds barred."

"What?" Richard stared at him flabbergasted.

"What? Do I have to repeat myself? Or are you scared?"

"I am not scared! Fine, I will meet you there." He stormed out of the room and disappeared into the darkness. Raven turned back to everyone.

"So tell me, who brought the brat in? Why is he here in our unit?"

"Because he seems to think he can cope dealing with us. Apparently, he's better than all of us lot," Christina replied. They knew her as Boom, considering her expertise was explosives.

"Who drafted him in, Boom?"

"No idea. It was probably Sarge. All we know was one minute we were all sitting here playing a game of cards when the door opened and he walked in. Started mouthing off when he joined us and you walked in about ten minutes later." Blade, aka Chris, said.

"Well then, let's go see what this puny punk thinks he's up against," Geek, aka Nick, replied, packing up their cards and putting them in his foot locker. They all stood up, grabbed their coats and walked out into the storm, luckily it had stopped raining at that moment though. Walking over to the gym in silence, they were all a formidable sight. All deadly in their own way, but none other than Raven himself. Luke was the first to admit his brother was stronger and a hell of a lot meaner than them when he lost his temper. He was their secret weapon, aptly called Mountain. Considering he was taller and wider than all of them. Although he should have been called Ghost, considering he was as silent as one. Boom barely stood five feet five. Geek stood at six feet. As did Blade. He himself was six feet three. He ushered them all ahead of himself and Raven, they walked into the gym and when they opened the inner doors, a loud roar escaped of people cheering and getting excited about the fight. How did people know about it already? But then he realised how. Richard. He had a gob on him and no doubt had already bragged on his way over and of course that spread like wildfire over the base. Shaking his head, he walked inside just as one of the Air Force announced into a microphone, well introducing Richard. Luke walked side by side with Raven and as they walked further in, they announced that Richard was against Raven. As Raven walked in just behind him, silence reigned over everyone, and it seemed louder than their shouting had been.

"Who the bloody hell are you?" Richard called out.

"You asked for Raven, you got him," Luke answered as Raven climbed up into the gym ring and cracked his knuckles. No one made a noise as the general made everyone step back from the ring to give it equal space all the way around. No one argued with him, considering he was the boss of everyone.

"But, I saw you in the barracks. You didn't tell me you were Raven!" Richard stammered, but Luke had to give the shit credit, he didn't back down and the plus, he didn't piss himself. Raven just looked bored. Luke knew what was coming, and he couldn't wait!

"You didn't ask. You were running your mouth, thinking you're the big man, when in reality, you're nothing but a worm."

"I am not a worm!" he screamed at him.

"Worm. Lowest of the low. You should have done your homework on who you actually want to run your mouth about."

"Fuck you." And then he did the wrong thing, he charged at Raven who didn't move a single inch. He let Richard get a hit in, but he only hit his chest. Raven went completely calm, which everyone that knew him, knew it was the wrong thing to do and someone muttered 'damn boy's gonna be sore when he wakes from whatever Raven is gonna do'. Luke noticed Raven saw him out of the corner of his eye, and the lightest flare of his nostrils let Luke know trouble was coming to Richard, and good, his cheek was hurting like a bitch at the moment from where the punk had struck him. Obviously, everyone knew not to hit him. Sure, in training, that was different, but for no reason, that didn't bode well for the one who did it. If they hit Raven, as he'd previously admitted to Luke, so what. He was used to it, could take a hell of a lot of 'punishment' and was always known to retaliate eventually, which was why majority of the time he was left alone and that was how he liked it.

"And now you will know why they call me the Mountain." Raven didn't give him any warning, just struck out with his right fist and slammed it into Richard's face, knocking the guy out completely in one hit. Richard hit the ground hard and Raven didn't bother acknowledging him, just climbed out of the ring and left the building, heading for a shower and then bed, leaving everyone behind in stunned, open-mouthed silence apart from Luke who wore a huge grin on his face that the bastard finally had what was coming to him.

Luke pulled out of the memory and saw Lexis was walking back to him, Alexzander again playing with Tairen. He looked down at Jinx as she wiggled against his chest where he was holding her and moved her to lay on his legs, her bum up near his stomach, legs in the air as he tickled her belly, causing her to laugh and smile up at him, her grey eyes twinkling.

"Alexzander OK?"

"Yeah, he's fine. He has a small graze on his knee but he'll be OK. Now where were we?"

"You asked about Raven and Richard."

"Oh yes, so go on, what happened?"

"Well, Richard didn't know it was Raven he was talking to. Raven told him that he would go get Raven and meet him at the gym and he'd then be able to prove that he was the better man. That happened, he realised the guy who he was talking to in the barracks was in fact the man he'd been slagging off, he then hit Raven in the chest. Raven retaliated and knocked him out in one punch."

"I'm not surprised. He's huge! When you left for the military, did they dunk him in miracle grow or something? I remember him as a scrawny sixteen-year-old who was as thin as a stick and smaller than the height I am now."

"No, they didn't throw him in miracle grow. Once he started eating regularly, he literally grew like a weed and when he was introduced to the regular workout as they require from us, he filled out to what he is now. But for his size, he's as silent as a ghost. Literally."

"How can he be as silent as a ghost when he's the size he is?"

"He's six feet eight. He just moves that quietly. Has since they began training us, they must have realised something within him, so used that to their advantage. Although his nickname isn't ghost, it's Mountain. Because at times, he is as unmoveable as one."

"Oh."

"Yeah. Now enough of that. What are the plans for today?"

"Set the swimming pool up, get the barbeque going. Get music going. Make memories."

"Sounds a plan." He grinned at her and handing Jinx over before standing up. Tairen and Alexzander walked over to them.

"I'll help you set up the swimming pool, Tairen. Then we'll get the barbeque ready, yeah?"

"Sounds like a plan." He motioned for Luke to follow him, which he did. They quickly grabbed what they needed and headed back to the garden.

Setting it up, Tairen quickly grabbed the garden hose and began filling it up. They sorted out everything, which took them about an hour. Whilst waiting, Lexis made them all a sandwich each, which they sat on the porch eating. Luke stared off into the distance and again the thought ran through his head of wondering if Raven was OK. And for that matter was Calista? What untold things had they found out there in the woods? Had they found the children yet?

Chapter Twenty-Nine

Calista woke up to the feeling of a rock-hard body wrapped around her, a heavy weight over her waist. She lifted the edge of the sleeping bag and saw it was Raven's arm. Her head rested on his bicep, and looking straight up his arm, she saw his hand was curled around a knife hilt, the blade pointing away from her, but she knew he would use it quick as a flash if anyone had come into their cave. Ever protective he was. She smiled at that, as usually it was she who was the protective one, well when she was working alongside someone. She looked past his arm and stared outside, the sky was lightening up, dawn was here and they needed to get moving. They had to cross to the other side of the swamp and then it was maybe half a day's walk to Fire Mountain. She moved Raven's arm off her and scurried out of the warmth of the bag. She hurried outside and made quick work of emptying her bladder. She went back inside and Raven was awake. He had his back to her, and was rolling up the sleeping bags. She knocked a rock with her foot and he swirled around, blade up ready to throw it if needed.

"Jesus Christ! Learn to make some noise when you walk woman!" He put the knife away and she grinned. Moving towards him, she made everything disappear apart from his backpack and the weapons.

"And what good would that do me? I'm a trained assassin. And says you, you move just as quietly as what I do."

"Good point. Guess I'm not fully awake yet. Where did you go anyway?"

"To pee."

"Oh. Well that explains why I didn't wake up with a warm gorgeous woman beside me. And speaking of peeing, my turn." He hurried past her and disappeared slightly out of view. She changed her clothes, made herself clean and began strapping her weapons to her body. It was a simple act for her, she'd done it every day since the moment of her 'birth' so she was used to it. As she was strapping on her axe to her back, Raven walked back in.

"Feel better now?"

"God yeah. So upon leaving here, how long do you think we will have before we reach Fire Mountain?"

"After we reach the end of the swamp, which will take the entire day, we will have to again find some place to rest for the night. Then it's about half a day's walk to Fire Mountain, and then we'll devise a plan on how to get in, get the kids and get out."

"I like how you are involving me in this." He grinned at her.

"Yeah well, we're a team. About time I had someone on a team with me."

"You have Nikki, Skyri and Draylan as your team though."

"They're my working team, when they join me, which majority of the time is a nope. I meant the other kind of team. If you want to try it that is."

"A relationship?"

"Yes, that."

"You don't have to ask me twice." He grinned again, pulled her against him and kissed her. She kissed him back, and wrapped her arms around him. They stayed like that for a moment or two before she pulled back before it got too heated.

"OK, come on, let's get going." She waited for him to shrug his backpack on, put his gun over his shoulder, machete in hand and blades attached to his thighs and inner arms. She made sure the fire and anything else they'd used was discarded until it was a barren cave again. Just how they had found it. Strolling to the mouth of the cavern, she gave one last look behind them to double check everything was gone, even the dirt they'd moved to allow for a smooth surface to sleep on had gone back to where it was before. Together, they began their trek down to the trees, careful of their steps so as not to sink into the marshland. Strolling through the trees, they kept their comfortable silence. Slightly ahead and to the left of them, Calista noticed a large mound appear and as they drew closer, she watched as Sarucha opened her eyes and stared at them, her head partly hidden under weeds.

"So, this means you are leaving now, yes?" she asked, rising up slightly to speak clearly.

"Yes. Will we see Apophis on our way out?"

"No. He's not here. Carry on straight ahead and you shall reach the edge by the day's end. I bid you well on your quest."

"Good tidings, Sarucha." Calista nodded her head in respect and they strode past her. Once they were out of view of the reclusive dragon, she looked at Raven.

"Walk behind me now, and step in each place that I do. That way you know it will be solid ground."

"Sure thing. Why not next to you?"

"Because if you step on marsh, you'll sink to your knees quickly. Whereas if I step on marsh, I can get out quicker than you."

"OK, that's reasonable enough for me, I won't argue. Plus, it means I can openly stare at your arse." She mock glared at him, which only made him laugh.

"Good thing I'm getting used to the sassy side of you isn't it?"

"I haven't even started yet."

"Then fuck! Someone save me from the arrogant man!" she cried out, causing him to grin at her as he stepped into place behind her.

"Get moving, woman. We have a mission to finish, then after that, I plan on keeping you hostage." She turned around to look at him.

"Hostage, huh?"

"Oh, yes. For at least a week in bed." He winked at her and she really tried not to be charmed by him, but it was hard.

"Oh, really?"

"Damn right. I plan on it." She shook her head and she waited until he was properly behind her, she took the first step to carry on the arduous journey out of the swamp. Ignoring the warm, fuzzy feeling in her lower stomach, as well as not allowing Raven to see how amused she was by his witty humour and the fact that she knew he wasn't afraid of her, nor scared to actually tell her to her face what he thought. As she trod around some bushes, she realised just what she had said back in the cave. She was indeed ready to begin and at least try in her relationship with Raven. She knew he didn't have long left to serve in the military and maybe she could persuade him to move here with her? Wait, what? Had she literally thought of asking Raven to leave 'Normal Earth' and move here to Mystic Being? Yes. Yes, she did and that was a scary thought as she had never needed, nor had to think of anything like that. Sure, Lexis was going to move here once she had finished her final year in Glasgow University, but that was more of her coming to live here with Tairen so that they could raise their kids together. But could her and Raven work? Considering their vast differences? Well, she would definitely try.

"What's that noise?" Raven's whisper in her ear had her snapping out of her thoughts and she listened.

"I'm not sure. Wait here and I'll go check quick." She looked at him over her shoulder as he nodded. She made him wait next to a tree, and he crouched down, obscured by the dense shrubbery. She disappeared out of his sight quickly and using her speed, raced to their left. A minute later, she slowed and blending into the shadows, saw it was a group of swamp nymphs playing together, whilst a little way from them was a male nymph rutting with a female whilst another sat on her face. They were nothing if not adventurous and uncaring in who they slept with, be it male or female. She edged away and made her way back to Raven.

"Did you find out what it was?"

"I did. It's swamp nymphs."

"I thought nymphs didn't reside in swamps? Only in the town together or in woodlands?" he asked, standing up from his spot and moving to her.

"Usually they do, but these are as their namesakes are. They very rarely venture out of the swamplands and keep to themselves usually."

"Ah, gotcha." They moved to the left and cut sideways from the nymphs, essentially going around them.

Wandering through the forestry in silence, careful to step where she did, Raven reflected on all that he had seen and done since he had been here in Mystic Being. He could definitely say it wasn't boring in the least. He'd seen and actually learned hell of a lot. And the best part, he'd fallen in love with an absolute badass who wasn't afraid to tell him how it was, nor was she intimidated by his size. But now that he'd seen some of the creatures here, he knew why. Take Gélio for instance, he was an absolute beast. And no wonder she wasn't intimidated by his size as she literally went nose to nose with the dragons, as well as other creatures here. Trust him to fall in love with the major badass. And the fact she could hold her own? So fucking hot! He chanced a glance up at the sky and saw that easily half the day had gone. Where the hell though? He could have sworn they'd only been walking a good couple of hours. Obviously not. Focusing back on where he was to put his feet, he noticed the sway of Calista's hips. Holy damn! He reached out and squeezed her butt cheek, causing her to jump. She whirled around and glared at him. He grinned.

"What was that for?"

"I couldn't help it. You have such a delectable arse. And it's been teasing me all day! I'm surprised I've shown so much restraint until now."

"Yeah, sure you haven't," she snorted.

"It's true. Cross my heart." He did with his finger and grinned at her. She rolled her eyes at him.

"Yeah, right. OK, we're about a ten-minute walk until we reach the edge of the swamp. Then we cross the flat land, through some more trees for the night where we will bed down in the canopy again, come the following morning, another half day or so and then we will be at the base of the Fire Mountain."

"Ok, so roughly a day's walk?"

"Give or take, yes."

"What will we do when we get to the base of the mountain?"

"We'll devise a plan on how to get the kids out as quickly as possible. The less people see us, the better."

"Can't you do an invisibility spell or something?"

"I can for myself, but not for you. Well, I can but they'd still see you if the light hits you just right. Not worth the risk."

"Why not?"

"Because we'll be in Fire Mountain. Loads of the walls are pure molten lava behind a thin layer of rock. All it would take is for us to stand in front of one and they'd see you."

"Ah, gotcha. OK, we'll devise the plan closer to the mountain base. Shall we carry on or have a break?"

"Let's carry on. Sooner we get up into the treetops and settle down for sleep the better. Unfortunately, Brynyfa is nearly upon us, so it's going to be dark easily within an hour or so tops." Whilst they spoke, they carried on their trek and he realised just how easy it was to talk to her whilst on this mission. Even in their silent bouts, it was comfortable.

"The day has literally gone nowhere," he grumbled as he followed her again.

"Unfortunately, that's what Brynyfa is like here. It comes in very quickly. So much so, that when it's highly set in, it will get dark around about three p.m."

"Blimey, and when does dawn break?"

"About seven to eight a.m. the following morning." He was amazed; it seemed it was dark here for longer periods of time than back in 'Normal Earth'. He didn't and couldn't really call it home, he'd never fitted in there. It was literally a place he existed in. Strolling through some trees he came across a vast wasteland, at least a football pitch wide and it went as far as the eye could see in either direction.

"God, how long does this go?" He looked first one way and then the other.

"From one end of the island to the other. It's never had life grow on it for some reason."

"Wow. Never?"

"Never. Now come on, sooner we cross the safer we will be. And you don't need to walk behind me anymore, we're out of the swamp land." He didn't argue, just followed next to her at a rapid pace. By the time they breached the other side, night had descended over half of the sky. They hurried through the shrubbery, being as quiet as possible so they didn't draw attention to themselves as there was no telling what was hiding out of their line of sight. Before he realised it, Calista had him flattened up against a tree, hand over his mouth. And just in the nick of time as well, as a horde of demons hurried past, lugging wild pig carcasses they'd caught, as well as a few had a couple of cows they'd obviously stolen, killed and were taking back to their homes no doubt to devour with eagerness. Once they'd both strained to hear that they'd disappeared, she finally removed her hand from over his mouth. Before he could think anything of it, he gave her a quick kiss.

"What was that for?"

"Felt like it. Plus, we're in a relationship, you can kiss me any time you want."

"Oh really?"

"Yep. All part of it."

"Good to know." She retaliated by giving him a quick kiss herself then she began climbing a tree a few feet from him. He grinned and quickly followed her up, after he attached the machete to his backpack and his gun slung over his head to give both his hands access to grasp branches. He quickly clambered up, shocked by how easily she scrambled up the tree. Once they'd reached quite a height, she motioned for him to stop, which he did and removed the machete, gun and backpack before collapsing into a heap on a solid branch. She sat on the branch just above him. He pulled a rope out of his backpack, effectively tying his gear to the branch so it wouldn't fall when they slept.

"How long will we be here for?" He gazed up at her and she looked back down at him from where she'd had her head tilted back, staring at the few stars that had begun to shine through the leaves.

"We'll get started at daybreak. We need as much of a head start as possible."

"OK, fair enough. You really going to sleep with your axe and sword attached to your back?"

"Yep. I'm so used to it now, it honestly feels weird when I don't sleep with them attached to my back."

"Fair enough. I wonder how everyone back at the house is coping?"

"Want me to show you?"

"You can do that?" He felt his eyebrows raise at that.

"Yep. You'll have to stand up though to see." He didn't hesitate, he stood up and because her branch wasn't too far a distance from him, and not to forget he was stupidly tall, he could easily see her hands as they were cupped. Actually his head was in perfect alignment with her breasts, but he wasn't going to think about that. He gazed at her hands as water pooled into them from out of nowhere. It began to glow, illuminating their faces. As he stared into the water, a scene unfolded. Lexis, Tairen and Luke were sitting around the table in the kitchen, eating dinner whilst a boy was in between her and Luke eagerly stuffing his face with chips. Tairen held a baby against his chest, rocking her slightly whilst she slept, hand tucked up under her chin, the other grasping his T-shirt.

"Who's the kids?" He chanced a glance at her quickly then back down at her hands.

"Lexis and Tairen's adopted children. Alexzander and Jinx. They are the reason Nikki didn't stay with me. I sent her to retrieve them from their previous address and send them to Lexis and Tairen."

"Fair enough." He watched as they laughed at something Alexzander did and saw Luke look over at Lexis, and because Calista had super wicked powers, he heard him ask how they thought he was faring. Lexis replied that she wouldn't be surprised if they'd teamed up together and Calista would keep him safe. If anyone could, it was her. Raven smiled at her confidence then stilled as Alexzander asked who he was. He watched as Luke turned to face the boy and with a smile on his face told the kid that Raven was his uncle. He was also Luke's best friend. Raven grinned as he watched the other two adults nod to confirm what he said.

"Thanks for that." He pulled back and Calista opened her hands at the side, the water rushing to the floor thanks to gravity.

"You're welcome." She settled back where she was and he got comfortable against the tree trunk again.

"So what are they then? The kids, I mean."

"Shadow Fae. Their mother was a shaoàluray."

"A what?"

"A prostitute. She was more interested in spreading her legs than feeding her kids. Hence, why they are so skinny. But I'm sure with Lexis cooking, they'll soon fill out as they're meant to."

"Damn, harsh for them."

"Yes. But luckily, Jinx is still young enough to know no different. And Alexzander knows he's got it good now. He doesn't even call Juliana his mother anymore. Lexis is."

"I couldn't think of anyone better for them."

"Me neither. As you can see, it hasn't taken her long to fall into the role of protective mother."

"She's always been like that. She has for as long as I've known her."

"Really?"

"Really. She mothered me and Luke when we used to come back to their parents' house, covered in mud, cuts and God knows what else from mucking around in the fields and woodlands that were near their home."

"What did you two do when she tried to mother you?"

"We thought it was really sweet. And she used to have a beaming smile on her face when she 'nursed' us. So we used to deliberately get a bit scraped up just to make her feel useful."

"That was nice of you both." He watched as she leaned her head back and closed her eyes. He wiggled slightly and moved into a more comfortable position.

"I suppose we had better get some sleep then."

"Yes, I'd advise it. I know it's early, but the best we can do is get as much sleep as possible. No one will know we are here. I've cloaked our presence."

"Good to know." He lay his head back and closed his eyes.

"Good night, Raven." Her voice whispered over to him.

"Good night, Calista." They settled into silence and sleep quickly washed over them, and they surrendered with open arms.

Chapter Thirty

The following morning, Raven woke up to the early morning sunshine beaming him right in the face as it shone through the leaves above him. Blinking open bleary eyes, he sat back really quickly, smacking his head into the trunk. Groaning as he rubbed the spot, he glared at Calista as she sat between his legs.

"How long have you been sitting there watching me?"

"Couple minutes."

"Why didn't you wake me up?"

"You needed the rest."

"I'm good to go. I'm used to minimal sleep." He stretched and as he drew his arms backwards, his shoulders cracked and he released a groan at how good it felt.

"That might be so, but I have no idea how much sleep you're going to get now."

"Yeah, good point. Now we really need to get out of this tree so I can empty my bladder."

"Definitely." He watched as she swung back on her feet and stood up in a fluid motion that he reckoned ballerinas would be envious of. He slowly clambered back to his feet and didn't move as he leaned back against the trunk. His legs were slightly numb from sitting in the same position for as long as he had. He gritted his teeth as blood rushed through his system again. Pins and needles were an absolute bitch. Soon enough they disappeared so he swung his backpack into place, secured the machete at his hip thanks to some leather strapping Calista had given him from God knows where which looped through his belt, slung his gun strap over his neck to dangle and they began the descent out of the tree. Once they'd touched ground he glanced over at her.

"Why is it that it always seems bloody longer getting down than it did going up?"

"Because you're desperate to piss."

"You're never if not blunt. Right, time to pee." He disappeared in the shrubs and quickly released his bladder, sighing happily as the pressure disappeared. He sorted himself out and quickly joined Calista who waited patiently.

"OK, ready to get going?"

"Yep, but don't you need to relieve your bladder?"

"Did it whilst you was asleep." She smirked at him and he retaliated by slapping her butt. She rolled her eyes at him and he chuckled, then wiped all the emotion off his face. Time to get serious considering they weren't all that far from Fire Mountain.

"Ok, so where to now?"

"Straight ahead and in about two miles, we'll reach the outskirts of the forest and then about two hundred yards on we will come across Fire Mountain, although we will see it from the outskirts."

"Fair enough. Let's get going then." He followed her as she turned around and took off. He noticed her weapons were back in place, she hadn't had them when he'd first woken so she must have got them when he was peeing. The axe looked sharper than usual though.

"When did you sharpen the axe?"

"Middle of the night. I didn't sleep much so kept a look out and sharpened the blade to give me something to do," she casually replied.

"Fair enough." They wove around some weird looking bushes and he felt a sting on his leg as he brushed past.

"What the fuck?" His outburst caused Calista to stop and look at him over his shoulder but he wasn't paying attention, he was looking down at his leg as a damn Flesher was again stuck to his jeans. He reached down and plucked it between his fingers, steering clear of that bloody mouth. He put it back on the leaves next to him and it scurried back a little bit to sit and wait for its next victim. It definitely wasn't going to be him again.

"You OK?" He glanced up at Calista.

"Yeah, it was a pesky Flesher."

"So you got bit again?"

"Yeah. But not like before. This one barely got its teeth into my leg before I caught it." They carried on walking whilst they spoke, no point in talking and standing around.

"OK. As long as it didn't pierce the flesh properly."

"Nope, all good." Again, they fell into that silence which gave him time to reflect on things that had happened. Yes, he'd already thought of it, but was it really too good to be true? Did Calista really agree to be his girlfriend? Or at least see where their relationship would take them? He really lucked out there as she was an absolutely stunning woman who didn't roll her eyes at his offbeat humour or moan at his sarcasm. And because he had proven himself time and time again, he could hold his own if he needed to. And honestly, he thought she respected that and that he wasn't one to rely on her constantly. Snapping out of his thoughts, he realised that they must have eventually walked a good mile or so before they came to a stop.

"What's up?" he asked, drawing up short.

"I thought I heard something. Not that I'm not surprised, considering we are on the outskirts of the mountain."

"So what do we do now?"

"We will carry on —" Before she could finish the sentence, an arrow head appeared from her stomach.

"What the fuck?" he yelled before looking behind her to find out who shot her. But he could see no one. He watched as she snapped the head of the arrow off, reached behind her and pulled the body out. Must have hurt like an absolute bitch, but yet, she said nothing. But then he remembered this would probably be a minor hindrance considering the previous injuries she had already suffered on this mission. As he watched her bring the blooded arrow around in between them, they were suddenly swarmed by at least two hundred or so Fire Demons. Calista turned to face the tallest of them all, giving him her back but he knew that she knew what she was doing. She was trusting him in a way to guard her back. And he wouldn't let her down, not without a fight anyway. He glanced at the biggest motherfucker there who stood at a good six feet nine, as he was just slightly taller than his own six feet eight frame. The big bastard had huge cloven feet. Huge black horns started above his ripped, pierced ears and curled back up above his skull, much like a typical demon's would. He had a muscular red and black body and Raven reckoned he'd throw one heck of a punch with his shovel-sized fists that were also tipped in black claws, if given enough leverage to get in a decent throw. He had serrated teeth that glistened behind his black lips. Red eyes surrounded by black stared at them.

"Well, hello Calista."

"Krr'ashlah." She sneered the word. Obviously, he was not friendly.

"Well, we know each other but who is this thing with you?"

"None of your business. Now why would Kharge want you to run his errands? You still his little bitch?" The resounding crack of his fist connecting with Calista's face was loud in the sudden silence after her question and Raven just about managed to keep the wince from leaving his mouth, and the emotions off his face. Not to forget the hard boiled rage that shot through his veins like liquid fire.

"Feel better now you've slapped me like the bitch you are?" Raven did smirk at Calista's remark then.

"You are nothing. You're no one special." And with that they all shot Calista with a dart gun. Needles quickly covered her flesh and the tranqs soon kicked into gear, causing her to topple to the floor in a heap. But Raven noticed it took all of those tranquilisers to get her down, and he was mighty impressed. Just showed how much it did take to take her down. Then he noticed everyone had their attention on him, but he outright refused to cower under their intense stare.

"So what are you?" Krr'ashlah glared at him.

"Someone that doesn't respond to you." He caught the guy next to him as he lashed out and using the machete they hadn't realised he'd slipped into his hand, free of the protective sheath, he lopped off the guy's head in a single swipe of his wrist, getting coated in the yellow arterial blood. Lovely. But he didn't catch the second fist that came swinging at him from Krr'ashlah. It spun him to the floor and before he could retaliate, some pounced on him and tied him up, effectively rendering him useless. He growled as he was grabbed onto his knees, his right eye already swelling from the force of the blow. He lunged at one of the men next to him who looked like he shot himself with steroids and sent the guy sprawling to the floor from the impact Raven hit him with. He wasn't going down without a fight, fuck it.

"What the fuck is he?"

"Human," he spat out before anyone else could answer for him.

"No way, humans don't hit as hard as you do," Krr'ashlah sneered.

"Then you've obviously not met a human like me."

"No, we haven't. But not to worry, it won't matter to us. We will find out soon enough what makes you tick." Krr'ashlah snapped his fingers and Raven was jerked forward, not by their hands but by spears jabbing into him through his clothes, so obviously they were going to take him and Calista to the mountain. That saved them having to find a secret way in then he supposed. He watched out of the corner of his left eye as the one he'd hit hauled Calista up onto his shoulder after they'd disarmed her of all of her weapons as well as the needles that had littered her body. Raven couldn't fight back as they also disarmed him before he was forced to follow them. They took all his weapons away from him, even his backpack was thrown into a small cart he hadn't noticed before that a small red demon covered in scars was strapped to the front of.

"Move it, Nomed." Again, another demon in pale red lashed out with a whip, causing Nomed to start forward, not even wincing as the lash cut into his back and caused puss green blood to leak out. Just how used to it was he? They were absolute fuckers and he vowed there and then he would kill every single one of them until either he went down or they did.

"Warden?" one called out and Krr'ashlah stopped and looked at the one who had spoken. So he was called Warden to everyone else but Krr'ashlah to Calista? Hold on, he remembered he'd read somewhere that to use a demon's full name was to have temporary power over them, so why hadn't it worked for Calista? Or was that only part of his name? Considering most were supposed to be unpronounceable to the human tongue because of the hard consonants and apostrophes. Not to mention some you had to literally roll the letters off of your tongue and only pronouncing it right was the way to gain control. Could that have been why Calista didn't get the control, because it was only part of his name? Or was it really all just a myth? He watched as one of the demons let out a cry of pain and smirked as he dropped Calista and she landed on her feet, a blade dripping in purple blood held in her fist.

"SHOOT HER!" Warden screamed and they all again shot her with their tranquilisers. It worked quickly as they realised the knock out drug shot straight into her system and she toppled to the floor. They roughly manhandled her into the cart Nomed was pulling, but they left the needles in her. Maybe not wanting to risk it again? He watched as Warden turned to face him.

"How did that get through her system so quick? We shot her with enough tranq to take down a dragon!" He got right in Raven's face. The only fucker to do so. Raven headbutted him.

"Should have done your homework."

"Tell me why!" Warden backhanded Raven and he just laughed.

"You hit like a little bitch."

"I do not!"

"Yes. Yes, you do, you fuck face fornicating fucker!"

"I am not that! You stupid fuck!"

"Sorry, I know I'm stupid but you see, I can't count past the number of fucks I give. I'm currently at zero." He laughed outright in Warden's face.

"FUCK YOU!" Warden shouted at him and hit him again. Raven spat out the blood that automatically pooled in his mouth.

"Ooo, I hope you're not allergic to nuts."

"Why?"

"Because I'm going to kick yours up your throat." That got the reaction he was hoping for. Warden punched him hard and as the ground rose up to meet him, Raven knew the guy's time was limited. He was going to rip his head clean off his neck and laugh as he did so. And if he didn't, he knew that Calista would.

Chapter Thirty-One
Two weeks later

Calista woke up from her light doze, her left eye now managing to open to about half way from where she'd been punched repeatedly from Warden. She was bolted to a wall somewhere inside Fire Mountain. The bolts that were used to hold her in place ripped through her wrists to lock in place on the wall. Chains covered above her breasts, along her pelvis, thighs and calves. Clearly they weren't taking anything for granted at the moment. She tried moving her head to look around the room, but because they had attached a thick collar around her neck which extended to a cage that covered the lower part of her face, it was virtually impossible to move anything but her eyes. A headband, as thick as her wrist, went across her forehead and attached to the cage by poles next to her ears, keeping her head upright at all times. It was torture, pure and simple. But she had dealt with much worse, so she could deal with the minor neck ache with ease. Thanks to her unique abilities, she knew it was high noon. Sweat rolled off her and dripped to the floor. Her body barely covered by the scraps of her bra and panties they'd left on. The rest of her clothing however hadn't stood a chance once they'd ripped them off her. She wondered briefly where they'd put her weapons. As well as what was happening with Raven. Was he OK? What were those fuckers doing to him? Before she could think anymore, the cell door opened and in rolled Warden and his battle-hardened bitch Salem, who kicked the door shut behind her. She was Krr'ashlah's woman. She had blood-red skin, splintered in places from scars in a paler red. Eyes as black as sin. She stood in a skin-tight black latex outfit. Weapons clung to all parts of her body. Black boots covered her feet. She was a tiny thing, no taller than five feet four or so, but she made up for it in sheer brutality and not one to back down either.

"So what shall we do to you today? Will you talk now?" Warden stepped towards a table that was to the left of where she dangled and picked up a scalpel. Moving back in front of her, she glared at him. She outright refused to allow them the satisfaction of hearing her scream out. He dragged the blade across her stomach, leaving a thin trail behind it which instantly weld up with blood. She watched as Salem stepped forward with a small vial of clear liquid. Popping off the cap, Calista breathed in. Now this was going to hurt. In that vial was acid, she knew it from the smell.

"I take it you already know what this is," Salam asked in her raspy voice, no doubt from where she'd had her throat slashed, as Calista could just make out the tips of the scars from where it was hidden by a thick leather choker. Shame they didn't succeed. But, oh yes, Calista knew perfectly well what it was, it was butyric acid. Or fermentation butyric acid which was also found as a hexyl esterhexyl butyrate in the oil of Heracleum Giganteum, a type of the Giant Hogweed plant that grew around here. She watched as Salam drew a pipette out of somewhere behind her, drew some of the liquid out and dripped it over the wound Warden had created. She clenched her teeth shut as it burned into her flesh. When that didn't get a reaction out of her, Warden opened the door and yelled out for his box. *Just what fun stuff did he have planned for her now* she thought. A minute or so later, in walked a slave demon, because of the collar around his throat and also around his wrists, along with the tattered bottoms he wore, not to forget the abundance of scars that littered his flesh, who dragged in a huge five feet wide by easily eight to ten feet long box. Well, it was more of a chest than a box. Once it was fully in the room, Salem walked over to it and flipped it open.

"You're dismissed," Warden snapped at the slave, who scurried out of the room as though his feet were on fire. Warden reached into the chest and pulled out six individual boxes of carved oak. He placed each one on the floor and opened the lid on them. Calista just about managed to keep the expressions off her face. She was in for a world of hurt now. Inside each box was a single whip. Not any type of whips though. These had all been modified with spikes all down the body. And razor blades flicked the ends. As she looked at each one, she recognised each individual one. They were the Bullwhip, the Snake Whip, the Signal Whip, the Stock Whip, the Cow Whip and last but not least the Bullock Whip. She watched as Warden pulled out the Bullock Whip and cracked it twice. Sparks flew from where the blades hit the floor.

"So are you going to tell us how you were planning on getting into here?" Salem asked, running a blade under her black claws and leaned back against the wall, all as calm as you like. But again Calista refused to answer her. Warden stepped in front of her and pushed a button from a small clip on his belt and the chains rattled as Calista's arms were moved to above her head instead of stretched out beside her. Once they were at a certain angle, Warden stepped closer to her, so much so she could smell the rotten stench that was his breath. It was enough to make her gag. Had the arsehole never heard of dental hygiene? Not that she was one to question that at the moment. She hadn't had a shower or anything in two weeks. Her hair was matted and clumped together from dried blood from where they had hit her repeatedly in the face and across her skull. Not to mention her mouth was as dry as sandpaper and her teeth felt grubby from not being brushed. Oh, how she missed the finer things of being able to brush her teeth and use mouthwash.

"Fine, you won't talk. We will beat it out of you!" He stepped back again and her eyed burned hatred at him. Did they forget they'd cut her tongue out so even if she wanted to talk, she couldn't? Not that she would talk but clearly they'd not thought it through. He stepped to the side slightly and Salem moved to stand next to Warden. She wouldn't let them know her tongue had already grown back, as she refused to open her jaws for them, and they couldn't prise them open either thanks to her facial cage.

"She won't talk, make sure you hit her extra hard considering that look she's giving us." She walked back to the chest and again rummaged through but Calista didn't bother watching her, she had her attention squarely on Warden. He flicked the whip expertly and it flew at her, lashing out across her stomach. Motherfucker that hurt, but again she didn't cry out. He did it again and again until she lost consciousness. But it didn't last long, a minute tops as water was thrown in her face. She opened bleary eyes and the first thing she saw was Salem's grinning face in front of her.

"Tender are we?" She reached out and poked at one of the wounds and Calista jolted. She hadn't used her hands, bitch used a knife, digging in the tip deliberately. Of course she did. Salem moved away again and Calista got a look at what Warden was holding. It was a serrated edged machete. Oh joy. She kept all emotion buried and watched as he reached up beside her and ran the blade along her arms, over and over again. Creating welts deep enough to have a small trickle of blood but not enough to cause serious bleeding. They were keeping it out as long as possible. She lightly wiggled her fingers as they weren't paying attention to her hands. All she needed was for one of the bolts to loosen up a little bit and she'd rip it out of the wall and then she would end them. As horribly as she could muster, if she could be bothered. She had Raven and the kids to save after all! Her head was suddenly thrown to the side from the force of a solid smack and she felt her eye socket rupture. She turned her head back slowly and glared at Warden who smirked at her. After they'd brandished more cuts and such over her body, Salem dotted bits of acid over the wounds. Warden lowered her arms again until they weren't directly above her head, and instead strung out like they were before and as they laughed, they left the room, but not before making the slave demon come back in, gather all the weapons and remove the chest. Breathing steadily through her nose, she closed her eyes and sent the last of her energy out and into one of her 'senses'. She found Raven. Knowing he was still alive sent a bolt of relief through her and she again succumbed to the blackness of unconsciousness away from the pain.

Down the corridor, in a small room carved out of the mountainside, chained and bloodied to the wall, was Raven. The only light that shone into the room was from a torchlight outside the door that glared through the small opening that people could see in. His hair had grown out a little thanks to not having a blade or anything to keep it the military short he had had for years. Fuzz covered his face as well, itchy and annoying, which was why he always kept himself freshly shaved. He hated facial hair, had since he'd first got it. His clothing was sticky from the punches he delivered to his face that had bust his nose and blood had poured. He stank as well. He was also pissed as anything. He moved his hands slightly, the only give he got from the chain that was wound tightly around his wrists and arms to keep him immobile. He also had chains across his chest, waist, hips, thighs and calves. He was chained so much because when he'd come to from being knocked unconscious, he'd ripped apart half a dozen of them before they'd realised he had moved. It took at least ten of them to pin him down and get him into this cell and chained up, although they'd not gone without injury. Or him for that matter. But it made them think of just what else he was capable of, hence their handy work to his flesh. Although, he did wonder how Calista was doing and how much damage had they done to her? And the kids, were they OK? As he was thinking that, he heard footsteps slowing down outside his cell. Wiggling toes inside of his socks, as the fuckers had taken his shoes, and rotating his ankles slightly in the chained restraints they'd given him, he luckily still had feeling in them considering he'd been standing for what had to easily be two or three days. Before that, he'd been chained to a chair for so long, his arse and legs had gone dead. Watching through his eyelashes, he watched as they opened the door and in walked Warden looking as smug as anything. He had blood on his hands and Raven barely managed to keep his nostrils from flaring as the smell assaulted his senses. Warden moved to stand in front of him and held up something in his hand.

"Ready for the next round?" Raven opened his eyes wider and glared at him before he realised what was in his hand. It was a mask that was designed to cover the lower part of the face, so Raven wouldn't be able to retaliate by either biting or spitting. He could talk but that was about it. Anything to save themselves. Absolute pussies. Couldn't they take him on one on one instead of chaining him up and then doing it that way? Or were they scared because of the way he'd gone through them before?

"Sure, why not. I'm still not going to break." He spat at him and the gob-full hit Warden square in the face. That rewarded him with a swift punch to the gut, but damn it was satisfying. Raven watched as another demon walked in. Oh goodie. It was Warden's right-hand man who was only known as Blade. Couldn't they have thought of anything more imaginative? Blade stepped up closer to him and taking the mask from Warden, put it against Raven's mouth and tied it up using the strap at the back. It cut into his face but he didn't give any indication that it hurt. He wouldn't give them the satisfaction. He watched as they lowered the lever against the wall that controlled the chains on his wrists, and he felt the tension leave his shoulders as his arms were given some rest. He waited with baited breath as to what they'd do this time. He was already sleep deprived, but that was nothing new. Not that he would tell them that. He was also ravenous, his stomach in continuous cramps from no nourishment. They barely gave him enough water to keep him going. So much so, his clothes now bagged on his lean frame, muscles wasted and everything. He used to be a big fucker, aptly named the Mountain, but at the moment, he might as well be called beanpole. He watched them as they conversed over by the door then Blade walked back to him and punched him in the face.

"Tell us what we want to know," he spat.

"Bitch please, I've been hit harder by a toddler." Raven laughed, knowing it would infuriate them both. And it did, both of them took turns punching him over and over again. Eventually they gave up as Raven wouldn't break and they swung the lever back up so his arms were taut again.

"Was that meant to impress me?" Instead, he just laughed at them. Over and over again until his throat was hoarse from it!

"Tell us what we want to know!" Warden fumed, getting right in Raven's face and launched a quick fist at Raven's balls, which would make any man cringe in pain, but Raven stammered through it, smiling sarcastically.

"What was that? Looking at your face is more hurtful than what you've done to me." He again let out a rich laugh, but it wasn't the deep belly chuckle, this was more of a sinister laugh, one that came from his chest. They backed up until they walked out of the room, muttering something between themselves. He just couldn't wait for their next get together. Lucky for him. He rolled his eyes and groaned as the pain finally assaulted his senses, and he also noticed they had left the mask on him. He sighed and shuffled a little bit, as much as the chains would let him anyway. Moving his legs slightly, he felt his balls loosen from where they'd been smacked up into his body, it hurt like a motherfucker, but he was not going to show them that it hurt him. He wasn't going to give them any leverage on him at all. He swallowed and felt the blood that built up in his mouth trickle down his throat. He had to give them credit, they knew how to throw a punch or execute torture, but what they didn't know about him was he was as stubborn as anything. They would never break him. And come hell or high water, he'd escape, get Calista, kill anyone that got in their way, rescue the kids and get out of the place. He was nothing if not determined. He wanted his woman back!

Chapter Thirty-Two
A further Three weeks later

Calista opened bloodshot swollen eyes, thanks to some meaty fists, and found herself in yet another room. This time she wasn't chained completely, instead she hung precariously spread-eagled in front of a blistering hot wall, by thick rope and chains with spikes stabbing through her wrists and hooking so they couldn't get out, not unless by brute strength and it'd still hurt. And the floor underneath her lay coated in razor wire; her bare feet just barely above them, also covered in chains to keep her in place. It was waiting, patient to lock into her skin and maim. She looked up as she heard a door open, and kept the sneer off her face as Scorcha, Kharge's daughter, walked in, like she had all the time in the world. It was the first time she had visited since her capture. Had she visited Raven though? Either way, it sent a surge of rage through her system. She had better have left her man alone. And yes, she openly admitted that now, Raven was hers. Completely. And she would kill those who had hurt him, she knew he'd been tortured and those responsible would feel her wrath as soon as she got out of this place, consequences be damned. No one hurt her man and got away with it. As weird as it sounded, being away from him these past few weeks made her realise just how quickly he had grown on her, and dare she admit it, she was even a little in love with him. Hold on, who was she fucking kidding? She was a whole lot of in love with the brute. Which was a first to her, but every time she had thought it over when she was left alone, it was always the same. She wanted her and Raven to live together, work on their relationship and see what happened from there. They just had to get out of the Fire Mountain first.

"Well, well if it isn't the infamous Calista strung up like waste in my father's dungeon," she taunted, her eyes flashing in obvious excitement. Calista didn't say anything as the young woman walked over to the weapons that lay upon the sole table that graced the room — the only piece of furniture — and it was welded to the floor. As Scorcha lavished over a knife, Kharge walked in and behind him were his personal guards. Warden and Blade, whose skin glowed from the lava that flowed like rivulets down the walls to disappear past the floor. No wonder the wall was scorching hot;

it was the only one that didn't have anything on it, but thanks to what ran down the other walls, this one got the heat from it all. Just her fucking luck. But luckily she wasn't literally against it, but a foot or so from it, not that it didn't help from the heat.

"Having a nice time hanging around?" Kharge sarcastically said and Scorcha turned at the sound of her father's voice, the knife forgotten as it tumbled to the floor. She hurried over to his side.

"So what's going to be done to her?" Kharge didn't answer, just snapped his fingers but continued looking at Calista. His guards from outside disappeared from view and returned a moment later dragging in an emaciated body. Calista's gaze flew to the body and knew the flesh in front of her. Didn't have to see the face to know it was Raven. And he was covered in blood and wounds, some new, some old. His clothes bagged on him as well. They'd obviously starved him, maybe hoping he would break? But she could tell, because they were still torturing them, that he hadn't given in, just as she hadn't. That was her man! The guards threw him to the floor where he twitched in agony. And then she saw the bite mark on the side of his neck. She knew what was happening; he was turning. She looked back to Kharge and saw the sick satisfaction in his gaze. Then she saw the vampire standing just to the left of him. It was Zuertich. Blood still coated his mouth and dripped off his chin. The satisfied look in his cold grey eyes made her want to rip his throat out and drain him dry. She half-listened as Kharge told them to chain Raven to the floor, just a little bit away from her. They did. They bolted the chain with huge clasps that sat melted into the floor. The chains hung from one place to another on his body. Wrists, knees, ankles and across his back were covered, leaving him in a kneeling position. Raven still hadn't looked at her. His black hair was matted and hung in clumps around his head. She looked back at Kharge and he nudged Scorcha; she didn't need telling twice what to do. She walked forward, crouched beside Raven and lifted his head up. Calista just managed to keep the emotions off her face! His face was a mess, well what she could see of it past the ragged black beard that had grown. Bruised facial features and big black eyes that were half open and he stared at her. The usual vibrancy of his eyes that seared her soul were now dull with pain. Mouth cut and bleeding slightly. Blood ran from his left ear and had run to his cheek. That long torture scar of his stood out stark white against his tanned flesh. As she looked at him, she saw a corner of his mouth raise in a semblance of a smile, so she knew her sarcastic Raven was still there. But how much more could he take before even that was taken away from him? Using what little energy she had, considering she'd been starved and barely had minimal water, she sent a warm caress over Raven and she knew he had felt it because his eyes widened slightly. She looked back up at Kharge when she heard the scraping of metal against metal. He moved towards her in a menacing slow walk. As if he had all the time in the world. He stopped when he was in front of her and raised the meat cleaver he had clasped in his palm. Big ass bastard it was. Thick shiny blade that looked to have been polished, but the edging was dull. It was blunt. It was really going to hurt. She knew it was. A new scent teased her senses and she sniffed slightly. Kharge had recently been with a woman, her scent clinging to him. Who was it? Either which way, when she got out of here, which was a when, not an if, she would kill the woman as well, who had obviously aligned herself with Kharge so she would have to go as well. Simple as that.

"Any last words?" he said.

"No," she said. The first word she'd said since her capture more than five weeks ago. And considering some of the hits and shit she'd taken, this was saying something. Plus, she still had that fucking mask on. So who knew when they'd remove it. Soon she hoped, it was fucking uncomfortable and itchy.

"Well, at least I asked, which is actually a lot more than you gave my wife before you beheaded her." He slammed the knife into her chest, and dragged it down until it reached the middle of her stomach. She didn't make a sound. She wouldn't give him the satisfaction of it. She looked down as much as she was able to, and watched as he removed the knife from where it was. Then these huge steel openers that surgeons used in 'Normal Earth' were placed in the middle of the wound and pulled the flesh open. Two demons moved to either side of her and took a part each in their hands, showing off her ribcage to Kharge, the white bone immense against the blood red of her organs and the blue of her veins. And thanks to her unnatural powers, etc., her blood didn't leak from her in a cascade of fluid, but rather just stayed flowing around her body. It was quite eerie for those who'd never seen it before. She, however, had seen it a few more times than she cared to admit. She looked back to Kharge and he now had a set of rib cutters in his hands, and he smiled a sick grin. This told her he was enjoying it immensely. But she'd pass out in a minute or so from the trauma her body was suffering; she knew she would. She just happened to stay conscious longer than anyone else. It was just her bloody luck. He pushed the rib cutters against her bones and snapped a couple away. Baring her heart and lungs to his gaze. He dropped the cutters, and put his hand around her heart, clamping down; but she still made no noise, just stared defiantly at him.

"NO!" Raven screamed, the sound hoarse and it made him cough badly. Kharge grinned and moved backwards, her heart going with him. The main artery, vena cavas, vein and aorta making a sick noise as they snapped and disconnected as the organ left her chest. Blood now poured out of the wound, down her and dripped to the floor. Her head fell forward, and her eyes locked onto Raven. The last thing she saw before the darkness pulled her under was Raven's tear-filled gaze locked onto hers as he struggled to get free. Then she saw no more.

Raven roared again as he watched Calista die. An unbearable pain went through his chest as he saw the love of his life hanging there lifeless, the demons still holding her flesh and ribs open. Kharge ordered them to let her go. They did and she swung listlessly. They removed the razor wire with gloved hands, and Scorcha, Raven noticed had the honour of letting Calista free of the chains. Feet freed first from their shackles, then the arms and she crashed to the floor in a sickening flop of flesh, head cracking off the solid floor. Scorcha kicked Calista's leg and moved past him, but not before putting the key to his own chains just slightly ahead of him. He heard her laugh along with her father as everyone left the chamber. Then he cried. He wasn't ashamed. He cried like a baby. Great fat tears rolled down his cheeks and landed on the floor. Then he remembered Scorcha had put the key down in front of him. He moved forward and just managed to reach it with his fingertips. He unchained himself and moved to Calista, and dragged her body onto his lap. But before he could fully move her onto him apart from her head on his lap, a massive pain wracked his body, worse than anything he'd been dealt with from his tortures. He dived away from Calista and screamed as his body seemed to have liquid fire ripping through his veins. He dug his fingers into the ground, the finger nails snapping off from how tight he dug into the slate floor; he snapped his neck back and roared from the pain. It must have lasted for a staggering twelve or so hours, the pains making him wish he would just die. But soon he stopped hurting and lay on his back, panting for breath. His clothes were in tatters on his body, not that he gave a shit. But as he held up his arm to wipe across his eyes, he blinked. He was bigger! Bigger than he'd been before he'd been starved, not loads but enough that he noticed it. Even his hands seemed bigger. That must have also been what some of the sheer pain through his body was from, that he'd grown an absolute shit ton. He supposed he'd have to ask Draylan when he got out. And he knew he would. They didn't call him Mountain or even Ghost in his unit for no reason. He might be a big bastard but he could move as quietly as a ghost when he needed to. Then he caught sight of Calista's body out of the corner of his left eye. Dropping his arm, he turned his head and looked at her. His eyes razor sharp. Teeth extended and deadly as a freshly sharpened blade. He crawled over to her, and noticed her heart sitting still near them and sighed. She was dead. No chance of happily ever after for them. He'd have to get free, rescue the kids and get back to the village. It was a nightmare. What was he meant to do now? Apart from rescue the kid's that is. But he wanted Calista, he wanted his woman for fuck sake! He pulled her body to his and clasped her cold flesh to him. He reached up and closed her sightless eyes and ripped that horrendous mask off her face as well, throwing it across the room. A raw untold hunger coursed through his system making him realise that he was starving, but he didn't care. He just cuddled his woman. There was no way he was licking up the spilt blood of hers that still resided on the ground. He also pulled the spikes out of her flesh, the ones Scorcha had deliberately left in, she'd only unhooked the chains and rope that had held her aloft. Yes, the spikes tore his woman's flesh but that couldn't be helped and he was thankful at least she wouldn't feel it. It had to have been a good twenty minutes he sat there for, when he heard a noise like a heart beating. He opened his eyes and looked down at her chest. And shrank back in horror, making her body thump on the floor. A tiny piece of muscle had come loose from where she'd been cut open and it was growing! He could soon make out what it was. An aorta. Valves. Arteries. Vena cavas. It was a fucking heart! Her heart was regenerating itself. But how? How did that work? Was it that small bit of muscle? Once the heart was pulled out of your chest, or it stopped beating, you were dead. Your body didn't give you a new one. Were her powers that great? Soon a normal heart filled the space where her other one had been. He glanced to the side and her other heart was still on the cold floor, completely still. He looked back at her, and watched as her ribs snapped back into place like they were on an elastic band and had been let go. They sealed themselves up, until they were perfect unblemished bone. Then her skin healed up until it was silky smooth again even where the spikes had been. Even the previous injuries she'd suffered had healed. But still her chest didn't move. It was seriously fucked up. He had to get out of there; he'd have time to grieve properly when he was away from this hellhole. Wiping the sweat from his face, fucking room was roasting, he staggered back to his feet. He didn't waste time in waiting; just threw himself into the door and soon smashed through it with his abnormal strength, not that he was complaining. He took a left and ran down a winding corridor, hearing laughter. He pushed a door open and it was full of demons that all turned to face him with astonishment on their faces. He'd have laughed if he wasn't so god damn hungry. He closed the door behind him so they couldn't escape and he attacked with a hell-bent vengeance, sating the hunger that beat savagely at him. Once everyone was dead, as the only way out of the room was through the door he stood in front of, he wiped the blood from his mouth, stole a pair of jeans and a long-sleeved black top from one of them, and shrugged into them, even if they were a bit tight, but fuck it. Then he disappeared out of the room again, his sock-covered feet slapping against the warm floor. For some reason, they'd left his socks and feet alone, not that he was complaining on that one. The rest of what they'd done to him; that he couldn't forget. Rich power pulsed through his veins, urging him on. His wounds healing themselves until he had unblemished skin. He did wonder if the scars he had before the change had disappeared but he would check that when he was away from the mountain and safe. He walked quietly down the winding corridor and heard a faint whimper. He stopped outside a door with bars at the top so you could look in, which he did, and saw children. The ones he and Calista had come to rescue. He knew it had to be them. He yanked the door off its hinges, not caring at all about the sound it made. Thanks to his now sensitive hearing, he heard footsteps coming towards them, so dived into the cell with the kids, and put the door back into place, but held it at a tiny slant. Looking at the kids, he held his finger to his lip and thankfully they understood what it was he wanted them to do. Once the four guards had ran past, he picked up the door and was amazed by his strength, quickly overcame it and threw it, hitting the guards, sending them straight to the floor.

"Stay right there," he said to the children, who nodded and huddled together, clearly realising he was there to rescue them. He made quick work of the guards, sinking his fangs into their necks and draining them dry of their blood. Magic, strength and even more power rushed through his veins and damn it felt good. He ripped his teeth out of the last guard and left the body to drop to the floor, threw back his head and roared. He whirled around as he heard a screech and caught the blade aimed for him. It was Scorcha and Lviana. He ripped out Lviana's throat with his claw-tipped hand and dropped her corpse, leaving it where it landed. It would have been too good using the blade for her. He threw it away and grabbed Scorcha who had tripped over her feet trying to run away. He sunk his fangs into her neck;

461

but her struggles didn't compete with the rage and hunger he was feeling. He drained her quickly and lobbed her body away, smashing it headfirst into a wall before it slumped to the floor in a messy heap. Not that he actually gave a fuck, she got off easy considering the rage that he was feeling. He walked to a guard and yanked off their boots they wore. Shoving his feet into them and tying them up military style, he was surprised that they fitted him perfectly. He raced back to the holding cell from earlier and shepherded the children out and they followed him. Not one of them blinking at the carnage he'd left. Just what had they seen that they didn't even blink at the mess? Either which way he didn't want to think about it and got them moving. They wove through tunnels and everything until he felt fresh air through a door in the shadows. He cautiously opened the door and blinked. Bright sunshine met his sensitive eyes. He walked out a little bit, and stopped up short; he saw a ledge just slightly ahead of him and just beyond that, was that lava river that flowed around the mountain. He looked back to the children and grabbed a hold of the littlest one. The one who was deathly pale and shaking.

"Hold on." The kid did, locking pale arms around his neck. He ran, and his foot caught the edge of the ledge and he leapt over the river, landing on the black stone embankment in one piece. He put the kid down and told her to wait in the forest. He repeated the action until all the kids were over. He jumped back and shut the door that he'd discovered and hightailed it back to the kids. He grabbed the littlest up into his arms again and they left, all without a backward glance.

Their nightmare over; his, just beginning.

Chapter Thirty-Three
Four days after Raven escaped

Calista sucked in a harried breath soundlessly through her slightly parted lips as her senses rushed back on board. Listening out for anyone else in the room with her, she only got the smell of decomposing bodies that assailed her sensitive nose. She opened her eyes and gently sat up, which took her two tries considering she had been chucked on top of a pile of bodies and had slipped in congealed blood and other body parts. Shaking her head, blood-matted hair dragged against her skull. Ignoring the slight niggling from it, she finally gained her feet. Sweeping an arm across her eyes, wiping away sweat, she braced her legs apart and took in her surroundings, aided slightly by dimly lit oil burners. Four bog standard walls haphazardly carved to create a room. To her left was a staircase that was barely wide enough for her to get up safely and not scrape her shoulders raw from. Blood, new and old, splashed up the stairs and walls. She couldn't see the floor from the amount of bodies. Gazing down at herself, she saw she was partially naked, lovely. Using the small amount of magic she had at the moment, she manifested a bra and top for herself, along with non-ruined jeans, underwear, socks and tight-fitting boots. Now she was comfortable and decent. Snapping her fingers and untangling her hair and conjuring up a hair bobble, she swept it up into a ponytail to keep it out of her face. But then she froze as she heard a slight scrapping noise and carefully turned her head as a small partition in the wall moved. Crouching down to minimalize being seen, she watched as long, skinny arms came out of the darkness. Emaciated fingers with yellow cracked nails dug into the walls as it pulled its body out of the pit. She watched as a head appeared. Features all sunken in to the point of it being more skeleton wrapped in a layer of flesh. Twisted, yellow and black teeth were visible past terribly thin lips. Eyes were black as night, no colour. A few strands of wispy hair coated the scalp. Calista watched as it reached back behind it and drew out a clump of flesh that really looked like an arm or something, not that she could really tell considering it had sizeable chunks missing from it. Great, she was in here to be its dinner. Not on her bloody watch! She watched as it emerged fully and just manage to keep from gagging. It stunk worse than the corpses and that was saying something! Clothes, if you could call them that, hung off the skeleton. Then she realised what she was looking at — a newly transitioned Feeder. It was like a Wendigo, only it fed off of the dead and didn't grow when it ate the flesh. And it wasn't contagious if it bit or clawed you either. This one must have been stupidly thin when caught and then starved more and was now being let out of the confinement to pretty much dispose of the corpses. She looked around slowly to see if there were any weapons she could use to defend herself, but saw nothing, just bones sticking out of flesh. Bare hands it was then unless she could snatch up a bone. She moved as slow as she dared over the body in front of her, but that must have caught its attention because suddenly it locked its eyes on her. Just her fucking luck. Now that she had its attention, she stood to her full height. The only wound on her was a faint trail from where Kharge had ripped her open, and even then, once she fed, that would disappear completely as would all the damage under the surface be repaired properly as well. The Feeder also stepped up to its full height, even though it happened to be bent over at an awkward angle, it still had to stand at a good nine feet high. It leaned down and next thing she knew, it charged at her, arms outstretched. They didn't care about anything unless it was food. She waited for it to get within literally centimetres of her before she let her knees go from underneath her, swept down and yanked on a bone that snapped away, leaving a nasty, sharp pointed end. Perfect for what she needed it for. As the Feeder sailed over her head, it landed in a heap but soon leapt back to its feet, its overgrown nails easily gripping body parts for stability. It charged at her again and as it got within range, she thrust up the bone shard as hard as she could under the Feeder's mouth and through to its brain. Letting go as arterial spray coated her, she watched it fall to the ground and twitch a couple times before succumbing to death. Grabbing the bone shard again, she made her way to the staircase, and turning sideways slightly, she slowly crept up them, careful of every step as they were slippery from blood and other remains. Once she had reached the top, she came to a black oak door. Putting her ear to it to see if she could hear anything, she couldn't so she carefully opened it. Darkness met her and she realised she was next door to Kharge's dungeon, if the horrendous screams were any indication. Taking a left, she crept along a damp corridor, only lit occasionally by a torch. Coming to a stop outside the first door she reached, she listened as demon's laughed and cheered about something. Listening closely, she heard what they were cheering about. Scorcha and Lviana were dead. Did that mean Raven had gotten out with no problem? And the kids? Not thinking anymore, she lifted her leg and sent her bare foot straight at the door, sending it flying open. The silence that descended over the room was magic to her ears. She entered and shut it behind her.

"Hello, ladies," she grinned and not wasting time, charged at them. She killed all of them bar one, the biggest fucker who hid at the back of the room, crying like a little bitch.

"Please don't hurt me!" he cried but she just laughed and dived on him, sinking her fangs into his neck. She quickly drained the demon and dropped its hollowed-out husk to the floor. Raw power rushed through her system as the blood went to work repairing the damage left behind from her torture. With the rich power coursing through her, she strolled through the rest of the mountain, killing anyone in her way. Stopping outside the room where she had been tortured, she followed her nose and found the room Raven had been held in. It was in shambles. Huge claw marks racked the walls, blood splashed up all sides and across the floor. Chains sat in a mess on a chair, the cufflinks stained with blood. A new surge of anger washed through her system as she realised Raven had been tortured horrendously. Time to dish out justice. Walking down another corridor, she saw it was the room the kids had been held in. It was sparse, with a few ragged blankets thrown on the floor, no pillows or mattresses. Obviously, the kids had been made to sleep on the hard floor and it was obvious Raven had gotten them out, thank God. The walls, however, were bare of marks and such. It was as if the room had been specifically made for the kids to be held in, motherfuckers. Moving past the room, she found the other demons in rooms, drinking and celebrating. She tore through whoever it was she could find, which only fuelled her as she drained their bodies of their life blood, leaving behind hollowed-out carcasses in her wake. She finally came across another room and opened the door. Inside were two bodies laid down on pillars, covered in wraps of white cloth. Candles graced the walls, giving light. Walking into the room, she closed the door behind her before she stepped up to the bodies and using some of her power, made the cloth open up, and she saw the corpses of Scorcha and Lviana. Lviana's head wasn't attached to the neck, the wound was ragged, almost as if it had been ripped off by someone of uncountable strength. Scorcha had the side of her neck ravaged and she was uncommonly pale for a fire demon who had just died, well it was a couple of days at least judging from the smell and colouration of their flesh. She leaned down and sniffed. A blooming smile crept over her face as she realised just who had killed them. Raven. That was her man! He had clearly ripped off Lviana's head and drained Scorcha dry, which meant his conversion over to vampire had been very successful. Which left one question. How powerful had he just become? He was already strong when he had been human, on account of the things she had seen him do, but now? Just what kind of strength resided in his body? Covering the heads back up to make it appear as though no one had touched the bodies, she crept back to the doorway. Listening through the door, she heard footsteps creep past so she waited to make sure the coast was clear. A minute or two later, it was clear, so she made her getaway. Taking a left at the bottom of the corridor, she kept her ears open for anyone around her. Reaching the end of yet another corridor, she waited for the sound of anyone approaching, heard nothing, so looked around the corner. To the right were more doors, locked with deadbolts, and to the left, yet another corridor which was slanted upwards. She quickly walked up it and it bent slightly to the right as she approached the top. She again emerged at another level which was just a black walled corridor, with no doors or anything along it. But it was wide enough for three fire demons to walk shoulder to shoulder through with at least an inch gap between them, so plenty of room for her to navigate as well as lots of head room. Which she was thankful for, considering she wasn't exactly small in height. Sneaking forward in absolute silence, she climbed some stairs that were badly lit from candles, but thanks to her oh so awesome night vision, it didn't bother her whatsoever. At the top of the stairs, she looked left and saw it was empty bar more doors and silence. To the right though, at the end and to the right by the sounds of it, was a lot of activity. She could just about make out angry voices but she couldn't quite hear what they were saying. Heading that way, she came across another door to her left, but silence was all that greeted her from behind it, but she opened it anyway. And grinned. Weapons of all kinds lined the walls and tables. On one lay her own battle axe and sword, which she quickly grabbed up with their straps and put them into their rightful positions. She gathered up other weapons and stashed them on her body, including some knives she placed into her boots, snug fit but nothing she wasn't used to. She strapped a couple more blades to her biceps. Turning her head to have a look at what else was around, she saw two long serrated blades with decent black-stained oak handles. She moved over to them and picked one up. Whoever had made it certainly knew their shit. She was impressed. Grabbing them up and using some Velcro that was sitting on the table next to them, strapped them to her hips, one either side. They were a waste of a blade just sitting there, and that wouldn't do, so she felt it was purely her right to take them, considering all the crap that had happened to her these past five or so weeks.

Moving back out of the room and closing the door silently behind her, she took a left and slowly began edging towards where the voices from earlier were. She came across a door. That explained why the voices were muffled. Leaning her ear to the wood, she could hear a male voice, someone who was majorly pissed. She could hear someone moving to her location from behind and using an age-old magic, made herself invisible. Magic bitches! She watched as a Fire Demon stumbled along, blood dripping from him in numerous places. Fang marks lined his throat, but not clean, almost as if someone had deliberately ripped their fangs from his flesh. One of his horns had been ripped in half as well, which must have hurt like a bitch considering the horns were sensitive and whoever had done it must have been stupidly strong, as the horns were solid. She perceived he was putting more weight onto his right leg, then saw blood marred his left leg, as if he'd been stabbed and the blade dragged down the leg slightly. Well, that explained the limping. As he hurried past her and into the room, she slipped in behind him before the door closed. And she stopped up short. The room was a lot bigger than she realised. High beams made up the ceiling, maybe to add character? Floor was sparse but instead of a mountain type floor as every other room she'd been in, this was rich black marble slate that reflected the light. Clearly someone spent a lot of time in here so wanted to make the most of it. The only light in the entire room was from the walls of molten lava running down and disappearing into the floor. At the end of the room from where she was standing, stood a high end throne. Made of complete bone stained black. Skulls lined under the arms and a huge armour-type back which was highlighted by what looked like vampire hands holding thick black candles on either side. A black cushion covered the seat for comfort. It was impressive to say the least. Next to it sat another throne, albeit smaller. It was black with spine legs and arm rests with a skull head, from a demon no less to separate the two. As well as demon heads marring the top of the throne, the ones at the top accentuated huge curling horns, mouths open on screams with candles inside lit, for added effect clearly. Again, a black cushion covered the seat for comfort. Obviously some had suffered to create the chair, maybe a prisoner or enemy used to make an example out of? It was hard to tell. But it wasn't her concern now so, looking past that, hidden into the wall almost, was a black oak-stained door, which opened and in walked Kharge. He wore black leather trousers and a muscled black T-shirt. Black boots covered his huge feet. Simple, yet effective attire. Red eyes were blazing like fire, so he was clearly riled about something. He was pretty intimidating with his height and size to those who didn't know him. To her? He was an absolute twat and she really should have killed him when she had the chance. But now? Now she would have that chance and she would obliterate him, along with anyone else that tried to stop her. Watching as he made his way to his throne full of confidence and thinking he was untouchable, the door opened again and a female standing at around about six feet one or two-ish, walked out. Her black and red hair was down in an array of curls and strands of it wrapped around a gold tiara that glinted with diamonds and accentuated her black horns highlighted with red glitter. She had jet black, red-rimmed eyes that were highlighted in black eyeliner. Full lips were coated in red lipstick. Pale pink skin gleamed, like she'd lightly dusted it with glitter. She wore a black corset that pretty much shoved her boobs up to her chin. A black scrunched up skirt covered her lower half, and was dusted over with a long lace train. Long legs, covered in fishnet tights were shiny, like she'd moisturised them or some shit and feet were encased in black boots with chains. In other words, she was trying too hard, or at least that was what Calista thought. She watched as this unknown woman sat next to Kharge on the smaller throne. Ah, so she was the new woman. Must have been the one she had smelt on Kharge when he had visited to rip her heart out of her chest. Moving closer, she watched as the limping demon moved to his king.

"My King and lady." He bowed before Kharge and this woman.

"So what is it you wanted to tell me and Braelynn? Disturbing us?"

"Well, as we know, Calista is in the decomposing room, ready to feed the Feeder that we have down there. And Raven escaped."

"Yes, I know. He killed my daughter and her best friend, along with half of the demons here. And the children I had taken to lure Calista here, before I could convert them to our side, or kill them if they didn't agree, that bastard took them! This is also why I sent you at least a dozen others to hunt him down, kill him by any means necessary, and bring them back to me. So, why is it, out of all of you mercenaries, it is only you who has returned to me?"

"He, erm."

"Spit it out already!" Braelynn snapped at him.

"He went through us all as if we were nothing my lord. He ripped most of our throats out with a single swipe of his hand. As he sucked the life force out of me, he stopped and told me to give you a message."

"And just pray tell what is that message?" Before the puny fellow could answer, in walked Zuertich, who moved to stand next to the demon and looked at Kharge.

"What is it Zuertich?" Kharge asked.

"Well, I was making the rounds, as I do, and well, everyone is dead sir."

"Dead?"

"Dead. Ripped into itty bitty pieces and others are completely drained of their blood."

"Who the hell could have done that?" Braelynn asked. Calista barely managed to hold back a snort. She wasn't exactly smart was she? But looking at her, she realised just who she actually resembled. She was the daughter of the demi-goddess Nightmarë who had fornicated with a fire demon which resulted in Braelynn. Well, that would soon end, as Calista planned on ending her life as well. As soon as possible, because she was pretty sure her and Kharge had been intimate a lot, so the sooner her life was taken, then there was a zero percent chance of a child being spawned. Yes, it wouldn't be the child's fault who their parents would be, but there was no chance of her letting these two leave here alive. Moving a little bit closer, she watched as Kharge reached over to Braelynn and took her black clawed hand into his own, fingers interlocking.

"We will have to find who it was," Kharge muttered, snapping his fingers and a slave stepped forward with a skull cup, no doubt full of blood or some shit.

"And as you were saying, slave?" Braelynn motioned to the demon who was waiting to speak again.

"Oh, yes. The message from Raven. He told me to tell you, my lord, that your days are numbered. He will come back for you and destroy you for what you have done."

"I highly doubt it. The male isn't dangerous enough to go against me." He laughed and drained his mug before handing it back to the slave who took it and disappeared.

"Of course, my lord. Is there anything you'd like for me to do?"

"Go clean your wounds. I'll call for you when I need you." The demon didn't need telling twice, he up and ran out that room fast enough to leave skid marks on the floor: which was impressive considering his wounds. Calista moved closer, she needed to get a good angle in so when it was the correct time, she would appear and it would still give her a good advantage for a strike.

"So what do we do now?" Zuertich asked, drawing Kharge's gaze.

"Round up the dead bodies, shove them down into the pit. Then we regroup and plan the downfall of the rest of the island. Those who are against us, die. Those not, join us."

"Understandable. What about those situated on the other islands dotted around?"

"We will have to convince them to join us. Again, those who don't are to die. In no uncertain terms, I will rule the entirety of Mystic Being, mark my words." Calista had heard enough. There was no way whatsoever that Kharge was going to rule the whole island. Bracing herself mentally for the shit storm she knew she was about to encounter, she moved into position, behind Zuertich and to the centre of the room. She closed her eyes, sucked in a deep breath and exhaled slowly and opened eyes she knew would now be battle hardened and emotionless. This was no time for fun and games, this was the assassin out in play and by God, did she want to play. She could almost taste the killing blow to Kharge, Braelynn and Zuertich.

"OK, so who should we start with? You know Attör will be one to take major convincing," Zuertich said and ran a blade between his fingers. Calista looked over at Kharge to wait for his answer.

"Raid the swamp. We will have to convince the two residing dragons there to join us first, then the swamp nymphs, then we go from there. And as for Attör, we know he won't join us, considering how close he was to Calista, so we will just destroy him." Calista's nostrils flared slightly at that. Not Attör. Not if she had anything to say about it. The poison dragon didn't hurt anyone, kept to himself ninety-nine percent of the time, so that was a no go, and not just because she had partially raised him. Actually, the entire island was a no go for them.

"Very well. We will have to stock up on our weapons then," Zuertich said.

"Of course. There is the main weapon room that can be used, as well as the small room outside of the door from here." Kharge stood up and stretched, and pulled Braelynn to her feet as well.

"OK. When do we head out?"

"Tomorrow morning. Get rested up. Drink your fill of blood, because guaranteed it's going to be a long day of rampaging." The two men grinned at each other.

"I don't think so." Calista made herself appear and the look of shock on their faces was absolutely comical. As was the look on Braelynn's face.

"You're dead! You're meant to be dead. They ripped your heart out!" Braelynn stuttered.

"Well, clearly I'm not, considering I'm standing right here, whole and very much alive."

"How?" Before they could ask, a demon rushed into the room, right for her, clasping a sword in his hand that he raised above his head, clearly intent on killing her. She didn't hesitate. Once he got within range, she yanked the sword from her back, and using countless years of experience and skill, lopped the guy's head off without breaking a sweat. She looked back at the other three who were standing there blinking at her.

"You should know I am not easy to kill." She twirled the sword around in her hand fluidly.

"But I ripped out your heart!" Kharge sputtered.

"You should realise it would take more than that to kill me. I've been alive for over twenty thousand years. Do you really think you'd be the first one to rip out my heart?" She laughed. Zuertich made a move towards her and she stopped all pretence of being happy and held the sword pointed to the floor as it dripped from the slain demon's blood. She dropped the blade and jumped on Zuertich. The momentum of her jump plus her strength sent the vampire crashing into the floor. Snapping her fingers out, she unleashed her inner kitty claws, razor sharp and sliced them into his throat, grabbed hold of his trachea and pulled it clean out. Zuertich stared at her with wide eyes. The blood draining out of his neck as she climbed back to her feet and dropped his flesh that landed in a plop next to him. Turning to face Kharge, she had had enough. Braelynn charged her, having lost the train of her skirt. She flew at Calista, claws outstretched. Slamming into each other, fists flew. For every punch Braelynn got in, Calista returned. Soon Calista overpowered her and threw hard punches to whichever part of Braelynn she could. Before she knew it, Kharge entered the fray so it was two against one. Calista held her own, defending off blows coming from the both of them. As she lashed out at Braelynn, Kharge took advantage and threw a right hook at her, which caught her right in the jaw. Laughing as she spat out blood, she returned the punch, catching him in the jaw and knocked a tooth out. As she'd done that, she felt a searing pain in her side and took a glance down, Braelynn had stabbed her in the side. What an absolute bitch. No more games. She turned full tilt to Braelynn and effectively ripped her throat out.

"NO!" Kharge roared and she watched as his horns elongated into straight points. Braelynn's body toppled to the floor in a flop, her eyes wide as she stared now sightlessly, head smacking off the floor. But Calista wasn't paying attention to that, she was watching Kharge. She watched as his body tensed, dropped the flesh of Braelynn's throat and then they charged for each other, bodies clashing in a thunderous boom. She slammed into the floor back first, the axe still attached so the handle dug rather uncomfortably into her spine, but she soon kicked Kharge off her and jumped back to her feet.

"I'm going to make sure you die once and for all you bitch!"

"Chitty chitty chat chat. Get on with it already!" she taunted, and he did. He dived for her again but she sidestepped at the last second so he sailed past her, but not before he sliced into her side with a blade he'd hidden in his palm. Blocking the sharp pain from the wound, she unleashed holy hell on him then. Using her untapped power she ripped into him, throwing punches and kicks into him until he finally fell to the floor in a blooded mess. She herself was not without injury. Cuts bled, bruises had already started forming from where he'd landed hard punches and vicious kicks. She even had stab holes in her ribs and one thigh from his bastard horns. She leaned over him, hand clasped on her sword she'd grabbed earlier from where he had thrown her across the room.

"I hereby bid you from this world."

"It won't stop you know, the evil."

"Maybe not. But I plan on ridding you from this world so you can no longer be in charge of it. And for everyone else who plans on taking over, I will rid them from this world as well for so long as I shall live."

"So sure are you?" He spat blood out of his mouth.

"Of course. Now you can join Braelynn, Tirana and your daughter in hell." And with that, she hacked his head off. Once his head had become detached, she stood up and sighed as her back cracked. Rolling her shoulders, they too cracked. Heaven. She moved away from the bodies and went through the door Kharge had appeared from earlier. Moving through it, she swept through the remainder of the mountain, ridding everyone of their life. Even those of the slaves, they would be no good to anyone outside of the mountain. Once she was sure she had gotten everyone, again fuelling up on blood from them, she made her way out of the mountain. Once she'd reached the outside, using her 'powers', she again scanned for life inside the mountain, she found two life forms in a room above her. Going to the place quickly, she stopped outside a door and leaning her ear against the wood, heard laughter. She reared back and using her booted foot, smashed through the door. Strolling inside she spotted Warden and Salam. She looked at them both who stared at her wide eyed with shock, both naked and very sweaty. The heady scent of sex hung in the air.

472

"Surprise, fuckers!"

"But, you're dead. We saw your body being transported to The Pits," Salam stammered.

"Obviously not. I told you I would come back for you."

"No! We were just doing our job. We're sorry!" She just shook her head, not accepting their apology. She wasn't that stupid, she'd read their mind. They got off on hurting people. And with that, she shut the door and then attacked. She literally ripped them both apart. Within minutes she was breathing heavy as body parts littered the floors. Blood sprayed over the walls, across the bed and over herself. She kicked Salam's head that was next to her. She left the room and left the door open as she strolled away. Again, using her senses, she scanned for any more life forms, but found none barring rats and other bugs. Which was fine by her. Using a spell she healed her wounds from the battles. Once she was completely whole and after another bone cracking stretch, she cleaned her weapons as she did so hate them being messy and blunt. Once completed, she planted one foot in front of the other to begin the arduous journey of going back home. She wouldn't make herself flash, it took up precious energy she didn't want to waste at the moment, anyway, she planned on spending a day or so with Gélio to go over everything that she had learned in the mountain. And she had to find someone who would take over Fire Mountain, after the bodies had been taken care of and it was cleaned up as well. After she had sorted that with Gélio, she planned on heading back to her home and convincing Raven to stay with her once he had finished the last six months of his service. Satisfied with that plan, she snapped from her thoughts, left the mountain but stopped up short as she came face to face with the Lava Lady who was dressed in a dress of molten magma.

"What did you do?" she asked.

"I killed everyone." No point going into detail, it had nothing to do with her.

"NO!" Lava screeched.

"Yes. Now I am going home." She snapped her hand out in a quick flash and sent a pulsing wave of ice-cold water washing over the woman. If she'd learned anything from her vast amount of years it was that lava did not win against a cascade of water. She hissed as it streamed over her in a tidal wave, rapidly cooling it down and it started bubbling. Calista didn't waste any more time. She jumped over the river and headed to the surrounding forest, not once looking back.

Chapter Thirty-Four
A week after Raven escaped

Lexis gazed out of the window as she cradled a glass of blood in her hand. Luke and Tairen were in the living room playing with the kids, but her mind was in turmoil thinking of Raven and Calista. Surely they should have been back by now? Just what had happened to them?

"Lexis, you OK?" She turned at the sound of her brother's voice.

"I'm OK. Worried immensely for Raven and Calista. They should have been back by now."

"Yeah, Tairen was thinking that as well. I'm sure they're on their way back. We just have to keep on hoping, even though it's been a long six weeks."

"Yeah, I know exactly what you mean. But hopefully, they'll be back here as soon as possible, considering we have to leave on Saturday for me to go back to Scotland and you two back to the army for the final part of your service." She rubbed her belly that was swelling lovely, with her son growing bigger every single day. She moved away from the window and followed her brother back to her fiancé and kids. As the kids looked up, she saw the happiness fade from Alexzander's face as he took in the worried look on hers.

"You OK Mommy?" He came over to her as she sat on the edge of the couch and put his little hand over hers, locking his fingers through her own.

"I'm OK, baby. Just worried about your Uncle Raven and Aunt Calista."

"I'm sure they'll be OK. They're tough, that's what you've told me." He smiled at her and she couldn't help but smile back. He had grown leaps and bounds since they'd adopted them. He smiled so much lately, as well as laughed. It was such a beautiful thing to see. Even Jinx was growing in leaps and bounds, so much so she now could say Mum, Dad and Lu-lu for Luke, which was impressive for a six, nearly seven month old. The next word she reckoned she would say would be something for Alexzander.

"How about we head to the town? Go sit down on the beach for a little bit?" Luke asked.

"Sounds a good idea." Lexis smiled, drained the last of her blood and took her glass into the kitchen to rinse it up whilst the men rounded the two kids up to change them into sensible clothes, as at the moment Alexzander wore just shorts and Jinx was wearing only a nappy. Once they were dressed properly, she put Jinx in the single buggy they'd brought and Alexzander was swept up into Tairen's arms, where he was happy to loop his arms around his dad's neck and hold on for the ride. Luke himself wore shorts and a tank top again, as did Tairen. Lexis had changed quickly into a pair of denim shorts, a white tank top and sandals. They left the house and Luke locked the door behind them. Blinking against the strain of the midday sun, they headed down to the beach. The town was busy, loads of activity. She smiled as she saw kids running about, laughing and playing catch or chasing each other. She made a pit stop at a shop and bought some lunch for them all. Once she'd collected what she needed, they headed onto the beach and settled into a spot. Tairen let Alexzander down and he took over putting down their towels. Luke took Jinx out of her buggy and taking hold of Luke's hands, waddled on her little chubby legs over the sand, squashing it between her toes and laughing as she did so. Lexis collapsed into a heap on one of the towels next to Tairen who was tickling Alexzander.

"Hi Aunt Lexis!" A giddy voice made her turn her head and she looked at who it was.

"Hi Ky. How you doing, kiddo?" Kylayn, more known as Ky, was a seventeen-year-old lad who was an extremely handsome vampire. Holding his hand was his sixteen-year-old girlfriend, Savannah. Only reason he called her aunt was because she treated everyone like her family, which they loved and why they all had respect for her and she had time for them.

"I'm good, thanks. I figured you'd be down here as it's a lovely day and all, and well, me and Savannah was wondering if you'd help us with our science homework? We just can't figure it out, the new teacher doesn't explain it as well as you."

"You teach?" Luke's voice drew her head up.

"When I'm here, yes. I'm the science teacher."

"Check you out!" He grinned at her, making her roll her eyes.

"Yeah, yeah. Ky, Savannah, meet my brother Luke. Luke, two of my students."

"Nice to meet you," Savannah said, her voice sultry smooth and her jade green eyes wide with curiosity.

"Yes, Savannah, he's human. As I used to be," Lexis said, understanding the curiosity.

475

"Sorry, I didn't know." She blushed and looked down at her feet.

"No need to be shy. I understand you wouldn't be sure about what I was," Luke reassured her. She smiled shyly at him and Ky got out his science book from the bag he was carrying. She patted the ground next to her and the kids dropped to their knees. Alexzander also dropped to his knees next to her.

"Ky, Savannah, meet Alexzander, my son. The little cherub with Tairen is our daughter, Jinx."

"Hi!" Alexzander smiled wildly at them.

"Hi." They both smiled back and nodded to Tairen who smiled back as he was feeding Jinx her bottle.

"OK, where did you get to that you're not sure of?"

"Here." Ky opened the book to where they were and she took the book from him.

"Ah, poisons. OK, what is it you're stuck on?"

"All of them?"

"Really? And how long have you been on this topic? I thought you were on venomous plants?"

"We were. We've been on this for one lesson and we're expected to research the list of poisons given to us. So we don't have much information about it, just that we have to work it out ourselves and hand in the paper in a few days' time."

"Who's the new teacher?"

"Mr Malgahorenly," Savannah replied.

"What is he teaching science for? He's the language professor." OK, that confused her.

"We know. But Mrs Kylandry was killed a couple of weeks ago by her ex-boyfriend."

"Oh crap. She was lovely as well."

"What happened to the ex?" Luke asked.

"Because Calista isn't here to mete out justice for Mrs Kylandry, Her Majesty Nixie stepped in as Mrs K was a fey. The ex was sentenced to rot in the dungeon until Calista is back and then he's to be sentenced to death."

"I'm surprised Nixie didn't kill him herself considering Mrs K was a fey and under her protection," Tairen said, joining in their conversation.

"I think loads of people were Tairen. But I'm sure whatever the case Calista will sort it. Can we get back to the work please?" Savannah said, ever the dutiful student. Lexis smiled at her.

"Sure. OK, so poisons. What are the ones you've been given to find out about?"

"We have been given cyanide, strychine, anthrax, conium, polonium, ricin, sarin and amatoxin," Ky said, reading them off the list Savannah was holding.

"Not many then. OK, shall we start with cyanide?"

"Sure." They quickly gathered their workbooks and a pen. She held the Book of Poisons out to them. Before they could do anything, Luke and Tairen stood up.

"We're going to go take the kids and get an ice-cream. Won't be long," Tairen said.

"No problem." She watched as they wandered off, Alexzander skipping alongside Luke and Jinx bouncing in Tairen's arms.

"OK," Ky's voice jarred her from staring after her family and back to the kids, "we know cyanide is a highly dangerous poison that kills by making the body unable to use life-sustaining oxygen."

"Very good. Now how long does it take to begin work on the victim?"

"According to the book, the effects begin to work within seconds of inhalation or within thirty minutes of ingestion."

"That's right. It's very fast which is scary when you think about it. Cyanide is also a chemical compound that contains the group $C \equiv N$. This group, known as the cyano group, consists of a carbon atom triple-bonded to a nitrogen atom."

"OK, got that." The kids wrote it down whilst she patiently waited.

"Got that?" Both kids nodded, but before she could carry on, more kids came wandering over to her, backpacks slung over their shoulders.

"Hey, Miss Blackwood, you teaching private science lessons?" one of the kids asked.

"In a way I am. I was just here with my family, but they don't mind me helping you guys out. I take it you've all got the poison paper to do yourselves?"

"Yeah, we do. We haven't got a clue!"

"OK, sit around here with me and I'll help you all out." They all dropped their packs and sat in a semi-circle around her, easily twenty or so students, but she wasn't fussed in the least. She loved it actually, which was why she volunteered at the local high school when she was here.

"So I take it you all have the same poisons to research?"

"Yes," Savannah replied.

"Ok, and did Mr Malgahorenly say you can all work together?"

"He did. Said it was to be a class project," she muttered.

"OK, that helps a lot then. Right, for those of you who have just turned up, we've started on cyanide. Savannah, can you tell them what you've written down so far as so they can do it themselves as well." She reached into her bag next to her and pulled out a black bottle that was full of chilled blood and took a swig. Waiting for Savannah to fill them all in on what she'd written down, she took in the appearances of the students, which ranged from demons to fey to Marbilians. And all of them were special to their own way and they were one of the science groups she loved to teach. All of them were eager to learn and it helped that she made it fun, so they soaked it up like a sponge. Once she saw they'd all caught up, and had opened their books to the right page, she put her drink down to carry on.

"OK, so we know that cyanide is highly dangerous, and one you do not want to mess with, correct?" They all nodded their agreement.

"OK, so what else does it say? Louisa, can you read this part for me?" She pointed to the tiny fey's book and she looked down.

"In inorganic cyanides, the cyanide group is present as the anion CN^-. For the salts such as sodium cyanide and potassium cyanide, these compounds are highly toxic. Hydrocyanic acid, also known as hydrogen cyanide, or HCN, is a highly volatile liquid that is produced on a large scale industrially. It is obtained by acidification of cyanide salts."

"OK fabulous. Thanks honey. So where it says the salts, sodium cyanide is an inorganic compound with the formula NaCN. It is a white, water-soluble solid. Cyanide has a high affinity for metals, which leads to the high toxicity of this salt. Its main application, in gold mining, also exploits its high reactivity toward metals. When treated with acid, it forms the toxic gas hydrogen cyanide. And the potassium cyanide is a compound with the formula KCN. This colourless crystalline salt, similar in appearance to sugar, is highly soluble in water. Most KCN is used in gold mining, organic synthesis, and electroplating. Smaller applications include jewellery for chemical gilding and buffing. However, potassium cyanide is highly toxic. The moist solid emits small amounts of hydrogen cyanide due to hydrolysis, which smells like bitter almonds. Not everyone, however, can smell this; the ability to do so is a genetic trait."

"Bitter almonds? Really?" one of the group asked.

"I'm very sure. Weird isn't it. Anyway, the taste of potassium cyanide has been described as acrid with a burning sensation, don't ask me how they know this, but I know it's been tried and tested. For some ridiculous reason."

"OK, so should we write this down?" another asked.

"Oh yes. Best to write it down, shows that you are eager to learn and study all sorts into it. Plus, you'd get extra points for putting in certain points and other little facts about it." She smiled at them all. They all then proceeded to write it down, with her repeating a little bit here or there for them, which she wasn't surprised about considering it was a lot she had just said. Once that was all completed and they were all up to date, she looked down at the book she had borrowed from Ky as he shared with Savannah.

"OK, who wants to read the next part for me?" One of the demon lads held his hand up.

"OK, Nyhlhoa, go on."

"Organic cyanides are usually called nitriles. In nitriles, the CN group is linked by a covalent bond to carbon. For example in acetonitrile, the cyanide group is bonded to methyl (CH3). Because they do not release cyanide ions, nitriles are generally far less toxic than cyanide salts. Some nitriles, which occur naturally as cyanohydrins, release hydrogen cyanide."

"Fab, thank you. Right, I'll read this part – so in nature, cyanides are produced by certain bacteria, fungi and algae and are also found in a number of plants. Cyanides are also found in substantial amounts in certain seed and fruit stones, which are usually found in those of apricots, apples and peaches. In plants, cyanides are usually bound to sugar molecules in the form of cyanogenic glysodies and defend the plant against herbivores. And for those of you who aren't sure what that is, herbivores are those who eat nothing but plants."

"Ah, but surely just eating plants isn't good for you?" Ky asked.

"It can be, as long as you mix it up with other things, not just plants. More so that of say, seeds, rice etc. It can be quite confusing if you're not one hundred percent sure of it. Anyway, cassava roots, which are also called manioc, which is an important potato-like food, which is also the base of what tapioca is made from, contains cyangenic glycosides."

"How do you know all this stuff, Miss Lexis?" Ky asked after he had finished writing down what she had said.

"Because I love science. I have ever since I was a child."

"Fair enough. OK, what else have we got to write down for the cyanide?"

"I reckon that would be enough for the moment."

"Looks like you've got quite the fan base." Lexis laughed at the sound of her brother's voice and watched as all the kids turned to look behind them at him.

"Everyone, this is my brother, Luke. He's here visiting me, along with his best friend, Raven."

"Then why isn't he with Luke if he is here visiting you?" Ky asked.

"Because he actually ran after Calista to go and help her."

"He does realise Calista is like the ultimate badass and won't hesitate to kill anyone who does get in her way?" one of the lads asked.

"Oh, he knows all right, but Raven is highly stubborn."

"Where did Miss Calista go anyway?" Savannah asked, packing the last of her books away, as did everyone else.

"She had to go rescue those children who were taken by Kharge."

"Surely she would have been back by now, then? They've been missing for some, what, six or seven weeks now?"

"Yes, but we're not sure what the holdup is at the moment. I am going to get Draylan to confer with Gélio and see if he can find out what is going on." She looked past the kids as she heard child's laughter and smiled as she watched Alexzander wrap himself around Tairen's leg and he exaggerated dragging the boy along whilst Jinx was clasped in his arms.

"Alexzander, what are you doing?" She shook her head as they came to a stop in front of them.

"Playing." He smiled at her as he climbed off.

"So why on daddy's leg?"

"Daddy said I could."

"That I did, kiddo. Show Mum what you picked out." That's when she noticed Tairen held a bag. Alexzander took it from his dad and opened it up. Everyone waited patiently for the kid to show what he had brought. Lexis smiled wide as he pulled out a small pair of jeans that were identical to the pair Tairen was currently wearing, a small black shirt and a mini waist jacket.

"Look at this, Mum!" He shrugged it on and turned around in a spin to show the different angles of the jacket on him. It was black with a velvet backdrop with mini chains and skull buttons.

"Honey, that's amazing!" He smiled as he took it off and carefully put it back in the bag. Then he noticed all of the kids standing around her.

"Oh, erm, hi." He smiled shyly at everyone. Savannah leaned down onto her knees and smiled at him.

"Hi, I'm Savannah. So you're Miss Lexis's son, huh?"

"I sure am! And that little beauty Daddy's holding is my sister, Jinx." Savannah glanced up and smiled as Jinx grinned at her with a small dribble of saliva out of the corner of her mouth.

480

"She's adorable."

"Sure is," Alexzander grinned and she noticed just like that, he was completely calm and at ease around everyone. Lexis walked over to Tairen and took Jinx from him. Luke pulled Alexzander up into his arms, causing the kid to laugh hysterically, his swim shorts pulled tight from where he was balanced across Luke's shoulder.

"Sea time!" Luke laughed and raced over to the ocean.

"No, Uncle Luke!" Everyone burst into laughter and Luke literally threw Alexzander into the waves. Lexis watched as he came spluttering up for air then dived at Luke, catching him unaware before sending him cascading into the waves himself.

"Miss Lexis?" She looked over at Ky.

"Yes, hun?"

"Since when did you have kids?"

"Ah, me and Tairen adopted them five weeks ago. But in a few months or so, I'll be adding to the family." She watched as it sunk in slowly as to what she meant.

"You're pregnant?" Savannah asked.

"I sure am. We're having a boy." She laughed, patting her rounding belly. She couldn't wait for him to be here so she could smother him in love and endless cuddles. Much how she was with Alexzander and Jinx.

"Congratulations you two!" Lexis hugged each of them as they congratulated her, and smiled as they all shook Tairen's hand, even the girls. It was just the way it was, no hugging the vampire males. More so when they were mated. Turning her head as she heard Alexzander let out a squeal of laughter, she saw Luke had picked him up and was walking back towards them, both dripping wet, but they had huge grins plastered to their faces. She had soon given up the negative thoughts that Luke wouldn't take to the kids, but it was as if they were of his own blood and for that, she would be ever thankful and grateful to her brother. They hung around the beach for another hour or so, and the kids she had helped drifted off to do their own things, until it was just them again. Luke collapsed next to her on the blanket, one arm slung over his face and sighed.

"You OK?" she asked, drawing in a mouthful of the orange juice Tairen had run to the shop to get her.

"Yep. Just starting to think about Raven again."

"I'm sure he'll be fine. He's with Calista after all," she replied. She glanced over at Tairen who was standing at the ocean border holding a giggling Jinx down in it so the water washed over her feet and Alexzander splashed her gently. She turned back to look at her brother.

"Honestly though Lexis, surely you have thought they would have returned by now?"

"Honestly, yes. But we have no idea what obstacles and such they've come across out there. But as I said, I'll get Draylan to confer with the dragons and we'll figure out something from there. That is all I can do at the moment."

"Reckon he will get somewhere with the dragons?"

"It could take some convincing, but I'm sure once Gélio listens to what he has to say, he'll send out a search party and inform us once he knows something."

"You reckon this Gélio will?"

"Yes. He was actually there when Calista was 'born', so he knows her pretty well. They're as close as anyone is to her, I suppose." she shrugged.

"Have you ever met Gélio?"

"Yeah. He's huge. I can honestly say I have never felt so tiny as I did when I stood next to him."

"How big is he?"

"Tairen, how big is Gélio?" she called over her shoulder.

"He's seventy feet long, fifty feet high. Why?" he asked, coming back to sit with her and Luke with the kids.

"Luke wanted to know, plus I've just said he was there when Calista was 'born'."

"That's an understatement and half. He was one of the reasons she was created in the first place, although they don't go into detail about it." He placed a now sleeping Jinx back into her buggy but moved it to shade her from the blistering sun. Alexzander plopped down next to Luke and leaned back against his uncle's stomach and fell asleep.

"I think someone is tired," Luke laughed as he watched his nephew's head fall back.

"I'm not surprised. Blistering sunshine, loads of laughter and play. It'll knacker all kids out."

"This is true. Reckon we should head back to the house?" Tairen asked.

"I think that would be the best. Get the kids out of the heat and I can start dinner." She glanced at her watch and noticed it was now four p.m. They'd been here for four hours already. Time really did fly when you were having fun. They quickly gathered all of their belongings and Lexis pushed Jinx off the sand. Luke carried their things and Tairen carried their boy.

They walked through the town to head back home, going around people as they carried on their daily business. It was a Saturday, so not many were working but they were out shopping, or taking their kids out for a run around and meeting up with friends to gossip. A typical village is what they were and honestly, Lexis loved every single second of it. She weaved around a couple of feys who were laughing with their daughter as she chased her younger sibling around their legs, and just before they headed up the hill to home, a deathly silence rained down on the town and all commotion stopped. She turned around at that, as did her family.

"What's going on?" Lexis enquired from Shrack, who was closest to her, holding his wife's hand.

"No idea. It just went deathly silent." he replied.

"Can you see what is going on?" Before anyone could reply, screams of utter joy rang through the air.

"Naomi!"

"Carl!"

"Sam!"

"Edira!"

"Crystal!"

"Kristopher!"

"Nekane!" As the last name was shouted out, Lexis recognised them. It was the names of the children who had been taken. Did that mean Calista and Raven were finally back?

"Tairen, wait here with the kids. Luke come on." She brushed past everyone and watched as one by one, through the trees on the outskirts of the town stepped the children who all burst into tears and ran to their parents who swept them up into loving arms and cried at being reunited with their beloved offspring. Lexis smiled at the sight, beyond thankful that they had returned safe, albeit a tad scruffy, until she caught the glimpse of someone coming out of the shadows of the trees. Into the lighter parts of shadows stepped a thunderous mountain of a man. Lexis blinked a few times. The guy was an absolute monster. Giant arms strained the black long-sleeved T-shirt he wore. Jeans barely held together over muscular thighs and calves. Longish hair lay straggled over the top of the head with bangs dropping into the eyes. Razor-sharp, ice-cold eyes stared out from the gaps in the hair, unblinking. A scruffy, unkempt beard covered the lower half of the face, barely hiding the hard slash of the mouth. A huge sword hung off of his belt, caked in old and some new blood of all colours. Hands rested at his sides, knuckles bruised and bloodied from what could have only been countless fights. Scratches marred the flesh too. Blood splattered over the clothes, but it didn't seem to faze the wearer. That was when she recognised just who it was.

"Oh my God, Raven!" She darted forward to him but stopped up short as she got a closer look at him. Gone was the carefree man she knew who had laughed and joked around with them at the beginning of this journey. This man in front of her was now a hardened killer who just stared at her with dead eyes.

"Raven?" Luke asked, gently walking up beside her.

"What happened? Is Calista with you?" she asked, not daring to move, he looked like he was ready to spring into action at any given moment. He didn't say anything, but just gave a simple shake of his head and took off for the house, hands clenched in tight fists. Everyone literally darted out of his way as he neared them.

"Did you sense anything about him?" She turned to her brother who watched his best friend walk away from them.

"I sensed something."

"Was that Raven who just walked past?" Draylan's voice caused her to jump but she quickly regained control over herself and turned to her beloved uncle-in-law.

"Yes, but I have no idea what is wrong with him. And Calista isn't with him. Do you think something could have happened to her?"

"Honestly, I have no idea. Let us go and join the man and see if we can get out of him what is going on and where Calista might very well be."

"Good idea. Although, by the looks of it, I don't want to press too much considering he looks about ready to rip someone's head off." She gazed up the hill as the black figure stormed up it.

"Let's get this over with." They headed back to Tairen who stood watching Raven, and thankfully the kids slept on still, completely oblivious.

"Tairen, I want you to take the kids back to mine. We don't need them around Raven at the moment, considering we have no idea what we are dealing with." Tairen nodded and walked off, heading to his uncle's without question. Before they could all move off, Lexis was called and she turned to who had shouted her name. It was the parents of the children Raven had safely returned.

"Yes?"

"Where did the man go who brought our babies back to us?" Melissa asked, gazing around.

"He's gone up to the house. Why, did you need him?"

"Yes, we wanted to personally thank him for returning them to us. But I must ask, where is Calista?" Kahlea, a jaguar shapeshifter said.

"We don't know where Calista is. And I don't think it would be a good idea to talk to Raven at the moment. He's about ready to burst. Once we've calmed him down and such, I will tell him personally that you all thank him," Luke replied.

"OK, we thank you for that." And with that, they all turned away and ushered their kids back to the safety of their homes. Lexis looked back up the hill and sighed.

"Let's get this over with." The men followed her as she climbed the hill after Raven. Before they could take more than a handful of steps, someone let out a petrified scream. Lexis whirled around and froze. A group of Wendigos had emerged. Clumps of saliva dripped from their panting mouths as they took a look around at everyone who had run away from them to a reasonable distance, all with fear etched on their faces. Before Draylan could do anything, a huge form whipped past them, causing everyone to watch with eyes wide open.

Chapter Thirty-Five

Raven took the children through the thick shrubbery but they all stayed glued to his side, having trusted him with their lives as he had proven time and time again that he was capable of keeping them from harm. More so considering the amount of shit they had come across since leaving Fire Mountain, which had to have been a good week ago now. Raven hadn't slept a single wink, preferring to keep an eye open in case of danger whilst the kids slept during the night when he'd found a safe place for them to bunk down. He was tired, hungry and just wanted to get them home as quickly as possible. He also wanted to shave; his beard was annoying him no end! The youngest girl, Naomi, kept a tight grip to Kristopher's hand, but the boy didn't seem to mind, which Raven was thankful for. He didn't need them clinging to him when he had to fight and he guessed they knew that as well. As they brushed aside some bushes, they could hear the beginnings of village life. They were now thankfully on the last part of their journey. The kids became excited at being back home again but they still refused to leave his side. Who knew what was lurking between them and the village. He shoved a couple of bushes out of their way and before they knew it, they were on the outskirts of the village. All that separated them was a couple of trees and again, more fucking bushes. He was sick to death of the fucking things. That was when he heard the people stop what they were doing as excited screams erupted as the kid's names were called, but they all looked at him to see what he thought.

"Go on." He urged them forward and they didn't need telling twice. They all dived out of the shrubbery and into their parents' waiting arms. Sobs of absolute joy burst out of them all as they held their loved ones but he just watched. Movement out of the corner of his eye had him turning his head slightly. It was Lexis.

"Raven?" her voice called, and he breathed in a sigh of relief that he'd already scrubbed the worst of the blood from him, lest he scare her. She looked radiant as ever and her belly had a bigger bulge to it, indicating her four months or so stage of pregnancy. God, actually how far gone was she now? He didn't know as he actually had no idea in how long he had been held hostage for. He didn't say anything as she came running up to him.

"Raven?" Another voice caught his attention. Luke. His best friend of twenty plus years.

"What happened? Is Calista with you?" Lexis's voice jarred him, but he couldn't speak. He was tense as anything and he had a niggling feeling in his gut that something just wasn't right at the moment, so instead all he did was give a simple shake of his head and took off for the house, hands clenched in tight fists. Everyone darted out of his way as he neared them. Not that he blamed them considering anger rolled off him in waves and he was a big bastard. He heard someone call out for Lexis but he didn't stop as he marched up the hill to the house. Where all he wanted to do was strip, crawl into the shower and wash away all the shit that clung to him, shave and then sleep for twenty-four hours before he had to face the world and the realisation that Calista wasn't coming back. As he reached about half way up the hill, a petrified scream erupted through the air, piercing his still sensitive hearing. He whirled around and saw the reason for the scream. A group of about ten Wendigos stood staring at everyone with mouths open with clumps of saliva dripping. Disgusting fucking creatures. Using his pent-up anger, he swept his sword up in his hand and charged down the hill. Rushing past everyone, he skidded to a stop just in front of the Wendigos, close enough to leap into action but not close enough that they could grab him.

"Not on my fucking watch!" he growled. The one at the front, obviously the leader, charged at him. He swept through them all with ease, his blade slicing through flesh like a hot knife to butter. Within minutes, he had dispatched them all. Whirling the blade loosely in his hand, he re-sheathed it and took off back to the house. Everyone just stared at him as he walked past them, but he was not in the mood to stop and talk. As he passed Luke and Lexis, they both stared wide eyed at him. He even noticed Draylan did as well. Moving past, he headed back up the hill and actually made it into the house this time. He moved through the home and disappeared out of the back door, taking a seat at the edge of the porch in the shade. He heard the door swing back open and out walked the siblings and Draylan.

"Raven?" He turned his head and looked at Luke.

"Yeah?"

"What happened to you out there?" OK, so this was how they were going to do it. One question at a time. He watched as they sat to the side of him, not completely surrounding him, which was good. He also knew his eyes were more cold than usual, the black ring around them making them appear colder, not that he actually gave a shit at the moment.

"A lot," was his reply.

"You seem different," Lexis said.

"That's because I am."

"How so?" Luke asked, drawing Raven's gaze to his.

"Like this." He opened his mouth and his fangs dropped down and his eyes literally glowed, fierce ice blue. Snapping his fangs back up into the gums, his eyes went back to normal, losing the vibrant glow.

"Holy shit! Did you know your eyes swirl when your fangs are out? And when the hell did that happen, you becoming a vampire?" Lexis stared wide eyed at him.

"No, I didn't know they did that. I got changed over when me and Calista were held prisoner in Fire Mountain."

"I have only known of one other vampire whose eyes do that when his fangs distend," Draylan muttered.

"Who?" Lexis asked.

"Lucian Cruorem."

"The Vampire King?" She turned incredulous eyes back to him.

"Yeah, he also happens to be my father." Raven stared at Draylan as he said that.

"What? How? Lucian has no children."

"He does now. Calista did a mind delve thing to when I was conceived. Turns out mother dearest wasn't so faithful. She had an affair with Lucian, which resulted in me."

"Could that be why they were as they were with you?" Luke asked.

"Yeah, that's what me and Calista thought when we spoke about it."

"Well damn, you know what this means don't you?" Draylan drew his attention.

"No."

"It means you're the prince of vampires."

"I'm no prince."

"Well now you are. And considering Lucian is going to hear about this, and I wouldn't be surprised if he finds out within a couple days or so, he'll be adamant that you go to the palace to see him."

"I can assure you, I'm not going to be a prince. Never will be. I'm not all that hoity toity type shit. I'm an army man for fuck's sake," he grunted.

"OK, so now we know that Lucian is your father, what else occurred when you were caught?" Lexis enquired, clearly wanting to keep him calm, which he could appreciate. He closed his eyes quickly before releasing the breath he didn't realise he was holding. He knew this was what would happen when he got back, so he sealed up his emotions and told them.

"We were tortured, in separate rooms, not that we gave them any information. Eventually we were put into the same room. Calista was strung up with chains and spikes and they'd placed razor wire under her feet. I was chained to the floor. I was changed just before being put there and just before the change hit big time, I watched as they cut her open, ripped out her heart and killed her, laughing as they did." He left out the part that he bawled like an absolute baby, cradling her body. That was personal between them and it was just something they didn't need or have to know.

"And then?" Lexis asked, tears in her eyes.

"They'd unchained her and such, leaving her body to drop and stay where it landed. They gave me a key, just out of reach of the chains before leaving the room, laughing as they went. I managed to grab the key, with some major stretches I might add, but I succeeded, then I couldn't think anymore as the change hit me full tilt. Think yourself lucky you had Calista do it for you Lexis as it is the worst pain ever to go through. When I eventually changed over, about twelve hours later, I broke free and went on a killing rampage. Got the kids out of the room they were being held in and now I'm here and they're home."

"You do know that Calista can't die from her heart being ripped out, right?" Draylan's voice caused him to snap his eyes to him.

"I saw it happen. She grew cold to the touch."

"Raven, I know you don't want to believe me, but trust me on this one. It isn't the first time she's had her heart ripped from her chest. She is alive."

"Then why isn't she here with us?"

"It can take up to a week to regenerate a new heart and for it to kick into gear. At least that was what happened last time. Give it time, she'll be back."

"If you say so." He didn't want to believe it. It already hurt too much from her not being here with him.

"Have you fed?" Draylan said, standing back up again.

"When I killed everyone in my path at the Mountain. Other than that, no."

"You knew how to feed?" Lexis stared at him whilst he also clambered to his feet.

"No. At first I didn't. I was just so fucking pissed off with everything that had happened, it was as if something inside of me snapped and I immediately knew what I had to do. I didn't ignore it, just did it."

"That's the instinct. How long had you changed over before that happened?" Draylan watched him with a curious gaze.

"About twenty minutes afterwards. When I had eventually caught my breath from the pain, I took one look at Calista's body and that must have been when it happened, when I snapped," he replied, which was the truth.

"Unbelievable. It's unheard of in new turns to get that instinct until a good few years down the line."

"So I'm a freak?"

"No. I reckon it is something to do with your father's genes. If you don't mind, when he does hear about you, let me be there with you and we can work it out?"

"Sure, whatever. But if he's that interested in knowing me, he can come to me." That was one thing he would not be deterred about.

"OK. Reckon I can go and let him know?"

"I don't see no problem with it, I suppose. It's bound to happen sooner or later. And I suppose it would be better him hearing it from you than someone gossiping."

"OK, I'll leave now. Lexis, do you want me to send Tairen back?"

"Yes please. About time Raven met my children." She smiled at Raven as she said that.

"Meet them in person you mean. I've already seen what they look like."

"Erm, how?"

"Calista."

"Ah, gotcha. Right, I will be as quick as I can. How long will you be here for?"

"We leave in three days," Lexis replied.

"OK. I'll go now and bring him back with me quickly."

"How are you going to get to him so quick?" Raven asked.

"Vampire speed. We have a heightened speed to run, etc."

"How fast are we talking?"

"Faster than the human eye can track," he replied before he literally disappeared from sight.

"Vamp speed. Good to know," Luke muttered. Raven didn't reply, just followed the siblings back into the house. Before he walked back inside, he looked over his shoulder and out over the vast landscape. Darkness had crept in whilst they were talking, the sky fighting with the darkness that was sweeping through with ease. Thanks to his enhanced vision, he noticed the Wendigos he had destroyed earlier had been removed from the town, but by who exactly? He didn't know, and quite frankly didn't care, just happy that they had been dispatched. Drawing his gaze out over the forest, he saw lights in the distance from small villages. Taking in a deep breath, he walked into the house, shutting the door behind him as he did so. As he looked up, he saw Lexis standing in front of him, holding out a black mug towards him. He nodded as he took the blood from her and downed it in a couple of gulps. She smiled slightly at him, hooked her arm through his and steered him to the kitchen before making him sit in a chair next to Luke who was nursing a mug of tea in his hands. He watched as she prepared another mug of blood for him and he nodded thanks to her as he drank it, thoughts again shoving through his mind, all of which were of Calista and their future that had been taken from them.

Chapter Thirty-Six

Draylan zoomed through the forest to the holding of the Vampire King after he had made a quick pit stop to Tairen to inform him to go back to the house with the kids who were now wide awake. About half an hour later after leaving his nephew, he stopped just on the outskirts of the solid twenty feet high brick wall that was surrounding the huge keep. Gazing upwards, night had descended to them, the sky alive with thousands of twinkling stars. Not a single cloud in sight. He never got tired of looking at the beauty of the sky. Something beautiful and tranquil about it. He didn't know what about it that calmed him, but he had done it ever since he was a babe in arms, and highly doubted it would end any time soon. Moving to the wrought iron gates that reached an additional five feet higher than the walls, they were a masterpiece. Huge gothic black works of art with pointed swirls highlighted by purple glass-blown skulls with fangs with black opal eyes that gleamed in the moonlight. They were beautiful and eerie at the same time.

"Halt!" a voice called from his left and he turned his head to see a couple of guards walking towards him. Both were of equal height, which was around about six feet three-ish, matching red eyes and muscular bodies. Only difference was one was black haired the other a deep chestnut.

"Yes?" he asked.

"What are you doing outside the palace gates?" Chestnut asked.

"I need to see Lucian."

"You call him the King, not by his name," dark haired retorted.

"Adrian, Cian, it's OK. I know Draylan." Another vampire stepped out of the surrounding shadows, just behind the duo.

"Forgive us Braeden, we did not know you knew this man."

"It's fine. I'll take him to Lucian. Carry on with your patrol." The men bowed slightly and strode past Draylan, not looking back at them. Draylan turned to Braeden.

"Good to see you again, old friend." He shook Braeden's hand. And it was good to see his friend again. As all vampires, they didn't age in appearance. So Braeden was as he has always been. Dark haired. Dark eyes that never missed anything. He was also muscular in the way a bodybuilder was when they were bulking and his mocha coloured skin was flawless as

492

ever. He had been a solider and worked out a lot before coming into his immortality at the age of twenty-five, which was the peak age. He stood at about six feet seven. He was what you'd also call a pure blood, but he was anything but. The man was so far laid back he might as well be horizontal, well until Lucian or his wife were threatened, then the animal that was hidden just below the surface was revealed — then you died. It was as simple as that. And considering that he himself and Calista had trained him, that was saying something.

"And you. How have you been?"

"Not too bad. And Luci?"

"Ask her yourself." He took Draylan through the gates and into the village that resided in the safety of the walls. Children scurried about, laughter rich in the air. Adults chatted or got on about their daily business under the gleam of the rising moon. As they strolled through the busy town, Braeden stopped at a hut that screaming was coming from. Before they could step closer to it, the screaming stopped and a healthy wail from a newborn erupted through the air. Braeden grinned at him as the door opened and a curvaceous woman walked out, her deep purple eyes sparkling as she spotted them. She had long black and purple hair that was swept up behind her in a ponytail, dreaded. Eyes were highlighted more by her black eyeliner, sparkling purple eyeshadow and long thick lashes. Lips painted a deep black. Cheeks were a rosy pink, strong cheekbones accentuated by a peachy type highlighter. She was a tall woman, about six feet two. She was dressed in a black halter-necked dress. Boots with chains covered her feet. She was a beautiful woman, inside and out. She pulled arm length blooded gloves off along with the blooded apron she wore and put them in a small pouch attached to her hip.

"Luci!" Draylan laughed and held open his arms and the woman let out a soft laugh before hugging him to her.

"How have you been, dear Draylan? I did wonder when you would grace us with your presence again." Her voice was sultry smooth, which was ideal for her job.

"I've been good thanks Luci. Yourself?"

"Never better." She beamed at him.

"Good!"

"Now, I know this is not a social visit, so why has my beast of a husband brought you here?" Braeden mock growled at her and tugged her to him, which only made her laugh and put her own hand on his which was

493

around her stomach. She was the perfect light to his darkness and Draylan was happy for them.

"No, it isn't I'm afraid. I'm here on business. I need to see Lucian. And Braeden is just walking me up here. I met him at the gate." Very few people got to call Lucian by his name. And because Draylan was kind of second in command with Calista, he was one of the very few who got to call him it, plus they had a mutual friendship.

"Well, I won't keep you. Go on with you now. But please visit again! And bring that darling Lexis with you next time you do visit." Luci smiled at him.

"No problem. Although it won't be her on her own OK?"

"How come?"

"She has mated with Tairen in the way of vampire. But we need to do a big wondrous wedding for her, the entire village is eager to help. You know how they adore her. She is also pregnant with their first child and they've adopted two others."

"Wow, she has been busy. And about time that nephew of yours has settled down."

"Oh yes. She's the perfect match for him."

"And Rayne?"

"I don't see her settling down any time soon. She's a wild spirit as you know."

"Oh, yes. She was here earlier actually. But no idea where she wandered off to."

"Probably back to her home. She's become quite a hermit at the moment. I'll have to find out why," he muttered.

"Might be a woman thing, us ladies like to have our own space now and again. Now go on with you. Go visit the king." She brushed a kiss to his cheek and with a quick hug he and Braeden left her to go see Lucian. As they walked away, Draylan took sight of the monstrous castle Lucian called home. It was built into the rock. Black stone. Tall formal front with sweeping black opal pillars held up a sweeping balcony. Gargoyle statues rested all over the place, always looking like they were watching your very move. Eerie yet wickedly cool, well to Draylan anyway. In front of the stairs, leading to the grand doorway, sat an impressive sized pond. Two black marbled pillars rose majestically from the centre. Enormous dragon skulls sat on the top, their sheer weight keeping them in place. Empty eye sockets filled in with uncut blood-red rubies, because Lucian was loaded, so why not. Mouths were open with silent grins and dyed red water gushing through silver coated teeth that glistened in the sunlight to cascade like a river of blood before splashing into the pond below. It was truly impressive. Walking up black stone steps to the main doors, of solid redwood. A good five inches thick and held in place by huge cast iron brackets, Braeden pushed them open and walked in, Draylan following.

"So why do you need to see Lucian?" Braeden was allowed to call him by his first name considering he was the King's second in command.

"I would prefer to just say it when I see him. I'm sure you'll be there when I do."

"Well, if Lucian lets me, that is." As they strode through the doorway, Draylan was confronted by a huge staircase with swirling, black, iron vines which split in two directions, dominating the entry-way, clearly the focal point as you walked in. Draylan was always impressed by it. At the top, where the stairs split, sat a huge gargoyle statue, front and centre, with wings spread wide and inch long claws digging into a thick slab, mouth open in a twisted smirk and eyes that seemed to follow your every move, all of it was perched high upon a plinth of polished marble to stop anyone from knocking into it. Draylan followed Braeden onto thick slated tiles and looked around. Dark walls held gothic oil burners, all of which were lit. Nothing else was there in the home that Lucian had built for himself.

"Robert, is Lucian in?" Braeden called out and Draylan looked to who he was talking to. It was a vampire with slicked back slate-grey hair, who was also impeccably dressed. Butler obviously.

"Yes, sir. He's in the room to your left."

"Thank you." Draylan followed Braeden into a room that Robert had pointed to and as he threw open the door, it was clear that this was the entertainment room. Well, it was more of a huge ballroom. Highly polished wooden floor. Oak-carved walls with high elaborate chandeliers with hundreds of white candles and slick old-fashioned oil burners clung to the walls with flames dancing along the tops. One of the walls held huge glass windows with wooden frames. It was obvious Lucian had held back no expense and honestly, Draylan would do the same if he was as loaded as the King was. Looking at the bottom of the room to where they were standing, seated upon a black and gold throne that dominated the room sat Lucian talking to a demon servant who held a clipboard in his hands.

"Draylan! Good to see you!" he called out and Draylan walked the length of the room to him.

"Good to see you as well Lucian." He shook his hand.

"What brings you here?" Draylan looked at Lucian and now properly looking at him, it was obvious Raven took after him. They had the same ice-cold blue eyes, long lashes. Strong features. Only difference was Lucian had taken to growing a beard, which strangely suited the man. Both were tall, including him who stood at seven feet tall. He even had the shoulder length black hair that was currently held back with a leather thong at the base of his neck. He was dressed in black jeans and a black muscle shirt with shit kickers on his feet. Casually dressed but he was one of the most brutal vampire fighters to ever live.

"I need to ask you something."

"Of course. But let us adjourn to the library and sit in comfort. Syanide, we will continue our conversation tomorrow." Lucian stood up and Draylan noticed the man was built like a brick shithouse. Not as much as his son, but still a big motherfucker. Syanide nodded, bade them all goodbye and disappeared out of a door to the left. Draylan followed Lucian in silence, along with Braeden and they soon reached the library. Walls were covered in books, shelves bowing from the weight of the leather-bound paper. The smell of old books perfumed the air and it was one that was pleasing to the senses. A huge stone fireplace stood against a wall, roaring with life. Leather couches, old with use were placed either side, one of which Lucian took and the two men took the other. A servant appeared, holding three goblets of sweet smelling blood on a tray that he offered them all. Draylan took a sip and kept the happy sigh inside. Warm, fresh blood was always the best but honestly, he was so used to the bagged stuff now, it felt weird drinking it this way, but as a treat it was perfect.

"So, tell me what is it you need to talk to me about?" Lucian's voice drew Draylan's gaze to him.

"Do you remember about thirty-two years or so ago you slept with a human?"

"Vaguely. Why?"

"Her name was Rebecca. And as you know, I'm blunt as anything so I'm going to come right out and say it. She was married. She cheated on him with you and well, your seed bore fruit. She became pregnant with your child."

"My child? How? She told me she was protected." Lucian put his mug down on the oak table in the middle of the couches, fists now clenched on his knees.

"She lied. She wasn't protected. Considering she gave birth nine months later to your son."

"A son?" he whispered.

"Yes, a son. His name is Raven."

"How do you know his name?"

"Raven is at Calista's house with my nephew, his wife and their children. Turns out, Lexis, Tairen's wife, her brother is his best friend."

"How is he? What's he like?"

"He's a good male from what I've known of him. He wasn't in my company long because Calista had to go and rescue some children who were kidnapped by Kharge and Raven followed."

"Is he vampire?"

"He was human up until about a week or so ago I think. He's literally just got back today from being with her. Apart from he was on his own and he is now a vampire. He's got some, shall I say, traits the same as yourself."

"Such as?"

"Eyes swirl when hungry or fangs are extended. Untold strength. Vast speed. He's also more unpredictable. When he was human he was a force to be reckoned with according to what Luke has told us."

"Luke?"

"Lexis's brother. Raven's best friend of twenty plus years."

"How was his upbringing?"

"Horrendous apparently. He left the family home at fifteen, never looked back. Has no contact with his parents or sibling. He hasn't actually long found out that you are his father. Do you want to meet him?"

"Of course. When?"

"Tonight? But if you do, then we have to go to Calista's."

"Why won't he come here?"

"Because he won't. Says the only way he will meet you is if you come to him."

"Surely you could have made him come here?"

"Ah, not really. He's a massively stubborn bastard and honestly, he swept through a group of Wendigos that had followed him into the village as if they were nothing but fireflies."

"How many Wendigos were there?"

"About fifteen or so. I've never seen anything like it Lucian. It was a marvel to watch, albeit quite scary with how easy he made it look."

"That is mighty impressive. Then let us finish our drinks and go and see my son." Draylan agreed and they all quickly finished their drinks. Braeden keeping silent as they spoke. Once their drinks were finished, the men stood and walked out of the library. Lucian called out for Robert to get his coat and the butler quickly hurried back carrying Lucian's trademark leather trench coat, which had a huge screaming skull on the back. The same one he had tattooed onto his back. He tugged it on and followed Draylan out of the palace.

"Quick question, Draylan. Just how tall is my son?" Lucian pulled Draylan to a stop.

"He's six feet eight in bare feet."

"Tall strapping lad then."

"Just as you were at his age, Lucian." The men shared a grin as they remembered what Lucian had been like at that age. What they had both been like. Absolute bastards, but caring as well to a degree.

"How will we get to Calista's?"

"Vamp speed. Braeden, are you coming along as well?" He looked over at the other man.

"If Lucian wants me to."

"Yes Braeden, you come as well."

"So he won't be home for dinner?" A voice called out to them and the three men snapped their attention towards the village.

"I'm afraid not, Luci. We're heading over to Calista's," Braeden replied to his wife.

"Whatever for?"

"To meet my son, Luci," Lucian replied.

"Son? Oh wow, your highness."

"Indeed. We shall see you soon."

"Good luck," she murmured and the men nodded to her and strode past, thankfully not being stopped again until they reached the gates and stepped past them, and then using the blessed speed of vamps, shot off back to Calista's so Lucian could meet his son for the first time.

Chapter Thirty-Seven

Raven sat on the couch, furthest from the living room door, nursing a mug of blood in his palm, stared into the fire that was blazing just feet from him. Luke and Lexis sat opposite him, watching him as he appeared lost in thought. He supposed he was in a weird way, he was thinking back to the time before he and Calista had got captured, the night they had spent in the cabin down on the beach from Dragon Hill. The night he had taken Calista's virginity as well as laughing together as well as being serious. It was perfect, or at least it had been until he had seen her heart ripped from her chest. The front door suddenly burst open, causing him to snap out of his thoughts and looked to the living room as a child's excited chatter reached their ears. It was time to meet the kids then. As he watched, Lexis jumped up from the couch and disappeared into the hallway where an excited 'MUMMY' was called out following by laughter. He glanced over at Luke, who had turned slightly and was grinning.

"What are you grinning about?"

"You're about to meet the two most adorable kids ever. My, no our, niece and nephew." And Raven smiled slightly at the excited look on his friends face. Before he could say anything, in walked Tairen cuddling a baby up against his shoulder whilst it snoozed in a black blanket with a skull on the back. Lexis trotted in behind him holding the hand of a boy. So that meant that the baby was the niece.

"OK, Alexzander, this is your Uncle Raven. He is the one Uncle Luke has told you about." She brought the small boy around the couch and Raven got his first look at the boy. He watched as the boy stared at him with storm grey eyes. Raven noticed Lexis had obviously dressed him in her type of fashion. He had on kid's ripped jeans with a black T-shirt with REBEL written in red across the chest and his feet were encased in converse. Smartly dressed to an extent. He also had peachy coloured skin with the overtone of a light grey tinge, but it suited him strangely.

"Hi," he murmured before hiding behind Lexis's legs. Raven understood why, he wasn't exactly someone to give the time of day to at the moment, considering he was still covered in blood from the Wendigos and from everything else that had happened.

"Hi," he replied, then watched as the kid walked out from behind his mother and headed to him, bypassing Luke with a high five. Raven stared as he came to a stop at his knees.

"So you're my Uncle Raven?"

"That I am."

"Awfully big aren't you?"

"I'm not that big." Raven's lip lifted up a little at the corner as Alexzander snorted with laughter.

"If you're not big, then I'm a fairy!" He grabbed Raven's hand and put his own against it. His entire hand fit into Raven's palm and Raven didn't so much as move as he felt the boy's skin on his own. Alexzander looked over his shoulder at Luke as he laughed at what the kid had said. Even Tairen and Lexis were chuckling to themselves gently.

"Uncle Luke, his hands are even bigger than your own!"

"That's right, he is bigger than me, fairy boy." Luke laughed as Alexzander growled and dived on him and they play fought, both laughing in merriment.

"Are they always like this?" Raven asked Tairen who had moved to the opposite end of the couch to him.

"With them two? Definitely. By the way, this is your niece Jinx." He pulled the baby off his shoulder and Raven was mesmerised. Peachy skin with the overtone of grey glitter that shone with health and accentuated more by the black baby blanket wrapped around her. She had a cute little button nose along with rosy cheeks. Long lashes lay as crescent moons against her cheekbones. Well, they did before they opened and she blinked tantalising grey eyes at him.

"She's a beauty," he replied and everyone agreed. Alexzander finally climbed off Luke and wandered back to Raven.

"Can I sit on your lap?" he asked and Raven picked the boy up, as gently as possible as he knew he was phenomenally strong now, and placed the boy on his lap. Raven kept a hand braced on the boy's back so he wouldn't topple backwards.

"Mum?" Alexzander drew Lexis's gaze.

"Yes, baby?"

"What's for dinner?"

"I was thinking maybe some chicken dippers and chips."

"YES! They're the absolute best. But you're going to need a lot." They all laughed as Alexzander grinned at them. Raven just made sure he kept still so as to not frighten the kid, or make him fall from his lap. He was still surprised the boy wanted to sit on him considering he was filthy.

"And why's that?"

"Because Uncle Raven is huge."

"I'm not that big!" Raven faked being shocked.

"Yes, you are! You're even taller than Uncle Luke!"

"Want to know my secret as to why?" Raven said.

"Yeah!"

"It's because I eat all my vegetables."

"Really? So if I eat all my vegetables, I can be as big as you one day?" He leaned forward and put his hands on Raven's bicep and squeezed slightly.

"Very well could be, kiddo. But it will take a long time as you've got to grow up first."

"That'll take forever!"

"Not really. But it will be worth it in the end. Just focus on eating your veg and being a healthy, happy kid."

"OK."

"Right, I'll go get started on dinner. Everyone wash up please." Lexis said, standing up with a stretch and Raven noticed her belly had begun swelling quite a bit since he'd left, but she looked so good with it. She literally radiated an inner shine with her pregnancy.

"I take it that's a hint for me to go and get clean huh?"

"Of course. I'm not having a messy bugger at our dinner table covered in blood. As much as I love you Raven, even I have limits." She grinned at him and he grinned back, the first proper smile since before he and Calista had been captured. He helped Alexzander down who scrambled after Lexis as she left the room.

"Come on, big guy. Let's go get changed before mother hen comes back in and hits us with the spatula," Luke laughed as they all clambered to their feet.

"She'd do that?" Raven cracked his knuckles and began to follow the two guys out of the room.

"Oh yeah. She did it to me yesterday when I walked in with grass stuck to my feet."

"Why did you have grass stuck to your feet?"

"Grass had not long been cut and me and Alexzander were outside chasing each other. Safe to say, Lexis was not amused that we were kind of covered in it."

"Doesn't surprise me with you."

"True that!"

"Good to see you're really good with the kids though."

"As strange as it sounds, I don't see them as Lexis and Tairen's adopted kids, they are theirs, so they're the nephew and niece I plan on spoiling as much as possible. I do love them unconditionally and I hope you'll grow to love them as much as I have one day too."

"You never know what will happen," Raven replied, and they then walked in silence up the stairs to the bedroom they had previously shared. Walking in, Raven cracked his neck. He sat in the old leather chair that had become part of the room and took off his boots, wiggling his toes.

"You want to grab the shower first?" Luke's voice jarred him from looking at his feet.

"Yeah, sure." He dropped his jacket into the washing basket before whisking off his T-shirt, then caught Luke staring at him.

"What?"

"You been working out when you were away? You're huge my man!"

"Nope, didn't really get a chance to considering we were walking through the forest to the Fire Mountain then we got caught and tortured for five weeks."

"Damn man, I'm so sorry about that."

"Shit happens. At least the fuckers who did it are now dead."

"By your hand I take it?"

"Hands and fangs."

"Good on you, man! So why are you so big? Not that you already weren't, but you are even bigger than you were before."

"No idea. I just knew when I was going through the change from human to vampire, I stretched out sideways. It was horrendous."

"That bad?"

"God yeah. Think of the puberty times a thousand!"

"Fuck that! Now go get a shower, you stink of blood and other crap." Luke grinned at him and Raven disappeared into the bathroom without argument. He quickly stripped and dumped the clothes in the laundry basket that sat by the door. He risked a glance in the mirror above the sink and gasped at what he looked like. He looked horrendous. His eyes were sunk into his skull, which made them practically glow. Nearly hollow cheeks. His hair had grown out from the usual military style and it had started to dread as well. Gross! And then he realised Luke was right. He'd filled out a lot more since being turned. A gene from his father maybe? Turning his back to the mirror, he leant into the shower stall and turned the water on, cranking up the heat to how he liked it. Once the room had steamed up enough, he stepped under the hot spray and sighed as the water raced down over his head and his body to disappear down the plughole along with dirt and blood that had clung to him. He washed his hair twice to make sure it was clean.

"Hey, Luke?" he called out. He'd never been body conscious, that was soon drilled out of him in the army and besides, Luke had seen him in all his naked glory plenty of times over the years.

"Yeah, buddy?" he answered, opening the door.

"Any chance of a hairbrush or some shit? I need to get these fucking dreads out."

"Yeah, give me a sec." He watched as he disappeared and sure enough, returned a minute later with a hairbrush and a comb.

"I wasn't sure which would be better for you so I got both." He handed them over.

"Thanks, man."

"No problem. And holy fuck, what happened to your ribs? They busted?" Raven looked down and sure enough, on the entire right side of his ribs and part of the left were huge ugly black bruises.

"They're not busted, they healed when I drank the blood. The bruises are just the aftermath of it all."

"Just how fucking hard did they hit you?"

"Hard enough to obviously crack my ribs in countless places. Not that I gave them the gratification of seeing it hurt."

"Of course not, considering you're a hard-arse bastard. What caused the last lot?"

"Me and my sarcasm."

"Really? Oh damn." Raven laughed slightly at the exaggerated look on Luke's face who knew just how bad Raven was when he let the sarcasm out.

"You should know what I'm like when I get going."

"Yeah, I'm surprised they didn't cut out your tongue."

"Yeah, they tried but turns out, I bite, hard."

"I wouldn't expect anything less. Now I'll leave you to the rest of your shower." And with that, Luke left. Raven brushed out his hair, not even wincing when it caught on the knots. Considering all the shit he had gone through, this was but an inconsequential hindrance. He finally completed his shower and stepped out, wrapping a plush towel around his hips, holding the ends together that just barely fit. Damn, he was going to have to buy some super-sized towels or some shit at this rate! He then shaved, getting rid of the crap on his face, and damn it felt good to get rid of the fuzz. He walked out of the bathroom afterwards and looked over at Luke who was sprawled on the bed, scribbling something into the notepad he had got from somewhere.

"I need to borrow some clothes from you, Luke. I have none."

"Yeah, you do. I made sure that you had plenty for when you returned. In the wardrobe to your right." Raven turned and sure enough, there was a double-sized wardrobe in stained oak.

"Which side?"

"Left." Luke didn't bother lifting his head. Raven opened the left side and sure enough, it had a small hang rail with some jeans hanging from hangers. And shelves held tops, jumpers, even the lower shelf had a coat stashed there, still sealed in a protective case. The top shelf held boxers, still sealed. Shit kickers lined the bottom.

"Geez, who got all of this?" Raven looked over his shoulder.

"Me and Lexis. She didn't want you to come back with nothing here. She's nothing if not stubborn and wouldn't take no for an answer." Luke looked up at that.

"I'm not surprised with her being stubborn."

"Tell me about it. And not to forget, she's got such a motherly instinct etc., with the kids, it's kind of surreal to watch at times. I still think of her as that annoyingly stubborn seven year old who used to follow us around everywhere or 'nurse' our wounds from us play-fighting."

"You and me both." Raven turned back to the wardrobe. He grabbed a pair of boxers, jeans and a black T-shirt.

"We got the biggest size that they had at the store. We know you're a big bastard, not to forget, stupidly tall, so we did the best we could."

"No, it's good man. Honestly." He dropped the towel and quickly got dressed. And of course, the clothes fitted, even if the top was a tad tight as were the jeans on his legs, but he didn't care at that particular moment in time. It was just nice to wear clean clothes now.

"You sure?"

"I'm sure. How did you find jeans to fit my leg length anyway?" Raven knew he wasn't the easiest person to find clothes for, considering his size.

"The store we got them from cater to everyone of all heights, shapes and sizes. I'll have to take you in there one day. It's immense! And they have things for everyone from designer dresses and suits right on down to work clothes."

"I'll take you up on it. You going for a shower now? And what are you scribbling down now?" He threw the towel into the laundry basket and sat on the edge of the bed. It felt so good being clean again. He didn't realise just how much he had missed it until he'd gotten into that shower.

"Yeah, and it's just a climbing frame I was contemplating building Alexzander and for Jinx when she's older, when we come back here."

"You want to come back?" Raven was shocked. Surely Luke would prefer to live on 'Normal Earth'? Find a nine to five job or whatever, settle down, marry and have a family.

"Without a doubt. Lexis has already decided after university she's going to move back here permanently to raise the kids. Tairen brought her this huge fucking house. It's actually really impressive and will suit them perfectly for their growing broad. I don't care if I never marry or whatever, I just want to be close to my sister and her family. And I was kind of hoping you'd come back with me too."

"I don't know, man. We'll have to figure out something closer to when we leave the army. I have no idea what will be here for me."

"Because of Calista?"

"Yeah."

"What happened between you two?"

"I'll tell you later. Right now, I can't go through the pain of talking about it."

"You really do love her don't you?"

"More than anyone will ever know. Want to know the biggest kick in the balls?" He breathed deeply at what he was about to admit, but that was the thing with him and Luke, they had no secrets between them.

"What's that?" Luke scrambled off the bed and sat next to Raven, looking completely serious as he looked at him.

"We were bedded down for the night, safe in this cave. She did the mind delve for me and saw what my parents did and why the old bastard was horrible to me. We spoke afterwards and well, she kind of admitted she had very strong feelings for me."

"Strong as in?"

"As in she loved me. And wanted to see how we could go with a relationship."

"Holy shit! That's a *big* commitment for you and for her!"

"Tell me about it. That's what the biggest kick was, knowing now that we can't go forward with the relationship."

"I know, man. Let me go shower then we'll head back downstairs. Have a look in the notepad and see what you think of the climbing frame etc. I'm sure you'll have an input in it." Luke laughed and disappeared into the bathroom. Raven stayed exactly as he was but reached back and brought the pad to him. Flipping it open, he was amazed at the detail in the drawings. Actually, no, he wasn't. Luke had always been fantastic at drawing. Looking at the design he'd done for his nephew and niece, it had monkey bars, four swings. A curling and a straight slide. Bridges with rope along the sides with a wooden floor. It was incredible. He flipped to the next page and saw that Luke had drawn the house along with adding in details of bushes along the porch edging and other small things. He was always fascinated by the detail that Luke put into his drawings. He heard the shower turn off and put the book down. Luke walked out a couple of minutes later freshly scrubbed, towel around his waist as he rummaged through the other side of the wardrobe, dumped the towel in the dirty washing and chucked clean clothes on.

"You ready to meet your father?" Luke asked, drawing his T-shirt on over his head.

"Ready as I will ever be." He sighed and stood up, rolling his shoulders as they cracked.

"Let's go then." As they walked out the bedroom, they heard the front door open and an excited Alexzander screaming out for Draylan, whose deep chuckle rumbled up the stairs to them. Time to get this over and done with. Sooner it was done, the better. Then he could focus on trying to sort his head out and what he was going to do with his life in six months' time.

Chapter Thirty-Eight

Calista rolled her shoulders as she walked through the gates of Dragon Hill. She was sore, tired and her temper was literally boiling just under the surface of her skin. One wrong thing and she knew she would snap and whoever was on the receiving end would not last very long. She walked past all of the caged dragons, all of them silent and watching her in the moonlight, all sensing if they said one wrong thing, she would eliminate them and she damn well would. She finally reached the main areas where fires were roaring ripe with life and dragons lounged around in all colours. Talking, eating or laughing as they watched their children running around carefree. She strolled through them all and headed to where the lords were sitting. When she finally reached them, the moon had moved higher and the moonbeam shone down on the lords as though caressing their flesh. She stopped on the other side of their pit as they stilled in their discussion and looked at her.

"Calista, we weren't expecting you here." Gélio said.

"I know. I came here to tell you I'm using the cabin for a few days."

"No problem. Where is the male that was with you?"

"Long story."

"Care to indulge us?" a red one said and she vaguely remembered his name as something like Gleregurn.

"Just Gélio," she replied.

"Why just him?"

"Because I only want to talk to Gélio. I don't answer to you lot." Rage shimmered in her eyes and lightning bolted across the sky, even though there were no clouds. They all stared wide eyed at her and she heard silence behind her as all activity came to a stop.

"It's OK everyone, go back to what you were doing." Gélio's voice boomed across the land and everyone slowly went back to what they were doing.

"Gélio, I will meet you at the cabin." And with that Calista walked off, heading down the cliff side and to the cabin she and Raven had shared. Sweeping across the vast vines, she strolled inside and set it to rights again. Two armchairs, roaring fire, bed at the back. She didn't need anything else.

Shrugging off her weapons, she left them on a small table she made appear. She wasn't one to just dump them on the floor if she could help it. The door opened and in walked a huge male who had to duck under the doorway to enter.

"Since when do you take human form?" She didn't bother turning around, she knew who it was. Instead she just walked to one of the armchairs and collapsed into it.

"Since it's easier to talk to you like this," Gélio replied, sitting down in the other chair. She looked at him. He still had those intense green eyes but in human form he was an astoundingly gorgeous man, even though he had green scaled skin. He was dragon after all. Thick rich black hair in a shaggy mess. Strong cheekbones. Pointed jaw. Full lips. He was what could be described as a god. But she felt literally nothing when she looked at him, apart from friendship. He was dressed in a suit of all things, but he was nothing if not classy when in this form.

"So what happened to you?"

"We were captured at Fire Mountain. We were tortured. Raven was changed over into a vampire and I had my heart ripped out," she replied.

"They do realise that doesn't actually kill you, right?"

"We know that. But obviously they didn't. Besides, it isn't the first time I've had that happen to me."

"What else happened?" She noticed he didn't comment on the fact it hadn't been her first time.

"Raven managed to escape, killing anyone who got in his way, but also managed to get the kids out of there that we were sent to get. I was thrown into The Pits as they call it. Bodies littered the floor, ready for a Feeder. I killed the one which was there. I escaped out of the room, killed everyone I came into contact with. I tracked down Kharge and his new bit of fluff, along with his right hand vamp. I also killed Warden and Salam."

"You certainly were busy."

"It was only fair that I got payback, considering the amount of shit that they had done to me."

"There is that. So all the bodies are still in the mountain?"

"Yes. I had no intention of removing them. The next person who wants the mountain can have that duty."

"Well, isn't that lovely of you. Clean up duty."

"They'll need a strong stomach for it considering there is also countless years' worth of blood staining the walls. Bodies literally left to decompose and skeletons left wherever they are."

"We will have to find someone who is wanting to perhaps take it over. How big is it inside?"

"Countless rooms. Huge throne room Kharge used a lot. Easily big enough for demons or whoever to settle into."

"OK, I shall put word out that it is up for grabs, but they will go through me for it."

"Understandable."

"Indeed. I am sure there are plenty of demons who would be willing to relocate from the villages and head into the mountainside. What will you do now?"

"Now that I am out of there and I'm here, I'll rest. I'm feeling really shit at the moment."

"Any idea as to why?"

"Apart from all the fighting and killing I've had to do since I woke up in the Pits? None whatsoever. What do you think it is?" And wasn't that a shocker. Her, asking Gélio what he thought could be wrong with her, but she trusted him unconditionally, considering everything they had been through since her 'birth'. He got out of the chair and knelt before her.

"Mind if I touch you?"

"Go ahead." For some absurd reason, if anyone wanted to touch her, they asked permission first. Apart from Raven, who just took what he wanted from her, which she had thought was a nice change and she didn't mind in the least. Gélio placed his hand on her shoulder, flesh touching flesh. He closed his eyes and breathed in deeply, both falling into silence. A minute or two later he snapped his eyes open and stared at her.

"What?"

"I know what is wrong. Although I am surprised you didn't pick up on it sooner."

"What is it, Gélio?"

"You're pregnant."

"WHAT?" She hadn't heard that right surely?

"You're pregnant," he repeated.

"But, that's ridiculous. I was always told I would never be able to reproduce because of all the different creatures used to create me."

"Well, it worked. Excuse me if I'm wrong or for asking, but was that why no one has ever seen you with a male?" Gélio got off of his knees and sank back into the chair.

"Maybe part of the reason. But honestly, I think half of the reason was because I never found a male worth my time in that sense."

"But then you found Raven, yes?"

"Yes." She didn't hesitate to reply.

"But how could a human male be worth the time?"

"Honestly, Gélio, I have no idea. There was just something about him that attracted me, so much so I fought against it at every turn."

"But he won eventually." Gélio was nothing if not brutally honest with her and that was one of the very few things she valued in her friendship with him, he wasn't one to beat around the bush.

"Yes. So much so that I've done something that I never thought I would ever do." She sighed.

"Have sex?"

"No, fall in love." She stared at him as she said this and watched as his eyes widened.

"And why does it sound as though that is the worst thing you would ever do?"

"Because he's human, he will die in forty or so years. A mere blink in our lifetime."

"But you've told me he was changed over into vampire. So he will live a lot longer than that."

"There is that. But he thinks I've died."

"Then go home, show him you're still very much alive. Show that male what he is missing out on. Settle down with him. Raise your child when it is born, and any others you're gifted with."

"I still can't get over the fact I'm pregnant."

"It is no doubt a shock to anyone when they first find that they are expecting."

"Yeah, I get that. Do you have any idea how far along I am roughly? But also look at me Gélio. I'm a highly trained killing machine, literally born for nothing but to fight against evil and keep Mystic Being secure. Who am I to know how to raise a kid?"

"I'd say six or so weeks. And Calista, all parents worry about that. You will be fine. You won't be alone. You will have your male with you as well as Lexis and her family. You will both know what to do. Take it one day at a time."

"Like you and Nyhkohl are with Murfy?"

"Exactly like that. I'll let you in on a secret, I was an absolute nervous wreck when we first got him. I was afraid to go near the boy half the time for fear of hurting him or something. But I'll let you in on a secret. Kids are made of some seriously tough shit, they bounce back quicker than what you realise."

"Maybe. So one day at a time."

"One day at a time. Now, get rest. Stay for a couple days, convalesce then go back to the main village and get your man back, OK?"

"Damn, check you out using the word convalesce."

"I know. I can use fancy words too you know." He snorted.

"Noted. And thanks for this, Gélio. I needed it."

"That is what friends are for. And don't worry, what was said between us, will stay that way. Now I have to get out of this form and get back into the dragon I am. Then I'm heading home to Nyhkohl and Murfy. I shall see you soon."

"Good bye, Gélio and thanks again. But when I leave, I won't go through the Hill. I'll just vanish and reappear back home."

"Of course. Until next time. And go and get your male!" And with that, he disappeared. She watched as he shut the door behind him and stewed over what he had said. He was right, kids were made of tough shit these days, she saw it every day in her line of work. Could it work between her and Raven? He had after all not left her side when trouble had started. In fact he had jumped in to help, even when she had a handle on things he still helped. And he didn't back down to anyone. She walked outside, stripped as she went and dived into the stream next to the cabin. Night had since fallen and she gloried in the light of the moon. She ducked under the water, submerging herself completely. Muck and other crap washed off of her. She shook her head in the water and came up for air. Crawling to the edge of the stream, she sat on the side with her legs in the water, and placed her hands over her belly. She was pregnant. With Raven's child. A huge surge of untold happiness shot through her as it sunk in. She knew without a doubt that she and Raven would be fantastic parents to their kid. And she would protect them with every single ounce of her being. She had never thought of herself as being a mother one day, as she didn't think she'd ever be able to become pregnant. Would she have a typical nine month pregnancy or would it be different considering her genetic make-up? She guessed she would have to wait and see. She got up and walked back into the cabin, naked as the day she was 'born'. Shaking her head of the water that clung to the strands, she snapped her fingers and she was instantly dry. She braided her hair into two simple plaits then climbed onto the mattress. She called forth two pillows and a thin duvet as it was warm. Curling up under it, she wiggled to get comfortable. Snapping her fingers, curtains then covered the windows, blackouts of course, and then the fire extinguished itself, dropping the place into avid darkness. Outside, she heard the vines creep back into place, to make it appear as though it was abandoned. In a few days, she would go back to the main village she called home and she'd talk to Raven, until then, she would sleep. Using an age old spell, she drew herself into the dreamless sleep. Essentially putting herself into a healing coma. Which would help considering the amount of shit that had happened the past six or so weeks. As sleep drew in, the last thought she had was she would do whatever it took to convince Raven to be with her again. Then she knew no more.

Chapter Thirty-Nine

Raven stood at the top of the stairs and stared at the man who was next to Draylan who was hugging Alexzander. He was tall, around about seven feet. So not that much taller than himself. He was a rugged man, with a beard that strangely suited him. He had the shoulder length long black hair that was currently held back with a leather thong at the base of his neck. He was dressed in black jeans and a black muscle shirt with shit kickers on his feet. And Raven noticed he also had a waist jacket on with chains from the pockets to attach at the back. He stared back at Raven and he had the same glacial blue eyes. Another man stood just slightly behind him. Dark haired. Dark eyes that never missed anything. He was also a big muscular bastard with mocha coloured skin. He stood at about six feet seven. Maybe it was his right hand man? Whoever he was, it wasn't important to Raven at this moment in time.

"Come on down, Raven. There is someone I wish for you to meet," Draylan called up, having seen him and Luke standing there. Raven walked down the stairs, Luke one step behind him. He noticed Lexis standing in the doorway of the living room, and Tairen behind her with his hands on her shoulders. Jinx must be down for a short nap before dinner. He stopped in front of Draylan and looked at the man with him.

"Hello, Raven," the guy said and even his voice was deep and rumbly.

"Hi."

"Who are you?" Luke asked, coming to a stop beside Raven, clearly offering his support. Not that Raven needed it, but he could appreciate it.

"Lucian Cruorem."

"The Vampire King."

"Yes."

"OK, guys, before this gets any more awkward, go into the living room where it is more comfortable, but please keep your voices down as my daughter is sleeping," Lexis called out, disappearing into the kitchen. The men did as they were told. And Raven glanced over at Jinx who was sound asleep in a crib next to one of the couch ends, which Raven took as he didn't trust or know the other man. Luke ushered him along so he could sit next to his niece, but he didn't mind.

"So what do you know of me?" Lucian asked, drawing their attention as he sat opposite them next to Draylan. Tairen had disappeared, obviously gone to help Lexis. Alexzander settled at Luke's feet, grabbing his crayons and colouring book.

"Nothing. I literally heard about you the first time when I had a delve done."

"You had a mind delve done? But they're very risky."

"Not when you trust the person who did it."

"Who did it?"

"Calista."

"Best one to do it." Raven didn't reply, just gave a single nod.

"So why are you here?" Luke asked.

"To meet my son," he replied.

"And what do you hope for from this encounter?" Raven wasn't one to beat around the bush.

"Lucian, would you like some dinner?" Lexis asked, poking her head round the doorway.

"Yes please." He smiled his thanks to her.

"Lexis, now isn't the time," Luke called out to her.

"And you can shut the fuck up. I wanted to ask, it's manners. You just sit there and stop being a bossy shit," she retorted before vanishing again.

"Someone found her balls." Raven grinned at Luke.

"The biggest of you all!" Lexis's voice trailed from outside, which made them all chuckle.

"And to answer your question, Luke, about what I want from this encounter is to get to know my son and see what goes from there." Lucian crossed his arms over his chest.

"What do you want to know?" Raven said.

"Everything!" How did he know that Lucian was going to ask that. He wiggled slightly in his seat and took a breath.

"I was born to Rebecca and Daniel Calhoun. When I was born, they turned against me and only raised me because the family knew Rebecca was pregnant. My childhood was horrible apart from the times I spent at Luke and Lexis's house. Half the time Rebecca and Daniel didn't even notice I used to disappear for the entire weekend until one time they found out I did and that I was at Luke's. I got back home and got the beating of my life, which for a twelve year old was horrific. But it was in places no one would notice, so any place on me that could be hidden by clothes. I left at fifteen and never looked back. I've not had any contact with them from

514

the day I broke Daniel's nose and walked away. I enlisted in the army at sixteen with Luke. Been there ever since. I finish my service time in six months or so, as it only counts when I am actually there and not away as I am now."

"And how long have you been away for?"

"We told them a month, but it's been longer. At least I think it has." He looked at Luke who nodded.

"We have been away for two months or so. You were away from us for seven/eight weeks."

"Where have you been?" Lucian asked.

"Me and Calista went to go rescue kids kidnapped. We were taken hostage at Fire Mountain. We were tortured and I was changed over."

"And Calista?"

"Heart ripped out. Killed and left in the room."

"And what did you do to escape?"

"I went on a killing rampage. Got the kids out and headed back here. Which took us about a week because the kids are slow and I didn't want to risk them travelling at night."

"Killing rampage?"

"Killing rampage. Lexis, can you take the kids out of the room? I don't really want them to hear this," Raven asked, and she nodded before ushering Alexzander out of the room with Jinx curled up in her arms.

"OK, so where were we?" Lucian asked.

"Killing rampage. I was turned when me and Calista were held in Fire Mountain. After twelve or so hours, or whatever it was, I escaped, killing anyone I came into contact with."

"Everyone?"

"Well, almost everyone. It was whoever I encountered in Fire Mountain that got in my way. I even killed Kharge's daughter and her friend as they tried to stop me from leaving."

"You do realise he will come after you in retaliation for killing his only child," the other guy said.

"Braeden is right. He will come after you."

"Let him," Raven replied.

"He's a dangerous bastard, Raven."

"And so am I. I'll take him on with everything I have inside of me."

"And what else do you have inside of you, apart from being a new vampire?"

"Follow me." He got to his feet and together the men walked outside. He motioned for them to wait on the porch and walked a small way from them. Taking a deep breath, he closed his eyes and he drew deep inside of him and pulled forth the glowing fire Calista had bestowed upon him the night they spent in the cave before their capture.

"Ignes interiorem lucem" Fire burst from the pores in his flesh, igniting his entire body. He had only tried it once previously, when he had escaped with the kids and they'd been sound asleep in a cave he had found for the night. He looked over at the men and all stood with mouths open in astonishment. He twirled his hands around in circles and the flames moved with him. It was super cool; but he knew how dangerous it was. He had found a carcass and using the flames, had seen what it would do. When he had finished, nothing but ashes had remained. Calista had been right, it was lethal.

"Penetralibus ignem," he whispered and the flames extinguished themselves as though they had never been. Nothing on him was marred, even his hair.

"How did you get that? I know of only one person who has that power," Lucian asked as Raven re-joined them.

"How do you think I got it?"

"Calista."

"Correct." He went back into the living area and collapsed onto the couch. They had of course again followed him and Lexis stuck her head round the door frame.

"OK to come back in?"

"Yes, Lexis." She disappeared with a small smile and an excited Alexzander ran in a moment later, waving a piece of paper in the air.

"Look at this, Uncle Raven." Raven just barely caught him as the kid dived on his lap and pretty much shoved the paper into his face.

"What is it, kiddo?" He pulled the paper back so he could make out what was on it. Scrawled across the top was family in a child's writing from where he had drawn over dots that Lexis had obviously written out for him and under them stood stick figures.

"It's all of us." The kid beamed at him as he showed off his drawing. And sure enough it was. A stick figure for each. Lexis and Tairen. Him and Calista. Luke and Alexzander. And baby Jinx with Draylan. It had a couple of trees on it as well.

"Great drawing, kiddo." Raven smiled at him and Alexzander gave him a quick hug before diving on Luke and showing him as well. Lexis peeked into the room again.

"Dinner is ready. Come and get it." They stood to their feet and followed the vivacious woman to the dining room as smells infiltrated their senses. The huge dining table was covered in food. All sorts of meats, vegetables, potatoes, etc. There was even pasties, still hot. They all took a seat and waited patiently whilst she handed them their plates and cutlery. Once she had seated herself, then they dug in with relish. A knock at the door stopped them all from grabbing food from different bowls.

"I'll grab it." Raven jumped up as he was the closest to the door and went to see who had knocked. Pulling the door open it was the last person he expected to see.

"Good to see you again," Skyri said, holding his hand out. Raven clasped it in his and gave it a quick shake.

"And you. So what do we owe this pleasure?"

"Lexis invited me to dinner. Not a bad time?"

"Nope. Just be warned, Lucian is here."

"The Vampire King?"

"The one and only. Turns out he's my biological father."

"Fuck. Really?" Skyri stared at him with wide eyes.

"Yes. But come on, food is dished up." They walked to the room where everyone was waiting.

"Well fuck, Lucian. Good to see you again!" Skyri said as he caught sight of the man.

"And you, Skyri. Been a while. How you been?"

"Not too bad thanks. Hey, kiddo."

"Hey, Uncle Skyri," he high fived Alexzander who grinned around a mouthful of mash potato before tucking back into his dinner — kid was an avid foodie. Skyri sat next to Luke and Raven took the head of the table again.

"So what have I missed?" Skyri asked, after thanking Lexis as she handed him a plate and he began loading it with food. Raven didn't say anything as Lexis brought him up to speed with what had happened since his return.

"So you got turned into a vampire, went on a rampage and Calista had her heart ripped out. She isn't dead, she'll be back soon." Raven looked at Skyri as he said that but didn't bother to comment, no point if no one listened to him. All of them were adamant she would return. But no one returned after having their heart ripped from their chest. He half listened as everyone talked whilst they ate. He gave the occasional grunt but really wasn't in the mood to talk. He soon finished what was on his plate and noticed Skyri put away pretty much everything else that was left. Must be the werewolf appetite. Glancing at the clock on the fireplace, he noticed it was seven p.m. Where the hell had the time gone? He watched as Lexis excused herself as she went to put the kids to bed. They all helped one another clear the table, wash everything up and put it away. No way were they letting Lexis do it after she had cooked it all. It wasn't fair. Once it was all done, they all got a glass of warmed blood, well the vamps did, Luke and Skyri got a can of coke each and they retired to the garden. Raven looked out over the vast landscape. To his right, the sea was calm and tranquil. The village homes all lit from within, as families settled down for the night. Mountains lay calm and quiet. The sky above them was a blanket of black velvet, with a huge, nearly full moon that was highlighted by a few thick clouds, and millions of stars dusted the sky that looked like firebugs. It was beautiful and actually quite soothing.

"So what happens from here with you two?" Luke asked, drawing all their gazes to him.

"I'd like to see you again, Raven. Get to know you," Lucian said and Raven looked at his father.

"Yeah, maybe. All depends on if I come back here."

"Wouldn't you want to?"

"Maybe. I don't know. I don't know what I want right at this moment in time," he responded honestly.

"I can understand that. Considering a lot has happened to you since you've been here." And wasn't that the ultimate truth. A short while later, Lucian and Braeden bid them farewell and departed their company. Skyri and Draylan followed not long after. Soon it was the four of them again, and Lexis let out a yawn.

"Tired?" Luke asked her.

"More than I thought I would be." She smiled and rubbed her belly.

"Why don't you head to bed? It's got to be late now," Raven said, stretching from his place on the couch.

"Yeah, I think I will. Knowing my luck, the kids will have me up at six a.m. again."

"Joys of parenthood, huh?" Luke laughed.

"Definitely. Good thing I don't mind." She smiled at her brother.

"Go to bed, I'll lock up," Raven said.

"Ok. Good night." She gave them a kiss on the cheek each and she and Tairen departed. Raven glanced over at the clock and was shocked to see it was ten p.m. now. Where had the last three hours gone? Probably because they'd been talking, so time passed quickly.

"Luke?"

"Yeah, man?"

"How long were Lucian and Braeden here for after dinner?"

"Two hours or so. We've been sat here for about half an hour. Why?"

"Just wondering, as I just looked at the clock and saw it was ten p.m. I didn't realise the time had flown by as it did."

"Yeah, mental how quick it's gone. Wonder what we're going to do tomorrow as it is our last day."

"No idea. I'm sure Lexis has a plan for us though. What time are we leaving Monday morning though?"

"I think Lexis said something about seven a.m. or something like that."

"Early then." Well, for everyone else, they were used to four or five a.m. starts.

"Yeah, because they're going to drop us off in America first, then head back to Scotland so she can finish the last of her course at university."

"Will she do it all before the baby comes?"

"Yeah. She said she's already advanced more than they had originally realised. She reckons she'll be finished by Christmas."

"That is quick. Three months to do the entire lot?"

"Or something like that. Her, Tairen and the kids will stay there until she is finished. Then come back here."

"And what about you?"

"What about me?"

"When we finish our time in the army, will you come back here?"

"Yes. I already said I would. Me and Lexis were talking earlier about it. When she's finished, they'll come to us for the remainder of the Christmas period, then we'll travel back here together. Will you come back with us?"

"Honestly man, I have no idea what I want to do at this moment in time."

"Well, you have a few months to think about it at least." Luke grinned at him and Raven couldn't help but smile back, but inside, he wondered would he come back? He didn't think he could want to spend time here now that Calista wasn't around.

"Yeah, true man. How about we head to bed ourselves?"

"Sounds a plan." Raven walked into the kitchen and drained another bag of blood. Better safe than sorry. Once that was done, together he and Luke made sure the doors were locked, lights were off and everything was secure. Once that duty was done, they trailed off to bed. Raven used the bathroom first, brushing his teeth, emptied his bladder and washed his face. He went back into the bedroom and changed over into some jogging bottoms and a tank top whilst Luke disappeared into the bathroom. He flicked on the lamps that Luke had put into the room and extinguished the main one. The room fell into a warm glow. He threw the curtains closed, huge heavy blackout curtains that fell to the floor. Luke came back out in jogging bottoms. Top half bare. They put their dirty washing in the basket by the door and crawled into the bed.

"Night, Raven. I'm glad you're home again," Luke said as he turned out the lamp.

"Night, man. And me too." Raven also turned his lamp off, sending the room into avid blackness. Luke quickly fell into sleep but it took Raven another good half hour, and the last thought on his mind before he slipped into nothingness was that he missed Calista and probably always would.

Chapter Forty
A few days later

Raven sighed as he slung his backpack over his shoulder and stepped off the plane at L.A. Airport. He was officially back on 'Normal Earth' and honestly, he hated it! He had never actually expected that he'd miss the place, but since being in Mystic Being, despite all the shit that had happened, he had strangely felt at home there. Their last day, Lexis had taken them to the beach and they'd spent the day there with the kids, gifting them with happy memories. He reckoned it was for him and Luke, to give them something to think about when times got a bit hard during their last months of employment in the military. He looked over his shoulder as Luke descended the steps and stopped next to him.

"Are you sure you'll be fine from here? We would have dropped you off closer," Lexis said, standing at the doorway.

"We're sure. Besides, it gives us a chance to ride our bikes as we didn't in Mystic Being," Luke replied.

"If you're sure."

"We're sure. Promise." Raven didn't say anything, just walked to the back of the plane that Tairen had lowered from the switchboard in the cockpit, walked up the ramp and began unchaining his bike from where it had been stored. He slung the big chain off from over the seat and then the ones that were locked through the wheels, even though they were secured with clamps. He wasn't taking any chances with the machine. Luke walked in and untied his own and together they wheeled them out. Once they were clear of the door, it rose up to lock back in place. Once they'd circled back round to the side of the aircraft, Lexis was waiting at the bottom of the stairs with Alexzander. Luke hugged his nephew whilst Lexis gave Raven a quick hug — he returned it. Then it was his turn to hug Alexzander, who stared up at him afterwards with eyes shimmering in unshed tears.

"Don't cry, kiddo. We'll see each other again soon."

"Promise?"

"I promise. I just have to finish my job and then we'll be together again," he reassured the boy.

"OK." Alexzander hugged Raven again quickly then slid off his lap to the floor and ran back into the plane.

"Please be careful you two, OK?" Raven noticed the worry in Lexis's eyes.

"Nothing here is anywhere near as bad as what I went through under the hands of Kharge. You have nothing to worry about Lexis. And you know I'll protect Luke with my life." He didn't wait for a reply, just shot off on his bike to the exit that would take them out of the airport.

"We'll be all right. I highly doubt we'll be sent out somewhere this close to the end of our service. We'll keep in touch, OK?" Luke hugged Lexis.

"You better or I'm sending Tairen here to kick your arse." She grinned at her brother.

"Yeah. Yeah. Now go inside the plane and head off to Scotland. We'll see each other again soon. I love you."

"I love you too." And with that, Luke followed after Raven, who sat waiting at the end of the runway they had to take. Before they could take off again, Raven's phone went off. Which was not surprising after he had turned it back on just before leaving the plane. He rolled his eyes as he saw who was ringing him.

"Yes, sir?" he answered. It was that arsehole, Captain Hawkins who was kind of their boss, but wasn't as they didn't really work for him. But they had to listen to him when they were on base.

"Oh, now you decide to turn your phone back on after nearly three months having it off?" Luke looked up as the booming voice echoed through the tiny device.

"We had some complications, sir."

"Complications involving a R&R you and Luke had? Really?"

"Yes, sir. We're on our way back to the compound now."

"Where are you both?"

"L.A. Airport, sir."

"Fine. It is 13:00 hours at this moment in time. I expect you both back here by 15:00 hours sharp." That was obviously plenty of time to get back to the compound as they were only two to three hours away tops.

"Yes sir." Hawkins didn't reply, just hung up.

"What did he want?" Luke asked as Raven put his phone back in his jeans pocket.

"Didn't sound believing at all about the complications we had. I can't exactly tell him I was tortured and turned into a vampire. I'd be sent straight into a padded cell."

"That's for sure. How long do we have to get back?"

"15:00 hours we have to be there for."

"Plenty of time. Shall we?" Luke grinned as he pulled out of the lot and turned right, Raven right behind him, but they didn't go far. Just enough so that they could watch the plane that Lexis and the other members of their small family were in, take-off. Once it was up at a decent height, they took off. A few hours or so later they turned onto a secured road that led to their military compound. Driving to the edge of the main building, they parked their bikes in the designated bike section. Tucking the bike keys into their pockets, they shrugged their backpacks onto just one shoulder and walked into the building.

"Well damn, I wondered when I'd be seeing my two adopted sons again." Kelly, the bases resident cleaner/part time cook beamed at them. She was a tiny woman who stood all of five feet with wild red hair and piercing green eyes and always greeted them with a motherly smile. She was also dubbed Grandma Kelly as she was about eighty but rocked an easy sixty. They knew her from when they had joined at sixteen, so much so they'd moved in with her when they'd hit twenty-two and had stayed ever since. And they'd been there since her husband Richard had passed from cancer when they were twenty. So much so, they'd given up their small flat to be with her.

"Hey, Mum," Luke laughed and literally bent in half to give her a cuddle. Raven bent even lower when it was his turn. They were the only two who called her mum. Everyone else called her Grandma Kelly. Her rules, not theirs.

"How have you both been? And Raven, you been working out? You're even bigger than before."

"We're good. And no, Mum, I haven't worked out. I just ate a lot."

"Good. About time you ate more for yourself. Not just enough to get by. Now, I'll let you both get on. Will I see you both later tonight?"

"Not tonight, we won't be allowed, so don't wait up. Bye, Mum." She gave them both a quick kiss on the cheek and then she disappeared into a side office, laughing at one of the office workers as they groaned jokingly as she walked in. Shaking their heads, they went to the Major's office.

"Here we go," Raven grunted as he knocked on the door.

"Come in." They walked in but didn't sit down. They never did unless given permission.

"Ah, the two wanderers return." Hawkins turned those beady brown eyes to them, but Raven realised something. He wasn't intimidated by this man anymore. He was nothing compared to what he had faced with Calista. The door flew open behind them and they looked over their shoulders at who walked in. It was General Wilson.

"Sir!" They saluted the man.

"At ease, gentlemen." They watched as he walked around the desk.

"When did you two get back?"

"Just now, sir," Raven replied.

"OK, so what has happened before I walked in?"

"Nothing yet. You didn't let me get to that part. They've been gone longer than the month you scheduled for them," Hawkins responded.

"And why is that?" Wilson asked, turning sharp green eyes to them.

"We had some complications we encountered, sir." Raven wasn't going to make them privy to what had happened, it was of no concern of theirs.

"Such as?"

"Personal things, sir," he replied.

"Very well, I know how much you keep to yourself. I trust no further complications will happen for the remainder of your service?"

"None, sir."

"Very well. Go bunk in and I will expect you both to be here come at oh six hundred." The men saluted them both and left the room. Raven had barely shut the door before Hawkins demanded to know what was happening. But Raven wasn't interested in what Wilson had to say about what had just transpired in what had to be the shortest conversation they'd ever had in that office, well him anyway. They didn't say anything as they headed to their tactical unit's bunk room. Walking in, they pulled up short. As there was usually only the five on their team which resulted in three empty bunk beds, they were shocked that they had now been filled.

"Well shit. If it isn't Mountain and TS back from their R&R," Boom laughed as she stood up from the chair she was slumped in. They knuckled tapped each other.

"Still the same badass Boom I see." Luke laughed.

"Fuck yeah. So where you two been? Could have used your help last week on a job." The men sat down in the chairs that were signed Mountain and TS. They had their own chairs, which helped considering Raven's was reinforced making an allowance for his monstrous size.

"Yeah, and what job was that? And who's everyone else?" Raven looked over at the newbies in their bunks, who all stared at him and Luke in curiosity.

"Transfers. Little badasses who needed a kick up the arse being on our team," Geek replied, briefly lifting his head up from a small compact he was tinkering with. Probably another handy invention he was mastering that would no doubt help in upcoming missions.

"OK, so what sort of shit did you get into trouble for to wind up with us?" Luke called out. A big bastard climbed off his lower bunk and glared at them with pale green eyes. He stood at a good six feet five or so, but Raven was completely unfazed by him. He had bulky muscles that made him appear larger. Nose was crooked as though he had been punched in it numerous times. Scars littered his arms and hands from where Raven could see due to his T-shirt. Combat trousers covered his lower half, along with their standard steel toe-capped boots.

"As if we answer to you," the guy sneered.

"Mike, you might want to control yourself. These two would rip your head off and not think twice in doing it," Blade replied, drawing a cloth over the hunting knife he was never without.

"Yeah, as if they could take me. Do you even know who I am?" Mike retorted, beefing up his arms to appear intimidating. Luke shot a grin at Raven who caught it out of the corner of his eye as he was too busy glaring at Mike.

"Couldn't give a shit who you are, boy," Raven said, and Mike's nostrils flared.

"Don't even think about it, Mike. It really isn't worth going to medic." Boom said, getting to her feet. She might only be five feet five, but Boom could hold her own like the best of them, hence why she was part of their team and one of the few Raven actually trusted to guard his six.

"Pipe down, woman, you shouldn't even be here. The place for you is in the kitchen serving your man." Boom's eyes flared at that and Raven had heard enough. He motioned for Boom to stay where she was and he got to his feet and walked over to Mike, who had to look up at him considering Raven towered over the man.

"Boom is more entitled to be here than you are, boy. You are to be a part of this team; therefore you treat each other with respect. If not, leave."

"How about you leave. You haven't been here for weeks. You know fuck all."

"Boy, I have seen and done more than what you can ever possibly know." Raven wasn't usually the one who got in other people's faces unless it was absolutely necessary, he left that to everyone else, but this time, he didn't give a shit.

"What, wiping your mother's arse," Mike laughed.

"I do not have a mother," he replied.

"Of course you do. Everyone has a mother."

"I disowned my biological parents when I turned fifteen." The door to their bunker opened and in walked Grandma Kelly.

"My God boys, I could hear you outside. What's all the bickering about?" she asked as she grabbed their bin near the door to change the bag.

"Nothing to do with you, old timer. Shouldn't you be in a retirement home?" Mike retorted and Raven snapped. No one talked to her that way, no one.

"Oh shit!" he heard Luke and Blade say as they scrambled out of their chairs to run at him. He didn't pay attention, just grabbed Mike and planted his fist into the guy's face, instantly breaking his nose. He beat him again and again until he was nothing but a bloody mess on the floor. He tried getting in a few punches here or there but Raven felt nothing but rage.

"Raven, let him go." Luke's voice shot through the red haze that had started too descended over Raven's eyes. It slowly lifted and he looked down at Mike who was trapped between his thighs. The man's face was an absolute mess. Shattered cheekbones. Broken eye sockets that were already swelling badly. Bust lip in three places. Blood covered his face and around his head. Raven climbed off him and looked at Kelly who stared wide eyed. He hauled Mike to his feet, where the man's head flopped. He grabbed his hair and held his head back so that he could look at Kelly.

"Apologise, or I'll hit you again!" he growled in the man's ear. Mike spat out a couple of teeth that had been knocked loose.

"I'm sorry." He didn't sound sorry in the least so Raven tripped him and slammed his head into the floor, instantly knocking the man out.

"Not good enough. You OK, Kelly?" He looked over at her again.

"I'm fine, sweetie. Come here please." He walked over to her and she pulled out a wipe from one of the many pockets of her apron. She ripped open the small packet and wiped at the plasma on his knuckles. The door burst open and Wilson plus Hawkins and a few others stood there with wide eyes as they took in the scene.

"What the bloody hell happened here?" Hawkins demanded, a vein popping up on his forehead, and if he wasn't careful, it would burst. God, did Raven hope that happened.

"Mike insulted Kelly. Raven taught him a lesson," Geek answered. Audible gasps resounded from the bunk beds at the mention of Raven's name.

"What did he say, Kelly?" Wilson asked the woman who had finished wiping the blood from Raven's knuckles as best she could. She turned to face the men.

"He said I should be in a nursing home," she replied and Raven barely managed to stop himself from going and pounding the absolute shit out of the guy again.

"Well I can safely say he won't do that again. Medics go and get Mike, take him to the base hospital, and treat him for his wounds. Raven, you need to get more control of your temper."

"I did," he replied. And he had, truly. The man was lucky he hadn't walked in on what Raven had really wanted to do. As in, he wanted to rip his throat out with his teeth and bathe in the plasma, and then rip apart the body with his bare hands. So, in all honesty, he had actually gotten off easy.

"You know this is to go on your report, right?"

"Sure." He didn't give a shit about a report.

"Kelly, time for you to leave. It's past time you went home anyway. Everyone else, lights out! Raven, we'll sort this out tomorrow." Raven didn't reply, just stood there like everyone left. Before Kelly left, she gave him a quick hug, a kiss on the cheek and a murmured thank you. He smiled slightly at her before she too left. Once the room had cleared out apart from those who were meant to be in the room, he turned around. Everyone was standing a small distance from him apart from Luke who was an arm's length away.

"Damn, my man. Talk about break the guy's face," Luke grinned at him.

"Shouldn't have insulted Kelly," he replied and moved to one of the single beds opposite the bunk beds. He and Luke had them considering there was no way they could fit into bunk beds. Well, Luke could with his feet hanging off but no chance for Raven. As he chucked his backpack on the mattress, he heard a shuffle behind him and whirled around. The newbies were all standing there staring at him, but at a safe distance.

"What?" he asked.

"Are you really Raven Calhoun, aka the Mountain?" one asked. He was about Luke's height, plain brown eyes and hair. Nothing special to write home about.

"Yeah, why?" Obviously his reputation had grown considerably since he'd left.

"Shit man, I can't believe I'm meeting you in person. Name's Charles, but everyone calls me Chameleon." He held his hand out and Raven briefly shook it.

"Why Chameleon?" Luke asked as he also dumped his bag.

"Because I'm good at blending in with my surroundings." Raven barely managed to hold back the snort. Sure, he might be good at blending it, but Raven was a master at it, which surprised a lot of people considering his height and size.

"If you say so, kid. Now go back to your bunk. I want to get some sleep."

"Sure thing, nice meeting you." And sure enough, they all went back to their bunks. Raven rolled his eyes at Luke who just grinned. Raven disappeared into the adjoining bathroom and took a quick shower to wash off the remaining blood Kelly hadn't gotten off him. Changing into his sleeping gear, he threw his washing into the hamper. He emerged and the main lights had been extinguished and small lamps had been put on to create a soothing atmosphere. Or at least that is what he thought, he would never be calm in here again. Not until he left for good. He crawled into his bed, put his phone on charge, placed his standard KA-BAR 1217 seven inch fighting knife under his pillow, handle barely peeking out from under his pillow so he could grab it easily. Turning his lamp off, he settled down to sleep. As he descended into the waiting arms of sleep, he heard everyone else switching their lamps off. He fell asleep to the sound of everyone's breathing evening out and Calista on his mind.

Chapter Forty-One
Two days before Christmas Day

Calista sighed as she stepped off the plane she had secured from Tasmania to get her over to America. She pulled her hood up so it hid her face and waited whilst Draylan followed closely behind. He had parked the plane up in a secure holding bay that would keep it there until they returned. She absently rubbed her slowly but surely growing belly that housed hers and Raven's daughter. She had waited with baited breath for the foetus to grow more before she had discovered the sex. They were having a baby girl, and damn if she wasn't going to be strong considering the kicks she delivered to Calista's ribs now and again. But thankfully, one touch of her hand to her belly and the baby stopped movement, as though savouring the fact its mother's hand was right next to it.

"How are we going to do this then? Do you think he'll accept that you're actually here and not dead as he has obviously thought?" Draylan asked as she dropped her hand and held them at her sides.

"Honestly, we have no way of knowing how he will react. We will just have to see that when we get there; and do not mention anything about the baby, let me tell them." Before Draylan could muster up an answer, a high-pitched squeal shot through the air followed by a loud, "UNCLE DRAYLAN!" Both their heads turned as an over-excited boy darted across the small parking lot towards them.

"Hey, kiddo!" Draylan laughed as he swooped Alexzander up into his arms. They watched as Lexis and Tairen waited for them to join them before they exchanged hugs. Jinx was sound asleep in her buggy. Calista smiled underneath the hood as Lexis held her belly with one hand. Calista realised they were both about a month or two apart, if that.

"How was the journey?" Tairen asked, as they walked to their small van they'd hired to collect them. It had to be big at the moment because of the buggy, etc.

"Wasn't too bad actually. No hassle or shit," Calista replied.

"Good. So how are we doing this for Raven and Luke?" Lexis asked.

"We'll go to their base. Talk to whoever it is in charge. Sort out something from there," Draylan replied as he clambered into the back of the van with Alexzander.

"Good plan. And it's good to see you again, Calista. It was horrible trying to convince Raven you were fine."

"I'm not surprised considering he saw me get my heart ripped out of my chest. Also, there is another surprise I have in store for Raven."

"What's that?" Lexis had tilted her head slightly in question. Calista gathered now was as good a time as any to tell her. She pulled the hood down and opened up her coat. She watched as it registered on Lexis's face.

"HOLY MOTHER OF FUCKING GOD! You're pregnant? With Raven's baby?"

"Yes, with Raven's baby," Calista smiled slightly.

"Oh my God!" Lexis laughed and hugged Calista, who actually returned it.

"So, as you now know, how do you feel about being godmother to the baby?"

"I would be honoured!" Lexis beamed as she told Tairen who congratulated her.

"So we will have another baby to play with soon?" Alexzander asked.

"When they're of a proper age, yes," Calista replied, which caused the kid to beam happily.

"So are you my Aunt Calista that Mummy has told me about."

"I'm Calista, yes."

"Are you Uncle Raven's girlfriend?"

"What do you think?" She wanted to know what this kid thought about it.

"Yes. You're the lady he was upset about."

"Upset, why?"

"He thought you had died. Obviously Raven had bumped his head as you're very much alive." The kid grinned at her and shoved a cookie into his mouth.

"He's way to sharp for his own good," Draylan chuckled as they all clambered into the car.

Calista sighed as she sunk into the passenger seat Lexis said she could have whilst Tairen took the wheel. They took to the road and all kept in a comfortable silence as Tairen drove them to the house they'd rented for over Christmas. Pulling up into a side road, Calista noticed the road was secluded and out of the way of others. Perfect. They pulled up outside the house and Calista looked it over. Typical four-bed rental property with a pretty white picket fence. White walls. Black stained frames around the windows. The front garden was tidy with the grass perfectly cut and a huge array of flowers in the beds. They all walked up to the house and strode inside. Living room on left. Doorway on the right led to a cupboard for coats, etc. Downstairs toilet was next to it. Stairs leading upwards directly ahead. To the side of them led the way to the kitchen. Calista strode into the living room and crashed down on the fabric-styled armchair. Looking around she realised it really was the typical holiday home. White walls. Basic wood furnishing. Open fireplace that would warm the place in the colder months. A decent sized TV sat above it. She looked out over the windows and one was looking out to the front of the house and the other to the back garden. She smiled as she saw Lexis had made it more hers for the Christmas period Calista knew humans were so fond of celebrating. A huge Christmas tree dominated the back corner of the room with twinkling decorations as well as baubles holding pictures of their family members, surrounded by vast amounts of presents in all shapes and sizes. Lights hung along the tops of the walls, currently turned off. She looked up as Lexis walked into the room holding two black glasses. She handed one over to Calista and she realised it was blood.

"Thanks." She took a sip and rubbed her belly slightly — baby had woken up and was kicking a good one.

"You're welcome." Lexis took a sip of her own and folded herself onto the couch.

"So what plans have you got for getting your brother and Raven here?"

"I spoke to their general. He said they're due back today from a stint he had them go on. So I can go and pick them up tomorrow at about ten a.m."

"Did he say what stint?"

"Nope. Classified. But apparently Raven has been an unstoppable force since he got back. They don't know he's obviously been changed into a vampire, but they're using his brute force and such for their advantage. I did get a text from Luke explaining that he and Raven were burned out. They asked for this to be their last stint."

"Thought they had six months left before they had that option?"

"Oh, they did do, but the general couldn't really say no to Raven considering everyone is apparently petrified of him now. More so now than before he left to go to Mystic Being."

"Unstoppable, huh?"

"You'd be mighty proud of him Calista. When he returned from bringing the kids back, once they were back in their parents' arms, he was walking back to the house when people started screaming. Wendigos had followed him to the village. All I remember was before Draylan or Tairen could grab weapons to kill them, Raven shot past and killed them all."

"How many were there?" She downed the last of her blood and put the glass on the coffee table.

"Ten or so I think."

"And he took them all on?" She was impressed, but then again, she had seen first-hand just how dangerous Raven could be when he set his mind to something. And that was before he'd even been turned into a vampire.

"Sure did. Once he'd killed them, he didn't say anything. Just turned around, walked up to the house and disappeared from view. No one moved until he'd disappeared, then the village workers got rid of the bodies and they all went home. It was eerie just how quiet it was in the village. Same as the next day, on the Sunday, we went to the beach to get their minds away from everything but everyone kept their distance from us. I think they were scared of Raven."

"This is understandable considering they saw him quickly wipe out the Wendigos. It leaves an impression which I highly doubt they'd forget anytime soon."

"Oh yes." Lexis drank the last of her drink as everyone else filed into the living room. Tairen plopped down next to Lexis whilst holding Jinx. Draylan claimed the other armchair where Alexzander climbed onto his lap.

"So when are the lads getting here?" Draylan asked.

"I'm going to pick them up tomorrow. I'll bring them back here and we will take it from there I guess," Lexis replied.

"And what about if Raven thinks it is a joke that Calista is here and flips out?"

"I'll take the kids into town when Lexis gets them. That way, they're out of harm's way and don't hear anything that will be said," Tairen muttered, moving a sleeping Jinx to the middle of him and Lexis.

"That would be best as we have no idea how he will react to us being here," Calista replied.

"Then that is what we will do. What time do you have to get them by?" Draylan asked Lexis, just as her phone rang. She pulled it out of her pocket and grinned as she answered it.

"Hey, big brother. What can I do for you?" Calista looked over at her from where she'd gazed out of the window.

"Just ringing in quick before we get out of range. You still picking me and Raven up at about ten a.m. tomorrow morning?" Luke's voice echoed through the phone.

"I sure am. I'll go to the main office for you both, OK?"

"Sure thing, little sister. See you tomorrow. Love you all!"

"Love you too." She pulled the phone from her ear as he hung up, he must have hit a no signal area.

"Mum, what's for dinner?" Alexzander's small voice drew their attention from where he was perched against Draylan, voraciously colouring in a small part of his new colouring book.

"Not sure yet. How about some dinosaurs?"

"Yes please!" He grinned excitedly and she smiled back as she got up to go to the kitchen. Calista glanced at the clock on the wall and was surprised to see it had already hit five p.m. They'd been back on 'Normal Earth' for four hours already! She rose to her feet and followed Lexis to the kitchen. It was quite big with white marbled counters. Oak cupboards. A decent electric cooker stood tall and proud. Coal black against the gleaming whiteness. A simple bar stood against the sides, creating a good sitting place whilst someone cooked. Family friendly and that whole kit and caboodle. Calista plopped her butt onto one of the stools and watched as Lexis rummaged through a freezer for things to cook for them all. She pulled out a couple of bags and plopped them on the counter.

"So how did you manage to get Luke and Raven here for Christmas?"

"I made a call to their general. When he heard what I had to say, he agreed they could leave earlier than the six months they had left."

"That is unlike a general to just let anyone go," she wondered aloud.

"We know that, but apparently he was quite eager to let Luke and Raven go considering Raven has literally been an unstoppable force since he got back. They're unsure as to why, and everyone is petrified of him apart from one woman who works there."

"Who?"

"Her name is Kelly. But they all know her as Grandma Kelly as she mothers everyone. She's a cleaner and a nurse maid if needed."

"Oh, right. So what else will you be doing for dinner?"

"Have you got any cravings?"

"Nope."

"Oh, you lucky woman! I've been craving the most unusual things."

"Like what?" Calista was quite curious considering she herself didn't crave anything out of the ordinary, for her anyway.

"Cheese-wrapped pickles. Bottles of vinegar on chips. Mars bars left in the car in the middle of a heatwave. Ice-cream with chilli sauce and I don't even like chilli!" Lexis laughed.

"Well, those are certainly different."

"Just a tad. You're so lucky you have none!"

"If you say so." She cracked her knuckles as the door opened and Alexzander walked in.

"What's up, baby?" Lexis turned her attention to her son.

"Can I have a juice box please?"

"Of course. Blackcurrant, apple or strawberry?" Calista just about kept the grin off her face as a hard look came over the kid's face as he thought hard on what drink flavour he wanted.

"Can I have strawberry this time please?"

"Of course." Lexis grabbed the drink from the fridge for the boy, pierced the top and gave it to him.

"Thanks Mummy." He dashed off out of the kitchen and back to the men.

"He's certainly come out of his shell with you, hasn't he?" Calista drew Lexis's gaze as she grabbed some frozen peas and put them in a saucepan.

"Unquestionably. And honestly, for how I feel about him and Jinx, it's as if I gave birth to them myself. Is that weird?"

"Nope. Not with you. As you are such a mum already. It's natural for you. Mothering instinct."

"You'll have it as well when your little one is born."

"Maybe. Who knows how I will be, considering I have very rarely been around children apart from rescuing them." She shrugged and accepted the glass from Lexis she had topped up with blood for her.

"You'll get the hang of it. And considering you will have us here to help you, you'll be fine."

"Well, I appreciate the help. We just have to convince Raven now to be a part of his child's life."

"And what about being a part of yours?" Lexis rustled the peas boiling on the stove to break up a couple that were still frozen together. Draylan walked in then and Calista glanced at him over the top of her glass as she drained the blood. That was one thing she had noticed whilst being pregnant. She had to take in extra blood but that didn't bother her. Instead of once a week, it was now four or five times a week.

"Lexis, Tairen asked any chance you can get a bottle ready quick. Jinx is waking up, so will apparently need her feed."

"Yep, no problem." And sure enough, she dived into making the bottle, using the microwave to heat the bottle up quicker than waiting for the kettle to boil. Calista watched as she used her wrist to test the temperature and smiled as she handed it over to Draylan.

"Here you go. Perfect temperature for her. Get Alexzander to show you where her nappies and clean clothes are as I'm sure she'll need to be changed as well." Before Draylan could reply, the kitchen door burst open and the whirlwind that was Alexzander came flying in.

"Quick, Uncle Draylan. Jinx needs her bottle." Lexis laughed at her son as he pretty much bounced on the spot.

"OK, I'll go take it in. Want to grab the nappy, wipes and clean clothes for her?" He smiled down at the kid who nodded with great enthusiasm and disappeared again, followed by Draylan.

"He likes helping with Jinx, doesn't he?" Calista asked.

"He sure does. No matter what we ask him, he's eager to help. Although at times, he can see we don't need the help so he just keeps her distracted whilst we change her. He's a great big brother to her, so I know he will have no trouble with the new baby." Lexis pulled out the chip pan that was tucked in the corner by the fridge and plugged it in to warm up the oil. Calista stretched in her chair slightly before she climbed off the stool and set about helping Lexis set the table in the dining room that joined the kitchen. Once that was done, everyone filed in whilst she and Lexis brought in the food and they sat down to eat together. The meal was filled with laughter and talks of everyone being excited for Christmas, as well as eager to see the kids filled with memories of Lexis's favourite day. Once they'd eaten, cleaned everything away, they all retired to the living room until bedtime. It soon hit ten p.m., and they all decided it was best to head to bed now, get in a good sleep for the big day tomorrow of reuniting with Luke and Raven, giving them a day to get used to being back with them again. Then the following day, they'd open presents and give the kids a beautiful memory. They had agreed no presents would be opened on Christmas Day until they were all up. Calista noticed Lexis had no need to tell Alexzander that 'Santa' wasn't real, he already knew considering where he came from and that there was really no point in convincing him. Lexis led Calista to the room she would be bunking in, a double bedroom to herself that was painted in a pale yellow with oak furniture. Simple and easy for the home owners to keep on top of. She got ready for bed and clambered in between the blue sheets on the four-poster bed. She willed the lights off and with a wave of her hand, drew the heavy duty curtains shut. Plunging the room into darkness. She lay listening in silence and could hear the deep, even breathing of the kids and Draylan whilst Lexis and Tairen themselves got ready for bed, talking quietly about their day with the kids as they did so. She tuned out and closed her eyes as sleep came in swiftly, sinking her into its open arms.

Chapter Forty-Two
The day before Christmas

Raven sighed as he, Luke and the other members of their squad walked into the base. All of them were tired, hungry and dirty. It was six a.m. and they'd just got back from a mission they'd been requested for specially from the president himself. Not every day they were asked for but the job they had been needed for, required each of their expertise. He shrugged his backpack onto his shoulder more comfortably as he drained his bottle of water. They all were about to walk past the big office when the main door opened up and Wilson stood there.

"How did it go?"

"They were rescued without injury. Only injuries they had were from their rope burns on their wrists and ankles. They'll make a full recovery health wise, mentally though will take a bit longer as to be expected sir." Luke replied.

"Very well, go freshen up and report back to me for the paperwork." He walked back into the building and shut the door behind him. He was nothing if not punctual. Raven rolled his eyes as he dropped his empty bottle into a bin near him. Rolling his shoulders, he cracked. Heaven. They all followed Boom as she headed to their bunk room. As they rolled in through the doors, they all beelined for the overstuffed chairs and each sunk into them with a sigh.

"You know, I'm quite envious of you two bastards," Boom said from her spot opposite Raven.

"Why's that?" he asked.

"You're officially off the books and shit come ten a.m. I have another five years of this shit yet," she grumbled and they laughed.

"At least you don't have to go out into the world and act like a normal person," Luke retorted and they all laughed at the exaggerated look of horror that went on her face.

"Oh shit, I didn't think of that. Can you picture me, normal?" She motioned to her face with her eccentric green eyes, three piercings in her lower lip, one in her nose. And loads of piercings up her ears. She had even gotten one done in her eyebrow.

"Lots of people would see you as normal, Boom." Blade laughed as he caught the knife she threw at him and tossed it back, which she caught easily and slid back into the sheath that was attached to her wrist.

"Yeah, but I'm anything but normal."

"You said it, not us," Luke replied, earning a grin from her. Raven rolled his eyes at the playfulness of them all. But it was to be expected after the shit they'd just gone through.

"So what do we do now?" Geek asked.

"Go check in with Wilson, get these reports out of the way," Raven replied and clambered to his feet just as the doors burst open to their bunker.

"How did it go?" Sam asked. Raven looked over at him dressed in all black that made his dark brown eyes appear black. Even his dark skin blended in well. If he used that to his advantage, he could literally become a shadow but he needed more training to master it. But again, that wasn't Raven's place to suggest it.

"Hell. The Amazon is an absolute shit fest for keeping its heat contained, but we got the job done," Geek replied.

"Awesome. How many you take out?" Sierra asked, coming up behind Sam. She was a tiny woman, about the same height as Boom but nowhere near as dangerous. Kid had a lot to learn still, but one day she would become a formidable force to be reckoned with.

"Both camps. Those kidnapped returned back with no problems apart from some scraps," Luke replied then downed a bottle of water.

"Mental wise?"

"Entirely different ball game. It was no picnic with what they witnessed," Boom said.

"Nice. Well, we'll leave you too whatever it is you're doing now." They both left without a word.

"Let's go get this shit over with then," Raven said and they all headed over to Wilson's office. Once they got there, Holly put them in a room to the side and they all took a seat at the table. A minute later, Wilson walked in carrying a laptop which he handed to Geek. Sitting down at the head of the table, he looked at them all.

"OK, so tell me what happened, and Geek, you write it all down as you're the quickest." Geek nodded and fired up a word document to begin.

"Who's going to start?" Wilson looked at each of them. Raven kept quiet, he never spoke in these meetings, the others were more capable to do it.

"We got to the drop-off point as instructed, donned our gear that we needed for this extraction but we had to wait for Captain Neale to meet us, which luckily wasn't long as he hurried to us carrying paperwork," Boom replied, stopping to take a gulp of her water.

"Anyway, he spread out the paper onto a makeshift table after he asked his second in command if we had arrived yet. So when he pointed to us waiting at the side, he motioned us over and we went over the map he'd produced for us. We went over everything for a good half hour before he was satisfied enough that we knew what we were on about. The only one who wasn't at the table with us was Raven, who had stayed by the wall watching everything and was sharpening his blades."

"Why am I not surprised at that one," Wilson replied, sliding a glance at Raven who just stared back at him with no comment. He was never one to look in on the layouts, he was their brute force and the most perilous of them all. All of which were openly admitted with no hesitation.

"So, Captain Neale had asked why didn't Raven join us in looking over the plans and Luke explained he never did. Raven is our muscle/killing machine. But he wasn't having any of it. He said as part of a team, he had to be in on the paperwork side too. And thinking he could intimidate Raven, got the biggest fuckers he had there to get Raven to join us. What they didn't realise with him sitting down was, well, Raven, you're a big motherfucker." Raven snorted as she shot him a grin before stowing away her emotions and turning back to Wilson.

"It didn't exactly go to plan on that. Luke tried telling Neale that it wasn't going to work, nothing intimidated him, but he didn't listen so we all just watched as they tried to get him to join us."

"And then?" Wilson jotted down something on his small notepad he continuously had with him. And Raven also noticed that he didn't contradict them for dropping the captain from the beginning of Neale's name.

"Well, we warned Neale to warn them to not touch Raven as that would be the last mistake they ever did," Blade said, joining in. They all waited a moment for Geek to catch up with him as his fingers flew over the keyboard until he gave a nod that he had caught up.

"So yeah, he didn't take that advice. Just told us to be quiet and let his men do their job. We watched as they tried using the coercion factor but Raven didn't so much as look up from sharpening his blades. So they resorted to putting their hands on him. We did warn Neale before to tell them to not touch him, but he didn't listen, and quicker than anyone could move, Raven had both men flat out on the floor, unconscious, and he just went back to his knives."

"OK, so both men are on the floor. Why didn't Neale take your advice?" Wilson asked.

"Honestly Sir, he was saying he was the one to give the orders and not us. We only warned him what Raven was like." Geek replied, not so much as missing a step on the keyboard as he glanced over at Wilson.

"OK, and then?" Raven rolled his shoulders from where he was sitting and shuffled his chair backwards more. He was too damn long to sit cramped under a bloody table.

"Ok, so once he'd called medics to treat the two on the floor, Neale turned back to us with a sour look and pointed to the map of where they believed those taken were being held. Once we had the idea of where it was situated, we rolled out. But not before Neale headed to Raven and tried reading him the right act in front of everyone."

"And what did you do when he did that?" Wilson looked at Raven for the answer.

"Told him to get off of my case, let me do my job as he wasn't in charge of me, asked Luke where in the forest we were headed so he showed me the map quickly and I headed off in the general direction. The team caught up with me," he replied.

"I don't expect anything different from you for that. OK, Christina, then what?" Wilson was the only one who got away with calling her by her given name, everyone else called her Boom, or found out the hard way why she was called that. Girl lived for her explosives!

"We followed Mountain with our gear and disappeared into the surrounding forest. We scouted for four hours before we heard voices and laughter. We backtracked a couple of hundred feet and got ready. All of us donned our black gear to blend in with the surrounding shadows, I did the guys war paint to merge their faces with our gear and I raced ahead to scout. I'm the smallest, so can easily hide better. I established we had about forty to fifty tango's in this one camp, but no prisoners. I scurried back and we devised a plan."

"And what plan did you decide on?"

"We were to take them out as quickly as possible. We did. Raven pulled up the rear then it got a tad hectic. Gun fire everywhere, people screaming out from injuries. As we got into the thick of it all, we hollered out for Mountain, because obviously we don't use our real names, just our code names so they wouldn't know. Raven came bounding out of the surrounding woodland and let me tell you something boss man, he was a force to be reckoned with! No one stood a chance against him. He literally bulldozed through the remaining thirty or so like they were nothing, and at a speed that was crazy. Once they'd been eradicated, we scanned bodies for anything to help us figure out where they were keeping those taken, when Raven dived onto this guy who had appeared out of nowhere. They crashed to the floor with Raven on top of him and somehow the guy gave us the location."

"And how did you manage to get the location out of him? Tangos aren't exactly known for giving in easily." Wilson again looked at Raven and he glanced up from the quietness in the room. He put his blade away he was using to clean under his fingernails as he looked at Wilson.

"Told him if he didn't tell me what I wanted to know, I was going to rip his spine out through his nose and beat him with it."

"And that made him give it up? Usually it takes more than that." It did, but Raven wasn't going to admit he had also flashed his fangs at the guy and told him he'd drain him dry painfully.

"I'm a scary motherfucker. He knew I wasn't joking."

"No shit. The guy literally pissed himself!" Luke chuckled. Raven rolled his eyes.

"So he gave up the location, then what?"

"I killed the bastard. We got to the next camp which was another hour away, destroyed them all as quickly as possible. Got the victims loose from the chains they'd put on them to keep them in place and we took them back to base. Then we came back here." Raven replied. Short and to the point. Simple and effective. Just how he liked it.

"Any injuries you sustain?"

"Nothing we can't handle."

"Still needs to be reported." Wilson replied.

"Couple of stab wounds. One bullet wound to the thigh."

"And you didn't say anything to us?" Luke gasped at Raven.

"No. I pulled the bullet out, sealed it shut with some stitches. Sorted," he replied, his voice holding a note of don't fucking ask again.

"The knife wounds?" Wilson asked.

"On my thighs, nothing I couldn't handle, sir." Again, bullshit but they didn't need to know.

"Fine. Go on then, you're all dismissed apart from Geek." They fled the room and shut the door as Wilson asked Geek if he had gotten everything.

"Well that was a load of fun," Boom said, cracking her knuckles.

"Just a barrel full," Blade snickered as they stepped out into the morning sunshine.

"Fuck me, its seven-thirty a.m! We were in there an hour and half almost!" Luke said as he glanced at his watch.

"Tell me about it. I'm feeling it in my arse," Boom laughed as she rubbed said arse.

"Should be used to minor comfort now. So what do we do now?"

"No idea about you fuckers, but I'm heading for a shower then have an hour or so power nap then head out to the field. Catch you later." She waved as she jogged off to join some women who were walking by.

"How about we hit the gym? Blow off some steam?" Blade asked.

"Sounds like a plan," Luke said and looked at Raven who nodded. As a single unit they headed to the camp's gym and walked inside to find it empty except for a few lads who were in the boxing ring working on their hand-to-eye co-ordination.

A few hours later

Raven cracked his neck as he pressed five hundred pounds of heavy gym machinery with his legs whilst Luke and Blade spotted him. Not that he needed it. It turned out he could handle a shit ton of weight thanks to being a vampire now. The downside, it was getting harder and harder to secure blood for himself. He would have to ring Lexis soon and find out a way of getting hold of some. He couldn't keep on going about it secretively as he was. He had quickly learned the usage of vampire saliva to seal the holes in his donor's throats, and the memory swipe to them so they didn't remember shit. Who knew he would have caught on so quickly. Yes, he'd fed when they'd been out on that rescue, but that was when he'd moved faster than they could see, grabbed a tango and drained them dry. He shoved the bar he was pushing back into its place and used his towel to wipe away the sweat from his brow.

"Damn, Mountain, I've never known you to press that much weight and not think it's a big deal." Blade was impressed, that was obvious by the tone of his voice. Raven shrugged.

"Is that the heaviest you have pushed so far?"

"With my legs, yeah. But I'm thinking of upping it eventually." He smirked at the shocked look on the man's face.

"Are you for real? Luke, please tell me he's shitting with me?"

"Pft, you wish, Blade. He's about as serious as you can get." Blade rolled his eyes.

"Raven Calhoun, Luke Blackwood, you've been requested to go see General Wilson." A gentle voice called across the gym from where they were. Looking up, they saw it was Wilson's secretary Holly, if Raven remembered correctly. She was one of those that was desperate to get into either his or Luke's pants but neither man was interested in her. She was a blonde who dyed her hair an even brighter blonde with a horrendous orange-type tan, fake tits and she was all of a size four she had squeezed into a small black dress. She thought she was God's gift to everyone and he was the first to tell her she wasn't and when he had done that she wasn't impressed at all. Not that he gave a shit.

"Yeah, OK. Thanks Holly. We'll be right there." Luke called out before turning back to Raven and rolling his eyes. He didn't like her either. Actually, did anyone apart from Wilson? She left and Blade looked at them both.

"Any idea why Wilson wants you?" Raven glanced at the clock on his phone and saw it was nine-thirty a.m. So they had half an hour before Lexis was due to collect them.

"No idea," he replied to Blade. Together he and Luke left the gym and headed to Wilson's office. No point in grabbing a shower when they were wanted now, plus he knew that was where the men spent all of their time when they weren't out or on the training field. They made quick work of crossing the base, following Holly who had waited for them outside the gym building. She walked towards Wilson's office and knocked on the door which was followed by a sharp 'Enter', which she did. Wilson was seated behind his desk, all smart looking, etc. as usual and paperwork in folders in front of him.

"Have a seat men." He motioned to the seats the other side of his desk and the men did.

"Do you need anything else, sir?" Holly asked.

"No, thank you." She nodded and closed the door behind her as she left them to it.

"So as you both know, you are officially off duty come ten a.m."

"Yes, sir," Raven said. And honestly, he couldn't wait. He was so done with all this bullshit now. He was eager to go out and do things at his own pace for a little while.

"OK, these are your discharge papers, so sign along the dotted line at the bottom then you get a copy as do we." Wilson handed them a pen each and they scrawled their names at the bottom. Wilson ripped the two pages apart and handed them their copies back in the folders.

"Any idea what you two will do now?"

"Go spend Christmas with my sister and her family. Then not sure after that, sir," Luke replied.

"Shame you two have come to the end of your service though. We need good men like yourselves here fighting for our country."

"Thanks, sir, but honestly, I've had enough of it now," Raven said, shoving his folder into his bag so he wouldn't forget it.

"Understandable. I did hear since you've come back, very few have come near you. I know you are more quickly to temper now though, Raven."

"That is true, sir. Which is why I spend minimal time around people at the moment." Raven wasn't going to go into detail about it. He refused to. The only one who know majority of it was Luke and he knew he wouldn't blab about it.

"Fair enough, I know you're a private person anyway so I won't push it." Wilson scribbled something down on a pad next to him then looked back at them.

"Any questions?"

"What will happen to the squad now, sir?" Luke asked.

"They will stay partnered up with each other and the newbies that were drafted in will be a part of their team now." Which was fair enough considering they'd all just come back from a job and Raven noticed they were all good at what they did. A bit more training with the others and they'd work as one without being told to. Raven snuck a quick glance at the clock and saw it was nine-fifty a.m. Ten minutes, and they were free men!

"OK, seeing as that is everything, you are free to go and I wish you all the luck in the world outside of here." Wilson dismissed them and they left. Leaving the office, Grandma Kelly was waiting for them, tears streaming down her face. Luke rushed forward and swept her into his arms for a cuddle.

"It'll be fine, Kelly. You'll find someone else to take under your wing," Luke reassured her.

"Maybe, but won't be the same as having you two under my wing." She blew her nose quickly.

"Maybe so, but you'll be fine, Kelly. You're a tough one." Raven smiled at her.

"I have to be to deal with you." She laughed and drew him to her for a hug. Raven crouched down so he could hug her properly. He released her and moved away.

"Will I see you guys again?" she asked.

"Probably not. We plan on moving to be with Lexis in Scotland," Luke replied.

"Right away?"

"No, we're going to take a week to get over the fact we're no longer military men. Then we'll figure it out."

"Very well, you both take care of yourselves," Kelly whispered, hugged them both quickly and disappeared into Wilson's office, who looked up from writing something and smiled at her. They left the building and pulled up short as their old squad stood in front of them.

"Ten a.m. You're officially free men," Boom grinned at them.

"Thank God for that. I'm fed up of it now," Raven replied as they all knuckle punched each other. They weren't huggers, not at all. No matter the length of time they'd all worked together, not once had they hugged, which he respected.

"So you're officially leaving then? Can't handle it?" a taunting voice called over to them. They looked over and saw Richard walking towards them with a smirk on his face.

"Man, did you not get enough last time when Raven knocked you out to not taunt us?" Luke snorted as he shrugged his bag on his shoulder more securely.

"I did. But why leave? Can you not handle it anymore? Has it all gotten to you?"

"Fuck off, Richard, we're not interested in hearing any shit you have to say," Boom said.

"Is that why you had to take R&R? Get too much?" Richard smirked at them over Boom's head, completely ignoring the small woman. Which he really shouldn't do considering she could wipe the floor with him.

"LUKE! RAVEN!" They heard their names being called and glanced over their shoulders and both smiled. Lexis was here and she huffed as she walked over, one hand cradling her belly.

"Hey, monster." Raven hugged her quick before Luke did, but he kept an arm around her shoulders.

"Who's this? Your girlfriend?" Richard passed an appreciative look up and down her body.

"No way. They're my brothers!" Lexis replied.

"Oh really? Fancy having a shot with a real man then?"

"Sorry, the only real men I see around here are Raven, Luke, Nick and Chris. You're just a snot-nosed brat who happens to think he's better than everyone else, when all you are is a bully and you try to intimidate people but you're nothing special at all," she retorted with a curled lip.

"Why you little bitch!" He slapped Lexis across the face causing the woman to cry out and Raven roared. No one touched her! More so when she was pregnant! Dropping his bag and not caring where it landed, he dived onto Richard, knocking the smaller man into the ground with a hard smack. He punched him over and over again, and no matter how many people grabbed him, he shook them off and continued pounding the guy's head into the floor. And because he was a huge fucker, and had filled out since getting back so he was bigger than his old weight and size, plus he was now a vampire, Richard didn't have a chance in hell. He gave a punch to his nose and felt the cartilage break under the impact. Blood gushed around Richard's head and coated Raven's knuckles. But strangely, the smell of it held no appeal to him. Again, no end of people tried to get him off Richard, but it was of no use, his anger was spiking higher and higher, and they just didn't have the strength to move him. Suddenly he was yanked backwards and sent flying a few feet. Jumping to his feet, he glared at the cloaked figure who had removed him.

"Raven, enough please!" Lexis cried out from where she stood next to Luke whose arms were wrapped around her protectively. Her cheek was bright red from Richard's slap and that set him off again. He took another step forward to beat the fuck out of the bastard again who had yet to get off of the floor, but was whining like a bitch and holding his nose. Blood leaked through his fingers which gave Raven a small bit of satisfaction, but he wouldn't be satisfied until Richard had broken bones in numerous places and didn't move again. Not dead, but knocked out. He needed that beat down bad, and he was the first in line to deliver it.

"RAVEN ENOUGH!" That voice drew him up short. Who the actual fuck? And then he got his answer as the hood was dropped and it was the last person he thought it would be.

Chapter Forty-Three

Calista waited in the car whilst Lexis went to get the men. Lexis was adamant that she go with her as it would be easier to get the shock out of the way a little bit and maybe her and Raven would be able to take a walk back to the house and talk about everything that had happened. Calista knew she was right in that way, but the million-dollar question was how would Raven react to it. Waiting patiently in the car with the window open to let the gentle breeze brush over her face, she heard someone get a nasty smack and then heard Lexis scream out. She dived out of the car and raced over to where she scented the woman. Before she stepped into view, she made sure her cloak was around her to disguise her features and rounded the corner and stopped dead. Raven was beating the holy hell out of a guy who was trapped beneath his thighs. Lexis, who's cheek was blazing red from a hand print, had Luke wrapped around her defensively whilst everyone else that was there tried to prise Raven off the guy. But it did no good, he was so much stronger than them. And damn if she was appreciative of the fact his jeans cut into his ass like a second skin. He was huge! Bigger than when she had last seen him, considering that was when Kharge had ripped her heart out. Changing into a vampire had clearly agreed with him, sectoring him back to his original size, but he had clearly been working out, adding even more muscle to his frame. She just managed to keep the drool in her gob! She noticed everyone realised their efforts were futile as they stepped back so she marched forward, yanked Raven by his jeans and threw him backwards a few feet but he quickly clambered back to his feet. She didn't turn around to face him though, just stayed facing the same way, but she knew exactly where he was.

"Raven, enough please!" Lexis cried out, one hand going to her cheek. She heard Raven take a step forward and knew the time was now or never to reveal herself. Everyone else was staring at her, wondering who she was and why she was so strong to remove Raven from beating the bastard on the floor, who she noticed had yet to move. She whirled around to face her male.

"RAVEN, ENOUGH!" she roared and that drew him up short. She felt everyone else take a step backwards as though they felt the power rippling through her. Which she didn't care about. She knew at this moment in time, she was the only one who would be able to stop him from doing something stupid, not that she didn't want to hurt the punk on the floor either.

"Who are you?" he asked and she saw blood drip from his knuckles, but he seemed unfazed by it. She threw her hood back and glared at him.

"You know damn well who I am!" His eyes widened as he stared at her as though he'd seen a ghost, which considering the shit he had seen happen to her, was understandable.

"But, how? I saw you die!" he whispered, just as the bastard on the floor gained his feet. He was unsteady, but he got to them. A door behind her opened up and a burly man in uniform stepped out, followed by a tiny, stupidly thin, woman with a horrendously fake tan and in heels she could only just walk in. She was everything that annoyed Calista. What the hell happened with being exactly as you were and not getting excessive surgery until all you looked like was a fake doll?

"What the fuck is going on out here? It sounds like a bunch of wild animals!" he said, stomping over to them. Calista looked at him over her shoulder and saw the exact moment he saw the handprint marring Lexis's cheek.

"Richard slapped Luke's sister because she wouldn't go off with him when he asked if she'd like to see what a real man can do," a male next to Lexis said.

"Is this true?" He glared at the man who must be Richard.

"She deserved it. Stupid quim should realise a real man when he's in front of her." Calista whirled around properly and got in Richard's face. Which wasn't hard to do as she stood eye to eye with him.

"Really? A real man? The person I see in front of me is nothing but a spoiled brat who should know better than to raise a hand to a woman who tells him no! And definitely a woman who is pregnant!" she hissed.

"Back off, bitch. I don't answer to you. All women should bow to us men." Calista drew her fist back and launched it into Richard's stomach. He grabbed it quickly and bent over as she winded him. But as he went down, she grabbed his shoulders and slammed her knee up into his nose, breaking it even more. He yelled out in pain and she shoved him to the floor onto his back as he grabbed for his nose to stench the new flow of blood, not that it did him any good, it leaked out through his fingers. She knelt over him, one hand on his chest to keep him in place.

"If you think for one minute that us women are going to bow down to a man, you are sadly mistaken. No woman *will ever* bow down to the likes of you. If you so much as think of hurting, or slating a woman again, I will come back here and I will show you just how dangerous I really am. I will skin you alive, rip you open with my bare hands and feast on your innards!" she growled and made her eyes change to her blood red and her fangs appear slightly as his eyes widened in fear. She quickly changed them back to normal and got back to her feet just as the repugnant odour of piss hit her senses. She glanced down at his trousers and saw he had pissed himself. That explained the smell.

"Who are you?" the guy in uniform asked. And by the way he held himself, she knew he was the one in charge.

"Raven's woman," she replied.

"The one who snapped at Hawkins at the beginning of their R&R?"

"One and the same."

"OK, good to know. Now, what the hell happened here?" Wilson repeated himself.

"Richard slapped Lexis, Raven beat him up, Calista stepped in and you saw the rest, sir," Luke called out.

"You seriously slapped a civilian? More so one who is pregnant? Where the hell is your head, boy?" Wilson fumed as Richard clambered back to his feet.

"My head is perfectly fine. She knew that she shouldn't have said no," he replied, wiping his hand under his nose, spreading the blood across his cheek. Calista whirled around and grabbed Raven as he started for the punk again. Only because she was so much stronger than him, was she able to hold him back.

"Raven, stop!"

"No. I'm going to kill the bastard!" he snarled and she growled back and because no one could see her face, flashed her fangs as well.

"No, you're not. He's going to get what comes to him," she said, squeezing her hands on his biceps more to know she was not going to be moved. She sensed Lexis moving over to him and she wiggled between them both. Calista stepped back, considering it would be a damn tight fit as they were both pregnant. She watched as Lexis reached up to cup Raven's face and was more comical considering she had to tiptoe, but Calista refused to smile at it.

"Raven, look at me, honey." He dragged his gaze down to her.

"What?"

"I'm OK. I'll heal. And besides, I think you and Calista put your point across to the shit. He isn't worth getting into trouble over, more so now considering you're a civ." Raven wrapped his arms gently around Lexis and cuddled her to his chest.

"Are you sure you're OK?" he whispered in her ear. Calista gave them privacy and looked at Wilson, who looked at her, but she noticed it was between her eyes. Why was it only Raven who could look her square in the eye? Oh yeah, because she was a trained assassin and everyone always said she gave off a dangerous aura. Go her!

"I'll get him away from here. I'm sure you're eager to sort Richard out for what he did."

"Indeed I am." She actually smiled slightly as she saw Wilson rub his hands together in glee.

"Right, let's go. Raven, me and you need to talk." She turned back to her man. Nodding, he grabbed his bag from the floor, and after a quick goodbye to his old team and Grandma Kelly, he followed her out of the base, using a sanitising wipe to clear the blood from his knuckles. Lexis and Luke got into Lexis's car after she said she'd meet them back at the house, but not before Luke took Raven's backpack from him and for once the big male didn't argue. Once they'd disappeared from view, she headed down the road, Raven quiet at her side. They didn't talk as they left the base behind. She reached an intersection and knew if she took a right, she'd go to the house, which she did do. About halfway there, she saw a small park to the side. Empty as children were tucked up at home with their parents watching movies and such, getting ready for Christmas. They headed in and sat down on the sweeping hill at the side. The grass was plush and thick and surrounded them as they sunk their weight into it. She kept her legs out in front of her as she couldn't put them up to rest her chin on them thanks to her belly. But because of the cloak, you would never know she was pregnant. She heard a sigh from Raven and looked at him. He was still a little sweaty and such from earlier, so she snapped her fingers and he was instantly clean again, not that he remarked on it.

"How are you here? This is real, right? I'm not dreaming?"

"No, Raven, I'm very real. You're wide awake. I know it's a lot to take in, but honestly, I'm really here. No fabrication of your imagination."

"How are you alive?" He looked at her and she hated the fact he had sadness in his eyes. She wanted nothing but happiness in them.

"You were told, it takes a lot to kill me."

"You had your heart ripped out of your chest!"

"I know, but it honestly takes more than that to kill me. I know what you saw wasn't pretty, and I'm sorry for that," she whispered.

"It broke me, Calista. Literally broke me. I didn't feel anything after that happened. Actually, I'm still very much numb from it."

"I know, I really am sorry. I truly wish you hadn't gone through what you did. Or saw what you did either. I hate knowing I was the one who got you in that predicament."

"Well, I was the stubborn bastard that went with you. So it isn't completely your fault. I knew what I was getting into when I followed you." He smiled slightly at her and she smiled back. It was a small step, but it was a step in the correct direction so she knew she was on the right track.

"So what's going through your head now?"

"What happened after I got out?"

"I was dumped in The Pitts. They dump all bodies they kill in there. They had a Feeder in the room they fed, which is like a Wendigo, but only feasts on dead flesh. I killed it, escaped the room and scoured the remainder of the mountain. I killed everyone I came into contact with."

"What about Kharge?"

"I slaughtered him as well. Including his second in command and new woman. I saw what you did to Scorcha and Lviana — nicely done by the way."

"Yeah, well, they got off lightly. I wanted to do more, but I knew I had to get the kids out."

"Understandable. Anyway, after that I went to Gélio. We had a chat about what happened and I put myself into a healing coma."

"How long were you in it for?"

"A month or so. It helped immensely considering I healed from everything. Then I went back to the village, where everyone took great delight in telling me what had happened when you got back." She moved slightly, before settling back in as she was before.

"What did they say?" He gazed at her and she noticed the sadness had ebbed some in his gaze.

"How you had gotten the kids back safely, albeit dirty but that was to be expected. And then you slayed fifteen Wendigos on your own."

"What can I say? I was pissed off." She laughed at that.

"No shit. I'm impressed though. And not many people would take on one Wendigo, let alone fifteen of the fuckers, and on their own no less."

"Yeah, well I'm an arsehole. I didn't give a shit as long as they were destroyed."

"I would never have guessed," she sarcastically retorted, earning her a snort from him.

"OK, so I really have to ask, why did you come back? Why here? Why not just stay in Mystic Being and forget about me?" And wasn't that the million dollar question. She moved to kneel between his legs which he had no choice but to separate, before she sat on them. And that was when she really appreciated the width of her man. He was all rock hard muscle that strained against the T-shirt he was wearing.

"I came back for you. I refuse to live without you, Raven. I know this is still a major shock and such that I am here with you, but I really am." She put her hands on his face so he would have no choice but to look at her. "I'm also a stubborn bastard and I refuse to take no for an answer. Come back with me to Mystic Being. Live there with me. What do you have to lose?"

"I'm broken, Calista."

"No, you're not. You're not broken, but I will give you chipped. But you know what, with some glue I can keep it from cracking more." And that got what she was after, he burst out laughing before he grabbed her and hugged her to him. But she made sure her belly didn't touch him, that could wait a few minutes more before she laid that whammy on him.

"Fine, so chipped. But it has to be damn good glue to keep it held together." She laughed from where her face was mashed into the side of his neck and damn if that didn't feel like home, which scared her as she had never felt like this before. She pulled back and he let her.

"I know the perfect glue."

"Oh yeah? Plan on letting me know what it is?"

"Love, Raven. Because I do, I love you." She sealed that with a kiss and he literally growled as he kissed her back. And damn if that didn't go to her head. The taste of him as he assailed her senses. The feel of him beneath her hands and on either side of her thighs as she knelt between his legs. He wrapped his arms around her to drag her even closer to him. All too soon they pulled apart from each other but she did notice he was panting rather hard.

"I love you too, Calista. Always be mine," he said, looking at her with steely conviction.

"Always."

"Good. You know what that means don't you?"

"What?" She sat back to look at him properly.

"You have to live with my cantankerous arse now."

"Just that? I think I can deal with that." She laughed as he tackled her gently to send her onto her back in the grass. He braced himself on his arms with a hand either side of her shoulders.

"Not just that, no."

"Then what?" And she rose up to kiss him gently just because she could.

"Marry me." And what did she do? She blinked. Just blinked.

"What?" she whispered. Surely she hadn't heard him right?

"Marry me. Take my last name. Make me the happiest man alive."

"Yes!" She laughed as he stood up and yanked her to her feet.

"I love you, future Mrs Calhoun!" He laughed as he spun her around.

"And I love you, Mr Calhoun. Cantankerous arse and all." She laughed as he playfully swatted her arse. She smiled as she saw happiness radiate from him, no more sadness in his eyes.

"I also have something to tell you." She knew now was the best time to get this over and done with, whilst they were alone.

"Oh?" And damn if it wasn't adorable, the small head tilt he did.

"Remember when we were in the cabin at Dragon Hill?"

"Yeah, that was where you gave me the best gift I've ever had."

"Well, brace yourself. I'm pregnant." And she watched as all sorts of emotions raced across his face until radiant happiness stayed.

"I'm going to be a dad?"

"Yes." She took his hand and placed it against her belly, where it was unmistakable.

"I'm going to be a dad!" he laughed in happiness as he again yanked her to his chest. She laughed and cuddled him back.

"So you're not angry?" She looked up at him.

"No. Never. I've always wanted to be a dad. But I did expect it would never happen, so I learned to live with the fact I would just be Uncle Raven to Lexis's kids and Luke's if he ever has any."

"And now?"

"Now our kid is going to know just how much their parents love them. I do know for a fact we're going to be ridiculously protective and such of them though."

"Well, obviously. Have you met the kid's parents?" She laughed as he grinned at her.

"How far gone are you?"

"Couple of months or so. Why?"

"Then we get married as quick as possible back at home. I plan on making an honest woman out of you, Calista. And plus, I don't want our child born out of wedlock, no one can hold that against them then."

"Back home?"

"Really, out of everything I said, that's all you ask? Yes, back home. Home as in Mystic Being. I am a vampire now after all," he grinned at her.

"There is that. OK, we'll spend Christmas here tomorrow with everyone and the day after, we'll go back home."

"Deal." They left the park to go to the house Lexis had rented for everyone and what shocked her the most, he held her hand the entire way back. As if they were just an ordinary couple out for a stroll. And that was a completely foreign concept for her — she was anything but normal.

"So you do know this means I've got to get you a ring and everything, right," he said as they rounded a corner that led to the trek up to the house.

"I don't need a ring, Raven."

"Well tough. You're getting one. Don't argue on this one, woman," he mock growled at her and she grinned at him.

"So how do you think Luke will take the fact I'm pregnant?" she asked.

"Honestly, I think he'll be thrilled. He's always said I'll be a dad one day, even when I started doubting it myself."

"Then I shall let you be the one to tell him. Lexis and Tairen already know."

"How did Lexis take it?"

"Like a champ. Said she couldn't wait for our kids to grow up together, be the best of friends as well as cousins. You know what she's like."

"Don't I know it." He laughed and stopped as they got to the property.

"What is it?"

"Nice house. But it isn't as nice as ours."

"And what is our house going to be like?" She gazed over at the living room window as Lexis walked past with Jinx in her arms.

"We already have it. It's the one on the hill. Everyone else can move out. I plan on having you to myself every night until our kid gets here."

"Well, we'll have to find Luke somewhere to live then if that's the case."

"Sure, he can move in with Lexis and Tairen. They won't mind. Live-in babysitter." He grinned at her and she laughed.

"Come on before they wonder where we are." They walked into the house together and headed for the living room where they could hear everyone talking. As they graced the doorway, everyone stopped talking as they looked at them.

"All OK?" Luke asked from where he was sprawled on the floor with Alexzander who was scribbling away in a colouring book.

"All good," Raven said and walked in to flop into an armchair.

"So no problems?" Lexis asked.

"Nope," Calista replied, plopping down on the arm next to Raven, who curled his arm around her waist and his hand fell over her belly.

"OK, fill me in. What the hell happened? Calista, how did you get that stick out of his arse?" Luke laughed as Raven threw a coaster mat at him from the small coffee table next to him.

"We talked about what happened. We're all sorted now though."

"Does he know?" Tairen asked, looking up quickly at them before returning his attention back to changing Jinx's nappy.

"He knows." Calista smiled as Lexis laughed.

"Thank God for that. I hate keeping secrets. It's bad enough I haven't told Luke yet."

"Tell me what?" Luke asked, sitting up properly.

"I'm pregnant," Calista said, drawing the man's gaze as it widened.

"You're what?"

"Pregnant," she repeated and pulled the cloak off, showing her small bump off.

"Ooh, you sly dog! Congratulations, you guys," he laughed, getting off the floor and high fiving Raven who sat there with a huge grin on his face.

"Thanks, buddy." Calista smiled as she felt absolute happiness radiate from him. Then they all burst out laughing as Alexzander grabbed Calista's cloak from the floor and put it on. Pulling the hood up over his head, he giggled as it completely covered him and about all of it dragged on the floor behind him.

"It's so cosy!" he gasped and wiggled where he stood.

"Want one for yourself?" Calista asked, which caused him to drop the hood so he could look at her as she got off the arm of the chair and knelt in front of him.

"Really Aunt Calista? I can get one too?"

"Sure you can. Take that one off for a minute." He did eagerly as she wove her hands together. Soon fabric began to form in between her hands, until it solidified as a small cloak. She held it up to him and after putting her own cloak on Raven's leg, he put it on. It fit him perfectly. It landed at his ankles and the sleeves dropped slightly over his hands, as her own did for her. She pulled the hood up and settled it into place. She also fabricated a pair of soft black fingerless gloves for him and helped him put them on.

"There you go. All done." She smiled as she gained her feet and settled back next to Raven who again wrapped his arm around her as they watched as Alexzander got giddy.

"Look Mummy! I have an awesome cloak like Aunt Calista!" He laughed in merriment as he swished it behind him.

"So I see baby. Calista, put yours on and let me take a picture of you both." Lexis pulled her phone out of her pocket. Calista rolled her eyes and put it back on. Pulling the hood up into place, she made sure it was all securely done up with the buckles then made sure Alexzander's was done up the same as well. They both stood against one of the white walls and Lexis took the photo. Calista actually laughed as she looked at it on Lexis' phone. She literally towered over the boy as he mimicked her stance. Legs spread, arms crossed over the chest and no features visible. Two black ghosts.

That Evening

Calista held Alexzander against her side as they sat on the porch swing in the garden watching the sunset, her foot against the floor to give it a small back and forward motion. He wanted to do it with her, so everyone else remained inside to give them privacy. He snuggled against her side and took her hand in his own. Well, his hand wrapped around two of her fingers. He was just that tiny for his age.

"How are you coping with all the changes, kiddo?" she asked him, drawing his gaze up to hers before he quickly diverted it back to the sunset.

"I'm doing OK. I love my Mummy and Daddy, but why did Juliana not want me or Jinx?"

"Because she was a bad woman. I won't lie to you, Alexzander, the world is full of harsh people like that. But you will also find the world is full of good people as well. It's a mixture of both."

"Will I be a bad person then?"

"No. Despite who your birth parents are, I know you will grow to be a good, strong male who cares deeply for those around him."

"Can you see the future?" She looked down at him at that question.

"Sometimes. I try really hard not to."

"Why?"

"Because it can change in an instant. I can see one thing happen, then a small occurrence happens and that path is changed forever. So I tend to not pry into the future."

"Well, I am glad I will be a good person. I don't like people hurting." And that right there was how she knew he would be a good male when he was older. Maybe it had also helped with the shit he had encountered before he came to live with Lexis and Tairen, but she had no trouble knowing he would be the perfect male for someone one day. She felt Alexzander move so lifted her arm but was shocked when he crawled into her lap and curled against her, so she wrapped both arms around him to keep him where he was. She soon felt him relax as sleep claimed him, one tiny hand on her bump.

"I'm glad you're my auntie. I love you Aunt Calista," he whispered before he drifted off to sleep and damn if that didn't do something inside of her. Since she'd admitted to falling in love with Raven, her emotions were all over the place. Yes, she was still that badass assassin but now, now she knew without a doubt she would be a fierce protector to this child and Jinx as well. And if Lexis and Tairen had any more children, or herself for that matter because she knew without a doubt she couldn't and wouldn't be able to keep her hands off of Raven. That male was just too damn good looking for his own good! But the plus side, he was all hers, so she could literally feast on him whenever she wished and she highly doubted he would complain.

Raven watched through the window as Calista sat on the swing with Alexzander at her side, both just watching the sunset and talking quietly. And then he smiled as he watched the boy climb into her lap and she wrapped her arms around him.

"Now that is something I never thought I would see." He looked at Lexis as she joined him by the window.

"What?"

"Seeing Calista snuggling with a child on her lap."

"First time for everything," he replied as Luke joined them as well with a beer for himself and two black glasses of blood for him and Lexis and they both nodded their thanks at him.

"Wow, is she cuddling Alexzander?" he asked, looking out of the window himself.

"Yeah." They watched as Alexzander said something to her and she tightened her arms around him slightly before looking straight ahead as all emotion went from her features.

"I wonder what he said to her," Lexis said.

"No idea. I'll go and ask her." He was about to go to the double doors that also led outside but Lexis stopped him.

"Give her a few minutes. She might need it. I wanted to ask you something anyway."

"What?"

"Now you know Calista is pregnant with your baby, does this mean you're going to come back to Mystic Being with us?"

"Yes. There is also something else we didn't tell you."

"Oh?" Luke looked at him.

"When we get back to Mystic Being, Calista has agreed to marry me, so we're going to get married when we get back." He watched as both of their jaws dropped.

"Are you serious?" Lexis whispered, looking over at Tairen who was equally as shocked.

"Deadly serious. I don't want to waste another minute of her not being my wife. And our child will not be born out of wedlock. She openly agreed to that."

"Wow! Everyone is going to be so shocked!"

"Good. And they will realise I will literally kill for her. No one will ever doubt what I feel for her."

"You do know the proper way to marry a vampire right?" Tairen said, getting to his feet and placing Jinx in the corner with a pillow so she didn't roll off of the couch.

"Calista isn't a vampire though."

"No, but you are Raven. You know what marriage to a vampire entitles right?"

"No. What is it?"

"It means eternity. Because it is eternity, very few risk it. They take a civil partnership which gives them most of the same benefits as a married couple, but they can separate. When you legally pledge your vows the vampire way, you literally become bonded to the other person."

"As in?" Luke enquired.

"As in soul to soul. Heart to heart. Blood to blood."

"Don't care, I'm marrying her. Simple as that. And if anyone disagrees, I'll slit their throats for them and we can carry on the ceremony." Raven was adamant in that. Nothing was going to stop him from tying himself to her.

"We know you're serious in that. But double check with Calista that she does know the risks."

"I know what the risks are, Tairen." They all whirled around as Calista walked through the patio doors, carrying a sleeping Alexzander in her arms. She put him on the couch and drew a blanket over him as he'd since taken his cloak off, only because Lexis had told him to for dinner so he wouldn't spill anything down it.

"We just wanted to be sure auntie," he said, drawing Lexis into his side and she snuggled into him, placing her hand over his own that rested above their son in her womb.

"I know that. I wouldn't have agreed to marry Raven if I didn't think it was worth the risk." She walked over to them and he wrapped his own arm around her waist.

"Right, before this gets anymore awkward, Tairen, help me take the kids to bed. We will be back down soon." Raven watched as the couple grabbed their kids and took them off to their beds for the night as it was eight p.m., bedtime. Maybe that was why Alexzander had drifted off to sleep on Calista's lap.

"So congratulations on the future wedding when we go back," Luke said, grinning at them and Raven smirked back.

"This means you have to wear a tux, you know."

"Oh, come on! Really? I have to wear a monkey suit? You know they make me itch!" Luke groaned which caused him and Calista to laugh.

"Yes, really. You're my best man, so suck it up!"

"Fine. I'll do it just for you. Gah, you owe me, dickhead!" Raven laughed as Luke disappeared out of the living room, leaving him and Calista alone.

"So you really want to bond yourself with me?" he asked her.

"You're not getting away from me that easily. Through thick and thin. Me and you forever, Mr Calhoun."

"Just making sure, Mrs Calhoun. I am ever your cantankerous arsehole after all." He chuckled as he drew her to his chest and kissed her.

Epilogue

Raven sighed as he paced in the hallway of his and Calista's home whilst she was upstairs giving birth to their daughter. He'd been banished from the room by Calista herself, as well as Lexis and their birth nurse, Luci. His father Lucian was waiting with him, along with his right-hand man Braeden, who also happened to be Luci's husband. Luke sat in one of the chairs they'd brought in from somewhere as they all watched him pace. None of them eager to stop him, considering his eyes were blood red and swirling and his fangs were out as he worried for his wife. As he paced, he glanced down at the black band around his finger. She was everything he could ever have hoped for and more. She was perfection. And right now, he felt like an absolute shit for having put her in this position. The front door opened and in walked Tairen with Alexzander and pushing the buggy that held Jinx and their month-old son, Carricke, who were sound asleep. Alexzander went straight over to Luke for a high five. The kid adored him and vice versa.

"Any news yet?" Nikki asked, trailing in behind Tairen. Raven looked over at her and blinked as two more people walked in behind her. Draylan and Skyri. He knew they wouldn't miss it for anything, considering they had become fast friends of his.

"Nothing yet." He began twisting the ring around his finger as Alexzander ran over to him. Raven stopped pacing, else he would trample over the kid and he really didn't want to do that.

"Up please." Raven picked the boy up who threw his arm around the back of his neck to keep in place, not that Raven would drop him. And once he had the boy in his arms, his eyes returned to normal and his fangs receded back into their normal position.

"Aunt Calista will be fine. She's a tough one." Alexzander smiled at him and Raven smiled back.

"I know, kiddo. But I'm still going to worry until it's over. That's what husbands do." Why couldn't her labour not be as long as Lexis's had been, only twelve hours! Whereas Calista's had been twenty-seven hours so far. Yes, she could take a lot of pain, but he still didn't like it. Why didn't she use her magic to speed it along? He would never understand women for so long as he lived. He cuddled Alexzander to him as the kid laid his head on his shoulder. Soon the boy wanted down, which Raven did and he ran off to his dad for his juice just as he heard an almighty *'I'm going to fucking kill you, Calhoun'* erupt from upstairs.

"Was that Calista?" Lucian asked.

"Oh yeah. I know those sounds of labour," Tairen muttered, which was true. They had all soon realised Lexis had a potent set of lungs on her during her own labour. Who knew a woman that small to them lot had lungs that made them literally wince. And the words she'd said? He was still shocked over the fact she threatened to rip Tairen's dick off! He was glad he didn't have to hear it often. Some things he just did not want to hear. Soon enough though, a door opened up upstairs and as they all looked up, Lexis appeared.

"Come on up." She was grinning so wide, he was surprised her cheeks weren't splitting, but she also looked tired. Which wasn't surprising. Raven didn't need telling twice. He shot up the stairs as quick as he could and hurried down to his and Calista's bedroom. Opening the door wide, he stopped dead. She was sitting up in bed, cradling a small bundle of pink cloth. She looked gorgeous considering the ordeal she had just gone through. Her hair was slicked back from sweat and Lexis had tied her hair up into a ponytail to keep it out of her face. Her eyes were literally sparkling in happiness. He blinked and moved towards her.

"Hi, beautiful." He kissed her softly then looked down at their newborn. She had a small tuft of black hair and healthy pink skin. She was beautiful, just like her mother. And then she opened her eyes and he stared, amazed. They were the same colour as his, but with her mother's thick, long black lashes. He knew she would be a heartbreaker when she was older, *if* he let her date.

"She's beautiful." He ran his finger down her cheek and she grasped it in her little hand. An untold wealth of love floored him as he stared at his daughter as she smiled up at him.

"She sure is." Calista smiled at them both and Raven kissed her again, he couldn't help it. As Calista ran her own finger down their daughter's cheek, Raven caught a glimpse of her wedding ring, same as his but with diamonds in it. Happiness shot through him as he saw it. He would never get tired of knowing she was his wife, his blood mate. Eternally bonded. She might be his Ťylaitosk, but she definitely meant so much more than that to him.

"So what name would you like to call the little lady?" Luci's voice pulled them both from the spell of their daughter. They'd had this chat over and over again since they had become married and moved here permanently. They had officially decided on naming her after the fey who had started it all off in the beginning by giving her foetus away to help them in the name of the good, and for that, he would forever be eternally grateful. So naming their daughter after her hadn't been hard to decide after all.

"Her name is Caliana Calhoun," he replied.

"Of course. A beautiful name for a gorgeous little lady." Luci bent to write it down on the legal document stating Caliana's birth plus adding him and Calista down as her parents. Everyone else came into the room then after a knock at the door he hadn't realised he had closed when he had arrived, and he took Caliana out of her mother's arms and brought her over to see the rest of their family.

"This is Caliana." He couldn't keep the wealth of pride out of his voice as he said that. The only one missing was Lexis, as she had stayed with the children downstairs, considering she'd been there for the birth and all, so had already met the little one.

"She's beautiful. Congratulations to you both," Lucian replied, staring in wonder at his grandchild.

"Want to hold her, Luke?" He asked his best friend after a smile at his dad.

"Damn straight, give me my niece." Raven laughed as he handed her over. As soon as she was safe in Luke's arms, who stared in amazement at her and she stared back, he walked back over to Calista.

"Hey, Luke?" Calista called out, drawing the man's gaze.

"Yeah?"

"Want to do us the honour of being her godfather? And you as well, Draylan?" Both men blinked at that, and Raven supressed the urge to laugh.

"YES!" Luke laughed.

"It would be an honour," Draylan replied and ran his finger through Caliana's hair and smiled as she grabbed his finger.

"Thank you," Raven whispered as he drew Calista into his side as he sat down next to her on the mattress.

"Whatever for?" She gazed at him.

"Giving me the family I have longed for since forever."

"You're welcome." She beamed at him.

"Together forever. Through thick and thin, right?"

"Damn straight. I told you already, you aren't getting away from me that easily." He laughed and kissed the tip of her nose. Luci came over and handed him Caliana's documents which both he and Calista signed.

"Thank you for being here Luci. We couldn't have done it without you," Raven said.

"You're very welcome. I'm glad I could help. Sorry for kicking you out earlier." She blushed.

"It's fine. I would have done the exact same if I was in your position. I know I wasn't good to have around."

"And that's the understatement of the century," Calista snorted.

"Well, at least you have a beautiful daughter out of it all. Although, I think it's going to be a bit of a fight to get her back." She pointed over to the guys who were staring at Caliana with nothing but love in their eyes. Raven laughed and knew that Caliana was going to be one very spoilt little lady. Soon enough, Luke brought her back over to them and handed her over to Calista who cradled her in the crook of her arm.

"We'll all leave and come back tomorrow. Give you both time to settle down with her. Congratulations again though, she's absolutely beautiful."

"Thank you," Calista replied, before staring back at Caliana. Raven walked Luke to the bedroom door, refusing to go any further.

"I'll see you tomorrow, yeah?"

"Damn straight," Luke laughed and they knuckle bumped before he spun on his heel and walked away. Raven closed the bedroom door as Luci followed Luke and looked at the bed. And as his wife looked up at him, she shone from within and radiated happiness. He hurried back over to them and gave her a soft kiss. He knew he would never be able to stop kissing her. She was literally his eternal life.

"Are you OK?" she asked.

"Shouldn't I be asking you that?" he laughed.

"I'm fine. It was all worth it in the end as we got the best thing out of it."

"Isn't that the truth. I love you, Calista."

"And I love you Raven, forever." He smiled as he kissed her, then cuddled into her as their daughter slept in her arms and she closed her eyes. And yes, sure, he was the prince of vampires now, having rekindled with his father, but looking down at Calista and his daughter?

That right there made him the luckiest son of a bitch ever.